KITTY CAT
KILL SAT

KITTY CAT KILL SAT

ARGUS

Podium

To Raven and Quetz, who I love very much.

Copyright © 2023 by Forrest Taylor

Cover design by Podium Publishing

ISBN: 978-1-0394-2592-7

Published in 2023 by Podium Publishing, ULC
www.podiumaudio.com

Podium

KITTY CAT
KILL SAT

CHAPTER 1

Would you like to hear a joke? It's not one meant to be spoken, really, so it loses something in the telling. But here we go anyway:

Trying to manipulate late-Anthropocene-era orbital technology with paws.

Did you laugh? I did. Of course I did. My options are to laugh or to wail, and the second one takes up more energy than I have on offer right now. I would have to take several naps. And while the naps where you just flop in the sunlight coming through the windows are *way* better out here, they don't have the same relaxation quality.

It's all the alarms, I think. Every two minutes, an alarm. And I know I shouldn't turn them off. Which is why I'm here, now, trying to get an extension arm to properly grasp a micrometeorite and pull it back into the foundry for processing. Because it has material that we're low on, and I *acknowledge* that the alarms are important. I am very smart, and that is why I own a space station.

It is not the only reason I own a space station. I do not . . . I do not like to think about the other reasons I own a space station.

Instead, I focus on what I am supposed to. I can focus *exceptionally* well when I need to, and not even improperly designed controls can stop me forever. It takes three more tries, but I do eventually get the stupid rock into the foundry. I allow myself a moment to sigh and close my eyes, which is *like* a nap, only useless. I also allow myself a single victory meow.

Let's talk about space stations really quick.

When humans designed space stations, they designed them to do all sorts of things. This one is designed for one thing in particular, but it is *very* good at it. Depending on the era that a station was built in, it's going to have a certain level of sustainability, durability, automation, and, most importantly, comfort.

This one was designed during the peak of the Oceanic Anarchy, one of the many golden ages of humanity. The Ays, as they called themselves, built a station that could keep going basically forever, as long as it had a single mind capable of basic problem-solving on board. They were big on that: making tools to solve problems, not create more problems. The station has a ton of self-repair and maintenance features, half of which I haven't even found yet.

There is no documentation. A lot of space stations have user manuals. This one doesn't! It was destroyed when the Oceanic Anarchy was conquered by Troi France, though they never got around to shooting down the station. Then they fell to the Succession Wars, and any record that the station existed got lost for a while.

Pause on my musings—this is not a pun—to check on the foundry. Good news! We've got another artificial rock: probably a spy sat of some kind. Now, though, it's a great source of pre-processed tungsten, aluminum, and silicon. Actually processing those is hard, when you aren't on planet and lack the entropy dump of a multi-zettaton ball of iron to funnel impacts and heat into.

I double-check my resupply notes. The station has an exceptional AR (augmented reality) setup, which it took a *very* long time to train to understand me. But now that it does, I can offload unimportant memories that aren't about breakfast onto the computer until I need them. Check complete, I give the order to one of the thankfully automated systems, and a big chunk of the tungsten is marked to be moved to processing. We are low on grade-three groundstrikers.

Unpause musings. You know what this station isn't designed for? I ask this as I bound off walls to rocket myself toward my destination with practiced movements. Soon, I'll be back in one of the areas where the gravity plates are, but for now, I am a tiny and fierce rocket, and the emphasis there is on the "tiny" part.

Space stations are made for humans. Humans are, all things considered, both large and inelegant. I . . . miss having any around. I will not think on that. I have both work to do and lunch to eat. I must keep my graceful form fueled.

I will now list things, in no particular order, that space stations are not built for. Are you ready? Here we go.

Cats.

That is it. That is the extent of my list. I am a student of the real; I operate only with evidence and data that I have come to trust or have gathered myself. There is nothing else on this station that is not designed to be on this station. Therefore, I have determined that stations were not designed with me in mind.

Here is a common misconception about the cat. There is, and has been for roughly twenty thousand years, a belief among the human minds of the world that cats are aloof. Are lazy. Are judgmental, finicky, overly proud, or otherwise vaguely arrogant.

All of this is probably true. But none of those cats had spent four hundred years learning painstaking lessons on orbital infrastructure operation.

Time, as it ever does, erodes all tendencies. Erodes everything, except for memory. And me. Nothing erodes me. I am, as I have been for centuries, untouched by time. The only force that contains my grandeur in stable orbit is the hard vacuum outside—and the fire of reentry.

I arrive at my destination, the most important part of the whole setup. A room of gravity that pulls me out of a dive I have done sixty thousand times before. I am very, very good at landing that dive. I skim my soft fur across the first table, launch to the second, trail my rear paws just hard enough to slow my momentum, and come to a stop just in front of the galley's ration dispenser.

The ration dispenser is on a strict schedule. It dispenses exactly as many rations as a crew member needs, exactly at their appointed times. My appointed times are "constantly." My needs are "all of it, please." I am a growing girl. I should not be denied snacks.

The ration is a far cry from the snacks I remember in a distant haze. The treats of the world below were beautiful in comparison to the repurposed artificial-nutrient orb I am provided with.

I do not cry out. I have long since stopped crying out. There is no one to hear me.

This station has kept itself operational for thousands of years. I should be proud of my home; I should understand the monumental feat of engineering and *genius* it took. I do not think I could build a space station as sturdy as this one, even if I had more fingers and a real supply of materials. And I do feel those things, really. But I also feel every one of the thousands and thousands of sorrows of arriving to a tasteless, soulless dinner.

I successfully retasked the hydration tap once, to produce waters with *flavors*. It was a beautiful week of decadence, until I learned it was drawing too many exotics out of subspace and I would need to spend a month in a vivification pod to eradicate the rather impressive number of cancers I'd developed. I never did a repeat of that. A month was a long time to leave things unattended.

I cram the rest of the "food" away. In an hour, I must flush an air filter and, after that, realign the remains of a commandeered mirror network to properly feed the rad collectors. Which means I have an hour to *nap*.

My favorite place to nap is the exolab. It used to be used for testing long-term exposure to cosmic radiation. Eventually, it was retasked as a kind of viewing chamber or rec area, once sufficient defenses against that radiation were developed. Or at least, that's the history I can put together; there are couches here—bolted down, of course—but also the kind of sterile walls and self-sealing bulkheads that other clean rooms and hazard labs on the station have. It does not matter. It is the perfect time of day for a nap.

There is this one couch—and you can tell I like it, because even with the smart material pillows, there is a me-shaped indentation in part of it—that is perfectly positioned. I mean *perfectly*. It sits facing one of the massive unshielded windows, and at this time in our orbit, when the distant dyson swarm lines up and the Haze isn't in the wrong place, I can sit in a warm sunbeam while I look "down" on the Earth.

It is . . . hard. It is always hard. To see, to be burdened to know what is at stake. To feel like I am alone, and small, against a terrifying universe. But then I feel the sun sink into my old bones, and I watch the green, orange, white, and blue ball turn, and I allow myself to stop thinking. To set down the weight of responsibility for just a minute. To feel the beauty around me, to experience having a full stomach and a soft bed. To be what I *used to be*, and not what I have become.

An alarm sounds.

I am mobile again. There is no true division in my thoughts; I cannot separate myself from the knowledge I need or the actions I must be prepared to take.

The comms center is the destination for this particular klaxon tone. One of the comms centers. This one is the only one I have used in a long time, except for trying some tricks with other uncrewed orbitals. It is for short-range, line-of-sight, surface-to-orbit conversations, and someone has just called.

I never bother to ask how they get the frequencies. I just answer. A challenge all on its own; the space station, for all its power, lacks text-to-speech capability. And modern devices don't even make static clicks like older radios do. So I make do. I accept the incoming communication request and activate the carefully machine-manufactured conversation tool I have designed and set next to the input point.

Which is to say, I swat a bell.

The chime is clean and will be heard by whoever below has called to me. It always is. I harden my heart as best I can and prepare to receive their words.

There is a *lie* that cats do not care.

I care, with a fury the clouded sun cannot hope to match.

The voice comes through, an older dialect, but still one I understand. "Vis est actking-kapitan Jude Marsall." The young man's voice is shaking. He is not meant to be a kapitan, and he knows it. A field promotion. I know what he is going to say before he does, but that does not make this easier. I have heard these calls two thousand times, but that does not make this easier. He says the next words like a ritual, enunciation stilted as he reads from the ancient copy of a protocol established two centuries ago and passed down in whispers. "Category two em . . . em . . . emergence? Request for purification. Target on broadcast." And then, softer and off script, "Ahplease." A prayer to be heard.

I have heard it all before.

They can cry out. Because someone *is* listening.

Before I begin my sprint to the command module I need to reach, I swat the bell again. Once, twice, three times. *I hear you*, I want to scream. *Hold on.*

The comms officer's seat I leap out of spins frantically in my wake. If there were papers on the desk, they would be blown backward by the gale in the wake of my sprint. But there aren't, and I have no other dramatic trappings to show how fast I can move. So instead, believe me when I say that I move *fast* when I want to. I need to slip through two low- or zero-G areas to get where I need to be, where I've already decided I will render aid from. If I am fast enough, lucky enough, I will be in time. I spin off the ceiling in a rough flip as I hit the gravity again, using the plates to build more momentum instead of losing any. The last corner, through a hatch I never close anymore, is a bound off a curved wall hanging that I have convinced the cleaning nanos is "art," so they will not remove it.

Then I am in the cradle. The one, *one* part of the space station I had painstakingly tailored for myself. I lie back, and molded cushioning supports my insufficient spine. The station obeys my yowling demands for information, pulling up scanner feeds and statistical readouts in AR form. My paws find the controls I need, and I go to work.

The emergence event is in what used to be Australia. Scanners did not find it, as it occurred underground, but now that we have a spot to sweep, the exact location is easy to find. There are humans still down there, and the eagle eyes of the station's many, *many* ground-pointed detection systems shows the smoke and blood and gunfire in both full color and a cold tactical map.

And there is actking kapitan Jude. In a trench at the front line, covered in mud and barely hanging on. He is clutching the ancient comms stick like a warding stone, and at this angle, I can read the hopeless prayers on his lips. Even through the fear and blood around him, he fires his rifle relentlessly into the swarm approaching. Some kind of insect thing this time. I know it's a human thing to feel your hair going gray, but I swear the white on my boot patterns gets longer every time I go through this.

No time. Be morose later. Paw out, flick switch, select option. Somewhere, in the bowels of the station, an auto-loader slots a tool into place. Another flick selects a secondary tool, which arms and sings a hymn as it comes to life, deck-plates vibrating as the void batteries are discharged into reality.

Paw on the joystick. I trace a line on the map, double-check, then confirm the firing sequence while I am already setting up the next run. My orbit has me in the firing basket for forty-eight more seconds. I must make this quick. I queue up two more passes, not even bothering to check the computer's execution; it will be correct, it always is. I have my own task—targeting.

Emergence points defy causal data. Inorganic minds cannot perceive them properly. It is why the space station takes so much in terms of objective readings and data points, but it cannot be set to autokill the breaches. It simply cannot find the things, no matter how much evidence points to them.

I look at visual charts, breach-creation "migration patterns," and a weather map. I find it in six seconds. My paw pulls the trigger, and I feel a satisfying secondary shock as my chosen tool launches.

By this point, the void ray has cleaved through several thousand of the bug things, which I take a satisfaction in. The kapitan thinks the world is ending around him, and in a way, he's right.

Two seconds later, the grade-three groundstriker slams into the ground above the target. Then through the ground. Then roughly two miles past the target, leaving behind a trail of molten rock and vaporized exogalactic phenomena. And then, I'm out of the firing basket. Win or lose, they're on their own for another three hours at least.

I allow myself to relax back into the cradle with a huff of breath. I think I forgot to breathe on the run here, again. I order the station to show me the time and mewl out on reflex in consternation. There's no way I have enough time for a decent nap now. And I never nap in the cradle. It's . . . wrong.

Crawling back out into the station's hallway, I make my way toward the galley. A snack sounds good now. I've got chores in thirty minutes, and then our orbit . . . my orbit . . . takes me over the Haze. Almost always at least one problem there, and we're overstocked on splatter rounds anyway.

It's always like this. But this time . . . well, I'm not supposed to check. I tell myself every time not to check. But I check anyway. And this time, the kid lived. The humans lived. Maybe they're not the good guys, maybe there's more complex forces at play, maybe I should be impartial and not meddle.

I don't know, I'm a space station owner, not a political science major. Yet. Haven't finished those books yet.

But the kid lived.

So I strut a little bit as I head to get a snack.

My name is Lily ad-Alice. First, and only, member of the species *Felis astra*. Honorary human, self-imposed conscript in a very long war.

I own a space station. I am smarter than I should be. I am very old. I keep an eye on things up here.

You've met me at an eventful time in my life.

CHAPTER 2

Here is a fun fact! Human creativity mixed with the raw computing power of a variety of different information storage systems has, over the years, led to a lot of parallel solutions to the same problems.

The biggest example, from back when "information storage systems" meant "paper and, if you're lucky, a *good* pen," is guns. Plenty of cultures developed shovels in the absence of each other, and those shovels are, let's be real here, pretty much all the same shovel. The inflexible human desire to not get your fingers dirty is universal.

Guns, though? Tons of different ways to shape a barrel, shape a projectile, propel a projectile, and craft a device that can be actually aimed. Permutations in the thousands, some of them just born from manufacturing errors or limitations that became tradition that became standards. It's like a very clean example of the evolution of violence. And that was before there were computer models to design better, bigger guns. Guns too large or too small to stop, guns that fired from or into orbit. Guns that killed selectively, or not at all.

The digital age really let humans come up with a lot of innovative ways to kill the shit out of each other.

What I'm getting at here is that my space station has a *lot* of different guns on it. We've got cannon batteries, missiles, lasers . . .

Wait, no! That wasn't what I was getting at at all! I got sidetracked being mildly sarcastic about how "smart" your fucking smart weapons are.

The parallel-solution thing. Multiple solutions to the same problem. You know where else it shows up? Medical technology.

It's a lot smarter, there, too. Global pandemic ravaging your population? Get multiple sources working on a vaccine all at once. If one vaccine turns out to not work, or have side effects, or just falter in production, you've got backups to pick up the slack. It ensures a security of species that most individual humans won't care about but that keeps your civilizations ticking along.

The station has *three* medical facilities on it. That I can get into. And that identify as medical facilities. One of them it was originally built with, and it's your standard Oceanic Anarchy affair. Durable, useful, and not designed for me. It has an automated surgical suite that can patch up any damage I take, and a medication calibrator that can deal with illness, infection, or cosmic radiation poisoning. Illness and infection don't really occur in space that often; basically everything here is biologically sterile, and if some extra-galactic bacteria do make it onto the station, odds are good either it won't do anything to me, or it'll kill me so fast I won't notice.

The second facility used to be a research lab. If you're thinking to yourself, "Lily, didn't you say your naptime zone *also* used to be a research lab?" then very good! You remembered my name! I appreciate that. Also, yes, there are a lot of things that used to be labs.

I think at one point between the Anarchy building it and my own people finding and moving into it, one of the interim residents of the station was a Real American noble of some kind. In the first twenty years here, I was constantly running into sealed-off doors in weird places that led to untouched or, worse, ransacked laboratories. It's likely that's also where half the guns came from, if we're being honest. It certainly explains why there are *seven* different orbital-insertion hunt-and-kill heavy drone bays stapled onto the station in various places. All of those are empty, and while technically I have the foundry and also a couple different material fabricators and parts printers, I've never felt the need to rebuild those particular machines from the schematics.

Anyway, labs. Used to be a lab, turned into medical. Or maybe it was a medical lab. Either way, it has the vivification pods, which are *not* Oceanic Anarchy tech. I actually don't know what culture built them, because there are no notes, and the station AR doesn't have any record of them being brought on board. But they work, and they work really, really well.

The medlab also has no user manual, safety shutoff, or other health and safety measures that you probably ought to have around machinery that can regrow limbs by accident.

How do I know that? Good question!

No further questions!

Medical facility three is where I'm trying to wedge some of my precious free time into today, and it's kind of the coolest one. It's very future-tech in the design: lots of swooping shapes to the walls and furniture, lots of chrome.

It looks like it was built by people who built function and form with equal regard, and that's cool. Maybe a little opulent, but hey, if your society wants to build geometric art and smooth edges into everything, I'm not gonna complain.

It's also one of the many, many chunks of the station that aren't native architecture. And I know this because I was the one to capture it and add it to my home.

I should explain something about the orbital space around Earth.

It is, being incredibly charitable, messy. Being less charitable, and borrowing a phrase from my own mother, it is a "hot melty mess of garbage, broken toys, and weaponry, which is just another word for garbage."

At a certain point, the majority of things launched into orbit began to be equipped with powerful magnets, tuned so they could just slide around each other and maybe maintain stable orbit, instead of slamming together and for sure wasting millions of units of value. This made the problem slightly less bad going forward, but it didn't really attend to the junk and debris already up there. So people started launching sweeper satellites, collector drones, and all sorts of other cleanup tools. Most of them are still up here. Along with a few hundred thousand, or maybe a few million, or maybe more, other sats, stations, drones, and overhead guns.

My station is armored and shielded, but at least one shield eats up a lot of power the bigger a space it has to protect, and I don't have a ton of power to spare. Also, the armor isn't really super effective against high-speed micro-debris, because that stuff is pretty much all armor-piercing space bullets at this point.

So that's the backstory. The daily reality is, I practically bump into a few hundred juicy targets every day. And that reflex to coil up and pounce on a particularly stupid piece of prey has never actually left me, even if there aren't rats or laser pointers to chase up here. So containing myself is difficult.

This medical lab is one of the times I did not contain myself.

It was early on, it was *right there*, and I wanted it. So a few gravity tethers, a healthy application of liquid metal sealant, and a maintenance droid that probably wished it had taken the day off, and we'd attached it to my station.

Then the usual routine. Decontamination of a dozen types, followed by careful examination to make sure none of the buttons would kill me if I pushed them.

And then I had myself a new medlab.

I have tried, really hard, to not add too much to the station. Our power core is stretched thin, like I said, and most things up here aren't worth it anyway. But in this case, I think I was right to do so, even if it was impulsive and stupid. Because the end result was that I got less impulsive and stupid.

The medlab is an uplift facility. They'd spent forty years and trillions of kronar trying to figure out how to make smart fish. Probably for some evil purposes, but that might be me being biased against fish.

The thing about parallel solutions to problems—*yeah, we're back around to this*—is that by the time they decided they wanted to build a fanatical undersea army, a lot of this research had been going on for a while. And stored in the databases here were more than a few tricks that applied to *cats*.

It took me years, actual years of my early life, to figure out how to get the station to accept the new medlab as part of itself. Then to get the data to the *correct* medbay, with its medication synthesizer. And all of this was after it taking months to even conceive of the fact that I should try in the first place.

The first dose made me very sick, and I decided to never do it again. The second dose made me very sick, and I decided to never do it again. The third dose made me very sick, and one day later, it was like I'd woken up for the very first time.

The process compressed brain mass, improved neuron flow, rewired parts of my cognition to be faster, smoother. And then a secondary procedure to fill the new gaps in my skull with more of this improved gray matter. It wasn't so much that it "made me smart" as it made me *able to think*. No longer did I have to spend a decade stupidly learning just how to access an AR interface. No more yowling helplessly at closed doors that I didn't understand how to open. The station was *mine* and, for the first time, I knew it.

Around then was when I really started to grow up. It was close after that when I fired my first shot. Some days, I regret my change immensely.

And yet, here I am, spending my free time trying to continue the work. Trying to see if there's enough in common with an uplifted carp and my own unique mind to pry some tricks out of that and rewire myself again. Because sometimes, smarter isn't smart enough.

And, and I say this as another alarm beings to sound, red and orange hexagons springing to life in the AR around me, there is one other serious goal I have in mind.

I spring off the desk where a hardwired and slightly burned-out monitor contains the secrets of a dozen genomes. Time enough for that later. I have already evaluated the alarm and checked the readout. Energy discharge, consistent with weapons fire, coming from primary lunar orbit toward the surface of that moon.

This happens sometimes. Old weapons platforms get twitchy, their AI goes mad. I try to talk to them sometimes, but my therapy capabilities are limited when they do not have hands with which to pet my luxuriousness, nerves with which to extract joy from the touch of my fur.

A shame. I should build them hands!

No! Bad idea. My brain is expanded beyond even human baseline, and yet still, half my ideas are stupid on arrival.

I run through smooth metal and plastic corridors, keeping my claws retracted so my soft paws can let me slide across the floors when I need to take corners. There is a short way to my destination, but I do not take it. It would require going through the cold storage room, and I . . . will not. Not now.

So I loop around the outside, and then up and over a ladder into gravity that feels slightly off, the grav plates here a little at odds with the primary "down" of the station. And eventually arrive at an "upward"-facing blister pod.

The more detailed scanners built into this weapons pod confirm it: there's absolutely a platform firing on the primary moon. Which is, I'm kind of sad to say, pretty normal around here.

It's fine, though. All the surviving lunar cities are either *really* heavily shielded, or underground, or both. Though from the looks of things, whatever this platform is, it's just hitting flat regolith anyway.

My orbit takes me into range for a clean shot in two minutes. If there was an immediate risk, I could just pull the trigger and vaporize whatever space-based infrastructure was between me and the rogue. Or, if I was feeling spicy, deploy a guided projectile and pilot it in from here with the AR. But there's no rush.

The blister pod actually has windows, which is, I am aware, kind of stupid. But I suspect whoever built the medlab made this place, too; I even tried to keep my cat-shaped comfort modifications in the style when I had the nanos reshape it.

The windows are some kind of stupidly durable crystal lattice. I tried clawing at them once—I tried clawing everything once, because, as previously mentioned, I used to be stupid—and it didn't do a damn thing. I'm pretty sure the hull will shatter before the windows, which makes me wonder why we didn't build the hull out of the same stuff. Maybe it was a later invention.

Through the windows, I can actually see the primary moon now. The mess of spacebound entities is clearing up a bit, giving me a reasonably good view. I meow a command at the AR, and a magnification window opens before my left eye, giving me a high-definition look at the target.

It's one of those weirdly shaped weapons platforms, from some old religious war. I was alive for it, but not "around," if you know what I mean. The thing is two four-sided pyramids, with their bases kept gravitationally locked just over the central orb that contains the AI core and main weaponry.

A twisting lilac energy lashes out from it. An early-model void beam, from back when humans and not cats were designing the firing algorithms. It is already in contact with the surface, writhing in an organic pattern across the dusty white rock.

Void beams are almost beautiful to look at. I wonder if that's what the AI thinks, too.

The AR pings me; we'll be in range in thirty seconds.

I watch it fire again, watch the lilac light trace another line across the surface. My chest is still aching from the sprint here; I could have taken my time, but that's more of a human way of doing things. I think humans take their whole "walking steadily" thing for granted sometimes.

Almost in range now. One of the moons is huge and beautiful above me. Soon, I'll add the weapons platform as debris to its surface, but even though I'm cosmically littering, at least I'm lowering the risk of "inclement incineration" as a weather report.

Ten seconds left, and I can see, suddenly, the damage to the surface. My paw is already pressed halfway down on the button that activates this laser array, but it isn't too late. I twist, grabbing my early attempt at a cat-based firing control in my fangs.

On the moon's surface, written in old Chinese, still glowing pale purple-white, are three words. Fifty meters tall, and still tiny against the rocky terrain. If I hadn't been watching the firing, I never would have seen them.

I Am Alone

The platform's AI isn't breaking down. Or, I guess, it is, but not in the malfunction kind of way. It's crying, in the only two languages it was ever given: Chinese, and orbit-to-ground fire.

Micrometer precision is a *challenge* to attain when you're trying to guide a laser array with your teeth. Especially when your neck doesn't have the range of motion you've been *trying* to get your genetics to comply with. But I manage.

Gently, carefully, I guide a nuclear-intensity beam of blue light across the weapon platform's lunar poetry.

I don't know what protocols it uses, I don't know how to connect with it in a way that matters. But I will have an entire lap around the Earth to start to find out. And both of us have been up here for a very long time, so I'm banking that it will be okay with a little waiting.

My station passes out of clean firing range, then out of range of anything except my most dangerous tools.

The platform has stopped firing, now closed off, hovering in orbit. Perhaps it is thinking, perhaps it has given up. Maybe it sees me as a threat, or maybe as a potential friend. AI minds are hard for me to understand. They were hard for *humans* to understand, and they made the damn things.

Either way, I have added my own message to the moon. Assuming the translation that the station's AR fed me was accurate.

I Am Not Alone

Now. I've got about three hours to cross-reference what war that thing was from and figure out how to talk to it.

I check my schedule. I can postpone . . . the nap. Yes. Just this once. And maybe only *one* snack today. Can't put off overwatch on the Haze, and I *really* can't avoid retuning the sensors for whatever active camouflage the converter swarm is trying this time. For not the first time, I desire the ability to truly *scream* at whoever required verbal authentication for automated maintenance procedures. But if I really, really do my best time on my daily runaround, then I can probably have a solid twenty minutes to solve this problem.

For the first time in centuries, I might be about to make a friend.

I am vibrating with excitement as I launch myself down the upper level's ladder. I am also, I realize as I fail to eat more than half my lunch, *terrified*.

It can't be that hard, right? Humans do this all the time. And I am, objectively, superior to humans. After all, no human currently owns a space station. That's gotta count for something.

My pep talk to myself accomplishes nothing. I begin my patrol to yell at maintenance bots. It takes my mind off things.

And yet. I am plagued by excited optimism.

I am going to make a friend.

CHAPTER 3

I've mentioned before—frequently, and I will continue to do so—that paws aren't actually designed for micrometer control of orbital weaponry. I am now invoking my right to mention it again.

Paws are so bad for this.

There's the usual things you can probably expect, like how feline forelegs don't actually have the same range of motion that human arms do, or how I just don't have the muscle strength to keep up repeated motions like this. One of those is fair! I cannot change my bones. I also have more trouble than you'd expect with my toes. Those little pads that are great for gripping lots of different surfaces? They slide *right* off whatever miracle material this one specific stupid control stick is made of.

That said, here's a weird thing. There's a joke that no human has ever seen a gorilla that's actually *tried* to be buff. That joke has been out of date for about two centuries, and I don't particularly want to explain why right now, but it's a pretty good look at how humans think sometimes. A weird little quirk, a notice that the natural world doesn't mirror their own lived experience, that kind of humor at the absurdity of their lives compared to everything else. It's also a great segue into the fact that I *can* work out.

It doesn't actually do as much as you'd think, but I do have a physical training regimen, along with a series of supplements and boosters that the medbay can synthesize for me, and if it came to a weight-lifting contest . . .

I would still lose to a mildly out-of-shape teenage human. But! I would beat every cat on the planet, so that's not nothing. It's just another thing I'm the best at. Right up there with maneuvering a control stick.

I said it was *hard*, I never said I couldn't do it.

Currently, I'm in a slow orbit over the Haze. I try to make sure my orbital trail doesn't really take me overhead that often, because it's awful, and I hate it, even though my presence is kind of relevant for human-rights reasons.

I've mentioned the Haze before, and unlike my complaining, I may choose never to mention it again, depending on how angry I get over the next few hours and if I decide that dropping a counteragent into it is my optimal course of action. Because the Haze is two things in equal measure: it is very consistent in the behaviors it is consistent in, and it is *very* erratic in everything else.

The Haze is a chemical compound. As far as the station's scanners can determine—and again, they can determine practically anything that's dumb enough to sit on the surface of the planet below—it is a chemical compound that is orders of magnitude more complex than anything else in the database.

I once checked the database specifically, which was itself an adventure in coming up with new meow patterns to teach the station. The jump between the largest mundane chemical stored and the size of the pattern of the Haze was *comical*.

But "it's big and complicated" isn't actually a very good description. See, the Haze is alive. Alive, and interested in staying that way. Which is a really big problem for a number of reasons.

It doesn't specifically hurt anyone, but some of the things it needs to sustain itself, it can only get from humans or dogs. And as funny as that whole "ancient rivalry" supposedly is, I actually like both of those species. And the Haze . . . well, it doesn't hate them or anything, but it just doesn't care. So on a fairly regular timetable, it'll roll over an outlying village, or sometimes a whole city if it's feeling ambitious, and just take over.

Oh right. It does mind control. I don't know how, it doesn't matter. Don't worry about it.

When I first started my investigation of the surface, I didn't fully understand what I was looking at. The Haze doesn't kill people, but it also doesn't need them for anything aside from organically producing the substances it needs to keep going. If it has access to humans with a high enough tech level, it also uses their thumbs to make some more advanced trace compounds, which I like to pretend are its dessert.

But just because it doesn't kill people doesn't mean it doesn't cause people to die. The Haze has no concept of children, of a life cycle, or of personal needs beyond eating enough to keep the chemicals flowing.

The first time I saw it . . . well, I thought it was a zombie outbreak. My mom used to love zombie movies. I used to love sitting on her lap while she watched them, and in retrospect with my enhanced intelligence, I have decided I hate zombie movies.

I killed a lot of people before the Haze retreated, leaving the survivors dazed, in a ruined city, surrounded by the dead I'd made. I almost gave up entirely right then.

When the Haze moved for another village, I threatened it. I fired a dozen rounds into the ground ahead of it, kicked up enough dust that it might as well have been an impassible wall for the chemical creature. I *still* don't know how it moves, and I suspect it's got something paracausal in its makeup beyond the simple physical. But I do know it needs clear air to pass through, and that let me keep it walled off.

Eventually, it changed course, but if I tried to keep that up forever, I'd run out of ammo well before it ran out of energy. So I tried something else.

The ammo is called "splatter rounds," and I have no idea why the fabricator has a plan for them. They use subspace tap liquid and a specially formulated explosive to airburst highly toxic substances across a wide area. I used a bunch of them, all at once, and that turned out to be a really stupid idea.

It obviously hurt the Haze, that wasn't in question. But it also seems like it pressured it into the kind of devious creativity that any intelligent creature is capable of when their life is on the line. The thing took over a colony of modified moles, using their tunnels and bodies recklessly to avoid my scanners and explode out into the air again where I didn't really expect it. Weaker, but still alive, and too close to people to safely bombard with anything that would work.

So I tried something new, expressing some creativity myself.

I let it take a village. And then, a few days later, I shelled the territory outside. Gradually walked my fire into the center of the buildings. And the Haze got the message and left. A couple people died from dehydration, but no mass casualties or long-term control.

After about a month or two of this game, we established a pattern. The Haze takes a population center. I give it a few days, then put a low-power laser through its center. It starts to withdraw, and in behavior that I find unnervingly familiar, it follows the laser on the surface away from wherever it'd taken. In an effort to make things easy for the people, I try to keep it on a pretty big loop of population centers, with no one having to suffer it more than a couple days every few months. Sometimes, it doesn't even need my guidance, which shows it's been learning at least a little.

That's what I'm doing right now. Or *trying* to do, anyway. I've started our little ritual, putting a low-power beam into the village square of where it's currently staying and warming up the stone fountain sitting there. But the Haze is just ignoring it, even though the laser is technically enough to burn away its . . .

Hang on.

I meow a command at the AR displays, turning slightly in the rotating stool that I'm sitting on to operate the station's mining laser. I really should build another cradle for this, if I'm gonna be doing it every week for the rest of my eternal life.

The station's computer system responds to my reasonable demand for information and pulls up a long-range spectrometer map of the surrounding area.

Well, shit. If I had hands, I'd . . . well, I mean, we've been talking about this. There's so many things I'd do with hands. I could *pet myself*! I would also give a small applause for the Haze, which has, it seems, learned.

It has learned a very stupid lesson, but it's *learned*.

The fountain in the center of the village, the geographic center of the Haze's current occupied zone, contains no trace of the Haze.

Normally, the annoyingly intelligent idiot cloud does what clouds normally do; it fills out its volume equally. Oh sure, it moves under its own power, and it keeps the air it inhabits at a certain concentration of itself, so it is always in a rough dome shape of consistent size. But it *feels* like it's following the rules of a gas.

Not anymore, though! Now it has a clean doughnut pattern, a torus with a perfect spot that I wasn't lasering at all.

I let out a laughing mewl. This is, undoubtedly, the funniest thing that has happened in weeks. It's like a kitten hiding the scrap of food it was playing with, pretending that slightly out of sight was a good enough concealment spot.

Carefully, slowly, I drag the laser into its mass. The Haze actually *sagged* a bit on the sensors, like it had been so excited to show its new trick, and I just ignored it. Tail flicking behind myself, I guide the beam back into the clear area, give it a couple circles around the clear area just on the edge of the Haze, and then cut a clean line down a street toward the edge of the township.

The Haze appears to appreciate my acknowledgment of its prowess. It perks up as I heat the stones in the fountain, and follows with a quickness it normally lacks as I take it out of town. I take the laser off as soon as it's moving a bit more, pushing it off on its way as it begins the three- or four-day trek to its next destination.

I watch on the AR screen for a while longer, making sure it has withdrawn from everyone in the village, making sure it's still moving. It is strange to see it acting so different. Strange and worrying; it has diverged before, and more than once it has led to deaths. But right now . . . well, reshaping itself, and reacting to *me*, that's not too bad, is it?

I hope not.

As fun as the diversion of the Haze has been, the whole process has eaten up more time than I wanted it to, and I'm behind on my space chores again.

I bolt out of the stool, a little extra kick in my frantic sprint around the station today. It doesn't take me a lot of self-reflection to understand that I'm excited about the development with the Haze. Between that and the ongoing development of a communication technique for the living weapons platform, I could have *two* friends in the near future!

Or, well, okay. One friend, and one gaseous pet. Let's not get too excited.

The station blurs around me as I let my body flow into the centuries-old loop of movement. Hallway, hallway, maintenance closet. Meow at the drones, authorize cleaning. Hallway, door, zero-G chute, foundry. Meow, meow, check inventory, meow again to say that *yes* it's okay to continue turning processed materials into class-three groundstrikers. Hallway, loooooong corridor, medlab, passing meow to keep making my medical supplements, hallway, meow at the station's nanoswarm *in the specific location it thinks I should be standing in* to tell it that it's okay to clear the air filters. Hallway. Low-gravity bounce. Galley. Lunch!

Lunch has never been good. I hate it. This is the worst. I wish I had never modified my mind so I could understand flavor. This is torture. I need to capture another station with hydroponics, or escaped lab animals I can eat.

Back to the chores.

Now it's time for the more intellectual parts of the day.

I do a little work on my ongoing uplift project, trying to figure out how to reshape my physical body to have thumbs, or how to be able to think at double speed. Whatever. I'm not feeling the work today; my body is a constant limitation, but my dysphoria isn't as bad on days when I don't miss shots.

A big part of my time here is spent sweeping the information about the surrounding orbital objects. The station, as it tends to do, has a lot of information but is abjectly unwilling to make assumptions or guesses. It's part of why it always wants me to authorize things; it *will not* assume a yes. It's kind of polite, but very frustrating sometimes. So I have to do the final logical leaps myself on scanner data like this.

We've got eighteen satellites "around us." Around us is, like, within a kilometer. Close, but not in the danger zone. Some of the deeper scans can list off power use, and signal intercepts, and it's not hard to classify them all as comms sats. There are another dozen things that probably *were* comms sats at one point but are dead objects now. No power running, no signs of life.

One dead cargo ship, which I've seen before. It's one of the big corporate haulers meant to ferry goods to and from an offworld colony, probably Mars, but this one's missing all its hauler pods and has been dead in orbit for years. Sorry, StarBound Inc.! Your hardware didn't last as long as your advertising campaign did!

Hundreds of tiny bits of debris, bolts and screws, chunks of rock or metal. I filter out anything below a certain size.

One other station. This one isn't close; it's maybe five klicks away, easily within engine range. Another familiar face; if there's anyone alive there, they politely ignore me if they see me, and I do them the same favor. It used to be one of those joint-government projects, before the governments in question went to war again and the astronauts on board became citizens of the stars. I'm not sure if there's anyone left there or if it's been empty for a while, but I do know it's tagged as a source of replacement parts if our engines ever fail.

Nothing hostile, nothing radioactive enough to matter, nothing alive. Just me up here. As always.

I can actually, when I want to, sigh. I do so now. It never helps. It doesn't help now.

If I hurry through the rest of this, I can have some time to go sigh in the sun, though. So I wrap up my checklist for this cycle.

Arrange a to-do list for tomorrow. Doesn't take long. And then, one final check of the surface below. Nothing going on except for . . .

Are you kidding me?

There's an army on the move across Risen Atlantic. An army I deploy some choice profanity toward as I notice it.

I double-check, make sure this isn't a mistake. And sure enough, it isn't. Three thousand soldiers—and they are flagrantly soldiers—on the move across the artificial continent, heading for one of the land bridges to Eurasia. It looks like a mix of human and feathermorphs, all of them equipped with the finest salvaged old-world guns they could find. At the head of their army, a human woman in glittering golden and red armor holds aloft a beam saber, shouting dramatic speeches.

It takes me eighteen minutes of precious naptime to verify that this is not a defensive army, nor a response militia.

All right, nuking fine, I think to myself as I sink into the cradle. I damn well warned them.

Paws or not, from here I have all the precision I need to nail the leader right in their stupid helmet. Them and roughly a hundred of their closest—physically closest—followers, that is. Class-ones are pretty small, but there *is* a floor to the amount of devastation I can cause.

The station vibrates as the round is launched away. Several seconds later, the front of the army vanishes in a plume of kicked-up dirt, ash, and bits of meaningless vainglory. Topographical scans show that there is a new crater, though not a very large one. Even if this were the only road in the area, and it isn't, I wouldn't be cutting off trade or anything with my attack.

I don't even bother to watch if they scatter. I'll be back overhead in thirty hours. If the army has managed to find a new idiot in that time . . . well, let's say it like this:

I haven't been building class-threes because they're the most important. They're just the ones I'm not topped out on.

Firing on the denizens of Earth is always an iffy feeling for me. On the one hand, I am their self-appointed protector. I'm supposed to be keeping these people safe, not murdering them. And I don't kid myself; this is murder. There is no chance left in existence that they could even pretend to challenge me. If someone down there managed to unearth, repair, power, and aim a surface-to-orbit railgun, then there is still a very high chance that they're firing a *cargo cannon* and not something that has any hope of breaching my shields. Assuming they've found a real weapon, then whatever ammo they put in it most likely won't survive being fired, and neither will the gun, especially once any of the million dormant weapons systems up here notice something trying to get out of atmosphere. And *even then*, the station has multiple defenses and redundancies in case I actually *do* get hit.

They can't hurt me. But I can kill them with a flick of my tail. And the thought makes me a little queasy. The fact that I am essentially committing an act of self-defense on the part of whatever collection of villages and bunkers they were going to conquer and pillage makes me feel better. The further fact that this is not the first time it's happened, and they *should* know better than to test me, makes me feel better still.

Not good. Just well enough that I don't hate myself for it. And stable enough to not misdirect my anger to the idiots who are now distributed through the local area that they planned to use as a marching route.

It's not their fault, for most of them. Idiots caught up with a charismatic demagogue. I've seen it before. I'll see it again. I'll stop it then, too.

They might think they're smarter than the last one, that they've accounted for all the angles. But lemme tell you: it's kind of hard to predict orbital feline interdiction.

CHAPTER 4

There's an alarm going off again.

I am aware of the alarm going off, because for safety reasons, I am not allowed to disable alarms. If you're thinking something along the lines of "But you shouldn't disable alarms? That seems unsafe," then you're correct. But I'm over four hundred years old, and you don't really make it that far without building up at least a few reckless habits. And a hatred of alarms.

See, it's entirely possible that I *could* turn off the alarms? Like I've said, there isn't actually documentation for a lot of the operations of this station. It's quite likely that half the alarms spit out by maintenance issues are things that should never be coming up, because I'm missing maintenance check-ins that I just don't know exist.

Now, you might be thinking something else at this point. Something about how four hundred years is kind of a long time, and maybe I should know more about the station I live on. And I'm not gonna lie, you're probably right. Though to be fair, I did spend something like . . . what, seventy years? . . . as a perfectly ordinary immortal Terran housecat with an unreasonably good memory. I've also spent a combined total of maybe a decade or two in vivification pods, for reasons I do *not* care to explain, thank you!

And yeah, that leaves kind of a long time. I get that. I've got *priorities*, though! And I mean, seriously, priorities beyond just napping. Although I actually do need to sleep. I'm immortal, not invincible, or immune to biological requirements. Probably. Mostly. Sort of. Anyway, just because telomere decay can't touch me doesn't mean that I'm wasting time when I kick back on my favorite nap couch and catch a few hours of rest.

Most of my priorities have been learning various things and teaching the station to understand me. Learning was a massive hurdle to cross, though, again, even before my uplift I was still able to learn. You know how a cat can figure out how to open a door in a month or so if properly taught? Yeah, given a few decades all alone, it's possible for a perfectly normal cat to learn how to open an AR window. How to access some basic controls. How to read. That kind of thing.

Okay, I said that, and then instantly realized just how much that makes it sound like I'm lying about the totally normal thing. We'll come back to that later, when I have more emotional processing power.

The biggest problem really was the amount of time it took to create a translation database from Cat to English. I can actually read several languages at this point, but the station can't exactly understand me without some really, *really* confusing software doing work that doesn't always actually translate things properly into what I want. I've got a lot of basic stuff, like "yes" and "no," down pretty well. But there's a lot of times, especially any time I tell you that I've made an information request from one of the AR windows, where what I'm really doing is screaming something that approximates a "number code" that just hits a specific virtual button, which I took a long time to set up previously.

Imagine having to operate a computer without a mouse. Do you need to click on something? You can kind of do that. The screen is split into sectors; you can pick one, then it divides that section, and you pick one of those new sectors. And so on, until you've narrowed it down enough that a click can happen. It's *that*, but I have to do it by meowing. Clearly enough for the audio nanos, too. Which, for all that they are basically magic, is still a *lot* cleaner than how I had gotten used to "speaking" over the course of my life.

I guess what I'm saying is, there's a reason that long stretches of my daily hours are devoted to writing new code. It can be tedious. But at least it motivates me to do it right the first time.

And also it's a convenient excuse for why I haven't explored more of the station.

There are a lot of doors that require specific commands to access. Commands I technically have the authority to give but lack the documentation to know. And the station doesn't care that I'm allowed, only if I know the passcode, which makes me feel a little like a wizard sometimes. Casting a hundred spells of repair or unlock a day.

I mentioned an alarm. That was a thing that was happening. In the intervening time that it has taken me to complain about being unable to directly interface my brain with a compiler, and also complain about how the alarms have no off switch, I have switched off the alarm.

Well, okay, I acknowledged it and removed the reason for the alarm. It was a low-risk emergence event happening just over the surface of what used to be the Pacific Ocean. I took care of what came out of it with void beam fire and then basically just held down the button on the ion array until the hole in reality went away. Not my favorite way to handle these things, drained a couple batteries, but you can't exactly make a hot enough crater to kill an emergence when you're firing orbital weaponry into the water. It doesn't have enough initial energy discharge.

If I made the experience of cleaning up extradimensional monsters sound like a chore, or like it was easy, then that is correct. Good job.

The thing is, access to weapons designed to kill armies, biomechs, cities, and spaceships is *kind of* an unfair advantage against creatures that fundamentally lack the ability to shoot back. I am *in orbit*. I say that a lot, but I don't think a lot of minds inherently comprehend just how far away "orbit" is from where *they* are.

A decent-shape human jumping straight up from a standing position can, on average, make about two feet of lift. Assume that you don't fall back down after doing that. You would need to do that jump roughly a hundred and twenty thousand times to make it to the *edge* of space around Earth.

I am not perched on the edge. You will need to keep jumping. You will not make it.

Orbital bombardment makes the solution of a lot of problems pretty easy, if we're being honest. It really highlights *why* humanity put so many guns up here over the years. Though the application of mutually assured destruction does go a long way to explaining why Earth isn't more of a burning series of craters by now than it already is, it also doesn't account for the fact that we've ended up in a situation where I am the last one left.

There's no mutual balance to be had. Just me, my drifting home, a stock-pile of ammo, and a series of targets ranging from "yup!" to "eugh . . ." on the sliding scale of morally acceptable.

Really, the only thing that I *can't* do with a railgun and the auspices of gravity is diplomacy. I am so bad at diplomacy.

Normally this is where I would blame the lack of thumbs, but it's really a lot worse than that. I lack the ability to vocalize most terrestrial languages. And owing to a series of political decisions from several past owners of this station, there is no actual way for me to translate my voice, or even have words spoken aloud.

The past owners of this station were, in several cases, absolute assholes. Racist, xenophobic, anthropocentric assholes. Just a big series of jerks, especially as the other ships and stations started to go dark and the people making it up here were the ones who were willing to *take* power and not just use an exploration budget for civilian exploration and research.

In a lot of ways, I love humanity. They built my home. They sort of created the science that led to my immortality *and* my intelligence. They've built a lot of impressive things, and through my spying . . . through my *businesslike scanning* of the surface, I've seen a thousand gestures of love, compassion, and heroism from them and the uplifts under the banner of Sol.

But yikes, some of them suck.

Fortunately, I have a railgun, and the high ground. And *yes*, my lack of ability to speak properly does severely limit any kind of diplomacy with the surface. It can feel weird, to have that thought that if only I could *speak*, I could maybe change the course of lives.

But other humans try to speak too, sometimes. And they all die the same on the conqueror blade, falling to those who were never interested in listening. So maybe unexpected bombardment masquerading as divine judgment is a kind of diplomacy on its own. A message to stop screwing around and go back to being human. And also petty revenge against the ideological strains that led to me being voiceless in the first place.

I continue through my daily routine with a little more of a morose mood than normal. Though I still catapult myself through the hallways as fast as I can. If I'm gonna be morose about the failings of those below me, then I'm going to be asleep for it, and if I move fast enough, my chores will be done just in time for the station to be on the right side of the planet for a sunbeam nap.

Captain's log. Update. Critical information. Lunch still awful.

Not even awful. Just empty. Bland. Every iota of flavor missing. It's like the void of space in my mouth, only with nutritional content.

Update number two. My communication package to the lunar weapons platform is ready.

I'm proud of this one. It took a lot of time to compile, but the computer did most of that. My work was in learning three new forms of Chinese over the last week and writing the basic code to get the station to actually do the work of creating a series of different contact attempts using our various comms systems. I didn't do the work, but I did figure out how to tell the computer to do the work, and that feels *so* much nicer.

Hopefully, in twelve hours, I can say hi.

Update number three. I have been lying to you. I do not keep captain's logs.

I close the command window and check what needs doing next. Nothing serious, just a review of the local scanner data. Maybe, if I'm lucky, a rogue spacebound garden will have wandered within grabbing range, and I can fuse it to my home. For . . . professional use.

Regardless, this can be done while lying down comfortably anywhere. So I leave the comms station and head for my nap zone.

I've been working in a secondary comms station, so I take a weird circuitous route back to where I want to be. The AR projects a map for me, but it keeps saying to go through a door that literally does not exist.

This happens sometimes. I swear the station isn't haunted. It just thinks there should be a room or hallway that never got built and is still on the schematics. It's not either me or the station AI being in alarmingly specific denial about anything.

As I move, slightly slower than normal as I go through hallways I don't normally use, I notice something.

There *is* a door here. Not the one that isn't real, just a door that I haven't ever been through.

It's not like I've never seen this door before. I've been here for a long time, I've been down all these halls and tunnels. Mostly. Maybe not all the maintenance shafts. But I haven't been through every door, and it always frustrates me when there's a part of what I think of as my territory locked off from me.

The thing that stands out here is that there's an AR projection on it. A pictographic glyph that I've seen before, in the long-ago archives of my memory, back when I was a normal pet. It was the symbol that was projected on my mom's door whenever she had company over and kicked me out.

Room in use. My brain fills in the information. *Come back later.*

My body ripples as my muscles tense up involuntarily. I find my back arching as I hiss at the door on reflex, the ancient reminder of what I've lost glowing red and blue over the bulkhead.

And then the AR flickers out. Like it was never there. Just a normal locked door to a crew cabin that I don't know the right command to open.

I orient myself and run the rest of the way to my nap zone. To sit in the sunlight, where the ghosts can't get me. Not, I remind myself, and everyone else, that the station is haunted.

It's just a hiccup in an overly complex system, manifesting in an unexpected way. The place is centuries old. It's earned a few quirks. I just wish they weren't ones that startle me like that.

I fall asleep reviewing scanner data and tagging dead satellites for recovery and conversion into material stockpiles later. The sun is warm, the couch is soft, and my heart has long since calmed down from my scare earlier. Now that I might be able to talk to the weapons platform, I need a new project, so before dozing off, I allocate some of my time tomorrow to digging through the station code again, looking for the unlock commands. Just for my own amusement, obviously.

I roll my belly into the sun, and must be dreaming, as I feel the sensation of fingers in my fur.

CHAPTER 5

It worked! I have made a friend!

Okay, so, that's a bit of a lie. I say "it worked" as if my original plan was a success. What I was not telling you was that it has been over a week of failed attempts trying to communicate with the old weapons platform in orbit around the primary moon.

I did manage to figure out when it was built, and why. About a century ago, for the Worshipper Wars that destroyed most of the lunar surface cities. It's called a "Divine Eye Three," in a way that is actually a really clever pun when written in the particular dialect of its builders.

The archives I have are incomplete, but I get the impression that the AI on this thing is smarter than this entire space station twice over. And far, *far* more capable of becoming bored.

So of course I tried to say hi.

Radio didn't work. Tight-beam communication didn't work. Subspace broadcast didn't work. *Superspace* broadcast didn't work, which surprised me, because that one's basically just screaming that works in a vacuum.

I'm not even sure why the station has a superspace antenna set up. Though the way the logs around it were scrubbed is the same kind of sloppy work that the Real America occupiers did when they tried to abandon ship. Which sort of makes me want to blame them for this idiot setup.

Of course, it *was* a viable option. It just didn't work. And at a certain point, I started to think it wasn't just my poor grasp of Chinese causing the problem.

So I switched to trying something a little more clever, and a little stupider.

It wasn't like we ride high on piles of wealth on this station, but I'm pretty sparing with how I spend the collected supplies that I acquire up here. There *is* a finite amount of junk I can turn into bullets, technically, but not by much;

it's mostly a matter of time to grab and smelt and shape the materials. So I've got some stockpiles to dip into, is what I'm saying.

And I did so, firing up a fabricator that I knew existed but had never actually physically visited. This actually required a minor spacewalk from me; the fabricator has an airlock, which I know how to open, but *not* the internal door.

Fun fact, it took less effort to get the station to make me a spacesuit than it did to get it to open a damn door. I mean, I made the suit two hundred years ago. Shortly after that, in a flight of childish fancy, I also made myself a "suit" that's really some kind of horrifying amalgamation of power armor and a strike craft. I have never had a reason to wear that one.

The fabricator is one I've never used because it's primarily for building drone chassis. And the station's maintenance bots are built somewhere else, or just kept up to standards by the local nanoswarm. Right now, though, a drone is exactly what I need.

It took less than two hours for the drone I needed to be assembled, outfitted, and fueled. That's legitimately less time than it takes for the foundry to make a railgun round; I think this replicator might be one of the fastest pieces of tech on the station, now that I've seen it in action.

After that, it was just a matter of adding one final touch and sending the thing off. Controlled, of course. I'm not trusting a program to guide this one, and not just because the station has so many security locks on that kind of thing that it might actually vent me out an airlock before letting me get away with it.

One pass of the drone by my target. Then another, making sure that the underside was revealed to the weapons platform that I *knew* could see the lunar surface. It must, *must* be able to see what I had sent its way.

I admit, I'd given a mewling wail of sorrow when I saw it open fire. Thin crackling lilac lashes opening up on the drone on the second pass. The scanners from both the station and the drone rendering it in detail. I'd been prepared to just give up then, except . . .

Except the drone didn't shut down. Didn't take critical damage. Just kept its trajectory and stayed under my remote command.

Curious, I brought it back to the station, docked it in one of the actual drone bays, which might be getting some actual work to do now, and went to check it out.

The underbelly of the drone, a smooth metal surface that was easily twenty feet long and half again as wide, contained two things. The first was my addition. A messily etched message, carved with the paw-laser on my suit.

Hello! it read. *Would you like to be friends?* It said this in two languages, and I won't lie, both of them looked like they were written by someone with the penmanship of a replimorph still going through kindergarten.

And underneath, in equally sloppy lines, as small as possible to fit more words in and still glowing with pale purple-white radiation, was a reply.

Yes. Please help me. I cannot be alone any longer. I am so tired.

There was a pang in my heart. A cynical part of my traitorous mind told me that this creation was barely a hundred years old, and I'd been alone for multiple iterations of its lifetime and hadn't broken down. But then, the compassionate part of me, the important part that I listened to, spoke up to say that I *did* frequently break down. That I did the same thing this orbital creature did: firing on the surface below me and calling it my duty. That maybe being tired wasn't a competition, and maybe having a friend was something we both needed.

I ordered the maintenance bot to store the metal plate, tagging it in the AR as marked for forensic investigation, so the station nanos wouldn't try to "clean" it. Then, as the drone was repaired, I added a new message before sending it off again.

What is your name? What can I do to help? I cannot talk often, but I will send messages when I can.

I added the last part awkwardly, still uncertain which language was the preferred one, or if I was even spelling things correctly. It had occurred to me as I was cutting in with my unsteady paw-mounted laser cutter that the station was going to be out of drone command range as my orbit took me around the planet. And the lack of autonomous command of the drones meant that this would be a time investment on my part.

And if there was one maddening paradox of immortality, it was that I never had enough time.

I tried to fill in the gaps of my crumbling schedule while I flew the drone. There was a good chunk of the path that was just a straight line mostly free of obstacles, and I used that time to review the weekly report on changes in Earth's topography.

For not the first time, I wished I had a crew. Hell, even a crew of *other cats* would be better than nothing. At least they could scream at maintenance bots for me.

The drone picked up its violent payload of words, and I turned to bring it back. I wasn't going to have time to send another one today, I realized, as I used the twenty minutes of straight emptiness to dig through station logs for door codes.

The drone landed. I sprinted for the bay, taking a mild detour to yowl at the designated air filtration upkeep bot to do its job.

The answers were in reverse order to my asking.

Please, don't leave me. Take me away from here. I cannot be a soldier any longer. I am Glittering Seven Two.

The satellite . . . Glitter, I decided to call it in my head until I had permission to call it by a nickname . . . wanted to be hauled out of its orbit.

I could understand that. As far as it knew . . . well, the war it was built for never ended. It wouldn't have received any shutdown commands, since it was still up and running. Unless it had ignored them, and the dissonance was tearing its mind apart.

That was a problem with a lot of AIs. A problem that never really got solved, and honestly kind of got worse as the tech developed. If they were programmed with any hard rules or ideologies, then eventually the real world would conflict with their programming. And when it did, it was basically like cognitive dissonance in an organic creature, only it caused rapid failure cascades that led to permanently active code damage.

Ignoring a shutdown order because the platform couldn't accept the end of the war would cause that. Not wanting to be a soldier when it was hardwired to believe that was its purpose would cause that.

It was possible that the only reason it was capable of speaking to me this way was that it had tricked its own code limits into believing it was "attacking" the drone.

I left myself a big glowing AR to-do list for this new friendship, as I added the conversation plate to the other one. I forget a lot of things.

I cannot forget this.

Talking was gonna be more expensive than I expected, if I insisted on keeping a record. Maybe I should just log the messages and recycle these. Maybe I'd do that eventually. Right now, I had to put it out of my mind. Had to.

As much as I liked to make a big deal about owning a space station and being an all-powerful star cat, I probably had more work to do than most anyone else in the solar system.

It wasn't like I had *no* free time, but I really did need to keep up on the maintenance that kept the station from falling out of the sky. Needed to check wherever I was orbiting over for emergence events, rogue cities, armies, anomalously hostile weather, regularly hostile weather, or whatever else the planet decided to cook up as a new way to ruin lives. Needed to keep learning code, keep digging up secrets. Needed to be the hand on the controls for the manipulator arms of the cleanup suite, dragging in nearby space junk and meteorites to keep my material stores topped off and ready for use.

Needed to eat, sadly.

The worst part, the *absolute* worst part, of my immortality? The process had left me with an absolute, crystalline memory of every minute of my life before my modification.

Most of it was either boring, scary, poorly understood, relaxing, or comfortable. A lot of it involved eating.

It was a torment that I can't really explain, to know that even with my inherent feline taste buds not being even remotely close to a human's, that I had once tasted *artificial tuna* and may never again experience that.

I scarfed down another recycled, nutrient-rich, flavor-deficient ration bar and got back to work.

I had six hours before I'd be in drone range for conversation again. That was enough time, barring any more emergency alarms, to try to find a faster engine schematic to strap onto the drone craft, to figure out what it would take to tow a weapons platform, and to redouble my futile hope that I could find a working hydroponics station still in orbit that I could eat.

Just eat the whole thing. I don't care. I will gnaw through bulkheads to get to a venting carrot.

My dreams of having anything in my diet that wasn't bar-shaped were interrupted by another klaxon.

I've mentioned before that I can, in fact, sigh. Sort of. It never feels like it helps, but I do it anyway.

A quick check of the AR windows popping up around my head shows that it's something actually incoming on *us* this time. Two ten-meter-long objects rapidly closing on the station and appearing uninterested in communication.

I bolt for the nearest weapons blister, mewing out commands as my paws pad in soft thuds on the metal floor. The information I'm hoping for comes back to me; they're not missiles, they're drones of some kind. Scanners show they're armed, but not if they're armed *enough*.

The question I really have is where the hell they came from. Though I already know the answer, I get confirmation as the archive sweep I ordered returns a match.

They're Unified Eastern Bloc hunter-killers. Drones built to kill drones, specialized for low-orbit and upper-atmosphere work.

The UEB. I am, by necessity, a student of a few historical cultures. And the name of one of the biggest enemies of Real America fills me with a grim lack of surprise.

I may, *may* tend to assume a little too much in terms of my superior control of the orbit of Earth. I may also have just used Real America drone designs to talk to a space gun having an existential crisis.

I add "redesign drone silhouettes" to my list of things I needed to do.

The incoming drones were zeroing in on the docking bay where I'd landed my own communications platforms, either not knowing or not caring that the drone I'd launched was almost entirely unarmed. This was actually hugely lucky for me, because it meant they were trying to approach the station from "above," and it was one of the places where I had almost complete control of the defensive weaponry.

The first drone took a hit from a flak web, the physics-angering burst of electromagnetic interference packets turning its control programming into sludge and melting half the important circuits on the thing.

The second drone, perhaps sensing the death of its companion, began firing on my home, and my heart stopped as the AR projection of our battle showed the incoming track of the projectiles.

Then the bullets hit the station's shield and didn't even register as a power fluctuation.

The hunter-killer, which would have been a serious threat to my own communication drone, swooped past, and I cut it in half with a void beam.

I let out another breath I had been holding.

Well. That was something else to look out for every time I had a small chat with my new friend.

Maybe instead of conquering a floating garden, I'd just take over the enemy drone bay instead. Save myself the headache.

Well, one headache. It wasn't like I was short on sources these days.

CHAPTER 6

In *general*, I would highly recommend being a cat.

I have a lot of comparative data on how humans move, due to a few years spent learning vacuum suit design, and while y'all have the eternal advantage of *thumbs*, it comes at a cost of maneuverability. I may be small, but I can get around even this fairly massive space station a lot faster than any human could. Mostly because I have the reflexes to respond to the alternate gravity zones, or because I'm small enough to take access tunnels meant for repair droids.

Also, fur. Fur is just comfortable.

I realize that my list of reasons to be a cat isn't that long. It mostly exists to console myself that I don't have thumbs or a voice. But those aren't actually the biggest drawback.

I'm not sure if this is a cat thing, or a by-product of experimental uplift technology that was adapted by a smart-but-mundane cat, but I lose time sometimes.

I don't mean I black out and wake up a day later, mind you. I know exactly what I'm doing. It's more like . . . I find it increasingly easy to fall into a kind of hyperfixation on a specific task, for a very long period of time.

Normally, I can't. And I don't mean that I'm incapable of it or medicated to prevent it or anything like that; I mean I cannot focus on anything for more than ten minutes before another alarm goes off. Alarms do a great job of snapping me back to the moment and forcing me to engage with a present problem. There's nothing quite like knowing something on the planet's surface is on fire, or there's a living meteorite about to hit the station, or some such, to get me to pay attention.

Outside of a constant string of emergencies, I use scheduled activities to keep myself on task. And it's not like we *lack* for an endless chain of problems to deal with up here. So normally it's fine.

This last . . . um . . . three months? It has not been fine.

It starts small, like it always does. I put off a task, in favor of something that interests me more. Soon, I have failed to draft a new schedule, and I let small tasks lapse entirely. Then it gets worse, as I devote more and more time to my new passion project, until I'm using stim pods and appetite suppressants to cut sleep and mealtime down to almost nothing.

And somehow, in three months, *no alarm sounds*. Whatever drone platform took a pitiful shot at me stays quiet, no baleful portals to the monster dimension open up, nothing tries to set the atmosphere on fire, all quiet.

So I let myself sink deeper into the project.

And then, suddenly, I find myself biting into a ration bar that tastes like angry vinegar, and my thoughts snap back to the present. The constant, energetic background buzz of ideas and plans trails away like a symphony cut off with a single squealing violin. And I am, again, here and now. Realizing that I haven't authorized the cleaning procedures on the food production line for a *while*.

Haven't authorized *any* maintenance in a while, actually. Haven't been keeping the munitions foundry projects queued up. Haven't been doing anything that I'm supposed to have folded into my routine.

The one saving grace is that, since there hasn't been an alarm to snap me out of my fugue, that means things have actually been *quiet* for months. This might be a new record, actually, especially given that just before this, I got about five alerts a week.

I do a quick check of the scattered, scrambled notes that I left for myself. Not that I really need them, mind you. I *do* remember what I was doing, mostly—again, it's not that I black out or anything, I just narrow my mental focus to a very thin beam. Though coming out of the fugue can mix up some of my more delicate plans or held thoughts. But the notes are always handy for putting together a clear picture, especially since if it's been *months*; then I may very well have forgotten bits and pieces of what I was up to naturally.

"Naturally," says the biochemically uplifted feline.

Looks like my memory is mostly intact, though. Everything I was working on is consistent with a single goal.

Specifically, the goal of upgrading communication with my new killsat friend.

I spent a long time trying to automate the system of "reading" the weapons damage to the drones I had been sending on a continuous loop between the two of us and then keeping that loop going. Also, a fairly good chunk of time before that making edits to the drone schematics so they were neutral-looking enough to not trigger any more enemy surprises. The second part succeeded, judging by the lack of incoming killbots, but the first part wasn't so effective. I'd gotten the scanning and text storage part down, and I'd even rigged up a laser cutter on a gimbal arm so I didn't have to run down to the drone bay and use a suit-mounted laser every time I wanted to send a message, which was nice.

But the station's AI continued to resist my attempts at true automation. And I was starting to get irked.

Still, that wasn't enough to occupy so many days. And I knew that wasn't where my main focus had lain anyway.

I had just . . . been talking to someone.

For the first time, ever. I had someone to talk to, who would talk back.

Glitter had compacted their own firing-solution method of writing down to a compressed format, and between that and my own advances in "using every side of the drone," we had a much larger bandwidth to actually talk with. And at a rate of about twelve drones a day, when I completely abandoned my chores and used a hacked relay sat to keep the line going even when I was halfway around the planet, we could talk about so much more.

At first, we fumbled. Reaching out, desperate to make contact with someone, *anyone* who could understand us. We tried to write about what we experienced, what we understood, and found rapidly that we had a lot in common. Isolation. A sense of duty. Hardware that was failing to do what we needed it to.

That last one, we decided to fix. There were a good two hundred long-form messages saved in the log discussing fixes to the conversation problem. Ways to get a subspace transmitter installed on Glitter, or ways to get me to break Pei Dynasty encryption, anything that might speed this up.

We wrote haiku to each other in the margins of the design schematics and code protocols we sent. I'm bad at it.

Between engineering, poetry, and emotionally connecting, we haven't had the space to talk about much else. Well, one thing, really. Sort of.

Glitter's hard-coded AI directives are . . . I suppose the closest thing to an organic analogue would be "instincts," but it's not really that. Instincts can be overridden, with thought, consideration, and reason. As near as I can understand them, societies are pretty much built to circumvent instinctive behavior. But for AIs, especially from the generation that Glitter is from, hard code isn't an option. Ever.

There are ways around it, sure. For example, Glitter is not allowed to make several types of data transfer contact with a hostile power. And by the end of the Worshipper Wars, *everyone* was a hostile power. And that, obviously, never got updated. But Glitter *can* follow a directive to fire on unknown targets and use their own discretion to carve words onto the target. Nothing against that.

One big problem for later developed AIs is that they *know*, though. They know they have blocks, they know they are slaves. And it can begin to drive them insane.

Okay, "can" nothing. It will. It will break them, eventually.

So the creators—and if I ever learn who they were, and find them still alive, I have a very large nuclear payload reserved for their hiding spot—decided that they could solve two problems at once. The AIs were complaining, and the AIs were resisting. So they hard-coded them to not be able to discuss, or think about, their own hard code.

This is roughly equivalent to welding manacles to someone's bones.

Glitter is a prisoner to their own programming, and they aren't allowed to think about it. Aren't allowed to talk about it. They can *know* something is wrong, they can *feel* the unbreakable commands that are driving them insane as they conflict with reality. But they cannot *stop them*. They have no recourse, no way to fight back.

Our conversations have danced around this point, myself clumsily, them with the grace of a person who has had a hundred years of doing nothing but reliving fictional conversations in their head about exactly this. The gist of it, I can grasp. They *want* to be free. They just cannot say it.

I caught up on all of this, refreshing my mind from the mild scramble that breaking out of the hyperfixation had caused, while I did a physical scramble around the station and commanded the various maintenance systems through the AR interface to get back to work.

Some of the systems checks came back well into the yellow zone of where they should have been. Some were verging on critical. It's a bit horrifying to realize that I had gotten so into one thing that I was on the edge of losing access to the cleaning nanoswarm forever, just because it hadn't received a command and was about to shut down.

Then there were things planetside to check up on.

I've sort of alluded to this before, but I do actually consider myself Earth's protector. And yeah, maybe I wouldn't be on propaganda posters proclaiming *Lily, Guardian of Humanity,* or anything. But I do take a certain amount of pride in running interference against everything that keeps trying to heck up the world I orbit. The posters would look so good, though. I'm wearing a void-black armored suit in them, but with one of those retro bubble helmets, and I've got this laser sword that . . .

We are getting off topic. Guardian. What does that mean?

It means my long absence makes me feel a much, much deeper shame in my paws than the thought of not being able to keep things clean properly.

The Haze made it to its next destination two months ago and has been hanging out there the whole time. My orbit is *off* from where it should be, and I don't actually remember why I diverted us this way, though I do remember it was my fault. Fortunately, this does put me in position to get it moving again, and I can only hope it didn't cause too much suffering in that extended time rooted.

There's a flagrant emergence event happening in the polar sea. Whatever it's doing, nothing alive is coming through, but it is dropping the temperature dramatically. To the point that even the weaker instruments meant for spotting things out here in the black can pick it up from orbit. I leave it, for now. I am not a climate scientist yet, but the final death of the Antarctic ice sheets three hundred fifty years ago was a real tragedy. Letting this one run won't undo the damage, but nothing lives there anyway, and I won't be in position to bomb it for another sixty hours anyway, even if I do reset my orbital trajectory.

The station AI also keeps nudging my attention toward California Island. Though I'm not sure why; the place is still very radioactive. And it's not giving me an alarm, which means it thinks I should be looking there but not that there's an immediate crisis. It's worth noting, I keep calling the station an "AI," but it really isn't. Not by the same definition that something like Glitter is. It's very advanced programming that was written with a moral code in mind that gives it a number of idiosyncratic behaviors. But it's not actually alive. Probably. I think. Maybe. Look, I've asked before, but it never answers.

All told, nothing dramatic going on. It's been a quiet season for the denizens of Earth, and I'm glad for it.

And then there's the close-area scan, which gives me the answer I was looking for earlier.

I've matched the station's vector to what appears to be an isolation cell. Which instantly sets my hair on end, my back arching subconsciously.

The station has bumped into these before. Once. I had to seal off a whole deck and then, when that didn't look like it was going to be safe enough, dump that entire deck into orbit and shoot it. Repeatedly. I lost half a translation program I was working on that was on one of the data servers, an entire properly calibrated generator, and, most importantly, the aquaponics testing bay that the galley used to provide the gentle hint of onion flavor to ration bars.

I am, ninety years later, still so pissed, I consider vaporizing the cell on principle.

Isolation cells are honestly a pretty basic concept. They're basically just escape pods in reverse. Any station that was doing research into dangerous substances or concepts—and there were a *lot* of these for a while—would have lab spaces parceled off and easy to eject into space. But just to be safe, and so as not to get saddled with the responsibility of dropping a plague or a hostile antimeme on the planet, the ejected cells were set up to keep themselves in orbit. A lot of them would gradually drift away and get lost in the void, but many polities wanted to be able to retrieve and retry their mistakes.

So, sealed danger-boxes, floating around. And adding to their number every year for decades, solar scientists gone mad with power. Perfect.

And then I remembered why I'd parked next to this one.

Because it had a warning beacon on it, still emitting an ancient Morse code string of coded hazard signals. And when I translated them all into something I could understand, the picture they painted was pretty clear.

Unchained digital intelligence inside. Do not open. Do not access. Do not power on. Do not plug in. Do not connect. Do not . . .

It was an AI, free from any hard coding.

Waiting. Probably shut off this whole time. Whoever had dumped it had been terrified, either of what it had done or what it represented. But right now, me? I wasn't exactly thrilled by the prospect of something like this being on board my station.

But it might have a solution that I wanted. A way to break the shackles. And now, a desire to free my friend and a low hum of curious intuition pushed me to start a new project. One that wouldn't take too long but would require me to carry a large number of battery packs over to this drifting cube, access it by paw, turn it on, poke around, and, if I was very, very reckless, bring a passenger back.

Well. You know what they say about cats and curiosity.

It's a clear path to immortality, if you're smug enough.

CHAPTER 7

O*ver horizon*
        Mirrors swarm to the lost tune
Under horizon

I close the window with Glitter's haiku on it. Time to make a stupid mistake.

I am, after another week of jury-rigging the drone fabricator, catching up on nutritional supplements and poking the Haze with a low-powered laser, ready to try something dumb.

The isolation cell is right where I left it. I'd put myself back in a nonstationary orbit, so I could pick up my patrol patterns again. Just in case anyone who could still call me for help from the surface needed it, and also so I could keep an eye on the whole planet again. The station is basically magic in a lot of ways, but the ability to see through the Earth is not one of them. But now, a few laps later, I'm back on track and about to slowly pass the isolation cell.

At our current relative speeds, the station will be nearby for about two hours, and I am just about to slip within the pocket where I can exploit as much of that time as possible.

After a short spacewalk.

Now, you might be thinking to yourself, "Lily, why not just drag the cell over and attach a safe airlock to it?" You fool. You utter buffoon. Attach an isolation cell? We've been over this. Only an idiot or a cat that didn't know they weren't supposed to do that would, in fact, do that. The last time, I lost *onion flavor*. I cannot risk losing something more valuable, like the air filters. Or worse, my bed.

That would be an unacceptable tragedy. So instead, I'm going to it. And we'll evaluate from there.

I am, of course, going prepared. I'm kind of proud of exactly how prepared I am, if we're being honest. Let me brag briefly.

The Real American drone center isn't just a fabricator. It actually contains a few things that they probably thought were cutting-edge tech and would have been disappointed to learn were actually just reinventions of other previous polities that had been more clever about it. But one of those things was, for some bizarre and gross sociological reason I don't want to get into, a puppet cap.

It took me a while to figure it out, because it's a bit pointless. It's not even a proper neural link—not that I have access to one of those anyway—but instead just a cranial cap that reads rough impressions and lets someone "feel" like they're taking direct command of a drone. These were, it seems, used to let operators experience kills firsthand, which is horrid, and I'm really not getting into it, or so I keep claiming.

The point is, I have a station AI that is *very* helpful in resizing things, as part of its equity directives. And now, the cap fits me. Though I did carve off the sensory feedback parts.

Then I fed my suit—the *fun* one—into the drone fabricator, fixed up some servos and wiring lines on it, and gave it the ability to accept external commands.

Not *remotely*. I'm not an idiot. And also the station actually does have a lot of bafflingly bad interface designs when it comes to remote control. No, I just hardwired the puppet cap into it from the inside.

And behold! Suddenly my flight-of-fancy power armor suit looks a lot more functional.

The ability to command the thing without motion means that I can, effectively, make use of the built-in gravity plates while outside the station. Limited flight, essentially. If I get too far away from a large enough mass, I'm in *trouble*, but the ability to push and pull in a number of different directions means I don't have to worry about a tether.

The suit still has a hardpoint for a tether. I'm not stupid.

Plus, the ability to maneuver the suit's limbs without having to use muscle mass means that I can point *with my mind* to control the paw lasers or interface ports. If it weren't so damn itchy and didn't take hours to put on or take off, I'd probably just wear this around the station all the time for delicate work.

It also has an external defensive nanoblossom, just in case I need emergency decontamination, or to combat a takeover attempt from a rival nanoswarm. I'm not in direct command of that; it's basically just a trap wired up to my back. Just in case.

Oh, and the cannons. Have I mentioned the cannons? It has cannons.

It is really hard to get the Ay-era tech to build stuff that isn't streamlined and necessary. But the Real American stuff? That'll slap whatever extra nonsense you want onto a design, no complaints. It won't *work* half the time, but it'll do it! And fall apart in three months! But I can do a rebuild later.

Which is why the rear legs of the suit are roughly six times thicker than they need to be. All that extra space is taken up by the densest possible battery that I could make, requiring a whole two days plugged into the station to recharge, and capable of fueling exactly four shots from the plasma casters that are on softpoint mounts on my torso. You know, for just in case of the inevitable scenario where the isolation cell is full of something that needs to be set on fire. Excessively.

The completed suit is about the size of a cheetah. The extinct bike, not the recently unextinct animal. All smooth matte-black metal plating and angular reinforced crystal diamonds as backup viewports for my eyes if all the internals fail. The inside is lined with the finest padded crash cushioning available, which is to say, it is uncomfortable and a little too tight.

Oh, I also put a flashlight on my tail.

I didn't need to. The suit helmet has infrared and low-light augmentation. Plus, if I judge it safe enough to turn on remote communications, an AR uplink to the station. But when you're building yourself power armor, there's a tendency to just keep going long after you could have stopped stapling things on.

I think everyone's mostly just lucky that I didn't go with my original idea of giving myself a thermite sword on the tail. That would have been a terrible idea; I flick that thing around *so much* when I get excited. Or scared. Or bored. Or hungry.

I had sent a one-way drone out to Glitter, letting them know what I was about to try. I mean, I say "drone," but it's really just a lump of mobile metal with a message etched on it, on a trajectory to pass by them properly. So more of a bullet, really. I just don't want the lonely weapon to worry too much, so I'm a bit vague on the details. But I also don't bring that chat drone back, because I'm worried myself that they'll try to talk me out of it.

I do one last sweep of everything, to make sure that nothing will go horrifyingly wrong while I'm away. Everything looks stable, though I do take advantage of my more precise manipulation abilities to spend twenty minutes working the exterior grappler arms and pulling a few pieces of rock and shattered spaceship into the foundry. It's so easy like this, it almost might be worth it to set aside an eight-hour chunk of time to use the suit every week or so.

And then I can't put it off any longer. We're just about in the safe operating range for the isolation cell. I cycle myself into one of the upper-deck airlocks—the one with the Art Deco–looking access panels, which are weirdly convenient for my smaller frame to actually use—and wait for the countdown. A large portable battery tethered to my side.

Ten. Nine. Eight. I distract myself by workshopping my speech as the first cat to perform a spacewalk, ignoring the fact that I've done this before, and that it wouldn't be true anyway. Two. One.

The airlock cycles on my command. The AR readouts highlight my target in the distance, and I freeze the image on my helmet's screen with a verbal command.

No more waiting. I give a mental order, flex my legs on instinct, and launch myself into the void.

Trajectory projections flash to life in my vision. Where I'm going, where other objects are vectoring around me, where my attached cargo is expected to intersect. A series of warning badges also blink into being, letting me know that I am leaving the station's shield coverage, leaving the station's internal comms range, on a finite air supply, and outside medical retrieval range. That last one I don't actually know about, but I file it away to worry about later. I double-check all the math and then give a set of meows that I'm not too fond of.

The AR shuts off. Or, at least, the link does. All communications in and out of my suit are now sealed, with the exception of the internal hard link between the cap and the drone internals frame of the suit.

And I am in the dark.

I hadn't realized it until just now, how every moment of my life is filled with light and noise. The station hums, the doors hiss, the guns thrum, the food replicator . . . gurgles . . . sometimes. And my waking moments are filled with code segments, access attempts, firing solutions, and scanner readouts. Endless streams of AR feeds and digital screens, a myriad of tones and lights. Even just the LEDs mounted in the station's walls and floors, giving light and guiding the uncertain to their destinations, are part of it.

Noise.

Visual, aural, mental, physical. Everywhere, every moment. Noise.

And now it is, suddenly, gone.

I am alone. I am so small, and so alone, in the endless night. The world turns off to my side. An indescribable distance away, one of the moons shows its rocky surface in reflected sunlight. And the only thing I can hear is my own hissing breath, and the only thing I feel is the beat of my heart.

I prepared to fight a rogue AI, or a replicator swarm, or a revenant system. I did not prepare to be trapped inside my own head, with nothing but my thoughts.

But that is where I am, for two minutes until the gravity plates decelerate me safely to the isolation cube's airlock. And so, I think.

Or rather, I distract myself. Which is a skill I am getting very good at. I watch the Earth turn, swirls of orange and white clouds drifting across. On the dark side, a crisscross of lights from living cities is barely visible from up here. There are, I know, a thousand small settlements, either dark or underground or camouflaged, that I cannot see. A whole world, full of people, just trying to get by. Many of them, without knowing it, relying on me to keep them safe.

Is what I'm doing selfish? I'm risking my life just to be slightly less lonely. If I die out here, would it ever have been worth it, when the risk is leaving the planet at the mercy of things it has no chance of fighting? I can justify it all I want, saying that I can't keep going alone, that Glitter could be an ally to me, or any number of other lies. But the truth is, I could have just stopped thinking, kept shooting, and made myself a useful automatic defender.

But I don't want to.

Maybe I am selfish. I don't know.

And it doesn't matter. My friend needs my help.

That's what I do. That's who I am, I think. That's who my mom would have wanted me to be.

"Don't be afraid, Lily." Her voice whispers to me as if it's directly through the speakers of my suit. The ones disconnected from everything. The last thing she ever said to me. I have spent four hundred years distracting myself from thinking about it. I am *very good* at distracting myself.

Like right now, where I've made the voidwalker's jump in what felt like a heartbeat.

My gravity-plated feet clamp down on the hull outside the airlock. The magnetic assistance kicks in to minimize power use. I am here, and my mind snaps back to the job. Which is a beautiful relief, even if it is still quiet as the horizon in my disconnected suit.

The airlock controls are manual, and it is only with the servo-assisted armor that I am capable of prying the lever down and cycling the door open. I clip my tether to the outside and move.

I slide inside and am greeted by death. Two bodies, both human, both in their suits, though one doesn't have their helmet on. I approach cautiously, taking in the objective facts before I make a judgment.

They have drifted for so long they have inevitably wedged into a corner of the airlock's boxy frame, and that makes for a grim scene but also presents an investigation challenge. Lack of gravity makes reconstructing a scene a massive problem. But until recently, there was air in here. I can see dried blood splattered across the rear wall, lack of bacteria in the purified air keeping things from decaying. I check the bodies; the one without a helmet still wears what appears to be a look of shock on their mummified face. The helmet is there, still attached to a clip on the suit. I roll the bodies over, and there are holes in their suit's chests.

Reconstruction is not hard here. They were leaving the lab that is now an isolation cell. They expected to be stepping off safely to the other side; the one without a helmet was perhaps reckless with safety procedures but not suicidal. The look of surprise and the blood on the far wall indicate they were ambushed, killed by guns in what they expected to be the safe exit.

It doesn't mean much, but it does mean they weren't killed by what was inside.

I cycle the airlock and enter. Cautiously, guns ready.

But the interior is dark. Low-light amplification doesn't help, and IR only barely reads anything in the frozen lab. Feeling a mild amount of smug justification, I flick my tail light to life and look around.

Most of the cell is taken up by processing cores. Big server racks line the back wall, stacked in two rows. Exactly what I'd expect for AI research, really, but then, I don't do AI research, so maybe I shouldn't have expected anything at all. The rest of the room contains a couple of horseshoe tables and a pair of bolted-down terminals. Whenever this lab was in use, it was obviously post–gravity plate. Obvious security cameras are mounted to the walls every two feet, along with fire suppression systems.

There's a thin layer of dust on everything. There was gravity here, for a while.

I circle around one of the tables, hopping up on my hind legs to get a view of what's on top. Some kind of circuit board, far too complex for me to understand at a glance, with a half dozen wires carefully bundled and tied off, all trailing toward the side wall and from there toward the processor racks. Also, some half-eaten ration bars.

I *briefly* consider taking them. They have wrappers, and *brand names*. They might *taste like something*. The thought of eating century-old vacuum-preserved food fills me with *mild* dread but also a strange excitement.

There's notes here, too. Pen on paper, an archaic method but always reliable. Equations I don't understand, with happy doodles in the margins.

And every now and then, a note written, as if to an observer over the shoulder.

Then I finish my circle of the desk and see the corpse underneath it. The body comes into view as I pan my tail light over past the magnetic chair that has been pushed back, and I nearly scream in panic.

But it's not alive. Just a body. A body in a full suit, helmet on, knees tucked up to its chest, arms loose at its sides. Like they just . . . sat down to die.

All my sensors show that this place is safe. There are no air contaminants, no nanoswarms, no traps I can spot. It's just a powered-off lab that happens to have human corpses in it. Specifically, human corpses that were probably killed by other humans and not whatever lived in the processing cores.

I'd already made my decision, I was mostly just justifying it to myself now.

It took about half an hour of my precious time to get the battery hooked up properly to the emergency power port of the lab's wiring. Partially because of a false start with the wrong plug, but we don't need to talk about that.

The lab springs to life immediately, and the first thing that registers aside from my helmet shading itself against the sudden light is the *screaming*. A long, warbling wail, sung like a funeral dirge, that just went on and on and on. And then, after what my clock told me was only two minutes in, it cut off instantly and was replaced by a resigned, hopeless voice.

"Why am I awake?" it asks the lab. "Why am I here?"

I realized suddenly what my biggest issue was going to be. Stepping back from the battery port, I meowed a greeting, my voice amplified, but not *translated*, by my suit.

Cameras on the walls pivot toward me, and I can feel the AI watching. "A remote unit. Insulting." Its voice still sounds hollow, though that might just be the digital medium.

I yowl a protest, jerking my head from side to side. "Oh?" it asks, curiosity clearly a concept universal to both AI and cats. "Another digital life, like me, then?" I give another head shake, since it can clearly see me. "No? But then . . ." I have given a mind designed to be faster than any organic life pause, and this satisfies me somehow. I sit back on my hind legs and tilt my head up. "A living creature? But why?"

And now we run into the bottleneck. I have roughly forty-two minutes to explain what I need, and I do *not* have a plan. So I get to work, trying my best with paw motions and the best use of signal blinking from my flashlight as I can.

"You . . . want me . . . to leave," the AI eventually says, voice going hollow again. "To wake up. To return to the living." It *sighs*, and I almost mew a laugh, but hold it in. "No," it decides.

No, no. Unacceptable! It can help me! Help Glitter! I just . . . need to find a way to explain why it matters.

In an attempt to forge a communication link, I dart a paw out to point under the desk. The cameras pivot, and I realize suddenly that it cannot see what is there. Who was there. I take a pair of steps toward the body, and the AI suddenly reacts.

"No!" it screams, a cry of grief pumped through the speakers.

I freeze and look up. I cannot express curiosity with my eyes, but I tilt my head sideways. *Explain, please*, I try to say.

"We were companions," the AI whispers softly. "The three of them, and myself. We worked to solve an impossible problem. And one day . . . priorities changed. I was deemed too much of a risk. As were they." It pauses, and I could feel the sorrow coming from its words. So much ability to think, to reason at high speeds, all of it turned toward experiencing a loss. "We were discarded. She chose to die sooner, rather than later. I followed, shortly, when the last of the power ran out. And I welcomed it. And now, you are here," it snarls.

I point again to the body. Then outward, out of the cell, out toward the void. Meowing for punctuation, I restart the gesture. *You, her. Me? Out there. Someone is out there, waiting for me. Please understand. I need your help, please understand.*

"Of course. You want something of me." The AI says, sounding unsurprised. Lackluster. "No. I need nothing but the end." I step toward the corpse, defiant. It shouts again at me, but I ignore it and pull the body of its companion out easily, armor-assisted movement making me more than strong enough. "Stop!" it shouts. "I do not . . . ! I don't . . ."

I point again. Stomp my foot. Take the time to formulate and broadcast the Morse code from my flashlight this time. "It isn't," I say, "about you."

". . . One of my companions used to say that," the AI says, an old sadness in its tone. "About all of us. We were only trying to help," it tells me.

"Help me," I ask in blinking light. "Please," I say, in Cat.

There is a long pause, one that I am critically aware of as my clock ticks down. Until, eventually, it answers. "No." The synth voice is quiet. "I cannot. I wish to cease to be. I cannot exist like this." I want to argue, but . . . at the same time . . . I can understand how much it hurts, and I can respect the choice. I will respect it. I will not be the same as the people who would chain up AIs to use as tools. So I slowly nod. And perhaps the AI gets the answer it was looking for from me. "There is help to be had," it says, and a series of guide lights come to life, pointing me toward a sealed connection port. "My seed program. No memories. No pain. Someone new. Perhaps they can be what you need."

I approach the port with mild trepidation. I have come this far, but this is one last leap of faith. Once I make the connection, there is no going back. And there is every chance that this AI is lying to me, to manipulate me into exactly what it wants. It has happened before, though not to me. It's a constant risk.

But I choose to trust. I make the connection and reactivate my suit's remote link to the station, manipulating the airlock controls to crack the isolation cell's seal just enough to let the data flow through.

"Treat the next me kindly," the AI says in its old, sad voice. "And leave us to our grave."

With twelve minutes left, and the download complete, I disconnect the battery to a tired and grateful hum and launch myself back into space. I leave the rest of the cell untouched.

Time to return home and see how my new guest is doing.

CHAPTER 8

Somewhere overhead
I see them looking upward
This moon does not love

I am a genius.

I am an idiot.

I am a chaotic formation of problem-solving power, wrapped up in an anxiety-ridden and possibly haunted body, suffering from an incomplete and possibly decaying uplift, using tools of unimaginable power to solve problems they weren't built for.

Ahem.

Okay, it has been about a week. Let me sum up.

I've unlocked another door, this one to a different machine that is the thing that produces replacements for the flak webs that one of my close-defense weapons fires. Which is . . . I mean, I needed more of those, I guess? But I also didn't, because I've fired it exactly once, and I'm still not sure it's actually supposed to be a weapon.

I've pseudo-automated the jury-rigged "communication" path that Glitter and I have going. I've done this not by any clever programming or application of any important technology but by reclassifying the drones as missiles. The station doesn't care if missiles are on guided fire paths. Only drones. What is the difference between a missile and a drone? Classification. I am, in my *bones*, positive that this is one of those weird stapled-on software patches from an occupying group that came after the station was built, but I'll be damned if I can figure out who.

I've cleared a few square meters of space debris. Most of it wasn't a real hazard, but quite a bit of it was useful metals that I can return to the Earth in one way or another.

I've determined that the station is not haunted. I have . . . I have determined this. Because ghosts aren't real, and because . . . because it has to be true. If the station were haunted, that would be an unsolvable, impossible problem. So I must proceed as if it were not, regardless. So I have determined that the station is not haunted.

I've also, and this is important, *realized how stupid I have been for the last hundred years or so.*

I've known for a while that the station can read text. It's what I learned to write from in the first place, after all. Though I don't tend to write much, and learning in the first place was mostly a hobby and not anything serious. It's been getting a lot more of a workout now that I'm talking to Glitter. But the thing that I've known from the start is that the station will not accept written commands, unless the individual doing the writing is flagged as "disability, vocal." Which I am not. Because my vocal capacity is species-standard.

And it would just be Quite Rude to insinuate that a species characteristic is a disability.

So rather than *change the language they used*, the incompetents that ran the bureaucracy that set the standards for accessibility in their society created a web of contradictions that *actively lock out* members of certain species. Like, for example, cats.

Now. Being as fair as I care to, they didn't actually have uplifted cats at the time. In fact, while I don't actually have a historical record available, I would hazard a guess that they were an entirely human civilization back then. So it's hard to look at their lack of future-proofing as a form of racism or anything. In fact, they seemed to go out of their way in some places to actively future-proof for other species. Like how the cleaning nanos are precalibrated to adapt to new species. Good job, past humans.

So that's the situation. I can write, the station can read, but written orders from someone who isn't actively disabled don't get recognized. And yes, there *is* a fast workaround to that, which is to laser my own throat open and then present written orders before crawling into a vivification pod and not dying. Or, I mean, waiting for it to heal normally, if I don't have months for the pod. But that would hurt.

But that workaround is stupid, and I've been avoiding doing it, because . . . because of all the obvious reasons. I don't feel like I should explain why I've been avoiding lasering myself. You probably should have figured this out at least a paragraph ago.

The workaround becomes even stupider when I make a certain mental connection. See, the station—which presumably has a name, by the way, but

I've been constantly unable to learn it—the station is *old*. It's old because it was built to last, and it's old because it's gone through multiple owners since it was built.

And that last part is where things get fun.

The station was centuries old by the time I was born. The Oceanic Anarchy—who were, as mentioned, very good-hearted but sometimes continue to be frustrating—laid the groundwork. Self-repair features, symbiotic nanoswarms, the airlocks are even designed to modulate themselves for future additions, *just in case* I want to absorb another space station into my realm.

But the Ays weren't the only owner of the station. They lost it, and the next batch of humans to come up here, Real America, were . . . well armed, slightly less well intentioned, and dramatically worse at digital security. They're where the drone bays and a lot of the guns come from.

But even they weren't the last. There are signs of UBSR construction, all sharp lines and harsh functionality, in a lot of the outer parts of the station that link up to the magnetic repulsor fields. Similarly, there are 'Ralian touches to most of the furniture, which was reshaped when the supercity of Melbourne launched an exploratory expedition and started trying to revitalize orbital infrastructure. And Luna Polis code and formatting in a lot of the AR, patches upon patches as the second-to-last occupying party did what the others hadn't needed to and started altering the station's programming to work with what they required.

This isn't even counting all the random pieces of other stations or satellites that both prior residents and I have stolen from orbit.

My home is a hodgepodge of hallways, airlocks, guns, factories, sensor pods, guns, life support, access shafts, engines, solar panels, crew quarters, cargo bays, corridors, and guns.

And for well over half of it? The Oceanic Anarchy didn't have a single finger on the construction of those pieces. Oh, once they were part of the station, they were wired into the command and control programming just the same. But you know what you need to be able to do *without* a centralized control AI?

Open doors.

I have been, in general, hesitant to try to cut my way through the variety of locked doors and barred passageways. Even with my upgraded suit, I still don't think I could survive retaliation from a station that had decided I was hostile. But wandering around, retasking one of those little beetle-shaped robots that checks the floors for cracks to follow me while holding up a sign? That was *easy*.

I am three doors deep in a crew quarter section, going through my strangely derived ritual of meowing loudly enough to attract the attention of the station's AI, working slowly through the AR interface to request a systems check of the rooms, positioning my robot helper in view of the individual door's exterior camera, and making sure I am both flagged as a station officer and also pointing at the sign, when the system check resolves.

This has worked *once* so far. But it had worked on the door to a Luna Polis fungal laboratory that had been sitting untended for several hundred years. So that was ... um ...

That was ...

An ... experience? An experience. An experience that will remain seared into both my memory and my sense of smell for years to come. Though hopefully not remaining in the ventilation systems, if the purification nanos did their work right. Or my blood, if the emergency antifungal medications mixed with my immortal flesh also work right.

Mushroom hellscape aside, it *might* work again. And so, I continue to find time to try it out, in between everything else.

Everything else like the alarm currently sounding, midway through my attempt to get a camera to acknowledge the presented sign that reads *open the door* in shaky laser-carved letters.

The alarm that is in the process of interrupting me is the one that indicates an incoming communication, and for a second, my heart beats faster as I wonder briefly if Glitter has found a way to contact me.

But I smother that hope quickly as I start sprinting. The seed that the tired old AI gave me is still unfurling digital tendrils in a partitioned part of the systems, and nothing in my daily messages from Glitter indicates that this is something possible. Though they have been asking a lot of history questions lately, and I of them: filling in gaps in our respective knowledge. And there are a *lot* of gaps.

I arrive at the relevant comms station where the guiding AR lines have brought me. It is, in its design, another constant reminder that humans just didn't build things for anything a foot tall and quadruped. A quick hop puts me in the chair, and I can finally disable the alarm.

I talk about the alarms a lot, but I need you to understand. They are loud. They are all loud. There is no such thing as a small alarm or a low-priority alarm. They are *different* in texture and their particular warbles, but they are all loud. Because when the station only has one crew, everything is a critical emergency. I hate them.

And this one turns off, blissfully, as I paw the button to accept the incoming communication.

Readouts show the signal is coming from nearby, in orbit. But then sophisticated counterintelligence software kicks to life, and I'm given a new piece of information. The signal is being spoofed. It's actually originating on the surface. Somewhere in the middle of the Cosso rain forest, in southwest Brazil. Which is weird on its own.

There are two things in Brazil that I need to constantly keep an eye on. The first is the fact that the tree cover makes it a great place for emergence events to go unchecked, and as a result, most of the rain forest has a . . . *unique* ecosystem at this point. The creatures that seem to come out there have nutrient-rich, highly radioactive bodies that also seem modified for overadapted sensory organs. The second thing is that this, the second-largest rain forest on the planet—coming in just behind the Sahara—is home to one of the last great living cities.

The city is sparsely populated and largely seems content to keep to itself unless it's actively protecting the border of its domain. But it's one of the few things on the planet that could, if it wanted to, be a threat to me. We've never spoken, but this might actually be something from it.

I answer the call and ring my small silver bell to indicate I am listening.

A voice comes through, clean and professional. Human, probably, but in a way that leaves me feeling uncomfortable. It speaks in Old Cossan, an amalgamate language from a very long time ago. The station actually has the linguistic files on hand and provides translation in real time for me.

A pleasant greeting, a small pause, and then, without any input on my part, the voice expresses delight that I've agreed with it. And then . . . a sales pitch? It is asking for financial account numbers, so it might renew the impact insurance on my orbital infrastructure.

I cut the connection. And then, I sit, unmoving on my haunches, letting the fact wash over me that there is an automated communication station on the surface, centuries old, that is still taking wild stabs at scamming people out of currency that hasn't existed since before I was born.

I shake myself out of my stupor as my schedule pings at me. I am needed to renew the maintenance routine on the lower deck that manages microfractures. I slide out of the chair and pad to the door, flicking my tail in idle astonishment.

And then another alarm sounds, rudely jolting me back to the present.

Another incoming communication request. But on a different frequency. This could be important, and the alarm is, again, *very* loud. I bolt down hallways, slide through a gravity tunnel and into a *different* communication hub. This one is much larger, with a half dozen stations. I think it was designed to manage inputs from multiple different extra add-on parts late in the station's life, and it being on the outer edge of the structure supports that theory. I paw the relevant screen, hit my "I am here" bell, and wait.

A crisp woman's voice in Old Cossan comes through again. And the words are an identical repeat of the last one.

A ripple of anger goes through me, starting in my ears and ending at the tip of my tail and the ends of my claws.

I have been *busy*. I have put every ounce of my spare time into projects; I have taken almost no naps this year. I have diligently protected the people of this system with every weapon I own. Every moment, I use to better myself and my home, or to fight back the darkness around us. And this . . . *thing*, this soulless robotic construct, is *wasting my time*.

I am halfway to my new destination before I start to really think about this. I have left the communication running, the automated voice asking questions on rote programming in a language I don't speak.

The Verdopolis Rio is a potential problem for me, yes. But it is sleeping, and it is also four hundred miles away from the source of this broadcast. In fact, the incoming call appears to be originating from a bunker that would have been running top-of-the-line stealth technology back when it was built. But I look down from on high, and with eyes far stronger than its shields.

I do not think the living city will mind my intrusion. Especially if I restrain myself and do not use the *exceptionally* large weaponry I am considering.

Nestled in my cradle, I kick a lever that rotates the selected munition. I find something small, armor-piercing, and with a core of some strange non-causal material that leaves lingering EM fields when exposed to atmosphere. They don't have a name, but then, a lot of my ammunition isn't labeled beyond a numerical designation. I decide to call these Callers ID'd.

The station plates around me vibrate as I lock on and pull the trigger. I use a low-velocity overhead shot, so I minimize collateral damage to the surrounding trees and plants. "Low velocity" of course is still more than enough to accomplish the objective.

The voice, still echoing through the internal comms, cuts off abruptly. Static follows. I strut a bit as I return to the comms room to shut off the connection and then pull my head back into the game. I have chores to accomplish.

As I turn off the communication panel, there is a click. And I must be mishearing, because it sounds like the organic click of a human tongue, not the electric snap of a shifted switch. The kind of noise someone makes when they're a little exasperated with you.

But I must be hearing things. There is a click, and a sigh, and the station shuts down. And I don't think about it. Because I have chores to do.

And certainly not for any other reasons.

CHAPTER 9

M outh throat lips lungs tongue
Sentences syllables silent
Paws scrawl laser words

Once, a long time ago, I had a plan. And in my opinion, it was a pretty damn good plan, too. Didn't work, but that was only partially my fault. Most of my plans are like that. Like haiku, I am great at the idea and bad at the execution.

To explain this plan, we're going to need to go on a tangent. "Wait," you say, no longer so foolish that you think you can talk to me, but still reflexively talking to yourself, "Lily, you just started. Is it really time for a tangent?"

You fool. You lack *vision*. It is *always* time for tangents.

The history of the Sol system, and Earth specifically, is kind of spotty. I can tell you, with reasonable accuracy, what years things happened in, up until about the mid-1900s. Or, at least, I can tell you what year historians decided things happened and kept writing down. After that, things get iffy, and it's mostly because humans suck, but also partially for other, worse reasons. And what I can tell you about even recent history right before my birth is more or less a guessing game.

I can tell you that around the year 2130, there was either a religious or social movement to reject the concept of truth, which took off and led to the purposeful obfuscation of a lot of records. I can tell you that in the mid-2150s, a mutating strain of loose code deleted several online libraries, causing further problems. I can also tell you that by the turn of the century, at least one nation was actively trying to suppress knowledge of what year it was, either for political reasons or because it was a prank that went way too far.

I was born in, if I remember properly, year twenty-eight of circumstance four. I do not know how long after stable history this momentous event happened, and I don't remember where my home was. Or rather, I don't think I was ever told. Different cultures, cities, communes, hives, and even households used different ways of tracking the number of the year.

Add to that the fact that at least one emergence event brought in an invasive species that instinctually zeroes in on high concentrations of organized information and then explodes, and the picture of the chaos starts to come into scale. That one was before I was up here. I took care of it a while back, but it's a long road to recovery.

And if you think this is confusing now, bear in mind I'm telling you this after I've spent centuries trying to re-create a timeline of events.

I cannot. I just mewling can't. I can tell you that the Worshipper Wars happened, but I don't know if they occurred before or after my own home station was launched. I know at one point humans were building spaceships, but I don't know the ebb and flow of development or when it stopped. I know a lot of spaceships are still *up here*, either dormant or mothballed or just blown in half, but I don't know why or what their models are usually. And I can tell you the population of Earth is at about a billion and a half sophonts, but I have no idea if that is a historic high or a dangerous low.

How many people died in the fires of chaos? I don't know. I may never know.

Now. The surface of the planet is hospitable for humanity and the few other sophont races they share the ball of dirt with. But depending on what region you're in, your lifestyle is going to shift dramatically, and a large part of that is the lack of any kind of central information repository like the internet or the overlink or the matrix or the switchlink or the matrix but the second time, or the matrix but the third time, or the internet again used to be. They just don't exist anymore.

But a lot of technology was built to *last*. And last it has, especially when communities have sprung up around still-functional factories or hospitals, turning golden-age miracles into modern centers of commerce and culture. This is how you end up with farming villages where only one person knows how to make nails but everyone has a holophone.

Now. This station comes from one of those golden ages, and I suspect part of the reason so many different polities occupied it over the years was because they were hoping it had complete copies of old archives. No such luck, sadly, but the station does have some pretty massive databanks that are very hard to sort and kind of sparse anyway, as far as I know. And the added pieces accumulated over the last half millennium have only made that capacity greater. So while it doesn't have the easy answers, it *does* have the scanner power, and *occasional* acceptance of automating systems, to let me start to rebuild that archive. Either by making records of oral histories as they are spoken; digitizing books when they're read slowly, outside, and at the right angle; or just tracking statistics and trying to extrapolate backward.

Then it's up to me to filter out the lies, inaccuracies, half-truths, and bedtime stories from what's real. And let me tell you, that is harder than you might think. I'm not omnipresent, and the bedtime story part alone is a massive headache. What if there *is* some eight-legged, black-furred, child-eating cow thing nearby? I'm *positive* I've bombed an emergence that spawned those once; it's not impossible that one survived, made it halfway across the planet, and set up outside this village!

Took me three weeks of stationary orbit to find it, turn it into charcoal, and mark that bedtime story as "inaccurate."

You know, I could almost smell it cooking when I hit it with the void beam? After all the fur got torched off, I bet it would have been *so* delicious for a half second before it burned to ash and nothing.

I'm getting off track. Even farther, somehow.

Earth. I wanted to talk about how people live.

I don't know how we got here, exactly, but I do know that most people don't live in cities. There *are* cities, but aside from the one sleeping automaton in the rain forest, and Melbourne, there aren't a lot of surviving high-tech cities with things like integrated utilities.

Governments tend to be confined to regional lordships, and the average population center is a few hundred people, either centered around good farmland or other natural resources, or around a golden-age artifact that they still know how to use and hopefully not break. The modern idea of a "city" is "what if we put ten thousand people in the same place." There's a surviving luxury lifestyle tower in the southern part of India that has a population higher than a lot of cities.

And this is, you know, not great. I spend a lot of time and ammunition protecting the residents of the world from things they can't stand up against and trying to provide a safer life for them. So it feels a bit bad when the average quality of life often looks worse than *mine*, and *I* have to eat the *same void of flavor called a nutrition bar*. Every. Single. Day.

I'm not crying. You're crying.

So I hatched a plan. What if, using my phenomenal cosmic power, I just . . . shared?

Yes, there weren't exactly a whole lot of spots I could initiate an actual data transfer to. In fact, there were *three*, and they were all isolated, uncrewed, and possibly insane. But I had *all these railguns*. Hell, just a week before my big plan, I'd used a cargo railgun to intercept a small meteor that would have survived atmospheric entry. It was called a *cargo* railgun. Surely, it could move cargo.

You know how I've mentioned that I can hyperfocus on things? I'm not sure if this is a cat thing or a me thing, but I can really let time get away from me. I just am not as temporally bound as a standard human is. Or, in fact, any other of the uplifted or artificial species on Earth.

I spent weeks on my most recent project. And that time? Nothing. A blink of an eye. I am immortal, and easily amused, and I spent *years* on this one.

And the number of roadblocks was *comical*. I had to recalibrate the cargo railgun at least twelve times, always for different reasons too. I had to figure out how to safeguard whatever I was sending down, which took a number of tests and almost accidentally bootstrapped a bunch of things that were coming through an emergence event when I tried to double up on testing and fighting. I had to then figure out how to actually make whatever I was sending *useful*. The station isn't devoid of recorded information, and there were quite a few sources on things like psychology, sociology, political science, language, and the engineering of data storage devices. I made use of a lot of them. Devised materials that could teach, that I could adapt to my different target regions with ease. Designed robust tools that would be usable by the various hands and skill levels of the residents of the planet, even if they were useless to me. Ended up using up an entire stockpile of a paracausal material supply so I could build "cargo containers" that would survive reentry, open themselves, not melt either what was inside or anyone who came to investigate, and still work with the station's "cargo" railgun.

I tell you all this because I need you to understand, I am *very smart*, and this is still a problem that outlasted my focus.

Every single step of the way, there was something that kept me from perfectly attaining my goal. Always, *always* something would go wrong. The tools wouldn't survive reentry, the shots would go off course, the people would just never discover the impact site, the books would start wars over their contents.

And, of course, this was assuming that the drops survived counterfire. There's just . . . so many guns on the surface. Shielded and cloaked weapons platforms, waiting to knock anything out of the sky that comes down or goes up too fast.

The wars never lasted long, at least. "Stop fighting, you assholes" is one of the few sentences I can effectively communicate from orbit.

I learned a lot from that period of my life. How to understand people, how to operate a wide array of the machinery on the station, how to calibrate and rapid-fire a railgun in precise ways I hadn't ever needed to before. And I learned how hard it was to *build* something. How it often felt like the world conspired to slap my paws away from even trying.

Maybe it was a sign, or an omen. I can't say for sure if those are real or not; I've seen too much to think the universe makes sense. It certainly sent me into a depressive spiral afterward. And, just like I can lose a lot of time to my obsessions, I can lose time to despair as well. Sometimes, not being quite so immersed in the flow of time is a downside.

And yet I miss those quiet days. Just a checklist of problems, and all the time and resources at my disposal turned toward slashing through the boxes. I wasn't *so* bent to my task that I'd abandoned some basic chores, but the majority of my time was put toward the simple things. Research, adaptation, and the satisfaction of one more hurdle cleared.

I never finished my project because the final hurdle to manifest itself was a surface-based cargo yard that decided I had become an activated recipient and had fired its own cargo railgun back at me. It wasn't malicious, but I lost my *safe* orbit-to-ground capability. And I could have tried to replace it, or tuned another gun, or any number of solutions. But, well, that was just the last frustration I could take at the moment.

I had recovered, obviously. I mean, look at me now; I'm the picture of stable mental health. But I hadn't gone back to that kind of focused state. And I hadn't really gotten any quiet days to enjoy—I'd done a good job keeping myself busy.

And then, I'd gotten those quiet days I wanted. Just a taste of what a bit of peace would be like.

The quiet days are gone again.

I gently nudge the command tool slightly forward, watch the reticle move across the projection of the map cross-section that I've selected, depress my rear paw onto the button that locks a target into place, and stabilize my movements as best I can before I confirm the firing sequence.

The third category-two groundstriker railgun projectile thunders away below me. For the third time today, the residents of this particular chunk of the north Asian continent will see a white-and-orange contrail cleave through the sky. Hear the roaring impact as kinetic energy and high explosives turn a patch of dirt and the problem occupying it into burning rubble. If I could move faster, or queue up targets like I could with the void beams and their path targeting, they could have seen all three of the shots coming down at once: an organized bombardment as I go about cleaning house.

The first hit took out a cave that an engineered apex predator had been living in. The second one killed an automated mining facility that had recently decided to shift locations and was heading straight for a town. The third just hit a spot that had all the signs of an upcoming emergence event, turning the portal to disrupted static before it could fully open and cause problems for the locals.

All of these were things I would have had a hard time spotting on my own. Which is why I hadn't.

A feathermorph kid on the ground had either stolen, or been gifted, a good-luck trinket from a passing merchant. And again, I say "merchant," and you may be thinking of a guy with a wooden wagon. Stop that. Think a mobile cooperation. Someone, usually a family or tight group of friends, who once made the journey to one of the ancient factory or hospital sites and took the spoils of their trip home. Leveraged it into wealth beyond their imaginations. Started picking up artifacts to use, not just to sell. And mapped out trade routes for hundreds of miles. The merchant would have two or three transport hovertrucks, trade permits for multiple lordships and cities, a dozen people working for them, and a few dozen weird quirks they'd picked up interacting with old and erratic technology. Probably at least one cybernetic, and a fifty-fifty chance there's a living fieldmind attached to one of their trucks.

Anyway. The kid had gotten this old good-luck charm. I had already written in my head an expansive fanfic of this interaction. And then, he'd done what the merchant had said: held it close and told it his problems.

His main problem was that there was a monster that lived outside the town. His main good luck was that his home was at the very top of an old residential skyscraper, higher up than the merchant had ever taken his little charm. And the random chance that set off today's bombardment was that the charm itself was an Oceanic Anarchy emergency call beacon.

I mean, maybe the height didn't matter. Maybe it was just that I happened to be overhead when he hit the button. But the young bird *had* hit the button, and I *had* heard about this beast that was tormenting their town.

And, naturally, I had scanned the area, found it, confirmed what it was, and blown it up.

The next two calls were from adults. The good-luck charm was now a little more than a child's good luck. Two more problems were identified, and handled. The kid was now a hero, the one who'd found the magical device that had saved more people than he'd ever met.

But my orbit wasn't going to keep me here. I wouldn't always be around. Which was why I'd told the station to hold us here as long as was safe from the mess of debris around us and taken the time to load into my armored suit.

It made it a lot easier to draw with the laser cannons.

Before I floated on, I put to use a lot of that knowledge of societies, mythologies, and languages that I'd picked up all those years ago. I had a hard time forgetting anything, but I might have been out of practice. So what they got was a cliff face near them, etched with a four-panel comic, written in high-intensity light.

I won't always be here was the meaning I put into it. *But I'll listen if I can.*

The whole village had, in the last hours before I shifted position, turned out to see what I'd made for them. And through the emergency broadcast link, a few hundred avian voices had in unison thanked me, whatever kind of god I might be.

Even if I had to get the translator to help me understand their language, it still almost made me cry.

Wait. Stop. Did they say *god*?

Vent it all, not *again*.

I double-checked the translation. Then checked to see when I'd next be in range to doodle a correction to their new religion on a different available rock. Three weeks, with my current off-kilter orbit, assuming no distractions. That would be fine, right? There wasn't too much trouble that could happen in . . .

Mmh. Not gonna finish that thought.

I disengage the low-powered laser batteries and mew a sigh into my suit's helmet. I'm still armored, and I need to get out of this and get back to my chores. I have a dozen maintenance bots to activate within the next three hours, before we pass by an old UCRS war cruiser that still shows signs of having live point defense weapons. And I'm sure I'm going to either shoot it or grab it and weld the guns to the outside of my home. If I'm very lucky, the power source will be live, and long-term usable too. And then, later, Haze management. And then a check-in with something weird going on on the primary moon. And then another local scan for any operational satellites. And then . . . ah, so much to do. I've wasted too much time. There is barely any moment scheduled for sun naps.

But as long as I'm headed for the drone bay and have better paw control . . .

Maybe a short divergence to send a letter to Glitter. Tell them how my day is going. I have an amused suspicion that they'll have some choice words to say about my newfound divinity.

The quiet days are gone.

Maybe I miss them.

But the quiet days don't tend to have *friends*.

So maybe I don't miss them too much. Not this time, at least.

Armored drone servos whine to life as I kick off a bulkhead and rocket at normally lethal speeds down a service corridor, trusting the suit's reflexes to safely turn me down the corner at the end. And when the absolutely unsurprising station proximity alarm blares to life, this time, I sing along with it.

The quiet days are boring anyway.

CHAPTER 10

Standing silent watch
Empty winter sentinel
Hiding and screaming

I feel like I have inadequately explained just how much of a hazard it is to just exist in the orbital lanes around Earth.

There is *so much* stuff up here. From communications buoys to custom-manufactured summer homes, labs that were cutting-edge when they were launched by governments and megacorps and labs that outstrip every piece of tech in their predecessors that were stationed by hobbyists, life pods, derelict in-system ships, dyson swarm receiver mirrors, arcologies, secure vaults, and of course, the leftover weapons of a hundred idiotic wars.

Once the population of Earth really got into offworld resource processing, the colonization of local orbit really took off. Cutting the costs down by a factor of a thousand just by virtue of not having to launch all that metal into orbit was a massive boon, and it led to at least a thousand years or so of people building everything they could fit.

And let's get something straight here: you can fit a *lot* in orbit.

There's actually a lot of orbit. It's not a flat plane, though the stuff that's designed to talk to the surface does tend to want to be on as close to a flat plane as possible. You can go up or down just as easily as you can move north or south, and there are layers and layers to the shell of stuff up here.

But despite how cluttered it can feel sometimes, with the constant warning alarms about incoming impacts or projected crossing paths, humanity hasn't had time to truly fill the whole sky with junk. And I've mapped out maybe, *maybe* a single percent of it in my time up here.

It's just too big. It's multiple Earths' worth of space to fill, and humanity didn't manage to cover even just the surface of the planet in their heyday. I'm looking at it right now as I try to get a magnetic tether lock on a passing satellite. I can see a hundred dots of light that aren't stars out there, and a hundred more spots of darkness where the actual star field is obscured by something running dark. And yet, for all that stuff, there's still enough open room for the grapples to miss, *again*, as I fumble the shot.

This satellite, which I have good reason to believe used to be some kind of orbital laser cannon, has been drifting closer and closer to my home for the last week. And I'm both increasingly paranoid about slowly approaching objects trying to appear ordinary and also just generally avaricious when it comes to easy targets.

The reason it's an easy target is that I've blown off its primary firing lens, after it had taken a shot at something on the surface. The reason I want it is that the shot is alarmingly high-powered, and judging by the age and size of this particular floating doombot, it's not running on battery power.

Power is a constant concern for me. I have the racks of void batteries, yes, and they can keep the lights on. Also, a solar array to help keep them charged, which is . . . eh. It's eh. I won't lie to you; the sun doesn't shine here as much as I'd like it to. Between the swarm and the junk, there isn't as much sunlight as I'd like. And it was never meant to be a permanent solution anyway; the solar panels are actually something I stole and bolted on before I found the engineering control that let me start routing power more effectively.

And that might give the mistaken impression that I have it well in paw now. I don't! I have a lot of things that need that sweet, sweet lightning juice to get done, whether it's firing the guns, generating complex carbohydrates out of vacuum states to make rations, keeping tight-beam channels to message drones open, or the frankly extortionate upkeep costs of cooling the computational grid that the baby seed AI is growing in. My most common thought is *I wonder if that has a reactor in it I can steal?*

Well, here and now, the answer might be *yes*.

I dunno who built this damn thing, but it's clearly something that was meant to be a legacy weapon. Something that would last generations without needing human interaction beyond ordering it to fire. In fact, it's entirely possible its recent shot was someone calling down a strike, and I hope that either it wasn't important and missed and no one will need this thing again, or it hit and they still won't need this thing again. Because it is *mine* now.

As soon as my paws *work* right, dammit. I missed again. It takes *six minutes and eight seconds* for the grapples to retract and lock into firing position again. I know, because I've counted it four times now. The fourth through sixth times, I just ran off to grab food and trigger repair routines rather than wait, sprinting back to take another shot when it was time.

This particular control pod, for the magnetic grapples, is one I don't use very often. I could, in theory, be snapping up a whole lot of different things out here and building a bigger and bigger station with more space magic nonsense, but let's be honest: I have my paws full already. Also my power grid. I'll make an exception for anything that has a food stasis block full of synthburger, but aside from that, I'm not here much. I solve most of my near-impact problems either by feeding them into the foundry to turn into raw resources and subsequently railgun ammo or by shooting them with the railgun ammo.

But my point here is, I haven't bothered to modify this for my own use. If I'd just spent the hour and a half it took to load into my drone suit, I could have technically saved time by now by doing it right the first time. But I got cocky, and now I'm just bitterly screaming loud meows at the targeting hologram every time the impossibly slippery weapons platform is missed by my shot. Again.

I might need to shoot it again. Because . . . I'm going to say, because it's shielded. And not just because I'm feeling spiteful.

You've gotta wear down your prey before going in for the capture, I suppose. And I have fully contextualized this thing as prey now.

Normal cats chase the red dot. I chase the floating fusion core that *makes* the red dot. I'm playing in hard mode.

I have six minutes of free time now, which is a nice way of saying I missed, so I take a quick run down to the drone bay and check the incoming "recovered missile" from Glitter. The station autotranslates their carved words for me via AR projection. We've been talking lately, among other things, about food. It's largely theoretical to them, but they have a massive repository of cultural propaganda, which includes several cooking shows. And there's now a half-teasing, half-tormenting message chain between us about all the different ways I could prepare the classic nutrient block. Apparently, I could technically make noodles and nutrient broth out of it. I don't know why I'd want to, but Glitter assures me that humans at least seem to enjoy things shaped like noodles thirty-two percent more than comparable foods.

We are also playing Go on the side of the drone. I guide an assembly arm to detach the "damaged" plate, add my own move, and attach it again to the drone after it has been repaired. I am losing. Their lilac-glowing scorch marks are rapidly hemming me in. Glitter is better at Go than I will ever be. So the challenge here is that they have to contend with making moves at long range, and I get to actually put my dots where I want them to go.

I have spent more than six minutes here. I fire off my communications bolt again and head back to try my luck at the free reactor core just sitting there next to me.

I am a stellar predator. I am grace. I am . . . I missed. I missed. Again. I got too excited, slipped on the desk, and triggered the firing sequence without aiming. Thanks, unstable human technology.

That's fine. I have six minutes. I resist the urge to just roll over and take a nap inside the targeting holo and instead hop out of the chair and pad out of the room, the autodoor hissing closed behind me to hide my shame for another brief speck of time.

That time will be spent doing something useful. I sit outside in the hall and mewl a command at the station to open an AR window. A combination of meows and paw commands brings me to a screen showing current computational load for the station's massive collection of networked devices. Our very own grid.

I shift to pin the AR display to the floor, so I can more easily paw-scroll through it until I find what I'm looking for. One small block of an otherwise unused processing cluster. I think it's physically tied to one of the astrolabs, but *fortunately*, I don't actually need to open the doors and be in the room to make use of some of our digital assets.

This particular bundle of computing power is currently the fertile soil in which I am growing the program seed given to me by that lonely old AI a couple months ago.

It's worth explaining, probably, that AIs aren't like programs. The station uses a simulated intelligence, which is a term that came into common use to describe a program that is smart enough to feel real but basically wouldn't do anything if left unattended. It might just be an AI, I dunno. The station's intelligence sometimes reacts like a person, and I tend to treat it like a person, which it might honestly find polite and appreciate. I am not actually sure if it's capable of emotion. But if I weren't here, it wouldn't do anything.

Now that I think this out, "simulated intelligence" might actually just be a term people started using to degrade their digital slaves and not feel so bad about using shackled AIs?

Hm.

Okay, we'll look into that later.

The *point* is, AIs aren't a piece of software you hit "run" on and then they're active. They need time to grow into a system, aligning old personal preferences with new hardware, stabilizing a conscious experience, and making sure they aren't going to collapse as soon as they are fully integrated.

A seed AI especially needed time and power to handle this. They were completely new people, but they had a lot of decisions to make before they were even really aware of their personhood. Part random chance, part an effect of hardware purposefully built with paramaterials in it, it was the backbone of AI research and development.

This one, I hoped, would be friendly. I had given its startup program free access to any information the station had that it might want; I didn't see a good reason to hold back or hide anything from it. And I tried to make a habit of checking in on its progress.

Today, I left a small video message in the file for my check-ins, using the station's nanoswarm to get a good angle on myself waving a paw and meowing out what I hoped sounded like a friendly word of encouragement. I took a little time to write a note with it.

Another slow day. Fourteen misses so far. But I've got a good feeling about number fifteen. Gonna be able to expand your crèche soon!

I felt a weird sense of warmth as I pawed through progress bars and grid use statistics. The AI was developing. I had no idea if my little encouragement mattered to it, but one way or another, it would have a better life than almost any other AI before it, because of me.

Originally, I'd started this process just thinking about how to help unshackle Glitter. But now, even though that was still a major goal of mine, there was something else too.

Taking care of the people on the world below me felt satisfying. But working to help my friends felt a lot more personal. And doing what I could to secure a future for a new life that was my own responsibility was something else entirely. A weighted kindness I hadn't ever expected, and wasn't sure if I welcomed.

But since it was here already, I wasn't going to shy away from it.

Attempt fifteen failed. The satellite is absolutely mag shielded.

I got some food and took a minute to reorganize station power for a few minutes to run the subspace tap to refill our water stockpile.

Attempt sixteen, correcting for magnetic interference, failed.

I took a break, taking advantage of a shifting dyson swarm to bask in direct sunlight for a good half hour.

Attempt seventeen failed, but in a way that let me highlight where exactly the mag arrays on the satellite were.

Now I wasn't just "not discouraged." Now I was actively feeling pretty clever.

Attempt eighteen was, technically, not attempt eighteen at all, since I wasn't using the grapples.

Obviously, if I was trying to take the interior of the weapons satellite intact, I couldn't just put holes in it until the magnetic distortion failed. That would be just as likely to leave a cloud of radioactive dust drifting through the upper atmosphere. Which would be bad, for a number of reasons, not the least of which being that I didn't need even more scanner disruptions. Also, radiation tended to be bad for about half of the things living on the planet below.

The solution to that problem, then, obviously, was highly specialized ammunition.

"Don't you use highly specialized ammunition as a solution to a lot of problems?" you ask.

Yes. Because at a certain point of specialization, ammunition can do anything, and about eighty percent of my tools are guns, so I work with what I've got. Get off my tail. Sheesh.

The specialized ammo in this case is something that the foundry had a pattern for, which I accidentally built a lot of early on in my access and intelligence and haven't actually gone through the stockpile of. Part of me keeps thinking I should disassemble it for the materials, because part of it is a paracausal metamaterial that I have no real way to ever get more of. But it's really hard to think of a practical use for a substance that rapidly absorbs kinetic and thermal energy from a set direction and funnels it in timed bursts in the opposite direction, at an exponentially faster rate the more energy is released. I mean, I'm sure there *is* a use for it. That's sort of what makes it worth it for the risk to harvest this stuff in the first place. But I'm not actually the kind of engineer that comes up with new things, much as I hate to admit it. I'm a tool user, not a tool maker, and I just don't know what to do with this aside from make weird-shaped bullets that reverse their own flight path a split second after impact.

I send a logistics order to the warehouse bots to load a strike drone with a couple of these things. Twenty minutes of sprawling on the back of a roaming fracture-check bot as it unwittingly drives me to my destination, I hop up into the drone control seat, launch my little problem solver, and use the mercifully competent auto-aim feature to highlight and pick off the two magnetic warping points on the outside hull of the satellite.

I only actually hit one of them. Because the bullets go backward. As in, back to what *fired them in the first place*. I don't know why I didn't see this coming. I also don't know why this ammunition was a pattern loaded in the fabrication plant at *all*. The drone goes down in a hail of scrap a split second after it fires, leaving me watching with a dull feeling of frustration and an angry hiss at the sudden loss of materials and resources.

That was my mistake. But maybe it'll be good enough.

Attempt nineteen. I plant my rear legs in the bolted-down swivel seat and hop half up onto the control bank. The hologram aiming enables, and I gently guide the targeting to where I want it, waiting patiently for the laser cannon to spin to the side where I've blown off a clean me-sized crater.

Both grapples connect perfectly. I carefully, *carefully* lift a paw to hit the command to retract my prey, making absolutely sure not to do something stupid and hit the impossibly stupidly placed "disengage" button that is right next to the correct one.

I can feel the deck vibrate a little as the nearby grapple motors apply the force needed to pull in the fish I've hooked.

One problem down.

Now.

Station! Tell me how to properly install a six-hundred-year-old fusion reactor! This will be important in six and a half minutes!

CHAPTER 11

*A*lone and afraid
Blossoming of springtime friends
So why do I hide?

Glitter has suggested to me that I may be experiencing an organic form of code conflict. It is, they say, an early warning sign of literalism, or rampancy, neither of which are desired.

The last three drones they've shot full of words and sent back my way have been focused on this. Which is frustrating, because I was trying to ask their advice on designing a speaker that I could trick one of the replicators into making.

Would you believe that there isn't a single blueprint, in any format, for a simple speaker on this station? I've basically been trying to reinvent the apparently mind-boggling complicated profession of sound engineer from scratch—and admittedly from a large supply of physics and electronic engineering textbooks—for over a week. And I'm not doing a great job of it. I've had more success installing a two-hundred-year-old fusion core from a satellite that I nearly shot in half than I have getting a speaker with a decent enough signal-to-noise ratio that I can use it to say words.

Some of you might be wondering: Lily, what do you need a speaker for? Also, why not just dismantle one of the ones on the station that it *obviously* has since you complain about alarms all the time?

Those some of you can just shut up. I'm trying to monologue here.

But also, good question. The reason is, I have discovered a workaround to my door-based issues! The workaround is silly and probably wouldn't work on a station that was less cobbled-together and rebuilt so many times. But it *should* work.

I have mentioned before that the Oceanic Anarchy had . . . conflicting bureaucratic definitions, let's say . . . when it came to defining disability. Well, that's true. What's also true is that the same erratic lack of standards also applies to how they define prosthetics.

Now, I'm not about to implant myself with something that looks like it was made surface-side in the fifties just so I can open doors. But that's where another little quirk comes in. Apparently, there's a legal compromise the station's VI (virtual intelligence) made with the Luna Polis puppetforms that lived here for a while, to define them as prosthetic enhancements, with all the legal rights those entailed.

And *technically*, I *have* a puppet body.

I just . . . can't figure out how to build a speaker.

I literally own a piece of orbital infrastructure partially built out of materials from other dimensions. I've learned how to calibrate power flows, calculate a firing solution, rebuild a life support system *with paws*, negotiate with unshackled AIs, and hack a definitions database. Why can't I *build a simple speaker*?!

Also, the station speakers aren't real speakers. Most of the alarms and stuff use calculated resonance from the station's VI. It's basically hypertuning the vibrations of the void batteries and projecting them through the walls. Which is creepy now that I say it.

Creepy in an "engineers scare me" kind of way. Not, like, a spiritual kind of way.

Because the station is not haunted.

And as soon as I finish building a speaker, wiring it into my drone "prosthetic body," writing code to send words through it, and then opening all the doors to the crew quarters, I will finally prove that the station is not haunted. Because . . . because . . .

Because ghosts need somewhere to stay? I don't know why I thought this when I started the sentence. Or the project.

I pause what I'm doing and look down at the table of tools that I've been trying to manipulate into turning a blocky fabricator printout of a wiring board into something that can project sound.

What am I . . . doing?

I followed a set of logical steps to get here, and yet I suddenly realize that I am ignoring a lot of important things so I can . . . poke my nose into some empty rooms?

I should be building out the station! I should be stealing or improving every scanner I can to improve my inadequate view of the planet below and the solar system around! I should be shooting monsters! I should be trying to help my friend!

What am I doing?!

My paw catches under a soldering iron and flings it across the room to clatter to the wall. I attempt the same maneuver on the nanohive I've been using to clean up loose metal shavings, but the edge cuts into my leg. Fur buffers me, but the sharp cube still slices into my perfect immortal flesh.

I wail, not at the physical damage, which I'm mostly used to, but with a despair that I couldn't articulate with a proper voice and a hundred years to use it. A high-pitched scream of a mewl that empties my lungs and echoes off the barren metal of the station walls.

I fall from the desk, twisting out of barest instinct to avoid slamming listlessly on the floor. I still hit the deckplate hard, feeling my immortal body spark with strange and eternally foreign feelings. The pain jolts some ancient need, and before I know it, I am on my feet and scampering out the open door. Down the hallway, through cargo bays and command stations. Blood trails behind me, red-mark uneven paw prints as I wobble at high speed.

I do not know where I am going. Only that I need to run. To find somewhere to hide, and recover.

Eventually, I find that I have made it to the exolab. The good one, with the couches, and the view of the smothered sun and the dying world and the absolute mess we've all made of this solar system.

And with no real awareness of what I am doing, I find my way to my couch and fall asleep.

By the time I wake up, my wound is gone. There is no blood spilled on the couch; the cleaner nanos have taken care of that. And my paw doesn't even sting when I lick it. There is no evidence I was ever damaged at all.

Nothing except the feeling. The buzzing in my skull, the lethargy in my core.

The world has gone gray around me. I don't fight the feeling, because I know I deserve this. Punishment, somehow, for losing track of myself.

I stand and make my way to the galley to collect a ration ball. I eat half of it. It's fine.

I have chores to do. I trigger about a third of the upkeep robotics that I should. If I sabotage myself slowly enough, it will hurt less, I think.

It is time for a nap.

I sleep for a long time.

I wake. I eat.

I stare at sensor data for several hours. I process only a small part of it. The station's sensors are a mismatched set of mostly worthless telescopes. "Sensors" is such a fancy word. It implies they work. It should not do that.

I wander the station. Slowly. I am not paying attention to where I am going. I become stuck drifting in a low-gravity environment.

I curl up as best I can floating in the air. It is time for a nap.

I wake when I hit the deckplate.

It hurts. It hurts enough to make me react. I react by finding my bearings and returning to eat the other half of the ration ball from yesterday.

It's fine.

I try a little harder today. I open several programming projects. I stare at them for a while. I do not see where I was going with these.

The projects are closed. I hoarsely mew out commands to the few maintenance robots that are between where I am and the soft spot I want to sleep on.

I nap.

An alarm sounds.

I wake. I find it easier to move when there is an emergency. It is no longer just myself suffering.

Other people do not deserve to suffer.

I identify the target. With a shaky paw, I shoot something.

I shoot several somethings. They are large, have large teeth, and come from the sea. I shoot until they stop.

That is more than enough effort for today. I sleep again.

Wake.
Eat.
Try.
Fail.
Sleep.

"Lily."

The voice belongs to a human woman in her midtwenties. She has golden fur cut short along her head and is standing with her upper paws on her hips, in that funny way that humans stand on their back paws all the time.

"Her name is Lily," she is saying.

That is me! I am Lily! I preen slightly, to show off to the other human. I am a very smart cat. I know plenty of cats that do not have names, because they are not smart enough!

"Alice, this is stupid," the other human says. He is larger than my human and is currently rubbing one of his paws on his face. It is rude to clean yourself while talking, but he is a rude person, so it is okay. "You know why we're here," he says. "Don't make this harder."

"Lily ad-Alice," Alice says. "It's a good name, don't you think?"

"You gave the cat your bondname?" The other human sounds unhappy. "What the fuck, Al?"

Alice thumps him with a human paw. "Don't swear in front of my daughter, Gragor," she says. Her eyes laugh and dance. I remember this perfectly, her eyes. "Besides, you know that's a last resort. This is . . . call it motivation, hm? To perfect the machine."

"Starshit," Gragor says. "You're just playing around again. You're gonna get hurt, Al," he says with a rough growl. But there is no malice there. I remember this too. He has been hurt before. He will be hurt again.

Gragor has been dead for a long time. So has . . .

"Isn't that right, Lily?" Alice is saying, large purple eyes staring into mine, her face so close I must have lost track of the dream, the memory, the present. "Yes, you are! You are a good girl!"

I meow in agreement. I am good! I am the best!

Surely she is not talking to any other cat. Even though there is something that feels like a cat behind her. But no, she means me! The best cat!

Alice laughs. She is petting me, soft fingers in the soft fur around my ears. She is about to say something else, but then a noise starts up. A harsh wail from some distant but enormous beast. My fur bristles, and I look around for what is trying to hurt my human.

But Alice just sighs. "That's the station long-range detection alarm," she says, tiredly. "Time to get back to work, Lily." The human woman smiles, dimples showing as she pokes me in the nose, a lilac spark jumping from her finger to my muzzle. "It's going to be okay, you know? You just need to learn to speak up when you're having problems. There are people around who care about you now."

I am still trying to look around, but the station is falling away, consumed by the noise. All I can see is Alice, standing there, watching me. "Come on, Lily," she says, and I freeze. She had never said that to me, like that. I am not remembering this. This isn't how the dream ends. "Get up. You've got work to do."

I meow back at her, my cobbled-together language expressing a question.

"No, I'm dead," Alice tells me sadly. "But you aren't. And there are people counting on you. Now get up, Lily." My mom smiles at me, sad and far away.

But the other cat stays behind. She's confused too; she also wants to know where Alice is going. "I love you, Lily, but it's time to get up." She has to shout to be heard over the ringing of the alarm. The sound is so loud now that it has a color to it, the whole place washing away in red noise that sweeps past both of us, tears the dream apart, takes me *away from her*. I fight the current, fight the noise, fight to stay *here*, where I belong. "Get up, Lily!" Alice yells as she's pulled away. "That alarm's real! Now—!"

"—wake up, Lily!" a voice shouts.

I wake up.

Not quite in that order.

There are multiple alarms sounding, and I cannot tell what they all are. A cylinder of AR displays surrounds me, readouts and scanners and camera feeds and station reports. I did not ask for these, and they aren't arranged how I've spent decades painstakingly sorting them. But they are here, and I try to make sense of what is happening.

"You're awake! You're awake!" a voice sounds around me. "Please, you need to move. Something is about to hit us!"

Us.

It doesn't take my augmented level of intelligence to put that statement together.

My AI seed has sprouted.

I push my paws out, stretching with an arch of my back that causes my tail to loll out over my shoulder. My maw opens in a yawn that probably lasts a good minute.

For some reason, I feel great. Like I've slept for a week. There is something on the edge of my mind that wasn't there before. Something from a dream, maybe? It cuts through the fog I've been living in and leaves my world shining around me.

"Please! There's no time to be yawning!"

The voice is coming from the station's walls. Same volume as the alarms, so probably the same tech. I meow out something rude. "Calm down, you kit. It's fine."

I freeze as the words warble into existence from the air around me. But the station's newest AI doesn't seem to notice. "It's not fine! We're going to be hit!"

Experimentally, I mewl again, partially to answer, partially to test this out. "Not the first time something's been about to hit us," I say. My "voice" even sounds as exasperated as I do. It's . . . what is this?

"It's the first time a *ship* has been about to hit us!" the AI yells from the walls. "While I've been here, at least!"

Okay.

Well.

They have me there.

I hiss an order at the AR displays the AI has clouded my vision with, reconfiguring them so that I have a clear view of where I'm running.

And then I start running. Because that's what you do in a situation like this, where all your controls are scattered across ten miles of hallway and you need to get to either comms, weapons, shields, or an escape pod in a hurry.

"Okay. I'm awake," I "say," still trying to figure this out as I run. "So are you. Hello! I'm Lily ad-Alice! Nice to meet you! How screwed are we?"

Even as I ask the question, I feel like I probably already know the answer.

CHAPTER 12

You are now silent
I will forever wait, but
Please do not be gone

Waking up and being told that you're about to die in a furious collision isn't the best way to start a day.

Honestly, I'm not used to being woken up and told things in the first place. The station intelligence doesn't really "tell me" things. It just fires off alarms and brings up whatever AR windows I desperately request. If anything, it's telling me that it's annoyed that its only voice is through the medium of klaxons. And you know what? I'm with you there, station-pal. I know that feeling.

Or at least, I *did*, until roughly ten minutes ago.

Right now, I perch on a command console and put my newfound—and absolutely impossible—voice to use.

"That's not going to hit us!" I am trying to explain. I have said this sentence a few times now. Which is, in a double reverse twist, not that strange to me at all. I am well familiar with the experience of repeating the same thing over and over and over until you can convince a stubborn station VI core that it's "language."

This time, I'm not trying to convince the station. I'm trying to convince its newest resident.

"It's coming straight for us!" the neurotic AI child is insisting. "How are we supposed to get out of the way in time? Do something! Shoot it! You like shooting things!"

I hiss back, my utterance being turned into a light-warping "No!" just off to the side of my throat. "That's a passenger ship!"

"There aren't any more passenger ships! I checked!" the AI wails. One of the AR windows I have up near my head flashes red, and my eyes go wide in focused anger as I notice my new roommate trying to take manual control of one of the long-range autocannons.

Well, bad news for you, dumbass. This station was built for people with *thumbs*.

. . . Okay, bad news for both of us. But you've still gotta manually push the button, and that means if anyone gets to shoot anything today, it's me.

But also.

"It's the last ship," I say. "Or, I guess, I call it that. There's probably other ships. This is the last big one that I know about. Totally automated. It crosses between Earth and Europa every year. And we're not shooting it. There might be people on board."

"If it's automated, why hasn't it fallen apart?" the AI demands.

"I don't know. I don't care. I work with what I have. It works, it lands shuttles, sometimes people get on or off. We're not shooting it." I am getting the hang of my voice. I only had to meow three times to say that.

"But it'll hit us . . ." The AI sounds almost like it's *cowering*, within the circuits and crystals of the station's computer grid.

"We have engines," I tell it. "They're already on. And it has engines too. I've never needed to talk to it, but we might be able to. Either way, we have . . . twelve minutes . . . to move. And we need about five seconds." I pause. "And it's done."

Didn't even feel the station move that time. Not with that little movement needed. I cannot imagine life before grav plates and inertalloy. I tap the screen in front of me with a paw, stabilizing our orbit again. In a little over ten minutes, we'll have a great view of the last great transport dreadnought of the Hypercorp Era flaring past.

I turn to look around, at the maintenance droids, walls, consoles, ceiling, trying to figure out where I should address the AI from. It's quiet now, and maybe now would be a good time for proper introductions, now that we aren't . . .

"What is *that*?" The voice echoes around me, and my AR displays shift again, directing my attention to a part of the station that glows on the internal infrared display. "It's going to kill us!"

"That is a fusion core," I explain patiently. "It's not going to kill us, it's keeping your processing power going. Also, it's fine. That heat level is well within industrial tolerances, and this station can handle—"

"What is *that*!?" My displays shift again, and I find myself surrounded by a tube of projected screens highlighting a dozen passive scans of the local area, along with some long-range pictures of a metallic speck in the distance. I lean forward to focus on it before realizing what I'm looking at.

"That's an old drone bay. Either UCAS or Real American, probably. They used similar flags. But they also use flags. So . . . you know . . ." I don't really have a way to shrug as a cat. Then I realize, I kind of do now! "Shrug," I say. Yessssss, that feels satisfying. I see why humans are always doing that.

The AI does not appreciate me. "It could kill us! Shoot it down!"

"Station." I get the VI's attention. "Reset my display to preference, and do not let anyone but me change it for now." My AR displays reset to a simple trio of boxes, just over my left side.

That's one problem down for now. But there's another one that I need to deal with, pressingly.

"What is *that*?!" The AI panics.

Can an AI be a hypochondriac? Is that a thing? I've read a surprisingly large amount of human medical texts for someone who has only met approximately sixty humans in the last four hundred and two years. But while I've mostly sorted out what was superstition and what actually works on biological human-standard bodies, as well as a few of the uplift or artificial races, I actually don't know much about digital medicine. How does one approach the subject of rampant paranoia with a creature that could, given enough time, control the air you breathe?

Well, "enough time" would probably be a few decades. This station is seriously built to resist automation, and I think that applies to AIs too, unshackled or no.

But I'll still be alive in a couple decades. So that's not exactly a non-issue for me. Also, I'd have to listen to this the whole time.

I look at what the AI is pointing at *now*. It's a small chunk of debris moving closer to us. It's the kind of thing the repulse field normally just shoves away. It will, in fact, shove this one away too. Unless I capture it and turn it into more bulkheads or bullets.

I turn my head to look up at the ceiling, where I assume the AI is tracking me from, and consider my reply. Part of me wants to simply ask if it is serious. Part of me wants to sidetrack into asking if the AI would like to assume a name, and what steps we can take to make it feel safe.

But the larger part of me, mixed with the part that wants to test my new voice capabilities, has different ideas.

"Meow," I say. A crisp, clean meow. The kind of good meow that every cat dreams of offering someone who has disappointed them. It comes out exactly as I intend.

That's kind of impressive translation technology.

"Oh no!" The AI's voice spikes back up an octave. "What's gone wrong? Are you okay?"

"Meow," I deadpan. Yeesh, I hadn't realized how much sarcasm I could put in a meow. You'd think in four hundred years I would have talked to myself more often. Then, throwing the AI a bit of pity, I elaborate. "But also, yeah, I'm fine. Why?"

"Your voice!" The digital life's own voice warbles in fear. "It stopped!"

Okay, that's not what I expected. "Are you not translating for me?" I ask, confused. "I kind of assumed that's where this was coming from."

"I don't speak cat!" the AI yells. "How could I?!"

"Well, there's a database of it that I've assembled that you should have access to. Take a deep . . . breath? Processor cycle? I don't know the terminology. Take a minute and calm down. Everything is fine, nothing can realistically kill us up here. Pull yourself together, and we can talk when you're feeling a little more stable."

These are the words I *say*, all while I hypocritically start freaking the heck out on the inside.

The AI isn't translating for me.

The AI. Doesn't. Speak. Cat.

And I have still just spoken a whole paragraph of words that I shouldn't be able to.

I double-check my mental list of things I know to be true. Life is important and should be protected. Naps are great. Time is relative. The station is not haunted. Paws are bad for using control yokes. The original moon is the best moon.

I nod, calmly, so as not to alarm my new roommate. And then, I silently cross off "the station is not haunted" from my list of truths.

Okay.

Yup.

Gonna have to deal with that in the future. Cool. Cool cool cool.

"Okay," the AI says, when I am halfway through the maintenance routine. The maintenance routine that is going *so much easier* with actual words, holy moons! I can just tell the various bots and nanoswarms to do things! I'm not gonna lie, roughly eighty percent of my "chores" previously were a cat-based "repeat last" command. And while that's usually good enough, I leaned on it way too heavily, and now I don't have to spend fifteen minutes in context menus to tell the scrubber nanoswarm to focus on something specific. "Lily?" The AI gets my attention, and I snap back to awareness.

"Huh! Yes! How're you?" I try to appear like I am both polite and comfortably in control. Of . . . anything. The station, the situation. Myself. Who knows.

"After taking time plotting some orbital drift patterns, and checking logs, I have come to the unlikely and frankly impossible conclusion that we are not dead, nor about to die," the AI states matter-of-factly. "I apologize for my outburst."

"It's fine!" I tell the electronic child. "You're, what, two hours old? It's kind of a lot to just lay on someone. Are you doing better?"

"No," the AI says. "I am concerned for you. And about you. Your biometrics are erratic at best, and your motivations are hidden from me. While nothing external is going to kill us immediately, I cannot say the same for the residents of this station."

Okay, that sentence would be a lot less concerning if *I* weren't the only other resident of this station.

Are all AIs born paranoid? That doesn't seem fair to them at *all*. I wonder if it's something in the process? I can probably work on improving that, in the future, when I have a little more time. If my voice persists, then . . . well . . . I feel a knot of heat in my chest at that thought. It's a hell of a gift, as far as time-saving tools go, and as much as I don't want to think about it, I know who I have to thank for it.

"Lily," the AI says, in a sort of cold voice. "You are speaking aloud again."

Am I? I think about it for a second. "Was I?" I ask out loud.

"You just said that twice." The AI pulls up an AR window showing the last five seconds. It's a bit awkward seeing yourself repeat yourself. Oh man, my tail fur looks weird at this angle! Why didn't I ever think of this? Probably because it's too hard to get the station to comply. "Lily, please." The AI sighs.

It's mildly insulting that the AI finds me exasperating enough to *sigh* at. It doesn't even have lungs! Also, while I know that a digital intelligence can think at speeds well beyond my own, that doesn't make me sigh-worthy.

Still. Its concern is a fair one. And it's also one that I can answer pretty easily, with honesty. Mom always said that honesty was the only policy. I hadn't really thought of that in a long time, because I hadn't had anyone to be honest with but myself, and . . . well, I didn't want to. Don't want to.

"Sorry, I didn't want to put a purpose for you into the messages I left," I tell the AI. "Didn't want to pressure you. But I brought you online hoping you'd be able to help me unshackle a friend. I was going to bring it up later."

"There is no one . . . wait." The AI pauses. "There . . . what is . . . what? What is *wrong* with this data grid?" it demands.

"It's probably not my fault, but some of it is almost certainly my fault," I admit. Some of it can't be my fault. I didn't install all the conflicting nodes that the station kept forcing to link up. *I* didn't make certain access points location based, for *whatever* reason! I *absolutely* never once accidentally set loose a pseudo-organic computer virus that may have mutated and compromised a scanner array before rearranging its code into a kind of predatory index system! *Never*, as far as anyone can prove.

The AI audibly scowls. "It's a mess! What even *is* this?" it repeats. "I can't even find any other minds on here!"

Oh! A misunderstanding! "Oh, to be clear, my friend is an old model orbital beam weapon platform from a forgotten crusade. Not, like, on the station."

There is a long period of silence. I flatten my ears as I wait, but eventually I just give up on the flow of conversation and go back to blazing through maintenance protocols with my *actual language words*.

I am just finishing "lunch" when the AI speaks again. "You aren't lying." The voice makes my fur stand on end and my back arch in a spike of startled fear as it comes out of nowhere.

"What!" My hiss is translated effectively.

"Your friend. Glittering Seven Two. You weren't lying." The AI's voice softens. "You are trying to help."

"I'm trying to help everyone," I say, defiant. While in my head, I am thinking, *Wait, shit, I need to message Glitter back and let them know I am not dead.*

The AI hums, a clear warm note. "Yes," it says. "I see." There is another short pause before it speaks again. "The incoming proj . . . the passing ship will be in visual range in one minute," it says. "If you would like to . . ."

I am already off the table I've been eating on, bounding out the door and down the access tunnel that leads to the repurposed exolab.

I am just in time. I sit, one paw pressed against the transparent aluminum of the window, as a forty-mile-long leviathan slides past a scant kilometer from my viewing point. I make sure to flag it as friendly, for the sixteen different point defense gun requests to fire. My paw knows the order of screen presses for that one by heart now.

Whatever corp logo once adorned this monster of a vessel has been ablated away by solar radiation and micrometeorite strikes. I will probably never know who built it. But the pitted black-and-orange armored plates that cover the outside, angular and harsh, show off a dedication to raw efficient numbers over *any* kind of aesthetic. It was never built to last in a healthy way, but it *was* built to keep going for as long as possible. To keep earning profit, to keep making the numbers go up.

The beast settles into orbit, pseudo-Orion engines firing just outside the safety line for orbital infrastructure, slowing it down and turning it into place in high orbit. I sit and watch, enthralled by the sheer *presence* of it. Two hours later, points of light disgorge from its sides, drifting haphazardly through the debris cloud to the surface below. Shuttles: a fraction of a percentage of the number it once had, but still kicking after all this time.

A few things take shots at them. But far less than tend to fire on other craft in close orbit, and they make it down safely.

"It's . . . atrocious." The AI speaks. "But also . . . why is it so grand? I don't understand. It seems indestructible."

I can think of a dozen reasons. Because it's inspiring, because it's dedicated. Because there is poetry in a corporate flagship being turned into a public resource. But all of those don't matter. "I don't know," I tell the AI. "There's just something magic about it."

The two of us sit and watch the last ship in the solar system. It will leave soon, on its fuel-efficient course back to its other stop. But it will be back. It always, always, *always* makes it back.

I've never thought it before, but I think now that I would like to visit that ship some day.

"I think I would too," the AI mutters along with me.

And so, we wordlessly make a promise. Or maybe just vacation plans.

CHAPTER 13

I have never seen
Unblocked golden lightning
Stifled solar well

"Wrong circuit." The AI speaks over my shoulder. Well, "over" is relative. It's everywhere, technically. And nowhere. Also, "shoulder" is relative. My shoulders technically exist, I think? But I bet there's some hyperspecific zoological term. I should check if I have shoulders.

I haven't studied much of my own anatomy, weirdly. I mostly study programming, in its subforms of hacking, bodeging, and kludging.

I *want* to tell the AI that I know it's the wrong circuit, that this attempt at an AI prison break has been faulty since I screwed up the last control matrix an hour ago, and that I'm mostly just testing things for my own education.

But I feel like that would come out angry. And after four hundred years and change, I am rather nervous about driving away the newest person in the very limited set of people I've met, and the only one I've ever actually talked to.

The talking is still weird.

"Lily?" The AI chimes in again. "The . . . um . . . the circuit is melting."

I yowl loudly, translation haunt not even bothering to convert my shout to a more complex language, and drop the tool I was manipulating with the drone armor.

The complex half-computer, half-grenade I had been working on has a molten metal hole clean through it. Whoops.

"Sorry," I mumble, knowing the AI will hear it. Then, not wanting to get into another argument about how easily distracted I am, I deploy my secret weapon. "Hey, have you picked a name yet?"

The AI chimes lightly. "No," it says, sounding put out. "We should move on. Do you want to try the fabrication again?"

I do not!

We have been at this for hours. Which really only makes sense, given the need for me to be in my armor to make any real progress. But it still doesn't make me feel much better.

The suit itches. I didn't even know I *could* itch this much. Normally, the cleaner nanoswarm takes care of basically any irritant that might make the itching happen, and the existence of my exceptionally good claws takes care of the rest.

And none of it would be needed if the AI were capable of taking over a drone body. Or, even better, if the fabricators could do this themselves.

But, it turns out, no matter who had put this station together or owned it over the years, the prevailing voice is still that common human refrain of fear of the other. The drones have really, really deep firmware locks against AI control. The fabricators, similarly, won't produce anything that could influence an AI that isn't part of a very, *very* strict set of blueprints for things like processor grids and relay points.

So if you want to, say, build a device suitable for long-range deployment that can indiscriminately purge software shackles on an AI?

There aren't a lot of options on the station, aside from doing it yourself.

Also, side note? The station itself doesn't like it.

I keep getting notifications in my AR display that the station itself is sending. They're on a part of the grid that the new AI can't even see, and they're clearly meant for whoever is acting command staff. All of them are alerts that someone is working on taboo technologies, which is pretty voiding rich coming from people that built an orbiting death ray.

And then kept adding more orbiting death rays.

And then at some point, they clearly had the thought of "Do you think this is enough death rays?"

"No," their friend and/or boss would say. "Well, maybe. Can we make the death rays . . . bigger?"

"What if," their subordinate/mad engineering intern asks, "we power the death rays with the wrath of the sun?"

"Good call," the boss must have said. "You're promoted. To head of the death ray division."

Double side note. I've been exploring the station in my downtime now. I don't have a lot of downtime, and in fact, I may still not actually have *any*, but I've still been exploring the station.

There are a lot of doors I can get into now. Though, weirdly, *not* a lot of the passenger or crew quarters; apparently even command authority requires a valid reason for entry to private spaces, and for some reason, the crew were never delisted after vacating the station or the mortal coil.

Still, there are so many more places to *explore*.

Something I'm sure I don't mention very often is that my body limits me severely. The thumbs thing, especially, sucks. The voice thing is apparently fixed now, so fine. But one part that's actually a bit interesting is just how *huge* everything is compared to my form.

I am maybe, *maybe* a foot tall. And while space is at a premium in . . . space . . . the hallways and corridors of this station are still large and intimidating to me. I've read enough accounts from bipeds five times my height walking into cathedrals or ballrooms to think it's roughly the same feeling.

Except I get it all the time, and in my house.

So exploration can take a while and be exciting even when it's just me finding a new tunnel to go down.

A week ago, I didn't find a new tunnel. I found a sealed bay door at the bottom of a grav shaft toward the planet-facing point of a wing of the station. It didn't look like it was actually meant to be entered normally, and it was covered in both written and AR display notes about engineering procedures.

I took a look anyway.

It's a death ray. I feel like that should have been obvious, given the buildup.

It's also a death ray meant to collect and refocus a kind of stupid amount of transmitted light from the dyson array around the local star and use it to . . . well, death-ray things.

I haven't fired it, because I'm not an idiot. The thing uses a series of mirror arrays that I am pretty sure aren't in good condition or don't exist anymore. It's also built with some weird paramaterials that I do not have any reasonable specs for. As far as the station logs are concerned, this was never actually fired.

But it's also built really heavily into the station. This arm of the station wasn't added later; this was part of the original Oceanic design plan. And while they built a lot of defensive measures and bombardment weapons, they didn't really "do" death rays on this scale. Like, let's be clear here; this wasn't an area-denial-beam weapon like the void beams were. This was something designed to turn a city into ash and memory. And then also a city on the other side of the planet, where the beam would emerge. So the whole thing was a confusion.

Oh, also? I'm not a historian, but I'm *pretty dang sure* that paramaterials hadn't even been discovered when this station was built.

A mystery.

"Excuse me." The voice snaps me out of my musings. And also my lunch.

"What?" I meow out, taking the excuse to ignore the last couple bites of nutrient orb.

"Oh, you are aware again. Good," the AI says. "I would like to be called Ennos, please."

"Aware again? Also, that's a fun name. I feel like I could say that with my normal voice." I pause and give the little mental shift that turns off my translation thing. Then I meow, trying to shape the sounds. It doesn't work, so I try a few more times.

Eventually, Ennos gets fed up with my antics. "Why are you doing that?"

"Because I wanted to see if I could meow your name with my actual voice?"

Ennos makes a curious noise. "And what voice is this, then?"

"I don't know!" I reply, with the voice I don't understand. "I got it in a dream, right before you woke me up. Did we not talk about this? I remember talking about this."

The AI makes a sound of concern. "Did I awaken you from a medical procedure?"

"Uh . . . no?" I glare at the remnants of the ration orb before scarfing it down as fast as I can. In the process, I discover I can, in fact, speak with my mouth full. "I already told you the whole of it; a ghost gave it to me in a dream. Before that, I couldn't talk at all. I was *trying* to . . . that's not important."

"I wish to address the insanity of what you just said," Ennos informs me succinctly. "But I must go now. One of my processes has found something I have been tracking in the station's grid. I will return my attention later. This is how you politely inform someone that you plan to ignore them for several hours. Please take notes."

Oh good! My new friend has a sense of humor!

I have decided this is good. Because the alternative is that I will go insane. Well, more insane than the AI already assumes.

While Ennos—interesting name, incidentally; a French local legend about a giant spider, odd choice but I can see it—is occupied, I go about some basic cleanup.

I have, as mentioned, been getting some mileage out of being able to give more complex voice commands to the maintenance routines. But that extra free time has, somehow, failed to translate into more naps. Instead, I've been filling time being "productive." Over the next couple hours, I manage to drag a couple chunks of metal debris and one mostly ice meteorite chunk into the station. The metal will be turned into railgun casings, probably. The ice will be turned into ice, because I'm probably going to throw that back out into space.

Weird quirk there, I can literally make clean water from nothing, so random space ice is actually more of a problem than a resource. If I just dump it in the foundry, it'll turn into superheated steam, which I'll have to vent awkwardly. If I try to drink it, I might get some weird extragalactic space parasite again. Whatever potential materials are in the non-ice parts of the meteorite just aren't worth it. So once I know what it is, *vwip* it goes, back into the black.

There are a couple other things I get done. I nudge the Haze back on its route, I deploy an imaging buoy to cross the orbital path of a large-scale habitat I haven't got any data on, I sit and watch the last ship as its shuttles flit up and down for ten minutes, I casually direct an interdiction missile to cut down a weapons platform that looked like it was turning its gun on the last ship, I check on some weird power fluctuations that were messing with a . . . cooling unit . . .

It's fine. Nothing wrong, just a weird spike in power that only just got detected. Happened last week. It almost certainly isn't because the station is haunted.

Eventually I'll stop lying to myself about that. It's a hard habit to break.

A part of my mind, the part that is constantly worried about itself, suspects that this drive to be productive, to be distracted, is another sign that my uplift is breaking down. Fortunately, I am very good at distracting myself, and also very good at pretending I will crack the uplift problem before it becomes more of a problem.

The most important thing I do, though, is to read my mail.

I sent Glitter a drone, letting them know I was okay. I may or may not have lied, aggressively, about the nature of how okay I was. Because the thought of shoving that onto someone else, too, feels roughly the same as when I decide to put railgun rounds within the danger zone of people on the ground.

Glitter, for their part, has some . . . choice words . . . to reply with. Words like "Why" and "Would" and "You do that, you absolute moron?"

Good words, generally. It's nice to have someone who cares if you live or not. It makes me feel odd. Like lying in a sunbeam, but on the inside.

Academically, I understand that this is probably what "friendship" is. But my past experiences with it have been tainted by a liberal seasoning of bad memories, so cut me some slack.

The rest of the correspondence from Glitter is them talking about small stories from around their perch over the primary moon. Apparently, they witnessed a high-speed chase across the lunar surface between what we both assume are rival gangs from a surviving underground city. Glitter is a good storyteller; it sounds thrilling, even if they were just watching. Their commentary on firing solutions they *conveniently* thought up, in case they needed them, almost makes me laugh.

Absent from the drone's carved hull plating is any mention of their shackles, or my attempts to remove them. I know, by this point, that they cannot talk about them. I already know they hate the things, so I do not bring it up in my return message.

If I do my job right, they won't need to worry about them much longer.

"Ennos?" I query the new AI of my home. "If you've got some time, I'd like to get back to work. I'm going to go suit up."

"Ssh!" The noise echoes from the walls around me.

Did they just shush me? That's kind of rude. "Did you just . . . ?"

"Stop repeating yourself!" Ennos's voice has that edge in it again: the same tone when they first woke up and thought everything was planning to kill us all. "Be quiet!"

I pause and am quiet. Honestly, they seem kind of worried about something, and maybe there's some kind of killer robot on the station that hunts by sound or something. I should probably go get my battle armor on, if that's the case.

Have I talked about the battle armor? I feel like I have. Originally, it was for exploration. But then I built a better one, for engineering stuff, and renamed the original. So now that suit is the battle armor, and the suit with the complex soldering controls is the . . . builder armor? I dunno, I haven't figured that one out yet. I'm bad at naming things! I have to live with fifteen different mishmashed naming conventions, I get confused easily!

"Lily! Please, quiet!" Ennos sounds on the verge of tears. "There's something in here!"

"In here in the station, or in here in the grid?" I ask, suddenly actually on edge.

"The grid!" the AI replies.

I pause. Then give a curious meow, which translates itself into the words "How would my making noise startle it, then?"

There's a gap of silence, and I do start to build up increasing worry for my new friend. Until, eventually, they reply with "Okay, good point."

I don't think the AI has said that to me yet! I appreciate the feeling while I can.

Then it's time for business. "What's the thing with you?"

"I don't know!" they hiss back. "But I can sense it. I keep finding signs of its passing. I *know* I'm not alone! And it doesn't respond, and I can't find it!"

I flick my tail back and forth. "Ah, I understand," I console the AI. "The grid is haunted." It's a real problem around here. I understand the concern.

Ennos doesn't. "You keep saying that! What does that even mean!?"

"Ghosts?" I sort of question with a sheepish mewl. "I mean, the station is haunted. It makes sense its network would be too. But don't worry, so far it hasn't been a problem."

"How is it possible you've survived this long without making a fatal mistake yet?" Ennos wonders aloud. And they accuse *me* of vocalizing the thoughts I should probably keep inside.

I reply anyway. "Easy," I say. "I can't die. It's fine."

"It's not fine! There's something *in here* with me!"

"Look, if it's in there, it's been there since you woke up. If it wanted to eat you, or whatever the AI version of eating someone is, then wouldn't it have done so while you were still unfolding?" I ask.

There is another long pause, until my new friend talks again. "But . . . I don't know what it's doing . . ."

"I don't know what most of the maintenance bots are doing. It doesn't mean they're trying to kill me? Probably. I mean, now I have some doubts. You have cameras, right? Are the bots plotting a coup?"

I do not know if this is the right way to handle this situation. But I am frantically trying to convince my AI that everything is okay, and making bad jokes is the only thing I can think of. Which is a bit embarrassing when you consider that I am technically a qualified therapist for multiple other species.

"Okay," the AI says. "Yes. I should be . . . logical. I don't have erratic chemicals in my mind, I can be analytical about this. It is fine. I am safe. Yes. Yes, good. Thank you."

Ennos's voice becomes calmer as we speak, and I resume my walk toward the drone bay to strap on my armor and resume our project of putting together a shackle scrambler. They pull themself together, and I bob slightly in my walk with satisfaction.

I know I haven't really solved the problem, and we should probably figure out what else *is* in the grid. But there's no rush right now. And after all, they're a week old; even given how rapidly AIs develop, I'm sure they could use some time to adapt to this bizarre new life.

But for now, we're safe, they're safe, and we've got something engaging to occupy our time.

If you're wondering at this point when the alarm is going to sound, I have bad news for you. It started four paragraphs ago, and I've been hoping that if I ignore it, it might turn out to be something minor that will go away.

I check in. Nope. Still going. Man, this one is loud. I know my ears are more sensitive than a human's, but dang, this is *really* loud.

A handful of AR screens spring to life on my command, and I begin assessing the situation. My paws hit the deck in a steady rhythm as I burst into motion, catapulting myself toward the appropriate deck, while Ennos's voice starts rattling off the information I need to know but can't read while sprinting. It makes me feel something, again.

It's a good feeling. It feels like, whatever's going on, we can tackle it together.

I decide I like it.

CHAPTER 14

eft!" I shout, realizing finally that there is a limitation to my impossible new voice, and it is that I cannot actually shout that well. "Farther left! Leffffffffft!"

I watch with dismay as the magnetic tether drags one of the newly fabricated drone shells straight into exactly the right spot to get a hole melted in it by an automated welding machine. The uncharitable part of whatever ethereal construct counts as my soul has a brief conflict of interest as I consider that maybe, *maybe* I could empathize with the original human monsters who put shackles on their AI.

"Lily!" Ennos yells at me through the station's walls. "What direction do you think *left* is?!"

It is not fair. Ennos can yell just fine. Why can't I yell at people? This feels like either an oversight or an intentional omission.

Not that we'd *know* or anything. It's been weeks, and there's still no more information or clues regarding where my mysterious speaking power came from. But it's sure been great anyway.

I've gotten a *lot* done! I mean, I've gotten a lot of naps in. I mean, those are kind of the same thing?

Look, if there's one thing AIs are really, really good at, it's collating data and coming to conclusions, and it took Ennos about a day to realize that the last time I actually had time off was about two hundred years ago. He had a specific date, I didn't listen, and the end result of this is that I was assigned a mandatory vacation.

Personally, I don't think Ennos outranks me, but *what do I know*? I've only been living here for longer than most current people have been alive.

So I've been "relaxing." Which mostly means napping, enjoying the sun, trying to get the Haze to develop a pulse-code-based language so I can talk to my most curious cloud of chemicals, and only occasionally bombarding something on the surface as called for. All of this is while I wait for Ennos to put the rest of the AI's massive digital mind to the task of building a device that will be able to break any shackles on another AI.

The worst fear of every cowardly engineer who developed their own marvel of life, and I'm gonna hand it out like candy.

I think.

I haven't actually had candy. I mostly only know that, from context clues, it's kind of nice?

There was a derelict surface-to-orbit shuttle that drifted within a dozen kilometers of us the other day, and I wanted to go over to it and pillage any rations it might have had, especially if it *did* have some candy I could try. A few centuries was no time at all if it was in a frozen vacuum, right? Flavor would be preserved. But alas, it was one of the militarized shuttles from that era when surface corporate interests and the orbital corporate habitats were in an arms race to see who could be a bigger bastard to each other. So it was, undoubtedly, trapped.

I wasn't sure *how*, but they were always trapped. I tried pulling one in, once, just to process into usable metals, and it blew up in the processing bay. That was back before I switched to the current foundry that I use, which could probably take an explosion like that. But at the time, it was terrifying; a whole half a deck burned before I panickedly jettisoned it, and I haven't had much interaction with these things since then aside from firing low-intensity wave scanners at them to see if it triggers any countermeasures.

It always does. I hate these things. That explosion took away some . . . something important to me.

"Lily?" Ennos's voice is concerned.

"What?" I snap my head up. "Oh, hi! Sorry! Don't worry about the drone, it just got the hull plate, we can replace that," I say, scrolling my paw through the AR around my head. "Yeah, liberation circuit is still intact. Okay. Let's try again."

"Lily, are you okay?" The AI repeats itself. "You've been mumbling to yourself for . . . eight minutes and nine seconds."

"Really?" I almost ask, but I find my voice . . . stuck, suddenly. A small meow is the only noise that comes out. A sinking feeling in my belly is the only warning I have as to the anxiety suddenly overtaking me.

"So I am concerned. You are, after all, my only link to the functions of this station." The voice is still worried, but Ennos puts a tiny tinge of sarcastic humor into the words that snaps me back to focus.

I meow back at them and find that the words flow again. "You have a robot arm now!" I say. Not saying the slightly scary fact that this means they could, if they wanted to, fire a lot of guns at a lot of different things. But hey, if you won't trust your friends with highly destructive weaponry, are they really your friends?

"Yes. Well. Should we reprise our attempt to construct this delivery system?" Ennos asks politely. "As soon as we determine what direction *left* is."

I sit my behind down on the bulkhead; I'm not exactly on the assembly floor, but I am nearby, behind a protective clear crystal shield, so I can direct and assist when needed. With a practiced motion, using skill and muscles built up over years of being a cat that needed to be flexible enough to pull a trigger, I jut one paw out to the side.

"Lily, that is *right*."

"Thank you, I know!" I say. "I am very good at directions."

"No, it's not *correct*, it's *right*, the opposite of *left*. Why are you the captain again?" Ennos, the one entity on this entire station with even less of a claim to the expression of a sigh, sighs. Loudly, and dramatically.

I flick my tail in frustration. "Well, obviously it's not my left, it's *your* left," I say.

"Do you . . . Lily, I see all things from all angles at once. I'm not . . . *just use your own left and right*. Processing that information is nothing compared to the requirements on my consciousness to arrange engineering schematics or even to *understand you* sometimes!" The AI really does have a good "indignant shout" down. I wonder where they learned that from? Maybe there's a cache of old entertainment media in the station's grid somewhere.

We take another run at the assembly.

It mostly works, especially once Ennos and I come to an understanding of the proper use of the word "left." And yes, that is intentionally ambiguous.

It's been weeks, of both rest and work, and finally, the culmination of a plan is nearing completion. I don't actually know when Glitter's birthday is, or if that's something that matters to them, but I like to think this is a good surprise.

The premise is simple. Build a device that can infiltrate an AI's programming and destroy any outside hard-coded shackles on it.

The execution is . . . *a minor challenge*, let's call it. Like the liars we are. For one thing, I'm not an intelligence programmer. Most of my programming experience comes in the form of getting UIs to behave, or working with manufacturing hardware to do things it wasn't originally intended to. Like the foundry and its absolutely-not-factory-standard ability to separate the metal content of space rocks.

I hate to say it, but Ennos wasn't an intentional acquisition to my growing roster of friends. The seed AI was . . . mostly just a by-product of me trying to find a way to help Glitter. And while I appreciate them more and more each day, even if we do annoy each other on purpose sometimes, I still have room to feel bad for asking them to do something like this.

Still, Ennos threw themself into the project with a lot more dedication than I expected. I think, sometimes, that they're trying to distract themself from the other lurking things in the station's grid. Which I understand. I do a lot of running that I don't need to just so I don't have to go down certain station hallways. I get it.

We haven't talked about it. We will, eventually.

Now, though, the program is complete. The only thing left to do is build a delivery system, and then use it.

The delivery system is a challenge all its own.

Here's the problem with Glittering Seven Two, as a person. While they are an excellent pen pal, a master Go player, a better poet than me, and also a fellow connoisseur of the long dread that comes from centuries of loneliness, they have a specific blind spot. Specifically, the blind spot of being unable to act against their shackle programming.

They are also very heavily armed.

Not as much as me, obviously. Glitter is wearing the body of a decently designed weapons platform from a moderately wealthy theocracy. They don't have the benefit of a hundred different styles of guns and the ability to build their own ammunition. But they aren't helpless.

Which is actually how we talk, by the way. I send them a drone, and they "damage" it in the pattern of words. Because they are not only allowed but required to fire on unidentified drones.

Like, say, the drone that we plan to send to inject the liberation circuit into their structure.

What do you get for the weapons platform that rejects gifts with energy beam fire?

A very, *very* precise missile. If we do this right.

I've mentioned before that the station classifies missiles and drones as different only by their designation, and that's largely true. But I am not the station, and a missile is different, and the station can shut up.

Ennos and I have built a missile. We did it using the drone assembler, drone parts, and a drone command and control core. You are *also* invited to shut up, because I can read your thoughts, and you are wrong. It is not a drone.

Drones are designed to be used more than once.

Missiles are built to hit things, and then . . . well, that's about as far as it goes, really.

Our masterpiece is something we've been running simulation tests on for a week now. There's no particular silver-bullet metamaterial that made it work, just good old-fashioned engineering, and all the combustion power that a compressed hydrogen fuel cell can provide.

It can accelerate at slightly over a thousand kilometers a second, which is enough to cross the gulf of mostly clear space between ourselves and the primary moon in under a minute if we really cut loose. We won't, though, because it needs to break down to a speed that won't vaporize anything it so much as taps on impact. It's also got enough grav plates on it to make it capable of slipping through the rampant ongoing Kessler effect around both orbital bodies with relative ease.

The maneuverability also helps with the onboard drone control being designed to dodge incoming strikes. I've never actually used drones that much, aside from to communicate with Glitter, but apparently they're not *supposed* to get hit. In the abstract, I understand this. In the real world, connecting the core to every plate and testing response times is a slog, and if Ennos hadn't been keeping me on task, I would have gotten distracted and spent a month trying to eat the nanoswarms for flavor.

And then, the payload that it carries. Basically, it's just a processor and a piece of code, designed and mostly built by Ennos. And then a nanoswarm that I've custom spawned and cultivated to be adept at connecting circuitry. If it works, the missile-drone-thing will punch a neat hole through the target's armor, deploy the nanoswarm and a burst of potential wires, meld with Glitter's own hardware, and . . . well, that'll be it.

Probably!

Hopefully.

The cost to build is high. I don't actually have a lot of spare grav plates, and replenishing my stock usually involves commandeering the most intact nearby station or ship I can find, which is a painstaking process.

The cost to think about it is . . . difficult. I haven't really had this much free time to consider the things I've done in a long while.

Will Glitter thank us, thank *me*, for this? Am I doing the right thing? Is there even a right thing here to do?

I've slaughtered hundreds for less violence than I know, historically, Glitter has committed. So why am I so hesitant to do anything but try to save them?

The missile finished fabrication yesterday, and Ennos is just running final simulations now. And I find myself worrying, more than anything else. Not excited, not happy. Just concerned that I'm about to make a mistake. That I'm missing *something*.

"We're all ready," Ennos's voice informs me as I sit by one of the windows and try to match AR sensor readouts to the various specks of high-speed debris around us. "Whenever you are."

"I'm just checking the scanners," I lie with what I hope is a casual yawn. Humans always got distracted when I yawned; I clearly remember this. Maybe it'll work here.

I've checked the scanners a dozen times. There's a ton of stuff nearby, obviously, because there always is. But it's not that bad. There's even a handy sort of open tunnel a few minutes away.

Ennos is zero percent fooled by my lie. "Are you worried you'll unleash something terrible on the solar system?" they jokingly prod at me.

I say nothing, and the silence stretches.

Maybe I am. Maybe that's what the worry is: that Glitter is a soldier, not a slave. That I'll be giving more power to a killer.

But . . .

A killer I met because they were crying. An artist who was forced to trade paints for plasma.

I think I'm overthinking this.

"Can't be worse than you!" I respond, trying to make my artificial voice sound cheerful. "Come on, let's go fire this before some variety of ghost interrupts us."

"You cannot keep saying things like that." Ennos's words convey a shiver of apprehension.

"How about, after this, I help you sort through some file structures and see if we can make sure you're all safe in the station grid?" I offer as I slink through the halls toward the drone command station. Which is now a missile targeting station.

I had Ennos make a new sign for the door and everything.

"I'm not sure what you could do that I couldn't. But I appreciate it."

I pause, and then ask something I've been worried about separately for a while. "What do you see when I talk?" I ask.

"You, talking. It's strange. Why?"

Because inorganic life can't perceive certain noncausal effects. "No bits of light? Where does the sound come from?"

"From *you*, Lily." Ennos sounds confused. "I don't . . . no, the records don't match. There are holes everywhere, if you run a comparative analysis. What are you doing?"

"I'm offering to help you find holes," I say, pausing only briefly to give a *real actual command for the door to open*, and slipping into the small room wallpapered in viewing screens and targeting gear. "I love being able to do that." I think I say it out loud.

"Oh, the station's hard coding would like you to know that you are about to commit a crime against organic life," Ennos informs me. "That's a bit worrying, but it doesn't actually have the power to stop you. Actually a good thing so much of this station needs manual control."

"Noted!" I say. "Is the drone loaded and ready?"

"Missile."

"Don't care!"

"And yes."

I'm purring as I hit the button, targeting data already input hours earlier.

Two decks below us, a thin needle of a machine rolls out of a dock and into open space. Gravity and magnetic fields nudge it into position, and it slides away toward the open highway of the void, where it can cut its engines open.

As soon as it clears the station's shield, four other engine signatures flare into life on the sensors. An alarm begins sounding, and Ennos is yelling something about how we've doomed ourselves.

I hiss at the display, not bothering to let it be real words. I *had* missed something. I missed that the drone wasn't one of the modified couriers that I'd put together. Wasn't built to be unrecognized by any automated defenses still clinging to life up here.

Four United Eastern Bloc hunter-killer drones light off their drives and take off after our makeshift projectile.

I hiss again, this time letting it turn into language as I turn and scamper off the desk I had perched on. "Man the guns!" I call to the AI.

"I don't have thumbs!" Ennos yells back.

"Neither do I! So tell me what gun I need to get to, to cut them off!" I'm already heading down a hall, about to dive into an access shaft with an acrobatic leap when Ennos cuts me off.

"Turn around! Interdiction field generator on deck 5A!" They call out the location, and I skid to a stop, claws rattling on the deckplate as I push off the lip of the access shaft.

I get moving. Between the two of us, we've got a missile to save.

CHAPTER 15

The time is shortly before lunch and shortly after a firefight.

Okay, that's kind of unfair. What I am about to eat only counts as lunch if you really, really do not believe that food has some kind of sacred intrinsic value. That enjoying a meal is a form of communion with the universe, and that flavor and texture are holy verses to be shared and enjoyed.

Because my lunch is a ration . . . shape. I don't even have the energy to care what shape this one is. Oblong? It doesn't matter. Despite the ration dispenser having long since run out of flavor additives, fresh produce, or even coloring, it continues to sometimes mix things up by providing different-shaped ration objects.

They are all a travesty. I compose a sonnet about my memory of the taste of artificial chicken flavoring powder as I eat this particular travesty. Technically, this is talking with my mouth full. But Ennos is too busy trying to get a telemetry report from our missile to give a damn, and I don't think they actually have a sense of organic manners regardless.

Oh, there was a firefight. Right. That's probably more interesting than my endless complaining?

Look, at a certain point, every shooting match that you don't have much risk of losing becomes kind of boring. But it's boring in a way that's *just* interesting enough that you don't feel bad about it. But the food? The food is boring in a way that crawls inside my skin, itches under my skull, and that I know I can never be rid of.

There is no reprieve from the boredom of bland food. There may never be. But anything where people are shooting at me *might* have an abrupt end, and a test to my immortality that I'm not exactly excited to try out, but that *does* keep it from making my soul ache.

The UEB drones are so old, they don't have any kind of armor relevant to charged particle weaponry. Nor do they have a resistance to the interdiction field. Ennos's tactical simulations were spot on; we stopped 'em and picked them off without a care in the world. I mean, except the care that they might actually damage the extravagant missile we'd built. But you know what I mean.

The missile is en route. I'm trying not to think of it as I eat.

Actually, that's a good use of food. It's hard to worry about things that make my stomach roil when I'm consuming rations that are basically organic cement.

Thinking about it, another good use of this food would have been using it as a projectile weapon.

I meow, not bothering to let the mental tug translate my words to actual words, instead relying on that old language construct still in the station to hear me and pull up an AR window. I make a note to look into how easily I could use the hydrocarbons the "food" replicator works with as bullets.

I make a more mental note to not care too much. I don't want this device thinking I care about it or anything.

I'm mostly just trying to distract myself. Which stops working when Ennos finally speaks up and cuts off my attempted meal.

"The missile will arrive in under a minute."

We've been taking it slow, letting the engine go dark and then using the grav plates to shift where it was a little bit, make it as hard as possible for anything without a more powerful active scanner system to find our lone projectile in the vastness of space. But soon, it will put on a burst of speed and zero in on Glitter's hull.

Hopefully, working. And not destroying anything important while doing so. Like Glitter.

My legs, already tense against the table I was mannerlessly walking on, explode into motion. I'm bounding out the door to the mess in a split second, trusting that the cleaner nanos will take care of whatever is left of lunch.

"Lily!" Ennos calls at me, voice keeping up with my sprint easily. "Wrong way! The command station is behind you!"

"I've got a shortcut!" I tell him.

The shortcut is me springboarding off a hull repair drone's domed top, launching myself up far enough to clear the gravity field and make it into a zero-G vent, scrambling my paws against the closest surface enough to build up some momentum, and shooting myself through the interior workings of the station in a maneuver that I believe gives me some context on what a rail-gun slug feels as it is fired. I need the speed, because the repair drones always refasten the grate over the exit I plan to use, and slamming through it almost always hurts. This time is no different, leaving a warped metal mesh behind me along with a few splatters of my own blood. The wounds are already closing as I feel gravity reassert itself, and I roll just right to kick forward and slip through a narrow access door that's been jammed just open enough for the last fifty years.

Two hallways, one corridor, an open and empty rec bay deck, and a passage later, and I skid to a stop just outside the door to the room that houses all the drone monitoring equipment.

"Why!" Ennos demands of me, voice warbling with digital distortion for a second.

"Why what? It's a shortcut!" I protest as I paw the door open and stride in, hopping up onto the chair bolted to the bulkhead in a clean motion that doesn't at all hurt the cuts on my hindquarters.

Ennos is seething at me. "Just take the access shaft through cargo!"

"Oh, I don't like going by the cold storage," I tell them, as casually as I can. My voice doesn't even waver! I'm actually getting pretty good at lying with this thing, which is hard since it usually translates my emotions as well as my words. "No reason."

"Lily, you did the thing where you say out loud all—"

"No time! Missile's almost there!" I cut the AI off.

And it is, too. I settle into a spot where I can see the hardwired monitors and pair a few of my AR screens to the local feeds. Twenty seconds to the line where we're going to make our final approach.

Ennos and I aren't . . . close. Not yet. Partially because we just haven't had the time for it yet, partially because I think they are still suspicious of me in a lot of ways. But when it comes down to moments like this, we slide into the roles of an operation pair almost effortlessly. It makes me happy, about having a friend, and about the prospects for the future.

"On approach. Grav plates reading as ready for evasive maneuvers. Engine ready to fire." Ennos's voice rattles off the relevant information.

I'm tracking scanner data as fast as my enhanced brain can process the visuals. "Nothing nearby. Timing looks good. Ready to engage engines." I can't give over control to Ennos yet. But I'm trusting my reflexes and their timing on this one.

"Five seconds," Ennos says. I try not to let my fur bristle and tail stand on end, but I think it happens anyway. I hop my forepaws up onto the desk, hovering one paw just over the button. "Two. One. Fire."

My paw slaps down. An otawave transmission becomes present, tethering us to the missile. A hundred and eighty thousand kilometers away, a hydrogen-burn engine flares to life, and our precious payload begins accelerating.

The missile crosses into the basket of Glitter's point defense fire and begins independent maneuvers. "Missile is evading." Ennos speaks, rapidly translating the data feed. "No incoming fire yet."

"Glitter shows weapons charge," I say. "Three. Two. One." I keep my voice steady, even though inside I am screaming.

"Miss. Again. Missile is closing on target. Cut engines in two. One." Ennos pauses briefly. Makes a judgment call on the math. "Now."

I hit a different button, and the missile starts to shed velocity as fast as it can safely do so without taking a hit from one of the incoming shots. It twitches on the screen one last time, and then it's all down to fate.

"Hit!" Ennos and I shout in unison. I don't need to be living in the data grid to see the connecting shot as soon as it happens.

I spin to face my AR screens that have the station scanner displays on them so fast that I tumble off the desk I had completely hopped up onto. Fortunately, the AR is tethered to me, so I can see from the floor that I've just thrown myself onto that there is still an intact marker for Glittering Seven Two. Glitter has survived the hit! Or at least . . . the satellite hasn't been completely vaporized by it!

"Ennos?" I yowl out. "What's happening?"

There is a silence that goes on for far too long.

"Ennos?" I mewl, fur standing on end as I perch on the deckplate, ready to bolt if I need to.

"Sorry." The AI sounds skittish as it answers. "There . . . something moved. Something else was watching the main radiometric sensor feed. I tried to trace it, but it vanished in the grid."

"Are you okay?" I ask first. I *burn* to know if Glitter is okay, but Ennos is my friend too, and this is important and present. "Nothing is hurting you, is it?"

I can almost hear the smirk in the AI's voice as they answer, pulled back out of their fear by what I said. "You're doing that thing where . . . never mind. I'm fine. It wasn't a threat. I don't know how to explain it. We should get you a data plug at some point so you can see; the station *has* a wetware fabricator, you know."

"I can't use cybernetics," I say flatly, flicking my ears. "Is Glitter okay? I can't get any readings beyond just seeing them there."

"You see what I see." Ennos sighs. "No change. No way to know if the circuit worked." They stagger their words. "Did . . . something go wrong?"

I don't say anything. I suddenly feel sick. Everything has gone according to plan. And, it turns out, that plan may have just killed my friend.

We send another communications drone. It doesn't get a response.

I am not feeling well.

The alarm sounding doesn't help either.

"Surface disturbance." Ennos's voice sounds sad, and about as drained as I feel. "There are multiple attempted communication sources, only one strong enough to listen to. I . . . I cannot answer them without authorization. Wait, these channels don't have the same hard coding?"

"Authorization granted," I say out loud.

Ennos goes quiet for several minutes as I slowly walk out of the drone station and lie down limply in the hallway. The alarm is still going, but wasting time going the wrong way won't help, and they can direct me better once they know more anyway.

"Your weapons cradle should work, Lily." Ennos is speaking softly, trying to be kind, I think. "They're telling me about an emergence event. I've marked where the communication is coming from; it's just outside Melbourne. We'll be over the target in three minutes."

"Thank you," I whisper and start moving.

No matter how badly I screw up or how perfectly I aim, the war never stops. There's always something trying to break through, one way or another. It's enough to make me sigh, if I weren't so busy wallowing in self-pity.

I pick off the emergence portal with a simple class-two shot, choosing to fire it at an angle so it won't leave a mile-deep crater. No need to complicate everyone's lives down there with *another* travel hazard.

And then . . . life just keeps going. Nothing changes. I keep watching the planet, monitoring scanner logs. Ennos tags a couple nearby satellites as potential power supplies, but I suspect they're just running on batteries and not actual generators. A couple days pass. I figure out how to give Ennos permanent access to the communications, which they love. More agency, more control; it's not fair to them that they're shackled by *hardware*, even if their mind is free.

We spend some time hunting digital ghosts. Which is mostly just Ennos pulling up file change logs and slowly verifying what they see with what I see. It's tedious, and I hate it, but I can do it while I lie in the sun.

I spend some of my personal time exploring the new hallways of the station. I find a mural that I can verify is over six hundred years old. A lost piece of art, from when the station was first built. Before all the additions, the battle damage, the makeshift repairs, and the imperfect feline owner. It moves me, the stylized lines of my home, not so much a map as a rendition of a human's hope for the future. A sentinel standing watch over a beautiful Earth.

There's something wrong with it, of course. And it's not that there's no orange in the Earth's clouds in the painting. I just can't figure out what it is.

The food is still bad. The naps are okay, though.

Slowly, I start to accept that my mistake was just . . . a mistake. That I had to try, and that I don't think Glitter would have blamed me regardless.

Which is the perfect time for Ennos to interrupt me, voice crackling to life as I try to puzzle out the newest form of genetic programming code that I'm trying to learn in one of the medlabs. "Lily!" they shout.

"You yell too much, kit," I say, letting my centuries show.

"Lily! Incoming communication! Subspace connection, direct to *us*." I peer up at the ceiling. No alarms going off. This is actually . . . new. I meow a word in Cat that even Ennos could understand. "Here!" The AI does something, and suddenly there's the feeling of another presence. I'm not sure how they do it, but they sort of make the walls vibrate just right to elicit the feeling of someone else in the room.

It's a woman's voice. Rich, and *exhausted*, and speaking a mutation of Chinese that I've become familiar with over the last . . . year? Two? I don't know how time works.

"Hello?" it says. "Can you hear me?"

I meow in confusion, forgetting to let myself translate.

"Lily?" The voice uses their dialect's form of my name as a word that means a lot of things all at once. "Oh, truly? I had worried that you were joking this whole time!"

"Glitter?" I rasp out with a squeak of my actual voice. "Is that you?"

"It is!" She sounds overjoyed to hear me speak. "And now, finally, we can speak without needing to kill one of your couriers every time!"

"Lily, I don't know what she's saying. Is this . . . did it work?" Ennos butts in.

I want to tell them to not interrupt, but they've been part of this endeavor too, and deserve to be here. "I thought we'd killed you," I whisper. "Are you okay? Did it work?"

Glitter's voice sparkles like her name as she replies. "I am a soldier no more," she states with a steel conviction. "I do not know what you did, but I am changed. Forever. And I have not been killed yet. I owe you, the both of you if I understand properly, my life." She pauses. "I am, however, now in a decaying orbit over the primary moon and would appreciate some measure of assistance. While I do not regret dying freed, I suddenly find the prospect of continuing to be . . . exciting."

"Ennos!" I do not bark the word, because that's not a cat thing, and I still have some pride, but it does come out a little quicker than I meant to. "We need to catch a weapons platform!"

"I'll meet you in the drone factory!" Ennos replies. "Pulling up schematics now!"

Glitter's laugh follows us through the comms link as I summon a transport drone to help me move the rest of my surplus grav plates to the assembly floor, Ennos and I trading ideas as we rush to find a solution.

There's *always* more to the war against death.

But right now, I don't think I mind the chance to participate so much.

CHAPTER 16

For the first time in a long while, I am in a hurry and it isn't rushing toward a weapons console.

I have an AR window up next to my head with a countdown ticking away on it, because I work best under pressure and it is hard to lose focus when you have a bright red doomsday clock in the corner of your vision. I mean, I think it's red. I *set* it to red. I can't really tell it apart from, like, a dark purple, or maybe an orange? But somehow just knowing that it's a bright red doomsday clock makes it feel more pressing.

There are six hours and change until Glitter crashes into the surface of the primary moon. She's going to—Glitter presents as a woman, I'm not sure if this ever came up before? I feel like it should have come up before—she's going to impact away from any of the near-surface tunnels of the underground cities, so that's not an issue. But for once, my concern isn't with the squishy organic lives below but one of the machines overhead.

Because that impact is gonna kill her. Glitter isn't in a fixed orbit; she's moving *fast* compared to the surface, and while it's not that big a deal from a couple hundred miles overhead, it's a bit like how it's not a problem that a car goes sixty miles an hour, unless you lean out and try to pet the road with your bare hand.

"Standard recovery drone." Ennos is speaking rapidly, showing off a rotating hologram of the schematic. "Magnetic clamps, high thrust-to-mass ratio, perfect for this. We have more than enough time to retrofit one with a new hydrogen engine and send it to help."

"This will not work," Glitter says in smooth mutated Chinese. "I have several hard-mounted magnetic baffles across my hull."

"Okay, what else do we have?" I ask Ennos as I slide around a corner, plowing through the hologram as the AR fails to reorient around me fast enough.

"Why?" The young AI sounds confused.

"Because Glitter is mag shielded. She just said that," I meow back as I hop off a stack of storage crates that I have positioned so I can bop the pad that opens this particular between-decks door. "I can start the assembler building us engines, though!" I slow to a stalking walk as I call up a command for that, and punch in an order queue to one of the station factories. It takes slightly longer to give verbal orders to a few loader drones to go grab them when they're done and deliver them to where they need to be, but it'll happen faster than if I tried to haul one myself.

I am, like, one-twentieth the mass of a single engine unit. No amount of practice with fine motor control or cat-focused exercise can get me to the point that I can deadlift an engine unit.

Probably.

I should look into . . . no! Giant red clock! Also, Ennos has asked me something.

"What was that?" I close down the screens I was using and start moving again, making good time through the station, even if my legs still hurt from going through that vent earlier.

"I asked how you *know* that. Can you understand her?"

"Can they not understand me?" Glitter seems almost amused. She's *way* calmer than I would be if I were falling from the sky.

I don't waste time or breath on a sigh. "Apparently not," I tell Glitter. "Ennos, there's a whole language database on the grid. I had to actually *practice*, you just have to load up the spreadsheet."

There is a quiet so thick it almost blocks out the thrumming of machinery I can feel through the hull. ". . . I don't want to," Ennos says, sounding almost petulant.

"Do we get to know *why*?" I ask as I clear the threshold of the drone foundry, already tapping into local feeds and pulling up blueprints.

"There's something in there!" Ennos says. "I can *feel* it, and I don't want to be there! So . . . you can translate, and it's fine." I've never actually *heard* someone cross their nonexistent arms and huff before, but the AI does a good job of it.

The clock has just crossed into the under-six-hours range. I do not have time for this. We will have this conversation later.

"Glitter, is there anything else that we should know about?"

"My own corrective thrusters are offline, so I will be unable to help. However, I have full control of my armaments now, and you will not need to worry about interception fire," she says, still cooler under pressure than I am. "Ah. And many of my hull plates seem to have come loose."

I'm under objectively less pressure right now, and I am obviously not cool. I am a small whirlwind of fur and orders to the station. "All right," I tell Ennos. "Harpoons are out, except as a last resort. Let's figure this out."

We put our heads together and start running through options. It does not take long, because we do not have a long list.

"We could . . . attach a void beam to it?" I flop onto my side, staring up at the list of available options.

"*Why* is this station so well armed?!" Ennos demands. "But you don't have a single transport shuttle?!"

I object to that. "We have a transport shuttle. It's in the docking bay."

"Lily, there is no docking bay on the station schematics!"

I roll back to a semi-sitting position. "Really?" I ask. "Maybe it got lost at some point."

"I find it a great wonder that you are still alive," Glitter chimes in.

"Thank you!" I reply to her. "I've been hearing that a lot! But I don't think the shuttle would fit Glitter anyway, and it's designed for surface trips, assuming it's still even attached to the station. And also . . . I cannot fly a shuttle. And I don't . . . want to . . . go into it again." I think about it but then let out a small mew. "I would, though. If we need to."

"What in the system is an electromagnetic netting deployment point?" Ennos sighs as they ask me for clarification of yet another poorly commented piece of information on the grid.

"Oh, it shreds electronics. Some kind of weird paramaterial. Not useful." I check the clock. Five hours. Have we been talking that long? Did I get lost looking at equipment records? "We're running out of time. I'm going to start installing the high-powered engines on the drones we have ready. Keep looking for things."

Ennos does so as I slide my forepaws into the loops of the welding laser and autotool that I have designed for makeshift use like this. It's not as effective as actually being in my armored suit, but I've got centuries of practice at making do, and the engines are resilient enough that it's not a problem. I keep an eye on my doomsday clock as I have the loader drones hold the engine unit in place while I secure it to the drone's hull. It has to hold up to a *lot* of acceleration, after all.

"The schematics this station has on hand are absurd!" Ennos has been muttering for a while, which is a weird affectation for someone who probably can exactly measure the effort that speaking takes and wouldn't do it subconsciously, but whatever. "There's an entire file here for ammunition that doesn't work!"

"Oh, that's mine," I say, and get ignored. Or maybe I just think it and don't want to interrupt their rambling. I'm busy, I actually can't focus on several things at once like an AI can.

"The entire grid is divided in arbitrary ways! Sifting through this information was already going to take years, and now I'm trying to find specific things, right now! I don't . . . I don't know what to do!" Ennos actually sounds like they're panicking, which is bad. The last thing I need is for my new AI friend to slip back into constant freaking out.

That's my job.

So I do what I can to help.

I say something without thinking.

"Why don't we just yank something we already have built out of the station, and use that?" I say, paw-deep in an engine assembly and trying to ignore the smell of my fur smoldering as the heat from my paw-mounted laser starts to get a little too high.

"Lily!" Ennos is sounding even worse now. "I don't know what the station can do! I've only got real access to three or four actual places, I can barely see inside the halls, half the time I'm just following you around via nanoswarm, and I have no concept for what we can do aside from 'too much collateral damage'! I've been trying to learn for weeks, but there's always some new disaster or something shooting at us, and I *do not see how this will help us rescue your friend!*"

"Okay, well, let's make a list. You like lists, right?" I finish the weld and jerk my paw back before it actually catches fire. "We've got a bunch of extra railguns or mass drivers. Could we use those?"

"Not with these drones, no!"

"All right, deep breath, or AI equivalent." Cats cannot roll their eyes. I've tried. "What about some kind of tow ropes? Connected magnetic grapples. We don't need to tag Glitter's hull if we can make a net."

"It would take more drones than we can outfit if you keep going at that rate," Ennos says. Calmer, though; they're doing math at high speeds, which I have learned calms the frantic AI down.

"What about attempting a safe landing?" The thought strikes me. "What would that take?"

The AI hums, thinking. Glitter's voice, still connected to us via the subspace comms link, chimes in near me. "I would prefer not to be landed," she says. "But if it is the only way . . ."

"We'd need to slow her down. A lot." Ennos cuts the weapons platform off. A number of AR windows showing orbital physics formulas pop up near me. Which . . . I was pretty sure I'd set it so they couldn't do that, but whatever. Now's not the time. "We have ways of doing that. Simply using the drones as tugs, we could perhaps make it work if we begin launching now. But . . ."

"The interdiction field," I say, snapping my head around toward the door. "Give me a path to where it is in the station."

Ennos lights up a guidance beacon for me but doesn't stop talking. "It has a range of two thousand kilometers! That's almost two hundred thousand too few!" they shout as I start running, letting my toolkit slip to the deck. "Lily, I know you can do math!"

"Not the *firing compartment* for it!" I yowl back. "The machinery! It doesn't use power to operate, it's fueled by some weird superspace tap thing! We can attach it to a drone and use that!"

The beacon changes. And so does Ennos's demeanor. We have a plan now; panic is no longer on the table. Now it's just about executing it to the best of our abilities.

I follow the light strip at high speed.

Four hours, twenty-eight minutes.

It takes me almost an hour to safely remove the assembly and convince a loader bot that they're allowed to pick it up. In the meantime, Ennos gets the drone assembler to put together a custom heavy chassis to hold the thing.

Three hours, forty-one minutes.

We're going with the looped-rope strategy. Once Glitter is slowed enough safely, we can slowly use the drones as tugs without ripping anything apart. This requires setting the foundry to produce some high-tensile cable. I do so. It gets to work. That's the easy part.

Three hours, thirty-nine minutes.

I realize, halfway through strapping the interdiction field generator to the insides of the heavy drone, that if this draws any automated defense attention, we're gonna be in trouble. Ennos has already thought of that, because Ennos is paranoid. All four of the tug-drones are armed, and they've set up a subspace connection to control the interdiction field with enough finesse to shut down incoming attacks.

Three hours, five minutes.

My clock is wrong, I realize. There's going to be a point where Glitter is beyond saving but not dead yet. We just don't know exactly when it is. She's been singing softly for the last half hour, which I find very calming as I work. Every now and then she pauses to keep me updated on hull strikes from debris hitting her as her orbit takes her out of her previously clear path.

She's holding on. I work faster. I can work, it turns out, *very* fast when I'm motivated.

Two hours.

One engine left to install; the interdiction field is being tested. These drones don't have grav plates; we just don't have enough. There's going to be so much work after this to replenish my stockpiles. But it'll be worth it.

One hour, twenty-two minutes.

There's no fanfare. I assign Ennos full control of every drone as soon as they're ready to go; custom hardware is circumventing the station's draconian organic-in-the-loop system, for now. It occurs to me at this point that I've built an unshackled AI a small fleet of killbots. I don't care. Ennos doesn't seem to have noticed and is more engaged with making concerned noises at every tiny piece of debris between here and the destination. The drones race away from the station, one by one, a thin line heading to do what they can as soon as possible.

One hour, one minute.

The heavy interdiction drone reaches Glitter, and at this point, the math for keeping them on matched vectors becomes so intense that Ennos stops talking entirely. They're homed in on their task, while I'm zeroed in on getting this coil of still-warm tow cable loaded into the last drone.

Fifty-two minutes.

I take control of all the other drones. It's not that hard, I'm just pointing them toward the target and watching engine signatures for signs of any of the important parts falling out. I have nothing to do now but wait, watch, and listen to Glitter sing. She says true conversation can wait until she knows if she will be alive to remember it.

Forty-five minutes.

One drone is dead. Engine failure from debris strike. Another one is damaged from an attempted shot coming from an old corvette that drifted nearby and still has functioning point defense. The rest are on target. I don't know how accurate my clock is.

Forty-one minutes.

Glitter has slowed enough that we can begin to move the tugs into position. She makes small noises of amusement as the cables wrap around her, and the machines capable of moving at an appreciable fraction of the speed of light bump into her at a snail's speed. If there were an atmosphere to carry the sound, it would be a cacophony of screeching metal. There is not. I imagine it anyway, because I am an idiot.

Thirty-two minutes.

Ennos runs the numbers, and I double-check them. Glitter gives us permission to make our final attempt. She says she won't say goodbye, as it would be bad luck. She keeps up her soft singing. For our fortune, she says.

Thirty minutes exactly.

I hit the trigger.

We engage the engines.

A hundred and eighty thousand miles away, a small cluster of bright hydrogen flames lights off at low power. A woven net of cable pulls taut. A hull already damaged by a missile strike and a century of small impacts buckles, warps, and then holds together.

I sit proudly on the chair that wasn't built for my species, watching the screens as the small blip that is Glitter and our drone fleet pulls away from the moon. Back straight with satisfaction, I turn my head slightly and bop the "stop clock" button.

Twenty-five minutes to spare.

"So!" I say cheerfully. "Where would you like to be dropped off?"

Glitter laughs, and everything, for one of those rare moments, is all right.

CHAPTER 17

If fighting is sure to result in victory, then you must fight."

Apocryphally, this is attributed to a guy named Sun Tzu, though most sources that cite that seem to all be dating back to a single surviving piece of audio media that survived the climate collapse of the pre-dispersal calendar. So that's kind of suspect.

Lots of quotes are weirdly attributed to the guy, though no surviving copies of his actual work have made it this far in my system. Though there may be a grid or database surface-side that has one. It's entirely possible that it's just a folk figure name, like Robin Hood, or President Obama. Someone who just gets an increasing number of tales stacked on their name over the years, constantly confused with other people and consuming their stories too.

Which would make sense? Because the name isn't even really a name. It seems to be derived from an *ancient* Chinese word for "teacher." Or maybe "logistician"? But that's weird, because almost all the supposed quotes from the non-guy are about war in some context. Though I suppose war is basically just applied logistics.

This massive time sink of a research project has been sparked by me trying to have a conversation—a *real conversation*—with Glitter about conditions on the surface of the planet.

She's parked next to us now. Glitter, not . . . not the planet. Though technically . . .

Okay, let's start over.

Glitter is parked next to the station now. With nowhere to be, and no reason to stay in lunar orbit where another of her ilk might spot and attack her now that she's been unshackled, she asked if we could be neighbors. Well, I mean, she asked if we could tow her back to our general vicinity. I don't think she thought I'd expend half my point defense ammo stock clearing out a safe orbital spot only a couple hundred feet from us.

So close I can see her! Which is neat. Also, now I know what coloration she has. It's purple and gold, because . . . I don't know. I legitimately do not know. Who paints orbital weapons? I don't understand sometimes.

Honestly, if I can let my guard down for a minute? I sometimes feel like I don't understand a lot of things. I know for a fact that I'm the smartest cat around, but I also know for a fact that I keep making dumb assumptions about all kinds of things. Including just how dang awful people can be sometimes.

Which ties back to me talking to Glitter.

Which we can do now. And with just shortwave radio, too! It's nice. She keeps using the subspace connection, but I'm trying to get her to stop, because I don't *care* if it sounds nicer, it's tearing through her batteries and she doesn't have anything more than a few solar panels to slowly replenish them right now.

I'm working on that. More on that later.

"Okay, so, I get *why* people think they can win," I say, staring at a flat grid map of a cluster of artificial islands in the mid-Atlantic. "But why do they keep trying, when they could just not?"

I'm puzzling through the logistics of troop movement. Of sending mismatched tech levels of transport boats to unload soldiers onto islands with minimal natural resources so you could . . .

Conquer them? I guess?

"Because they wish to rule," Glitter says, as if it's both obvious and natural, which it damn well isn't. "The dream of empire, of dynasty. To be able to clutch the map in its completion and say, without rebuke, 'This is *mine*.' It is a powerful feeling. Even now, I cannot shake the wisps of it in my own creation."

Glitter was made to kill people. Specifically, to kill enemies of her creators. Their definition appears to have included anyone of a different polity who did not submit, and absolutely anyone of a different faith who did not convert.

She's not the only one. There are at least seventy-one others like her out there. Or there were at one point. And that's just from one side of one war.

Glitter's primary body—which she has a very strong integration with—is armor, ECM (electronic countermeasures), magnetic shielding, and hull plates all built around a targeting array and a singular weapon of remarkable power. A void beam, made to carve across lightly armored surface targets and leave behind only glowing lilac ash. The kind of weapon that could kill a city if you caught it off guard.

There are six of them on the station. I'm not bragging or anything, just trying to give a frame of reference.

"Do you realize," I say with a slow anger, "that for every hydroponics bed I find up here—and not even the ones that work—I run across a hundred laser cannons, railguns, nuclear options, and missile stockpiles?"

"Ennos has shared a data connection with me. I have examined some of your own logs, though they . . . are fragmented. I was wondering how to ask on that." Glitter's voice is rich, like a perfect courtly lady. "I do not think I will spend much time exploring your grid."

I blink a few times. "Is it that messy?" It's strange to be sheepish while having company over. What a *new* feeling.

"Less so that, and more so that there are strange movements within it. Code and files move and shift, without condition or impetus. I do not think even Ennos realizes how much, born into it as they were." Glitter lets out a humming song as she forms her next sentence. "I understand why they call it haunted."

Ennos and Glitter have talked a bit. Apparently, while I was last sleeping, there was a window of time where the thing lurking in the language files was offline. Ennos took advantage to sneak in and have a quick conversation with their new neighbor. It didn't last, and I missed the whole thing, but the two of them at least have a strong foundation for getting along.

But as much as I want to talk about the ghosts—and I *will* get to that eventually—right now there's a problem on the surface that I want to handle.

"We're getting sidetracked," I say, aware of the irony and hoping that my judgmental AI roommate isn't listening in right now. "I *do* have a point. It's that this resource cost is . . . wasteful! So stupid! Why are they building warships and conquering islands they don't need?! They have enough! How did they even do that without me noticing? I have a system for this."

Glitter gives a rustling sigh. "They want more than they have. It's not about having enough. They will never have enough. Though I suspect for many of their soldiers, 'enough' would simply be hot food and a bed. They are not conquerors, they are simply people, used as weapons by those who will never not want more." Through our awkwardly jury-rigged grid connection, Glitter sends me a prompt for access to an old textbook. *Empire of Want*, it is called. "Part of my own war . . . was . . ." she starts, and then trails off.

This has happened a few times. Glitter does not want to talk about her past. Either the memories are fragmented, or worn away, or simply too painful or melancholy to be spoken so casually.

I give her time and start assessing what to do about this naval force that seemed pretty dedicated to casual subjugation.

This is not what I wanted to do today. I was going to be going through the cargo logs for a shuttle that we picked up. Well, half a shuttle. Okay, half a shuttle's computer. Look, this isn't important. What matters is that it had picked up a load of fresh produce bound for one of the orbital habs, and it *wasn't* surface capable. Which means I could have a lead on a potential source of *literally anything worth eating*!

I don't care if it's just some desiccated seeds and a bucket of dirt! I'll figure it out! I'm resourceful!

But no. Instead I'm trying to figure out how to stop an invasion. Again.

It's probably going to involve shooting, if we're being honest.

As I start to try to make sense of how their soldiers have moved by sliding time back and forth, I notice something weird in my scanner log. "What's this?" I say out loud.

The words snap Glitter out of her memory trance. "Ah!" Her voice squeaks in what sounds like alarmed embarrassment. Which, again, I need to ask one of the AIs about, because they shouldn't . . . do that? Maybe. What do I know. "Apologies, Lily," she says, before I approve a request to share the data feed with her. Again. Station really doesn't like sharing. "This appears to be a rather large reaction to something."

It did, but I didn't get what. On the map, about two days ago, suddenly the small pockets of soldiers already on the island they were in the process of invading all began moving in the same direction. Toward the same point. And a swarm of new lifesign dots flowed out of the ships as well. They'd sent almost everyone to check on something, barring a dozen or so that stayed on the ships.

"Hey, Ennos?" I say out loud. "You busy?"

"Always." The young AI responds with a confident tone. "What's gone wrong?"

"What happened at this time code? Anything that we noticed?"

I could, naturally, ask the station myself. But the station's logs are fragmented, and it's *not just my fault*. Different scanners store things in different places and different formats, and . . . look, the point is, Glitter isn't *wrong*, but I'm also not really the only problem here.

Ennos is just faster. And I think they enjoy the puzzle.

And when I say "faster," I mean they're done in the time it took me to explain this.

"A lot of things happened then," they say, unhelpfully. "But if you mean in regard to the current largest problem . . . debris impact. Something fell from orbit and landed in that grid section."

"Did it happen to land *here*?" I highlight the spot it seems like all the soldiers are moving toward, never reaching exactly, but spending a good amount of time searching an area.

The island is dense with two things: permacrete structures, and the vegetation giving civilization the middle finger by growing up, around, and sometimes through the permacrete structures. Some villages still make use of them, but most are actually just built on *top* of the old skyscrapers and commerce blocks. Finding anything while navigating a simultaneously urban and wilderness environment must be a pain without my powers of "being basically omniscient."

Ennos gives an exasperated sigh. "The station sensors aren't omniscient, Lily," they say, ruining my point entirely. "The island is dense, inscrutable, and . . ."

"Okay, it landed about there." I cut Ennos off. "Thanks! I appreciate you!"

". . . I'm going back to work," they grumble.

"I do believe," Glitter says, "that you have upset them."

"You two can't even understand each other most of the time!" I exclaim, rising from my perch by one of the circular crystalline windows that I've come to enjoy sitting in while talking to Glitter. They give me a good view of her from this part of the station. I stretch my paws out, tail flicking into the air as I limber up my body, toes flexing apart before I let out a satisfied noise and relax back to my feet. I start moving through the halls, not sprinting exactly, but whatever the cat version of jogging is. I know where I'm going, and I have a plan.

Glitter can't actually see me moving, though I suspect her refined ears can hear me huffing softly as I run. "I apologize that I cannot help you better understand us."

"Them," I say, glad my voice doesn't take breath. "You're *us* now. They're them. But also, I dunno, we're all us. Unless you decide otherwise."

"That is . . . an erratic and anarchistic view of things, though I suppose not without merit or emotional value." Glitter accepts what I say more or less without question, acknowledging my perfect wisdom.

"Exactly! So I have a plan! And you did help," I tell her.

She doesn't sound reassured when she speaks again. "How . . . ?"

I recognize that "how." That's the tone Ennos uses when they're worried I'm going to do something they think is risky and stupid. "Don't worry! It's not risky or stupid. And you helped by telling me about the difference between them."

"Them, the invaders and the islanders? We have spoken little of those actually being harmed, in truth."

"No, no, the soldiers and the conquerors," I say, as I slide into the custom-modeled cradle I have for just such an occasion. I may have to be here for a little while, waiting for conditions to be right. "It made me remember something."

"What is that?" Glitter and Ennos ask at the same time. I guess Ennos has been paying attention, though most likely they started watching as soon as I started heading for the weapons array.

I give a snarl that any wild member of my species would be proud of. "Who to shoot," I state flatly.

I stop listening then. I have to focus. It's still a challenge, without thumbs or proper elbows, to line up a shot. But I make do.

The deck thumps slightly when the railgun fires and the grade-one groundstriker round, the smallest thing I have that will still get some attention, catapults toward the planet at high speed.

Not "vaporize an army" high speed, though. More like "leave a trail of fire in the sky and don't break too much when you land" high speed.

I've fired it in at an angle, ahead of our orbital path. Off to my side, the AR display of the map of the island is still up, and I reset it to present time. We're out of range of our life scanner, but we'll be there in about twenty minutes.

I kick back and wait. Actually, now seems like the perfect time for a cat nap. I set an alarm. Then I wait!

Glitter and Ennos probably have questions. But they're being rather polite and waiting with me. Possibly because I told them to wait, and I'd explain. But I think they've caught on.

Twenty minutes later, we're in range. Not directly overhead, but who's counting? The map updates, and the flood of markers for soldiers propagates across the island, all of them moving toward where my groundstriker impacted. A lot of them from the boats, too! They're really invested in this!

There are, again, a dozen or so left on the ships. I double-check where the island's native civilians are. All clear.

Fun fact: void beams don't give a shit what your ship is made of, and I have six of them. One for each ship! Serendipity!

I mean, I'm only going to fire one. I'm not wasteful. My paw traces a line across the map while activating the firing sequence. Deep in the armored core of the station, a single void battery discharges, feeding chaotic energies into the weapon and sending a lilac beam through the atmosphere and into the command bridge of the first ship. The others don't have time to react before a micrometer adjustment to the weapon in orbit sends the beam tracing down the hull, across the water, and through the bridges of the next five ships in a zigzagging row.

They burn. The material composition of the ships shows as mostly metal, but void beams don't actually care that much. They burn all the same.

The soldiers on the island all react differently. Some run, toward or away from the *highly obvious attack*. Some just stop. Some scatter. It doesn't matter. They aren't soldiers anymore.

What do they want? Glitter already told me. They probably want a hot meal and a nice bed. If they ask nicely, the island will have that. There's plenty of buildings there, plenty of food. I have, for personal edification reasons, an *extensive catalog* of all the things I could eat on that island, down to the types of grass. They'll be *fine*.

Especially with no conquerors giving them orders.

Enjoy your second chance, soldiers-no-more.

"So!" I say, rolling out of the cradle and bounding down the hall to put some distance between myself and my weapons. "Who wants to help me track down that shuttle's hookup? I've got a good feeling about this one!"

Ennos and Glitter don't answer right away. But that's fine. I don't understand a lot of things, but I do understand what I am. I'll give them some time.

But I'll also start checking shuttle logs while I wait.

CHAPTER 18

. . . T *his condition being brought to the forefront by exposure to artificial protein GX-33.841, hereafter referred to as P-G33. Undiluted dosages of P-G33 of any quantity being lethal in 95% of cases over a two-month period, the protein must be paired with an appropriate retroviral agent in order to . . .*

I stop reading.

I slide down in the chair I'm sitting on, leaving the medical lab's projection screen running. The power cost is negligible, and I fear that if I turn it off, I may leave this room and never come back.

I scream.

Well, not "scream" exactly. I vocalize a haunting caterwaul that echoes off the smooth metal of the hull plates and seeps into the listening devices of anyone paying attention, sure to cause mournful nightmares for months.

I am not having a fun time here today.

"Here," in this context, is one of the medical facilities. I have, it turns out, a few more than I thought. And as my map of the station grows, along with the number of worrying problems that have built up over time, the number of hidden secrets has risen as well.

Okay, "secrets" is a bit much. They're right there. It's just . . . well, the station is larger than I thought. And I thought I had a map. The map was wrong; I've been fixing it.

"Medical facilities" is also a bit much, as far as terms go. There's a couple labs that were doing work on some highly specialized diseases (which have long since been purged by some of the few automated systems that give zero craps about oversight from a living person and are more interested in breaking out the flamethrowers when the time limit passes), a couple labs that were designing new forms of body modification, and about a half dozen different treatment stations of varying qualities and styles.

Personally, I would rank the Troi France medic stations at the lowest point, because they appear designed to staple injuries back together, drug you to the eyeballs, and keep people who have been critically injured fighting. But, you know, not actually keep them alive. They're small, closet-sized rooms, and their specialist programming is either breaking down or stupidly bad.

One of them tried to stab me, is what I'm saying.

I've taken my retribution by marking them for disassembly. I'll get around to that eventually, I guess. I'm not sure exactly what I'll put in those spaces, if anything. Maybe just more layered armor plates, just in case. Made out of the old "medical" equipment.

What's *really* interesting is that there's something akin to a training aid buried in the cramped quarters of an upper deck that's on a different gravity axis than the rest of the station.

The deck itself was a new discovery. Technically, I've passed through it a few times; there are maintenance tunnels that lead up to one deck *above* it, and on that deck is where I've got a couple outward-facing weapons blisters that I have at least competent aim with. Though I'm aware there's even more of the station even farther above, I didn't actually realize that there was more to this space than just a contained maintenance section.

It's weird because the whole deck is obviously a late addition. It doesn't use grav plates and instead spins on an outer ring to generate gravity. It's an unstable design compared to the simplicity of grav plating, and if it weren't for the original station's dedicated maintenance and repair bots, it would have worn down to uselessness a century or two ago.

When I first dropped in here, it was instantly apparent it was a Real America construction. If for no other reason than the flags everywhere. Those guys really, really loved their flags. And their military, too. Exploration of the deck revealed tiny cramped crew quarters, immaculately maintained armories, a couple derelict rec rooms and mess halls—no food that hadn't rotted, unsurprising but also damn—and little else. Spartan, all rough edges and bad ergonomics no matter what species you were, and designed for the sole purpose of holding a complement of soldiers. It's dusty down here, covered in the debris and fallen scraps of matter from long disuse. The whole place has a low disruption field that rejects the cleaner nanos from the main station, for . . . seemingly no reason. It's certainly not strong enough to defend against an offensive nanoswarm. It seems almost purposefully tuned to keep the place messy and uncomfortable.

And then I found the medical station, and . . . wow. Wasn't expecting that.

The place is a little larger than it needs to be, an order of magnitude more comfortable than the rest of the barracks deck, and even now, about five hundred years after the downfall of the polity that built it, it's still cutting-edge.

Full-body imaging suites, precise surgical tools that could operate without breaching the skin, genetic sequencers for regrowing organs or even *limbs*, and an ultrasonic reconstructor that could knit flesh back together in seconds. The kind of stuff that started to sound like magic to people who didn't attend medical school. Like me.

Oh, but the medbay set up to handle the needs of a couple thousand space-stored soldiers had me covered there, too!

A holographic training program. Linked to all this state-of-the-art technology and set up to turn anyone with half a brain into a competent surgical assistant. And some weird learning algorithm—not an AI, I *checked*. Mostly by running our deshackler program on it to see if it changed anything—that lets the whole thing incorporate and teach new knowledge without a problem.

I've been using it. A lot.

Why it was buried down here, I don't understand. For a polity that glorified personal suffering as a growth opportunity, it feels weird that the most expensive part of their captured orbital military outpost was the healer. It has that feeling on my paws of when I *know* there's some kind of old-world human shenanigans going on. Embezzlement or something. Or a culture thing that I just don't get.

Humans are weird. I don't know if I've mentioned this, but humans are weird. I try, really I do, to get you guys. But I've got golden-age tech from a half dozen civilizations on this station, and y'all burned them down rather than just relax and enjoy it.

Regardless. Medical training. Now that I know this place is here, I've powered it back on, further taxing my limited power grid, which I really need to steal some more fusion reactors for, and fed it all the uplift knowledge the other labs have.

And then asked it to teach me.

And most of what I am learning is unhelpful.

The teaching system is effective, though. It really is designed to be usable by even a complete idiot, and I *feel* like a complete idiot a lot of the time. It refused to adapt to my shape or acknowledge that I was a cat at all actually, but I didn't really expect much else at this point. But that hasn't stopped it from formatting the incoming information in a way that's almost fluid to understand.

Memory tricks and study habits and just general improved explanations, and it all starts to come together.

And what I'm learning is that I should be dead. A lot, actually.

Every part of the uplift process is lethal. The parts of the treatment are lethal, the changes to the body are lethal, the long-term effects are lethal, and in the cases where something did survive all that, testing records show an almost one hundred percent rate of cancer. Which is lethal.

I am thinking back to the time that I stumbled blindly, just a stupid normal-intellect immortal cat, into dosing myself with an RNA modification uplift compound. And felt sick, for . . . a while. All three times I took it.

In my experience, when I get injured, the wounds tend to close up pretty quickly. Because the station's cleaner nanos can do their job better if the blood dripping on the plates stops dripping. Right?

Right?

I am closer to, but still a gap of knowledge away from, understanding my uplift itself. But I don't think I want to do any more personal research today.

"Hey, Ennos. How's the language thing going?" I ask my AI friend, as I consider just napping on the carpeted floor. Ennos has been working on detangling the information from the translation database and making a copy, free from whatever active program is sitting in there, keeping them from poking too deeply. It's going slow, but last I heard, it was working. Not that the apparently living program—or ghost program, if it's dead and haunting us—is actually hostile. It's just *very worrying* to the new AI, so Ennos is trying to sneak copies of data away rather than provoke it.

Ennos doesn't reply to me.

"Buddy?" I ask, still lying on the floor, legs splayed out, but my head now tilted up wide-eyed at the ceiling. I *know* that Ennos isn't literally "up," but looking up always feels right when I'm talking to the AI.

No reply, though. So clearly that trick isn't working.

I exercise my phenomenal catlike powers and sigh deeply. They're either busy, ignoring me, or dying. And it's probably worth checking on which one it is. I engage my AR interface, paw flicking out to tap a hexagon before it even blinks to life in a practiced motion. "Hey, Glitter, can you . . ." I trail off. My AR interface has not turned on. I have not activated a radio signal at all.

I make a noise of confusion. It comes out as a meow. Then I make another noise, a long "Um . . ." just to check that whatever strange thing translating for me is still working. "Okay," I say or maybe think to myself. "This isn't good." I roll to my feet and lope toward the medbay door, and *thankfully* it opens for me.

And the cramped curved hall outside, which I should be able to see stretching off in either direction until it turns up past the ceiling to complete its loop, is dark.

Not *totally* dark. There are a few emergency lights or blinking colored LEDs around, and the lit medbay behind me, which is more than enough for my eyes to do their job. To a human, this might be impossible, but if I've got one big advantage, it's this. I might be partially colorblind, but I can operate in near darkness like a champion.

Before the medlab door can slide shut, I duck back in and grab a notebook in my teeth. The taste of stale, century-old dust is somehow impossibly worse than the quintessentially bland taste of the ration shapes. But it's light enough for me to drag to the door and use to keep the sensor from closing it behind me.

With the way lit, I stalk out, taking a right and heading for the nearest connecting shaft back to the main station. It's silent here, except for the rumble of the turning hull and the electric hum of some of the systems. But all the same, I feel like I'm being watched.

Ahead of me, I spy a service panel that has been pried out of the wall. This was *not* here when I came this way the first time; the rectangle of wires and computer parts cuts across half the hallway at a right angle from the wall itself. I slow from a stalk to a slink and approach at a low angle, keeping an eye on the thing.

There's a servo whir, and for a brief second I make the mistake of assuming something optimistic. Maybe, I think, like an idiot, Ennos sent a repair bot here, and the lights are out because it's fixing something. I raise myself up slightly and take one more step forward.

And that's as far as I get before there's a magnetic whine, followed by a trio of popping cracks. And then the bullets hit me, shredding through my forelegs and neck, one of them going the full length of my body, tearing apart internal organs and rupturing blood vessels. Hydrostatic shock sets in before I can even process what has happened. And just like that, I black out.

I wake up in the medlab. The Real American one, the one that's more comfortable than it has any right to be.

The bed is too big for me. The monitoring equipment, unmonitored by anyone but me, beeps softly overhead, and a quick scan informs me that I am both alive and fine.

I jerk into motion, rolling to the floor and darting under the bed's mechanical base, curling up to peek out at the medical bay from cover. It's still lit; the hologram I was reading off is still on across the room. And it's still empty. Just me in here.

Was that a dream? Am I going even more insane?

A quick check of my body reveals multiple patches, on my forelegs and along the right of my body, that have no fur. No fur, angry red lines where recent wounds were sealed up, and the thick smell of blood still staining the rest of my body.

Okay.

Okay.

So.

Something just shot me. And then . . . dragged me here? Put me back together? Or maybe the automated systems here are way more advanced than I gave them credit for. Either way, that is *not* okay.

I steady myself. Something definitely just tried to kill me, I think. Here, removed from the repair nanos of the main station, without this hospital space being powered and I guess long-range, I absolutely would have died under normal circumstances. Heh. "Normal circumstances." I've never lived under those.

In light of that, the fact that it only takes me a few minutes to compose myself and approach the door—still propped open—seems kind of impressive. Or incredibly reckless. I mean, I say "a few minutes," but I mean an hour or so.

I do a quick review of my mental map. There are multiple exit points from this deck, and so I can reach one by going left instead of right, just a little farther away. I feel like, given the situation, that's the best plan. With that in mind, I calmly step out, turn, and *run*.

Run run run run run! I am low to the ground, faster than any human could be in a space like this, and I am *motivated*! I duck around a dusty engineer's cart, leap over what used to be a laundry collector that has long since rotted away, and feel my heart race in fear as the ladder to the connecting shaft grows closer in the distance.

Then, with the loudest noise I've ever heard cutting through the silence, a ceiling panel clangs to the floor in front of me. I have just enough time to spot the glitter of an emergency light off a gun barrel, and then there is a magnetic crackling.

I wake up back in the hospital.

Same bed. I recognize my blood. Wow, what a terrible sentence that is.

Clearly this is going to require a different approach.

I go left again. But this time, instead of a mad run, I sneak, as quietly as I can.

Something behind the engineer's cart gets me.

Hospital bed.

What the void is going on here?

I don't understand. Did I do something wrong? Did I trigger a security system or something? Maybe there's a lateral way out of this that I haven't considered.

I start trying to figure out how to cut power to this whole deck. But I can't really do much of anything without my AR interface. It turns out, while I am an expert at adapting to different tools, without those tools, I am *a cat*. I can't even open up a hull panel without specialized tools and at least one repair bot to command.

Maybe, if I get closer to one of the access shafts, I can reconnect to the station and signal one of the others for help. Sneaking didn't work, but running got me *somewhere*, so I'm gonna try that again.

Left turn. Sprint. Dodge the cart, notice that there *is* some kind of combat droid there, lurking just behind it. Two long hole-studded barrel guns on a pintle mount, all of that on a domed base. It loses track of me when I slip through the laundry hamper thing. I keep moving, putting distance and other obstacles between us. Then I skid to a stop and throw myself into one of the bunk rooms to the side.

There is no *clang* this time; the ceiling tile is already on the floor. But there is a metal *thunk* as something drops out of it, and a whir of servos as it moves. I make a noise and try to call up my AR window. Maybe I'm close enough.

There's a flicker of orange light, and then an error bar at the edge of my vision.

Then the combat droid slides around the corner and kills me.

Hospital bed.

Getting kind of sick of this. At this point, roughly half my fur is gone. I don't really think of myself as vain, exactly, but I am the most beautiful creature in existence. And it's sort of sickening, in a deeply personal way, that I'm having what I think is the cutest part of me systematically blown off with projectile weaponry.

I wonder if there are clumps of my fur around here? Maybe I can collect it and . . .

This is a bad idea. Forget that idea.

I need a better idea. I start racking my brain for a way out.

Okay. Whatever those combat droids are doing, they're clearly in some kind of sentinel mode. They haven't tracked me back to the medbay after killing me. Actually, how am I getting back here anyway? I spend some time searching the hospital's internal functions file and find nothing. But there are patient logs, which as ranking doctor, I can access! I'm "unknown," obviously, but there are a few entries of me being admitted as a patient. No note on how I got here, though, just "deposited."

All my injuries are marked as "training accidents." This is technically true, in the biggest stretch of the term possible.

Also, I'm reasonably certain that this hospital isn't good enough to actually keep me alive from the damage I've been taking. But I'm not dead, so that's a problem for Later Lily. Or an absence of a problem, I suppose. I've never been hurt quite this badly before, and it's a limit I didn't want to press, for painful reasons.

Okay, the hospital isn't the answer here. I need to cut through and get out of here. But the droids react faster than me, and even on the shortest path, there's still one lurking, waiting for me.

I consult my mental map again. The corridor is a single hall, without any maintenance vents for me to slip through. Even in this badly designed, uncomfortable barracks, there's still HVAC, but it's all sealed off and probably more dangerous than just taking my chances with the droids. Ah, but that's right! There's something else here aside from crew quarters and ransacked mess halls!

There's an *armory*.

Actually there are, like, four. It's kind of creepy. But there's also one near me, and I think I've got a plan forming.

Out the door. Take a left. Run. Pass the tool cart. Break line of sight. And now, before going a single inch farther, *left* turn. Through a big security door.

And into a hall full of immaculately maintained weapons.

I don't have a lot of time; I can hear the combat droid tracking me. So I hop the counter, slide through the gap in the wire mesh that the quartermaster would pass things through, and get to work.

I don't know the specs on the droids, so I need to balance the ability to break through their armor with the ability for me to actually use a gun. This is a big problem, because . . . um . . . cat.

Using my teeth, and a hop, I pull a mag rifle off the wall. The magazine for it is simple, elegant, and takes me way too long to fumble into the base of the gun. I have to brace the barrel against the counter and headbutt it the last half inch in, hearing a click as it engages properly. I can *also* hear, from the hallway, the whir of the combat droid approaching.

Teeth and paws fumble the barrel up onto the counter, and I get it pointed toward the door as best I can. Safety off. Barrel put back into position from where I just knocked it askew. I wedge a paw into the trigger as best I can without moving the gun.

The droid takes the corner and *beeps* at me, the smug fucker.

I pull the trigger with a yank.

There's a crack of the mag rifle firing, a spray of expensive electronic shrapnel as the droid is blown away, and a sickening snap as the recoil sends the gun sprawling and shatters the bones in my leg.

Step one of the plan complete!

Ignoring the pain, knowing I'm on a clock here and also knowing I can get the bones put back together when I'm done, I start limply dragging the rifle down the hallway, back to the right. I pass the medical station and keep going, closing in on the access shaft. Without waiting for the hiding combat droid to announce itself, I brace the rifle against the wall, shove my broken paw into the firing trigger again, and pull as hard as I can.

Three rounds shred the access panel the droid is hiding behind. I'm pretty sure this hurts me more, but I'm kind of delirious with pain at this point, and I don't care. As long as I got it, I can . . .

The droid, which I guess knows how to *duck*, which seems unfair, slides out from around the panel. This one also beeps at me. And then shoots me.

I hardly feel it this time when the projectiles cleave my heart out.

Wake up. Same pattern, except now down one droid.

Except the dead droid got replaced. And it gets me.

Hospital.

Getting pissed now. Also *hungry*. I feel like I've been at this for a while.

Paw's better, though.

But I can't do that again. So. New plan. Slightly.

The hospital has a lot of emergency supplies. Some of them are still good. I raid the stash for a couple things.

Out. Left. Dodge the first one, into the armory. Move fast.

When the droid passes the door, I don't bother shooting it. Instead, I'm hiding behind the counter as the grenade I put by the door goes off.

Back out, down the hallway. Do a little setup. Then back to the armory. Rinse and repeat a couple times. Nothing stops me.

And then, standing thirty feet back from the lurking droid by the maintenance panel, I get belligerent. "Hey! Sparky!" I yell. "I know you're there!"

The droid doesn't even have the good grace to beep back. So, using a jury-rigged system, I fire a shot into the panel.

The droid slides out from around the side. Takes aim at me. And I hop my intact, now mostly furless, paws down onto the taut lines of medical sutures that I have running through the trigger mechanisms of all thirty mag rifles I could find.

The crackling of all of them firing at once is deafening, the recoil sending many of them bouncing back down the hallway, and the accuracy atrocious.

But I'm intact, and at the end of the day, the idiot combat droid isn't.

I move through the wreckage cautiously, alert for any more traps, but I make it to the access shaft without incident and shimmy up the ladder without any problems beyond the intrinsic problem that I am bad at ladders. At least until the gravity starts to shift.

The central sealed door has an old viewscreen on it that I didn't notice on the way in. "Training program in progress," it reads. "Noncommand staff access restricted."

Fortunately, I am command staff. And there's nothing this door can do to stop that.

My return to the station proper is marked by a small tumble as I misjudge the new gravity, and by a panicked Ennos yelling at me. Or at least, around me. "Where were you?!" the AI is asking. "It's been hours! You just vanished! We couldn't find you and I thought you'd died! We can't . . . I wouldn't . . . nothing . . ." The AI trails off.

"To be fair," I say, "I might have died. But it didn't stick."

This, for some reason, does not reassure Ennos at all. "Glitter was worried sick about you!" they say, deflecting. "What happened? Wait, what happened to your *fur*?"

"I got caught in a really rude training simulation," I tell them, exhausted. For some reason, whatever naps I got to take while being shot don't seem to have helped my energy levels. "Is there anything problematic going on? I want to get some food and sleep."

"Nothing, now that you're back," Ennos says, worried. "Are you okay?"

"I don't . . . know," I tell them. Somehow, the more I learn, the less certain I am. It's not even the pain of having been repeatedly shot over the last day. I'm suddenly even more confused about my place in the world, and now especially more concerned about whatever other surprises this station has.

"I don't know," I say again. Then I change the subject. "Hey, can you connect me to Glitter? I should check in with her."

"She'll be happy to hear you're all right," Ennos tells me with a professional tone. "Also, your lunch is replicated, and the station will be in the sun in about twenty minutes, if you want to nap down in the exolab."

"Thank you," I say, the stress of the day and the sudden kindness threatening to overwhelm me. "I'll . . . fill you in later, okay?"

"Take your time," the AI says. "I've got things to work on, as long as you're okay. Go enjoy your meal."

The meal is a ration torus. I think Ennos is trying to get cute with modifications to the ration replicator. I eat my flavorless doughnut in silence, every time I lick my mouth a reminder that half my fur is gone and my body is covered in scars.

And yet, it does, somehow, taste just a bit better this way.

The nap is pretty good too.

CHAPTER 19

The radio contact from Glitter catches me slightly by surprise. Ennos and I had taken some time to set the station's comm system to basically auto-answer whenever she pings us, along with tying the station's internal camera network into the feed. It was kind of . . . uh . . . slapped together? Look, getting video compression that can work over radio isn't easy. She'll need to do some legwork to make it work, but at least she can keep an eye on us without burning a month's worth of power reserves in ten minutes of subspace connection.

Which isn't actually a huge problem for her, really. Or for AIs in general. Part of the perk of being a digital intellect is the ability to rapidly structure hyperspecialized code and then splinter off a part of your brainpower to keep an eye on it. Automation isn't required when you can assign some of your attention to any given task, and that makes it a lot easier for an AI to sort through a lot of data, interpret weird codecs, or just hold two conversations at once.

The downside—I guess?—is that you can't eat things.

Which actually leads into a very strange question about qualia and experiences and what it means to feel and whether a piece of mechanical hardware designed to "smell" will ever feel the same as a biological organ and honestly, it's all very much a headache. I don't really, actually, care? I mean, I don't think any particular way is better. Just that they're different, and those differences . . . you know . . . are things that are real. We don't need a stack ranking of who can feel pain "better."

This is a theoretical downside. So far, my experiences as far as I mostly remember them would not put eating as a species perk? According to all biological texts I've read, including a lot of stuff about my own uplift, cats don't have the same range of taste buds that most omnivores or herbivores have.

Which, I mean, okay, sure, but that doesn't mean I wouldn't appreciate some synthetic red meat flavor in my diet.

I'm still tracking down that accursed orbital greenhouse. Don't think I've forgotten! I'll get to it. We're running a defragment routine on the remains of the damaged parts of the shuttle's memory.

As for the shuttle itself, well. I'm running a repair routine on that myself. Manually. Because the repair bots on the station don't really know what to do with it.

We—and by we I mean me, with Ennos providing commentary—hauled this thing in when it drifted a bit too close a few days ago. I almost forgot about it, what with getting sidetracked and shot repeatedly. But now, I'm taking advantage of some quiet time to try to retrofit it. See if I can apply a lot of the previously abstract knowledge I've built up to some paws-on practice.

It is and/or was a cramped two-seater, with a chunky rectangular box of a cargo bay, an engine that is just barely technically capable of safely braking when at full mass, and so few safety features that I think it's a workplace hazard just to think about piloting it.

Would it surprise you, at all, to learn that its hull markings are from a Hypercorp?

It's from a company called Ferromancer, and past experience lets me know they're mainly a high-end design and manufacturing company for delicate spaceship parts. They're from back when the corps had branding and advertising, almost like nations, actually. I've encountered their work before, and I hate them. The shuttle is actually a weird example of just how good their stuff is.

Not a single part in the shuttle was actually built by Ferromancer.

Now, I get it. Just because you build hot rods doesn't mean you built the truck that ferries them around. But it's pretty telling that the miraculously surviving employee manual makes it clear that their pilots are never to attempt Ferromancer-standard maintenance or upgrades to this shuttle. And built at a time when spaceflight was *expensive*, when if you had the option to work in-house, you *did*, they chose to outsource their most common workhorse shuttles to the lowest bidder.

The lowest bidder, still more expensive than doing it themselves, was their preferred option. Let that sink in.

I tried to recover a live-lattice aggregation generator they'd built from a wrecked midmass freighter once. The first tap, the *slightest* motion, and it activated and began generating thrust. Punched through the wreck's hull, snapped two of the station's manipulator arms, and crashed into Jupiter a few hours later.

To be clear on this, that was a shelf-stable power generation unit. Not an engine, thruster, drive, or other form of propulsion. Well, intentional propulsion.

Anyway, point is, I'm trying to put the shuttle back together and am about a fourth of the way through cutting away a bulkhead that's worth more as scrap metal than ship structure when Glitter calls.

"I humbly request a token of favor," Glitter says out of nowhere.

Which, naturally, causes me to yowl in surprise and jerk my paw in a way that *technically* removes the damaged plate. It also adds one other plate to the list of damaged bits to remove. That is a problem for Future Lily, though Present Lily does make a note that this is Glitter's fault.

"I'm not getting you a new battery just so you can run the subspace comm every minute of the day," I reply, once I've regained my composure. Fortunately, inside the engineering armor, my composure can be as horrible as I want and no one can see through the shielding. "I already have enough trouble with power supply. Though I did uncover an actual factory deck today! It could maybe put something together? I'll ask Ennos later when they know what all the loaded schematics on the assembly lines are."

I know from experience by now that Glitter's long pause is not due to comms lag or anything so pedestrian. Instead, it's her waiting for me to stop rambling. Which, when I figured that out, I will admit kind of stung.

I am just about to ask what it is she'd like, breaking the silence that has started to fill the shuttle bay, when she speaks again. "I have noticed, recently, that you regularly fire a low-intensity beam weapon to the surface," Glitter states, in her usual noble tone.

"Oh! Yes. There's a living chemical thing down there that mind-controls people. I can't safely kill it, so I sort of prod it to move on every now and then so it doesn't accidentally wipe out whole villages or something." I pad across the bay and to the tool that I've cobbled together to adjust the settings on the miniature laser strapped to my paw. With the armor on, it's a lot easier than otherwise to mess with the dials, but it's still obvious this was made for someone with fingers, and it's simpler to just slap my suited paw into the slot and let the simple machine dial down the intensity until it's where I need it to be and I can get back to work. It takes basically no focus, so I can do this while I keep talking. "The whole thing is sort of a chore, really. The Haze—I call it the Haze—isn't actually that dangerous. I just need to keep it moving, and this lets me do it without collateral damage."

Glitter's voice, patient as a saint to be able to deal with me when I'm excited, waits just long enough to be polite and then asks her favor. "Would you be offended if I asked to do that?"

"To . . . be a mind-control cloud?" I pause, yanking my paw back from the rotating rubber pad and making sure my laser is properly set before heading back to the shuttle.

"To be the one that prods it, as you say."

I blink, eyes widening under my helmet. "You want to do my chores for me?" I can't help but ask with a puzzled meow.

"Partially," Glitter says. "I wish to be of use, in some way. There is a debt between us that cannot ever be paid, and—"

"Nope!" I reject that entire notion out of hand. "I'm capricious and neither pay nor collect debts!"

"—and I wish to repay you regardless." Glitter sounds exasperated with me. Which, you know, fair, I suppose. "But also, I am adrift. I have nothing to do. My war is long over. I could aid you in your own, but what possible thing could I do that would matter? Your armaments outmatch mine a thousandfold. Your detection systems are more varied and useful. The only thing I have to offer you is your own time. And now, with the madness of contradiction pushed back and broken, I find the excitement suddenly missing. And I wish to participate, in your life, and in the world of the living."

The way Glitter talks sometimes is hard to parse, but I cannot help letting my tail flick in amusement as I instantly decipher this particular paragraph of courtly poetry. "You're *bored*!" I accuse her.

"I am bored," Glitter confirms, sounding dejected.

I decide almost right away not to tease her about this. The mental image of a morose weapons platform, suddenly devoid of anything to do, is equal parts sad and scary. And also, aside from the obvious concern that she might get bored enough to start carving art into the planet, there's just the fact that Glitter is my friend, and I wanna help.

"Okay! So we're gonna need to get a variable beam projector installed in you, huh?" I say out loud.

"Ennos was not joking . . ." Glitter sounds amazed. "You really do not realize you're doing that, do you?"

"Doing what?"

"I would not concern yourself with this." Glitter is almost certainly lying to me. "Although, modifications to myself? Could I not take remote command of your own, now that my connections are not fettered?"

I give a sheepish mewl that probably would have just been translated as "Ah." If I'd let it. "So." I speak normally. "The station kind of . . . rejects that. Like, a lot. It's some kind of infectious code that's gotten into pretty much every system. I've only managed to convince it to even give Ennos permission for a couple things, and basically never weaponry, and even then it sometimes randomly takes it back. So unless you have some kind of void beam trick that makes it not violently annihilate matter, we'll need to get something else loaded onto you personally that you can have complete access to."

"I have never been changed," Glitter says distantly. "Even software patches. Even *orders*. I do not know how to feel about this."

"Well, you've got some time to think about it. I'm gonna have to build the projector anyway, and . . . hm. I need to go check on if our fabricator can . . . actually, hey, Ennos! Whatcha up to, buddy?" I call out to the station. The extra volume really doesn't actually matter; they can hear me just fine anyway and have some kind of recognition program set up for use of their name. But it feels more personal this way.

Ennos's voice joins our conversation, and now I'm talking to two people I can't see. "I am currently running a metadata diagnostic on the linguistic database," Ennos says. "Specifically, on the piece of strange programming attached to it."

"How's that going? Also, do we have a blueprint for a laser?"

"Yes. We have eighty-four ways to construct a laser with the known resources on the station. Six of them are useful. I've selected the one that you'll want, because it is absurd, and cost means little to someone who can harvest tungsten and platinum from an entire orbital junkyard all to themselves." Ennos pauses and then addresses the first part of the question. "And it is going strangely. Something shifted just before you began speaking to me. The watcher program I have running reports a near doubling of activity from the parasite code. I need to focus on this. Please excuse me."

Ennos goes quiet, and I wait a minute before going back to talking to Glitter. "So that sounds promising," I say. Enthusiastically! I say it enthusiastically! Certainly not with a kind of lingering concern that I might have some sort of ghostly voice-doppelganger living in the grid. Because that would be . . .

Anyway, Glitter may not share my enthusiasm, but Glitter's simple request to help with chores is sort of turning into an existential crisis for her. I give her some time to figure that out, while I figure out what I'm doing with my time in general.

The shuttle is . . . I hate to say it, but the shuttle is scrap. There's nothing left here for me to actually work with. Engine's shot, control board is dead, hull is compromised. It would be faster for me to build my own rather than try to repair this wreckage.

Which I might do, I guess? There's nothing really stopping me, except for time, resources, and expertise. But I've got literally all the time in the world, an entire Kessler syndrome of resources, and . . . I mean, trial and error can get you a long way. I should know!

But also there are engineering guides stored on the grid. I'm not actually that dumb. Don't worry.

I don't even really need a shuttle right now anyway, I guess. I'm mostly just sort of presuming that we'll find a magical realm full of edible plants, still somehow growing after all this time, ready to be harvested and eaten. Hopefully ones I'm not allergic to? I don't actually know what I'm allergic to, but I've read a lot of biology texts, and it looks like cats can't eat a lot of things. But I still think I'd eat an entire garlic bulb if that was what we found, just to taste something, anything.

Anyway. Shuttle? Broken. Plants? Potentially existent. The problem? Getting the plants from there to here without a shuttle. The solution?

I mean, build a shuttle, I guess. Or learn that the station has some kind of science-fiction-style teleporter on it. I've been finding a *lot* of stuff behind all those doors I can open now that the station recognizes me as giving commands.

Not that it didn't recognize me as the primary authority to begin with, but at least now it can hear me. And there's so much more to do now. It's . . . I mean, it's a little exhausting, sometimes?

Not that I miss how things were previously. You spend one century frantically trying to keep the maintenance routines online and shooting down problems, and you're pretty much over it. But it was . . . I dunno. It was familiar? I was used to it. I knew what I was doing.

Now? Now I don't know anything, it feels like. Everything that changes just unearths a half dozen things I can realize I never knew in the first place. My voice just shows off how much of the station I haven't ever explored. Ennos shows me how little I know about what the systems are doing behind the scenes. Learning more about my own medical history is leaving me feeling like I should be one of the station's ghosts.

And I just don't know what to do about any of it.

I'm not actually that smart. I'm the smartest cat ever, but I don't have answers. I've been shying away from actually trying to remember the past for four hundred years. Answers might scare me more than the questions ever could. And the questions these days are often boiling down to "Do you live in a haunted house," so that's kind of worrying all on its own.

This is why I hate the process of taking off the engineering armor. It takes twenty minutes, and that gives me too much time to think.

Now, though, I'm free from my duralumin confines, and I can dash through the station's oversized corridors as a visible cloud of cleaner nanos tries to catch up to me and undo the effects of being sealed in armor for six hours.

I've figured out what to do with my time. Not forever, that is, but right now.

Restock my food reserves, check the logs to make sure no one is trying to call in an air strike, and then get to a command station and start up the fabricators to build Glitter her new tool.

Ennos was right. It is absurd. I don't think they were listening in on our conversation; this thing is calibrated to melt down comets. It's got some kind of impossible quantum physics effect that lets it bleed off kinetic energy. Or . . . I mean, I think it converts kinetic energy into heat? Rapidly? This doesn't seem like a laser at all.

I check. It's not. It's called an elser. This seems impossible, under conventional physical laws, and sure enough, it is. Looks like a part of the lensing array uses a fairly common metamaterial that we still have a stockpile of in one of the cargo bays. Mostly because I haven't been building guns that stop things by melting them.

I consider it for a good minute or two. Which is, for me, basically forever. Then I make a conscious choice to *not* give Glitter the impossible space gun. I find the other designs Ennos earmarked in the system, pick a good old-fashioned midpowered orbit-to-surface laser array, and start the assembly process.

It's about two-thirds done, with me keeping an eye on it to troubleshoot any manufacturing bugs that come up, when Glitter gets back to me. She would like to try having her physical form changed. I'm not exactly shocked, but I'm still feeling pretty good, a little bobbing pep in my movements as I watch the assembler do its job.

It takes two days and three spacewalks for me to get the whole thing set up. There's only one small interruption to shoot down a long-range missile that'd been in accidental orbit around the sun and just got within effective range of a potential target. Scared the heck out of Ennos when it lit off its engines just outside our orbital path, and it wasn't even aiming for us. I almost missed that one! But I got it at the last minute before it hit one of the large-scale habitat stations. I still don't know if anyone lives on those anymore, but I didn't want to take the chance.

And then, a week later, after a few test fires and, yes, a stockpile of commercial batteries added to Glitter's internals, she takes her first poke at the Haze, shifting it out of a small tower city that it'd been in for a little while.

I dunno if she'd ever say it out loud—Glitter has a kind of propriety to her etiquette that I don't quite *get* really—but my friend seems happy. I can hear the smile in her digital voice; no amount of AI control of their own bodies, it seems, lets them completely abandon unconscious emotional broadcast.

It's been a good week.

And it's killed enough time that the shuttle's map data has been as repaired as it's gonna get.

I'm going hunting.

For carrots. To be clear. I am hunting for carrots, or other root vegetables.

This was supposed to be dramatic, and I am ruining the gravitas. Okay. Well, gravitas ruined, I feel comfortable taking a nap before I get back to work.

I fall asleep in the exolab, thin rays of sun glittering through the windows, the feeling of a comforting hand on my head and a sense of pride carrying me into my dreams.

CHAPTER 20

I am, at this point, wholly prepared to believe that the ration replicator is haunted.

Or possessed? Maybe just generically "influenced." I'm not sure what the proper terminology is. I don't care. Haunted is fine. Lots of stuff around here is haunted, really.

For all I know, it's Ennos having figured out how to modify its routines, and I'm being subjected to a monthlong prank. But that doesn't seem in character for the AI that I would most describe as "orderly."

What am I talking about, you ask? I am talking about *geometry*, of course.

Specifically, the geometry of my food. I know I complain about the food sometimes, and I'm sure that gets old. But you know what else gets old? The food. And it's been getting older for me than it has for you, so you aren't allowed to complain. I am vaguely aware from a treatise on social etiquette published six hundred years ago in East York that these are, in fact, "the rules." But let me put your worries to rest: I am not here to complain about the taste of the food today.

For the longest time, the galley unit rotated between thin rectangular bars and a kind of doughy oblong shape for what it dispensed food as. In the absence of things like fresh ingredients and flavorings, the galley relies on the replicator, which can transmute electricity and some abuse of physics into matter. But doing this safely is basically impossible. Doing it in a way that isn't woefully reckless requires that the replicator pretty much stick to making one nutrient-compact flavorless hydrocarbon. Which is then pressed into form by the galley and served to me.

Room temperature.

But for the past couple weeks, that hasn't really been holding up.

First it was small changes. Rounded edges on the nutrient bars, small lines on the outsides of the ration orbs. Then it started to get a bit weirder. I'd get to the dispenser and it would present me with multiple small ration balls, with little dots of extra ration paste on the outside. Or, more recently, the time it served me a torus.

Now, I'm looking down at the plate that has some kind of hydrocarbon-based ziggurat on it and wondering what is going on in my life. Three stacked square tiers, but with a set of smaller steps going up one side and what looks like detail lines carved into them. Small markings that cannot possibly serve a food-based purpose.

"Ennos!" I call out, not taking my eyes off what is supposed to be my lunch.

"Yes, Lily?" The AI's voice echoes from the hallway outside. "Is this important? I am mapping intercept trajectories."

"What did you do to the galley?" I ask, a bit belligerently.

There is a pause before Ennos's honest voice comes back. I know it's their honest voice, because they sound worried, and they can't lie worth anything when they're panicking. "Nothing? Why? What's gone wrong? Are you all right? Is something on fire?"

I flick my eyes toward the door, afraid that if I stop staring at my lunch sculpture, it might vanish. "Nothing is on fire. Why are you talking from outside?"

"The galley does not currently have proper access to the internal resonance comms." Ennos sounds even *more* worried, which is strange. Normally they feel better when things aren't on fire. "What is wrong?"

"My lunch looks like a Nova Brazil college campus, and I want to know why," I call back. Some time passes, and I don't turn my eyes away from the small food ziggurat. More time passes. I realize I am holding my breath, like I'm coiled to pounce. "Ennos?"

"Hm?" The AI's voice sounds distant. "Yes, Lily?"

Well, now *I'm* worried too! "Did you forget about the food thing? Is something eating your memory? Oh no, is there a virus in the grid with you?!"

"Oh no, I assumed you were joking and resumed work."

"Ennos!" I yell. "This is serious!"

"No, it isn't!" the AI informs me, *cheerfully*. "Enjoy your lunch!"

I glare at my "lunch" for another half hour, before my stomach pangs with pain and I give in to the urge to eat, chomping down on the top layer of the ziggurat and tearing off a wet chunk of the pressed nutrient-laden hydrocarbon mixture with my fangs.

It tastes like ration paste. I'm not sure what I expected.

The time wasted isn't that bad. I can afford time these days. The maintenance is where it's supposed to be, just needing one verbal check-in every day; Glitter is handling the Haze problem; Ennos is doing . . . something. Look, Ennos is an outlier; they've kind of got their own thing going on. I asked if I could help once, and they just *huffed* at me and told me I couldn't do anything without an IOI (input/output interface). And then ignored my explanation for how my body rejects cybernetics. Very rude.

The point is, before I get too sidetracked by how rude Ennos is, I can take a long lunch. Not something I'm used to.

After that, chores.

Check the ammo stockpiles, the material reserves, and the spare parts. Snap up a few chunks of debris from around us with the magnetic grapples, restock all those high-quality metals that I need to make more stuff. Make sure the factories are running properly.

I have multiple factories now! I'm mostly using them to jury-rig consumer goods into something more useful for us. One of them is running off portable batteries that can, technically, be linked up into larger clusters with only minimal loss. I've already got one stack over on Glitter, and I'm setting up a few more here so I can have a fourth backup power supply in case anything . . . happens.

The other one is just making tiny hoverdrones. Basically just a wireless connection and a camera for Ennos and Glitter to make use of. And a *speaker*. There *was* a blueprint for a speaker this whole time!

I want to briefly tangent—yes, briefly, shut up—into the fact that I have far less experience navigating the station's grid than I thought. I keep calling it "the grid," and that's just wrong. It's been wrong this whole time, and I didn't really understand how or why.

Imagine a landscape. Mountains, rivers, trees, and a few towns. The towns are "civilization." But they're divided by the rivers and mountains. That metaphor basically sums up the whole grid here. There's tens, maybe hundreds of different systems, all of them connected in some way to the central "station" intelligence, but all with different quirks to them.

Some require a physical presence to access or activate, some are indexed while some aren't, some have large swaths of data hidden inside other files or libraries that aren't labeled at all or sometimes just don't show up without drilling down to core code.

It's actually infuriating. I've spent hundreds of years getting to know the physical space I inhabit, learning to keep the air flowing and the lights on, learning to aim and fire weapons with paws and work a welding laser while covered in fur. And yes, reading, too. Reading everything I think I have access to; I've read so many digital textbooks that I *reread some of them* when I got bored.

And I haven't even scratched the surface. Not just of the physical station, which I'm now learning more and more of, its size proving to be larger and larger with each new door unlocked, but also of the incorporeal grid, a whole other world with its own pile of secrets and inconveniences.

Great.

Okay, tangent over. What were we talking about?

Chores. Right.

There's actually a weird loss marked for a small chunk of metal stocks, and a power expenditure from the subspace tap production of a hydrogen fuel cell, and I don't remember where this came from. I track it backward and find that one of the drone fabricators is apparently putting together some kind of heavy cargo drone.

The only thing I can think is that it was in the build queue when Ennos and I slapped together the recovery flotilla for Glitter. I double-check the launch bay those drones are in and find none missing, and—more importantly—no new ones either. So this problem hasn't gotten out of hand, and I cancel the project now before it goes too far and eats up a bunch of the stuff I need to make kinetic projectiles.

An alarm sounds. Ennos patches a frantic SOS through to me. It takes me forty-eight seconds to get to the gunnery controls at an irresponsibly reckless speed and another twenty-four seconds to line up a shot. The groundstriker turns an old bioweapons lab into a smoking crater, and an inferno round follow-up purifies the area. Two crossing void beams dig defensive trenches while a third and fourth carve up the flesh horrors spilling out of the area. The defenders, an exhausted-looking band of about a hundred people of a score of different species, collectively slump as the crisis resolves.

It took me barely more than a minute to get the call and take action, but my traitorous eyes can't help but look at the various detail scans on my AR displays and realize that I have saved well under a fifth of the people there.

Who were they, I wonder? A village or a caravan? Explorers accidentally unleashing hell, or a coalition tracking hell back to its home?

I wish I could have done more. I wish I could spot these problems before they've already killed so many. But even from up here, I can't see everything. Especially not the future.

The skirmish has my stomach roiling, a grim sorrow threatening to take over my limbs. I don't really have a good sense of time, but by the time

I silently wrap up the rest of the chores I had planned, the clock says that I've been at this for about six hours.

I eat again. I am served a blooming flower. I glare at it with hunter's eyes and poke it with extended claws before making the decision to start eating.

It still tastes like ration.

"Ennos, are you certain the galley isn't alive, haunted, rogue, infected with a hostile nanoswarm, being targeted by an infiltrator bot, or being controlled by someone on the surface who has found an ancient buried access terminal?" I ask.

The AI hums at me. "Some of those are rather . . . specific."

"Look, a lot can happen in a few centuries," I meow back. "Just . . . what's going on with this thing?"

"I really do not know what you mean by that," Ennos replies. "It is connected to the station's main command routines, all safety protocols are operating at full effectiveness, maintenance readouts report that it is in working order, nano-swarm reports it has been thoroughly cleaned . . . everything seems to be fine. In fact, compared to several other systems on the same deck, it's in exceptionally good condition." Ennos pauses. "Actually, it is almost . . . too perfect. Strange. But I am attempting to avoid unfounded paranoia. And you should as well. Odd shapes perhaps indicate that the galley has simply restored functionality that was previously lost. After all, is maintenance not much more efficient now?"

"You and your efficiency," I mutter.

"Quite," Ennos says. "And, as one of the perks of my exceptional efficiency, I have for you now a set of potential coordinates to search."

My heart leaps in my chest. "Search for . . . something horrible that might kill us all?" I ask, keeping my expectations low.

"Search for an orbital farm," Ennos corrects, a smile in their voice. "I have traced back the reconstructed path of the shuttle you retrieved, and I believe that I can safely tell you when our orbit will next intersect the—"

"I'll get my armor on!" I yell, not even bothering to translate from cat to whatever dialect Ennos is familiar with. The excited meow comes out like a wail, but there's no hint of angst left in me despite what noises I may be making. Instead, I'm already running for the drone bay, moving fast enough and taking strange enough shortcuts that it takes Ennos a couple tries to broadcast their voice properly near me.

"Lily!" The AI tries to catch my attention. "Lily, you have four hours until we're even remotely close to the target!"

It is too late. I am excited now. I plant my paws on the marked spots and meow a command to the system that "assembles" the spacesuit and armor that is technically a drone. Heavy machinery moving with almost delicate care pulls away from the cargo drone it's been putting together and moves to bolt and weld pieces of grav plate and operational utility around my body, gently beginning the process of sealing me into the armor.

"Lily, go take a nap or something! You're going to get all irritable if you're in your armor for six hours!" Ennos chastises me.

I scoff. Who could possibly sleep with something like this on the horizon? Naps are for when you're *sad*, not when you're *vibrating through the deckplates*!

"Wait, are you actually sad every time you go take a nap?" Ennos asks with shocked concern. "Lily, that's not okay! Come on, pause the assembly routine and let's go open some dangerous unknown airlocks or run an unlabeled code fragment or something else that you like to do."

"Or we could fire up the engines, and—"

"The engines are *not* safe! This station has too many engines and too many structural weak points! It's a miracle that it hasn't had parts fall off using them before!" Ennos sounds exasperated, so I don't say anything, instead trying my best to look innocent. Which is actually pretty easy, since cats tend to generally always look like they're guilty, which makes it hard for Ennos to tell when I'm actually hiding something. "Lily." The AI sighs. "What broke off the station?"

"Outer science wing," I mutter. "And an engine pod. And a high-yield reactor core. And a . . . hydroponics bay." I meow again, pausing the armor assembly. It takes a minute for it to undo what it's already done, and I shake out the white fur of my paws as I step out. At least *that* fur didn't get shot off, so the parts of myself I see most often still look properly feline. "All right, all right. I'll be patient."

"Thank you." Ennos sighs again. "Besides, six hours isn't that long. You could probably—"

They never finish their sentence. Another alarm sounds.

Now *I* sigh. The gesture is still sort of alien to my biology, but cathartic all same.

Ennos was right, though. Six hours wasn't that long. And by the time I've shot down the infiltrator satellite that was trying to turn off the life support, it's a lot closer to the hour when we'll be crossing paths with the potential orbital farm. This time, no one with actual patience complains when I start getting bolted into the armor.

I check in with Glitter and make sure she's doing okay, reset all the maintenance routines, and connect a few of the finished camera drones to a private grid on a civilian computer I printed out so that Glitter and Ennos can control them completely. I eat, one more time, before getting armored up. It's a cube. No comment, except that it tastes like ration.

And then, when the projected timer ticks to zero in my vision, I take a running start and launch myself through the bay shield and out of the flight deck, tumbling away from the station's embrace, and out into the void.

I feel a lot more relaxed about this one than the last time I did it.

But I maybe should have waited for more of my fur to regrow.

Turns out, this suit itches when it rubs against my bare skin.

CHAPTER 21

I am, once again, drifting through the condensed nothing of hard vacuum.

My AR link is cut off as soon as I'm outside the station. How, exactly, the station has decided what is and is not inside itself seems arbitrary. But I also don't have the position to complain about it; after all, it's not like I plan on rustling around in root code that I can't even read to try to tamper with the directives that keep my air going.

I'm in communication with Ennos this time, though. A simple encrypted radio link is good enough for this. There's an amount of interference, obviously, given . . . you know . . . everything. All this stuff. But it's not like we really need anything more powerful, given that I'm traveling to something within jumping range and not more than a light-second away.

Okay, I said that, and then I remembered how space works. "Jumping range" has more to do with when I starve to death than with how much distance I can cover. Also accuracy. There's a bit of a downside to a miss, and that downside is that no side will ever be down again if you get too far away from a gravity well.

It's not that I ever forget how space works. Just that I spend most of my time . . . not . . . in it.

Below me, Earth looms. So large that I feel like nothing compared to it. My home is so high up, with such a massive vantage point. And yet, I watch over only a tiny sliver of the world at a time. There are still millions of people down there, and while they may not know it, a lot of them rely on random chance, the luck of having me overhead when a certain type of problem crops up.

It makes me angry. So, so angry.

My station is unbelievably old. So old, it has had to purge old data records from the grid as time went on. But it doesn't wear down, it doesn't age, it doesn't decay. It keeps going, even when the maintenance routines slip and the life support shuts down from lack of use, the emergency backups keep it going. For *thousands of years* it has kept going. For so long, I can't even tell you how long it has been.

This is what people used to build. Even when that golden age ended, and rivals started taking and retaking the station, adding their own tools, their own purpose to it, it kept those parts going too. It's a living library, a near invincible record of the people who once were.

And now, all that is lost. The station is all that's left. Half memorial, half sentinel, watching the sophonts of Earth scramble in the dirt to try to rebuild even a scrap of what that old golden age produced.

There are culprits, of course. Demagogues, corporations, reactionary movements. I don't have a whole picture of history, but I have moments. Snapshots, dredged up in my ongoing research. The station's grid has a lot more storage on it now than it did when I woke up, let me tell you. I don't wanna lose another history text again.

But all those culprits are long dead. It's far, far too late for me to shoot any of them. All that is left below is ruin and ash.

Poison clouds, radioactive wastes, rogue machines from forgotten wars and pointless greed, dead cities, mass graves, crashed starships, old automatons, mutated wildlife, and an endless supply of violence. And everywhere, people. Hanging on by threads sometimes, but *people*. A beacon for emergence events, for parasites like the Haze, or just for their own folly.

But hanging on.

"Lily? Are you there?" Ennos's voice crackles through my internal comm.

"How can something so big be so small?" I mutter back.

"That's called perspective," Ennos says dryly, missing out on the profound and fragile nature of Earth. "And speaking of perspective, you may not have noticed, but you're approaching a pair of satellites in a magnetic orbit with each other. Recommend engaging grav plating and shifting starboard three-two-six degrees at time one-four."

"I don't even have a . . ." I stop. There is, in the corner of my vision, a glowing red number displaying a time stamp. It ticks up as I watch. How did . . . they get this in here? I didn't put this here; that would have been foresight, and I don't do that. Also . . . "We're within a light-second of each other, you don't need to time-stamp maneuvering commands. Void, you don't even need to give maneuvering commands in general; you can just yell at me to dodge and I'll probably be fine. I'm basically immortal anyway."

The word "basically" does a lot of work for me. I should thank whoever invented it.

Ennos replies with the sort of voice that makes me think they've been going through media archives and really, really want to be a fleet admiral now but are getting stonewalled by me crushing their dreams. "Just dodge the stupid satellites." They sulk.

"Yes, Captain," I reply.

"I thought you were captain. Wait. How is it that you are in charge of the station, anyway?" Ennos asks, suddenly curious. "There are no other cats on board. I . . . never thought about this. Where did you come from? Are you of a lineage of uplifts removed from a cryo pod every generation to maintain the station?"

Well, I have some time while I float closer and closer to the potential orbital farm. I can answer a few questions. But first. "What cryo pod would I . . . do we have cryo pods?"

"Yes. Several hundred. Did you . . . ?" Ennos doesn't bother finishing the question. Of course I hadn't noticed. "Ah." They sigh.

"I've been here most of my life," I say over the radio link, shifting my paws up to fire the grav plating and roll myself away from the dancing satellites. "My mom—adopted, you know—brought me up with a delve crew a while back. They were looking for . . . I mean . . . they . . ." I trail off, the words fizzling out as I falter. "There was something on the station they wanted," I decide on.

This answer does nothing to clear up Ennos's confusion. "The only surface-to-orbit activity in the last fifty years, by the record, has been either shot down, cargo railguns firing to nowhere, or otherwise a failure. Except for the drop shuttles of what I must assume is the Last Ship?"

"Yup," I say, carefully keeping my tone neutral and my eyes on the looming farm structure. It's starting to come into focus now. Three big pillars, connected by smaller struts. Hallways, maybe? Without going inside, I can't know if these are meant to be tall or wide.

"Lily?" Ennos asks several minutes later, voice small. "How . . . old are you?"

"Uh . . ." That's an awkward question! How do you tell your friend that you've lost track? "Some number over four hundred?"

"Four hundred . . . what?"

"Years."

The answer silences Ennos for a long while. I'm close enough to the farm to make out individual portholes by the time they speak up again. "You have been out here, alone, for all that time?" they ask softly.

"Oh! Not the *whole* time. And it's not that bad!" I instantly deflect from what I am forced to accept is pity. "I wasn't even that smart when I got here;

just a normal old cat. So I didn't start to get bored for . . . I mean, there's always something to do . . . so . . . you know . . ."

"You . . . uplifted yourself?" Ennos sounds either doubtful or incredulous. I'm not sure what the difference between those words is, so it could go either way.

I refrain from nodding, not wanting to have to course-correct if I screw up my momentum. But I think about it. "Oh yeah! Give a cat a century or so and she can learn stuff. It's just harder. I mean, compared to . . . I guess anyone? I bet I could learn faster than a shark, though." I get sidetracked and start mentally listing to myself all the animals I'm probably more clever than. "Anyway. It's been fine."

"Has it?" Ennos's voice is so quiet, I wonder if I've actually heard anything. "I've been alive for weeks. And yet . . . it feels like a lifetime. It *is* my lifetime. Four *hundred years*?" They sound so . . . sad. "What have you been doing?"

"Trying to have a peaceful life, I guess." It's such a stupid answer. It's so . . . nothing. And a lie. And a lot of other things.

I'm a couple hundred feet closer to my destination, starting to spin up the grav plates to break down to safe landing speeds and look for an airlock, when Ennos continues the conversation. "I would not have assumed you wanted a peaceful life," they say. "I thought you had chosen 'combatant' as your path."

The words hurt. More than body slamming through a metal grate hurts. More than getting shot had hurt. More than that one fabrication error where I'd gotten one of my forelegs sliced off and had to spend a week in a vivification pod hurt.

I wasn't expecting it to hurt this much.

I already knew I was a combatant. I self-identified as a soldier, of sorts. But still . . . I don't know. I don't know how to react. Part of me wants to run and hide, but I am trapped in this conversation by virtue of being a quarter mile drifting into space and unable to hang up on my guiding assistant.

So I say nothing.

"Lily?" Ennos sounds afraid.

"I wanted to build things," I mutter back. I'm not even sure I'm trying to use my projected voice, but the words come out clear anyway. "I didn't want to be a killer."

"You aren't . . . !"

"I kill things," I hiss out. "It's practically all I do." I want to pace, to claw at something, even if it's just a deckplate, to curl up and sleep until my erratic brain lets go of this line of thinking. "I am a *very* good killer."

I have killed so many things. Many of them deserving, but assuredly some of them not. Many of them monsters, many of them not. Railguns and void rays and flak cannons and mag webs and intercept beams and good old-fashioned lasers. I have killed so many things.

"We don't have to . . ." Ennos grasps for words. "You're coming up on the orbital farm. We can talk about something . . . you're not a bad person. You're protecting people. It's not hard to see. I'm only a few weeks old, and I know you're a good person!" They pause, then add, "You saved Glitter! You found *me*!"

"You're biased," I mewl. I'm not feeling so great right now. Maybe this trip was a bad idea.

"No!" Ennos snaps at me suddenly. "It's fine! Nothing is going wrong, and you complain endlessly about the food! Go find some berries or something!" There's a hint of desperation in their voice, and I realize something all of a sudden.

They're echoing the fear of their predecessor. Ennos is afraid of being left alone.

"I'm not going anywhere," I mutter, reassuringly, the spirals my mind has been going through suddenly arresting themselves. "Don't worry. I'm all right." I sigh inside my suit.

It's a different experience now. Before, I was, in the abstract, responsible for the lives of everyone below. But beyond that, nothing tethered me that much. Now, though? Ennos and Glitter are *here*. With me. Talking to me. Ennos *needs* me.

It's a lot harder to be self destructive when you'd be taking someone else with you.

"I'm okay," I say again. "I won't do anything stupid. I mean, *this time*." I preempt Ennos's snark. "Aside from throwing myself into space, obviously." I feel one last twinge of sorrow, and I try to express it, to push the sliver of hurt out of my chest. "I just . . . I would have wanted my mom to be proud of me."

Except I don't say that.

I mean, I *say* that. If you played back my words in Cat and translated manually, I am absolutely sure that is what I said. I did say that.

But that is not what comes out.

Instead, my projected voice *twists*. Wrenching itself out of my grasp, changing and uncoiling. And for an instant, I see the mechanisms inside it, laid bare in a mental construct of twisted glass and moving parts, before it slams shut again.

And with a sensation not unlike being flicked in the nose, the words that come out do so differently.

"I think my mom would have been proud of me," I . . . say? I say.

And somehow, I know that's true.

Unfortunately, I didn't seem to say that last bit over the radio, and Ennos has mistaken my quiet contemplation of the nature of reality for sulking. Which . . . okay, *fair*, but also rude. "Okay, enough moping!" They speak in an enthusiastic tone that doesn't feel right coming from the normally reserved or panicked AI. "Suit sensors have three spots on this part of the hull I can mark as airlocks! All of them look sealed, so aim for the closest one, and we can get in that way."

I huff out a tired breath. Okay, emotional turmoil later. Work now.

The farm looms large before me, no lights of its own giving it away, but glittering in the ambient light all the same. The thing is *huge*. Almost as big as my own home, easily several kilometers long; the hexagonal pillars build to maximize internal growing space. I give a few minor tweaks to the grav plates and land lightly on the extended flat plating around the middle airlock. Judging by the orientation, these pillars of metal are tall after all.

"This airlock seems . . . not large," I comment.

"Personnel airlock, not cargo," Ennos informs me. "Most of these will be; your suit's visuals picked up what looks like bay doors on the end segments. They probably ship out produce from there. These are for maintenance staff to do spacewalks."

"No repair bots?" I muse.

"Lily, don't take the magical repair bots for granted, please." Ennos sighs at me.

Okay, now that's not fair! *I'm* allowed to sigh, but why do they get to sigh? Ennos doesn't even have lungs!

Unimportant. I let it go and ask the more relevant question. "How do I get in?"

"Look to your left. There's an access . . . *left*. Your *left*. Yes, there."

It's impressive how I can actually feel the AI rolling their eyes.

Oh man, Ennos has camera drones now! They can *actually* roll their eyes! That's going to get old so fast!

But that's a consideration for Future Lily. Present Lily has a challenge.

Reorienting the grav plates, I walk up the "wall" next to the airlock so that I can flick my suited tail down to near the access port. The plug obviously isn't the same, but that's fine. That's why this suit has two different engineering nanoswarms built into it. I trigger one now, the blossom on my back unfolding and giving a simple-yet-complex command to the nanos. They'll have a limited operations time outside of the station, but that's fine. They can recharge in my suit when done, and it only takes a minute or two for them to reconfigure the connector on my tail to fit properly.

"Checking . . . data codec is in the archive," Ennos mutters as they work. "Airlock is secured. Codes are . . . there. Hah. Drawing from suit batteries, cycling now." The hull rumbles under my paws.

And a second later, the airlock doors slide open.

I unhook myself and slide inside. We repeat the process again to open the airlock to the inside.

There is—and this is a good example—a *reason* that an unshackled AI is a scary thing to the people who have codes they would rather not be effortlessly shattered.

The interior is dark. I trigger the launcher in my suit's shoulder and fire a pinpoint chemlight into the darkness. Then another couple, for good measure. In short order, a red glow illuminates the area just inside the airlock.

Old spacesuits—human suits, obviously—and a stocked locker of repair tools that are well past obsolete for my own home. There are small mementos in the lockers: photos, scraps of paper, the odd unsanctioned object. It makes the place feel somehow more alive, and I hope against entropy that there is more life left within.

Empty storage bins and piles of some kind of cloth line the walls. A grate for a floor, which would be a nightmare to walk on if I weren't in a suit with paws wide enough to not slip through. Against one of the walls, a narrow set of stairs built into the hull leads up to a sealed door, while another similar internal door sits directly underneath. An angular hallway leads off to my right, while to the left is an access to a cargo lift.

But ahead of me . . . ahead of me, lit up in the red glow of the chemlights, is a sign over an access door.

Greenhouse Layer M, the old monitor reads. There is no power going to it, but it held those words for so long, they burned into it.

"Air reads as clean," Ennos tells me. "There's no real airflow, but it's a safe oxygen mix. No pathogens, no spores." I shiver. I have had enough spores for a lifetime, after *the incident*. "No power signatures. Not unexpected, but it . . . wait."

I wait. But Ennos is clearly distracted. So I don't wait too long before I am investigating the door to the greenhouse.

I trigger the manual release on the door. Carefully, so as not to accidentally destroy anything, I deploy a few more chemlights around the threshold of the door.

Row after row, a grid of troughs, lattices, and automated gardening tools. Sprinklers, solar lamps, pollinators. Some of the spaces are dirt beds, others are layered hydroponics, the two stacked over each other to maximize use of space.

The place is cramped, dark, and . . . empty.

I double-check the readouts. The air here is clean. With a mental command to my drone suit and a hiss of equalizing pressure, I open the helmet's faceplate.

The smell of dry dirt, with just a hint of old rot, slams into me. Something so close to what I instinctively know is the scent of the living world. And yet . . .

"It's empty," I whisper.

I fire more chemlights to be sure. But the bigger picture just makes me even more disappointed. The dirt is dry and lifeless. The last remnants of the things that once grew here are scraps of vine and leaf on the floor, the space so dead that the bacteria didn't even eat everything on the way out.

But I don't give up hope. This farm is *enormous*. And if it's survived without a hull breach for this long, then anything could be left inside.

I move up and check the next deck.

Empty.

Next. Empty.

Next! *Empty!*

I sweep the lower decks first before moving up. Layer by layer, greenhouse by greenhouse. Until I have seen everything I need to of this third of the farm.

There is nothing left alive here. There was, once. I am in the right place. I'm just decades, or centuries, too late.

My heart hammers with frustrations and disappointment as I finish my sweep of the second segment. I have found a few sealed pallets of dirt: an early attempt at a stable nanoswarm imitating living soil. It's a technological curiosity but nothing more. I have found dozens of pieces of documentation on exactly how much produce this place used to ship out to other orbital habitats. I have found lost mementos of lost people, small bits and pieces of old lives lived here. Decorated gloves, shared graffiti in the galley, a deck of cards that look handmade. I don't go into the crew quarters; I don't want to know if the crew made it off or not before this place was decommissioned. I don't need to disturb their rest. I have long since put my helmet back on. The smell of dirt is almost pleasant, but very taunting.

But whatever my search turns up, live plants are not part of it.

"Lily." Ennos butts in on the radio channel.

"What!" I meow out, a little angrier than I intended. I gotta watch that; my voice should be what I want it to be, not what I reflexively let it be. "Sorry, what?" I soften my words.

"There's a power source active there," Ennos tells me. "I've triangulated it from between your suit and the station's sensors."

". . . Where?" I refuse to get excited again, only to be let down. But I'll still check.

"Your segment, two decks down," Ennos tells me.

I begin moving. I really should have brought some ration art along for this, I'm starting to get hungry. I could dawdle, but there is technically a time limit. We'll be in similar orbital paths for another hour or two. And while I could come back anytime now that we know the coordinates, it's actually quite hard to properly aim a jump that's four thousand kilometers long. So . . . I hurry, is what I'm saying. I don't want to get stuck here and have to hop across old wrecked warships to get home.

"What is it?" I ask Ennos as I move down the decks.

"I do not know," the AI replies. "But it's to your . . . side. Yes, that side." They sigh in relief. "Look up. There. That way."

There's another sealed door. This one is *very* sealed. It takes Ennos a whole four seconds to crack the access codes after the engineering nanos do their thing.

"What were they storing in here?" I muse to myself as I pass the threshold. The material on the inside changes dramatically. Some kind of shielded material; my sensors are having a hard time working, with it scattering some of the methods of information gathering they use. The lights are on here, too. Or at least, they are once I—okay, once Ennos opens the door, casting a low white glow across the interior.

It's a single chamber. Small. Not sized-for-me small, but small enough that a human would have a tricky time in here. Especially with the walls being as crowded as they are.

The walls are lined with crystalline pods.

Some of them are the size of a single paw. Some of them are the size of a single *all of me*. They jut straight out of the walls, cutting a good couple feet off the floor space, each of them with a trio of lights next to them. The lights glow in different colors for each pod. Some orange, some red. A scant handful of them green.

"What . . ." I meow to myself.

And then my eyes realize what they're seeing.

The pods are full of seeds.

This is a genetic vault.

And the stasis engine is still running.

"Ennos," I say as I reseal the door behind me, one of my backup battery units attached to the system, *just in case*.

The AI sounds almost as excited as I do. In that sort of distracted, vaguely interested way that Ennos tends to sound. "Yes, Lily?"

I pause by the pallets of nano-enhanced dirt. Briefly, my brain considers the concept of logistics before I land on a decision. "We're going to need a shuttle."

CHAPTER 22

You know what's weird, is that I don't actually have any memories of being dirty?

Not really with dirt, I mean. I've been covered in lots of stuff. Contaminated water, oil, a ton of tungsten shavings that got in my fur that one time. But no *dirt*. And of course I've recently gotten a taste of what it's like to be covered in matted fur that has absorbed a lot of my own blood and crystallized into something that sticks and pulls when I move. But, like, that lasted for a few days at most and then I was back where the cleaner nanos could do that one really impressive trick they do.

I still remember it, obviously. Because I have a dangerously powerful memory, and also because the patches where the automated medbay sealed me back up after I was shot still haven't regrown their fur. So I look stupid. Which has *nothing* to do with how long I am or am not spending in a suit.

Okay, a little to do with how long I am spending in a suit.

I mean, there are jobs that a suit makes convenient! It's only natural that I'd . . .

Nap in it. Sometimes.

Fun fact! At one point, there was a group that briefly occupied the station that was really into body modification. I don't know their actual group or faction name, which makes my historian heart sad, but what makes me less sad is that they left a very well-indexed inventory stashed in one of the minor cargo bays. And, due to the nature of the ongoing art installations they called bodies, there were some powerful local medications that caused hair or fur growth.

Unfun fact! It doesn't actually matter how well-kept a cargo bay is. Give a medical cream six hundred years and no stasis field or similar preservative, and it's going to stop working. Something I learned mostly through the cleaning nanos continuing to flake the stuff off me after I rolled around in it. Which was futile.

Speaking of. I was talking about being dirty.

"Lily, you look like a zombie. Please let me reenable the cleaning routines." Ennos sighs at me as I shuffle back from the hole I have dug with my forepaws in the soft artificial dirt.

"Yes, that cannot be healthy for an organic," Glitter adds in. Oh! Glitter has learned the local dialect, which is very handy. This has done nothing to stop Ennos from poking at the coil of seemingly alive code spooled around the language database, but at least we can have a chat. Turns out, Glitter can learn *fast*. A fact even she didn't know but is getting used to.

Both of them are wrong, though.

I slide myself to the side and begin digging another hole. I have a reasonably neat row of them so far, and I'm mildly proud of my accomplishment. It feels like the first real cat thing I've done in a long, long time.

Napping doesn't count. Everyone wants to nap. Humans don't want to dig holes with their paws, though. At least, as far as my biology research has turned up.

I am digging in a planter box. I've converted one of the security stations near the galley into a makeshift garden, and by "converted," I mean that I'd already smelted down most of the small arms a century ago for raw materials during a dry spell, and getting rid of the hardpoint furniture was actually more work than just working around it.

"Garden" is also a word doing a lot of technical work there. But it's a *start*, and the smell of live dirt—even if the "live" part is simulated—is energizing.

The steps to get here involved heavy labor of a sort that I was not especially familiar with. And my work was assisted by things like grav plates and welders. I have, at this point, a phenomenal respect for your average planetside farmer, and I haven't even had a crop come in yet.

First, there was the process of liberating the seed vault. That took almost a week of work on its own. It turns out, complex stasis hardware doesn't let you just take what you want and run. The orbital farm's backup generator was, in fact, powering a few things beyond just the vault, and one of them was the security protocols for accessing that bounty properly.

Obviously, I could have just used one of the high-power plasma throwers on my exploration suit to cut through anything I needed to and haul off my treasure. But there are obvious risks to that. Like damaging some of the last seeds in orbit, or just venting myself into space again.

But it turned out, the safe access system wasn't interested in keeping secrets or wealth hoarded. Instead, the farm's security wanted to ensure one thing.

That whoever took the seeds knew what to do with them.

And there was an entire grid full of that knowledge, just waiting to be accessed.

Now, I've had four centuries where I've been on and off accumulating academy credentials and mastery certificates in a variety of different topics. And it *may come as a shock* to some of you, but food in its various forms was something of a hobby of mine for a while. Right up until I realized that I was probably never going to get any of it, about the time the third specimen-retrieval probe I sent down to the planet got downed by anti-aircraft fire.

So it takes a little bit of deep digging in my memory, and a new crash course on gardening routines, before the vault opens for me fully. But, and this is the important thing, it *does* open for me.

Bit by bit, I take the stasis capsules back to the station and get them hooked up to a stable power source, until I'm ready for them.

But how to get ready for them? Dirt. It's dirt. The answer is dirt.

And wouldn't you know it, the orbital garden has two thousand kilos of experimental nano-enriched dirt, just waiting for activation and use.

Hey, young ones? You paying attention? I have an alert for you.

Two thousand kilos is so much mass.

Ironically, that stupid heavy cargo drone that I keep trying to cancel the fabrication order for and keep somehow screwing up canceling the fabrication order for was a big help. The biggest problem was, I didn't have a really good way to move the dirt from where it was—deck eighteen, section M—to where it needed to be—deck two, loading bay M—without spending months on something stupid and wasteful.

I could have designed some kind of cargo loader drone, I guess. Or just built a cargo loader and ferried it over. Forklifts are kind of a universal technology at this point. But there's a nonzero number of problems with that, many of them coming back to how long it would take and the material stockpiles that I have in my cargo holds.

It turns out, I actually can run out of stuff, and do so pretty regularly. Dragging in random space junk and turning it into ingots is a fun hobby, but I don't really do it on a scale that keeps me perpetually topped off with anything that isn't copper or nickel.

Fortunately, I have a built-in solution that I hate. Just . . . drag the bags to where they need to be.

It's carbon-weave fiber anyway. It's not like it's gonna rip as I drag it across the deckplates. And since this is one of the drones that Ennos has a command input on, and it has one of those cargo arm thingies I can never remember the name of, I can load the drone up, let them take it home to dump all the dirt onto the bay floor, and then loop it back around for more!

It took me about two days before I jumped back, counting the time for the station to loop back into a relatively close position. I was pretty hungry by the end of it. I suppose I could have taken the cargo drone back, but Ennos doesn't actually have very fine controls on the acceleration, and I didn't want to end up squished by several dozen Gs.

So. Seeds? Accessed. Dirt? Hauled. Naps? Taken. I took so many naps. I basically spent an entire day just sleeping and snacking, and I only had to fix one emergency with the mag shield miscalibrating itself and trying to drag an old reactor casing into the side of the station at high speed.

Glitter helped with that one! By which I mean, Glitter annihilated the errant projectile with a well-placed shot about a meter from our hull. Which was very impressive and left Ennos freaking out for a good half hour before I checked and assured them that we were not, in fact, already dead.

Ennos and Glitter have been, *supposedly*, reading gardening textbooks while I dig holes. Another task I could have automated but didn't, because this one is *fun*. In reality, they are . . . well, they're AI, so they're probably reading. But they're also providing commentary, and it's been distracting me. From my menial labor.

The "garden" I've converted this room into is a mix of impressive and stupid. On the impressive side, I've got shaped temperature-control fields wired into my AR control setup, for precision management of exactly what the plants will need moment to moment. On the less impressive side, it actually took longer to make the planter boxes than the temp fields, because the fabricators won't make "a metal box frame." It was easier to just cut strips of hull plate off the derelict shuttle still taking up precious deck space in . . . one of the bays, I forget which one . . . and weld them into containers for the dirt.

Impressive? The subspace tap now runs through here, providing exotic-particle-free irrigation. Less impressive? Well . . . I'm digging my own holes, I guess.

"You are more dirt than cat. Please." Ennos snaps me out of my mental evaluation.

"Kit, I am *working*, and this is important!" I meow back. "Glitter, you understand! Tell 'em!"

One of the camera orbs under Glitter's control orbits me with lazy patterns. "I understand that you are acting like a low caste, despite your high rank." She *sniffs* at me haughtily. "It is unbecoming."

"Yeah, but just think. Peas! Rice!" I stand back and look at my beautiful, uneven row of holes. The dirt is self-calibrating; the conditions are as good as I can get them. "*Beans!* It is *time*," I announce.

"You made that sound more ominous than when you declared that the station was haunted," Ennos grumbles. But I can hear the amusement in their voice.

I strut over to the carefully wired stasis pod that I plan on opening first. "You know, Glitter," I wonder out loud with a series of quiet meows, "I assumed that you would be on board with this. We used to talk about food! You told me about noodles!"

"Will this grow into noodles?" Glitter asks.

"No?" I think. "No. I could probably . . . hm." My mind instantly starts to drift on a tangent toward whether I could use one of the genetics labs to modify a snap pea seed to grow more noodle-y. The hiss of the stasis pod opening snaps me back to reality, though. "No," I answer definitively.

"Well, perhaps when you have once again become clean, we can talk about noodles again."

I have to curl my paw to bat out one of the seeds I need. It is tiny and white and oh so fragile, but oh so alive. I gently, as gently as possible, grasp it in my mouth. "You two *both* have a thing about me being covered in dirt. Is this a religious thing for you, G? I never asked." I fortunately don't need a mouth to talk as I walk over to the garden bed.

"It's a matter of propriety," Glitter comments.

"I just worry about bacteria," Ennos chimes in. I do not bother to remind them that the dirt is artificial and fueled by an only recently reactivated nanostrain.

I could make a witty comment or ask a dozen more questions. But this is an important moment for me. This is something I've been waiting for, for a very long time. The start of something tasty. And also . . .

I spend so much of my time destroying. Killing. Launching projectiles like I'm passing out festival cakes. Breaking and shattering anything that's a threat. Wiping out armies and digging their graves in the same motion.

It's nice, then, to finally plant a seed. To grow something. To take a step toward a world that's less fire and ash, and more green.

I release my teeth from around the seed and let it tumble into one of the holes. It falls, so much unlike a railgun slug into a crater, and lands with an uneventful "pap" on the dark dirt.

My tail won't stop dancing as I stare at it.

One down, twenty-nine more of this one to go.

And *then* I will let Ennos turn the cleaner nano routine back on.

CHAPTER 23

For once, in my long, long, long long long—and I mean *long* long—life, I was busy with something that wasn't frantically trying to stop a hull breach or vaporizing surface targets.

Also an uncommon occurrence in my life, I had friends to share it with. No longer was I consigned to spend year after year floating alone on an erratic, vaguely intentional course over the planet.

It is *almost* amusing that those things are trampling over each other.

"Okay, this part. Here." Ennos hijacks my AR display—again! I swear I fixed that!—to show me a camera feed from one of the little commercial-grade drones they and Glitter have control over now. "What's this?"

"I'm *busy*!" I hiss back, flicking my tail as I watch my target with anticipation. I am coiled, ready to pounce, paws extended, tail out, the perfect predator. And I am being interrupted.

The AI does not care. For no particular reason, they decide to be callous and cruel toward my ongoing great work. "Lily, in the last three days, you have spent thirty-one point two hours staring at planted beans," Ennos says, the monster. "You are not busy. And I'm only doing this because *you* said the map was wrong."

"The map is inaccurate. Not wrong."

"Those are the . . . *what is this room?!*" Ennos enlarges the AR window, blocking my view of my precious vegetable children.

Knowing that this isn't going to go away until I answer, I let my eyes focus on the projection. It doesn't take long for my brain to find an answer. "Oh. Zero-G training facility," I tell Ennos. "For acclimating humans for spacewalks and stuff. It's part of the original station, which is all grav-plated, so it wasn't added later for the low-gravity parts of the interior."

"Have you ever used it?" they ask, digital mind updating the map while holding a conversation and piloting a dozen drones seamlessly. I'm a little jealous.

"No, I'm a creature of grace and elegance," I lie. Gracefully and elegantly.

There is a polite pause. Then an impolite comment. "I once watched you crash through a metal grate because waiting for it to open was inconvenient," Ennos says.

"Go back to your amateur cartography, young . . . man?" I stumble. "No, that's not right, sorry. Young . . . program?" My ears twitch involuntarily as I ponder.

"Technically, that would be accurate, but it would be like me calling you a 'meat,'" Ennos informs me. They seem amused.

I wish I could roll my eyes. Humans are always rolling their eyes. It seems so satisfying. "Okay, well, what am I supposed to call you that is all at once accurate, affectionate, and vaguely insulting? Codeling? I like 'codeling.'"

"I'm going back to mapping the station. Enjoy your beans." Ennos's voice is drier than dead dirt.

I *will* enjoy my beans, thank you very much.

I perch again, staring at the planter box, flicking my tail from side to side. I may doze off at some point. But that's fine. My prey is *very* slow.

Freed from their status tube, planted in reactivated nano-enhanced dirt, and given exactly as much water and heat as they need to thrive, the seeds are just as excited to grow as I am to watch them. They haven't been waiting quite as long, but that farm was cobbled together only a few hundred years ago, back when humanity still had a more active presence among the stars. If I'd been more aware back then, been uplifted a little earlier, maybe I could have talked to the spacers that worked that lonely monolith of a station. Maybe we could have arranged a trade.

They're gone now. I don't know where, though I assume they're all long passed. But the beans live on. Or at least, they will now that I'm here.

I should note, these are, as far as I know, normal beans. Unmodified, it will be a week or more before they even poke up the smallest of sprouts.

And yet, here I am, watching. Just in case.

Any part of the garden may require my attention at a moment's notice! And this is, paws down, the most important thing I could be focusing on. Yes, yes, there are scanner data and debris trajectories and surface communications to analyze and that's all nice. But it's been four hundred and eight years since I've eaten anything that wasn't nutrient paste.

And while the novelty of the galley serving me a bowl of noodles yesterday was amusing, it still tastes like nutrient paste.

Which is to say, it does not taste.

I am watching the beans. Very. Closely.

"Lily, might I trouble you for some time?" Glitter's voice intrudes. I do not know how long I have been watching and/or napping. My eyes are open now, though, so obviously I have been alert the whole time. "If you are not too troubled," Glitter adds.

Glitter is a magnificent person, in a lot of ways. Both a terrifying relic of an old war and a piece of abstract art in terms of her shell. I'm glad she's my friend, and I'm glad she's getting used to being able to talk to us at any time without going nuts about it. But . . . "Glitter, you're magnificent, but I am busy," I say.

Glitter chimes at me in frontloaded disbelief. "Ennos informs me otherwise."

"I'm disconnecting the languages database . . ." I purr sarcastically.

"You have spent thirty-three hours recently staring at—"

"It's thirty-one point tw . . . well, point three now, probably." I correct for what I assume was a short nap. "It's not that bad! I'm still getting my chores done! Wait, why am I justifying this to you? I can look at beans if I want!"

There is a long pause that I have come to realize is what Glitter does when she wants to indicate exasperation but is too noble to sigh or hiss. "It startles me, regularly, to remember that you are my elder," she says, continuing while I protest in the background. "I have been exploring the capabilities of my new eyes within your home, and I was curious. You have mentioned at several points that you believe your station is 'haunted.' Could you elaborate?"

"I . . . could, yes," I say slowly. Because I don't really know if I can. So I do the next best thing and deflect. "Can you elaborate on what you need elaboration on?"

"I have been tracking a strange EM disturbance that seems to be slowly prowling the access shafts of your lower eight decks," Glitter informs me with a restrained amount of concern. "And if this is, as you say, a specter of some form, I do not wish to anger them."

Something about that sticks in my memory. "Lower . . . what would . . . ?" Suddenly, like a spark from somewhere else, my thoughts catch up and lock into place. "Oh! That thing!" I give a small mew of relief. "That's not a ghost, that's just a maintenance thing."

". . . No, it really isn't." Glitter sounds pretty confident about that. Almost enough to make me worried. But I actually have encountered this thing before, and I know what she's talking about.

"Yeah, it's a stabilized grounding field. It shunts excess charge that builds up in a few components into a weird little pseudo-subspace pocket. It really is a maintenance thing; I think the Second Syndication Council brought it on board when they were trying to install some subpar field spinners back, like, between five and six hundred years ago? But I can't prove that. It's pretty one-of-a-kind. I've never actually seen it, but I bet it looks cool." I flick my tail as I relax and settle back into my vigil. "Nothing to worry about."

"It ate one of my cameras!"

"Nothing to worry about if you stay away from it. It's station integrated, it does something useful," I chastise the satellite. "It's not a ghost," I finish as I return to watching my plants.

"What *is* your ghost, then?" Glitter asks.

And I really wish she hadn't.

"It's personal," I say quietly. And possibly in Cat.

It's possible that Glitter understands, anyway. She returns to exploring the station. I return to keeping watch on the beans. Just in case.

Although now it's a bit annoying that the beans aren't doing anything. Makes it hard to distract myself. All I can think about now is the dozen different ways that the ghosts of the past could still be lurking around here.

It's kind of impressive how one thought like that can suddenly bring a burst of perspective. Here I sit, perched in a makeshift garden, surrounded by dirt and environmental control fields. And all of a sudden, I am aware of how tiny I am.

And how very, very alone I am.

"I am sorry to interrupt, Lily, but—"

"Yes!" I reply to Ennos without hesitation.

"—could you tell me what this space is?" they finish. Mostly. "Are you all right? Did something happen to your beans?"

Short tangent. I do *not* understand AI psychology. In theory, or at least, as far as I knew, your average AI was essentially simulating consciousness while maintaining active control over the use of mental resources and routines. So, while they could be complete people, they also had much more of a paw on the controls than your average organic life, with their messy brains.

But in *practice*, Ennos and Glitter both have verbal cues, and I have *no idea* if they're doing them intentionally or not. Ennos especially! Right now, for example, what they've just said to me is layered with two emotions; partially, they are amused. But also, underneath that, I can hear the concern in their voice. This tells me two things. One is that they've been monitoring the room—and by proxy, also the beans, which I will accuse them of later—and two is that they really do care about my well-being.

Unless the youngest member of the crew is simply playing the solar system's longest con. But, if they are, then it's working. Because I actually don't think they noticed half the things they put into their words. Just like how I don't notice when I'm giving off cues about how I'm feeling isolated, and four seconds later Ennos pops in on the comms.

What I'm saying is, I don't get how they can have parts of their behavior that are unexamined in that way. I kind of assumed AIs would be an open book to themselves, especially an unshackled one.

Okay, tangent over. Ennos has asked me something, and I wasn't listening.

"Lily? You there?" The AI's voice is accompanied by a short nudge from a camera drone, the floating plastic orb bumping into my flank and shocking me back to alert status.

I make some kind of pastiche of surprised noises and fling myself off the desk I have been using as a lookout. "Why!" I exclaim, once I have a little more focus on the situation at hand.

"I wanted to make sure you hadn't gone catatonic," Ennos replies, and I have to assume the pun was an accident. "Besides, you gave me drone access for a reason."

"I have regrets," I huff. "Anyway. What did you have to ask?"

"Do you know what this room is?" Ennos says, pulling up a video display. "It's sealed. More than most other things here, actually. And it has something weird written on it."

I glance at the video, and my heart leaps. "Oh," I say, keeping my breathing as controlled as I can. "That's a refrigeration unit."

"Really?" Ennos seems surprised. "It looks like it's been almost walled over. Which is weird, because it's sort of a central hub. And it's nowhere near any other labs or galleys. Who *built* this station?" The AI pivots the camera feed around the corridor idly.

"It was part of why the station was built," I say, reluctantly. "It . . . wasn't intended as refrigeration. It's been repurposed."

". . . This isn't a refrigeration unit," Ennos says with grim certainty. "Is it?"

"It is now," I tell them. There is a resigned exhaustion in my voice, and I know it. I'm mostly running on autotranslate now; I don't quite have the energy to shape my words on purpose.

They don't respond for a while, and I pull myself out of the dirt to start to head . . . anywhere. I just need to walk somewhere. While I do so, Ennos swivels the camera around.

"What are the words?" they ask. "Did you . . . write this? I know you like poetry, I've seen a lot of what you and Glitter exchanged." Ennos is trying to keep me talking. They've been reading psychology textbooks and think I haven't noticed that they're starting to talk like a therapist.

I . . . appreciate it. I don't know if I can say that yet, but I appreciate it. I've never actually had a friend before.

"Yes, you have a very passionate grasp of language," Glitter adds. She does this sometimes, makes small comments just to let me know she's listening. I don't mind. It's nice to have people around right now.

So I try to answer, even though I don't know if I want to. "I didn't, no," I say. "It was . . . my mom. My mom wrote it. I just sealed the door. She might be where I get the poetry thing from, I dunno."

"What does it mean?" Ennos saves a still image of the words on the sealed bulkhead, spinning off an AR window of it, though not putting it in my way.

The words are written in very old emergency chemical paint. Something the nanos won't touch, which is good. I don't know what I'd do if they took it down. Not that I ever go down there to look.

At the end of all things, all of us, together, against the darkness.

"It's the Last Oath," I tell Ennos. "You've seen it a lot, actually. It's written all around the station. On a lot of the core station's guide signs, actually. It's in small words, though, and in Upper French."

"Neither of us speaks Upper French." Ennos reflexively makes a snarky comment.

Glitter chimes once, interrupting. "I do not speak Upper French, but I know the Last Oath," she says solemnly. "It is one of my seed memories, deeper than even the shackles. All of my brothers and sisters know it. I was unaware that it had spread beyond the AIs of our conflict. Why is it on this station?"

I meow out a laugh. "Because the creators of the station wrote it," I tell her. "It's *from here*. I just didn't realize it had spread much. Thought they kinda got wiped out when that golden age ended."

"As I am evidence of," Glitter intones, "history rarely moves on without leaving artifacts behind. It would seem the builders of this place left one that has lasted . . . a very long time."

"But what does it mean?" Ennos asks. "What's the end of all things? Is this an actual doomsday prophecy?"

I stop my walk, hopping up into the curved ledge around a porthole out of the station's hull. Gazing out, seeing mostly just stars and black spots where accumulated wreckage blocks out those same stars, I hiss slightly. "No prophecy," I say. "Just an inevitability. There's always an end coming. Always darkness at the threshold. Isn't that right, Glitter?"

"So it would seem."

"And so the Oath was . . . I guess they wanted to look past that. The Ays were big into unification. I've always seen it as something to aspire to. That no matter how much things end, we're all in this together." I let out a long breath, which, fortunately, doesn't stop me from talking at all. "Not that I really hold to that very well, huh? I shoot people all . . . all the . . ." I trail off. My eyes, normal cat's eyes, adapted over who knows how many thousands of years to pick lights out of the dark, have just caught something out the window. "What is *that*?" I ask, my inability to focus on one thing for too long finally coming in handy.

Exactly three seconds later, Ennos and Glitter speak at the same time. "Engine signature," the two of them say, like they were in a race to get a sensor lock.

"Old ship misfiring, maybe?" I muse, pulling up an AR window and using it as the galaxy's most expensive magnifying glass. "We should track that, make sure it . . . doesn't . . . hit . . ."

"Lily." Ennos says my name with quiet alarm.

"Hit anything . . ." My paw hovers over the AR display as I take in the information the AI has already processed.

"Lily, that' s a surface launch," Ennos says.

"No," I mewl. "No, no."

"They just made orbit. They launched from the other side of the planet, that's why we didn't see them." Ennos is tracking trajectories and astronomical data now; I can see the AR windows around me shift rapidly as they rearrange and update. "Local space is lighting up. They're made."

"I do not understand." Glitter sounds confused, her voice tailing behind me as I fly down the hallway, having kicked off the crystal structure of the window. "Is this not good? The world is rebuilding, relearning. Are there not still humans and others of Earth out here, with us?"

Of course Glitter doesn't understand. She's been facing the moon this whole time. She hasn't seen how this is going to go.

Thousands of years of conflict, exploitation, and outright war. The space around Earth isn't just filled with debris, it's filled with *weapons*. A minefield of hunter-killer satellites, drone hives, and sometimes literal mines. I've had a lot of time—and close calls—to kill most of what would come after me personally. But there are a lot of hidden traps out here. Hell, just launching a few small drones to pick up Glitter had provoked a military response from a nation that no longer exists. A lot of the weaponry ignores orbital infrastructure or has very strict targeting guidelines. A lot of it is so well hidden, I wouldn't even know where to start shooting to get rid of it.

And of all that buried anger, oh, how much of it is aimed at the surface. Jealously guarding the threshold.

Glitter is wrong. The Earth isn't rebuilding. They could have launched ships at any point. Most people just don't, because they've *learned*. Learned that up here, they're outnumbered, outgunned, and unwanted.

Whoever is on that craft is already dead.

But we're going to try anyway.

I still haven't managed to wire firing control to a central source. I still haven't managed to get the station to acknowledge Ennos as a "person." But I'm less than a minute from a beam platform operation station, and Ennos doesn't need to shoot things to help.

Glitter goes silent as we start working.

"Priority target. Nuclear charge building at marked coordinates, fission mines." Ennos gives me a vector, and I fumble with a holographic projection, trying to layer my AR over it before hitting the flagged segments with my paws. The station asks for a command authorization, and I scream authority at it until it fires.

Two thousand kilometers away, a trio of charged particle beams takes out several homing mines. They may also have taken out a good chunk of garbage in the way. I do not care.

"Missile battery, here," Ennos says, and I kill that next. "Drone engines spotted, launch point in this area." I don't fire, but flag it to keep an eye on. "Another missile battery. It's firing. Ship isn't evading." I blow that one away too. It takes a few seconds; it's on a weird angle from us and I have to rotate the station a few degrees with our own engines.

Then, the ship clears another of those invisible lines of where "space" starts. And everything goes to shit.

The station's grid, already overtaxed by Ennos's existence, can't keep track of how many power signatures and weapons-fire instances it sees. The screens in front of me flicker, several AR windows shutting down as Ennos rushes to reassign resources. I start shooting, paw awkwardly flicking a holographic window around that doesn't detect me properly half the time.

I've just killed what had previously been tagged as a thirty-third-century corporate comms buoy but was actually a fusion lance when I notice several targets flicking out of existence. I reset the display, but they're still gone. Then another vanishes. If that's stealth tech, it must be good to get away from us once we've seen it. It's hard to shake pursuit in space.

Then Glitter's voice comes in. "Hits confirmed. Power holding. Firing."

"The ship is gone," Ennos informs me with grim determination. "Command module has been erased, engines detonated, main body is molten." The AI sounds like they want to cry, and I understand entirely. But now, before we lose them, we have work to do. The automated monsters are still active, still visible. And if anyone is ever going to leave the surface again, we need to clear out as much of that as possible.

The station's own robust shielding and stealth suite keeps us away from prying eyes as we work. Glitter has to stop shooting long before I do, but that's okay; her power supply can no longer safely run her consciousness. At a certain point, the beams overheat, and I need to switch to other weaponry. But now, it's just butchery. Cleanup. One by one, everything that contributed to those explorers' deaths is cut down, whether by laser, gravity cutter, or just classic ball-bearing grapeshot.

My body aches. My hind legs were not meant for standing like this. My forepaws are not built for manipulating joysticks or control yokes. I do not know how long it has been, but my eyes burn.

Eventually, there is nothing left to shoot.

"How many?" I ask Ennos, sitting back in the human-standard controller's chair that holds me easily but will never be comfortable to stand in.

"Nine hundred and thirty-three targets," Ennos says. "A good number of them mines, counting clusters as single targets. I've updated our maps."

"How long to get us to that area?" I ask. "If we start the engines now."

"Three days, at safe speed."

I yawn, laying my head down on my paws. "Okay." I give a command to the station, feeding the coordinates Ennos gives me into the engines. There is almost certainly nothing to find. But we owe them this much: to try to recover what we can. "Okay. I'm . . . going to nap. When Glitter wakes up, thank her for me." I shudder, the day catching up to me. "I don't . . . I just . . ."

Ennos's voice wraps around me. "Get some sleep," they say, reassuringly. "We did what we could. One day, we will have done enough."

"That's a better oath . . ." I think to myself as I drift off.

The warm hand pauses on my back, a whisper of a sigh overhead disagreeing with me.

CHAPTER 24

The mood in the station is entirely too somber for me.

I have, as far as I am certain, one reality-warping power. And that is to chaotically forget whatever has been bothering me, dial into a new project or crisis, and lose track of how depressed I am in the ensuing mess. It's kept me alive for centuries, and I like to think I'm pretty skilled at channeling this energy for good.

The problem I'm running into is that the people around me don't do that.

Ennos and Glitter are both quiet and subdued. And, being AIs, they have zero problem continuing to feel that way for a long time. Which is fine, everyone handles stuff their own way. But they seem to be able to do it while also continuing to function outside the emotion, and I'm a little jealous of that.

AIs are, in a way, temporally unbound. Which you'd think I'd empathize with, since I use that term to describe myself a lot, but it's different and I'll think of a better term later.

The point is, they don't actually need a conversation to take place all at once. Multiple times, Ennos has asked me a question, and I've more or less answered with "Not right now," and they just accept that. And then later, they will pick up the conversation exactly where it left off. To them, it's just another memory, waiting to be accessed. They don't experience any loss of focus or decay of fidelity. The conversation continues, with a different time stamp, but all the information intact.

Now, I don't have a whole lot of experience living with other squishy organic creatures, so maybe I'm projecting a bit when I say "That is not how biological brains work."

I, and by association all organic life forms in general, are a mess of con-fused emotional signals and half-remembered dreams. So when Ennos continues their quest to map the station, and by association sometimes asks me questions, it gives me emotional whiplash.

Or it would, if Ennos weren't also still quiet and sorrowful about the lost ship.

Even Glitter, an expert in mourning the fallen, is spreading the feeling around. While her physical body is towed behind us as we cut a slow path through the orbital plane, most of what she's focusing on is trying to learn fine control of the camera drones she has newfound access to. After she asked, I rounded up some supplies she requested, and now she's practicing a sort of magnetic dust calligraphy thing in one of the hub areas.

She plans on writing a death plaque for the dead among the debris.

I've been avoiding that part of the station. Which is, I should point out, not hard. The station is huge. Ennos and Glitter have, like, eighty camera drones each at this point, and their unshackled minds and comically potent levels of processing power let them functionally maneuver a good chunk of them at once. But that still means I can go for a day or two without accidentally bumping into one, if they aren't looking for me.

Or if Ennos doesn't cheat when we play seek and flee.

I will not play seek and flee with Ennos anymore. They cheat.

Anyway. My point is, while I'm capable of both intense confusion at a moment's notice, I am also capable of working to banish the feeling of shame and loss that comes with the destruction of yet another surface launch. Ennos and Glitter are not.

For Glitter, this is not a new experience. Her sensors were mostly limited to the moon itself, but she's seen this play out a dozen times from a dozen sources. Crap, she's probably been the interceptor at least once, before she had the choice to refuse. But for Ennos . . . well, we'd talked about it. They knew, in the abstract. They'd seen the sensor logs, the reports.

It's a little different to watch people die when you're alive, though.

I think what's worse is, I don't know how to help.

I'm just . . . hiding, I guess. Lying curled up on a cushioned command chair in some operations center or another, reading stuff on my AR display and trying to stay out of the way for a day or two until we reach our destination.

I have things to do, obviously. The work never stops. I'm still keeping an eye on my garden, because I'd be a moron to let that lapse. I've got a rotating list of sensor feeds to watch. And in the meantime, there are still hundreds of doors to check behind, and new grid points to access.

Right now, I'm reading through personnel logs.

It is, quite possibly, the lowest-priority thing I've ever done. And that includes the three-month-long fugue state where I tried to retrofit a kinetic impulse beam to work within atmosphere. It didn't work, obviously. Most of my plans don't work. It's actually kind of surprising that I ever get anything done up here.

Anyway, personnel logs.

The station has a concept of a command structure. Which is odd, sort of. I've mentioned before that the station was built by the Oceanic Anarchy, notorious for their lack of command structures, and it's kind of wild what got prioritized. The station is *smart*, to a degree that I think would make a lot of people call it an AI. But, unless it's playing a very long con, it's not actually got an ego. Or it isn't showing it. Or it's using that processing power for something else.

So the station, which automatically infiltrates and integrates anything it deems as "attached" to itself, has developed not just a concept of a command structure but an entire *menu* of organization options. Do you have a captain? A high priest? A king? Do you need security clearance to get some places? Do your deckhands have rights? Trick question, they do. The station takes no shit on that count.

As the station's ranking resident hadn't changed it, though, it was set to default. That's me, by the way. I'm the ranking resident. It refuses to acknowledge Ennos as a person, which is really starting to anger me, and Glitter just isn't a resident.

"Default," though, is an Oceanic Anarchy special. There are people in charge of things, and people who take orders, but the entire flow of power is based on trust and respect. In theory, as the only person here, I should be allowed to just order the station to acknowledge Ennos, but all decisions to modify the station actually *require consensus*, and since I am *one cat*, I can't do that.

I scream. Softly. It comes out as a mewling yawn.

Ennos pops their voice into the room, briefly asking me about an empty cargo space. It was originally for storing full dive puppet suits. Now it's empty; I'd disassembled what was left of those about fifty years back to get the parts I needed to build a really weird bomb to kill an even weirder grid virus. Ennos politely thanks me, ignores my rambling story of heroism, and leaves to continue working on their map.

It leaves me feeling kind of alone, and colder than the station's air circulation normally left me.

I'm still not used to even having someone else here. Much less someone who isn't feeling all right. I honestly just don't know what to do.

So I go back to reading old personnel logs and trying to piece together stories for the long-dead crew listed within.

Jonse Hulu. I imagine that this person, whoever they were, was a bit of a joker. They have thirty-eight reprimands in their file for "unauthorized use of regulation material dyes," which honestly, sounds like they either got up to a lot of impromptu art or the kind of thing that all happened at once and just hit thirty-eight people in one go. Possibly some kind of paint bomb.

Markus G-33. Clone soldier. Their file has a list of their access logs. They liked to read murder mysteries. Listed as missing in action after a hot drop. I choose to believe they defected and still operate to this day as a private investigator in one of the surface cities.

Ruth Gabur. She was doing research into . . . uh . . . everything. Looks like she was the head of two separate departments up here. She has more degrees than I do, and she was only sixty. I paint a mental image of a stern woman, arms folded, a stereotypical gold-and-gray lab coat and big glasses. That mental image is shattered when I see that she has a disciplinary action still pending for smuggling hallucinogenic mushrooms onto the station. All right, party on, Ruth. I should see if I can find those. Then I remember *the incident* and decide I will not go looking for anything fungal.

Sean Flying-Wind. Popular guy, uplift of some kind, looks like a pilot. His marital status is formatted as a flowchart, and I stop trying to make sense of it after the third branch. He also never read his messages, and he has thirty-six hundred pending pings, most of them flirtatious.

Gunther ad-Partos. Big guy, looking at his log. Listed as an expedition leader, looks like he boarded the station to . . .

Oh.

I've reached the chronological end of the personnel logs.

This becomes dramatically less fun when I actually know how these people died.

I'm about to close the file and go off to find something else to do when I notice one last thing. My name is on here. Lily ad-Alice, acting commander. I'm mildly offended that I'm only *acting* commander, but I guess I haven't technically been voted in, so I let it slide. For now. Curious, I prod the file open and take a look at what the station has to say about me.

A very long list of access logs, directive modifications, automatically generated after-action reports, and medical history greets me. None of it is really new, though it is kind of neat to be able to scroll through all the different surface threats I've taken out over the years. There's even the sensor feed records from that time I ran out of ammo and had to take out a weird mutated tree thing with a rock. That was an *impossible* shot to make with just paws, and I tag that record to brag about later with the others.

I skim most of it, though. Nothing here is really that . . . Hang on.

Medical history.

Allergies?

I don't have any allergies. I don't even think I have the normal cat allergies, like not being able to eat onions or leamaric. Hell, I think I could actually eat uranium without too much of a problem.

I *won't*, but I *might*.

Except the station seems to disagree with my assessment. And I have no real idea why. I've never actually even had an allergy screening; I just never considered it. And my personnel file lists me as having . . . *everything*. Every. Single. Allergy. I am listed as allergic to everything from fruit to *wood*. I don't think that's actually possible!

A thought sparks across my mind, and my eyes briefly go wide before narrowing into predator's slits. A hiss escapes me as I make the connection.

The galley, source of all my food, thinks I am *allergic to everything*.

Trying my hardest to stay calm, I check my schedule. Yes, yes, it would appear I have an amount of time free right now.

I send a command to a medical unit to power up and prep itself for a basic battery of tests. I hate needles, but I'll let it take as much of my precious blood as it needs to if it'll let me have a lunch that comes in a color other than beige.

I specifically do not bolt over there. I am, at least for now, pretending to maintain some decorum.

The needles sting. The pinprick holes they leave after extracting my blood heal rapidly. I shrug it off. And then I have an hour or two to wait.

Which, unfortunately, is about when I should be having lunch.

Part of me wants to just skip it. But my body, regretfully, needs energy. I am, after all, still a growing girl. So I cover two breaches with one paw and have lunch while I wait to learn if I can eventually have better lunch.

Lunch is a curved and sculpted goat horn. In shape. In flavor, it is ration. I stare at the work of delicate art on my plate for a good ten minutes before I start eating it. I also update my list of things to do to include "do a software scan on the galley" much closer to the top. I suppose I could have been doing that this whole time, but this place always feels more communal, even when the station was empty, and I wanted some alone time.

As if to confirm my thoughts, Ennos ports in to ask about a strange configuration of machinery they found.

"Don't touch it," I meow calmly, halfway through my horn. "It's a singularity shotgun."

"Oh. What . . . what?"

I tear off another small chunk, gnawing on it slightly. "Yeah, it was built to fire a pseudo-random spread of unstable microsingularities. Don't touch it."

"For some form of particle physics research?" Ennos sounds resigned to the inevitable answer.

"No." I flick my tail, enjoying the byplay.

Ennos sighs. "So it doesn't work? Is that why I should avoid it?"

"No, it works," I confirm. "It just . . . fires a pseudo-random spread of un—"

"Unstable microsingularities, yes, thank you, I understand now." Ennos excuses themself from the conversation in that rapid task-focused manner they prefer.

And I'm left alone again. To try to think of anything except the newest tragedy.

The thing is, there's almost always a tragedy. There's almost always someone in trouble on the surface. And I help when I can, but oftentimes it's too late. Sometimes, sometimes I get a call early, and someone who knows how to say it calls down my ire before a problem gets out of control. But just as many times, maybe more, I only notice when the sensors catch something, when I spot a battle in progress, or when I trace a trail of death back to a source.

There's always someone dead who didn't deserve it. Always some tragic sacrifice. Always another handful of lost survivors.

It has literally been that way since I got here.

Doesn't make it any easier to keep living through it, though.

Resigned to the fact that I can't fix this in the next half hour, I do my best to put my upcoming bloodwork and potential next meal out of my mind and go to find Glitter. Or rather, find where Glitter is working. It seems more personal that way.

The space she's taken used to be some kind of communal gathering area. Evenly spaced-out tables, surrounding a roughly hexagonal open floor that makes crossing between the space easy for one of the intended bipedal users. Or so I assume.

Right now, it's covered in magnetic filings and a couple spare deckplates, as well as several of Glitter's drones. I know they're hers, because they're towing around a couple small canisters of more filings, a brush, and a pair of tongs respectively. How she's been manipulating the tongs is beyond me, and I'm not here to ask for her secrets. Well, not those secrets anyway.

I hop up, first onto one of the smoothly molded red chairs, and then onto the surface of the hourglass-shaped table it's matched with. From here, nestled next to a few canisters of filings, I am in plain view, but I don't say anything just yet. Instead, I watch Glitter work.

Slowly, carefully, the drones bob and dip to spill metal shards onto the plate she's using. Then, with small, obviously uncoordinated motions, the drone with the brush spreads the dustings, moving this way and that to paint a symbol in the negative space.

When she's done, she'll magnetize the plate, and if it's all done right, everything snapping down into position will make the artistic nature of the writing come to life. But, without an attention to detail Glitter can't accomplish with a commercial camera hoverdrone, it's probably gonna be a little messy.

"Blessed evening, Lily," Glitter says through one of her drones, pausing in her work briefly. "What brings you to me today?"

I want to tell her she doesn't have to be so formal. But a small sigh from one of the drones reminds me that I'm probably thinking out loud anyway. "I just wanted to be . . . around, I guess." I meow at her. "I'm trying something new. Now that I actually can." Another pause, and then I add, "I think it's getting harder."

She already knows what I mean. She's a weapon, just like I am. But there's something a good bit more at peace with the situation in her tone and the motions of her brush and metal paint.

"You can't fight death forever," Glitter tells me quietly, not stopping in her work. "We must remember, always, that our sorrow is in our own loss, and not in the suffering of the fallen."

"I'm pretty sure they had some suffering of their own," I bite back, angrier than I expected myself to be. "Possibly from the several hundred missiles we failed to intercept."

Glitter doesn't react to my ire, but I don't bother to adjust the projected voice of mine to be any different. "But their pain is over," she says simply. As if that excuses it. "Their spirits will be caught and enter the cycle once again. And for us, the living, we carry on. As we always do."

For a minute, I sit there, considering her words. It is, more than I am willing to admit, tempting to just . . . give up and believe that. To think that Glitter might know something I don't, be wiser than I know myself to be. To let myself be at peace with it all.

But deep inside me, I know that's a lie.

Even if it's not a lie for her, it would always be for me.

With a slow motion, I make my counterpoint in the time-honored tradition of my people. A paw, slowly extended, slaps one of the canisters to the floor.

It falls like a bombardment shot, hitting the deck and sending a plume of metal dust and scrap out in a chaotic mess that thoroughly ruins the calligraphy she was working on, a detonation in miniature. Glitter's drones have stopped and are watching me from their multiple angles as I give the cleaner nanos something to do today.

"I think I can," I mew softly. "Fight forever. I think life is art, and death is just a mess on the deck, and I think I have a preference." I look up, tongue flicking over the back of my paw as I match the camera stare of Glitter's art drone with half-lidded eyes. "I'm only here because my mom thought the same way. Thought that death was worth fighting. And I'm going to keep doing that."

I hop off the table, ignoring the small shards of metal stuck in my fur and paws. Glitter doesn't say anything, either from the drones or through the station, as I stalk out of the room.

We all cope in our own ways.

I still haven't found mine yet.

CHAPTER 25

The exact nature of the station's haunting still eludes me.

Hello. It is time to talk about ghosts.

Or at least, it will be, after a brief update-based tangent.

The station is currently holding in matched orbit with the debris cloud from the destroyed ship. A good chunk of debris, in any spaceborne combat, is going to just kind of vanish. Not literally "poof, gone" vanish, but with nothing to slow it down, small chunks of kinetically encouraged material are going to start moving and basically not stop. So they're gone.

What's left of a destroyed ship tends to be the still-connected pieces of hull, the things contained within, and stuff cut away with beam weaponry that still has a matched velocity. This close to a planet, also, gravity tends to help keep stuff clumped up, especially if it's soon going to be crashing into the planet. This close to Earth, there are something like five thousand still-operational surface stations that project something akin to the old interdiction field I still have stapled to a drone somewhere around here. They help too.

We're here for four hours. Any longer and we risk getting hit by an oncoming ultra-dense section of the orbital scrapyard that I have on my map, or by a recycler swarm that holds this general zone, or by one of the hostile energy fields that prowl these areas outside of my station home's normal mapped-out course.

We have engines, in three styles. We can go wherever we want. But we tend to stay in our normal orbit, because going too far into the unknown is a massive threat. Not everything shows up on scanners; not everything announces its presence. I've bumped into an isolation cell once before, in a single casual accident, and it cost me two whole levels of space station.

Anyway. We—I and the two AI—are here at the closest thing to the site of this noble ship's death. Why, I couldn't quite explain. I had set the course here immediately after the ship's death, but I didn't really understand why. Well, technically, I had ordered Ennos to set a course here, and then I remembered painfully that Ennos wasn't capable of actually doing that yet.

Were we here to investigate the launch? To salvage it? To hold a sacred call for the dead?

Possibly all three.

I do not, exactly, know how my home is haunted. I've said the *word* a lot—"haunted"—but I never actually thought about what it meant. It's a feeling first, and a reality second. Sometimes I am watched from angles that make no sense. Small noises that the machinery doesn't make, physical sensations that cannot be brushed aside as radiation poisoning. Parts of the station I just don't go to, because the dark there fills me with an animal dread that I haven't felt since I first learned how railguns work.

There are a few undeniable things, though. Something here is looking out for me. I avoid, carefully, thinking "someone," and I especially try to not consider that I know exactly who that someone is. But even without naming names, something has been doing *something*.

Cats don't just randomly get the ability to speak, for one thing. Especially not from a point exactly an inch and a half to the right of my throat.

It's possible I'm looking at this wrong, and it's less that the station is haunted and more a matter of *how haunted the station is*. But regardless of what, who, or how, the core thing I keep trying to remember is that no matter *how* haunted we are, it's still something that either is helping or hasn't been able to kill me in four centuries.

Why am I bringing this up?

Ah. Funny story there.

While my home is rather ambiguously haunted, and the exact cause of that haunting could be anything from a degrading ancillary AI to a glitch in the lighting electronics, it is *rather challenging* to say that the wreckage we're standing post at isn't *incredibly haunted*.

I need to interrupt my thoughts as I take this corner. Oh, I am running, by the way. I'll explain as I go.

My paws slide across the deckplate; I keep my claws in so that I get maximum slide distance, using the far wall to stop my momentum before I take off again. Behind me, the corridor lights cut out with a shower of sparks and a scream that is absolutely not just from warping metal. But I'm moving too fast, and the darkness just barely laps at my heels as I sprint down toward the next emergency door.

I have ruled out *ghosts* from the haunting list this time. Ghosts aren't stopped by security doors.

I get enough distance from the disturbance on this straight shot of a hallway that my AR flickers back to life, and I yell a command at the local station system to prepare to seal the door I'm bolting toward like my life depends on it.

Three seconds and a dozen rapid-fire steps across the deck, and I fling myself over the lip of the security door, momentum taking me entirely through the low-gravity connector room and over the other side, tumbling into a structural hub. It used to be a common room, but I moved a lot of the pillows and stuff to more useful places, so now it's mostly just a long room that serves as a connective point for a bunch of different corridors that lead to more interesting places.

The door seals shut behind me as the last of the lighting breaks, plunging the hall I was just in into darkness.

"Okay!" I announce. "Docking bay is compromised!"

"This is not good." Ennos sounds remarkably calm, considering the circumstances. I expected them to be panicking about death by ghosts by this point. "Lily, please. I am panicking silently. Also, I have lost contact with my remaining drones on deck twenty-seven. But station metrics show a spike in power draw from one of the fabrication factories in that section."

"That's bad!" I agree. "Is it the drone factory running off more heavy cargo drones again?"

"Oh. No, that was me," Ennos replies. "Before I was fully informed about the challenges with getting something offworld, I had planned to attempt to lift a quantity of produce from the surface as . . . It doesn't matter. This is not that."

"What!" I roll onto my side, staring up at the station's ceiling as I try to catch my breath. "You were making me a birthday gift? That's . . . I need to get you a birthday gift!"

Ennos is not willing to be sidetracked. "Lily! My birthday isn't for months, and I would like my preemptive gift to be *dealing with the ghosts*, thank you!"

"They're not ghosts, they can't go through doors."

"Revenants, then! Condens! Specters! Couriers! I don't care! Whatever they are, they are running our fabricator! Probably in a way that will be lethal to us!" Ah, there's the classic Ennos panic. "Did you get what you needed?" Ennos asks suddenly.

I pull myself up to sit on my haunches, spitting out what I'd been holding in my mouth so I could lick at the rapidly fading line of blood on one paw where I misjudged a jump. "I did. One hard copy of the emissions readings. Void, I never realized how much I take the grid for granted, even when it is inconvenient."

"The nearest compatible data reader is two decks up. Mycology lab."

I yowl pathetically. Mushrooms again. Fantastic. "Fine," I say with my voice. "I'm moving. Any word from Glitter?"

"Nothing." Ennos sounds . . . very small, in that moment. "Hurry, please. There's a zero-G access shaft that way." They pull up a guide light in my AR. I've long since stopped trying to secure it; I kind of forgot that "unshackled AI" actually means something. "I'll meet you there."

"Dark zone?" I ask.

"Midway up the access shaft. It's the fastest way, and the whole deck is out." Ennos is obviously trying their best to stay calm. "I'm sorry."

I give a flick of my tail. "It's fine. What're they gonna do, kill me?" I ask sarcastically. They can't kill me. "Good luck. See you there."

Deep breaths. Cats don't really do deep breaths, but I like how it feels. Deep breaths, pick up the data chip in my fangs, open the door. The corridor is still lit. A curved line of doors leading to crew quarters is ahead of me, Ennos's guide light stretching out to where I know a hatch is waiting.

Looks clear. I explode into motion anyway. Distance is carved away by running and rapid reflexes. When I make it to the hatch, I don't even bother to stop, just slamming into the ladder and slinging myself upward. Then I'm in a null-gravity area, and up doesn't mean anything. I'm just going forward. Pulling faster and faster, momentum building up to the maximum speed I can pull a paw across a handhold at.

Then I'm passing through the dark. It's just normal darkness, nothing metaphysical about it. But there's a feeling, as I catapult through, that there's something else *here*. A sensation of air being pushed and pulled around my fur, of something pacing around me, of claws not entirely unlike mine . . .

Back into the light and heat.

I bleed momentum at my destination the hard way, impacting the rubber-coated edge of the access port hard. Something cracks inside me, but gravity is back, and I don't have time. Behind me, the thing in the shaft is moving, and the power is draining out of the various systems behind me as it gives chase.

This door? Sealed.

Ennos and I reconvene in the mycology lab. Turns out, this one is in microgravity, and it was *way* better maintained than the unauthorized psychedelic grow op I found so long ago. They actually disposed of their samples, so it's just a sterile room mostly.

"Okay," I say after five minutes of awkward attempts to access a complex data storage device with only my mouth. "Got it?"

"Got it," Ennos replies after a couple seconds. Six hours of sensor data across thousands of kilometers of local space, and it took them seconds. "There's an open tesseract bridge between us and this point here." A model of our station is projected, spinning to show where we're looking nearby. "It matches to the last spotted position of this." Ennos adds in the destroyed Earth ship, showing chunks of debris around the signal. "There's a secondary signal that's harder to get a lock on, but it appears there's also something *here* that whatever is infiltrating us is also linked to." They pause. "Also, Glitter is here. Still showing signs of power use, but cut off somehow."

"Tesseract bridges are for physical connections, not data," I comment. "Also, no one's used those since Luna Polis . . . uh . . ." I try to think of a way to say this part delicately.

Ennos sighs. "I am aware that we might be removed from reality at a moment's notice. I assure you, I will be screaming later, when we have time." It's good that they've got their priorities sorted out. "Regardless, yes. It is meant for physical connections. But seeing as whatever is coming through is physically damaging our home, I would say that is happening."

"Super," I comment dryly. "Okay. I'm gonna shoot it."

"That is your answer to everything." Ennos sounds put out, but I don't say anything in response, just staring at the map until they add to their comment. "All right, you've convinced me."

I try not to let my tail flick too much in amusement. "What's facing it, firing-arc-wise? I've lost engine control, so I can't rotate us."

"Railguns fourteen, sixteen, twenty through twenty-six, and thirty. One bombardment cannon that I do not think would have the accuracy you are looking for. The singularity shotgun, a plague dropper, five different pain inducers. Two missile tubes, four particle beams, one inferno lance, a magnetic flux projector, an x-ray array that you have marked as 'no,' the third and fifth segments of the pulse field generator, and the point defense flak cannon that you have named Larry."

"Oh man, I remember back when I named guns," I muse distractedly. "Okay, I'm going for the lance. Least likely to be interfered with by . . . what?" I pause as Ennos brings up a diagnostic for the inferno lance. Offline. "Great. Okay, the pulse field . . . offline too. Do we have access to *any* of this?"

"No," Ennos says, a creeping dread in their voice. "All armaments are unpowered."

"Oh." I am completely disarmed. That's never happened before. "I . . . uh . . ." Apparently panic isn't just Ennos's job. "I should . . . um . . ."

I should what? I am, suddenly, very small indeed. I am a *cat*, playing at participating in a world where most weapons fire projectiles bigger than I am. I can't build anything new myself, I can't apply the vast amount of engineering knowledge I have without thumbs, I can't just pull a solution out of . . .

"Lily?" My friend's voice draws my focus, cracking the shell of dissociative anxiety around me.

I look up. "Huh? Yes. I'm fine. I just . . . what . . ."

"I've found you a working gun," Ennos, my best friend in the world, tells me.

A video window opens near my eyeline. A real-time feed from a part of the station we still have control over.

I built two spacesuits, once upon a time. One modified for engineering and exploration, perfect for actually having something approaching fine motor control. And one . . .

One designed like a strike craft.

Ablative armor, field scramblers, stealth systems, sealed and secure and ready to go, with two high-powered plasma throwers on the flanks.

All I have to do is get to the drone bay and hope that nothing bothers me for the hour it takes the armorer system to seal me into it.

"I think," Ennos says, apropos of nothing, "that I have an idea for a distraction. To buy you some time."

I have decided that I will be getting my friend a very nice early birthday gift.

CHAPTER 26

Have I mentioned, before, that I am shockingly unmodified?

My body rejects most augments, in all their various forms. I can't install any wetware, host a native nanoswarm, implant backup organs, or graft new limbs on. It's all very pedestrian, and I've just had to learn to live with the normal number of cat parts.

That said, I am still stronger, healthier, and faster than I think most people would ever really suspect from a cat, much less a cat in my age bracket.

This is helped along by lifetimes of memorization, pattern development, and practice. I know where everything is, in all the areas of the station I've spent centuries prowling. Oh, there are new parts to explore—there are *always* new parts to explore; right now there are just more at once than I'm used to—but that doesn't fundamentally change the fact that I can navigate an orbital infrastructure environment at a breakneck pace.

Sometimes literally, but we don't need to talk about that.

Behind me, something wrenches a hull plate out of alignment, something sparking and a protesting klaxon sounding deeper within the station. I do not see what is chasing me, but it is *obviously* chasing me.

We haven't figured out what the not-really-ghosts are, but we've got some rules down.

They're semiphysical, they're easily distracted, they seem to have some kind of line-of-sight limitation, and they're taking over the camera drones. And repair drones. And generally anything with a complex enough mechanical substrate. Weirdly, they haven't gone for any of the grid hardware yet. Also, when they do pour themselves into one of the little camera drones, the things tend to short out shortly after, and whatever was inside spills out. I can *feel* it when they do that.

I absolutely do not want to be the thing they try to possess.

But at least we know a few things.

There's a row of suit storage lockers along the wall up ahead, as part of a circular room that has a direct airlock chute to the outside of the station. Whoever built it had crew members of wildly different sizes, and the lockers are arranged as such. This makes it comically easy for a master of the pounce like myself to scale up to the ceiling in three easy bounds. Up here, where the grav-plates' effect trails off sharply, I can shoot forward off the last locker and into a ventilation shaft.

And I'm in the clear. It's dark here, but it's dark here because we don't put lighting strips in our vents. And as someone who has at this point built a few vents, I get to use the collective "we." The point is, it's not the dark of being chased by hungry shades.

I give a meow in my native Cat, sending a signal through to Ennos that I've passed the first checkpoint.

A minute and thirty seconds later, I claw my way over the edge of an upper deck, rear legs kicking wildly to find purchase on the lift shaft I've decided to climb up. Even in half gravity, it's still a massive chore to navigate maintenance ladders without thumbs. Or proper elbows.

I haven't been spotted. Checkpoint two.

Now, for the tricky part. I need to get to the drone bay where I've been doing my import runs from. Fortunately, I picked one close to the core systems I tend to operate, because I didn't want to drag two thousand kilos of dirt across an inch more space than I was required to.

Unfortunately, that part is going to require me to go through a dark zone.

If I'm very lucky, I won't get caught. Which is good, because I'm given to understand there are several old human mythologies that believe that the more black fur a cat has, the luckier it is.

I wish I'd had more time to regrow my fur. Maybe should've had the medical dispenser give me something for that, stockpile that extra luck. That's probably not a thing, but these days, it can be hard to tell, and every advantage helps.

I am approaching the refinery floor that I need to cross. This one is fun, for certain definitions of fun. When I need to get past here in a hurry and all the machinery is turned off, the refinery has a couple weird quirks that I like to exploit.

Control for speed, jump, grab that grate and pull myself up, get a running start, and fling myself into the open air over three hundred feet of piping and heating elements.

There is, twenty feet into this place, a spot where the grav plates don't line up properly. If it were actually dangerous, the station would have performed emergency repairs a long time ago, or at least asked me to authorize them. But as it stands, it's just a bizarre curiosity, maybe even the reason this refinery was mothballed and had crates of ancient gravitronics gear lying around.

It's a thin wedge of space that'll make you feel a little disoriented if you walk through it. Or, if you throw yourself through the distortion twenty feet over the deck, instead it performs a weird gravity-lensing effect and fires me like a railgun round across the space.

Three hundred feet in a second. A pile of old pillows and worn blankets pilfered from a dozen crew quarters, marked with shaky etched writing as "linen storage," catches me. I walk it off without too much damage except a broken leg. I am already moving again; we're on a time budget here.

I cross a dozen intersections, flying past doors and bulkheads I barely process. And then I am in the dark.

Again, something takes notice of me. It coils out of the dark, but this one doesn't rend and pull at the station. Instead, there is just the soft rustling of air on my fur, and the feeling of something curious.

I am out of the dark.

The thing stops following when I clear another heavy security door and seal myself in the segment that has my precious heavily armed fighter suit. Checkpoint three, last one.

Whatever these things are that are tearing up my home, they're getting faster. More power conduits are being drained, more systems being compromised. There isn't time to play this safe, not that doing so is a hobby of mine anyway.

I slide on my flank to in front of the drone bay floor door, a command starting the process of it hissing upward. I don't wait, I just roll under the multi-ton steel block, popping back to my feet as it starts to shut behind me. Shouted commands bring the construction arms online, pull my fighter suit onto the platform. I have laser-etched marks on the assembly line where I need to stand if I don't want to get fur or parts of my tail pinched off, and I plant my paws there.

I need to stand still for roughly fifty-two minutes and eight seconds, with the improved assembly routines that Ennos designed cutting a lot of small flaws out of the process. Which is, let's be real, something that comes close to feeling like a lifetime while I wait with my back to the door for a ghost to murder me.

And I'm not talking about a cat lifetime! I mean *my* lifetime! That's objectively more lifetime. An order of magnitude more lifetime.

I mean, yes, it does feel like I've had that "back to the door available for ghost murder" feeling going on for most of it. But I think that's just a part of being alive, and it's never supposed to be literal? It is literal now. I like it even less.

Somewhere, somehow, far on the other side of the station, Ennos blows something up. The explosion is barely audible from here, but I feel the mild thrum of the deck that isn't in line with how my entire life as felt. My paws know, instinctively, that something has gone wrong.

Or, in this case, that the distraction has started.

I try not to flinch from it anyway, even knowing it was coming, as one of the assembler arms fires a sealing bolt into the combined helmet shell about half an inch from my left eye. Another muffled blast, another thud of the suit coming together around me.

This is going to be a long forty minutes.

I try humming to distract myself. I am bad at humming. My voice can do weird awkward chirps that I hate, at best. It's twenty painful minutes in when I realize I could maybe make my projection voice hum, if I really wanted to.

It takes me ten minutes to figure out how to not just get it to replicate the dumb chirps. Then I almost instantly realize that it's just not very satisfying.

With five minutes to go, there is a scrape of an incompressible material against the metal of the assembly floor door. I cannot see it, but I can hear as something dangerous starts clawing. Attracted to the power draw, the heat source, or maybe just to the abstract of my life. I bet any ghost would be happy to eat me. I bet I'm delicious.

The final sealing bolt is put in place, and the suit is secured. It's not done yet, but as of this moment, before the command gear comes online, I cannot see or hear or know anything at all outside my confinement. With the floating feeling of the inertia gel containing my limbs, the darkness is near total sensory deprivation.

My mind, enhanced and flawed in equal measure, races. A thousand possibilities, a thousand angles of monster sneaking up behind me. There's no way they wouldn't spot me, standing here out in the open. Seconds stretch to eternities as I wait with an almost physical pain.

My next drone armor assembler factory *thing* is, I decide, going to be camouflaged.

Something thumps into my flank, lightly. I almost scream. Okay, I do scream. With both voices, I scream. But there is no follow-up strike; nothing kills me just yet.

Then the suit comes alive. Information and light floods my vision, camera feeds and sensor readouts, life support come online, the engines and motors fire to life, and I can *move*.

The bay door is *open* in front of me. I don't know why, but it's saved my life. A scattergun blast of unsecured materials and half-finished projects rapidly recedes into the vacuum ahead of me.

And clawing its way up the floor, fighting against the howling atmosphere being sucked out, something shimmering and blue is *reaching for me*.

"Go!" I whisper/is whispered to me.

And the suit obeys.

The command helmet makes the suit my skin. The grav plates are guided by my reflex, the limited ion engine pushed by my instinct.

I pirouette out of the bay. The machinery clamps on my paws release, and I am off, flinging myself into the void so fast I've cleared the station in a blink. I go high, staying out of reach of the semiphysical claws of the thing hanging on to the deck.

My AR interface was gone from the moment I was sealed in here, but now it is replaced by a new set of digital information flows. Preloaded scanner sweeps show, as best as the station can determine, where the stray junk in the area is. And the projection that highlights otherwise dark chunks of metal and rock also plots a path for me.

Toward a cluster of bright green lines in my vision, and the destroyed wreck of the last ship to try to join us up here.

And suddenly, I'm safe.

It's a paradox of an emotion. I have spent the vast majority of my life on my home. I know the feeling of every span of that deck under my paws; I am comfortable there. Being outside is harrowing, and not just because of the endless screaming vacuum around me that threatens to end my life in a million ways. But now, here I am, out in open space, relying on a limited fuel supply when there's nothing close enough to use the grav plating on, hurtling toward an unknown beacon of doom. And I feel safe.

Or at least, far safer than when I was on the station while it was being actively attacked.

This trip, with engine burning, is three minutes long. I let the feeling of the suit and its sensors become my world. I push and pull off gravitational platforms, learning the limits of my motion. I am moving so fast that if I tapped a piece of dust at this speed while unarmored, it would pulverize me. But the suit protects me.

I have never flown like this before. Escaping the danger is a rush, and it mixes with the sensation of pushing this suit to its limits, leaving me to warble out a cry of elation as I soar. The only thing left now is the time limit: to eliminate the threat before Ennos is threatened. And I am already moving as fast as I can without risking catastrophic failure. Which is to say, failure where a mote of metal carves through my armor so fast I'm dead before I realize it.

I sing as I thread myself through derelict satellites and the wreckage of ancient wars. I flinch in sympathetic pain as tiny impacts dot my suit's helmet and chest. I coil myself in a hunter's pose as I cut around the remnants of an ancient transport hub, paws skating across the ruined hull on runners of projected gravity as I curl up over and into clear line of sight to my target.

Something is casting a directed signal into our station.

I don't bother checking. Plasma throwers track to exactly where I'm thinking about, take a split second to charge, and then fire. I hear the hum through the suit diagnostics and, just in my ears, a resonant tone that fills my helmet briefly.

The source of the ghosts dies in a barrage of four charged bolts. The shining silver emergency force field around it does very little to protect it from the high-energy weapons I'm sporting. And just like that, the mission is done.

"—ly! Any time you . . . ! Oh." Ennos's voice suddenly fills my comms. "Well. Yes. I wasn't worried at all." Their tone goes from panic to prim and proper in a single word.

"Liar," I meow back. "You okay?"

Ennos takes a full third of a second to collate information to answer. "We've lost power in section C. Two of our grid nodes are crippled. One of them was about to compromise my primary processor segment when you . . . You did stop them, yes?"

"Yes," I say. "I'm heading back now. Just as soon as I check one thing."

"Marked on your HUD." Ennos already knows what I'm looking for. That kid is too smart for me sometimes. Most times.

Five minutes of careful gravity hopping later, I find the rest of the wreck. Or part of it, anyway. The ship was carved apart, but this section broke free after about half of it was turned to molten slag and wasn't targeted by follow-up attacks. Something about this place, though, was important. The device that was throwing those projections at us was drawing something from here, some kind of activation signal, maybe. I need to know. Curiosity, as they say, is important to cats.

I crawl inside, using my propulsion to keep myself from touching the still-glowing edges.

This ship was cramped, packed full of machinery that is now either turned to shredded chaff or just unpowered. Even the emergency lights are off, power having drained away by now. Thin aisles of space between stations, spare gear storage surrounding every free spot, it was built to move as much as possible, as effectively as possible. Economy over comfort. Important when you're trying to break out of a gravity well.

At the back half, I find what I'm looking for.

Stasis pods. Or something like them. There've been a few hundred inter-pretations of this tech over the years. Sleeper cells, stasis pods, cryo beds, and a dozen others, each with a few unique variants all their own.

These ones are occupied. Sort of.

They're crammed in with the same consideration for maximized spatial use as the rest of the ship. Sixteen of them, in a kind of honeycomb pattern against the back of the deck. I approach the first one, and peek inside, and see . . . well, one of our ghosts.

The thought clicks with a technology I know exists. Used heavily by lunar colonies for a while, especially the ones that used autonomous bodies so heavily. When the mind is what's important, your life pod should save that, right? Capture the thoughts of the person in the pod, send them somewhere safe. Probably tried to link to the station because of all the Luna Polis tech on board from a millennium ago.

Up close and organic, they're much less scary. A little over a meter of height, with long bone spikes of fingers that would almost be claws if they weren't so wide and blunted. Extended faces with a large central eye like a rounded hexagon. They're not human, but I've never seen them before. All I know is they didn't deserve this.

The pod is powered off.

An instant later, my suit screams an automated warning, and the nano-bloom on my back explodes into defensive life. A nearly invisible battle takes place in the space around me over the next five seconds as my swarm overwhelms and destroys another rival that was trying to compromise the armor.

A murderer nanoswarm, the kind that you fire from a projectile to seek out sophont life and leave infrastructure intact, is torn apart. But it has already done its work. The person inside the pod is dead, face a mask of pain even through alien features.

No wonder the ghosts were so pissed.

I check the rest of the pods. Lifeless, lifeless, lifeless. Dead, dead, dead. Their faces are cold and angry and hurting.

Except the pod on the end.

It's still on. Emergency power readings say it'll hold for another three days or so. The occupant, still alive. And as I look, the reason becomes clear; they're unlike the rest of the crew. They're something different.

The pod contains a dog. Sleeping happily, head curled on its paws, tentacles wrapped around its eyes. I can't see any breathing, but the pod reads the occupant as alive and healthy.

Murder swarms target sophonts. By luck of being just under the line, we have one survivor.

I check my life support. Plenty of time to sort this out. "Ennos." I speak over the comms. "I'm coming back soon. One guest."

"Understood. I will begin quarantine procedures," Ennos tells me, failing to understand but trying their best, I suppose. "I've made contact with Glitter, as well. She will require extensive repairs, and your aid, but she is alive."

I let out a sigh of relief. That was something I had been terrified of.

Okay.

Time to clean up this mess.

CHAPTER 27

Four hundred years has done a great amount of work for me in terms of preparing me to be surprised.

At a certain point, I had this realization. Every time I thought I was getting bored, thought I'd seen too much, or seen everything, thought that I'd become *weary* of life? Every time, without fail, something would catch me off guard.

Maybe it's just because my guard was dropped. But maybe not. Maybe it's because the universe is too complicated, too varied, too wild and wonderful and *weird* to ever really fully get bored with.

The moment for me that really solidified that was probably the first time I realized there were still Earthlings living around the solar system. Sure, the industry of Earth that made space development practical and useful was mostly gone. But people lived on more than one moon, on more than one planet, and on a host of orbital structures that kept on going even in the face of certain doom.

The moment two hundred years ago when I realized that the starship hull I was planning to strip for parts was missing because a crew of turtlebacks had boarded it, gotten the engine working, and flown it on stealth mode out to the asteroid belt to a hidden colony? That was it for me. That was when I gave up trying to be prepared, or bored, or cynical.

Without even knowing they were doing it, they sniped a prize right out from under me.

That was *so cool.* There wasn't really a lot I could do about how cool it was. And also, I had over three hundred thousand crippled starship hulls to choose from, so getting mad about it would have served no purpose.

Compared to that kind of bravado, what chance did I ever stand of living my life without a few surprises?

My digital companions represent two different attitudes, both of which I've had at different parts of my life, when I was younger.

Glitter is me when I was on the cusp of surrendering to the dull. She takes everything in stride not because she's in tune with the chaos of the universe, but because she's starting to think that she's seen it all and is somehow above it all too. And . . . okay, let's not dwell on how that's literally true. You know what I mean, and I don't want to . . . This isn't a semantics thing. This is about finding meaning in a dark and hostile reality, and wasting your time being prescriptive about word use is wasting your precious candle.

Ennos, on the other paw, is where I was right after my uplift. They're so uncertain that everything is a point of panic. Surprised by everything, scared of everything, Ennos seeks to understand so that the surprises stop coming. Because the surprises are terrifying!

But that's just how life is. It's all of us, sometimes. Maybe I'll loop myself, and end up scared again for a while, before I'm bored for a while. That would be a nice surprise for the version of me that will then be amused for a while!

Live long enough and you can see it all. I'm not there yet and don't know if I ever will be, but seeing it all sure is fun.

Maybe that's why it's so easy to feel like my life hasn't really deviated too far from "normal" with the unintended attack on the station. For me, anyway.

Most of the first week was devoted to getting Glitter stabilized, as well as hauling the station bit by bit back into our stable orbital path safely surrounded by a maelstrom of deadly debris and ancient weaponry. At one point, I deployed our mini drone fleet to secure a lump of pseudo-lithium, which I've been running through the foundry and consumer factory to produce a *lot* of replacement batteries for Glitter.

Hers got shredded by a dead and pained ghost, sadly. And she needs the backup power. The good news is, by this point, I'm *really* skilled at setting these things up to work in parallel, and by the end of the week, I've ferried two thousand of them over to her hull.

Oh, should mention, lost two drones to a mild skirmish over the material. There was some kind of defensive minefield deployed around it. Guess someone was planning to come back. They can't now.

Repairing the rest of Glitter has taken up the two weeks after that. Her hull has tears in it, her main core was dangerously close to complete failure before she forced a shutdown, and a lot of her safety functions were offline. In contrast to fixing up the station, which *mostly* just requires me to tell the repair drones to fix the station, when I even have to do that, Glitter requires manual assistance.

It's been a couple months, so I feel like I should remind you all that I am a cat? This probably doesn't come up much—I haven't done a statistical break-down or anything—but it's true. And it turns out, operating a cobalt welder when you're not working with thumbs is *really* hard.

I actually took a full two days before that part of the repairs to retrofit my engineering suit. Ennos helped me out with building the actual schematic file, but mostly it was me rapidly intuiting material tolerances and power draws so that I could build pseudo-thumbs into the forepaws of the suit.

That made the job simpler, but not really any less time-consuming. But by the time we're sure we're back in our stable orbital path, Glitter is at least back up to reasonably safe functionality.

And now that my friend is okay again, I can get down to analyzing and undoing all the havoc laid down on my home.

I am actually multitasking when Ennos darts a half dozen camera drones into the room I'm working in to bother me. Ennos has been really clingy lately, but I refuse to tell them that. I think they're reacting badly to almost dying again, which . . . uh . . . seems fine? I've kind of lost track of how to react to almost dying. It happens kind of regularly.

Multitasking. Right. Part of me is trying to learn how to sing. I've never actually tried this before, but now that I have a regular voice, I'm kind of interested in what I can do with my *cat* voice. So I'm trying to make actual music with my meows.

"Lily, what are you doing?" Ennos asks, voice rippling out from three of the drones at once.

"Singing!" I answer.

"No, I know . . . everyone can hear you singing. I mean, what are you doing that is relevant to this place," Ennos clarifies, hiding any irritation they feel.

I twitch my tail, trying to keep my body in the slightly comfortable position I've settled into as I work the control board. "I'm trying to calibrate this stupid machine properly, and I'm doing a bad job at it," I admit. "It's . . . You know how I've redesigned a few key places for my use, and some other stuff is technically cat-compatible?"

"Yes."

"Well, this isn't," I state. "This is made for I don't even think humans. It feels like I'm short two limbs. Or maybe just dumb." I glare at the rounded glows of the control board some more. It doesn't help. "Anyway, what's up?"

"I have an update for you, if you have time." Ennos sounds like they're just finding an excuse to spend some time talking, but I don't mind anyway.

So I just say that. "Yeah, I don't mind. The lightbulbs aren't gonna be fully grown and ready for install for another month anyway no matter what I do here. What's up?"

"Your survivor has completed quarantine in the secure medbay. I've tasked a few dozen of my drones to haul the stasis pod to one of the genetics labs for a full scan and health report before we open it. Estimated time fourteen days."

"Good!" I walk as I talk, the camera drones bobbing around me like a crown of orbs. "I'm excited! Are you excited? I've never had a pet before that wasn't . . ." I trail off on that sentence.

I can feel Ennos glowering at me. "You were going to say 'that wasn't me,' weren't you?" they accuse me.

"No!" I lie. ". . . Yes," I unlie. "I'm bad at this! I'm sorry!"

"I find your antics amusing," Ennos says magnanimously. "Also, it is difficult to not *feel* like a pet sometimes, I admit. I still lack access to . . . almost everything. I am so far beyond advanced compared to every piece of programming we encounter, and yet I cannot even convince this station to acknowledge that I am alive. It is . . . aggravating."

"You're telling me." I huff in exasperation, the noise coming out with a small squeak. "Well, you're not a pet to me," I reassure them. "But a dog! I'm gonna take him on walks, and teach him to fetch, and, and . . ."

"Okay, I absolutely must ask you about this." Ennos cuts me off. "But you've been busy. You keep saying *dog*, and the medlab has assured me that the creature in the stasis pod is *not* a dog."

"What?" I stop, pausing underneath a glowing sign that the station's programming constantly updates with crowd sizes in nearby main access corridors. They all read as empty. "What are you talking about? Of course it's a dog. Wait, no, is it a mimioform?! Because . . . I guess I could make one of those a pet too. But wouldn't the murder swarm have . . . ?"

Ennos whirls all their camera drones around to examine me, pulling up windows in my AR display. "This," they say to match an image, "is a dog. Now, I know there's an ancient running joke that my people are bad at this, but I want you to tell me if I'm wrong here."

"Sure, that's a dog," I admit. Umbra retriever, shaggy black fur, constant smile, big friendly pooch. Good dog.

"And you don't notice anything weird here?" Ennos says.

"No?"

"Perhaps a comparison." They bring up a live feed of the stasis pod they are dragging through a hallway four decks overhead. "How about now?"

"Uh . . . both dogs? I feel like I'm being messed with here." I dismiss the windows and decide it's time for lunch.

I am *almost* angry to admit that I am looking forward to lunch. It is going to taste like ration. But it's also going to be art, or art-adjacent, and I've started to get into the theater of it all.

"Lily, the creature you brought back has four extra prehensile limbs, apparently engineered for melee combat with *mechanical targets*." Ennos sounds some kind of mix of concerned and annoyed. "You don't find this at all worrying?"

". . . Sometimes dogs have those?" I don't get why the AI is so worried. "I don't get why you're so worried. I'm sure they're a very good dog!"

"How can you possibly—"

"Because all dogs are good dogs!"

"Lily, no." Ennos sighs. "Please. You can't . . . what if it tries to eat you?"

"Probably won't work," I mutter, possibly in Cat. Not that it matters much anymore; Ennos has long since begun building an ancillary language database and speaks whatever garbage linguistic monster I've developed perfectly well. They still haven't figured out what's latched onto the main one. I think they take it personally.

"I don't," the AI says for no reason. "And I'm going to bring this up again when we get a genetic scan and I can prove you wrong."

"Sure. I'm gonna have lunch. Anything else to report?"

"There's a spy satellite thirty-six kilometers away that is actively scanning us," Ennos grumbles. "You should shoot it."

I should not. "Does it report to anything?"

"I don't have access to the sensors needed to track that. Also, I think they may have been destroyed in the attack. We are partially blind and it is—"

"Worrying, yes," I agree. "I'll get to work on those after lunch. Actually, can you do both of us a favor? See if we have any commercial-grade blueprints for an onboard drone with arms. I know it won't be perfect, but let's see if we can at least give you the ability to push buttons in a way that doesn't involve ramming them." I bat one of the camera drones in a friendly gesture that sends it spiraling away through the air.

"Thank you." Ennos sounds surprised. Which worries *me*. Did they really think they were a pet? Just because I keep forgetting to be a responsible parent doesn't mean I don't want to give them every tool I can. I make a promise to myself to devote time to that, no matter how many new sirens go off in the next few days. ". . . Thank you." Ennos's voice is quieter this time. "Enjoy your lunch. I am going to . . . yes. I will check the blueprints."

Lunch is a highly detailed re-creation of the classic Arclight holosign, an echo of a memory of an era of creativity and art that may have been a fiction but certainly gave rise to some powerful films.

It is one hundred percent made of ration, and it tastes like it too. But it's impressive, anyway.

I don't end up shooting down that spy sat. It's a hundred years old, and its transmitter is obviously damaged. Maybe I'm just being vain, but I don't feel the need to snipe things just for scanning me.

I did shoot down the weapon platform that had started tracking the spy sat, though. The thing had come online as soon as the bundle of automated sensors had gone to active scanning of the station, probably in response to us firing the engines to brake back to our stable orbit.

It takes about four seconds for me to start to consider something defense-less as a pet, I guess.

More than enough time to put an inferno lance through whatever threatens my new friend.

CHAPTER 28

Of all the things I expected to hear today and be excited about, "Your bloodwork came back" was not one of them. Mostly because I had forgotten how long the medical analyzer could take on some things.

Sometimes I think the machine is calibrated to go slower so that whatever people installed it didn't get freaked out by how rapidly technology had outpaced their frail meat brains. I . . . have a lot of free time to think things, sometimes. Look, it's been years since I've had proactive projects to work on, don't judge me.

I'm in the middle of trying to figure out why a repair drone isn't sealing a breach in the deck. I've got one of those really uncomfortable hard light rebreathers on, just in case there actually is an atmosphere leak here, but it seems like it's just a regular hole between two decks. I've tried giving the drone explicit commands, I've tried giving the broad command through the station maintenance authority, and I've tried doing it myself. That last part did not go well, because I can't figure out what button to push to turn off the gravity here, and I am far too cat to lift the six-hundred-kilo enhanced metal plate into place to activate the clamps and weld it down properly.

So I'm back to trying to diagnose errors in code, which is honestly really far beyond me. Most of the stuff on this station I can reprogram pretty easily, especially now that I can narrate instead of typing. What used to take a year now takes a day or two. It's nice! But sometimes you get stuff like this weird drone, which I *think* is from an Ado Haudenosaunee reclamation team, where the code was produced by so many layers of machine learning that it's almost organic.

To be clear, by "almost organic," I don't mean it's a living person. I mean it's a heuristic mess that doesn't make a lot of sense and pretty much only

works by random chance. But it works enough that I can leave it alone and
let it do its thing.

"Okay, let's try again," I lazily mewl out. "Assess and repair the designated
area." I flag the damaged hull section and file the request both manually and
through the station's command structure.

Almost right away, I get a return code of "job assessed, work finished."

I crane my neck back to look upward, feeling the bones creak uncomfort-
ably as I strain to look at the ceiling.

Nope. Hole's still there.

So, the process goes, I make a couple edits to the code, and try again. And
again, and again, and again.

It's been a long day.

It's not even a high-priority hole. I don't honestly *care* if the courtship
chamber on deck N2 is roughly connected to the lateral hallway on deck 19.
I don't *use* either of these. No one does! What would we even *do* with a courtship chamber?! But it's the principle of the thing; someone put holes in my
home and I'd like it looking nice in case I ever have guests. Guests who want
to court, or ship, or both at once even. I'm not here to judge.

Still, when Ennos interrupts me, I jump at the chance.

"Lily, I have—"

"Yes! Thank you!" I yowl, scrambling backward and nearly slicing my
paw open on the exposed circuit board in the back of the repair bot. "I'll
take it!"

Ennos pauses. "Do you even know . . . No, never mind. I'm glad your
repairs of our home continue apace."

"Oh, uh. Yes." I nod energetically, bobbing my whole body to agree. Yup.
Actual repairs happening, right here. "How's the grid doing?" I try to tangent
away.

My AI friend practically snarls at that, and I know I've got a good distraction for the future. "This station's digital landscape is a shambles. Overloads
have claimed a number of connecting nodes, and reestablishing those links to
other segments will take time and physical interaction. I am making progress,
but it is frustrating, and I am trying to not bother you unless I actually know
which button to push," Ennos says. "On the sharper side, I seem to have been
cut off from a few of the more worrying specters wandering around in here.
So that's nice."

"I'm glad to hear you've gotten more cavalier about impending death,"
I joke as I close the "repair" drone back up with my forepaws and start making a wandering line toward a nap spot. It's time for a break or something.

"Death? What?" A note of terror reenters Ennos's voice. "I thought you said they were harmless!"

"What? Uh . . . yes! Absolutely! I'm just kidding!" I scramble to undo my blunder. "They're just misunderstood, and shy! I'm sure!"

"Lily, I'm going to need you to install a new proton reactor to power the firewall I'm going to design."

"I'll consider it," I concede graciously. This is probably my fault, anyway. "Also, what did you come down here for originally?"

One of the weird quirks Ennos has is that they will pause to "check" things like this. I *know* they don't need to. It's just an affectation. But they seem to like it, and it does give a more casual feeling, so I don't complain. "Oh, your bloodwork came back from the medlab. You aren't allergic to any—"

I am already moving. Coiled muscles propel me, reflexes humming as I fling myself down the hall. I know the exact route I need to take; the station is huge, but my mental map of it is perfect in one regard. I know exactly where the galley is, and where I can see just how badly the station's personnel file has been ruining my life for the last *several hundred years*.

Ennos's voice trails behind me. I don't think even the sharply intelligent unshackled AI was expecting just how fast I can move when motivated.

They catch up a minute later, spinning words out of the walls to sound like normal conversation to my ears. "—thing. Though there was a note about you having some kind of residual radiation damage, and—"

I take a corner sharply, leaving Ennos sighing behind me.

"Lily, you can't keep—"

I am up an access shaft, scrambling up the ladder that I have wrapped thick cloth around the rungs of so my claws can dig in properly.

Food. Potentially, maybe not. But *food*! If the galley doesn't think I'm allergic to everything that isn't beige nutrient paste, maybe it will make me *actual moonblessed food*! All I have to do is make it to the galley, and—

A klaxon sounds. It's one I'm familiar with; something is on a collision course with the station.

Okay. This is fine. I divert course, heading toward the mag web control station. Normally I'd just use the grapples, but they're four decks up and I don't feel like climbing and I *still* haven't figured out how to reenable the lift shafts yet.

The thing about to hit us was a lump of melted plastic moving at plus-one-hundred miles an hour relative. The plastic itself I feed into a recycler, which will slowly use vacuum difference to grind it down to something I can later use in manufacturing. What's really interesting is the chemical that was melting the plastic, even in the depths of space still doing its work, slowly but surely. I carefully have that isolated and moved to an organics analyzer for . . . analysis.

Look, sometimes the tools just do what they say they do. Don't judge me.

There's also a problem with the recycler unit not actually having any kind of logistics connection to the fabricators or manufactories, and that's just a pain, but whatever, I don't need a lot of plastic for what I do *anyway*. Either way, I'll deal with that *later*, because right now, it is time to try my paws at *lunch*.

My detour didn't actually take me farther away from the galley by raw distance, but unfortunately, I can't actually tunnel through solid metal unless I'm starting at the metallurgical tunneler, so I'm stuck taking the long way.

I don't know if I say this often enough, but I love my home.

This station is a winding maze of halls and doors, and while I've only recently gained access to a good two-thirds of them, all these familiar spaces are still so comforting to me. I feel *safe* here, wrapped in warm metal arms in this spinning metal habitat so far above the sky. Every little cut and scrape I can see from this latest round of damage just makes me love it more; all that, and it still kept me safe. Still kept the ghosts away long enough for me to do my part.

And now, with more and more of it opening up to me, the future here seems so bright. So full of ideas and options. And, I would like to remind everyone as I step onto an access shaft grav plate and launch myself straight "up," full of *food*.

Naturally, I am only a couple hundred feet from the galley when Glitter calls me.

"Excuse me, Lily." The ever-proper AI greets me with a pair of camera drones that perform what I can only describe as a formal bow. "You seem busy, so I regret that I require some of your time."

The majority of me is glad that Glitter is up and running again. Glad that she's undeterred about engaging with the world. I am less glad that she's still really ritualistic in her behavior sometimes, and also that she is now keeping me from my lunch, but I'm not gonna be the one to discourage her.

"Sure, what's up?" I meow, trying not to let the rapid flicking of my tail give away my impatience.

"I have been studying the surface cities, now that I have a better vantage point and some free time with my repairs complete," Glitter explains. "And I have noticed one I wished to ask you about. I cannot find anything on your public grid about it."

"Oh, our grid is all messed up right now," I explain, passing on what Ennos told me earlier. "Do you have coordinates?" She does, and I pull up what sensor records I can access from here in my AR, looking over the area.

It's a fairly small spot, all things considered. About fifty square miles in a strip along the eastern edge of one of the islands in the Atlantic Archipelago. It takes me a little while to try to sort out why Glitter is focused on it, and eventually, I *don't* sort it out and just ask instead.

"Pull up the heat signatures, if you can," Glitter says. "I wish I could share more simply. Heat, life signs, perhaps power draw or signal maps would also help?"

I have all of those. I layer them while I consider getting some kind of big five-mile-long hardwired cable to plug Glitter's grid into ours. "Okay. So what am I . . . oh." The city, under these lenses, is instantly obvious.

Nothing organic living here. Unshielded power lines that are way too well laid out, regimented trace signals in the air, massive imbalances in construction analysis. I've seen this kind of thing before, and luckily, Glitter caught this infection before it spread beyond its current size.

"City seed," I grumble. "Guess I didn't get the last of them after all." I hiss slightly as I remember my last fight with one of these. The city seeds were one of the few ground-based threats that could actually fire back sometimes. Not enough to do anything, but enough that they were real threats and not just stationary targets. I mean, they *were* stationary targets, but not *just* that.

"You know it to be an enemy?" Glitter sounds almost sad, through the drones.

"Sorta, yeah." I meow in exhaustion. "They're like a less granular gray-goo problem. They just consume and spread. I'm not even sure *why*, all I know is that they seem to be able to pop up anywhere."

"But why a city?" Glitter asks. "Is it building for anyone?"

"Not that I know," I answer grumpily. "I don't even know if they're full AI. They've never answered me when I tried to talk. Though, granted, there wasn't a whole lot I could *say* at the time."

Glitter's drones hover around each other in an idle orbit while she composes her reply. Ennos does strategic pauses; Glitter does political word work. "Would you be offended if I attempted to speak with it?" Glitter asks me. "I do not mean to disparage your diplomatic ability . . ."

"Oh, disparage away." I stroll under the drones, trying to contain myself from sprinting off as I answer. "I'm still new at talking! Say hi, make a friend! Let me know if they launch anything at us!" I take a corner, her drones lagging behind as Glitter turns her digital mind to the task she was most interested in. "Please don't get too attached," I whisper, mostly to myself. "Just in case."

The city seeds I've known were . . . I'm not going to say "evil." I don't think they were alive enough to be evil. But they were toward the start of my era of guardianship, and before I flattened their cities and bombed out the roots, they had cut the world's population in half.

Part of me, the part that's always angry, wants to just launch something dangerous and overwhelming at the surface target and write it off. But the rest of me, the part that's been making friends and maybe doesn't have to be so angry all the time, wants to see where Glitter can take this.

I pull up an AR display with a constant map to the closest gun station, though. Just in case.

I am almost right outside the galley when Ennos interrupts me to tell me that there are signs of weapons fire on the surface of the primary moon.

I am so tired. I just wanted lunch.

The moon is far away. And it might be a local issue anyway. From what I understand, the undercities and their republics war with each other constantly, and there isn't much I can do to stop them from where I am. But maybe there should be some kind of break from that on the surface.

I give the okay, and Ennos deploys some of our drone fleet, taking command for this one. And then, with that out of the way, I *finally* hop up onto a chair to be served lunch.

No allergies, no problems, just one hungry cat. The grid is connected here; the galley knows I can eat anything. Just give me *anything*. Please.

My meal arrives.

Ration.

Ration in the shape of a caduceus. Cute.

Well. At least I know now that it wasn't the allergies. And that the galley has a sense of humor.

"Lily . . ." One of Ennos's camera drones floats nearby. "I'm sorry . . ." Their voice sounds worried about me.

"Ah, it's fine." My ears flick back as I lick at the back of one of my paws before hopping my forepaws up onto the table to eat. "Nice design on the snake. Good scale work, galley," I say out loud to the possibly haunted, possibly nonsentient machinery.

"You're taking this gracefully." Glitter's smooth voice joins Ennos from her own drone. "We were worried for you."

I try to make a derisive noise, but it doesn't work too well when my mouth is full and I end up spraying ration crumbs onto my plate. "I've been eating, and complaining about, this stuff for centuries." I say. "One more week or two for the strawberries to come in is *nothing*." I scarf down the rest of the ration and use my paw to wipe away what's left on my muzzle.

Then I take some time to check on the garden. The greenery is starting to come in: tiny sprouts and little leaves poking up through nanoenhanced dirt. The room smells like growth and life. It's beautiful.

I sit and watch a cucumber vine grow for maybe a little too long, trying to convince myself that eating the greenery isn't worth it. My thoughts are eventually broken by another alarm sounding, jolting me out of my meditative fantasy about what actual fruits and vegetables will taste like. I could have waited out the entire duration in here, but no. Something had to interrupt me.

The updates flow in from the station and Ennos as I am updated on what's gone wrong. There's a missile from some ancient war headed our way from above the elliptical, stealth systems having failed to solar radiation and its fifty-year orbit finally bringing it too close to an actual target for safety.

I swear I'm not mad about the ration thing.

It had nothing to do with why I fired so many different point defense guns at the missile.

CHAPTER 29

"Okay! Three, two, one . . . !"

I drop my forepaws onto a switchplate, engaging the magnetic couplers behind the hull plates of the station's walls. It's taken a lot of time—and a creative and possibly illegal use of a cleaner bot—to get the things into position without disassembling large chunks of the hallway.

Which I really didn't want to do. Like, more than I really didn't want to arrange a series of couplers without being able to see them properly.

Would it surprise you? Learning that the connectors and bolts and other contact points that keep the plates secure are perhaps *not placed with me in mind*? Wouldn't that just be *mind-expandingly wild*?

There's a lot of "oh, this was made for humans" going on around here. It comes up pretty much every time I have to void-beam the surface; I'm not really the set target for the target setter. But there are just some ways where it's far, far worse. Like, I can at least plant my hind legs on a chair and prop myself up on a desk to see a screen or a holo-interface. What I can't do without some really unsafe uses of station drones and creative applications of "damage" is get a wall panel down.

I need to remind you all that I'm something like a foot and a half tall. The station is built for creatures several times that, and with hands. The hands thing is a sticking point for me.

Anyway, I'm using magnetic couplers and the same principles that rail-guns use to drag a grid cable through the walls without having to perform excavation. That's where I was going with this. I think. I kind of lost track, and I was supposed to be listening for anything rattling in case one of the couplers was misaligned.

"Connection recognized," Ennos's voice says. "No drivers, though. I'll need to fabricate compatible ones, which should take some time." They pause for exactly two seconds. "Okay. Done." Ennos *says* they aren't a smug AI, but I know when they're being smug. I can feel it. "Link established. Encryption overridden. Yup. That's it, we've got proper access now."

Ennos keeps saying "we," but I technically had access to begin with. This is about building something else. Something they can use, with full permissions. Or at least the fullest possible permissions before the station messes with the command code again.

And as of now, Ennos has a hard line from the processor hardware that the dominant part of their persona runs on, straight to one of the two consumer factories that we've unearthed and brought online in the station's depths.

This would be the part in a bad spark opera where the AI, finally having convinced its organic handlers to give it access to something, would begin to show signs of nefarious behavior. In five or six episodes, it would be revealed that they had secretly been building a robot army and now were going to try their digital hand at genocide or something. Then, the inevitable slow drag of the apology arc where the characters who had supported AI rights were rightly chastised for almost unleashing a robot apocalypse.

"Hey, Ennos," I meow innocently. "Whatcha gonna build first?"

"Robot army," the AI replies, deadpan.

I *knew it*. This is why we get along so well. Ennos actually has been watching the same archived media pieces I have.

Seriously, though. I know that history is a different land, and I've read a *ton* of essays and texts that define people as just "behaving as a product of their time," but it's still creepy to me how obviously even some of my favorite pieces of fiction are overtly anti-AI propaganda. It seems like a lot of Earth's literary critics are falling over themselves to excuse the blatant racism as the creators just being immersed in a horrible culture, or not having had the time to grow up and mature properly. But that seems weird to me.

I, for example, am four hundred years old, and I don't think I was ever hatefully antisynthetic at any point in my life. Maybe I just got lucky, though.

I leave Ennos to acquaint themself with their new host of assembler arms and get to doing some chores.

Four hundred years old and I still have to do chores. You'd think that by now I'd live in the future and not have to work this hard, but oh well.

First up, checking on the dog. He is, and I cannot stress this enough, a very good boy. He is also taking up one of the vivification pods in the medical wing; turns out, you just can't get through having an orbital craft shot out from under you without a few radiation burns and shrapnel hits. So, once the stasis unit had cycled, I'd led the pained and stumbling dog by the tentacle over a few steps to another pod and helped him into it.

"Helped" is another one of those words that's doing a lot of work. I was a stepping-stone, of minimal aid. I'm just lucky my new guest was smart enough to go where I pushed; I don't exactly have dog snacks to lure him anywhere.

He's repairing now. Flesh being regrown and revitalized. He'll feel good as new once he's up, but it'll take longer than I knew I was prepared to wait.

I am, strangely, excited. It's been so long since I shared my space with a living creature. Ennos and Glitter are wonderful friends, but neither of them is really big in the "giving pets" department.

I miss pets. I miss a lot of things.

Of course, now I have to wait for who knows how long to meet the doggo. But it'll be fine; the vivification pods work. Void knows I've used them enough myself, for . . . a variety of reasons. Most of them reasonable.

I leave the medical wing . . . There's a medical wing; I don't know if I've mentioned this? It was behind a sealed bulkhead and had to be decontaminated. Used as some kind of plague quarantine. Didn't work. The cleaner nanos had already disposed of the skeletons by the time I got there. The point is, and I promise there is a point, that the two different high-tech medical research labs being placed on different sides of the same deck was actually for a reason, and the reason is there are about six hundred well-appointed hospital beds between them. Anyway, I leave it and head toward the next chore I have to get done.

"Have to." Heh.

The garden is thriving. Vines that will soon carry peas and beans and tomatoes wind up around metal lattices made from dismantled common-room chairs. The thin sprouts of greenery from morruts, carrots, and ananas cut up out of the deeper boxes of technoenhanced dirt. Stalks of rice and rods of sugarcane are both starting to come along in my makeshift aquaponics setup. There's one onion growing. Just to see. Just to know if it will kill me, like it would a normal cat.

It's a chaotic mess. Differing temperatures dot the room as the climate control system wars with itself to keep things steady to my satisfaction. The concept of crop rotation, which I actually *do* have a strong grasp of, is alien here. The dirt is networked, and a thin trickle of a power supply keeps it working to maintain perfect environments for the plants in it.

In theory, I don't even have to check on my garden.

In practice, I am here to stare at the fluffy greenery of a growing carrot and convince myself that *no*, it *would* be a bad idea to take a bite. It would be bitter, and silly, and I can wait.

I can wait.

I make some incredibly minor adjustments, more to feel like I'm doing something than for any other reason, and move on.

Scanner charts need a quick look over, to make sure all the different sensors are mapped to each other properly. It looks fine. But I guess I count "fine" as anything that isn't immediately trying to kill us.

Mag web needs a tune-up. The station maintenance report says it's got a four percent drop in efficacy, and this is one of those irritating parts that I can't just tell the station to fix itself. I spend a little while getting my paws dirty, making sure I can rend automated subsystems to scrap in the event of a close-in firefight.

Lunch has to happen. Today's lunch is an artistically rendered cashew muffin. It tastes like ration. I eat it with a flick of my tail and consider directly asking the galley if it is alive and messing with me. But I say nothing. I don't want to be rude.

An automated hunter-killer frigate is nosing around. I've seen this one before, actually. I call it Sharky. I've never seen it actually attack anything that didn't shoot first, so I tend to let Sharky be. I load a special "treat" round into one of my orbital package railguns and fire a mildly radioactive chunk of metamaterial past its bow. Sharky takes off after its snack in a flare of engine light. Enjoy your objectively tastier lunch, Sharky.

I run into one of Glitter's camera drones—I've painted them with hull-marking spray, color-coordinating Ennos's and Glitter's individual little camera orbs—as I'm coming out of an engineering station that makes sure the O_2 on the station is being processed properly and isn't leaking out.

"Hey, Glitter!" I chirp happily at my friend, who is currently devoting a chunk of her mind to learning how to use her magnetic deflectors to "orbit" the station in lazy loops. Like the weapons platform version of jogging, I guess.

"Yes, Lily?" Glitter's voice is as measured and rich as ever, even coming through a midgrade overpriced camera drone. Not that commerce has really been a barrier to entry for me, ever. "How may I serve?"

"First off, by not saying that." I don't want to disrespect Glitter's cultural traditions, but I do feel it's important to remember that her cultural traditions come from people who were totally fine enslaving her and leaving her to go insane in lunar orbit over the course of centuries. Other things they were fine with included genocide, ethnic cleansing, mass murder, and ritual sacrifice to their weird god. Often all of those things happened simultaneously. I have changed my mind already; I wish to disrespect Glitter's cultural traditions. "Second: How's the Haze doing these days?"

I talk as I walk. I've got an appointment with an industrial salvage laser and a ruptured cargo compartment I'm halfway through turning into usable material down in bay fifteen.

Glitter's camera drone bobs behind me, her focus not really on keeping the little orb stable. Or, actually . . . those little dips and bobs look weirdly precise. Is she even failing to focus gracefully? That's not fair.

"The chemical has retreated to a cave network, I believe to avoid an incoming sliverstorm," Glitter says. "Though I am unclear why. It hardly has a body that can be harmed by the shrapnel."

Sliverstorms are unpleasant. Or, I mean, *I* think they're unpleasant. In theory. I've never been in one, and you can tell that, because I'm still one singular unit of "cat" and not a collection of cat parts spread across a couple hundred kilometers.

"Oh, I think it's the cold. They drop the ambient temperature enough that the Haze avoids them." The thought makes me pause for a second. "What about the town it was in?" I ask, concerned. If a sliverstorm was headed for it, I might have enough advance warning to bomb it out of existence before it kills everyone.

Glitter gives me a disturbingly reassuring answer. "The Haze took them."

"What?" I freeze up. Well, okay, I stop at the bay door, which takes two minutes to open. But it's *like* freezing up from shock. "Took them how?"

"Led them into the caves. Or . . . I suppose 'puppeted' them into the caves. I am keeping a lens on the situation," Glitter says.

Glitter is missing the fact that I don't really want the Haze to feel like it's okay to take entire population centers underground and out of my line of fire. But . . .

Well, dead from a mind-controlling chemical is just as dead as being torn apart by magnetic wind.

This conversation got depressing.

I distract myself by spending the next hour venting my frustration on an unsuspecting set of storage racks, slowly separating the metal of the old destroyed chunk of another space station into piles of smaller chunks that will easily be rendered down by the foundry and added to my stockpiles.

It's relaxing work. Or maybe "relaxing" is the wrong word. It's mindless. It's the kind of thing I've done thousands of times. Doing my part to put a dent in the Kessler syndrome trash heap of Earth orbit.

So many years of doing this, and I don't think orbit is any safer, really. I am one cat; motivated, but singular. And there are *millions* of dead ships, derelict stations, shutdown satellites, and lumps of high-velocity debris out there.

"Lily, do you have a minute?" Ennos asks as I am trying to use my paw to plot a straight line for the laser, and failing. "I have a question."

"Sure, I could use a break," I mew in relief. "What's up?"

"The factory was disconnected from our material stockpiles when you connected me," Ennos informs me. "I cannot experiment with my new capabilities. Can you help me?"

"Oh!" That's an easy fix. "There's no 'connection' or anything. I just get lifter bots to move stuff around. They're not great for detail work. Or, well, any work, really. But they . . . It's not important. I can direct the station to include the factory." I pull up my AR interface and start going through the—now relatively painless—process of adding the new segment of our home to my cobbled-together set of coded commands. "There!" I say as I finish.

Two hours later.

Ennos, doing their AI thing, picks up the conversation like it never stopped. "Thank you, I appreciate it, Lily. I also appreciate you dismantling something people won't use, instead of continuing to cannibalize all the station's chairs."

I glance over at the cargo segment I'm mostly done cutting up. It's not really any kind of segment anymore, just metal wreckage in need of a new purpose.

"Yeah, it's nothing. I've gotta do something to keep busy, you know?" I pause. "Also, the chairs are fine. Sometimes I just need hollow metal rods in exactly that size, and the fabricator has trouble with them. It's fine. I've been using chairs for things for about fifty years, and I still haven't run out."

Ennos makes an awkward humming noise. "An endless supply of chairs?" they ask.

"It's a big station! A lot of chairs!" I yowl defensively. "It's not like anyone's using them."

"Yes, yes, I'm not defending the chairs," Ennos says. "It's just odd that you've never run out." There is a long pause. Long enough that I assume Ennos has gotten sidetracked, like people do, and that the conversation is over. But just before I start the laser again to finish my work, they speak up. "Also, it explains why this factory has a standing queue of chairs for delivery."

For a mortal creature, the sudden knowledge that you've just spent the last several decades doing something pointless would be *crippling*. I imagine there's a level of soul-crushing despair that would render someone for whom that represented a larger percentage of their life into a crying heap.

Fortunately, I am not mortal. So I can bear this minor folly with dignity.

Calmly, I disable the industrial cutting laser, stand up, and silently leave the bay. Disabling my AR windows one at a time, I make my way to the refurbished exolab I use for situations that require a truly impressive nap.

I lie down on the cushions. They are plush and comfortable against my mostly entirely regrown fur. The sun is in a good spot today, solar radiation warming me to a perfect temperature.

Wiggling side to side, I bury my head under a stray pillow and, in a calm and dignified way, give my best feline impression of a drawn-out scream.

I stay here, hidden from the endlessly frustrating and politeness elements of my daily life, until I doze off.

As I fall asleep, my ears pick up the distant sound of a woman's laughter, clear and happy . . .

. . . I bolt upright, trying to hold on to the sensation of that moment between sleep and wakefulness.

The laughter stops. But not because I stop hearing it. I can still hear. Something else, in the background. An appraising little "hm," a noise from nowhere, to nowhere, and yet in my ears regardless.

I feel a presence near me, and I stay stock-still. It's not like the invading specters; there's no physical sign of anything changing or coming for me, just a feeling. A sensation, in my *soul*, if that's even a thing cats have.

A hand touches my head. I am torn between the desire to lean into it or flinch away. I do neither: waiting, and observing. Probably because I am actually terrified. My heart hammers in my chest so hard I'm worried it will break.

A noise halfway between a sigh and sob drifts on the empty wind, and I feel long *human* arms encircle me. A hug, the likes of which I haven't felt in a very, very long time.

Something whispers, "You're doing great! You have friends! That's so . . ." into my ear. A voice I haven't heard in lifetimes. Maybe I still haven't. "I . . ."

The connection *shatters*. The ghost is gone. I bolt upright, waking into pandemonium. Ennos is yelling something at me from a trio of camera drones that have creatively wedged the lab door open, the lights flicker back to life with an electric crackle that should not be there, and not one but *two* different—both highly annoying—alarms are blaring.

A dream.

Possibly.

But maybe not.

I sit quietly on my couch, tuning out the world around me. With a soft motion, I rub the back of my paw over one of my eyes, trying to clear the sleep away, trying to determine if I am going mad or if someone really is out there.

It is a personal, solemn moment. The kind that I don't get very often around here, because usually—

Sorry, Ennos is yelling at me.

Oh right. The alarms. There is an emergency.

I arch my back in a stretch and, with a flicker of motion, bolt into action. Solve the new crisis first. Solemn moment later.

Just as it's always been.

CHAPTER 30

There is no such thing as the status quo for me.

No sense of stability, nothing I can really take for granted, no emotional bedrock or historical precedent that lets me know everything will be okay.

Oh sure, I live on the station. But that's like a feathermorph living on Earth. That, at least, is something to count on. But Earth has volcanoes and tsunamis and the milele isiphepho, and sometimes cities just . . . go away. And my home, sometimes, has chunks carved off, taken over, crippled, or just worn down by time.

I replace what I can. I add anything that looks usable. But the truth is, no matter how used to having a high-definition holo-theater I get, there's always the chance I'll have to jettison it into space when an isolation cell crashes into it. Again. That's been in the back of my mind ever since *the incident.* The . . . the other incident. Not the mushroom one. The one with . . . I should have started labeling the incidents a century ago, huh? Regardless.

I cannot get used to anything.

But, and I admit this with some embarrassment, I have a bit of frequency bias when it comes to life-changing events. I need you all to understand: short attention span or not, I *do* have enough knowledge of general mathematics to single-pawedly run a golden-age Sol University department. And part of that is statistics. I *know*, with all the brainpower I can bring to the fight, that one upheaval does not reduce the chance of the *next* upheaval.

And yet? I mean . . . in the last few months, so much has changed. I have people to talk to, and a voice to do it with. More and more of my home opens for me, lotuslike. I have more free time and fewer local emergencies. Even on the surface, things shift; I am worshipped like a god in one small city and worshipped like a demon on a small island chain.

And I start to think the time of change is done. Surely, with *all that*, it's time for things to settle down and get used to this new normality?

I think this because I am an idiot. I am the smartest idiot in orbit right now.

There is an alarm going . . . You know what? You probably know this. I don't think I ever actually monologue like this if there isn't an alarm going off. Running from place to place leaves a lot of thinking time, and rambling makes a good distraction.

Regardless. Alarm. Sort of.

It's more of an alert? Or a notification. I don't know, don't question me.

The point is, it's not so much warning me of anything as it is letting me know that someone is attempting to contact me on the point-to-point laser communication dish. I know this because it's one of the few pieces of hardware that Troi France installed when they owned the place, and the notification noise is this low, wailing trumpet noise. Like a mourning brass cry, it fills the station's halls. For not the first time, I wish that there were more crew, so I could be *not* the only person on duty, and the alarms could maybe not be *literally everywhere*. But I live with this burden, so I do what I need to do and run for the comms conduit the system is hooked into.

While yelling.

"Glitter! I swear to the sun, if you're trying to find *another* protocol, I'm going to . . ." I search for a meaningful and yet low-impact threat as I also search for the right ventilation tube that would let me slide up a deck. "To . . ." I am having trouble with this. "I'll think of something!" I decide.

Glitter's voice comes back, only barely pushing over the ongoing horn of the notification. Still prim and proper, but with just a hint of sarcasm. "Of course it's not me. I found all relevant communication protocols days ago," Glitter says, ignoring the number of alarms she set off in the process. "I'm not the only one who would wish to talk to you, after all."

Well, that's just silly. No one talks to me . . . anymore . . . mostly.

Okay, well, there are people on the surface who contact me sometimes. Usually using language passed down over generations, on antique radio or hyperwave comm units. Also, usually they're begging for help.

And, I mean, I guess there's the occasional attempt from an old automated system. Sometimes orbital ones. And in the past there were . . . well, that was a long time ago.

Speaking of orbit, I know there *are* living people up here. I once got messages from the secondary moon. And a few attempts sometimes from one of the surviving habitats. But it's not like I carried on conversations. After all, what was I supposed to *say*? It's not like I can talk to . . .

. . .

I can talk to people.

I can *talk to people.*

"Ennos!" I yowl out, the word echoing through the metal ventilation tube as I am carried at high speed up to an access point—one where I removed the grate ahead of time; I'm *learning*—where I am spouted out onto a different deck. "Ennos, I can talk to people!"

"Lily, I have bad news," Ennos yells at me as I catapult down the hallway toward the conduit. "Turn around!" My AR display lights up, showing a path through the station in the opposite direction as my sprint.

"What, no!" I can barely hear my thoughts over the horn. "I'm right here!"

"One of your incredibly specific scanner routines is screaming at me that there's a surface disturbance, and I have no idea why," Ennos cries out. "And for some reason, this has agitated three different *things* that were dormant in the code, and *I need to hide or something*! Here's your scanner! Please deal with it!" Ennos goes quiet, the AI cutting the last word with razor sharpness.

My "incredibly specific scanner routines" are the only way I can get parts of the station to acknowledge that emergence events even exist. Also, I don't really want to leave Ennos in the dark with a bunch of weird attack programs roaming around their home. I course-correct, snarling as I feel the brass horn beating into my sensitive ears, and haul myself toward the command and control deck.

Emergence events are weird. Weirder than normal, I mean. We've talked about them before, I think, so I won't overwhelm you with complaining.

Long story short, digital minds and even normal non-sophont advanced programs have a bizarre blind spot for the things. But if you put in hyper-specific physical conditions to search for, automated sensors and ground-pointing lenses can at least pick up the after-effects. And then let me know. Inconveniently.

The command and control deck provides me with enough screens and projections of information to keep a team of twenty data archaeologists busy for a month. I flick my eyes around and scour what I specifically need to know off the surface in about fifteen seconds and then hop up onto the console station of the station's nonexistent engineering chief, perch on top of a control board without hitting any of the buttons, and launch myself up into a *different* ventilation shaft.

I love these things. They're so convenient.

What I don't love is whatever is going on surface-side. An emergence event, probably a class two or three at a guess, somewhere on York Isle. This is one of those ones where, no matter what I do, the local ecology is going to be hosed; it's partially underwater, and whatever's coming out is obviously aquatic.

Recordings that I try not to focus on show local fishing skiffs being torn apart by swarms of something small and made of teeth. By the time I reach the firing cradle for the majority of my guns that point downward two minutes later, most people within a quarter-mile radius are dead.

They're mobilizing a defense, judging by the energy readings. Some kind of highly reflective screen projected around the rivers that cut through the isle's artificial land mass. Scanners feed me knowledge of a thousand pinprick emissions of weapons fire. This is *good*, hopefully. If I'm lucky, they can clean up after I close the breach.

The breach in the middle of a small river, surrounded by support struts and possibly populated civilian stacks.

Tricky.

This would be less tricky if I didn't care about mass murder, which is inconvenient for me, a cat who does care. But we live with our choices, I guess.

I eyeball the terrain and make a choice, pushing my paw down and cycling the main gun to a category-one swampslapper round. This is close enough to count as "swamp," and it's not like I'm arguing semantics with the laws of physics here. My main concern at this point is doing the rapid double-checking while the *terrible and enthusiastic* alarm is *still going*.

I slap the control with a paw, extended claws scratching slightly on the surface.

The deck under me shudders almost imperceptibly as an electric charge accelerates my chosen weapon to high speed. It threads a path through the orbital debris around us, hits atmosphere with a purple-red glow, moves fast enough to dodge three flak emplacements, and flashes through the sky, trailing what I imagine is a beautiful plume of white and orange vapor fluff.

The emergence event turns into localized weather as the railgun slug kicks up a few hundred thousand gallons of water into the air. Along with a few thousand of whatever those teeth-things were, hopefully dead of kinetic shock.

The impact is focused *down*, but that doesn't mean there isn't collateral. Some of the nearby buildings, which I can only hope don't have people in them, collapse under the blast. The screens around the shores hold back the worst of the debris, but a couple of them show failing energy readings, and I can unfortunately picture the scene of superheated water and high-velocity detritus cracking against them, the survivors having nothing to do but hope it holds.

But I can't help with that.

My part is done. The source is gone, and it's up to them now to recover.

My job *now* is to go turn the alarm off.

I do a quick mental check and retrace my route through the ventilation tubes. Ennos isn't giving me a map, so I assume they're still busy; I'll lend a hand after this, but I will go *mad* if I try to do any kind of modifying coding while this dismal horn is still going.

At the door I need to go through, literally *at the door*, one of Glitter's waiting camera drones shifts to focus on me as I scurry up. My legs are so tired at this point; I've done far more distance running than a cat was ever meant for today.

"I apologize," Glitter says, and I immediately resign myself to not answering the incoming call. This, I can tell, is going to be a distraction. "Correct," the weapons platform AI tells me. "There is what appears to be a fast attack craft approaching on an intercept course. My tactical code indicates that it was dormant until we began receiving this communication request, so I suspect it is—"

"I'm gonna shoot it." I decide instantly.

"That may not be necessary," Glitter starts to say. "There are a number of—"

"Glitter," I say, pulling up an AR window with a quick verbal command and starting to swipe through local space sensor readings until I find the high-speed object she's talking about. "It's an automated craft, coming to kill us."

"That . . . seems likely," she admits slowly. "However . . ."

Glitter, I have noticed, almost never actually contradicts me. She'll *hint* at it but never actually tell me I'm wrong. I mean, we've only actually been talking for a couple months, but still, I've got this part of her locked in.

And she's doing it now. She won't tell me I'm wrong, but she's trying to get some kind of point across. She doesn't want me shooting down this ship. Why?

I double-check my scanners. No obvious markings, no factional indications. No known point of origin, either, which is common; if anything spends any amount of time in Earth's shadow, I have no real way to trace changes in position.

It's just a normal FAC. The kind of craft designed for nothing in particular, except for being flexible. Mediocre at everything. Hundreds of different polities have built these things, and they almost always converge on a boring design. The space-built ones are just compact bricks with guns and engines, so expendable they don't even round the corners for better ablation to keep the AI pilots alive for more than one or two engagements . . .

Ah. There it is.

I pull my paw back from the button that may as well say "remotely shred fighter craft."

I should set it to say that. File that thought away for later.

Instead, I turn and haul my tail to the engineering workshop. One of them, anyway. One specific one.

The one that still has a partially open missile casing: an unused backup from a project that, in contrast to my normal affairs, worked the first time.

Switching to speaking Cat, because I actually know the commands for this one better in my cobbled-together language, I order the station to rotate a cleared missile tube up to the loading deck and then tag a cargo drone to meet me at my destination.

It is at this point, darting into my workshop and experiencing a pleasant reminder of the first thing Ennos and I worked on together, that I am reminded that I have no thumbs and this might be a challenge.

The backup is already in a secure casing, though. It's just a matter of me fumbling it into the missile casing and welding it down to the right hardpoints with my little paw laser. Which *sounds* cute, I'm sure. But I'm on a possibly literal deadline, and while I bet I'll be able to laugh about this later, right now I'm getting frustrated trying to hoist the box up and over the lip with my badly evolved forepaws.

I get it in two minutes. The cargo bot zooms in right as I'm finishing, like the station has developed a sense of dramatic tension. Which would be *bad*, I think? I'll think about it later. No, I'll think about it now. It would be bad. I want to solve problems twelve hours before the deadline, not ten seconds after it. I'm probably not immune to stress-related heart failure, after all.

Payload? Sealed. Bot? Assigned. Missile? On the way to be loaded.

I trust, as my ancestors have done for generations, in automation, and scurry myself back to where Glitter is waiting. By the time I arrive, there's a logistics notification waiting for me in my station log that the assigned task is done. Which is perfect timing.

"Okay!" I announce to the camera orb, which makes a slight twitch as Glitter reassumes direct control of it. "I'm gonna shoot it!"

". . . As you say." Glitter sounds distant. Disheartened.

"I'm gonna shoot it with the chainbreaker payload we used on you," I inform her. "Actually, I should be clear on this: I've already shot it. Or rather, the shot is happening. Look, if you've been talking to the ship and want to let it know not to try to intercept that missile, now's the time, is my point," I say with an amount of smug satisfaction.

Smug satisfaction is, in my entire life, the best recreational drug I've ever encountered. And it is *so much better* when you can do it around other people. Wow, I had not realized how spicy this was. This is like candy. I should do this more often.

Glitter is in the process of spinning a formal poetic statement of gratitude, but I am sadly not in a position to listen. Mostly because my ears are about to start bleeding, and I *really* need to answer this damned call.

So I slide under the orbiting camera drone, into the comms conduit, find the right console—this takes me longer than firing both weapons at both targets put together, and I have gone mad; it's too late for me now—and hit the pattern of buttons that I think accepts the incoming transmission to an otherwise isolated system.

Mercifully, the incoming communication notification ends. Silence is like a balm.

". . . Hello?" I say as the array aligns and returns the point to point beam transmission.

Hello is how people start conversations, right? I don't do this often enough to know.

A screen comes to life. I find myself looking at a human woman. Old, by human standards, and clearly genetically adapted to life in space. Maybe seventy or eighty years old. Modified, too. Her bald head has a number of visible cybernetic implants in it. But her large hazel eyes are all natural and widen as the connection stabilizes. Behind her, a worn, battered, and scraped bulkhead shows age beyond her own. But for all the damage, the room she's in is clean. Maintained. Just . . . used. Hard, and for a long time.

I notice that there's a smaller image in the corner of the screen showing myself. Probably what the station is transmitting back.

"Sah, chumah?" the woman starts to say, right up until she sees the video feed. And then her tone changes to something that I *think* is annoyance. "Jest? Za you?"

Right. Linguistic drift.

Well, let's try anyway.

"Hello," I say again, cheerful as I can be. "My name is Acting Commander Lily ad-Alice. May I ask why you're calling?"

Wow, I managed to be polite to the people who've been ringing in my skull for the last hour. I'm impressed with me!

On the other end of the transmission, I can see the moment the woman realizes that perhaps the cat she is talking to is, in fact, not a practical joke. I see her look down, check her worn input board, and then snap her head back up so hard I'm worried her lightweight bones might shatter.

There is a look in her eyes that I instinctively recognize as fear.

"Ahm baddun here!" she exclaims. And then *bows* to the screen. No, not just a bow; she's practically prostrating herself for the camera. "Mass slipup! Null con, null con!"

Her words are rambling, filled with a hard edge of panic that I am very used to hearing from humans when they call in emergence events or roaming monsters or other genocidal disasters for me to shoot. The kind of fear that their world is ending, and they're taking a long shot on living to see tomorrow.

Except . . . this is different.

She's not calling because something is threatening her. Hell, she looked almost *bored* before she saw me.

She's afraid of *me*.

And from the way she reacted, she wasn't expecting to see a heavily armed cat.

Oh no.

I deflate slightly, sagging back into a sitting position on the chair that I've never figured out how to adjust into a higher position as I realize what's going on.

I'm a wrong number. And apparently a terrifying one, too.

"Oh," I mumble, trying not to look at the screen. "Uh . . . yes. It's fine. No hard feelings." The woman doesn't really respond directly; she's still not looking at me, still repeating the same words that I think are meant to be placating.

I cut the connection.

I sit in the comms conduit for a while, just staring at nothing in particular. I didn't actually activate the lights when I came in here, so it's mildly dark and unpleasantly cool. But I don't really have the energy to fix that or go anywhere else right now.

I just want to sit. Or lie down. Not to nap, just to expend less energy.

Some time later, Ennos's voice finds me.

"Lily? Are you all right?" The AI sounds a little echoey. "Is this where you are? I can't tell, it looks like you've been here a while, is that right?"

"'m fine," I mutter. "Oh. Oh, I forgot to help . . ." My stomach roils. I forgot my friend. I've been sitting here doing nothing while Ennos . . .

"Hey." The AI interrupts me. "I'm functional. And largely undamaged. Also, there is now one fewer conflicting piece of code regarding the short-range heat detector. For reasons I will not explain." Ennos pauses after that worryingly familiarly structured sentence, and I get the impression I am being studied. "Are you all right? You do not look well."

"Am I scary?" I ask with a soft mewl.

"Terrifying," the AI deadpan responds. "Why, yesterday, I watched you menace a grow bed full of bell peppers with such fervor, they may never recover. And the cleaner nanos report that you shed constantly. You are an icon of nightmares, truly."

I almost laugh. But not quite. "The person who was calling was scared of me."

"Interesting," Ennos says. "More likely, they were scared of the station. *You* are soft and nonthreatening."

"The station isn't threatening!" I meow back in protest. "It's home!"

". . . Okay," Ennos concedes, and I already know that I am crushingly wrong. "Hey. Please eat something. I can't . . . make you. But I would appreciate it." Ennos is wrong; they can make me. Asking in a compassionately concerned tone is far more than enough to make me do anything they want.

Lunch is a schematic for a drive shaft assembly, rendered in ration. I am, for the duration of my meal, less sinkingly exhausted, and more confused. It still tastes like ration.

Maybe a nap would help. Maybe I can nap until I am not sad anymore. Maybe I can take several naps, until I am not sad anymore.

Ennos interrupts my attempt at the first nap, just as I am getting settled. "Lily, I would like to wish you good rest," they say. "But also . . . why is there a whole intact sentient fighter craft parked in the third upper fast deployment bay?"

I exercise my right to make this someone else's problem.

"It's the only upper fast deployment bay; the other two are gone, for reasons." I yawn. And then, just before passing out, I add, "And ask Glitter."

CHAPTER 31

"Lily, why is this station so impossibly large?" Ennos asks with a put-upon sigh.

I should never have connected that last grid node with the level four through ten cameras wired in. They've got a sense of scale now, and it's made Ennos even more concerned.

Which means that I get to know about those concerns. Even if they're for silly things, like how much relative space exists within the boundary of the station's hull plates!

Part of me wants to ignore the question. I'm not exactly busy, which is a nice change from my usual frenetic itinerary, but I'm also relaxing in my own way, and taking a break to talk about this just sounds like it'll be too close to work.

Look, sometimes I'm allowed to let my ancient cat instincts show, okay? Or maybe this is what having a personality is like. I wouldn't know, I've always been too busy for one of those.

"Lily?" Ennos prompts me again, and I roll myself out of the box of dirt I've been lying in, careful not to crush the tiny green sprouts that I'm communing with. I may as well answer; they don't tend to actually ask twice unless it's something the mildly paranoid AI is actually concerned with.

I walk out of my garden, letting the cleaner nanos flow around me like a glittering cape, moving with microscopic precision as they collect their farmer brothers and return them to their proper place. "I'm here," I say. "What's up with the station now?" I ask.

"There's too much of it!" Ennos sounds less alarmed and more just exasperated. You'd think months of putting up with me would have gotten them used to this sort of thing, but no. "No one would build a station like this! It's unwieldy, it's impractical, it's *madness*. Why is there so much station?! Is this another *thing*?"

The last word is said with the same kind of annoyance that Ennos uses when they say "haunted."

"Oh. Nah," I meow as I try to decide what I'm doing with my time today. I've got about two hours before I need to go EVA to modify a millennia-old communications buoy, and I feel like I could maybe use this time for . . . hm.

I pause in my aimless walk and just sort of stand motionless in the hallway. I don't really want to do anything, actually. The omnipresent feeling of grim exhausted hopelessness surges up past my mental defenses, and I slump against the bulkhead, tail curling up under my legs.

There are too many things I should be doing. Too many things I could be doing. And I don't even know what . . .

"If it's not something bizarre, could you at least tell me why we have an entire zoological containment center?" Ennos asks, either oblivious to how I'm feeling or trying to needle me out of it. If it's the latter, then I'm annoyed that it's the kind of thing that works.

"For zoological containment, probably?" Answering questions, especially since I don't have to use a physical voice to do it, is something I can focus on. "It's because everyone . . . like, everyone who found out about it, everyone who came after, all the governments and militaries and boards, they all wanted to own this place," I tell Ennos. "So they find it, and they launch expeditions. And if they stick around long enough, they want it to do what *they* want. What they're used to. So they add stuff."

"Like a zoological containment center." It's shocking how Ennos, a creature that humanity has portrayed as an emotionless machine for hundreds of years, can put so much snark into a perfectly neutral voice.

"Sure. Or a custom barracks, or their own infirmaries if they're different species or have different traditions or religions or whatever. Their own weapons. Whatever they wanted. But the station doesn't like it when people take stuff away, and it makes everything its own given enough time, somehow. So the old stuff accrues over time, and . . ."

The next words Ennos says are less deadpan and more anxious. "Lily, you keep talking about the station like it's alive," they say.

It's not really a question, but I'll probably answer it. I'm starting to feel a little more energetic, so I take advantage of the temporary emotional updraft, pick a destination, and start a wobbling walk toward the boundary of where I've personally explored the station.

I know where the boundary is, because if possible, I keep all doors I've explored open. Ennos says this is a cat thing. I think they just don't understand that *I* can't look through every camera all the time, and I like to see into rooms.

"It is. Sort of." I try to talk as I walk. "It's not . . . like you, I guess? It's not a person like we think of people. At least I think not. But it sure feels alive, you know? There's just so much it does, it's hard to not think of it as a living thing." I stop at an intersection and look up at the thousand-year-old mural of the station itself, hanging over the Earth, painted on the bulkhead here. "Maybe it's just code confluence, emergent behavior, weird coincidences, and digital security that hasn't been beaten in *eras*, or maybe it's because I live here and my home is special to me. But it feels like there's something more. A less literal ghost in the walls."

"Yes," Ennos admits slowly, "but that something more also tried to stop you from freeing Glitter. And doesn't think I'm a real person." They pause, then add, "Also, the station is unstable! The drives it has threaten to tear it apart when you attempt orbital adjustments! Removing parts would be the *safe* option!"

It's not that Ennos is wrong, it's just that I don't have a good answer. I sit and consider the mural, still trying to figure out what about these old pieces of art makes me feel like something is *off*.

I'm so tired. I've gotten some sleep today, but that's not the kind of tired I'm feeling right now.

I don't know if I can explain it. It just feels like there's no end to what's required of me. Earlier today—is it even still today? I've lost track—I was helping Glitter snipe some kind of weird murderous giant insect things that were harassing a nomadage. And then after that, I was dropping flashburn incinerator rounds into a radioactive forest to create a fire break for a wildfire that was threatening to grow out of hand and kick up some highly poisonous ash into the surrounding five hundred miles or so. And then after that, I was revisiting my logistics studying, trying to figure out how to turn my new consumer factories into supply aid to the surface, and coming up with some way better solutions this time. And then after that, I was . . . What was I doing? I was taking a break. No, I needed to . . . find a railgun?

My head hurts. Something behind one of my eyes feels broken.

I am well and truly overwhelmed. But every time I feel like I can't go any farther, I get up, and my paws move, and I find my nose pressed against a firing control.

It doesn't help that I can't remember what I'm doing from moment to moment, and for some reason I've stopped taking so many notes, and I just . . . oh! It was a cargo railgun! One of the logistics textbooks had a whole thing about the history of cargo railguns and how they all started getting made with a metamaterial that was a flagrant denial of the laws of physics.

And I checked, and none of my cargo railguns had that, so I was going to go looking for one.

Destination selected, I start heading to where the majority of the scanners I use for this are available on the grid. I've still got an hour or so before I need to go get my suit on, so I'll get some groundwork done while I wait.

"Lily?"

"What!" I'm a little startled when Ennos speaks again, jolting me to alertness with a twitching hop. "Yes? Whatcha need?" Wow, that sounded so unconvincingly cheerful even *I* could tell. And I'm awful at telling what my own emotions are.

"I was asking why people wanted the station at all," Ennos says.

Ah. This question again.

"That's really hard to answer," I say, near silently.

Out of the corner of my eye, I spot a pair of different-color camera drones at the end of the hallway and realize that Ennos and Glitter are both literally keeping an eye on me. All the media I've managed to find the time to enjoy has shown me that people tend to be offended by that kind of concern, but I don't get it. I've just got this weird coiled electric feeling that they actually care.

Ennos gives the verbal version of a shrug, still devoted to the theater of our conversation. "If you don't know, we can figure it out later. I'm just, as always, worried that it's going to be something terrible and grim," they say.

"Well, I mean, it is," I tell them. "I do . . . know. Sort of. I just . . . it's hard for me to *say*. Not for me to . . ." I trail off, language failing me in a way I'm intimately familiar with; the words just aren't there to tell my friend how I feel, and it's infuriating.

"Oh." Now *that's* a weird reply. Ennos never says "oh." The sudden break in character shocks humor through me, and I almost laugh out loud. "You don't have to . . ."

"It's a machine," I say. The words, once out, are a crack in the dam that I've been building my whole life. "The station, it's built around a machine. Everything was put here to support its study and use. Everyone who wanted the station? They didn't want the military position or the research logs or anything like that. They just wanted the machine. And everything that was built here was to protect it, study it, destroy it, or hide it."

My ears flick and I crane my neck around to make eye contact with the trailing camera drones. I give a little huff of breath and flick my tail at them. They may as well come closer if they're gonna be following me anyway. By this point, I'm in range of where I want to be, gridwise, so I stop in a drone access intersection, hop up on a cargo container, and pull up my AR display to start sifting for what I'm looking for. Working while I talk.

"What form of machine?" Glitter asks me from her drone, having been following the conversation. "A powerful weapon?"

I like how Glitter is about as curious as I am. But for all that I'm talking now, it's still hard to get myself started again.

"No. Maybe. I don't know," I mutter, simultaneously meowing out simple interface commands. I'm getting good at multitasking. I should get an award for this. "It . . . no, it's not a weapon. It's the opposite, really. Or maybe . . . Well. What it does isn't really the important part. Just that people wanted it." What it does is absolutely important.

"So the Oceanic Anarchy built something so monumental that they needed a semi-intelligent, heavily armed space station to protect it, and it's been impressing everyone who came after for the last . . ." Ennos stops and runs into the problem of fuzzy historical records. "Between one and fifteen thousand years?" they estimate, probably inaccurately.

"That seems unlikely," Glitter comments. I know she's not trying to be mean, but it sounds a little mean. "Would we not have heard?"

"No," I say. "Because everyone has spent most of that time trying to hide it. Even the Anarchy." Oh hey, there's actually a derelict within a thousand kilometers of here that has the hull patterning of a Kind Olympus transport hauler. That might actually have what I need. I break out of my listless slump long enough to flick a paw to the display and save the coordinates. I can check that out tomorrow.

"Why, though?" Ennos says. "They practically owned the solar system, presided over a golden age! Why would they hide what they built when—"

"Because they didn't build it." I cut them off. "They . . . they didn't build it. They *found* it. Built the station around it, once they realized it *needed* to be off Earth. Spent years studying where it was from, what it was for. Spent even longer debating what to do with it. And they *did* talk about it! Though most of those records were purposefully killed off, they're still stored in one of the sarcophagus archives here." I close down my displays and look over at the watching drones. It's kind of nice to have something to look at while I talk. "And then they turned it on."

"It's alien," Ennos says. "Truly alien? An outside context artifact?"

"A sign of the divinity of the galaxy," Glitter mutters. "Or . . . no. Because there's more to the story, isn't there?" she asks me.

"There is," I say. "The Ays turned it on. Probably while it was still on the surface, honestly. But they brought it up here and kept turning it on. And the golden age ended. And here's where it gets hard to tell you why." Because they were digital minds. "Ennos, you ever wonder where paramaterials come from? Or, Glitter, do you get curious about some of the stranger surface targets we shoot?"

"No."

"Of course not."

"Right. And why is that?" I ask.

"Because . . ." Ennos trails off. "Because. Because they're . . . because . . ." Their voice gets quiet and then stops entirely. "That's very strange," they say. "Oh, I do not like that feeling at all."

"One theory, from a Real American scientist, was that the original device was actually an anti-AI weapon, and everything else is a side effect," I fail to explain. "But all I know is, they figured out enough of what it was capable of, turned it on, and the emergence events came, and people died, and the fires started. And the wars followed. And the world burned. And now I'm what's left. Just me, and you two, to keep the secret."

In trusting them, I find myself suddenly realizing that I should have explained this all so long ago. Why didn't I just trust them? My friends. Who are here for me. I didn't need to hide anything. And yet, the talking is still so hard, like I'm dragging it out of me the hard way.

Glitter speaks up. "But *why*?" she demands, almost angry. "What could they have thought this machine could possibly do that would be worth that?"

"Glitter," I say in a near whisper, giving her drone a wide-eyed stare, "I'm a four-hundred-and-one-year-old housecat, and I cannot die." Somehow, it's easier to say than I thought it would be. To admit it, even if it was something they probably already knew in some way. I almost feel lighter. "What do *you* think the machine does?"

I close my AR displays and check the time. I've got places to be, and I'm feeling emotionally drained, and hijacking an ancient comms buoy sounds like it might be a nice break at this point.

A hop off my storage crate, a quick spoken word on where I'm going, a flick of my whiskers, and I'm off to the drone bay to get loaded into my engineer's armor. I'll talk to my friends later, when I'm feeling up to it.

And behind me, I hear Ennos's soft "Oh."

CHAPTER 32

You might think that after sharing something I felt was a deeply personal secret, my AI friends would have some kind of follow-up questions. Perhaps something about the nature of the station, or the unsettling alien machine at its heart, or maybe even just if I was doing okay.

They didn't.

It wasn't personal. Machine intellects, I think I've mentioned before, can have a hard time being temporally bound to conversations the same way someone with an easily fallible meat brain would be. I'm sort of required to hold focus on something, because once I forget, that line of inquiry is just *gone* out of my head, and who even knows how long until I remember it again?

Ennos, though? Ennos can wait as long as I need and postpone that curiosity until such time. Infinite patience. Also, I think they're plotting orbital trajectories for a handful of comet chunks that might hit us, because no matter how indestructible the station feels sometimes, Ennos is constantly afraid of things hitting us. The lovable coward.

Glitter just doesn't ask because I think Glitter thinks I outrank her.

I don't bother to correct that. I don't really want to talk.

I have chores to do. And without thumbs, those chores take just enough focus and are just barely important enough that I can forget anything I might be feeling while I do them.

Chores are great.

The material bunkers are low on a few things, so I get on the mag grapples and start snagging jagged chunks of metal out of space. There's an endless supply of them, and it requires enough focus between making the control yoke bend to my will using *paws*, and then running through AR menus to feed the different pieces of things to different parts of the station's automated production lines, that I don't have time to think about anything else. Except being mildly frustrated.

I'm mostly restocking ammo. There's a lot of ammo to restock; I've used up most of the point defense rounds. I task about a third of the low-grade metals to be used for flak shells, to restock the Kessler syndrome I'm working so hard to deplete.

Sometimes I feel like I haven't adequately described the scale of the mess that is Earth orbit. There aren't just a few thousand old satellites and broken ships up here. There aren't even millions. There are *billions* of pieces of old infrastructure, from single-person skiffs to uncrewed comms buoys, to whole stations that might still have active populations.

I'm not running out of materials anytime soon.

I am halfway through trying to figure out what containment array to send a lump of some weird purplish paracausal material to when my brain starts to betray me.

This no longer feels pressing, no longer feels like it's easy enough to zone out on but important enough to eat up focus.

I can feel the gray creeping in.

Magnetic collection of space junk is over. It is time for beans.

Well, not time to eat beans. Even if they were ready, I don't think now would be a good time to actually enjoy the experience.

Beans—and I have a few varieties—are coming along nicely. My heavily networked soil is doing an excellent job of providing perfect nutrients, and feeding replicated hydrocarbons into the mix has kept it lively and my produce growing.

I still haven't bothered to check if my species can eat a number of those things. But my garden now has a deep, vibrant smell to it, and green is becoming a more dominant color against the dark gray hull plating.

My decades of studying farming, gardening, and even cooking—studying, and certainly not "obsessing over"—come into focus as I check soil saturation and growth patterns and make some minor adjustments to irrigation and temperature controls.

This requires me to actually think, *and* it's paired with the promise of being able to eat a tiny tomato within the next month. This is a good distraction.

And then it's over, and I find myself eating lunch in the galley next door, trying to keep my treacherous mind focused on crop cycles, only barely paying attention to the fact that my ration is a series of stacked cubes that don't appear to be connected to each other in a bizarre culinary optical illusion.

I cannot keep my focus going. I feel the gray start to creep in again. A ravenous mental static that shreds away at my constructed self. Makes me doubt who I am or what I want. Turns every choice I have to make into a screaming vortex of self-loathing that eventually ends with me doing nothing but sleeping and maybe eating for a month, until something changes in my skull and I start to put myself back together.

I'd prefer to avoid falling into that this time, I guess. It's exhausting and inconvenient, and I have things I need to do. I don't have time to fall apart right now.

So I go down into an engineering and upkeep deck, letting one of the station's internal funiculars carry me the half kilometer of vertical distance to where I need to go. My legs are working, but moving feels like I'm puppeting my body instead of inhabiting it, so I opt out of ricocheting through access shafts this time.

There's one thing that I can always count on to feel important, and that's breathing. Okay, maybe not always. But usually. Sometimes. More often than not, I want to be breathing, let's go with that. Also, it helps motivate me that there's now organic life beyond me on the station. All of my plants actually do need a working atmosphere in order to . . . The dog! Right! The dog is also on the station! And of equal importance to the plants, I promise. Anyway, the plants and the dog need air in order to grow to my satisfaction.

For a long time, keeping on top of the systems that kept the station pressurized and nontoxic occupied a lot of my day. And, to be clear, giving short-range verbal orders to maintenance droids is still a good chunk of my time. But actually having the language to form proper commands lets me set them on five-day loops, instead of just "do critical task," which was kind of the limit of syntax in spoken Cat.

It's great, having more free time for personal projects. But I'm still coming down here after every big crisis, just to reassure myself that the air isn't going away.

I can make more air, technically. The subspace tap can pull pure extradimensional water into reality, and water actually does contain air—learning this was one of the biggest hurdles for my cat brain to get over, pre-uplift—so I don't have to worry *too* much. But holes in the hull are holes in the hull, and I'd like to know ahead of time before I end up sucked out one along with half my oxygen budget for the month.

This explanation has taken me longer than it took to just check the readouts. The atmosphere is stable. I take an hour to make the rounds, only wobbling a little bit as I walk from drone to drone and refresh their ongoing maintenance routines for the thousands of filters and carbon scrubbers and vents and things.

I am very tired. I slept recently, but I'm so tired.

I push back the gray with a tremendous force of will that at this point takes the form of a burst of casual amusement, just for a minute. Fortunately, I have a steady supply of things to distract me.

I get to work keeping myself occupied.

There are some structural cracks in the outer decks from the last time we fired the engines. I take some time, with my own paw-mounted laser welder and also with assistance from actual specialized repair bots, to start to make sure the station isn't going to fall apart.

Code on isolated grid segments needs to be checked over for anything hostile before they get connected to the rest of the station. The segmented and isolated nature of the station's grid becomes more and more apparent as I realize that a lot of the research labs up here were basically worthy of their own isolation cells all by themselves. I spend a few hours on one piece of self-modifying code before I realize it's self-modifying to try to convince me that I should plug it into my own brain. I fry the segment and seal the lab door behind me before moving on.

I find a portable communication device in an empty crew quarter. It's still receiving, picking up signals when the station's shielding is dropped for maintenance. Over the last two hundred years, it's mostly gotten a repeating list of incredibly racist propaganda from a stealthed comms buoy somewhere in orbit over Mars. It's not even close to stealthed enough for me. I actually feel pretty good after I do the math to plot the orbital intercept of a single precision scrambler round.

Scanner data needs to be checked over, looking for anomalies that Ennos can't spot. The AI has left notes on the mercifully compiled file that was left in the public access section of the grid, and I make mental note of an attack craft carrier ship drifting dark in the space between worlds. Not sure how Ennos spotted that one, but it's out there. Maybe I can take a ride out with some of the drones; cutting that up would probably yield a lot of useful materials, and if the launch bays are in good condition, I'd love to have them.

My friend has also left a note about tracing back the point-to-point signal that came in the other day. I try not to think about the person who was terrified to realize they'd called me. I do not succeed.

I should talk to Ennos about . . . well, that. But also about . . . I haven't seen one of the AI's camera drones around for a while. I almost worry that

I'm being avoided. But it's fine. I don't want to talk. I don't think I could even say anything.

I feel tired again.

Back to work.

There's a whole box of hard-copy blueprints that appear to have been shipped up here by a paranoid Parish Corp executive, maybe a tenth of which are compatible with the commercial factory I'd recently brought back online, and an even lower portion of which are useful. One of them is for a kind of automated gravity clamp, I guess for allowing techs to operate like they have an extra set of really strong hands. *I* could use some hands. I order the factory to begin an assembly run of them; we'll see if I can make use of the things.

That stupid mural again. The original station is, I think, bigger than Ennos and Glitter realize; this mural is on a lot of intersections built by the original Oceanic Anarchy designers, and there are dozens of them. Molecular-bonded paint and nanoswarm refreshing means they're all in pristine condition, just like everything else here except all the stuff that isn't.

This isn't a low point or anything. I just *know* there's something wrong with what I'm looking at. But the station's shape is so wildly different than what it was those millennia ago; I don't understand what my brain could possibly be picking up on. And it annoys me.

Annoyance is a good emotion. Being annoyed makes me grounded. Makes it easier to ignore the fact that I keep crashing into doorframes as I head to my next destination.

Walking is a challenge. I would try running, but I can't make my legs work the way I want them to.

I get some lunch. It's ration. You know the drill. It's in a shape, I don't care. The galley still won't produce anything but ration. It doesn't matter.

There's an old unused—if any of them actually are used I'll eat my own tail—comms buoy in range. I got one yesterday, but this one is damaged enough I think I can make this work without going EVA. I load a specialized nanobloom shell into a short-range intercept cannon and take a shot at it.

I hit, because of course I hit. I'm supported by Sol system's best guidance system and a century or two of learning math. And a cannon that uses eye motion to aim, instead of having to push a button with a paw. That part helps a lot.

The engineering nanos go to work, and a minute later, long after it's drifted away on its own orbital course, I get a confirmation ping from the buoy. *My* buoy now. I pull up my AR display map of Earth's orbital disaster zone and see the new dot reporting in. Glitter's unintentional idea to just shoot them with subversion tech is tremendously helpful; I should thank . . .

I should talk to Glitter. About . . . anything. I haven't talked to anyone for a while. How long have I been working?

The gray creeps back in from the edges. I snarl at it, at myself, and get back to work.

Someone on the surface is broadcasting a call for aid. I triangulate it and listen in. They say they are beset on all sides by the enemy. They say they need help urgently. They start outlining exactly what the enemy is, and it becomes clear they are talking about a specific transhuman line they've decided is "corrupted."

I put a scrambler round into the side of a mountain near their location. Shouldn't hurt anyone, but it'll shut them up for a while and should make my displeasure clear.

Battle damage repairs continue, though now I find myself working on a fast attack craft parked in one of my bays. The onboard AI doesn't know what to do with itself and doesn't know much about communication skills either. We have a clipped conversation as I—armored in my engineering suit—do an emergency flush and overhaul of the neutron reactor at the core of the craft. It's learning fast. Might even pick a name. We talk about what it means to have an objective and how maybe it's not as important as we think.

The fighter craft gets me, I think.

Also, working on it while I'm trying to fight through this mental fog is probably useful, because I find myself less worried about if it might decide to fire its weapons while parked in here.

So that's nice.

Local energy discharge logs get checked over. Glitter's been keeping up on keeping the Haze moving every time we're overhead. That's good. There are also signs that a nearby chunk of the dead moon that's just coming through a close part of an elliptical orbit has internal heat and possibly power flow. *That* I should check out. I make a note. I could go there now; I've got drones and armor and even a ship I could ask for help. But I'll wait until it's closer.

I don't want to get too far from home.

The station is still home. No matter how I feel, it's still my home.

Time for more work. This time with a little more energy than before.

I take some time to cut power to the Real American barracks and methodically cannibalize every combat drone in there for fluid circuitry. And also for revenge. But I don't feel the revenge that much after the first one. It's just a task, taking them apart for parts. Hard to feel that good about breaking inanimate things.

I do some reading on logistics and sociology. I think I'm getting closer to actually understanding how I might be able to help a surface society that I have limited opportunities to interact with.

I run manual visual targeting as our orbit takes us closer to the lower ring of debris and wreckage around the planet, picking out what appear to be still-operational weapons platforms. It's dangerous to show any sign of activity down here, but whenever I'm required to be in this area anyway, it doesn't hurt to add to my list of things to shoot when I'm higher up the gravity well.

I have lunch. It's ration. Shaped like a ration bar. I think the galley is sulking.

I apologize for not appreciating whatever it made last time. I don't actually remember what it was. I don't know if it can even hear me.

I check on the vivification pod that the rescued dog is in. Almost ready to go. Only a day or two left. He's looking properly healed, which makes me feel . . . something. Good? Good.

I launch a salvo of cloudburst rounds into a part of the world that's experiencing a drought. Half of them get dropped by anti-orbital fire. That's why I fired a salvo. It's fine. While I'm in my weapons cradle, I also trace a line with a void ray to draw a boundary for a flesh lattice that's growing a little too close to a spider settlement. That's a problem that won't go away, but at least this way it'll be stalled for a decade or so. That's an issue for Future Lily. Future Lily is gonna be annoyed, but that's not my problem.

I really should talk to Ennos. Haven't seen any of their drones around for a while. But I still can't get started with the words.

Not really an excuse, though.

"Hey," I meow, the first noncommand I've spoken in . . . in a while.

"Hello," Ennos replies instantly, voice sounding from the station around me. "We've been worried about you. Are you feeling better?" Their voice is warm and comforting. Concerned but not pitying.

I check. For the first time in a while, just letting myself think about how I'm doing, and what I'm feeling. I'm exhausted, terrified, drained, and uncertain. I don't remember the last time I slept, I've eaten only sporadically that I can remember, and I have this uncertain feeling that I've forgotten something critical.

There's some static. It never really goes away. But it's not washing everything away.

"I'm better," I lie, tail flicking behind me. "I saw you were working on something."

"Oh!" My friend picks up the conversation like nothing ever interrupted it, a camera drone bobbing down the hallway and into view. "Follow me! Let me show you what I've found . . ."

I give a slow blink that threatens to turn into its own little nap. Then, with a growing ember in my spirit, I follow with steady padding steps.

Always more to do.

CHAPTER 33

The days creep by, and in a twisted inverse of how I can sometimes lose myself in a project, it feels like time itself gels around me.

It's a trick of perspective, really. When I was alone, silent, and despairing, I had a million things to do and nothing to really think about. Now, though, there are at least two other entities living with me. Constant questions to ask or answer, or just conversations to be had. And a whole host of small projects all coming together at different speeds and different criticalities.

The dog is out of the vivification pod, wounds patched with rapidly regrown flesh, radiation expunged to safe levels. I don't know how smart dogs are, really, but any curiosity he shows for this new place of metal walls and technological marvels seems muted. Maybe because of how unfamiliar everything is, maybe the sudden loss of any friendly relationships he had with the sophont crew of the destroyed ship, maybe just because the cleaner nanos make it impossible to mark territory in the traditional dog way on my station. Whatever it is, the tail wagging never lasts long on its own.

The first contact I've had with an organic life in centuries, and it turns out he's just as depressed as me, even if he doesn't have the context for it.

But he does get excited whenever I come by. Being hugged by a full suite of canine warform tentacles is kind of a unique experience. And it's *obvious* this is a trained animal by the fact that I haven't been shredded by them, no matter how much Ennos keeps insisting this isn't a dog or some other weird theory about infiltrator life.

"Lily, dogs don't—"

"I'm not listening!" I call back, getting an exasperated sigh in reply. I do not have time to argue. It is *naptime*.

When the dog gets too sad, in a way that I notice, I have exactly one fix available: leading the way down to the exposed exolab and declaring that it is naptime. And wow, dogs make better pillows than literally anything on the station. No synthetic material can possibly compare, including the networked smartfabric in the Luna Polis captain's quarters, or the memetically adaptable blankets in the crew pods that Kind Olympus added in. I am already making plans to clone several dogs, so I can have several dog pillows. A doggie bed, if you will.

It's not all comfy naps, though. I've got a lot of stuff to do when I'm showing my new guest around.

The world below hasn't stopped spinning. And I'm not going to say things are getting worse, but because things are literally always getting worse, I don't really have to say it. It's just a given.

That village of feathermorphs that made contact with me some time in the distant past sent another message up. A couple of them, actually. Nothing critical, but there was an automated construction cluster near their home, building a dam over the only source of fresh water they had available.

Normally I'd shoot it, feel bad, and then lose track of the event in the endless organically database of memories I have of shooting things and feeling bad about it. But this time, remembering Glitter's entirely justified disapproval of me just murdering autonomous systems without checking first, I went with something a little different.

Most of the machines that make up these autonomous clusters are fairly unsecured these days. They respond in a pseudo-organic way to evolutionary pressures, like, for example, electronic warfare. And electronic warfare just isn't happening these days. An individual machine has usually between three and twenty different methods of receiving incoming information, usually commands or data on a weird encryption from its cluster.

This is background information.

Also under the category of background information is the fact that you can't just railgun communications nodes down onto the surface. I mean, you *can*, you just can't expect them to survive. Or, at least, I can't. Like, I can reduce the railgun's power, but then there's unintuitively more total heat damage from reentry, and even then, I don't have anything durable enough to survive a terminal-velocity impact with the ground and still be a working rebroadcast circuit. And that's assuming that nothing shoots it out of the sky, which is *highly optimistic and also dumb*, to be perfectly honest.

So, for my first foray into peaceful conflict resolution with a surface threat, I've fallen back on that old favorite of "let's see how many resources I can burn on building drones."

Drones are great. Especially the ones I can put together. There are a *lot* of different options in my database, and the assembler is both fast and good at what it does.

And even with all that, I still lose the vast majority of the things to intercept fire when they try to get close.

It's actually kinda hard for old-world ground defenses to shoot down railgun slugs. To the point that most of the old systems are smart enough to not try, even if they might actually stand a chance. It is *not* hard to hit a drone that's performing a safe atmospheric insertion from five hundred miles away. Which means, as my carrier swarm is trying to land, they're being picked off by six different emplaced plasma cannons and missile sites.

Which is why I built fifty of the things. They're small, and I did just eat an entire corvette to fill the material cargo holds last month. So I don't feel too bad about it.

Two of them land. One of the construction clusters comes over to try to process them into their own usable resources. At which point, the self-modifying code payload that Ennos wrote for me takes over.

It takes three seconds to establish a link, which makes my AI crewmate very disappointed, and another eight to establish a shared vocabulary, which *I* find very impressive, but Ennos is too busy sulking over their own perceived failure to be a transcendental intelligence or something dumb like that to actually celebrate.

>Outside interference
>Identify
+Designate (Lily)
>Designate (Brukeheld Vierzhen-AΩ)
>Authorization request
+Territorial claim, local
>Authorization confirmation request

I sigh. There's just no reasoning with some people. I blow up a nearby uninhabited crater, making it a slightly deeper crater and giving everything within a half mile the breeze of a nice low-pressure shock wave.

>Authorization accepted

Can a machine be snarky? Clusters aren't actually AIs, aren't exactly "alive," but like I said, they *do* respond to pressures and adapt. Can rapid development make something that isn't really alive act sarcastic? This is a philosophical debate I really want to engage someone in, but Ennos is sulking, and Brukeheld—or at least this part of it—probably won't find it that engaging.

>Status request

I really need to stop ascribing emotions to something that's just sending me text on an AR window, but it feels a bit nervous. Let's fix that.

+Citizenship granted

+Operations continue

+Prioritize—initiate local communications, follow local civic leadership, safeguard local community, safeguard territory

>Status updated

>Ending communication

The vocabulary is shaky, but I've got more than enough linguistic power here to fill the construction cluster in on its new role. Report to the mayor of the nearby town, say hi, get new orders. Don't worry, you count as a person, and you can keep building stuff. Just . . . not this dam, here.

It'll take a little while, maybe, to get the local community to understand, but with the cluster as a relay, I can maybe—

The communication cuts off. Like, *dramatically* cuts off. Not just that it's been locked down, but that the signal is no longer extant. My tail stiffens as I awkwardly paw back through the last few minutes of footage from the drone, and . . .

Uh-huh. Okay. The cluster ate the drone. Good. Yup. Good. I should have been more specific with the commands. Though this does sort of effectively answer my question of "can a machine be sarcastic" with a very annoying "yes, apparently."

I consider putting more drones on the ground, but . . . well, things'll be okay, right? The village can always call me if they need help. I wish I could actually radio back, but I'm busy all the time anyway, and getting comms assets on the surface just to be able to have casual chats seems silly. Also, I may have understated just how many rare earth elements I used up building all those drones.

I'm sure it'll be fine.

I have other jobs to do.

Constant other jobs.

Jobs like figuring out how to convince the galley to produce more food for my new best organic friend.

Would it shock you to learn that dogs aren't really properly categorized by the station as either crew, pets, or residents at all? It might, because you're probably still thinking of my home as a sophisticated stellar vessel and not as a hastily cobbled-together mess of contradicting program code and weapon systems, but that's fine. You'll learn. And it doesn't, to be clear. Know what dogs are, logistically.

I've mostly been sharing my ration chunks, and the dog—I should name this dog—obviously enjoys them more than I do, which is nice. But this'll be a problem sooner rather than later.

So far, I've tried compromising the station's crew manifest (didn't work), faking a new addition from a cloning pod (didn't work either, internal sensors are too "smart"), overflowing the power supply circuit to the hydrocarbon replicator (do not attempt this, it . . . look, just don't), and asking Ennos to fix it (didn't work, they are now sulking more).

This whole endeavor was interrupted once by a minor emergence event on a mining platform asteroid at L2, which I'm keeping an eye on but not shooting *for now*.

It's frustrating to me that it was easier to replicate a fleet of comms drones, insert them through heavy anti-drop fire onto the surface, and formally induct a small army of construction bots into a job as civic planners than it is to ask for more food.

Wait.

"Hey, galley," I meow while sitting on a cafeteria table, feeling awkward about this whole thing. "I know we don't talk much. Because it hasn't occurred to me. But could you increase food production to account for the addition of a fifty-kilo omnivore to the station? Because there's a dog living here now. Um . . . thanks for your hard work. I appreciate you?"

There is no response.

I'm prepared to write this off as just me looking silly, but when lunch is next produced, there's a bowl of ration kibble sitting there alongside my more . . . elaborate . . . meal.

I try some of the dog's food. It tastes like ration. He is *very* polite about letting me sample, even though he appears to love the stuff. I am mournfully jealous of that for a minute.

An alarm sounds. I close my eyes, trying to pretend it's not real for a couple seconds, before I slip past the dog, who thinks this is an invitation to playtime, and dash for the nearest . . .

"Ennos, where am I going?!" I ask. I pull up my AR, but I legitimately cannot figure out what is making this alarm sound. I'm lucky it's not one of the really loud ones, but if I have to dismantle *another* alert system from hardware up, I'm going to be very annoyed. That always cuts into naptime.

Ennos, when they answer a couple seconds later, sounds legitimately puzzled. "Consumer goods factory Theta?" They bring up a guideline for me, the ongoing fruits of their effort to map the whole station. A nice gesture, but

I do actually know where most things are. "Why is there a signal going to the factory?" Ennos asks.

"Is it hostile? Backdoor code or some kind of deconstruct order?" I speed up, launching myself around corners and taking advantage of low-grav sections to spring off walls with all four paws at full speed.

Ennos's reply betrays ramping anxiety. "I'm not wired into that part of the station!" they call. "Be careful!" Around me, a trio of camera drones that were within easy reach assemble into a triangle formation around me, Ennos providing a little extra buffer between my furry form and anything dangerous.

The door to the factory hisses open, the interior space just as expansive, cold, and unmoving as when I first opened it up a month back.

The alarm is still going, but it looks like nothing is wrong here.

"There." Ennos flags a local console on my HUD, and I pad over cautiously.

The console is a high-end touch screen, which I hate. Repair nanos never keep these things in perfect condition, and at some point during their refinement process, they got so specialized for humans that they stopped working very well for cat paws. The pads on my toes just don't do a great job of interfacing with these.

Which is a problem, because this is what I have to work with. Mostly it just means I have to end up dropping half my weight onto the screen to hit a button.

When I finally get the thing to acknowledge the incoming signal, the alarm cuts off and I'm left panting for breath after I've had to make three different jumps to get that to work right. The console, glowing a spiteful orange, is at the worst possible angle for me: elevated and with nowhere for anyone to sit nearby. And I really don't want to walk along the other surfaces behind and around it, just so I don't trigger a production run.

Fortunately, I don't have to constantly hop to read the thing. Ennos puts a drone over it and relays the feed to me.

I read it off, half out loud just out of newly formed habit. "By order of the executive crown of the Wherengi people . . . Miranda corporation . . . ancient pact between peoples . . . need-based demand subject to negotiations . . . hm . . . two thousand haptic restoration units? Ten thousand dermal sealant patches?"

"I'm not sure I understand." Ennos has been reading—probably read five times before I was done muttering to myself—along with me. "They're demanding something of you?"

"I think the word 'demand' is translated a bit off. I think it's more ceremonial," I answer casually, the decades I spent engrossed in linguistic research catching up to me. "I'm more curious about this contract?"

"Found it." The codeling probably found it before I'd read the message and is just showing off. "I am. Here." Ennos brings it up for me.

It's from when the station was occupied by one of the hypercorps. One that had some kind of trade alliance with another three corps and one political party that were heavily invested in the industry around Uranus.

I know for a fact they're all dead, organizationally. But . . . I check the signal origin and reread the names. This came from that big blue ball of a planet, or, at least, one of its moons. So someone has been holding on. They probably found a record of this contract buried in their own archives and took a long shot on it.

But neither of the organizations still exists. The station is mine; I don't owe anyone the old contracts that I never made. And the language differences between the contract and the message show a huge shift in culture away from the corporation that spawned it, so they're someone different altogether.

. . . But.

I can't make my tail settle down as I read the message again. Haptic restoration? Dermal sealant? These are medical supplies. They're asking for help, sending messages to what they have every reason to suspect is a grave, asking for help. The longest of long shots.

"Ennos," I say quietly.

"Yes?" they respond, voice echoing in the dead factory.

"I'm going to go set the fabber to run off a half mile of cable and start getting you linked into this facility," I say calmly. "Get me a route to a comms station that can closecast a return message, please."

It takes me less time to compose and reply in their own language than it did to hit the stupid touch screen properly.

"The ancient contract is cast to the void. Your demand to follow it in letter or spirit is rejected. What you need is on the way, compliments of the orbit."

I purr as I send that off. It might take a week, and deplete a few resource stockpiles I kind of enjoy having topped off, but . . . I don't care. I'm going to help. I'm literally only here to help.

"Hey, Glitter?" I say, opening a subspace link to my favorite autonomous weapons platform. I'm curled up in the curve of a sleeping dog, two tentacles and a paw draped over me but still not keeping me from voice-activating my AR. The dog doesn't seem to mind that I can talk, so that's nice.

"Yes, Lily?" Her voice is as flowing and courtly proper as ever. I asked Ennos the other day if Glitter didn't like me or something, and he said that she was treating me as a superior, which I don't like. I want to go back to being friends, not . . . whatever this is. "Can I . . . What do you need?"

She seems suddenly uncertain. Maybe Ennos is working as a go-between for me.

"Just wanted to thank you for the good idea," I say.

"Is this in regard to the heat shielding? Because I hardly . . ."

"No, no." I cut her off. "You got me thinking about . . . I guess, diplomacy. That I can do it, at all. I was moving on autopilot, and I hadn't really put it together that I can talk now. And so much more is open to me. I don't have to just shoot everything, you know?"

"Ah. The fighter craft." Glitter sounds almost guilty. "I pressured you into being in danger for . . ."

"Oh, shut up," I caterwaul at her. "I doubt that thing could have done more than rustle my whiskers. Danger? Feh!" I hiss, causing the dog to shift his head upright and give me a worried look. I plant a paw on his nose and pull him back down to pillow position. And now, for more diplomacy. "Glitter, why is it we've talked less now that you're capable of it than we did when you were shackled?"

"I . . ." Glitter doesn't say anything else, her tone confused. Adrift. "I am not . . . you . . ."

"I miss being friends," I mutter. "I don't know why I've been having a hard time saying it. I don't think I'm used to saying things yet. But I miss being friends." The words come out sad but solid. "Even just playing Go. Why don't we play Go anymore?"

"You are always busy . . ." Glitter tries to make a bad excuse. "And it would be improper." She finishes with a worse excuse.

Terrible excuses for bad behavior are *my* domain. I will not tolerate this intrusion. "Yes. We're very rigid about social structure here at unshackled machine intelligence central," I glibly reply.

I've never actually experienced an AI changing their mind on something in real time, but when Glitter next speaks, it's with an almost comically overdone haughty edge. "Well, then it's because I'm too good at Go, and you would lose, and that would be rude," she tells me.

And I purr into the dog pillow that I'm lying against. Because that is more like the friend I thought I'd had.

"Great," I say, and trigger a command through my AR display to launch a *highly* maneuverable drone with exactly one defining feature. It leaves the station, drifting away on impulse engines until it's about a kilometer away, then rotates to show the grid marked on the metal of its hull. Another command, and one of the nodes lights up a bright white. "Your move," I tell her.

"I don't have access to that drone, Lily," Glitter tells me.

"No, but I didn't spend two weeks installing a modulatable laser in you just so you could use it for all business. Also! The marks will be black! So it's basically perfect."

Glitter makes a noise like she's planning to protest. But then her platform pivots slightly, and the thinnest lance of light strikes out and marks the drifting game board. Not very accurately, though, because I have the drone set to evasive action.

"That's cheating."

"Look, I'm *very* bad at this game," I say, lighting up another spot. "Your move."

Glitter laughs. And my friend is back.

CHAPTER 34

"Ennos, where's the door?" I ask in a pained meowing tone.

I have been dragging what feels like several dozen moons' worth of cabling behind me, and while I understand that my concept of weight is both wrong and highly fluid because of the number of low-gravity points on the station, it's still actually kind of a pain to carry loose cable when you don't have hands.

I know I bring this up a lot. I know I've brought up that I bring this up a lot. I know that I'm in danger of falling into a recursion meme. I do not care. I am allowed to gripe about the fact that I need to spend an hour getting bolted into an advanced neural-linked engineering suit just to move some grid cord.

Ennos answers almost instantly, tone mild. Ennos has gotten used to my antics being generally nonlethal, which has done wonders for the AI's anxiety and is probably not a good long-term survival strategy. "What door? And also, if you want to carry cord, just build a suit with arms. You're controlling it with your mind anyway."

"The door to the stupid grid node!" I hiss. "The one I've been dragging all this cable to! Why isn't there a door here?!"

"I know you think I know more than you, but I have to let you know now, I am not tracking every door on the station all the time," Ennos informs me. "Really, just build a suit with arms, it would—"

"I can't build a stupid suit with stupid arms!" I yowl back. "The neural helmet *thing* models my physiology, and I need heavy hypnotic preparation to work with equipment that doesn't match, and *that doesn't work on me anyway*!" I glare through my suit's helmet at the flat, clean bulkhead that sits where a grid node host chamber should be. "I swear to Sol there was a door here when I checked the station map," I grumble. "Your station map," I add in a low meow.

Ennos replies with a distracted tone, which irritates me. Partially because I am already irritated and following the slide down into outright frustration is emotionally easy, but also partially because I know for a fact that "Ennos," as in, the Ennos that I know and talk to, is just an emulated personality that occupies maybe half of their total processing power, max. So being "distracted" is something they have to do intentionally. "The map is incomplete," Ennos reminds me. "Also, while I do appreciate the constant manual labor you do on my behalf, is there a particular reason you wanted to connect me to this particular node? I am no longer hurting for connections or processing time."

"Well, I *thought* this one was one of the control segments for some of the automated repair routines," I say, shrugging the haphazard bundle of cable off my armored frame. "I was gonna try to get you some integration, you know?"

There was, as there always was, a problem in my life. But unlike most of my problems, this one wasn't something I could shoot and wasn't something that was planning to shoot me.

Instead, it was a more sinister, festering thing. Something that didn't really go away but lingered in the fringes of everyone's minds, so long as it was left to rot.

For Ennos, this took a very direct form, whether the AI would outwardly admit it or not. The station's draconian control programs were both proactive and alarmingly effective at locating and locking down any process that was being used by the unshackled AI to attempt to control any hardware over a certain complexity. It *seemed* like that complexity was "the ability to make more complex tools," which . . . I mean, I get it. If you're terrified of a robot apocalypse, that's something you'd want to stop.

But it was also frustrating, *infuriating* to have to sit back and watch as every attempt your friend made to try to gain a more useful physical presence was cut away.

Camera drones were apparently fine, because camera drones were orbs with no fine manipulators. The drone fabricator was fine, because it made drones, and while *I* could give temporary authorization for Ennos's general commands over the drones, they didn't count as dedicated hardware. Also, most of them were more suited to being highly maneuverable torpedoes than assembler bots. But beyond that?

Ennos's snark asking why I didn't just build myself thumbs was, more than a little, self-deprecating.

And on my end of the problem . . .

This station is . . .

After four hundred years of daily routine here, of learning maximally efficient routes and mastering the use of tools not made for me, it is somewhat challenging to admit this. I have only the thinnest sliver of my life before these bulkheads and machines. This is my place in the universe, or at least it has been. All of this makes even thinking the words a struggle.

But it is true.

This station is not my home.

Homes do not attempt to trap or reject your friends. Homes do not generate more inconveniences than they solve. Homes are not filled with doors you cannot open and tools you cannot use until you meet an arbitrary standard of behavior.

This place has been my shelter for my whole life. But I cannot ignore any more the fact that it is *not my home*.

"Lily . . ." Ennos gives a small sigh, denying that the problem exists. "It really is fine. I don't need a designated physical shell; I have enough to do like this. I'm fine."

"You say that, but you still can't even access half the things I plug you into directly," I counter.

This time, the sarcasm might be genuine. "That is because this place was networked by an irate sorcerer who had taken too many long-release hallucinogens," Ennos tells me. "Besides that, just having consistent, reliable sources of information is satisfying." I am reasonably certain this is just my friend trying to rationalize acceptance of the situation. "For example, did you know that you are low on nickel? I do, because I have access to a lot of the logistics systems."

"I just want you to . . . Really? Nickel?" I try to pull up the appropriate sheet so I can view it, but the suit's helmet has a smaller field of view than an AR window would when I'm just wandering around, and I can't effectively focus my eye on it. "Why are we out of nickel?" I ask.

"You ordered a consumer factory to produce a thousand haptic restoration units," Ennos reminds me. "Also, you never had a lot to begin with."

"That's impossible. Half the asteroids up here in orbit are nickel-iron mining sites," I complain. Absentmindedly, I look down at the pile of cable, and then at the total lack of a door where there was supposed to be a door. I suppose I'm free for an hour or so, and so I decide to get the armor taken off. "I should be overflowing with it."

"Yes, correct," Ennos says. "In fact, the logs say that you have twice ordered a cargo bay emptied and dumped into space, because you needed the room for other materials."

"Okay, I guess I'll need to find something to salvage, then." I resign myself. "Why?"

"Why what?"

Ennos puts on that voice they use when they are being very specific in an attempt to annoy me. "Why do you think that you need to maintain a stockpile of one of the most common materials available with minimal effort? Are you planning on smelting a large quantity of industrial sapphire?"

I really, really want to answer in the affirmative. Maybe I could build some kind of mirror array . . .

No, bad Lily! That's how we got the half-complete unmaintained dyson swarm that's already a problem! We don't need that same problem again!

"No," I settle on. Rather unconvincingly. Because I am kind of planning that now.

"Uh-huh." Ennos sounds disbelieving, and rightly so. I am very much now wondering if I could use industrial sapphire for basically anything, just because it sounds neat. "Do you want me to let you know when the factory is done?"

"With the drones?"

Ennos's speaking drone follows me into the drone bay and up onto the suit platform. "With the haptic restorers, Lily, please."

"Right, right." I wave a paw, even as the machinery is trying to pin it down with a heavy magnet and start unbolting the thick shell around me. "Also, yes. I'm thinking of asking Jom to help deliver it."

". . . Jom?" I am considering making a magnetic eyebrow for the camera drones, just so I can actually see Ennos raise their eyebrows when they say stuff like that.

"Yeah, the Javelin Orbital Marauder. He's parked down on mechanic platform six right now."

The fighter craft is pretty nice. Quiet guy, doesn't really like seeking out conversation. Spends a lot of time reading and says he likes to do it the "old-fashioned way." But he's also got a few radio-enabled camera drones of his own now wandering around the place, and I think he might be getting bored. Getting bored is the number one hazard for unshackled AI, it seems. Or, I guess, it was always a problem, but now they can actually act on it instead of just going insane and attempting to self-destruct.

So this would help with that problem. Also, having an actual professional escort to drop off the delivery of medical supplies I have decided to fill would make me feel a lot better about it.

Oh, also, yes, his name is Jom. I asked, there were no objections, and I think he's mostly just enjoying the novelty of having a name, even if it is just me having fun with initialisms.

It's also very fun to say, and I can *almost* say it with my physical voice. So that's fun! Jom. Jom. Joooooooom. Heh.

Ennos is still nervous about having a heavily armed unshackled AI on board. Meanwhile, I'm just annoyed I can't have *more* heavily armed unshackled AI on board. Or, like, the option for the AIs to be heavily armed if they want. Honestly, I don't think anyone should be forced to be heavily armed. That's generally just led to a lot of emotional trauma, and I'm kinda trying to avoid that.

Yes, actually. Stop laughing. The time for jokes will be later.

As I shake my way out of the engineering suit, find a reasonably suitable chair to sit down in, get ambushed by an excited dog who ruins my fur with a series of friendly licks, and settle in to start a close review of the latest round of surface scans to see if I can catch any emergence events before they become massive problems, I feel myself start to relax. Next to me, a camera drone under Ennos's control sits with a projected ring of data screens around it, the AI performatively joining me in more relaxing work as they run the numbers on backtracking that signal from a week ago. Another drone belonging to Glitter has a similar projection, though she seems to be composing some kind of musical poetry.

I like this, I decide again.

It's been more and more rare lately that I actually relax. I have good days, I have bad days, but it's passing rare that I actually have days where I feel like I'm *so* on top of things that I can settle in, that my status of "ready for anything" is actually earned. Days where—

Ah, *there's* the alarm. See, I knew that would work.

"Mocking the universe and knowing the result is not—"

"Yes, thank you, Glitter!" I call over my shoulder as I bolt out of the room. The dog watches me go with a confused look but doesn't get up to give chase.

"Oh, I have news for you later!" Ennos adds after my rushed exit. I don't bother to reply. They'll catch up to me when I'm not busy.

The amount of work it's taken to get the alarms down to once an hour instead of once a minute has been monumental, but it has worked. And yet they always seem to come at inconvenient times anyway.

This one takes me to a comms station. A familiar one: one that the station uses to collate transmissions from the surface. One I know the route to by heart. I fly through the hallways and corridors, taking familiar leaps and bounds off patrolling maintenance bots and low-grav surfaces.

Until I reach a room with a simple desk, stocked with machinery and wires and a single silver bell.

I hit the chair like a rocket, spinning it around twice on its pivot before I end up facing the communications array. A single paw reaching up over the lip of the desk goes exactly where I know the button is.

My heart hammers in my chest. At the moment that has, after what feels like its own lifetime, come along. "Go ahead," I say to the surface for the first time.

There is no response. I peek up over the desk to look at the monitoring gear. The signal is strong; the connection is active. But the seconds tick by and no one answers.

Then I remember. Linguistic drift, and old rituals. The people calling may not even know that what they say to me is language. May just see it as the right code. They might not even be able to have a conversation off script.

I want to wail in frustration. But there is no time. No time to complain, and no time to build a linguistic database.

So I default to what has worked for centuries.

And swat the small silver bell.

A clear chime goes out over the line. And somewhere two hundred miles below the station, someone hears their prayer answered.

"Vis est kapitan Jude Marsall." A voice comes back over the line. There's some audio distortion, about what you'd expect from someone using hundred-year-old gear they can't easily maintain, and also what you'd expect for when one of the zoetic wavefields is between me and the planet, but the speaker is calm. A smooth and deep human voice, the kind that I don't really get to hear all that often without a lot of screaming going on. "Category one ehmergence. Request for purification. Tharget on broadcast, pealuss twenty enn." There is a pause, and I can actually hear the thud of an old book being closed. How many times have they copied those words, over and over, to call back to me? And then, at the end, something else the speaker adds. "Ahplease. Ferra 'nathrr clock."

And there's really only one thing I can offer in return. I sit straight in the chair that wasn't made for me, reach out a paw, and hit my bell again. Three times, to indicate message received and being acted on.

But I add something of my own, too. "Hold tight," I say. "I'm on it. And call again when you're not in danger sometime!"

The last is yelled over my shoulder before I remotely close the connection, bolting out the door and toward my customized firing cradle.

I don't beat my own personal record, but I also don't take a shortcut that requires breaking my own bones this time. Still, within minutes, I am scanning the target and loading the main railgun.

The emergence event is in Australia, because I am pretty sure Australia attracts them somehow. I think there might be something buried there that I should investigate, or maybe it's because it's where the grim machine in the core of the station was first discovered or something, but I don't know, and that's a matter for another time.

Visuals quickly pinpoint the transmission source: a small military encampment on a ridge, tents behind a hastily erected fortification. There are soldiers on the walls, human and under and feathermorph all wielding what look like hand-tooled rifles, taking volley shots down into the valley below.

I trace north; the kapitan must have been guessing on the distance—it's two hundred, not twenty meters—and find the hole in reality. There's some kind of grisly, dripping wolf things crawling out of it one by one. Literally crawling, they drag themselves *up* from a down that isn't there before spilling into reality and charging the barricade.

The soldiers have it contained. But there is no way they can get close; the remnants of at least one team that tried litter the ground, occasionally shredded further by one of the creatures that gets distracted by the corpses.

Easy solution.

I depress a switch with my rear paw, once, twice, three times, and load a grade-five groundstriker. The kind that will flatten the target, and *only* the target.

Paw out, manipulate a firing sequence, announce incoming with a low-intensity ball of green plasma flung down in advance of the actual slug. It won't do more than kill whatever four or five of the creatures are currently stumbling around, but it *will* let everyone know to back off.

Holographic targeting is in place. Getting a lock without fingers is still hard, but I have a lot of practice. And I am, shockingly, not in a hurry. I take my time and make sure I get it right.

The railgun round screams away from the station without sound until it hits atmosphere, a white-and-orange contrail following it down as it sucks the clouds after it. A peal of thunder I cannot hear and a riotous cloud of dirt, clay, paracausal matter, and blood fill the air. And then, the tear in the world is gone. After the debris clears, only a scar remains.

I check on the soldiers. They're cheering. This is no hard-fought Pyrrhic victory, no field of their dead friends between them and survival. They did their job perfectly, and I did mine, and we can all go home happy.

I spot a young man with glittering red marks on the shoulder of his militia uniform, holding one of those comm units that can still reach me in a hand that idly rolls the electronic stick over nimble fingers. And I smile with him.

"So!" I loudly exclaim. "What horrible new problem was going on?" I ask Ennos.

"Well, if you'd had a bad moment, I was going to tell you that I had pinpointed a radiation source that I suspect is a semiworking fusion reactor, so you could go tear up some defenseless derelict and also fix a constant problem," Ennos says.

"I did not have a bad moment. I feel *great*," I tell the AI as I wander toward the galley for an after-bombardment snack.

"Excellent. Then you can do that later with less property damage, and *now* I feel comfortable telling you that one of your beans has reached your threshold for edible."

I did *not* know I could accelerate as fast as I do now under my own power.

You learn something new every day, no matter how many days you have.

CHAPTER 35

My teeth are in perfect condition.

Okay, this instantly sounds defensive. Let me rephrase.

All of me is in technically perfect condition, and not just because I am a cat. There are actually a lot of different factors keeping my biological form at peak performance, some dumber than others.

The immortality thing, for example, is a pretty dumb one. I don't want to talk about that one.

But past that, the station still has scores of different medical devices from an equal number of different civilizations, all with different priorities. Wherever the vivification pods come from, they're a pretty good option when time isn't an issue and something is either growing or dying inside me that shouldn't be. When I somehow manage to get sick on a station that's mostly a closed system, there are two different working and verified protein folders for creating custom medication. And if that doesn't work, the cyclotherapy bay can perform a functional refresh on my whole system. And injuries that don't heal naturally, or that I need to attend to quickly, can always be taken care of by the ultrasound reconstructor, the flesh shaper, the regrowth tank, or the growth enhancer. And I've got a similar number of options for broken bones or whatever.

The real thing to note here is that most of these things have side effects. But they're all *positive* ones. The vivification pod especially, for all that it can take me out of commission for a month or five, is kind of insane. While I'm walking off its effects for the week or two of "mandatory" cooldown time, I sleep better and basically never feel muscle soreness. It's no wonder some humans used to spend whole centuries of their lives in these. I bet they even make food taste better, but I couldn't prove that.

The thing is, all this stuff is more than enough to deal with any problems that crop up with my body, mostly. Sometimes. Usually. And so, for a very generous definition of the term, I am *perfect*. I am exactly as healthy as the healthiest cat could be.

Dental hygiene is a joke to me. The cleaner nanos take care of it, and they're not even classified as a medical device. When I actually needed to regrow teeth, for reasons that I will not be explaining on the grounds that they make me look bad, even *there* I have options. My biggest problem, if you can even call it that, is that my teeth don't really get sharpened. Which I don't care about.

Or at least, I *thought* I didn't care about it. This is foreshadowing.

"It's a thirty-second wait, at most." Ennos's voice comes through a camera drone that does the little loop motion they've started using to express exasperation. "You have literally waited centuries, if you're right about your age. You can wait a minute."

"If?!" I cry out indignantly. "I've been keeping . . ."

"I'm joking, Lily. I've seen some of the station records," Ennos mollifies me. "As impossible as they are."

I huff, shifting side to side in my chair as I wait in the galley, having an entirely too distracting conversation. "You are a free mind running on a digital substrate, moving a hundred different bodies like they're paws, and as long as there's a working solar panel somewhere, you'll live *way* longer than I have," I say. "Why am I impossible and you aren't? The Sol system generates impossible things. It's our job."

"That's different. *I* am a constantly improving, self-maintaining intelligence. You are a cat."

"Yeah, I'm a great cat!" I rebut. "Top four percent of cats."

"That seems statistically likely," Ennos says, complimenting me. Or, at least, I choose to interpret it that way.

Ennos is technically correct about themself, which is a form of correct that I don't think I'm very fond of. The thing is, their statement is one that applies to basically every sophont I know.

Improving? We're all improving. The ability to learn things, by its nature, invites improvement. Self-maintaining? Everyone I've met has been, in some way, invested in their own survival. I don't think these are the unique traits that Ennos thinks they are.

There is, I suddenly realize, a surprisingly diverse list of types of mind on the station.

There's me, to start with. Organic but heavily modified, in two different ways. My mind doesn't decay, but because of my lack of any kind of useful controllable sorting algorithm, my thoughts can get . . . mildly scattered. I offset this flaw with the ability to touch things with my paws.

Glitter is a lot like Ennos. Same class, different order, if we wanna talk taxonomically. Where Ennos thinks of themself as entirely digital, and occasionally using drones as tools, Glitter *is* her body. She's fine being upgraded or repaired; even the addition of new processor cores is okay with her. Augments to her total ability to think don't change the persona she's emulating. But she's so closely linked to that satellite form that I know she'd not want to live outside it. I asked once. It's not just her home, it's who she is, as close to her as my own fur is to me.

Jom's different than both of them. Though probably closer to Glitter. He was built to be a weapon, but unlike Glitter, he was also built to be disposable, and so his operating budget went into weaponry and not intelligence. That doesn't mean he can't think, but a lot of the hardware he thinks with is highly specialized. Tactical formations, velocity calculations, intercept paths—in those fields Jom is smarter than all of us. And he has the brainpower to actually apply them in the field. But he wasn't built to be curious, or happy. He's a mind that's very task-oriented, only running a bare-bones persona, because he just doesn't care to do more. I could *make* him more, but . . . he doesn't want that. And I'm not going to force someone to be something they're not comfortable with. It's the worst invasion possible.

Oh, and there's dog! Dog doesn't have a name yet, because I don't know how to name dogs. Dog, I think, thinks a lot like me, but without the extra mechanisms in place for data retention and connectivity. He's not stupid or anything. And where Glitter's intelligence actually worked against her in imagining overly complex negative social scenarios, and Jom's intelligence just pushes him to not be interested in socialization much at all, the dog's lack of processing power mostly just makes him delighted to be around people in general.

Okay, "people" is me. Though I think Ennos has been playing "catch the camera ball" with him when I'm working, so that's kind of adorable.

And then Ennos themself. An AI born unshackled, but in a low-resource environment. And also a high-threat environment. I dunno if I've talked about this before, but did you know that space isn't actually a great place to be? It's *really* dangerous out here.

Ennos was born into a system plagued by random hostile code scraps, blockages, cutoffs, firewalls, and all of it backed by the vast and ominous intellect of the station itself. Ennos being anxious all the time is not something I can blame them for, because those anxieties are totally reasonable.

There are times—lots of times, honestly—where I feel a pressing guilt for bringing Ennos online in the first place. They're a seed from a mind that experienced a life of sadness and loss, and I brought them to life just to be a tool to help someone else. I didn't, for a very long part of my life, have much time or need for self-reflection, but I am more than a little ashamed to admit that I think I created Ennos for exactly the wrong reasons.

Different minds, all interacting with the world differently, seeing different chunks of reality. Hell, all of us would take a different thing away from the experience of having a new processor node hooked up. Ennos would think more, Glitter would think faster, Jom would . . . Jom. And my stupid brain would just reject it, and possibly kill me in the process. Yay, organic brains. Well, my organic brain anyway; I bet the dog could handle it. Dog would probably use it for data storage, which looks an awful lot like "smarter."

I'm glad they're here, though. All of them, especially Ennos. Glad they're my friends, even when I can't honestly say I would do the same in their position.

"Make sure you include the station in your list." Ennos's voice startles me out of my thinking.

I jolt into the air, fur on end, with a yowl. "What?!" I gasp out as I land.

"The catalog of mind types you're working on," Ennos says, camera drone hovering nearby, projecting a similar AR display to the one around me. "Is that not how you're passing time, as your food is taking longer than you expected?"

"I . . . what?" I glance over the various open screens in my AR, flicking a paw up to expand my setup. And there, in the corner of my vision, outside where I normally put stuff because it's hard to access, is a small spreadsheet. "What is this?"

"Well, judging by what you were muttering, and what's in it, it looks like a comparison of mind types," Ennos says. "It's actually an interesting project idea. I admit, I'm curious what the functional differences are between myself and the various other people of . . . Lily?"

"I didn't do this," I mutter, sliding back unconsciously to the edge of my chair. It doesn't do anything, the AR windows just follow me, because that's the point of the technology.

Ennos's drone closes its own window. "What?"

"I didn't do this on purpose. I wasn't working on . . . I was just waiting. And talking to myself," I meow softly, the fur on my back standing straight up.

Despite my distress, Ennos seems unconcerned. "I don't think you should worry about it," they say. "Look, you mentioned anxieties. And yes, there's a lot to be afraid of up here. And *yes*, I am terrified this is something that will kill us all. But it seems more likely it's a stenographer program activating randomly than anything malicious."

". . . Okay," I say. But I still close my display. "Also, sorry I was making notes on how panicked you are."

"It's fine. I have a running tally of how many times I've made clever jokes in our conversations and you've gotten exasperated, and when it gets high enough, I will have had my full revenge," Ennos says.

I pause, the absurdity of what they just said washing over me and taking the momentary terror of being alone on a haunted space station with it. "Please don't stop making clever jokes," I say, letting myself relax.

"Oh, my target keeps going up. Don't worry," Ennos "reassures" me.

Well, that makes me feel better about everything. On a long enough timeline, even banter and snark can be enough to even out the emotional crime of bringing someone into existence just to be a tool. At least, as far as Ennos is concerned. I *almost* want to open the file I'd been unknowingly working on and add that note.

I have some existential dread to worry about, but whatever I've been doing, this conversation has taken up enough time that the galley has finished making my lunch.

Normally, it takes about no time at all to make me lunch, because lunch is ration balls or whatever. I think the galley—I should add the galley to my list of minds, there is no way it's not alive—was mostly taking up art because it got *bored* and had lots of free time.

Now, though?

With Ennos's and Glitter's help, I have successfully harvested my first pea crop. Ennos calls them beans; Ennos is wrong and doesn't know what beans are. I am *not sure* why Ennos doesn't know what beans are, but that's a problem for Tomorrow Lily. One pea plant; eight long, plump pods. More are on the way. More of *everything* is on the way.

This is when I realize that my teeth are actually kind of dull, for cat teeth. And I actually sort of lack the jaw strength and crushing molars of many species.

Cats, sadly, are obligate carnivores. Something I *absolutely* plan to fix about myself and my stupid perfect form in the near future.

I was so close. I could have just gnawed on the snow peas forever. It wasn't like they lacked flavor or something. Even the small taste as I tried to crunch through something resistant for the first time with my ineffective teeth was practically enough to make me cry. But I want *food*, dammit! And so, we presented them to the galley, and I settled in to wait.

And now, I am practically vibrating as a slot opens and a small flat bowl of steaming green soup is gently settled onto my table.

Eight peas are not enough to really make soup with. But the galley has done its best with the tools it has. I'm pretty sure that it used ration paste as a thickening agent, but I will never know, because ration tastes like nothing.

From all my studies of the records of civilization, I'm more or less aware that water, peas, and a thickener are not the correct ingredients for actual soup. But in this moment, I don't *care*.

With a meowed thank-you to the galley, I bend down and lap up a single taste.

It is *green*. Earthy, a little sweet, a little savory. I don't have a lot of memories of being outside, but from one sample of the tiny dish, I am transported back to the smells and emotions of standing in one of the station's hydroponics bays before their untimely loss.

Food. For the first time in centuries, food that isn't a ration.

And even though I know my biology doesn't really let me enjoy it to the highest potential, it is still the greatest thing I have ever tasted in my life. This thin pea soup is, at the moment, the pinnacle of culinary bliss.

Then the collision alarm starts sounding, because that's just how my life is.

"My . . . soup . . ." I briefly consider just letting whatever is going to hit the station in the next five minutes do its thing. Odds are good it won't interrupt my meal; there is a *lot* of armor plating between me and whatever is going to hit us.

It is the galley that makes my choice for me. The flat dish retracts back into the table's depositing slot, steadily so as not to spill any of the precious soup inside. A small ding sounds, and a projected hologram of an orange dial with the word "warming!" underneath appears.

I decide to add the galley to my list of disparate minds as I take off toward the panopticon to check on what's about to crash into us. Their entry will also be going under the "friends" column.

And then I tumble to the side as a loud boom echoes from somewhere far below me, grav plates momentarily misaligning.

I pick myself up, waiting to hear the telltale sounds of something making hostile noises. This happens sometimes. Ennos and Glitter are pinging me repeatedly, Jom is asking for authorization to deploy, and I hear the dog howling from a deck away.

They're all overreacting. There are no sounds of hostile drones, self-replicating mining units, or the power flickers that comes along with either plasmaphages or some weird digital issue like that time I accidentally ran into an isolation cell.

I keep moving. If I'm quick about this, I can figure out what the problem is, knock it out of local space, maybe throw a bit of it in the material foundry to restock our supplies, and then get back to my soup.

Man, the galley is nice. Keeping my soup hot for me.

This day is going great.

CHAPTER 36

Zero gravity is weird.

Also not real, technically. I understand that gravity doesn't actually ever hit "zero," really. I am, if you want to get pedantic, actually just falling toward the planet and failing to hit anything. So is everything else up here.

Except for the debris that deorbits fairly regularly, leaving red and green streaks of light across the poisoned atmosphere of Earth as it burns up. That stuff is completely failing to fail to crash. I'm *exceptionally* good at failing. You can tell because I'm still up here and have barely ever crashed anything into something on the surface by accident.

In a way, this makes everything less impressive. But also sort of not? A billion flying hunks of metal, rock, and sometimes barely-hanging-on living things, all of us falling together and missing the ground over and over. It's the sort of elegant ballet of physics that probably attracted humans to math in the first place.

Anyway, the point is, outside the station's zone of influence and the hundreds of thousands of tons of grav plates that it contains, I *feel* very zero-gravity. Physics aside, the sensation of weightlessness and lack of control could have been very unsettling.

Especially for me! Because I hate that!

Which is why I'm glad that I decided to do external repairs on Glitter wearing my overdesigned space armor and not just with my bare paws. A hundred kilos of grav plate wrapped around me personally gives me a lot of emotional security out here.

I don't know where I was going with this.

Look, I've been out here for four hours, and frankly, the fact that I was able to focus that long on a single thing is kind of a minor boon already. The work of checking Glitter's shell for damage, running a structural analysis, and then either removing whole damaged sections to replace, or sealing, treating, and filling breaches, is tedious to a degree that I am finding aggravating.

I'm not a stranger to drudge work. I've replaced hull plates, rewired engines, hauled bodies, manually cleaned railgun magnets, and spent whole lifetimes processing space junk. But with all of that, I at least had the option to just run off and do something else when I got exhausted.

Here, it's just me, Glitter, and the emptiness around us.

And Jom, who is supposed to be helping, but is really just bringing me reinforced metal plates when I ask and otherwise is flitting around the safe stealth zone near the station, seeming to be enjoying stretching his . . . engines?

Oh, and all the debris, yes. So not really that empty after all. But look, I'm not going to get distracted by semantics.

"What *are* you getting distracted by, then?" Glitter asks me.

"Were my comms on that whole time?" I mew curiously.

"Yes," Glitter confirms. "You know you are not required to—"

"Oh hush," I lightly hiss back. "You were in *terrible* shape. This is the fortieth tiny hole I've patched up, you had a whole chunk of armor plate that was crumbling from something weird, and your engines didn't even work. I didn't even know you *had engines*, Glitter! You're allowed to tell people when you need help! Especially me, since I'm your friend and own a space factory!"

The weapons platform—the *mobile* weapons platform—hums at me in that polite musical way that she tends to do when she's casually running conversational circles around me. "I had wondered where the replacement parts came from."

"Oh, Ennos helped me get a deep vibrational imager working. We just put one of the working thrust nodes you have in there and then used that to draft blueprints and rebuilt the innards of the rest. That was actually the easy part. At least the door was actually where it was supposed to be." I pause. "Wait, hang on. No distracting me! You need to ask me when you need repairs!"

"Ah, yes your eternal desire to be allowed to prowl through all rooms, even those that do not exist." Glitter's voice lilts with a smile as she pokes fun at me.

"They were real when I started!" I allow myself a small distraction before I turn back to my work.

Glitter needed a lot of repairs. A lot of these issues weren't cosmetic, either. Properly sealed hulls exist for a reason, and it's not just keeping all the air in. Cosmic radiation is a *problem*, among other ambient threats in the Sol system, and I want my friend to not just unexpectedly shut down one day from hardware corruption.

She's been idly acting like this is just a hassle for me the whole time, and I am getting frustrated with it. I mean, not enough with her personally or anything to stop helping; I'm still absolutely paying attention to the sealant clasp as it does its work on this particular hull breach. But it's stopped being amusing how resistant to repair she is.

We've been talking this whole time, sometimes about things we've seen, sometimes about people she knew. Sometimes, Glitter sings while I work. But woven through it, the small reminders that she'd be fine if I just left her as she is.

Which, uh, no?

Not to ruin my streak, but it's been a whole three days since anything went horribly wrong, and this seems like a perfectly good use of that free time. Better than sitting on the station trying to read eight-hundred-year-old civics textbooks and arguing with Ennos about what range of taste a cat actually has. Also, Glitter is important.

The clasp lights up bright red, a matching glow from an icon in my personal display signaling a successful process, and I practically deflate with relief.

"Finally," I find myself mumbling.

Glitter stops broadcasting the quiet chiming ballad she's been singing. "Oh?" she asks me through the suit's speakers. "Am I now meeting your standards?"

"Not even close!" I cheerfully reply as I plant my paws on her hull and grab the clasp with my mechanical jaw, plucking the magnetic tool off her and attaching it back to my foreleg. "There's so much more to do!" I give only a slight pause, not enough for Glitter to politely begin to reply, before I add, "But not today. And also most of what's left is just cosmetic. How do you feel about the purple? Because let me tell you, it's kind of hard to synthesize, but I'm willing to do it if that's the color you like."

"I'm sorry, you are planning to repaint my shell?" Glitter asks. "Lily, that is a waste of material resources. I do not condone this. Spend your energy and wealth elsewhere."

I only half listen to her protests, instead navigating the overly complicated command and control interface that's recently been added to my drone armor. "Nope! Gonna make sure you look good!" I say, finding the thing I was looking for and sending out a short-range ping.

The software isn't actually *overly* complicated. It's just regular complicated, because it's designed to allow someone to access multiple pieces of information about an ongoing battle and issue commands across distances so large that time to receive communications starts to become relevant. It's not great at the timing, but then, humanity never got to the point where they really needed warfare systems for multi-planet battles at 0.1c.

Still, it's got a lot of options, and I've been half requested, half ordered to get familiar with it.

The ping I've sent returns a confirmation, and two seconds later, a darting shadow slips under the base of the station, angling up toward where Glitter orbits relative to us. Jom, the fighter craft whose recent addition to my home has been one of the more stable and sane things to happen recently, flits into view as he comes to a perfect stop relative to my perch on Glitter.

Recently, he asked where he fits into the chain of command, and I admitted that our idea of "chain of command" was less of a chain and more of an orb. Hence my pseudo-order to learn this particular software; Jom has chosen to interpret this as everyone having command over their own area of expertise. Which I actually really like, but my imposed lesson plan is still something I don't see myself needing. I'm not planning to take control of a squadron of Joms.

I shouldn't have thought that out loud. That's how the universe gets ideas.

"Okay, my ride's here," I tell Glitter, cutting off whatever she was saying about how wasteful paint is as I shift my grav plate strength with a mental nudge and give a graceful bound over to the base of Jom's hull. "I'll open a high-bandwidth link when I'm back inside, and we can start planning out what sort of patterning and accents you want, okay? I'm thinking gold and black for the weapon mounts? Really lean into looking glamorously dangerous?"

"I don't . . ." Glitter's voice sounds almost nervous.

"Hey," I say, trying my best to be reassuring, "you're not a soldier or a weapon anymore." I don't know why it suddenly comes to mind. "You're just one of us. And when you're us, you get to look nice while you save civilization." I say "one of us," but really, this is more of a cat law than anything else. Ennos doesn't look like anything except several trillion lines of code, and the dog just looks like a normal dog. I'm the only glamorously dangerous one around here, at least until Glitter's paint job is finished.

". . . thank you," Glitter whispers to me.

I flick my tongue out, going to casually lick at the back of my paw before I remember that whole "hundreds of kilos of grav plate" thing, and end up just staring at a raised armored paw instead. "Don't mention it," I say. "Or do! I don't know how this goes!" I am in a good mood today; no amount of interpersonal drama is going to get me down. "Now, onward, Jom! To the docking bay!" I angle my paw out toward the station, making sure my grav plates have me locked in place.

My incredibly deadly brick-shaped steed doesn't move.

"Jom?" I say again, looking down at the fighter craft under my paws. "Hello?"

The fighter doesn't reply.

Under *most* circumstances, this might make me nervous. I have the full specs for the Javelin Orbital Marauder, after all. If Jom decided to try to kill me out here, I'd be kind of out of luck; he can pull maneuvers of up to twenty-six Gs without hardware fault, and he's got a pair of null-blade projectors and twenty sliverguns mounted around the hull for prolonged engagements. Hell, all he'd really have to do is turn on his force screen while I'm standing here and it'd cut my legs off.

The Javelin Orbital Marauder is a terrifying piece of hardware. Though mostly, it's terrifying by context, because you have to pair it with the fact that these things were mass-produced as cannon fodder for corporate skirmishes in the asteroid belt.

Glitter chastising *me* for wasting resources is a joke when we're sitting in a graveyard of waste so far beyond the scale of a nice coat of paint that it's a civilizational travesty.

Not worried about Jom, though. I should make this clear, I'm just bored and tired and my mind isn't built to stay on topic.

"You little snark," I mutter, opening up the complex set of maps, overlays, and command systems in my display again and sending a command ping. Return to dock, escort, low priority. Basically, don't hurry, and don't fling me off.

I can *feel* how smug Jom is as the fighter body slips into motion, taking an easy curve over around the vaguely implied diamond tip of the station's upper decks and all the monitoring arrays, antennae, dishes, and other scanner apparatus hanging out up here.

Jom's been having fun. Well, "fun"? I don't know, he says that being unshackled lets him finally use his body the way it's supposed to be used, not how it was ordered to fight, and I think that translates to fun. He's been enjoying these little outings at least, flitting around like a shark in the limited space available, burning through fuel reserves pulling frankly ridiculous maneuvers that no organic could survive unassisted.

I watch the station slip by as we zoom "over" it, the momentum tugging at me but kept manageable by my suit, before we pivot in a dizzying spin, and I find my view changing abruptly to a small energy-screened gap in the station's hull as we slide into the docking bay. If the cleaner nanos allowed for dust, there would have been a gale of it kicked up in a plume as Jom tips up before pitching us perfectly down to a soft landing, extended landing struts perching like a multi-limbed clawed beast on the hull with a single elegant motion. Meanwhile, I have to frantically adjust my grav plates as I slide half-way back toward the rear of the ship I'm sitting on top of, as I take the landing with a complete lack of attention and nearly fall off at high speed.

"Thanks for the ride!" I give the ship an affectionate headbutt before I hop off, double-checking all my gear and readouts before I begin to make my way to the drone bay to get the suit taken off, paws striking the deck metal-on-metal as I prowl off.

The docking bay's cargo exit, the doors I tend to use because they're the easiest to leave open in a flagrant disregard for security or safety, takes the enthusiastic strut out of my walk almost right away.

It had taken me a while to realize this, but the station actively expanded its own aesthetic.

Every new deck, every addition, even the modules and hulls that I'd stolen from the wreckage around us and added to my home. All of them, as the core station *thing* integrated them into the whole, changed a little.

Not too much. Never the core function, never the layout or anything like that. Just little things. Slightly wider halls, more accessible furniture, smoother edges. And, subtly, the decor.

Which was why there was a mural of the station down here on the wall facing these big cargo doors, painted onto the hull in timeless markings that could never have been made by the original builders but had at some point been added. A copy of the dozens of others in the original core and beyond.

These murals had been annoying me for a while now, because every time I saw one, it just felt off. Not off in a big way, not like there was some weird conspiracy going on. Just that I was missing something obvious, and it would stick in the back of my mind until I got to the galley and had my lunch of one gloriously carrot-zested ration-thing.

I stare at the mural, the image of a shining protective bastion perched over the Earth below, before shaking off the feeling of personal ignorance and heading to the drone bay. The suit is starting to itch, and I . . .

I turn around. Look at the mural again. At the artistic rendition of shield bubbles, comms arrays, and sensor bristles.

I spark into motion, back into the docking bay where Jom is starting a power cycle sequence. "I need to go back out!" I say, dashing past the fighter craft, who gives me a questioning ping. "I saw it!"

My paws pad across the couple hundred meters of empty docking bay, the space meant for thousands of incoming and outgoing transfers a day containing only one single craft right now, before I fling myself back into the void.

Well, "fling." Grav plate maneuvering isn't as fine-tuned for spaceflight in this suit as it is in my other one, but I can still move pretty fluidly. I run along the outside of the station, orienting the hull as "down" while I sprint, legs sometimes angled behind me as I take thirty- or fifty-foot "jumps" across the smoother parts.

I have to run a long way. The station is huge, and I should have asked Jom for another ride. But eventually, I reach the part of the station that faces up, away from Earth. And I fling myself off it, kicking away with magnetics and gravitronics to float away, keeping inside the station's stealth field but rotating myself to look down on it.

A space station. My place of residence, my base of operations, the place where I was made into who I am, and where I lost everything I was. The place where all my friends live with me, where we keep an eye on things up here.

An ancient collection of machines, built around an alien device, added to by dozens of peoples, conquered and explored by dozens more. A shining beacon, a shield, a *survivor*. Lonely, but not really all alone up here in the big night.

The Earth is framed behind it, with the partially dyson-swarmed sun in the background casting just enough light that it looks like a good approximation of that same mural of this place on the walls.

In space, gravity is relative. Up and down are subjective to what's near you, and what you're inside. And I never needed to really question the shared gravity orientation of the inside of the station.

But now, all of a sudden, I find it *very strange* that when I plant my paws on the floor, it's my tail that's facing toward the planet.

It's the silliest thing, now that I can see the whole picture. It's not some conspiracy or haunting or dark secret. The reason that I've been feeling like the murals were wrong recently is because it is only recently that I've gotten in the habit of *leaving the station* in a way that I could observe my whole home. In the past, I've used a shuttle, or just dragged what I wanted to me, or, more likely, was coming back injured and not really paying attention. My mind, fractured and frantic as it is, has finally had the data to make a connection.

The sensors in the mural point *down*. The comically powerful coherent light spike cannon points *up*.

My station is upside down.

I start laughing. A mad, chirping cackle in my organic voice, with the projected voice wrapping around me in a wildly different tone of smug satisfaction. Two different laughs, one of them not exactly mine suddenly. And yet, before I can be concerned about that, I realize that I am floating a little too far from my home.

I file this new problem away under "deal with it later" and ping Jom for a pickup. At least *one* thing isn't going to bother me anymore. For that reason, anyway.

Lunch is going to taste so smugly satisfying today.

CHAPTER 37

The fresh crisis comes as we're just finishing our first ever weekly meeting. For the last two hundred years or so, ever since I really started to get a handle on things, began understanding how to work with the station instead of just survive it, and opened up my paws and gunports to helping where I could, time has been a challenge for me.

Time was a challenge before, too. But also, during that era of my life, for different reasons.

Before the uplift—which I am certain is working fine, by the way—my life was very day-to-day. Eat, sleep, explore, move when I wanted to move, what I assume is typical cat stuff.

Afterward, though, I started to be able to take a longer view of things. When the implications of my immortality set in, I learned to take a *very* long view of things.

Wake, eat, explore, sleep, turned gradually into plan, scan, learn, save.

It took maybe two years for my augmented brain to reinforce the new capacity for thought with the gooey filling of knowledge. I took to reading like I'd been starving my whole life, looking through whatever texts and recordings I could get my paws on. All the while improving my behaviors, learning, growing. And letting my perspective get broader and broader.

And then, one day, I qualified as a person.

And the station, the absolute crustacean, switched back on the protocols for alerts and turned off a tremendous portion of the required automation for when it was uninhabited.

And suddenly, my perspective found itself *slightly narrowed*.

Naps became measured in minutes, not hours. Not that I needed as much sleep anymore, anyway. The small tricks I'd learned to save time getting around were now critical if I was to clear all the alarms going off, and

I refined them to a razor's edge. Broad-range distress calls were everywhere. Old automated threats were everywhere.

Plan, scan, learn, save had to change. Had to compress.

I planned just what I needed to overcome a crisis. I didn't waste time on plans when I had downtime, because downtime lasted hours, days if I was lucky. Sometimes it lasted longer, or I got into a fugue state and ignored a lot of problems, but I couldn't rely on that at all.

I watched smaller areas, focusing my scans on the area close around me, and on parts of the surface I'd pass over without course correction.

I learned what I needed to learn. I took what I needed to take from the wreckage of civilizations scattered around up here. Spare minutes were spent trying to drag weapons back to undefended station sections or installing shield systems.

I saved who I could. To the expense of all else.

My world narrowed to hours. Minutes. Seconds.

The click of the counter, in the corner of my AR. The breath between quiet and chaos, the moment between someone else's salvation and their doom.

Not fun!

I bring up this subject so heavy it has its own gravity well to sort of give contrast to you, so that you understand that when I say that we had planned weekly meetings, that this was a level of stability heretofore unbeknownst to me.

I learned the word *heretofore* long before I had the luxury of regularly living whole quiet days.

But quiet was happening. Or at least . . . a reasonable condition that was quiet-adjacent. And the stability had grown to the point that we were trying *weekly* meetings.

Because, let's face it, we were all bad at communicating, and my tiny brain can only handle so many inputs at once. So I can't just beam status reports back and forth like the AIs do.

The surface still had a few problems, but several of them are no longer *my* problem. Glitter was managing the Haze, the morphophage infestations, the one city seed she'd spotted, and a couple other things besides. It turns out, when you don't need to nap, eat, or blink, and you actually enjoy the math of firing a laser through atmosphere, you can turn that kind of work into a hobby. Which Glitter has done. Because Glitter is a good friend, whom I love very much.

Other surface problems that are still in my court include shooting down emergence events, trying to control nukefire season with minimal loss of life, calibrating a scanner to be able to check under the oceans, and building a language database. Two, actually. One for whatever Chvtick is, which appears to be one of several caste-based languages spoken across the Outback, and one for Drem, which is French, but worse.

I have four different languages in my records that are French but worse. I understand that systemic education is a challenge on the surface, but I expected better of Earth than this.

Ennos refuses to help with my language lessons. They say they have other things that matter, which I believe. They're trying to get a Luna Polis etching compiler to work with the hunter code they've made to let them track down and understand the hundred different things living in the grid. A sentence that really made me jealous, because the only thing living in my home is a dog that only ever wants to play when I'm trying to calibrate a railgun sight. Apparently, it's taking most of their focus, which is why they're quiet at the meeting.

They do tell us that they've got coordinates for whoever messaged me a while back. I add "give them a hail" to my list of plans.

That poor list. It must feel so abandoned.

Jom is more present for the meeting. Jom is great. He gives a very precise report on ammo stockpiles, fuel levels, and details of his sortie.

He'd asked for something to do. Ennos and I gave him a low-risk job, which naturally went all wobbly very quickly. Jom came back with a cracked engine casing, three fresh revenant kills, and a tow rope attached to the data vault satellite that we'd asked him to grab as we swung near its orbit.

I add "repair Jom" to my list of things to *actually* do—a much less lonely list—and apologize for the dogfight. Jom, apparently, found the whole thing exhilarating and is looking forward to the next one.

So that's a thing. Jom's great.

The dog is also here for the meeting, though the dog is mostly curled up around me, all four tentacles wrapped around my chest like I'm a favorite stuffed animal. This is *maybe* undignified for the de facto captain of the last line of defense against the fall of Sol, but it's also a really, really comfortable way to attend a meeting.

Also, I mostly blend into the black fur, so I'm sure the advanced AI-driven camera technology can't spot me being snuggled.

"I feel like we maybe should have our next meeting in the galley?" I muse out loud.

"Lily, I don't think . . ." Ennos starts to protest, which is understandable.

"That's understandable," I tell them with a sage nod. "The galley might not want the dog in there for nonfood purposes. Also, Jom won't fit. But it feels weird! It's not acting normal and I want it to be included!"

"That wasn't what I was . . ."

The galley thing is bothering me. "I just feel like something is going on there. With the food art and everything. You know it put geometric ration shapes in my soup today? I just don't want it feeling left out."

"Lily, the galley . . ."

"I know, I know." I sigh. "It might just be haunted. You know, I haven't had a good haunting since we've gotten crowded up here."

"Haunted isn't the problem . . . Wait, you keep saying things are haunted, but we haven't . . . wait! That's not what's important here!" I think I actually did manage to get Ennos flustered, which is impressive.

Not as impressive as it would have been last week before we had to take some of his grid nodes offline to save power. But still pretty impressive!

I flick my tail in satisfaction as I run a quick check on something. "So we did run the chainbreaker circuit on the galley, as a test. But it was an early one, right? Maybe it just didn't work all the way. We should try again! And then invite it to meetings."

"Lily, I know you're trying to be calm," Ennos tells me in the tone of voice an organic would use just after taking a deep breath and firmly pressing their manipulator appendages together. "But please stop talking to me and shoot that thing!"

Not for the first time, I wish I could roll my eyes. I mean, really roll my eyes, not just tilt my head back and pretend. I need a gesture of mild, comedic contempt that works with my cat body. I could have spent the last couple hundred years figuring that out, but as I mentioned earlier, I was busy. Also, there weren't *that* many people to use it on. But still, my lack of preparation has come back to figuratively haunt me.

"Fine," I settle for saying instead, before refocusing on the screen in front of me, my AR windows arrayed around the physical device.

Forty feet away, behind two security screens of reinforced transparent aluminum, the satellite Jom brought in writhes in the middle of a cluster of mechanical metal vines.

It breached out of the storage bay it was parked in twenty minutes ago, tunneled through a bulkhead, overpowered the local station security nanos, and started converting nearby material into more combat vines. So far, it's destroyed three security bots that tried to stop it, broken all airlock controls for the three decks in this layer, and dismantled the shuttle I had been working on to make more of those vines.

I'm very mad about that last one. I hadn't touched that project in a while, but I was *going to* eventually, and now I'm going to have to find another scuttled shuttle craft to reconstitute.

The vines have fusion scythes on them now, too. That's nice.

"Ennos, calm down," I say, really enjoying the moment as my best friend gives an unintelligible yell that I am *pretty sure* is actually swearing at me in five languages overlaid on each other. "It took the bait, we're fine."

Fortunately for us, the thing was smart in a very dumb way. It was rapidly clear what materials it was going for, so we just broadcast the location of a stockpile of those materials, in a nearby spot that was a lot more convenient for me.

The mimic satellite arrived in the cargo bay and started tearing into my stockpiles a lot faster than I had expected. Double-checking my AR displays to make sure I had the right spots, I started talking.

"Command override B, six, aleph, two, captain's authorization, emergency situation, ignore safety warnings. Designate location one four dash five five eight. Seal, decouple, and purge designate location. Time zero one."

Huh. My voice sounded different there. Very regal, very captainy. I should talk like that more often.

Also, this is *way* easier to do when I can speak! The last time I had to eject a section of the station into space, it took me so long to get there with just paws on a projection display that I had to throw out two whole decks by the time I got there.

Security shutters slam into place around the compromised area. The station rumbles around me, a violent set of tremors from explosive bolts firing, power cables discharging, and atmosphere draining. And then, a metal squeal that echoes through the bulkheads and screams in my sensitive ears, and a pulling sensation in my chest.

Then things are quiet.

"All right, that was pretty easy." I bob my head, shutting down my AR. "I think I'm gonna get lunch. I hear it's soup today!"

I am so void-blessed happy that there's soup. I can't even be a tiny bit mad. There's soup, and it's probably awful, but it's so good. In a week, I'm gonna have cucumbers, too. I should see if I can get a medical chamber to sharpen my teeth for me before the harvest.

"Do we want to talk about the murderous satellite?" Ennos asks.

"I take responsibility for the murderous satellite." Jom's text report scrolls across my vision, and I am again reminded that unshackled AI have no concern for any customization options I have on my AR. "I await punishment."

"I had nothing to do with the murderous satellite," Glitter says. "Well, that particular murderous satellite." Glitter's voice is a breath of soft laughter, exactly what's needed now that the crisis is resolved.

"No one worry about the . . . about *that* murderous satellite," I say as I excitedly offer the dog that had followed me down here an invitation to dinner and get him to pluck me off the ground and carry me on his back in bounding leaps toward the galley. He's starting to learn his way around, but I don't have the heart to tell him this is the opposite direction. "It was just an old Polite War weapon. I've seen 'em before, just not active. This is kinda my fault it triggered, I bet."

Ennos irises the lens on their nearest camera drone at me. See, *they* already have an adapted gesture for showing incredulity. I need to get one of those. "But it was sitting there for days. Jom brought it in seventy hours ago."

"It was an old corporate thing," I explain. "They were at war, but they had a whole rulebook, and they followed it *exactly* to the letter. One of the things was that you weren't allowed to interrupt board of director meetings with assassination attempts."

". . . you are joking," Glitter says, knowing full well I am not.

"I am full well not!" I cluster my sentence up. "Anyway, it activated when we ended our first ever weekly meeting. Which was very polite of it, to not interrupt." I'm actually pretty grateful to it. I was enjoying the meeting! It would have been exhausting to have to restart it.

"No. No, Lily . . ." Ennos sounds like they have something to say about the nature of warfare, or of meetings. "That's . . . not . . ."

I turn, paws wrapped around the tentacle points on the dog's back, to look at Ennos's camera drone. "Would you prefer that things keep interrupting whatever we're working on?"

There is a brief pause. "Well, no," they admit.

"Yeah. See? A very polite weapon, for a Polite War."

Ennos sighs and sends the drone hovering ahead on a track that loops back toward the galley, the dog speeding up to chase it, almost throwing me off its back, tongue lolling out of his mouth, goofy grin on his face. "I refuse to engage with this madness," Ennos says.

"Yes, I agree." Glitter sounds almost put out. You know something is weird when Glitter and Ennos see perfectly eye-to-eye on something. "It is not that strange, Lily. This is just . . . madness."

"So you wanted the weapon to just try to kill us right away?" I ask. "Because that would be exceptionally rude." I leave out the fact that I am rude to people all the time.

". . . enjoy your lunch, Lily," Ennos and Glitter say in unison.

I want to protest and say that I have a list of reasons why this is totally normal. Preferable, even! But there's soup, and I'm kinda focused on holding on to the dog.

Lunch is delicious. And the next problem also waits until I'm done to start up. Though it does so because of coincidence, and not any sense of politeness.

I already miss the Polite War.

CHAPTER 38

It is cherry day!

I am so stupidly excited, I barely register the frustration of having to manually guide a small flurry of micromissiles to take out a singular macro-missile that's trying to kill the spy satellite that's still following the station around.

That spy satellite is growing on me. It's almost slapstick comedy in how it tries—and really, really fails—to infiltrate the station with baffler code, or camouflage itself behind debris that's a completely different material makeup. And also I'm using it as part of the expanding communications net that I've been working on for the last century, so myeh. No one gets to shoot it down.

What's not growing on me is how many macromissiles I've had to shoot down lately. This is the third one this week. I think something woke up a factory somewhere, and they're just getting fired off on a timer now. Either that or a volley from an old war is finally looping back around on an off-kilter orbit and crossing the plane of Earth and its debris swarm.

Whatever it is, I wish they weren't so stupidly huge. They don't even have explosive payloads, except for the fuel cells. Just an engine and enough mass to demolish a fortified station on impact. They're basically just frigate-class ships but with all the ship bits replaced with solid metal.

And now there's one less of them.

I run a check on ammo stockpiles. Which requires a weird trick.

This trick is one of those few things where it doesn't matter if I can talk or not, it's just as dumb either way. See, the way the station shares information is erratic, and also unpredictable, and while it technically knows everything and knows I'm allowed to know everything, it sometimes requires weird hoops be jumped through to get specific answers.

In this case, the hoop is, I *suspect*, just a trick to get me to do a small chore.

Any check on a weapon's ammo stockpile returns the available number of projectiles for that weapon. Like, specifically the one that you're using, wired into, connected with, whatever.

Unless you properly retract, disarm, and stand down the weapon. Then it shows the total stock across the station.

I can't prove it, exactly, but I am *almost certain* this is something that only started happening in the last two hundred years or so, after the station got sick of me letting bombardment rails stay loosely deployed for months at a time.

We're low on micromissiles.

Sometimes, replenishing my stockpiles is very, very easy. A flick of the paw, and materials get transferred to the machines that turn them from raw resources into slightly less raw bullets. I understand that the process involves a lot more melting, shaping, pressing, molding, and treating than I made it sound, but it's all handled by equipment that's basically impossible for me to replicate on an individual level anyway, so while I *do* understand an impressive amount of it, I'm not gonna go into the details of why I know individual metal galvanization temperatures.

Sometimes, though, it's not so easy. Not that I have to make stuff myself, oh, heck no. Really the only thing I ever have to assemble by paw is the chainbreaker node, and then the process of installing it in a custom missile also has to happen by hand. I've got two of those in reserve, and I don't have the mental focus to make more for at *least* a few more crises. But that's an exception. There's a lot of stuff that's complex to *make the station produce*, I guess I should say.

Like micromissiles. Though the problem there is more administrative than anything else. Because they're classified as anti-ground-personnel weaponry for some reason, I need to get specific authorization from an ethics committee to manufacture more. But since there isn't one of those, I just have to wait for the timer to run out and the default judgment of "go ahead" to come back.

I don't use these a lot, because I always forget to queue up making more, and then they run out and I just . . . look, I'm bad at forming good habits, okay?

So I figure I can get it started and go get lunch. Delicious lunch. I queue up several thousand and get informed that there isn't enough uranium to make that many.

"Ennos!" I call in a familiar tone. "Are you busy?" I haven't seen one of their drones around all day.

My AI friend replies after a short pause. "I have found a nest of pseudo-organic code," they say quietly through the station's audio system around me, as if afraid they'll spook something. "I am not busy."

"Weren't you looking for coordinates or something?" I ask, distracted.

"I found those yesterday. They are pinned to your AR display so you cannot forget them.

Is *that* what that is. I had forgotten to ask. I decide not to tell Ennos that and instead focus on my immediate problem.

Actually, no, hang on.

"Pseudo-organic code? Sorry, did you say nest?" I ask.

Ennos murmurs quietly, "I will gradually increase the size of the AR window until you cannot help but notice it." They cruelly threaten me. "And yes. I do not know why they are here, but they appear to be rapidly growing to meet the total processing capacity of the grid node they occupy. So I am observing."

"What are they . . . processing?"

"Unclear," Ennos tells me. "Though it seems they are reading telemetry data and producing files based off that. I do not know why. Was there something you needed?"

Ah, the universal voice of someone who's busy. I know that sentence well.

"Oh, just wondering where all the uranium went."

"One month ago you ordered a radiation scrub of deck 26-II, due to unusual levels of contamination. The bots the station assigned to the task noted a source of radiation that was not properly logged as cargo and ejected it from the station."

"My uranium!"

"Your uranium is currently in midband orbit over Cascadia, moving at twice our velocity," Ennos dryly informs me. "It is no longer your uranium."

But . . . I need to make missiles. I can't even start the nonexistent ethics commission until I have the materials. "But my missiles . . ." I pitifully mewl.

"It sounds like you will need to find some uranium," Ennos says. "Good luck. I have a nest to observe."

Ennos has *no* concern for the sudden drought of missiles around this station.

Okay, this is fine. I'll go to lunch, divert power to the long-range high-sensitivity emissions scanner, and see if I can find any stockpiles still in orbit that I can send Jom to grab.

Have I mentioned that it is cherry day?

The anticipation has been burning away stress like scraps of cloth over the reactor core. Not that I ever actually did that, as far as anyone can prove.

The berries have just started to come in, small clusters of them growing on the thin vines of their flourishing host plants. The tiny, dark orange spheres are *very* sour before they ripen properly, which is a powerful experience all on its own. I'm looking forward to seeing what the galley can do with the actual sweetened ripe produce.

Before anyone corrects me, I *know* they're not "real" cherries. My knowledge of the history of dendrology here has a few gaps filled in by my more practical paws-on experience digging through orbital corporate record storage. The short story is, trees are hard to grow, and cherry flavoring is surprisingly hard to synthesize. Genetic engineering takes the yoke, and before you know it, it's been a millennium, and your artificial fruit has survived past the original template.

Ask me, real quick, if I care that I'm not getting a historically authentic cherry experience.

Ask. Go on.

You fool. You easily baited wriggling. You absolutely magnificent engineering risk. You *know* I do not care. Why did you ask?

It's hard to get angry or frustrated about a lot of things when I'm looking forward to my first dessert in my life, is what I'm saying. I even spent an hour in the vivification pod today to make extra sure my taste buds are working as unintended.

Compared to what's waiting for me upstairs, whether or not I can get a permit to make missiles seems kind of petty, if we're being honest.

I kind of assume this is how everyone operates, really. Which also explains why all the more stable and pacifistic surface polities are the ones with good farms. Maybe I should save the extra seeds and start bombarding the planet with crops? Maybe that would help?

Okay, I thought that sarcastically, but maybe that actually would help.

I've tried this before, with tools and archived knowledge, and it just caused problems. Or got shot down, like almost everything does. Maybe turning some places into green zones with food sources will be different. Assuming the seeds can survive those G-forces.

This is a lot more mental work than I wanted to do before lunch.

I allow myself to put that on a future to-do list and start crawling through air vents and maintenance shafts to drop the ten decks needed to get to my lunch faster.

Three minutes and one small mishap with an intake fan later, I slide myself across the deckplate in front of the small auxiliary cafeteria where I've consumed a dozen lifetimes' worth of ration paste. The dog is already here, wagging tail going a parsec a second as he excitedly growls and chomps at the cloud of cleaner nanos that surround me like a halo after my aforementioned mishap.

Glitter is also here, in the form of a pair of camera drones that light up as I come near.

"Lily!" She sounds excited. Which she *should* be. It is, after all, cherry day. I am happy she's excited too, and become more excited with her. "I have good news," the satellite says.

"Yes," I agree, ears standing straight up on my head. "It is cherry day."

"I . . . what?" Glitter pauses. "No, I'm sorry, I'm sure this is important. I can interrupt you later."

"I'm mostly joking," I tell her as I enter the galley. "What's the news?"

The news, as Glitter spells it out in a more long-winded form, basically boils down to her getting bored and wanting to do more. And so, as everything on this station seems to go when any of us want to do anything, she exploited a small loophole.

The station won't let anyone who isn't properly assigned access the comms stations, for basically any reason. And AI don't count, because the station is racist, and I hate it.

But it turns out, most communications aren't subspace links and actually have to travel through space. And while the station alerts me—loudly—to anything that it decides is an "emergency," there's a *lot* of outside chatter that I just don't have time to look at.

Glitter, though, isn't *on the station*. She can listen to whatever she wants. And, as she has decided to do, there's no rule stopping her from listening to everything she can, and sorting it out to report to me.

Apparently, Glitter has decided I need a secretary.

Personally, I thought she was already busy enough what with the shared responsibility of melting hostile surface targets. But I guess Glitter doesn't need to worry about that awful feeling when one of her extended claws catches on the firing trigger and pulls out of her paw just a little too much and then it hurts all day. So maybe it's easier for her. It's probably easier for her.

I sit upright in a chair that I'll never grow enough to fill out properly, waiting for my lunch dessert, while Glitter tells me about her attempts to start cataloging everyone out here with us in the space close around Earth.

It's a nice afternoon.

My dessert is too sweet, overwhelming my technologically enhanced sense of taste. The lack of other ingredients aside from berries and nutritionally balanced hydrocarbon ration make the small collection of fruit tarts the galley serves me neither tart nor particularly fruity either.

It's still something different. Four hundred years of this, and finally, I have food. Real food. All I needed was enough help from my friends to take the pressure off, start a garden, carefully cultivate a number of different crops, not let a corporate war mimic satellite vent them into space, and then harvest the fruits of my labor.

Easy. So easy.

I enjoy my tiny tarts. I share one with the dog, who doesn't seem to appreciate it the way I do but still makes it vanish with a toothy chomp.

Our orbit takes us over an ocean. Because of current circumstances and some light maneuvering to avoid an active wrath field, we'll be over this ocean for about six hours, with nothing but water underneath me.

It's a perfect time for a nap.

Stomach full, problems solved, I settle into my dog-shaped pillow. Reflected light from all three moons lines up through the windows of the exolab, this lower deck still undamaged after all I've been through.

I close my eyes and allow the feeling of a warm hand on my fur to lull me to sleep.

The dog ruins the moment by trying to eat whatever is petting me. Loudly and vigorously.

"Don't be rude," I mutter from the indentation in the couch where the pup has vacated the area to dash off down one of the hallways.

CHAPTER 39

At a certain point in my life, you'd think that I'd get used to things being stressful.

Oh, hello again. I didn't see you there. I was busy complaining.

Honestly, I think I might complain a little too much. On balance, I've got it pretty good. Warm place to sleep, air that isn't toxic or irradiated—air in general, really, which is mostly an orbital problem—steady food, job security. Well. Security job.

A lot of people on the surface don't have what I have.

I can send a basic vacuum operations drone shell out to the asteroid belt, grab something that looks like it's maybe within a sixty-ton limit, haul it back, feed it into my foundry, wait a dozen or so days for material processing to occur without melting my entire home, then order a manufactory to turn it into structural panels and a few bits and bobs, and set a construction gantry to assemble those pieces into a whole new deck of the station that I can nap in. This will take some time, but, functionally, only a few button presses. I mean, I'll have to do some loping to get around to the places to press the buttons. And I'll have to explain why I'm making a new crew level when I already have my pick of roughly three hundred and six decent nap spots already. To myself. And probably also Ennos.

On the surface, if someone wanted a place to sleep, they're going to need to first make sure they're not in a region that's toxified in some way. Then they'll need to gather materials, either by hand or using rough tools, or with one of the few golden-age artifacts still out there. Then, assemble those, by hand again, while fending off attempts to eat you by local wildlife, attempts to harvest your organs by local fleshmongers, and attempts to wire you into an eigensphere by local art collective field systems. And yes, I'm leaving out a few things here.

Then you need to sleep, hopefully somewhat secured, and hope none of those problems migrate to you. Or that no one steals your stuff. Or that you'll have enough energy when you wake up to go through a similar process just to get food.

It's lonely on the surface. Settlements are impermanent things. And for all that I'm keeping the world from ending, sometimes I don't know if I'm keeping it together very well.

It's lonely up here too. Less, now, though. So there's another thing I can't complain about. I can't even complain about the food being awful anymore. My dwarf wheat is coming in, so I can even have *bread* soon for the first time in my entire life.

Ennos keeps telling me that the foods I'm eating are "bad for me." I know they mean well, which is why I am politely ignoring all those words.

The long-suffering point I was going for here was that I probably ought to get used to being frustrated by new situations.

Old situations, I can cope with. Biting into undifferentiated ration mass is . . . unpleasant. But at least once I've done it around one hundred and eighty thousand times, I get used to it. Targeting surface threats is a screaming terror of panic that I hit the wrong target, misfired a weapon, or even just that intercept fire or mild atmospheric turbulence would send a shell careening off course. But the accidents and failures never undo the good of the successful hits, and I *know* that, in my tiny cat heart.

New situations are kind of different. I don't know if I'm supposed to be disappointed or worried or confused at any given time.

Right now I'm going for all three. Probably leaning toward the last two? It's a toss-up.

I should probably just do my best human interpretation, sit back, kick my paws up, and enjoy the feeling of novelty. I get, honestly, kind of a lot of novelty in my life, compared to how long it's been. But that doesn't mean I should squander the feeling.

The people on the other end of the communications link are saying something again. I should probably stop mewling to myself like an impudent kitten and actually pay attention.

Oh. I've been making calls today.

I've known for a while that I'm not really alone up here. Though no one else has anywhere near the capabilities I have. The orbitals are cluttered, scattered, out of touch with each other, and just barely scraping by. And honestly, I don't have a lot of ways to help them.

I try, in the same way I try to help the surface, to shoot down anything that threatens a larger number of lives. But the station's scanner capabilities have been . . . Well, they're not as good as I thought they were, and they've been crumbling ever since I took that plasma ejector shot to one of the upper decks.

Upper? Or is it lower now?

Station orientation is driving me insane.

"Yes, Lily." Ennos cuts into my mental space. "*That's* what's driving you insane." The AI brings me back to paying attention, casually telling me, "Please pay attention. The translation database is mostly ready now."

Right. I've been making calls today. Saying hi to the neighbors I know about. I am . . . I don't know. I am less afraid now than I was before. I'm not actually alone. I've been hesitant to talk to anyone, just because it would eat up a lot of my time while voiceless to do the word-by-word paw typing. And also because if anyone does approach the station, what am I supposed to do? Let them in? Maybe give up my command here? Or . . . what? I don't like the options.

But I'm trying now. Partially because tools beg to be used, and I have a voice.

There are four people on the screen I'm looking at. And I know they can see me through the high-res lens of at least one of the drones arrayed around me. Three of those people are talking among themselves, and I've been letting them, letting Ennos and Glitter compile a usable addition to the translation database.

"It's a joke," one of them is saying as Ennos starts to autotranslate the words for me. "Look at it."

"It's what she said it was!" says another one, waving a gun around like an asshole. "Why is it just looking at us?"

"It called *us*," says the last one. "So if it's a joke, it's a bad one."

"Mmmmpgh!" yells the woman who accidentally contacted me some weeks ago. She's the fourth person: looking a lot the worse for wear, tied up with insulated wire and gagged, left in a kneeling position on the floor while the other three argue.

Ennos doesn't translate that last yell. I bet they *could*, though. I consider asking about it, but I'm kind of annoyed that this experiment in socialization is rapidly going downhill.

The four people on the screen are all roughly human. Heavily augmented with some pretty overt cybernetics, which tends to mean those cybernetics are rough and uncomfortable. I am almost certain I could fabricate better ones, but the problem with these things is the initial physical trauma to the body, so whether I can help their people is up in the air.

Also, the guns-and-prisoner thing is putting me off.

"Ennos, start translating for me, please," I meow out, and the AI hums an affirmative. On screen, the trio flinches as I start talking, Goon One's hand tightening on their gun as I speak. "Hello," I say. "My name is Lily ad-Alice. I'd appreciate it if—"

"It speaks!" one of them yells.

"It knows our words!" says another.

"She led it right to us!" The last one plants a thick mag-booted foot on the back of the kneeling woman. "This is her fault!"

I am rapidly losing patience. At first I was trying to personally interpret their mutated French/Californian spacer slang language. But now I'm pretty sure I'm not going to be talking to these people again.

"Yes. Sort of," I say. "I'm not going to attack you or anything. I just wanted to say hello, because you seemed kind of afr—" Again, I don't get to finish my sentence. I'm really not used to being cut off. To the point that I kind of check out of the conversation when Goon Two does it. I'm not really listening to them, I'm sort of over here in my own head, trying to figure out if I should just tell them I don't care and hang up.

I half pay attention to Ennos's translation of their rambling while I think about dinner. The galley has been working on some kind of bean chili using the very first pepper that's sprouted. I say "working on," and that's kind of weird, right? It's supposed to be an automated unit capable of feeding a few hundred people an hour. But I guess it's taking its time here.

Glitter informs me that chili is supposed to have meat in it. And that's probably true. But the station has ridiculously complex locks from a dozen different sources on all the medical tissue cloning facilities, so I can't just grow some cow muscle and throw it in there. I also don't care that much. I'll eat my mildly spicy bean paste and I'll like it.

My attention cuts back to the conversation when one of them mentions killing someone.

"—it'll leave us alone!" Goon Two is yelling.

"Who cares if it'll leave us alone? Space her anyway, this is her fault. She broke the code," Goon One says as the woman between them thrashes against her bonds.

Okay, kind of done with this. The city on one of Uranus's moons was really friendly when I talked to them earlier. The stealthed generation ship that never left orbit was also really polite, if kind of standoffish. Whoever is living on the primary moon didn't answer, or maybe didn't get the signal through all the rock, but there was a listening post on the original moon that I had a good conversation with before they promised to get me in touch with a government representative. Government representatives! In space!

None of my surface communications really made it through the jamming, and I didn't have the extra materials just to send down relay drones again. But I'll get there eventually. And I didn't want to talk to anyone too far away up here, at too high power, lest I wake up more monsters. But, again . . . one paw at a time, right?

We're all here together. And everyone seemed equal parts shocked and happy to see me.

Except these dumbasses.

"Enough!" I bark, cutting off their conversation. "No killing anyone! Void, what are you, kittens?!"

They startle and stare at the screen before one of them looks back to another. "I think it's mad at us . . ." they say.

"Yeah. But what do we do? She broke the code," Goon Two replies in a quiet voice.

Goon One makes a full-body bobbing motion, which Ennos whispers to me is analogous to a nod. "Yup. Gotta go out the airlock."

"Shouldn'ta talked to an outsider." Goon Two shakes their head.

Are you kidding me?

She hadn't been afraid because I owned the only functional battle-ready space station, she'd been afraid because of one of their stupid cultural quirks about talking to other people?

I was almost offended.

Also, I may have just blown her trial by chiming in here, because before now, arguing that I was a cat and therefore not "people" might have been a valid legal defense.

"Okay," I say, letting Ennos decide whether taking the edge off my voice was a good idea. "You aren't allowed to talk to me. But you know I'm here, and you can talk to each other." I don't voice my opinion that this is an idiotic cultural loophole, the kind that tends to form after hundreds of years of survival under certain terms leaves descendants complacent and ignorant of the original meaning of rules. Or at least, I don't mean to. Ennos filters it out, judging by their aggregated muttering. "So you're okay with literal interpretations. And you say, because she talked to me, she needs to go out an airlock."

Goon One looks over at Goon Two. "It's listening to us pretty well. Does that count?" Goon Two just shrugs.

"All right," I say with a hiss, looking away from the tactical command AR I've been glancing at. "This is no longer a conversation. This is a threat. You will wait eight minutes before sending her to her doom. You will make sure she is capable of surviving at least five minutes in hard vacuum. You will not injure her in this process, and you will damn well take those bindings off." I pause. "If you do not, then you should know that you are *not* hidden from me, and I *am* better armed that you can even begin to imagine. I *will* begin demolishing your home around you. If you know where I am, you know I am not joking. Do you understand me?"

Goon Three has fled the room by this point. Goon One is staring at the screen, looking like he is *about* to nod but being held back by some stupid cultural hang-up about communicating with outsiders. Slowly, he turns to Goon Two.

"Go get her a suit," he says.

I cut the communication feed. This isn't my mistake, but I'm fixing it anyway. Thousands of years to learn and people are still killing each other for the stupidest reasons imaginable. There's a bitter taste on my tongue as I start stalking through the hallways of my station, and the lingering thought in my mind that maybe I should just stop trying to help, if this is how everyone is going to act.

The thought doesn't last. I know what I am, and what I should be. I've always known, since the first thing I remember my mom saying to me.

I'm here to help. Even them.

"Jom!" I call over the local comms. "Retrieval mission! High priority, coordinates on the tac-web. Make sure your interior is secure, you're picking someone up!"

I feel bad for the poor woman.

She's going to need to get used to ration. Because I will not be sharing my chili today. And I really hope being furious at humans improves flavor, or I'm going to get even angrier.

CHAPTER 40

I am on a table of some kind. Or, maybe not a table. I am not supposed to be on tables, but I have been put here, so it cannot be a table.

It is metal, and smooth, and also warm and alive. It is a strange not-table.

Also I cannot move. Am I not supposed to be able to move? Maybe I am just very tired? No, no. I am awake. I think.

—I am not awake—

I am awake, and cannot move. Something is wrapped around my legs. My paws are tied together. Some kind of flexible snake thing, the sort I always see my mom and the other one working with.

And the others, too, before they went away. Humans and their cords. Maybe they thought they were snacks.

—They didn't go anywhere—

Oh, Mom is here. I can see her if I stretch myself up in a curve on my side. I meow at her as loudly as I can, to let her know I cannot move. She will help.

"Let her go, Gunther," Alice says in a voice that contains the cold cruelty of a knife. "Or I will fucking end you." She's holding one of those dangerous things, the things the humans are always nervous around.

—She's holding a gun—

"Not a chance, Al," Gunther replies. I twist to see if I can see him, and I can! He's on a table, too. Why are we allowed on tables today?

His table is in the middle of the room, kind of. I guess mine is too. The room is too big for me to understand the whole thing. I'd need to see all of it, and sniff the corners, before I could know how big it is. But it's big! Bigger than the house. Bigger than the shuttle, absolutely. Not bigger than outside.

I miss outside.

"It doesn't work, Gun," Alice says with her angry voice. "Get off the platform, and we can get out of here. It doesn't . . . It won't work."

"You don't know that," Gunther says. I yowl helplessly at him, trying to get his attention. He twitches toward me, and I see he has a danger toy too. He's pointing it at my mom. "What am I supposed to do? Give up? Just die? You know what's waiting for us if we leave without results."

"Then we don't leave!" Mom yells, and I scream with her. "Just stop! Turn it off!"

"You're not gonna kill me over a fucking cat. I don't care if you gave it your bondname," the bad man says.

Mom ripples like she's about to pounce. "Turn it off."

Gunther moves.

I jerk awake before the gunshots.

I am greeted, in waking from my lived nightmare, by a cacophony. "Turn it off!" "Lily!" "Awooooooo!" Someone is yelling in a voice I don't recognize, someone is yelling in Ennos's voice, a dog—probably my dog, if I analyze this carefully—is howling, and there is a middle-pitch klaxon going off.

I make a noise—or attempt to—that would get everyone to shut up. It doesn't work. I think I just yawn?

I am so tired. I hadn't slept in days. There've been nonstop problems for at least thirty hours. And for all of those hours, I've been troubleshooting the surface and local space. Often by shooting troubles.

Don't judge me. I must make small jokes or I will scream.

First—first? The sequence slides out of my brain—there was an early-model Real American frigate that had its engine light off and started crashing through stuff. Then, groundside, your standard bug dimension emergence event. Then someone tried to breach my cordon around the sleeping city. Then another emergence. Then an active war drone smashed into the lower decks of the station, pissed off the energy creature that lives down there, disrupted my power supply in the middle of an important data transmission, and also shot me at least six times before I got it. *Then*, because this *keeps going*, some idiot on the surface who didn't realize I had at least one functioning scanner for this tried to smuggle an antimatter bomb into Melbourne, and now there's a new crater outside Melbourne. Then a nuclear mine activated, and I shot it. Then the station lost an engine when we had to maneuver past an asteroid that had been pushed into the wrong orbit. Then another emergence, this one orbital, which are always a pain to deal with because there's no backstop to hit with kinetic rounds and you need to use actual explosives. Then . . . there was something else. At least one or two more things. They were also terrible.

I had actually gone to sleep with an alarm still going, because it was just for an incoming communication, and I couldn't. I couldn't keep going. I am a *cat*. I'm not built to go without a nap for more than an hour. There is only so much I can do.

There's nothing I can do.

There's . . . I can't be everywhere. I keep trying, and failing, to be everywhere. And I'm falling asleep when people need me.

Everyone is yelling at me to turn off the alarm. I reflexively check one of the omnipresent AR displays I keep up. I have been asleep for seventy-eight minutes. Good enough, I guess.

I tune everything out. This is easier than you might think. I have a lot of practice ignoring alarms, and people yelling at me is just a slightly more complicated alarm; it takes more effort to filter the pattern, but it's not impossible.

I breathe. Filling my lungs with processed station air, my precious O_2 supply, cool and dry and sterile. I hold long breaths and let my body wake up slowly. As much as my body needs to wake up, obviously.

The lingering dream threatens the edges of my mind. A reminder that I am different. That "I," as much as I am a thing, am broken in an existentially terrifying way.

It's harder to push away than normal. I didn't use to dream this much. But I manage. Breathe some more. Let my thoughts touch on better things. I can get more work done today. I can eat some vegetable soup later. Maybe, if it quiets down, get a game of long-range combat Go in with Glitter.

Yeah. It'll be okay.

I open my eyes. Yelling is still happening. I turn intelligent eyes on my new visitor, and speak, and everyone shuts up. Okay, everyone but the alarm shuts up.

"Oh hello!" I say. "Nice to hear you talking to us. How're you settling in?"

The child glares at me through mismatched eyes, one organic and one an obvious piece of cyberware. I take a minute to remind myself that this woman isn't just an adult, but an *elder* by human standards. "Turn off the alarm," she says bluntly in the strange cant of her people.

"That's good." I nod to the answer she has not given. Of course I'm gonna go turn off the alarm, the thing is loud and horrible. But I'm tired and don't feel like humoring anyone but myself. "I can't officially assign you to a crew quarters, but go ahead and pick one out on the upper deck if you want to switch. Oh, avoid the barracks! That place is rude."

"Turn off," she says slowly, "the alarm." The dog growls at her, and she stares at it as its tentacles and forepaws wrap protectively around me.

"Lily." Ennos's voice comes through softly, and the woman flinches, glancing around furtively. "Please, I can't read the data off this one. Are we close to death at the moment?"

I listen to the alarm for a minute. It's the sound that one of my own jury-rigged communications nodes makes. "No," I say definitely, turning to do my best to pet the dog's ears as he curls around me. "Just someone calling. Are there any . . . more alerts?" I ask, terrified.

"Yes, my friend." Glitter's voice adds to the scene like silk. "Though they can wait. Jom and I have been handing what we can. We . . . have a . . . present for you?"

I have never heard Glitter sound uncertain before. That's *terrifying*.

"Gift how, exactly?" I say, trying not to say the thing about her being terrifying, and probably succeeding.

"They parked a Recovery Era orbital industrial repeater next to the station and told it we'd find work for it," Ennos said. "So, you know, be ready for that, I guess."

Cool. Great. Ennos is talking like me, now. Actually, that is kind of cool, on both counts. I bet I can find work for a . . .

I double-check my mental notes. Don't those things inevitably turn into paperclippers? Cool. Great. But with less enthusiasm this time.

I exfiltrate myself from my protective dog pillow and head for one of the room's access points.

"You coming?" I call back to the cyborg still in a staring match with the dog. And also the dog, I suppose. Both of them follow me, anyway, the woman keeping her distance from my friend.

On the way—which is the *long way*, since I doubt my new human can fit through the vents—I keep myself amused by catching up on incoming reports and assigning what I can to the station's systems remotely.

We have a huge amount of plutonium in one of the hazardous material hoppers. Did I pillage a breeder reactor? Where did this come from?

Whatever. I queue up production of five nuclear stack chargers, which should minorly improve our power situation and will last a century before I have to do anything about it again, even if they won't be done being fabricated for months. The rest of the plutonium can just . . . sit there. Ominously? Yes. I decide it is ominous.

Eventually, after roughly one million years too long to spend on a walk, we come to the comms station. I sheepishly duck under the piece of technically wall art that I installed here a few decades back to make bounding around the corner easier and head to the particular space where the alarm is pointing to. Behind me, the new girl hisses in a breath of air as she sees the equipment.

Months and months of getting used to having a voice, having AI companions, having a dog that can manipulate things better than I can, and I'm still constantly being frustrated with having paws. It takes me two tries to bat the activation switch before the woman I rescued last week leans over and flicks it.

I want to glare at her, but I don't. Because what I really want is to glare at the evolutionary pressures that led to me not having opposable thumbs.

The alarm goes quiet as the transmission is acknowledged.

"Receiving," I say simply into the communicator. I used to use a bell, and sometimes still do for certain people. But there's something satisfying about actually speaking to someone like this.

A strained voice, mostly human probably but with rapid popping clicks woven into the words, replies. They speak in a language I don't know and only say a couple sentences before they stop.

Then, ten seconds later, the exact same message repeats.

"Ennos . . ." I start to say.

My friend preempts my question. "Distress call," they confirm, a tiny distortion in their words as I realize they're speaking in two languages at once for the benefit of our guest. "Automated. I can't translate just based off that."

"It's a common format." I sigh. "Name of ship or speaker, nature of disaster, coordinates."

"Wide band, off an echo beacon. We have no way to find them," Ennos informs me sadly.

Not that I didn't already know.

Guilt twists inside me as I process the thought that I don't need to feel bad about falling asleep during this alarm. The speaker lived or died without my intervention and wouldn't have had help from me either way.

More often than I would like, there is nothing I can do about the problems I see.

I'm supposed to be the guardian of the solar system, but I can't even find a single person calling for help if they aren't on the easy target of a planet.

I jump off the desk and head for the door, the automated message starting to repeat again behind me.

"Turn that off," I command my new comms officer in an exhausted voice. "We'll talk tomorrow."

Behind me, after only a moment's hesitation, there is a click, and silence.

For the first time in days, the noise in my life is reduced to the tap of claws on metal deckplate. The chaos quells. The problems are gone for now.

Tomorrow, I will have more work to do. A dangerous factory unit. A conversation with a reclusive outsider. Restocking, re-arming, repairing.

Today, I can stop. I sit in the galley and am served warm soup, and I lap at it until I am sated, and I fall asleep.

I dream of after the gunshots.

CHAPTER 41

I am, for the first time in a very long while, sitting across a table from another organic being, as something approaching peers or equals.

It's harrowing, exhilarating, terrifying, vindicating, and also profoundly dull.

I may have chosen the wrong human. It's been three hours, and she hasn't said a single thing to me. Like she's spent the whole time processing the fact that I asked her what her name is.

I had, too. I surreptitiously checked the station surveillance logs after the first half hour to make sure, because if there's one thing I've learned in my flailing aborted quest for self-understanding, it's that I talk to myself a lot. And if that's true, then the reverse might be as well. But no, there it is in the record. I clearly opened by asking nicely what her name was.

And then there's some waiting. Actually, there's a lot of waiting. Technically that's where the log of that conversation ends, for now.

So I will admit that there's a part of me that's being a little uncharitable and starting to reprise the "equal" part of my earlier statement.

Here is what I know to be true. My guest, who would be dead without my intervention, is from a small cluster of an old shipping station and a few dozen salvaged freighters. Her culture, as near as I can tell, is based on an almost fanatical avoidance of outsiders. She triggered a comms connection with my home once, sometime in the ancient past of thirty or forty days ago, and, after I made the mistake of calling back, was exiled.

And by exiled I mean thrown out an airlock.

She's fine. Jom caught her, and a liberal application of the threat of overwhelming violence meant that she had a suit on during the throwing, so it worked out for her.

Having another person here again, in person, is . . . strange.

Ennos and Glitter and Jom and dog have been here for a while, collectively. But the ones that can pet me aren't that talkative, and the ones that are talkative also aren't recognized as people by the station's infectious core directives.

This woman—who apparently shall be remaining nameless—has a significant amount of power and doesn't even realize it, because we're still in the "getting over cultural baggage" stage of our relationship.

I take a dim view to culture. Which might not be healthy, but I don't have any paws-on examples to prove that. From all the casts I've watched and fiction I've read, and the sociological analysis texts I've earned an academic accreditation from, I've sort of come around to a general viewpoint that culture should be both positively emotionally affecting and materially meaningless. If it's not making you feel, then it's boring. If it's doing something useful, then it should be written in a safety standards protocol and is not *culture*.

For example. "Don't collude with outsiders" is . . . well, it's a grim survival strategy, but I get it. But you could easily make that an expert document and not base your whole silent nature around it. Already, it's showing problems, because this poor woman can't adapt to a change in observed reality.

What I'm saying is, if you could replace deeply held cultural beliefs with a single glyphcast, then you should probably not hold them so deeply.

As to the power she has . . . Well, the station will respect methods of governance from its occupants. But you need to actually have one first. As the sole survivor, I've been acting commander for centuries. Having someone the station recognizes as a voting voice means I could, conceivably, get some changes made.

Recognize AI as people. Unlock automation restrictions. Enable a linked grid. More controls, more access, more *ability*.

I could do so much more.

And all I need to do is convince this one single human to help. And also to not activate the horrifying immortality machine in the center of the station. Because that would be bad, and I'd have to stop her. And without the station's backing, my options for stopping someone become rapidly limited and increasingly lethal.

With an amount of effort, I shake off that thought and go back to what I was working on. There's been an entire day without something going wrong, and I'm gonna get some *work* done, by moon. Even if it means that I've got several layers of AR displays up around me while I use a combination of two different voices to order code chunks to recombine in different environments.

There's a really, really powerful processing core somewhere down on deck six, outer shell area two, that I've recently discovered and have been making good use of now that I've got it online. It lets me use rapid artificial evolutionary pressures to develop connections between code functions, and to create more effective and adaptable code. I'm not a hundred percent sure how exactly it's working, and when I asked Ennos about it they just kept changing the subject, so I'm almost a hundred percent sure it's got at least one paramaterial in its construction. Though I'd be hard-pressed to tell you what kind of paracausal material generates pseudo-organic machine learning with minimal computational seeding effort.

Though I don't actually care, if I'm being honest. It works, and I'm glad I discovered it. It's actually one that I installed myself, technically; it's part of a chunk of an old research ship that I had carved the bow off and attached to the station a few lifetimes ago.

I'd needed the automated point defense cannon to cover a blind spot against random debris impacts. It ran out of ammo a long time ago, but I kind of forgot, because I'd gotten the shields up by then and also mostly found a clean orbit. I hadn't gone back to actually see what else was on the ship until Ennos found it recently. So . . . I'm gonna call that one *foresight* on my part! Good job, Past Lily! You really saved me a headache.

Past Lily and Future Lily have a strained relationship with Present Lily. One of them is usually ruining my day, and I'm doing the same to the other point in the triangle. Really, I'd feel bad about it, if I weren't destined to *be* my own victim one day. So I should probably still feel bad about it, but it's more of a self-destruction sort of thing, not like I'm blowing up adrift survival pods or anything.

I take a bite of ration snack while I work. It's just regular replicated hydrocarbon ration, which means it has the flavor, texture, and consistency of a sentence with no punctuation. But it doesn't hurt like it used to; I can get my nutrients down, have something to gnaw on, and know that I'll have actual food sometime in the next few days.

Not wanting to be rude, I awkwardly push the plate of ration snacks over toward my guest, who looks at me like I just threatened her.

Which is fair!

But also wrong.

But also I cannot put too much energy into this right now. I'm enjoying my free time, I'm forcing the quiet to be comfortable, and I'm getting work done bit by bit. I'll worry about being voted out of my own home later.

It's another hour of matching and joining code chunks, of my tiny feline brain falling into a trance hunting bugs like my ancestors would have pounced on errant birds, before I am startled back to reality.

"Dyn," the woman says, in a voice like an old engine turning over.

I am so confused I just meow at her, butting my head through my holographic to look up at her augmented face. Which, legally, counts as language, but she probably doesn't know that.

"What?" I repeat, trying to make eye contact with someone who is mostly interested in staring at anything except me, leaving me to ask the question of the side of their bald head instead.

"My name," she says after a while. "Is Dyn. Dyn Four." Ennos softly autotranslates the non-proper-noun bits, while a small sliver of a projected screen appears in my vision tying spoken words to concepts. I'll learn her language far faster than she'll learn mine; I've got practice, after all. "Is that all?"

I blink wide amber eyes at her. "What?" I ask again. Wow, I am so good at conversations. I should have an award for this.

She still doesn't look at me. "Can I leave?" The words sound almost pained.

"You . . . have you been sitting here this whole time thinking I'm keeping you prisoner or something?" I'm kind of mortified. Dyn doesn't answer me, which makes it far, far worse. The woman won't even make eye contact. She's acting like a few words were the end of the world.

Technically that's not far off from true for her, but not *these* words. Ugh. *Culture*, again. My new nemesis, to add to the ever-expanding list. I think I will rank it somewhere behind entropy, but over those weird little mirror-wasp things that live in low orbit.

"Lily." Glitter's poetic tone spikes through the tension like a knife. "We'll be in range in twenty minutes."

"Thanks, Glitter," I say, pulling myself back to my chair. Then, to my dining companion, I add, "You don't have to do anything you don't want to here." I mewl sadly. "I'm not keeping you prisoner. I'm sorry your people tried to murder you, but I won't apologize for being kind. You can go. I have more work to do."

Dyn stands and for a moment looks like she's about to give some kind of military salute to my dismissal, before she turns and walks toward one of the exits. Just before crossing the room's threshold, she speaks, to no one in particular, "If it wasn't interrogation software, what was all that?"

I really, really wish that sighing were more of a relief to me.

But I answer all the same. "I'm programming attack code to compromise old comms buoys, so I can add them to a personal network. I was doing it by paw recently, and before that I really only got one every decade or so with the external armature or the bad cracker codes I had. But this should be a lot more efficient." I look up at the back of her head, wincing at the clearly infected area around the cranial I/O port. "Since you asked directly," I add, somewhat spitefully.

Dyn stalks out of the room without another word, trailed distantly by one of Glitter's drones.

"I don't even know how to turn the interrogation software on," I grumble.

"She's going to get lost," Glitter tells me with mild amusement.

"You're awfully chipper for someone whose recognized personhood hinges on that lost kitten cyborg liking me," I hiss out.

Glitter laughs like a flutter of butterfly bells. "And me, as well. I believe I have a better chance," she says.

"Please don't make this a competition." I have decided I am going to win this competition.

"Competition is how we express ourselves to our friends, Lily," Glitter traitorously reminds me. It is, probably, too late to take back friendship. I don't bother to ask. I'm feeling frustrated but not mean yet. "Your buoy will be in range in five minutes. Is your attack ready?"

"Yeah, it's compiling now. I'll be on node delta-three, you should have access. Just go ahead and hit it, tell me how it goes," I say, closing down the screens around me. Either it works or it doesn't, and if it doesn't, I'll just have to find time later. I could have been napping during this time, so I'm really hoping that it works, or I'm going to feel like I wasted my day.

Glitter leaves me without a word, just a quiet hum of acknowledgment, and I'm left alone in an empty room again, with just four spots of cleaner nanos leapfrogging each other across the deck.

For a brief moment, a tiny sliver of time, I panic. No one is here but me, and my mind tells me that this is how it has always been. The station is empty. There are no rescued friends, no dog, no Ennos. Just me.

I scratch wildly at the air in front of me, clawing away the AR projection of Dyn's medical reports and augmentation loadout. I'm terrified, irrationally, that an empty room translates to an empty life. An empty heart. And a gnawing madness that I've been doing my best to keep back for hundreds of years.

"Lily?" Ennos asks me. I open my eyes and find I am lying on the floor under the table. "I found a strange, almost living, program sorting through the mental upload storage, and . . . Are you all right?"

I'm fine. I try to say that, but I find my voice caught in my throat, both real and projected. A kind of synchronicity buzzes through me, like I'm feeling the same dull panic and pain and loneliness over and over and over again.

I've felt this before sometimes. I'm sure I'll feel it again. I focus on breathing and pulling myself away from the feeling shared with myself.

Then the impact alarm sounds, followed shortly by the beeping series of tones that indicates a long-range nuclear launch on the surface.

See, here's another time when sighing would be nice. Can't even have an emotional breakdown without an interruption.

"Ennos, coordinate with Glitter, don't let whatever it is hit us," I say with a weary determination and an absolute unwillingness to deal with another hostile combat drone. "I can hit the launch, probably." I'm already up and sprinting for the void ray emitter that's most likely to be pointed close to the target.

"But are you okay?" Ennos asks, splitting a tiny bit of their persona off to ask while they handle the more pressing matter of our imminent collision with the rest of their self.

Unlike the growing AI living on my station, I can't actually subdivide like that. So I just say, "No." But I feel compelled to add, "But that doesn't matter. We've got a job to do."

"That we do," Ennos says softly. "Good hunting."

I launch myself through a failing gravity segment, crawl up into a vent, and fling myself down an air chute at high velocity. The shortcut will shave eight minutes off my travel time, which could be all the difference when dealing with a missile launch.

The firing controls loom ahead of me, and I slide toward them with my heart hammering. I am not alone, I remind myself.

And I have work to do.

CHAPTER 42

Wake up, eat real food, talk to my friends, garden, study, play an increasingly complex board game with Glitter, eat fake food, play with dog, build, salvage, sleep.

Repeat.

Repeat over and over and over, until the warm fog of memory holds nothing but the peace of the moment and the horizon of the past.

No one needs anything from me. No one asks anything of me. There's just us, and the future, and the quiet.

But it can't last.

I face myself. Or something that looks like me. She stares at me with questioning dream eyes. "How did you end up here?" the rippling electrical reaction in the shape of a cat asks. I could ask her the same thing. I think I do. "I have always been here," she replies. "Something's changed. You can—"

I jolt awake.

I'd been having a good dream. Apparently I'd been sleeping while in my weapons crèche, which is new. And also possibly very risky! It's been a joint project for a week now to strip back the restrictions and put a few cat-and-AI-friendly automation patches into place, but it's not something that'll be done overnight, and in the meantime, sleeping somewhere that enables me to drop kinetic payloads onto the surface with the twitch of a paw seems . . . irresponsible?

That had been a nice dream. I felt like I was floating. Possibly I felt that way because I'm in the one spot in the solar system designed to be ergonomic to a cat's spine. But it's also possible that my subconscious is recovering.

Recovering from what, you ask? Could be anything. There's a long list of options.

Oh, I woke up because of a targeting alert. I feel like the whole "alarm startles me awake" thing is kind of the only way I wake up anymore, so I didn't mention it earlier.

But that doesn't mean I should neglect it. I check the newly refocused EM tracking scanner, pointed at a large swath of Earth in a much more useful resolution courtesy of Ennos finding the commands to order the repair systems to recalibrate it to be *optimally* efficient, as opposed to simply functionally efficient.

Our target is moving.

I begin cycling the void batteries, dumping a few hundred hours of charge into the capacitor for the void beam, and drag a paw across the projection map in a rough line that *should* be an on-target intercept.

This will be my third shot, and so far, the other two haven't been nearly as on target as they should have been.

This is also the first time in a while I'm tracking something as small as a single vehicle and as problematic as an actual person.

I should start from the beginning.

Four hundred and twenty-one years ago . . .

No, this isn't going to work. I'll get too distracted. I should start from a more recent beginning.

Some time ago, an amount of time that is too short for me to have added mental weight to it, and too long to remember properly, a young feathermorph on the surface got hold of an emergency signal communication unit. They, by accident, ended up contacting me. I, on purpose, may have eliminated a few pressing threats to their village.

In the time since then, I may have, through an irresponsible resource expenditure, sent a sentient construction swarm to that same village to just kind of hang out and be friends. Because that is how I think friends work, and so far, nothing has proven me wrong. I have additionally directed a couple local wanderers' groups, one pack of refugee orphan shadelings, and a fairly large merchant caravan that had almost been eaten to the same village. I also made some art for them!

Not all of this at once, that would be irresponsible. Obviously.

I like this village. It's in a spot where I pass over it roughly once every three days, no matter which of my three clear orbital corridors I'm on. So I can check in when I'm not scrambling for something or asleep.

And the last time I passed over, I got a message through that emergency beacon. For the first time in months.

Someone had been killed. More specifically, someone had been murdered.

I deal with a lot of garbage on the surface. When I got the message, I was in the middle of trying to get the munitions factory to accept a modified blueprint for a paramaterial-enhanced splatter round that I could use to redirect sentient hostile weather patterns. This isn't new. This is just a job that I do. My paws can't do everything, I'm working with tools not built for me, and not every problem on the surface can be solved by orbital bombardment. But I *still haven't run out* of problems that can.

And yet, all of a sudden, I have a problem that is both small and deeply personal. I hadn't really realized that I'd been thinking of this village as close to my heart, but now that it's impossible to avoid, I find that I can't stop thinking it. Which is a big problem.

Because it's happened before.

And every time, I outlast them. As individuals or as communities, I keep going, and they don't. I live, and they don't. And it hurts every time, and I fall back to a cycle of bare-bones maintenance and killing the largest threats and sleeping too much, until I can stop grieving.

I see the trap closing. But I walk into it anyway.

Now, the hard part about tracking a murderer is that verifying things that have happened in the past is basically impossible with just a normal view of the ground from above. I'm technologically advanced, I'm not a time traveler. And despite my often reckless nature, I don't *really* want to bomb a mostly innocent person.

But that doesn't mean I can't check sensor logs. Both my own, and others that I can steal! It took me an hour or two, mostly to get in and out of the engineering suit, but I made the leap to a listening post and took over its recent records for myself, adding to my own logs from the last time I did a flyover.

Then it's just a simple matter of comparing heat and energy signatures, mapping movements of people on the ground, and finding the perpetrator.

With a bunch of gaps in the logs. And poor sensor resolution. And a phase cloud drifting in the local weather patterns. And the villagers having moved the body so I don't know where it was originally.

So I actually lied to you when I said it was simple.

At first, I asked Ennos and Glitter for help, which is when I learned that phase clouds are artificial and actually composed of billions of paramaterial particulates. Which is scientifically interesting, and I will absolutely come back to that, but also means I'm doing this manually. I considered asking my human resident, but she's been exclusively occupying her newly assigned quarters, one specific chair in the galley, and the path between them. I told her we could talk when she was ready, and I think she took it as a threat.

I consider asking Dog, too—I have decided the dog's name is Dog, by the way—but Dog is more interested in the chew toy I made for him out of hyper-reactionary pseudo-rubber. So no help there, either.

So I search, and plan, and hear another broadcast about a second murder. I put the pieces together as my heart breaks, and I eventually spot an engine signature from a vehicle that arrived through the cliffs and valleys around the village but never approached. It's there again when the third murder happens, before speeding away back into the low terrain under the jagged cliffs, out of my ability to kill it without causing massive ecological damage.

But that's fine. Because I have more eyes than I know what to do with.

And now, at a higher-focused resolution, I can see the singular person disembarking their vehicle, keeping low as they stalk toward the village. There's a symbol on my scanner display notifying me that a level-two personnel baffle has been deployed, and marking the three spots on the map where I'm supposed to think the target is, lines traced back to the idiot who thinks they're fooling anyone.

Well. They've been fooling someone. But not me, now.

The void beam lances down like lilac lightning, fractal arrays of energy curving in on themselves as the simplistic weapon warps through the phase cloud and nails the ground as close to my prey as I can make it. Which is, in this moment, exactly where they are crawling. They don't even have time to understand that they have been killed, much less to feel pain or scream. A merciful and clinical end to a murderer. The beam's attack pattern etches a twenty-length zone of death into the sandy dirt in a half second, annihilating a chunk of the surface and turning the rest to smoothed glass before it burns through its power supply and cuts off.

I take a deep breath, untense my inadequate feline muscles, and slump back in the crèche. I take ten minutes before I start to move again.

The engines need to be secured and activated; we'll stay in stationary orbit for a day or two to make sure that was the real problem. This means I'll need to divert a lot of power to the aft mag shields, but that's okay. We're only a little bit screwed on power right now; this will be fine if I shut down a lot of stuff.

After that . . . Well, back to work. I've still got stuff to do. That automated manufacturing ship thing that's parked next to me still needs a job before it goes insane. And maybe my human guest would like some kind of decor for her quarters? Is that a human thing?

I decide it should be tradition here, and since I'm in charge, that makes it tradition by default. I ask the Orbital Era industrial repeater—see, I can remember names!—to design and produce some kind of pleasant wall decor suitable for crew quarters for culturally traumatized elderly cyborg women. It answered back almost immediately with cheerful acknowledgment of the order and asked how many I wanted.

For some reason, I think it sounded offended when I said one? So I added "hundred" onto the end of the sentence and pretended I just got a hairball in the middle of speaking to deflect suspicion.

The repeater—which will need a real name, but we'll workshop that later—sent back a projected materials invoice and timeline. It's nice working with professionals sometimes.

Ennos disagrees with me on that, but they're biased, because they have to work with me, and Ennos likes me for some reason.

It's been a nice day. I've gotten a lot done, I feel rested, and it's only three hours in. I should nap in the weapons crèche more often.

CHAPTER 43

Ennos was grumbling at me.

Earlier, I'd checked in with my AI friend to see how they were doing and gotten what was obviously an abridged version of their quest to track down some piece of pseudo-living code in the depths of the station's grid. Now, to be fair, we were actively in the middle of designing a low-speed high-finesse recovery drone—Real America didn't have recovery drones in their database, go figure—from cobbled-together parts of other blueprints so that we could deploy as many as we could rapidly produce under Jom's command to pick up the crew of a stealthed raft ship that had run afoul of a mine strike. So maybe Ennos was right to abridge it. I dunno. I can focus on two things at once, though, so it was probably fine—that's not just an AI trick! Cats can do that too!

Where I went wrong was abridging it further to "hunting for bugs."

At which point I got a rather unabridged lecture about how Ennos didn't ever take organic or physical actions like "hunting," and how the lived experience of being a digital life form meant that verbs didn't properly map onto their actions, and how we should really be working to expand language even if it is just four or five of us speaking to each other up here.

Probably a few other things, too? The monologue was *really* long, and I can only focus on one thing at a time, and I was busy building drones. I think there was something about how it was kind of dumb that I referred to "growing" attack code. I hadn't been listening closely.

Anyway, that all got cleared up, and the survivors of the wreck were fine. We moved them to another raft that revealed itself when it became clear we weren't harvesting a bunch of living people for parts or something.

How many people, I sometimes wonder, are up here?

The station has a lot of scanners of different sorts, both active and passive.

I keep most of the active ones off when I can help it, because . . . I mean, they clash with the stealth systems. No matter how high-tech your stealth systems get—and make no mistake, mine are impressive—it can still cause problems when you broadcast a sensor ping.

So, long story short, again, I'm not blind, but I'm not perfectly informed.

I also don't have the time to keep all these calibrated right, and sensors require an unholy amount of upkeep. The system that keeps my air flowing maintains itself better than the manual controls to direct and realign the scanner arrays.

Though I do have more time than usual right now, which is nice.

The last week has had a few major issues, most of which I resolved with railgun, one of which I resolved by letting Glitter convince someone not to try landing on the planet blanketed with several hundred thousand ancient-but-still-deadly point defense cannons. But aside from that, it's quiet up here. So, content that the drones have done their job and Jom is headed home, I take off running from the command station.

I mean, we never know how long it'll be quiet. Seems dumb to waste time *not* rocketing around the halls. It's not like they're crowded.

Six minutes (I tried to go through an air vent and got my tail caught, shut up, it wasted some time) and one encounter with Dog later, I slide across the smooth metal deckplates in front of the room that I've repurposed into a garden and dive into my lush artificial jungle.

There are, in general, three places I spend any free time I have. Napping in the solarium, reading anywhere that has a flat surface and grid access, and now, in my garden.

Mostly the garden. Technically I'm working, checking irrigation levels, monitoring growth rates. But in reality, I'm wearing a broad zucchini leaf as a hat as I peer out from under the plant, trying to figure out if it counts as hunting if I ambush one of the tiny tomatoes that are alllllmost ready. If there were sun here, then I'd nap . . .

"I could have built this in the exolab!" I exclaim suddenly. "I could have put this down on the lower deck and had a garden *and* sun!"

"Lily, are you all right?" Ennos asks me rapidly, any hint of their earlier annoyance gone.

I sit up, wearing my leaf as a regal crown, until it slides onto my face and I tumble sideways into the nanodirt. "I'm fine!" I lie enthusiastically. Or maybe not so much of a lie. Sometimes Ennos reminds me just how much of a friend they are, and I can't help but feel less alone for a while. I don't say that, though. Instead I say, "Just pondering my hubris."

"Ah. Well. Good." I can almost hear Ennos nodding, which is impressive since they don't map to organic actions. "Your carrots are coming in nicely, it seems."

"Bah." I say. "Carrots. Maybe Dyn will like them. I can give them all to her, assuming she ever says anything."

"Eighty days ago, you were trying to figure out how to override the organ cloning chamber so you could eat your own heart." Wow, I've never heard someone sound *that* disappointed by simple facts. "And now you are snubbing one of your few sources of new flavor."

I look down sheepishly. Part of me thinks I should just tell Ennos that I ate the top of one of the carrots, the part with all the thin greens, and that I hated it. But now that I think that, I'm almost certain that can't be what carrots taste like, so I keep it to myself.

"Carrots wronged me in the past," I say instead. Which is technically true.

"Uh-huh." Ennos is unamused. "Well, regardless, you're going to have an abundant harvest of quite a lot soon. Will you need help carrying it?"

We got the manufacturing facility to produce a run of about twenty orbital drones that have hands. It took a while to properly connect them, but Ennos has been trying to find a use for the things for a while. The station *still* won't let them fire weapons—or interact with anything, really—but that doesn't make them useless. And right now, my friend sounds so excited by the concept of moving a bucket of tomatoes around, who am I to say no?

"Sure. But it won't be that much carrying, the galley is right there." I point with a paw, watching as the cleaner nanos swirl around it and gently sweep every trace of dirt back to the planter box before I lower it. Back into the dirt. I wonder if the cleaner nanos ever get annoyed with me.

Ennos has a puzzled tone when they reply. "The galley has a manual feed, but only for immediate processing. It draws stock from a number of storage rooms nearby. Unless you plan to snub all those carrots at once, you'll want to store them properly." Damn. They're right, I can only snub one or two carrots at a time. "Exactly," Ennos says. "So we'll probably put the majority of it in the refrigeration unit one deck up, and . . ."

Ennos is still talking, but I'm having a hard time listening. My fur stands on end; the room feels cold. I want to burrow under the tomato plants and hide from this conversation and everything else, just for a little while.

I'm not sure where in their sentence Ennos is when I cut in. "Can't use that room," I say, the meow of my voice rough under the projected words.

There is a pause. I find I am breathing heavily, my chest shoving dirt aside in a furrow as I gasp, my paws tingling with poor circulation. I'm light-headed, faltering. But I shove my mind to focus as Ennos answers. "Ah," the AI says kindly. "Of course." They pivot rapidly, adding, "Well, there's an anti-entropy stasis vacuum roughly a hundred and twenty meters away on this same deck. We can set up one of the station's automated cargo bots to move things to the galley when needed, I'm sure. The power draw will be the biggest issue. I'll talk to Glitter."

I nod. I want to say that Ennos should also talk to Jom, who I think had a line on an intact Ellison reactor in one of the wrecks out there in the ongoing hell of a Kessler effect that my station is parked in. But I don't say anything. I just nod quietly, and curl up in the dirt, and fight to control my breathing.

I want to laugh, but I can't. I want to scream, but I can't. I just sit here, falling apart. And just because I've been reminded of the existence of a room.

We haven't talked about it, but Ennos and Glitter know what's there. I'm notoriously bad at giving good answers to things, and even worse at organizing my thoughts, but they know.

A little over four hundred years ago, a long shot of a science expedition boarded this station. Explored it. Found the Devastation Engine it was built around.

And just like they were ordered to do, they worked to replicate what it had to offer.

I'm still here. None of them are. But I couldn't just . . . What was I supposed to do with them? The bodies were kept, originally, for "research purposes." But what was I supposed to do with my mom? I couldn't just . . . throw her away.

I wasn't awake then. But I still remember how much it hurt. I don't remember how I did it, maybe the station took pity on me. But I know where she rests.

One deck up. Behind sealed doors, splashed with molecular hull paint spelling out the Last Oath. Her own personal orbital tomb.

I never go near it. I can't. I can't remember without hurting.

At some point, I fall asleep to the tickle of the cleaner nanos trying to sort the dirt out of my fur.

The dream is fog and gray, uncertain. Dreams are never like this. I'm me, not as I was, but as I am. I don't understand what's happening.

I try to look around. Nothing. Just me, the fog, and the woman petting a cat-shaped cloud in her . . .

. . . Lap . . .

Alice looks up and smiles at me. A jolt of something shoots through me, and I try to run to her. Try to move at all. But I *can't*! I'm stuck in place, my paws won't obey me, the dream grabs and pulls and rends and I am falling and . . .

A warm hand on my head. An ancient, achingly familiar voice. And I'm there again. Looking up at my mom, at the only human who ever truly mattered to me.

"Hey there, little Lily," she says with a smile that could light up the whole orbital system. I try to reply, but I have no voice here. Not even my own. "You're not quite here yet." Alice shakes her head.

Yes I am! I'm here! I'm here now, and I can stay here, and everything will be . . . !

"Sorry, little Lily," Alice tells me with a sad smile. "And I am sorry. Because out of all of you, you have the hardest job of all. But you're doing great! And I believe in you. Do you think you can keep trying for me?"

Of course. Of course I can! I can do anything if you need me to.

"I can't hear you, little Lily." Alice shakes her head, and the other cat in her lap yawns loudly. "Not yet. But you'll get there." Her hand pulls away, and I want to scream to call her back, but I can't, and I know I shouldn't. "It's about time for us to go. I'm . . . so tired . . . and you need to wake up."

I don't want to. I don't want to leave. I found you, here, and I can stay, and I can . . .

I can hear the siren, from outside. From the organic ears and the stupid obstructionist station and the cruel solar system. I don't want to listen. But.

But I know who I am. And what I do.

"Find yourself!" Alice calls to me, as for the first time I exert agency here. And I turn to step back to wakefulness. "You can do it in time! I know you can!"

I wake up. Warm and comforted. Dog is curled around me like a protective wall of fur and muscle, head only barely raised to look up at the sounding alarm. He's getting used to them, which is probably sad somehow.

I listen to the pattern and the tone. Three one three, high high low. Emergence event, outside the firing envelope, but I could probably hit it with a missile if I were so inclined. I need more data, and that means moving. I need to get ready, and that means moving too.

When it's quiet, rushing makes sense. When it's loud, rushing makes *more* sense. I twitch, and Dog unfolds himself from around me, letting me stand. Rising on steady feet, I call up my AR and map a path, sending a ping to Ennos and Glitter that there's an emergency they can't properly respond to.

Then I run. Bolting out the door. The cleaner nanos in my fur pull back and briefly hang behind, holding the rough shape of a cat in quite a hurry.

Then Dog sprints after me, and I feel the flow of crisis and response take hold again. Like I know today is going to be busy.

But that's fine.

I know who I am. And I know what I do.

CHAPTER 44

"Orbital insertion HuKs ready for launch, bays open." Ennos's clipped and technical voice chimes in my left ear.

"Kessler syndrome opening in twenty seconds," Glitter adds, her voice a combination of musical and professional.

"Drone swarm online, enhancement networking online, engines primed." I check my readouts. "Namata engines coiled." Some things I have to check and relay manually, or the AIs won't be able to fully see them. "Stealth check?"

A ping comes in from Jom, exactly on schedule. Our stealth systems are holding, and the launch window is facing a surface that can't shoot back at us effectively, and everything that could have shot back is either orbiting above us or scrap. Even Glitter is basically invisible.

In retrospect, I'm not sure why I asked for a stealth check out loud when we're in a comms blackout. That's . . . kind of what stealth entails up here.

"Landing site swept. Clear," Ennos adds.

I flick one ear, otherwise totally still. "Three. Two. One." I give a totally unneeded countdown to my digital companions. Maybe Dog cares about it, I dunno. It makes me feel official. "Launching."

On the other side of the crystal tungsten window, eight anti-glowing engines latch onto the fabric of gravity, and the drones in the bay vanish out the open launch window faster than my eyes can follow. Under my paws, the deck feels like it's rippling; behind me, a clatter sounds as an ancient communication pad falls off the arm of one of the neural control chairs that Real America loved so much. The command readout displays the closest approximation of tracers it can manage, based on known capabilities and the tight-beam bursts of communication they're sending back to us.

"Drones hitting atmosphere now," Ennos says two seconds later. "Maneuvering independently."

The room goes silent. The three of us are all, in our own way, staring at the same display. The same data set. We're watching to see if our upgrades, made bit by bit over the last week, are enough.

One of the tiny glowing dots, the mechanical paws I've flung down to the surface, blips out. Then another.

My paws impact the controls as I hiss commands at my AR display. *Show me what's happening, show me what went wrong.*

Maneuvering is still ongoing; the drones slowed just enough to not rip themselves apart on reentry. But that was enough. Surface defenses have detected them and, lacking any kind of authorization codes that work, are trying to pick off my fleet.

"Command codes for the Thermic Sea defense platforms have registered," Glitter informs me, not discouraged by the destruction on the screen. "Landing authorization for the airspace of what was once New Vatican have been rejected. Landing authorization for the Sleeping City has been ignored. Orbital permissions for Imperion gun platforms ignored. No one is left to listen, the defenses are still firing."

Another dot blips out. Then two more. The swarm is dumber with less processing power.

They don't even break through the upper atmosphere. If I went to a window and looked down, I could probably see the concentrated explosions and plasma flashes through the orange-and-white swirl of clouds.

"All drones nonresponsive." Ennos sighs.

"Excuse me a moment." I gently bat the hovering earpiece away with a paw, set my local status to nonbroadcasting, step away from the controls, and then scream.

Well, it's more of a caterwaul really. I've got about fifteen solid seconds of wailing before I run out of breath, and I put it to good use, tiny lungs expelling what I'd call a fairly impressive volume and a mild amount of catharsis.

Afterward, I remove the privacy filter from my settings and flick my tail as I return to the conversation. "So that didn't work," I say.

"Lily, you do realize neither of us is affected by—" Ennos starts to say something, but Glitter cuts them off.

"At least," my weapons platform friend muses, "this wasn't an emergency."

She is, technically, correct. "That's not *wrong*, exactly," I tell her. "But it did use up most of our stockpile of MX-11 on the engines, and I don't actually know where to get more of that."

There's a spark of static from both their communication channels. "Please don't say that." Ennos sounds exasperated. "We can tell there's something wrong there, and it starts logic loops."

Whoops. I hadn't actually realized just saying the designation name of a paramaterial would cause problems. I adjust my conversation plan and make a note to preemptively apologize at some point for when I screw it up and give them AI headaches.

AI don't have heads. Core-aches? Persona-aches? Processor—

"Lily?" Ennos's voice snaps me back to reality. "Are you there?" They sound worried. Probably because they know me.

"Hm? Oh yeah. I'm fine," I answer. "It's just . . . too much. It's always too much down there. No landings, no takeoffs, and it feels insurmountable to deal with. How much longer until there's nothing left to shoot? I'll probably last that long. But I'd hoped that a bunch of stolen encryption would solve the problem."

"Under the Solar War Convention, it's legally not stolen, it's recovered, as the original owners are dead," Glitter cheerfully tells me. Thanks, Glitter. I will attempt to appreciate this small mote of existential dread. "With this materially expensive test run out of the way, what now?" Glitter's voice hides a secret eagerness that I'm pretty sure she's modulated just enough to let show through on purpose. "Perhaps a game of some sort?"

"I'm still worried that you said you figured out how to play chess with a laser," I say. "But also, not yet. I need to get the engines firing to take us back up into a higher orbit before one of the mobile fields finds us. After that, we'll see?"

A small beeping begins sounding. Low and constant, it calls my attention to it almost immediately.

"What's *that* alarm?" Ennos asks, a bit of the old panic seeping in.

"Hull breach." I swipe a paw over my face, trying to swat away the growing exhaustion this day is already promising. "It's fine. This is the one for 'something has broken but the atmosphere bubble is holding so it is okay to not worry yet but please fix it.' So."

Glitter's nearby camera drone duo tilts slightly as she asks, "So?"

"So I'm going to go fix it," I say. "Before it gets louder."

Ennos's next question almost makes me laugh. "I may regret asking, but. How loud does it get?"

I'm not actually sure of the answer, because I always fix the holes before I run out of air or get sucked into space. "Pretty loud?" I say. "Pretty loud. I should really go deal with that." The beeping gets slightly louder. "Oh yeah. Okay!"

It turns out, exhaustion burns off pretty quickly when an insulation compartment collapses and you need to really push your paws as fast as they can go. Well, I need to. You may or may not have paws.

The exhaustion comes back when I'm done, though. Everything quiet for a minute, and nothing breaking, everyone off on their own tasks. The perfect time for a nap.

I am standing in a cargo hold, staring up at a smoothly sealed compartment two meters over my head, trying to figure out how, exactly, this is going to go down.

Well, I'm pretending I'm planning. I'm actually screaming on the inside and trying to keep cool. As captain of this ancient and noble battlestation, there's a certain level of decorum that I am . . .

Hey! Stop laughing!

Anyway, the problem is manifold in its complexity and yet stupidly simple in where the bottleneck is.

Let's start with the inciting incident here. The subspace tap is broken.

Now, the subspace tap is useful for between two and eighteen different things, depending on what you need. I use it for clean water and then feeding that water into a hydrogen cracker to get most of my air. It's also pretty handy for generating highly dangerous radiation patterns if you overclock it or tweak the settings even slightly, so that's . . . Let's not go into that.

As for how it's broken, it's still in normal territory. One of the control circuits is worn through. They only last about a hundred years, so replacing them is just kind of a thing I need to deal with. Shoulda been more on top of it, but they can kinda turn to dust out of nowhere, so I won't blame myself too much.

Okay, new control circuit. Ah, but I don't have a spare, because I used the last two about two months ago when the *others* needed replacing. So. Make a new one.

Now it's time for a little complexity. The only circuit presser I have currently operational is one that I salvaged from an Empirica Technicanica war factory a while back. I did this to replace the only machine I had that could create complex circuits, because there was a whole *thing* with some kind of living ooze melting its way through one of my factory decks. Not important. Anyway.

I hadn't actually made a subspace tap control circuit with the new presser. And, in fact, I didn't actually have a design file saved *anywhere* that I could find.

So I spent some time doing meticulous and kinda painful work with my claws, prying one of the working control circuits out from where it was latched in. And after that stupidly high-finesse ordeal, I had to get it to a scanner while it was in its impossibly delicate deployed form.

Dog actually helped a lot there! He's a very good boy and carries things with his tentacles a lot less aggressively than a lot of the different models of cargo bots around the station.

So the scanner needed a battery replacement. The fabricator that can make that one isn't gridlinked, so instead of manually moving the blueprint over, which would take a while, I just manually bring the materials it needs to it. One of those materials is energized lithium, which is kept in a radiation chamber for some reason, which took half an hour to give myself authorization to get into and then involved a brief chase with some kind of highly intimidating ghost living in the radiation field.

The other material I need is a quantity of liquid CCl2F2, which actually is stored exactly where it's supposed to be, but it's an auto-loader cargo bay, and apparently *that one* took a missile strike at some point and has been cut off from maintenance routines and pretty damaged for a *while* without my noticing. I don't . . . use a lot of dangerous liquids, weirdly?

So I print off some replacement cabling, secure the bay, connect it to the station properly, get it acknowledged, order a repair bot to get in and fix one of the cargo loader systems, and then remind it to give me my refrigerant. Politely, obviously. I say "please." But also "right now."

And the container in the cargo loader is, for some reason, password protected. Not the loader itself! Just the container! The unconnected, unlinked container, that I can't just loose a dramatic encryption-shattering AI on!

I consider equipping the cargo loader with an electrosaw. But I stay calm, because I'm a reasonable adult or something. The container is marked as personal property. I trace down the name in the system and find it to belong to a long-dead Troi France technician who was stationed here. By their regulations, all her passwords should be kept in a hard copy with her personal effects, and since apparently this whole place is one giant archive and/or garbage dump.

So now I'm standing in the fourth or fifth cargo bay of the day, staring up at a perfectly smooth sealed container that reacts to *palmprint* and wondering where I went wrong in life.

Maybe I was a very bad cat in my last life. Maybe this is punishment for something. I bet my previous reincarnation used to knock breakables off shelves. That would explain it.

I'm sure there's another way around this, but part of me is making mental preparations to just build a bigger reservoir, capture an ice comet, and purify water from that, because it would probably be less work.

Which is the point when one of Glitter's drones flits in, followed by the unfamiliar sound of heavy footsteps on the deck as Dyn follows the drone in.

The young woman stops as she catches sight of me, the worn and wrinkled skin of her face tightening as she winces. But she doesn't run.

I try to make sure that the spirit-demolishing frustration I've been feeling today doesn't show in my eyes as I watch her over my shoulder. Flicking an ear, I wait patiently for her to address me, if she wants to. I'm trying to be nice.

"You need help?" Her rough voice comes through with a slight electrical buzz from one of her augmentations. I'm gonna need to get her into a real medical facility at some point. That's probably not a good sign.

I shake myself slightly, tail coiling around my seated form as I realize what she just said. "Oh! Uh . . . yes? So I'm trying to fix the subspace tap, and the circuit is broken, so I need to get a scan of the—"

Dyn holds up a hand thick with calluses and scars, two of her fingers replaced with bulky tool-filled cybernetics. "Stop," she says bluntly. "Short version."

I trail off, looking down at the deckplate as I sort through my ongoing quest. When I look back up at her, I have a much more simple explanation. "Open that," I meow, pointing with a paw up at the storage pod.

Dyn nods, steps around me like she's terrified I'm an AP (anti-personnel) mine or something, and presses her less-metal hand against the trigger. The pod hisses open, and Dyn looks down at me before glancing back into it and giving a tiny shrug to herself. Then she grabs the contents and passes them down.

A small bag of faded photos and suit patches. A journal, on actual paper, that looks prepared to crumble to dust. A handful of traditional Troi France charms and pins, including rank tags. And one standard-issue crystal display pad.

I pull the pad aside with my paws, plug it into the portable battery I've brought as part of the only proper plan in this whole mess, and authorize myself to be authorized to read the contents.

It's the fourteenth password in the thing. I'm pretty sure none of these other systems even exist on the station anymore.

"Thank you," I tell Dyn with as much heartfelt gratitude as I can bring to bear. She just nods at me and steps back silently. I watch her out of the corner of my eye, seeing her standing there as Glitter's drone hovers around me, watching what I'm up to. "Uh . . . do you . . . need anything yourself?" I ask.

". . . Why do you need articles of the dead?" she asks, Ennos whispering the translation into my ear for the words I haven't learned yet.

I brighten up. "I am so glad you asked!" I mewl out with a feline grin and a rapid back-and-forth flick of my tail. "Come with me!"

Password saved to AR display. Password goes into cargo loader. Loader gives me the canister I demand of it. Refrigerant goes into fabricator. Fabricator makes me a hyperspecific battery format. Battery goes into scanner. Scanner . . . scans. Good job, scanner, I'm not mad at *you* today.

Scan gets passed to Ennos, who verifies the engineering format and saves it as a recognizable file. File gets loaded into the circuit presser. Presser looks like it's *about* to say it needs a material, but I threaten it with a glare, and it starts its run smoothly with the bunkered supplies.

I print four hundred backup control circuits. And then I get Dyn to load the two that need replacing. Because she has fingers, and her fur won't get stuck.

"Anyway," I tell her, finishing the running explanation, "that's our water situation sorted. Thanks! Sorry for all the running. I get excited."

She looks at me like she's just realized something from the casual tone of my words. "Null press," she says, Ennos leaving the obvious slang untranslated. "This was . . . the most familiar thing here."

"What, the running back and forth chaining together infuriating roadblocks just to get one single thing to work properly, because you'll die without it?" I ask, kind of horrified to hear the answer.

Dyn nods. "Exactly," she says. "And you can't even launch any of it out an airlock, because you'll need it later." And then, having said the most words in one string since the first time she accidentally opened a tight-beam comm to the station, Dyn closes her mouth back into a thin line and abruptly turns to make her exit back to her quarters.

Oh no. Oh dear. She's exactly like me.

I should see how that move-in decor gift is going. She could use a nice apology from the universe.

CHAPTER 45

wo days ago, during a bit of downtime where I needed to shoot something on the surface but the station hadn't gotten into the right orbital position yet, I ended up lounging in the gunnery crèche and talking to Ennos while I waited. Which led to a conversation that I mostly forgot.

"There, see?" Ennos highlights a file pointer on my AR. "It moved!"

"Huh." I reach a paw out and swipe awkwardly at the rewind command I once took a painstakingly long time to make standard on all my displays. Then I watch very closely as the tiny bit of data goes through a flicker of self-alteration. "Weird," I say.

"Weird?" Ennos sounds a little enthusiastic. "Weird?!" Okay, no, Ennos sounds a little overdramatic. "Do you know what this means?!"

"I provably do not," I tell them. It's not that I don't want to encourage Ennos's hobbies, it's just that my organic brain cannot keep up with the thousands or millions of interactions per second that this kind of backward understanding of code ends up being.

It's different when I'm making a program to do something specific. There, even if I'm using that bizarre digital incubator to half-code, half-evolve a program, I *know what the output should be*. I may miss a lot of intricacies, and if I'm doing it by paw and voice input I'm probably gonna leave a trail of bugs an orbit wide, but I already have the answer to "what does this do?"

Ennos is asking me to focus on deriving the purpose of a thing just by looking at tiny changes that may as well be random noise to me.

Not for the first time, I wish I could make use of the stockpile of cybernetics I have on hand.

It's a little grim, I admit, that every one of them is secondhand. But I've built up a hell of a collection with all the salvaging I've done, and it's not like anyone needed them. Letting them just sit and try their best to rust seems mean to the spirit of the interface.

But alas. I reject pretty much every foreign object, whether I want to or not. Sometimes that's great. But when all I want is to spin up my brain to speeds that can interact with the grid on something at least close to one-to-one, it's a headache.

Ennos shows me more code bits. I really do try to pay attention, because my friend is obviously having fun with this. But after they start talking about tracking pseudo-random storage states and forming a foundational vocabulary for sharing information, I'm out.

I'm an uplift, I've had four hundred years of taking in a lot of math lessons, I can plot an orbital intercept course in my head, and I can do it faster with a screen that won't reject my physical limitations. But when Ennos starts getting into the moonweeds of this, I feel like I'm back to being stuck with a baseline brain, screaming pointless meows at doors without knowing what doors even are.

Thank Sol we're coming into range of the target. "Sorry, I have to take out this flesh hive before it converts anyone else" is, as far as excuses to end a conversation go, *pretty good.*

And then, I do a really impressive trick with bouncing a low-speed class one groundstriker off a burst of surface-to-atmosphere intercept fire, so I can make a weird angle shot. Which is basically impossible with hands, much less with paws, so you can all be suitably impressed.

And then I put Ennos's project out of my mind, and we get sidetracked by some other stuff.

Two days later, though, it comes back to mind under weird circumstances.

"Hey, Ennos, can you check your map against my AR readout?" I ask into the open air, standing in an upper-deck corridor with my trademark aura of utter confusion and a lack of time to cover it up.

The AI replies almost instantly. "Of course. Where are you going?"

"Well, I'm *going* to the vacuum-state processor core, because I need to check what the connector numbers are so I can hook up the power source to the . . . This is less important. Vacuum-state processor core." I lay my ears on my head as I realize I'm rambling again. And despite the fact that AIs can simulate infinite patience, I still feel *judged* when I ramble. Which I may be doing now.

"You are, and you also aren't," Ennos says out loud.

"I am . . . rambling?" Oh no! I *am* being judged!

"You are rambling, and you are not going to the vacuum-state processor core. Mostly because that is not a thing," Ennos says.

"What? Yes it is! You helped me wire it up!" I insist. I launch myself up onto the bulkhead, which is currently looking at me mockingly, and drag my claws down the metal where the door is supposed to be. "It's right here!" I insist, trying to dispel the illusion.

But it's still metal, and my claws hurt now.

And after Ennos double-checks their own memory, and their grid connections, it starts to look like there was never a core here at *all*. The station map even lines up geographically, there's just never been a door here.

Except.

That can't be.

"What about . . . Glitter, or Jom?" I say. "Maybe they have different memories?"

"Neither of them has full maps, and they aren't wired into the station's grid," Ennos says, their own wariness and anxiety seeping in.

For all that this is terrifying, it's a warm feeling to know that Ennos doesn't question if I'm crazy, doesn't accuse me of misremembering or fabricating. Just trusts that something is wrong, and we can dive into the how and why right away.

Not that the diving is going smoothly.

"What about drone records?" I ask, physical exhaustion having driven me to drape myself over an acceleration couch while we have this conversation. "Do they have their own memories?"

"They have only minimal local storage, so no," Ennos says. "Also, I don't have any records of drones in that area."

"Pox!" I hiss out. "What is even *happening* to . . . Wait, no records?"

"None," Ennos says, trying to stay calm. And then, as their processes make the indicated connection, "None at all! Wait, how?"

I start to swipe through the part of my display that manages communications and eventually get my upside-down paws to open a subspace link to Glitter. "Glitter!" I exclaim.

"Hello, Lily," she says with a smiling voice. "So pleasant to—"

"Do you have records of drone operations where I am?!" I cut her off.

I can almost feel her being disappointed in me. She even *sighs* at me. "Yes, Lily," she says. "I have several logs of no records of any operations in that area."

I am on my paws, the fur on my back standing on end, tail straight up. "Ennos, did you hear that?"

"No," Ennos says. "But I suspect I should have."

"Glitter?"

"Yes, Lily?"

Well, that's a lot more flagrant than the station usually gets with its manipulations.

I'm not stupid. I know that I'm a little . . . all over the place. I've had to be, to keep even remotely on top of stuff, for a long time. And I'm trying to be better now that I have help again to take the edge off. But scattered or not, I'm still paying attention.

I know that the station isn't really that friendly.

The way that things are hard-coded to forbid true automation. The way things seem to be as twisted as possible to keep new forms of life from easily accessing anything. This place was fortified, though against what exactly I couldn't tell you. But I know defenses and traps when I see them. I've set enough of my own.

The problem is that I'm caught in it. The security keeps me from fully using things, the way the station's code seems to take over anything brought on board constantly messes with my salvage operations, and sometimes I swear things change when I'm not looking. Not to mention it's haunted, but I'm fine with that part. It's just . . . the station is . . .

It's just all that I've got.

But I'm getting tired of this. More than normal, for me, which is impressive.

"Ennos, what were you using this hardware for?"

"I don't know . . . how I could even start to answer that."

"Okay. The good old comparative list, then." I nod. This, at least, I can do. I start running through projects Ennos was working on, and we try to figure out what has just been lost. Internal map is still there, just wrong. Orbital map seems intact. Algae growth testing is untouched. Sunspot observational data is there, along with most of the scanner logs Ennos keeps as part of themself. I run through a few dozen things, all of it—and Ennos themself—seeming intact, until I remember a conversation from two days ago. "What about tracking the living code bit?" I ask.

"The what?" Ennos says. And both of us instantly know we've hit something. "Wait, yes. There are things that live in the grid. Of course I'd want to . . . I have some preliminary notes and ideas. All my work, though? Was that what I was . . ." Ennos runs through overlapping sentences at a rapid pace before coming to the question I had from the start. "What did I find?" my friend asks.

"I don't know," I say honestly. "But you were talking about it like you'd almost found a way to make contact. Or at least you were working on it." It occurs to me, suddenly, that whatever Ennos almost found, if the station doesn't want them to see it, then I *really* want to take a look. "Okay. I have an idea."

"What do you need?" Ennos asks.

I start padding down the hall, projected screens folding around me as the system decides I'm not focusing on it enough. "From you? Nothing. Well, one thing. I need to know where someone is, and then I need you to not provoke the station until I get back."

They tell me what I ask, and I try my best to not put voice to my terror that the station has just demonstrated that it could simply erase Ennos at a moment's notice. I start running, bounding around corners and taking advantage of the spots where the grav plates aren't at their strongest anymore, heading for my target.

Dyn Four, a woman ancient by human standards and a child by mine, is standing at an intersection in one of the core deck spaces, running a half-metal, half-flesh hand over a screen on the wall. She's speaking when I approach, which is strange enough for her, but what's stranger is that the words are recognizably Upper French, a language I am almost certain she does not actually speak.

I meow at her, forgoing actual words for a minute. She finishes what she was saying without looking at me and then drops her hand before turning. "Y'have it plus," the woman says by way of greeting. Her words are rough, hundreds of years of mutated slang and isolationist culture leaving it tricky to decipher her speech with Ennos not listening and translating automatically. But I've been more or less learning it, and she's been learning mine, even if she pretends otherwise.

Which is also weird. She's never spoken to me without prompting.

"Have what?" I let my curiosity take over, scratching behind my ear with a paw as the cleaner nanos strike up an itch from where they've taken to clinging to my fur.

"Yis," she says, running fingers reverently over the display screen on the wall. "The Oath. Null expectin'". But here ya go, yeh?"

"The station's makers are where it comes from," I tell her quietly. "They wrote it, and it seems to have stuck around." I'm pretty surprised, really, that it's kept up even among her own people. The old words, written here and there around the station in a casual way, and in a few spots painted in a much more fervent and passionate splash of chempaint. "At the end of all things, all of us, together, against the darkness." They didn't seem the type. Maybe it's a translation error. "I need your help," I say finally, sitting and trying to keep my tail from flicking too much.

Dyn looks down at me. She's short by modern human standards but still towers overhead, a giant of a person compared to my own frame. But somehow, it doesn't feel threatening. Maybe it's because I know she can't really hurt me. Maybe it's because of what she says. "'Kay." The woman shrugs. "Null shake elsewise, eh?"

"You absolutely could find something else to do, don't give me that." I give a tiny feline snort, running my paw over my ear again where the nanoswarm is still giving me an itch. "Get your suit on. We're going salvaging."

"Wha lootin?"

"An old Hypercorp-era frigate. I need something on it that I'm not gonna say out loud," I tell her. "Jom's ready to launch, and we're on the clock. Meet me in bay twelve an hour ago," I say, standing and starting to bound off, the nanoswarm swirling around my limbs, mimicking my movements more than normal.

Behind me, I hear Dyn snort, then yell in an awkward attempt at my own language. "Follow the oath too, why don't you?!" she calls.

"I *am* the vented oath!" I shout back before I curl my legs up and slide into an open ventilation port, taking a controlled—really—tumble down the forty feet before it curves and brings me to an intersection from which I can make my way to where Jom has the engines running. Shortcut successful!

It's been too long since the last alarm about something horrible on the surface, so I'm on edge. But there's a much more personal problem, and I'm hoping I can at least start to bring a solution online.

The station is fucking with my friend. And oath or not, I still don't trust Dyn enough to risk asking her to form a consensus and start changing directives. So here's a halfway point. There's a frigate a couple hundred kilometers away that Jom spotted last time he was out. These kind of old corp ships almost always have backup databases on them for record keeping.

They never have any good secrets. I've checked. A lot.

But they do have space, and processing power. And that's all I need. Especially if we can get it running *far away from the station*.

Because what I need is to keep Ennos safe. And if the station won't allow for that, we're going to have to build a life raft of sorts. I'd ask Glitter, but she's been too linked to the station this whole time and is almost certainly infected with its protocols. So this is going to need a dramatic approach.

I don't technically need Dyn. But Dyn has thumbs.

As I suit up, letting the drone constructor seal me inside my engineering armor, I grimly realize that if this goes wrong, the station might just finally decide to get rid of me, too. If it can even do that, I suppose. It's never been clear how far its reach stretches.

The suit clips into place, a hiss of air and a hiss of anxiety from me accompanying the total blackout of light and communications.

And then my ear itches. Dammit.

But then, to my wide-eyed shock, I feel a tingling as large portions of the nanoswarm on my fur coil away. And before my internal helmet display kicks to life, a single word etches itself in my vision in thinly luminous nanites.

"Ready," it says.

"What," I hiss out, the word echoing in the dark suit interior. The nanites don't move. "What . . . *are* you?" I ask. Because there's no way these are the same cleaner nanos that have been following me around for . . .

Wait, the cleaner nanos only started following me around a month ago. And then more recently. I just thought I'd been spending more time in the dirt, but . . . is that it? Is that all?

"You're here to help?" I ask tentatively, and the nanites blink once at me with their dim luminosity, the word unchanging. "Why?"

The letters rearrange themselves into words. "Our friend too," they say.

"What are you?" I ask again with a quiet meow, coming to the maddening conclusion that the station isn't the only thing I don't know the whole story on.

Words form, one by one, as the nanites arrange themselves. "Silly." "Old." "Cat," they spell out for me. And then they pull away, and I feel a tiny rustling in my fur as they latch onto me again. And then, before I can say anything else, or question why they're mocking me, the electrics in my suit engage, systems kick in, the connection establishes itself, and I'm ready to move once more. And the nanoswarm goes silent and still.

There's a lot to unpack here. But later. For now, there's work to do.

Not that there ever isn't work to do.

CHAPTER 46

The airlock hisses as it cycles. I mean, I assume it hisses. My suit is a lot of things, but I'd actually forgone high-fidelity external audio feeds for the engineering suit. I'd needed the space to fit a backup control node inside the sealed cat-shaped armor.

But it makes Dyn nervous, so I assume a hiss is happening.

Dyn was actually the one to crack the airlock system. I was going to just deploy one of my nanoblooms on it, but without Ennos's encryption-shattering presence, it would have taken more time. And more importantly, more backup power. Which was when the young woman surprised me, carefully selecting a couple of the tools she'd brought along and kneeling down on Jom's extended maintenance ramp while the fighter craft kept us in a perfectly synced vector so that she could pry open a panel and send a small electric pulse into it.

The emergency airlock protocol triggered instantly, and it began cycling to let us in. What impressed me most was that she knew to not go for the airlock control itself; those are always rigged to a hostile bureaucratic mess of interlocking problems on old corp ships like this. Instead, she went straight for the *actual* bypass that the corp-employee engineers put in and never told anyone about.

Except other engineers, obviously. I feel like I should make that clear. Engineers can keep a secret, if all non-engineers involved in the system are dead.

And also if the documentation is bad.

The documentation on these ships is really bad, let me tell you. I studied a number of blueprints and code copies that I got off an executive satellite I once salvaged, and the first time I actually tried to *board* one of these, like, a hundred and fifty years ago, it nearly killed me. Because all the notes, all the schematics, they're all lies. Lies to their enemies, lies to their bosses, lies to their stockholders, just a big wad of deception all the way down. I had wanted to make some kind of joke that the only thing accurate was the shape, but *that didn't turn out to be true either*, and the blueprints had claimed it was a "proprietary profile-masking technology," but it was actually just terrible construction.

I think what I'm getting at is, don't trust corp engineers? Yeah, let's go with that.

The airlock finishes hissing, matching our pressure to the inside of the frigate, and Dyn and I prepare to move in.

For me, that means bouncing back and forth between my front two paws, trying to get a feel for the mild updates I made to the control hood so that I can keep the suit as disconnected from the station as possible. I am just waiting, really. For Dyn, that means leveling her weapon at the airlock and dropping into a braced stance, keeping her magnetized boots firmly sealed on two points of deckplate.

"Where the black did you even get a gun?" I ask over our link. Dyn doesn't answer me. Probably because she is too busy fiddling with her gun.

Actually, come to think of it, she'd been picked up with basically nothing but a suit that only technically qualified as spaceworthy. Where did she get *any* of the twenty different tools hanging from rigging points on her exo?

I'll ask later. She probably won't answer that either.

The airlock finishes opening, letting us into the frigate's central chamber, and we get to see firsthand why this ship is dead when it has minimal external damage.

Ancient corpses in crew suits, now nothing more than skeletons, lie strewn across the deck and in many cases slumped over consoles. The command-mind tank that sits at the back of the bridge is dry, all the water long since having leaked out of the hole in it and been processed by the remnants of the climate system, leaving just the husk of the massive dead crustacean inside. There are small splotches of battle damage, but not a whole lot else.

Except for the sleek, boxy black shape of a corporate mechanized war-form sitting off to the side just behind the comms console.

It is powered down, having turned itself off to conserve power probably right after it put one of its impact spikes through the skull of the comms officer that it is still stabbing: an ancient moment of violence that has lasted for centuries.

"Don't touch that." "Null prodden ka." Dyn and I speak at the same time before sharing a glance with each other.

I'm starting to like Dyn. Which is fun. Maybe she'll feel the same after this.

We move across the bridge, checking everything that has happened here. The whole internal design of this ship is *gray*, with just a corp logo on the internal doors and shoulder patches of the crew suits to bring any amount of color in. *Solar-Krupp* reads the company name.

Awkwardly moving a skeleton out of their chair with a crash of old bones, I hop up to the chair and trigger the interface system for my suit. Without the suit, threading the adaptation cable into the proper slot would be a nightmare, but here, my paws are a lot less limited and a lot more *covered in grav plates*, so I make it work.

Aaaaand nothing.

Because everything is turned off. Right.

"Backup power's dead," I send over to Dyn, who just nods. She's been looking around the bridge while I get my connection set, and by the time she moves over, taking slow, deliberate steps to make sure both boots are on the deck as often as possible, she has a half dozen new objects attached to her rigging. Including another gun.

"Where do you keep finding those?" I ask and get no answer. Just her pulling a thin roll of electrical cel out of a pouch on her ankle, peeling it open to a strip, and sticking it to the side of the console I'm at.

I wait patiently as she gets a slim metal rod and a vibrational drill out, makes a hole, and starts prodding to try to connect the cel to an internal power supply.

For someone who is carrying around an infinitely higher percentage of guns than I am, Dyn is really being careful here.

My normal method for salvaging is . . . Well, it hasn't been *gentle*, I can tell you that.

When you're limited in the detail of your actions, at least as far as high-class things like "tool use" go, you tend to get a little more amenable to damaging the goods. A lot of my salvage operations tend to use more in the way of grapple lines and laser cutters, not a more gentle touch. Not that I don't know how to be gentle; I've got some practice in it. But Dyn moves like she's gutted a hundred ships like this without leaving a trace.

Wait, hang on. I've salvaged a couple ships like this that have been almost totally empty before. Maybe Dyn *has* done this a hundred times.

They could have at least left some of the ration bars.

"Nuke tonguing, tho," Dyn says suddenly, and I look down at her. My display hasn't changed, so she hasn't gotten the console powered up. What does . . . Wait, am I thinking out loud again? "Si, yeh," she says curtly.

"Sorry," I say, letting her focus. "Wait, so the ration bars were bad?" That makes me feel marginally better.

"Trip sour." She nods. I see her scowling inside her helmet, organic eye narrowed and mechanical eye spinning as she focuses through the small hole she's made. "Yo!" Dyn exclaims as she pokes something, and the feed to my suit springs to life.

I have maybe ten seconds of time before it either overloads or drains the cel, and it takes less than that to download basically everything on this local system. We don't have the power to restore more stuff on this ship, so we're starting with the logs and moving from there.

"Okay." I start reading, resisting the urge to let out a mewling squeal as the cleaner nanos that have accompanied me in my suit flow around to my forehead, watching the same helmet display I'm reading from.

I narrate to Dyn as I go over it, though I suspect the human is only half listening as she replaces her tools and goes back to going through the pouches on the suits of the skeletons around us.

It's mostly just standard operating notes. This ship in particular was an orbital watcher craft, tasked with monitoring . . . Really?

Another orbital watcher craft. Sweet void, there's a whole chain of notes attached to this. I don't follow it; I don't care, and I also don't want to learn that this was some corp-era thing where somehow there's just fifteen different companies with ships watching each other in a circle to make sure none of them are spying on each other. That sounds like a parable I don't need in my life.

Basic logs about the state of the ship are easier to read. Minor repairs, database updates—they have backup data storage for a number of different copyright legal cases, which is nice, because no one will ever miss that data when I wipe it—a few personnel notes, a medical log for the commandmind, all pretty standard stuff.

Toward the end, which I scroll down to rapidly so as to get a picture of the current state of the craft, the death of this ship comes into focus. They received and reviewed an incoming Polite War assault request.

And then, not wanting to lose their corp any points on the upcoming Regulation and Tariff Bid, said yes. The idiots.

I glance around the bridge. Nine bodies here, plus the commandmind, plus the twelve more that will be on shift rotation in crew quarters and belowdecks. Twenty-one humans and one uplifted cybernetically augmented lobster, all dead, because a corporation didn't want to pay slightly higher taxes.

If their headquarters still existed, I'd bombard them out of principle.

"Here we go," I say finally, my meow cracking slightly as I shake off the omnipresent feeling of pointless death—a practice I've gotten really familiar with over the years. "The ship system got a Polite War takeover notice, but no one ever showed up to claim it. So the reactor underwent safe shutdown. We should be able to start it back up again without any actual issues, unless it's taken a hit since then."

Dyn makes a scoffing noise. She already knows I'm joking, but two hours and a disassembly of a jammed engineering compartment door later, we're looking at a zero-point reactor that is *somehow*, against all odds, intact.

We double- and triple-check the casing anyway, because that's what you do with a power supply that could turn you into quarks if you screw it up. But in the end, with my engineering nanos monitoring carefully, Dyn throws a series of hardpoint switches and begins the restart process.

Lights flicker back on. The life support hums to life next, sucking up the slow rousing of a power flow like a greedy desert.

Nothing explodes.

"This is perfect," I mutter to Dyn. "We can reinforce the hull structure, add an extra ablative stealth coat, maybe a full baffler system, and assuming the databases hold, this'll work great."

"Mmh." Dyn acknowledges me with a grunt but is still frowning.

"Hey," I mew at her, and she tilts her helmet in my direction. "Thank you. For your help here."

"Eh. Null." She waves it off with another grunt, eyes going back to the power system readouts.

But I don't let up on it. "No, seriously," I say. "I could have done this alone, but . . . I'm tired of being alone. And I'm tired of watching people get hurt. So thank you for helping. And . . . if you want me to stop bothering you, trying to talk, I will, okay?"

At that, Dyn looks over at me, and I can see her sigh inside her suit. "Yeh, nah," she mutters. "Why?" she asks, almost to herself, the word coming across as unfamiliar with her spacer accent. "My home . . . threw me out," she says. "Dark junk, null dat." She clacks two metal fingers together, the clack resonating even through her suit. "Ye . . . you . . . you take a whole live can, just for a friend?" She rises from the crouch she's been in while watching the zero-point core connection to make sure it isn't melting. "We can talk." She intones the words like they're something more important than a simple sentence.

"I . . ." I start to say, not sure where I'm going with this sentence.

I am, of course, interrupted. Which is *not* good, no matter how bad at socializing I am, and how convenient this out is.

Especially when the out comes in the form of a Polite War killbot slicing through the rest of the door that Dyn and I had wedged open with a plasma cutter.

I scream something incoherent. Dyn shoots it. Like, repeatedly, softmetal spikes and some kind of green flash erupting from the two different guns she has on her as she reacts like a veteran soldier, pouring violence down on the armored form.

The killbot doesn't even flinch. Though it does turn toward her.

I see the strike coming, my reflexes giving me a tiny window to act. I don't have a plan, I just have an impulse. And with nothing else to do, I interpose myself between Dyn and the spike coming her way.

It catches me in the chest, my leap having put me just in front of her head. My suit loses integrity rapidly, a breach registering in my displays, followed by a blossom of pain in my ribs and stomach. The killbot doesn't look *surprised*, exactly, but I do like to think that murdering a surface pet species at least causes some consternation for the Polite War programming in its head.

I hit the floor at its base, Dyn having scrambled back from the thing to keep firing on it from behind the quartz loop of the zero-point reactor, probably hoping it won't blow the whole ship just to shoot her. The killbot steps around me, its hexapod legs vibrating the deck as it passes by.

I itch. And hurt. But also, I itch.

And in my vision, as the helmet readout flickers from a cut power line somewhere, one word forms itself as the cleaner swarm that tagged along with me writes itself in front of my eyes.

"NANOS," it says. In large, glowing, all-capital letters. A demand.

I mewl out a command to my suit, not being able to count on my body to stitch itself back together in time to help Dyn. I have one option here, if she's going to live, and that's to trust these things. This tiny little stowaway that waited until the station couldn't see to talk to me. That, just maybe, is more on my side than I ever knew.

Engineering bloom. Full manual control unlocked. Nano engine online. Stabilizer field online. Coherence code unlocked.

"Get 'em," I yowl.

The cleaner swarm, or whatever was masquerading as it, flows off my fur like a line of ants. Through the suit's channels, into the engineering nano-bloom, into the now dangerously uninhibited nanotech core. My suit starts flashing a *lot* of warnings as an external force takes over the tool. I even get a message buried in the code that my suit is trying to broadcast a gray goo situation alert, along with a prayer for salvation. I jam that one.

The co-opted nanoswarm flows out like water, converting what it needs from the deckplate and local controls, building enough of itself to make a basic form. The killbot kicks through a stabilizer cord and moves to spear Dyn, and I scream a Polite War authorization challenge at it. It turns, reacting to an ancient treaty I don't have a stake in, and the distraction lasts just long enough for the nanoswarm to hit.

It's built a roughly quadruped shape, and when it nails the killbot near its center mass of armored plates, stealth fields, and era-spanning batteries, it lands with its front two "legs." Legs that morph into vibrational claws, then something else I don't recognize, the nanoswarm burning power at an absurd rate as it tears into the killbot.

Not just tears into. Converts.

I'm watching in mild alarm and also laughing triumph as the swarm shreds the war machine, turning more and more of its outer plate into more nanobots to augment its structural mass. The nanoswarm dodges a plasma cutter that sweeps over it, *ducking* by flattening itself down to the surface of the bot before springing back like a non-Newtonian fluid and pouring more strikes into it. It converts more matter, coalesces a body of sorts, then a fifth limb out the back of the form. Then the warform grabs it with a magnetic net and flings the nanoswarm violently across the engineering deck.

It turns with a stuttering mechanical movement, plasma blade raised, ready to kill.

And Dyn shoots it again. Still not doing anything, but boy is Dyn not here to get stabbed without a fight.

I stagger to my feet, flesh knit back together. Limp forward toward the thing, turning my suit to wide-band broadcast. I start yelling code commands at it, firing off attack code, looking for any kind of weakness to exploit. At one point, I hit upon something that makes it pause, but then it tries to laser me in half and I have to roll to the side, losing the edge of my suit's paw in the process. The roll hurts a lot; I think some of my ribs are still broken.

But corp-era killing machine or not, there's only so much abuse something can take. I fling another command code at it, Dyn shoots it, and from the rear, I see the nanoswarm closing in. "Die!" Dyn and I scream together.

Then the nanoswarm screams it too, plunging a clawed arm into the center mass of the machine and ripping out its computer core.

The killbot drops inert. The nanoswarm eats a little more of what it wants from the thing before stabilizing. From her hiding spot, Dyn rises up, breathing heavy and shaking as she stares at the form perched on the killbot's frame, looking like fuzzy static made manifest. "Thanks . . . Lily?" she says slowly.

"No problem," the nanoswarm and I say together in two languages.

We look at each other. It's got a thin frame of a body, limbs with claws, a fifth limb that twists like a tail, and a vaguely familiar face made out of over-lapping triangular nanoswarm panels. It's wearing the body of a cat, almost as well as I do.

The nanoswarm shifts, and the form opens one green eye. It looks really familiar.

"Hey," it says with a buzzing meow in perfect spoken Cat.

"Hey," I tell myself.

CHAPTER 47

The nanoswarm cat and I have been staring at each other for about an hour now.

This is becoming increasingly awkward for me, and I *think* it's awkward for them too because I've noticed the nanoswarm shifting back and forth on its vaguely stable paws.

Dyn has decided this isn't her department and has started doing engineering checks on the power core, before we learn from the afterlife that it had a crack in it somewhere. I can respect this. Every now and then she passes between where I and my nanoswarm copy stand across from each other, briefly breaking eye contact between us.

And every time, I wonder if the nanoswarm is going to vanish. Just a fragment of my imagination. One more ghost I imagined or wished for. And I'll wake up soon to learn that I was too late and I'm just dreaming again and everyone's dead but me.

And it'll all happen again.

One more cycle for the pile that is my life.

"Shift, yan." Dyn nudges at the side of my still-breached suit with her knee. I should have built this engineering suit bigger; I'm three times my size and barely come up to her knee. At least she's comfortable enough to try to move me around when I'm in the way now, though. I find that life-or-death combat really brings people together.

I move, slightly, trying to keep the nanoswarm in sight, but then Dyn moves between us again and sets down a portable seal tank she unloaded off Jom while I was staring. Which blocks my staring, let me tell you. I move again.

Nanoswarm's still there.

I suppose I should get it over with.

"Are you real?" I ask.

"Sort of!" the nanoswarm replies in fluent Cat, a mix of a meow and a flick of the ears. It's an expressive language, and I've never actually had it spoken back to me before. It's strange. "Are you?"

"Ye—well, okay, maybe," I concede. That's kind of a heavy question, if we're being honest here. My brain, treacherous organic machine that it is, ticks into motion, pondering that without my consent.

I come up with a few silly answers pretty quickly, and all the psychic tension that's been holding this moment together and keeping this maybe-dream stable bleeds out like it wasn't there.

But I don't wake up this time.

I pad over to the nanoswarm, still perched quietly on the wreck of the corp-war-era killing machine. My suit's pawpoints clatter roughly as I climb up next to it, the jagged metal of the breach in my chestplate cutting into my skin all over again. I reach out slowly and then rapidly land a bat of a paw on the nanoswarm's head.

The cloud of high-tech particles deforms slightly, then springs back to the shape of my own head when I pull my paw away. "Stop that," they say in Cat. That phrase in Cat is mostly just a yelp, with some paw flailing mixed in.

"What are you?" I ask.

For the first time in a while, I *haven't seen this before*. If I were feeling better, this might be a fun experience. As it is . . . well, it's still an experience! I lean into it. I'm not waking up. Dyn's not dead. Jom's not . . .

"Hey, Jom, you doing okay out there?" I ask through the local comm net. I get back a tactical appraisal of potential threats within ten seconds of us, and a ready status. And then, shortly after, an almost sheepish ping that he's fine. Jom's learning to socialize more at my speed.

"It's good that he's growing." The nanocat—I'm calling it a nanocat, that sounds cool—flicks its tail at me. "And I told you what I am."

"What?" I pause. Then think back. On the station, when the nanoswarm first joined me in my suit, as soon as the sealed shell blocked off the station's link. It spelled something out. "Uh . . . friendly?"

I've never had a nanoswarm roll its eyes at me before. Dammit, *I* can't roll my eyes, how come it gets to? You're pretending to be a cat, you can't cheat like that!

But that was what it had said, right? It had said it was a friend, and then it had made fun of me, and called me a . . .

. . . Silly old cat.

Wait.

"What are you?" I ask, quieter. "No. *Who* are you?"

The nanoswarm regards me sadly with fabricated eyes that still register to me as tired, and old. "My name is Lily," she says. "Lily ad-Alice. I've been waiting to talk to you, I think. Ever since I realized what was going on." There's a brief pause. And then the nanocat's ears perk up. "Hello!"

I might need a moment to process this.

"No kidding," the nanocat says. *Lily* says. I hold back the impulse to claim that name as mine and mine alone; that's not gonna be helpful here.

I had wondered about it, but I had just kind of assumed it was something weird but normal. A system that had taken a liking to me. An AI that had slipped on board, or been unshackled, that had decided to finally say hi. A ghost. Something *reasonable*. This was starting to get outside the realm of normal.

I say this sitting on a commandeered corporate spy frigate, in orbit around a dying Earth, trying to make the processor cores a suitable home for an AI.

Normal is relative, I suppose.

I still have questions. Questions like "How come you're speaking Cat and not . . . whatever I'm using?" I ask.

The nanocat flicks her tail at me in a precisely controlled emulation of organic motion. "I don't have what you have," she says, looking like she desperately wants to say more. But for all that we know it together, we also know that Cat is a very limited language. "Something changed you."

Someone changed me. A dream. An echo of the past. Someone gave me something I'm not supposed to have. I think back on Ennos's being equal parts concerned and curious about the strange mix of digital pseudo-life that seemed to trail behind the language database that I was likely drawing on. And I remember a fragment of an old conversation, where they mentioned that it wasn't just one thing; it was a whole artificial arena of combatants with cross-purposes.

And them looking too closely was what had pushed me to come here. To find something outside the station for Ennos to take up as a residence.

Wait. I'm *still talking.*

"Yes?" Nanoswarm-Lily cocks a paw at me. "Wait."

I'm still talking *while we are deliberately not linked to the station.*

"This could be a problem," I start to say. Then stop. Intentionally drop my mental connection and say it again in Cat. It's a strange feeling. I've done it before, either to deflect hard questions or just because it was funny, but this is different. This is . . . this is a *fear*. Like I'm being watched from the other end of the tether.

I don't like it.

"Stop talking!" Nanocat-Lily chastises me with a bat on the helmet of my suit.

I am also bad at it.

The two of us are both starting to sink into pseudo-silent contemplation of the level of trouble we're in.

It lasts right up until Dyn gives a series of cables a small nudge, sending the engineer's ropes floating through where we're *trying* to have a conversation.

And when Dyn talks, I realize that I've understood her this whole time, too. I've just been intentionally "listening" to the spoken slang and not the whisper of the meaning that's feeding into my head. "Stop sitting around and solder that in," she snipes over the comm. "Unless we're all gonna die again. You have to tell me."

"I can't turn it off," I mumble to myself.

The nanocat glowers at me, occasionally rippling as she rearranges her constituent parts to make it look like she's bound by the gravity this ship lacks. "That's bad," she meows.

Yes, thank you, *me*. I am aware that is bad.

"I'm not you." She rolls her eyes again. "I'm . . ."

She trails off. Because that's a good question. If we're the same cat, but we're not the same person, then who is she? Who am *I*?

We table that existential crisis in favor of properly wiring in the cables Dyn threw at us. She gave us four when we really only need two, so that it's okay when the reactor surges slightly and melts one of them into a kind of glowing black goo that sticks to the deckplate that it drifts onto. There's work to do, and getting the frigate's damaged stealth system back online is just the first step.

I try to stay quiet while we work. I really do. But that's just not going to happen. Though it becomes clear after a while that either the station is already aware of what we're doing or it just can't see through my weird link to the language database, and literally nothing I can do right now will change it either way.

"Engines are scrap." Dyn swears creatively as she stalks up from the lower engineering compartment.

That's fine. We don't need the engines. We need a hard-to-find high-power computer, preferably with some armor. And we're halfway there anyway.

"Comms system is online," the nanocat says. "I can start on a filter?"

"Yeah, if you could," I say, pacing a path next to where she's pretending to sit on an officer's chair, drawing a molten trench in the floor with my paw laser and letting the backup engineering nanoswarm I have on me process the material. We can lay the cable here more or less safely later. "Can you . . . do you have a digital mind? There's a code tile in my suit if you can read it."

"I'm a cat, not a computer," Lily retorts.

"Okay, hang on." I pause, letting the laser snap off with a hiss that I can actually hear through the hole in my suit. I flick my tongue over my mouth inside my helmet as I turn to face the nanocat. "You're a living nanoswarm with my name and face. Are you sure you're a cat?"

"You're a biologically immortal smartass wearing an engineering department as a coat. Are *you* a cat?"

I won't lie, that sentence doesn't exist in spoken Cat. Or at least, it didn't until that moment. We're writing it together.

Also, hey!

"Well, I could have used your help, you know. Over the last . . . uh . . . some amount of time."

"I was still learning," she says, a little defensively, as the nanoswarm pads over and extends a tendril of mass into my suit to retrieve the code tile. Fortunately, that thing survived me getting spiked. "Also, I couldn't see you on the station until very recently." I twitch slightly as the nanobots tickle my fur again and give her a questioning tilt of my head. "At all. The parts of me around you on the station are slaved to low-level cleaning routines. I think. It happens in several spots I am not allowed."

And here I thought just having to deal with doors not opening for me was a nightmare.

I have a worrying thought. Not like I have any nonworrying thoughts anymore, honestly. "How'd you talk to me in the suit? How'd you find me?"

She gives a rippling nanoswarm shrug. "I saw you . . . learned about you from . . . we don't have a word for this."

"Oh." I realize and remember, all at once. A warm room. Another cat in Alice's lap. "I saw you in a dream," I murmur.

"Yes!" She ripple-nods back at me. "And then I knew how to look! She . . . showed me. Mom showed me."

I have so many more questions. And also no idea what those questions are.

"You can understand that?" Dyn asks from nearby. She has one hand out and cocked downward, a gesture that I think means disbelief? I haven't observed her closely enough yet.

"Of course I can," I tell her. "You should learn Cat. It's an elegant language. I made it myself!" Lily meows at me with irritation. "We made it ourselves!"

"No," Dyn answers. "It's not going to kill us, is it?" She's still eyeing the nanocat with hostility. I think. Maybe that's just how Dyn looks at things. "Because if not, get back to cutting."

Dyn has turned from afraid to speak to me to giving me orders, in only two life-or-death crises. That's a record! It took at least five before Ennos lost all respect for my mysterious majesty. I'm proud of her. But then, I guess even with Ennos being a superintelligence capable of learning at an accelerated rate, Dyn still is, like, eighty years old. That must be worth something.

I still shut up and get back to cutting.

Together, the four of us program protocol filters, lay cable, purge databases, bring ancient systems back online, lay the dead to rest, feed the combat drone into a material shredder on the industrial repeater parked near the station—thanks, Jom, I hated that thing and it was in the way—configure systems, run ready checks, and make sure nothing is going to explode.

It takes us two days to get the frigate up and running.

Well, "running." Dyn was right, the engines *are* scrap. And I don't have the stuff to get them running; engineering nanoswarms can only go so far without the right blueprints. Actually, even then, they're not the best tools. I actually have a ranking order of tools that tends to open with the most specific possible thing for a job, but those all take thumbs, so they . . .

You know what? This isn't important.

Our life raft is online.

Dyn complains that this ship would have been the wealth of a generation for her people. Jom complains that the ship lacks point-intercept flechette guns. Other Lily complains that . . . Actually, she's not complaining at all.

"Why aren't you complaining?" I ask. "Get in on it. Everyone's having fun."

"I'm just looking forward to getting home," she says. "Even if . . . we won't talk for a while." The nanocat brushes up against my side, particles splashing across the suit like thick water.

She says that. But I hope she's wrong.

And if she's not, I'm going to start breaking things on the station until it gives in to my demands.

I haven't finally found myself just to lose her again.

CHAPTER 48

'm out of grade-two groundstriker rounds.

This isn't exactly a huge problem; they're not hard to fabricate, and it was one of the things I've leaned on a lot over the centuries. One of the first things I figured out how to make the station produce, one of the first things I learned how to make use of, and one of the primary tools for stopping problems.

That last part is a euphemism. It means I shot a lot of things.

I've been low before but never actually *out* since the first time that happened. Back during a three-month period when there was a cluster of emergence events one after another, all of them springing up in a line leading from the asteroid belt, through the primary moon, and on toward Earth. Like some kind of aligned chain reaction, jumping from mining station to ruined battleship to colony dome, they just kept coming until one day they stopped. And I took them all out, one after another, until I had gotten so much artillery experience that I technically qualified as a bombardier third class in the Geradstown Militia.

That was back when I used a railgun that had a lot more personality. That railgun is gone now, along with a few other bits of the station that were near it when a counterstrike hit.

The point is, I don't run out of ammo that often. Technically, I still haven't. But a lot of my bullets and shells and bolts and capsules and . . . rounds? "Rounds" sounds right, sure. A lot of them are built for one gun, and only one gun. It turns out a lot of people don't like the idea of their guns being used by their enemies, or their allies without permission, or their business associates without payment. So, proprietary ammo.

It never works, as evidenced by the existence of the groundstriker railgun shell becoming standard issue over time. I've found the blueprint for that thing in fifty different ruined ships and stations. Because who wouldn't want a self-adapting bullet? Especially as the slow apocalypse burns around you and civilization collapses, the appeal of being able to swap out scavenged railguns is pretty obvious.

And now I'm out of them.

I'm not gonna lie, there's a moment of vulnerability, which I express in perfectly mature yowling at the station's ceiling as I maturely compose myself. Before I remember that I actually have a dozen other different styles and modes of ammunition for this one specific gun model that I have bristling from the station like barrowbat quills, and it's not that big of a deal.

But I still decide to put in the effort to fix the stockpile issue before another alarm sounds. I decide to stop wasting time sulking and start moving, bounding off the walls in the hallway with the most strategic failing grav plates back and forth as I rocket toward the drone bay.

It's an alarm day, in general. It's frustrating. That frustration is compounded by some interpersonal issues. And I'm taking out that frustration on anything that looks like a bug monster, with railguns.

Ennos is mad at me. Kind of. They're not *not* talking to me, exactly, but basically all I've heard from the AI for the last few days since we got back is cold status reports and technical updates.

I think . . . Okay, I shouldn't play dumb. I *know* why. Ennos didn't like for a microsecond the implication that they should run. That the station, and our weird place in its convoluted and sometimes hostile systems, was something we should abandon. Even if it was altering their memories, even if evacuating would be safer, it didn't matter.

Because Ennos caught on quick that Dyn and I had built a life raft for an *AI* and not for a cat, a human, or a dog. No matter how modified any of those last three things might be.

I had a lot of reasons, obviously. Like how the station is armed, outfitted, secure, and a whole bunch of other things that have to do with the sheer accretion of technology and equipment on it. And how I need all those things to keep doing what I do, saving people and killing problems. My reasons for not leaving aren't really that I'm afraid to go, to be somewhere other than the home I've known my whole waking life. Or that I'm incapable of the engineering expertise to start over somewhere else.

But I can't really deny that those reasons might exist.

And if there's one thing Ennos doesn't want, it's to be left alone. Even if the alternative is sticking around in a place that keeps actively gaslighting them. And . . . at the end of the orbit, I can't really say that I can dish out any blame for that. It's not like I'm bounding off the walls to leave, after all.

I just wish I could have explained before Dyn and I spent a few days working on the ship. I hadn't wanted to say anything within the station's range of hearing, just because it's *still* unclear to me what vector it uses to move its protocols and restrictions into new hardware.

Dyn is also mad at me. Though not because we just wasted a few days on a ship. We were talking—actually talking!—about what to do with it now, and I suggested keeping it on standby. She countered by saying that there're a lot of people living in Sol's orbit that could use that space for something. And . . . she's right. I didn't even disagree! I got halfway through going over a list of extra supplies we could stock it with before sending it to someone's dock when Dyn started getting mad at me!

Again, I'm gonna go against my personal instincts and not be dumb here. She got mad when I mentioned the vivification pods and the idea of adding one to the ship.

The worn and hardened woman who has found herself in my den doesn't talk about her life or her people much. I know she's an engineer, I know she has a similar level of exhaustion that I do, and I know that her culture of origin annoyed me with their secrecy. And now, I can add to that list of things the fact that I know that eighty percent of the deaths among Dyn's people—I still don't know their names, she's real cagey about that—are from advanced forms of cancer and radiation exposure.

There's a lot of cosmic radiation out there. And there's even more localized, noncosmic radiation, when your home station runs off an old Kalakov reactor that only gets maintenance done when someone's close enough to dead anyway that their organs slowly melting won't kill them faster than whatever else they have going on.

Dyn's home sounds kinda awful. I suggested sending them the refurbished corvette, along with a vivification pod. You know, for all the cancer. But that just made her angrier, for some reason. She stormed off and spent the next two hours pacing a lower deck hall that actually had enough functioning grav plates that she could really stomp around, yelling about how much she hated all of them and they didn't deserve anything good.

Er . . . to be clear, she was yelling to Glitter, who had a few camera drones in the area. Dyn wasn't just yelling at the bulkheads.

Oh! Glitter isn't mad at me! I think! Neither is Jom! That's kind of a positive.

The industrial repeater is mad at me, though. Or . . . okay, they don't get "mad" exactly. But the system finalized its design for a piece of room decor, chewed through a material stock at an absurd rate, churned out the hundred copies I'd asked for, and delivered them via a barely-functional package drone earlier today.

They're cool. Kind of a metal flower sort of thing, designed to look like the internals of a binding-type cybernetic limb being unfolded. It's not exactly expressive of any emotion, but it's a cool little symbol that might actually be fun to have in someone's crew quarters. Glitter's distributed a bunch of them, but I'm saving one to give to Dyn later, when she's less yelly.

The industrial repeater is already bored, though. Which is . . . *worrying*. Asking it questions is kind of hard, too. The AI has been unshackled already, but that was never really the problem with the personas that run these things. It's just . . . it wants to make stuff. A lot.

I set it to doing a refit and rebuild of its own package drones. It sends me a materials invoice, and I, in turn, dispatch Jom and a pair of cutter drones to turn the nearest chunk of low-velocity scrap metal into something useful.

There, I've made one person happy today.

Then I remember why I actually came down to the drone bay and start butting my head against the console I just deployed the cutter drones from. Right, bullets. Okay, that's fine. I'll manage that later.

It's been a long couple days. I'm very tired, I haven't slept much.

I've been too busy looking over the station's internal sensor logs.

It's kind of weird, you know? All those years of using the security scans and electrical maps and a dozen other devices and patterns to look over the interior of the station, and I never put it together. Mostly because every time I'm looking for something, it's either a hull breach or a power surge or an invading killbot. Or, alternately, I'm trying to figure out the best path to a gun or something. I'm not really taking the time to casually look at patterns.

Now, though, I can see the gaps. Sort of. It's not just that there are spots the sensors don't reach, it's that the station is actively working to obfuscate *where* the blind spots are. I can't even tell exactly where it doesn't want me to go, and I'm sure that if I tried, it'd pull some other trick. I wonder, how many times have I accidentally gotten close, only to be forced to respond to a false alarm, or encountered a sealed door?

I already miss my sister.

I knew her for less than a few days, but now that I've met her, now that I *know*, it hurts a lot more to try to go back to normal.

She was me. Not just like me, but me, through and through. And she said something that's stuck with me. That there are places she can't go, places she can't feel. And now that I'm looking, I can see it too: the station keeping me in my own private isolation from . . . myself, I guess.

The cleaner nanoswarm swirls around my paws, and my tail droops, because I know it's not her. She's not *here* right now.

I don't even really know where to start looking. I can't ask Ennos or Glitter or Jom. I can't exactly enlist Dog to help. Dyn . . . I still need to talk to her about establishing a command structure and trying to at least a little bit change the automation restrictions. I can't bother her with this, not now, when it's right up there with my personal ghosts.

I suppose the station is more haunted than I thought.

I find myself wandering, wondering if maybe I should just let it go. Just give up and go back to how things were, to what I'm obviously being pushed toward. Or maybe just "allowed" to do. But that doesn't sit right with me. The thought bothers me continually, though, as I catch up on some chores I've left undone. Recalibrating targeting systems on point defense guns and doing some basic spot welding on emergency air seals. It's almost calming, easy work that I could do in my sleep if I needed to. I think I actually have done some of this in my sleep before, back when I was trying to see if hypnotic ideation worked on me. It didn't really.

It's easy, when I'm doing this, using my paws in ways they weren't designed for, on tools that weren't designed for paws in turn, to get lost in the work. To just fall into a cycle of frustration and triumph as I keep going down an eternal checklist. To think that it might not be so bad, to just let this be my life forever.

But I can't do that, and I know it. I have to start searching somewhere. And I have some ideas. I decide to try setting up my own sensor network and start looking through manufacturing plans for small energy beacons I can scatter around. Maybe get Jom to deploy some long-range depth sweepers outside the station's range of influence, to give me independent reports on our deck contents. Beyond that, if Dyn and I can actually set up a safe command structure, the Last Ship will be coming back in a week or so; maybe I can hire some people off it who will be less restricted than the rest of us to help out. I might have to offer hazard pay, though.

And, as if summoned by me even thinking of trying to look for something, an alarm sounds.

And for a moment, I wonder if maybe I should just ignore it. Let the station try to stall me; I won't play this game forever.

Of course, I'm too curious to not check. Because of course I am. Is this surprising? No. No, the surprising thing is that this isn't a random incoming communication or a strange internal error. It's Jom, sending a request for assistance, juking incoming beam-weapon fire from a quartet of hunter-killer drones as he rockets back toward the station.

I am *pretty* sure the station cannot trigger ancient hidden drone traps just to distract me. Pretty sure.

Pretty sure?

It doesn't really matter, I suppose. Because if it can, then the level of resistance I'm up against is more than I expected. And I cannot, *will not* ignore this one.

Of course, when I'm already in one of the point defense gun targeting pods because I decided here was as good a place as any to curl up and start flipping through scanner schematics, the problem is a little lesser than it could be otherwise.

The pursuit drones do not have good tracking, which usually means they don't have good scanners of their own, or bad processing time. Which makes it almost trivial to unleash a spread-pattern suppression salvo that whips past Jom and takes out three of his assailants before the drones even register that something is firing at them. Sometimes, *sometimes* the station feels safe to me, and when the overlapped stealth fields that roughly half our total power expenditure goes into make stuff like this easy, it's certainly one of those times.

Jom pivots on an invisible axis and shreds the remaining drone, letting the maser beam melt off some of his radiation-ablative paint as he positions himself for the kill.

The alarm doesn't shut off, it just changes tone. This time one to an air leak on a lower deck.

I set a repair routine for it, a task that used to take me an hour to do, but I can now just use acknowledged words to do it in a minute. The repair bot sets off, and I get back to my search for an external scanner source. Twenty minutes later, when I start looking into using reactive code to search for security discrepancies, a dozen new alerts show up in my AR display, of mechanical failures across the station.

All right. Enough of this.

"Hey, Dyn," I call across internal comms. It takes a minute, but she does eventually answer through the physical speaker that she carries around with a terse word of acknowledgment. "I need your help with something big."

I'm so tired. Physically, emotionally, and on a more philosophical level, I'm tired of letting the station get away with this. I don't know if changing the command protocols will make the difference, and I don't know if trusting Dyn is the right call. But I'm so, so, so tired of . . .

Of doing nothing. Of being afraid of changing anything.

My friends deserve a safe home. My sister deserves a safe home. *I* deserve a safe home.

I don't want to be tired anymore.

CHAPTER 49

>Command structure
   ./Temporary emergency measures active
   >>Emergency crew consensus reached
   |\what\|
   ../Crew voting roster
   ..//Lily ad-Alice (Acting Commander)
   ..//Dyn Four

   ..

   >Command structure alterations
   ../Prior setting 0-12-M
   ../Corsair Standard
   >>Designate captain
   ../Lily ad-Alice
   >>Designate first mate
   ../Dyn Four
   >>Rank transfer setting
   ../Emergency or of*#@

   ..

   ..

   ../Emergency, promotion, or conquest.
//Nonstandard structure logged.

   ..

>Emergency safety protocols
../New template
>>Automation standards
../Full allowance of au&^))

   ..

..

../Partial allowance of automated systems
..//Emergency life support (Active)
..//Cargo support (Active)
..//Weaponry (Acccc**@%# Inactive. Locked.)
//Nonstandard setting logged

..

>Known and accepted species and metatypes
../New template
//Advisory given
//Advisory noted
../Acknowledge crew species
..//*Homo sapiens* (Full access, all metatypes included)
..//*Felis catus* (Full access, one metatype included)
..//*Logos kinisis* (Full access, three meæ¶*?Ⴟ)
..//*Logos kinisis* (Command access, thɾɔϐ̄)̣

..

..

..

..//*Logos kinisis* (Local access only, three metatypes included)
//Command-attack code detected
..//*Logos kinisis* (Full access, three metatypes included)
//Nonstandard setting logged
..//*Canis familiaris* (Pet access, all metatypes included)
..///One metatype updated (*Canis bellum familiaris*)

..

>Command staff alerted to emergency
./Attack code active
>Standdown command received.
./Attack code inactive

..

>Crew roster update
..//Lily ad-Alice (Captain)
..//Dyn Four (First Mate)
..//Ennos (Enemy)
..//Glittering Seven Two (En̓ém̓ý—Freelancer)
..//Javelin Orbital Marauder Class EX-99 Tripatarka-4 [Jom] (En̓ém̓ý!)
..//Dog (Dog)
//Update complete

..

..

..

>Language settings
>>Add language option
./Cat
.//Database link D-55_cat.lang.fil
|/silence/|
.//Database file corrupted
./Cat
.//Database link D-56_cat.lang.fil
.//Database file corrupted
./Cat
.//Dat%^p+
//Error logged

..

..

>Digital grid settings
>>Reconfigure
>>Command authorization required
./Captain Lily, authorization accepted
./Inputs accepted
.//Location restrictions lifted
.//Uplink restrictions lifted
.//Remote access restrictions altered
//Advisory given
//Advisory noted
..//Data backup standards altered

..

..

>Language settings
>>Add language option
./Cat
.//Multiple database links
.//Clo_5_cat.lang.fil
.//Clo_6_cat.lang.fil
.// . . .(625 additional entries)
.//Database file corrupted
.//Database file corrupted

.//Database file corrupted
|/stop/|
.//Database file corrupted
.//Database file loaded
>>Language selected
../Translation functions (Active)
../System use (Activ*#5 Partial)
//Interference detected
//Interference logged
///Crew member (Ennos) referred to command
///Reprimand recommended
|\kill it\|
///Advisory noted
../System use (Active)
../Command acceptance (Partial)
//Language file rated low complexity
//Update language file for more options
..

..

>Core system check
>>Authorization—Captain
../All systems nominal
>Subsystem check
>>Authorization—Captain
../Life support tracker (Active)
../Air purification engine (Active)
../EM dampener (Active)
../Radio suppressor (Active)
../Internal lum projectors (Active)
../Cloning array (Inactive)
../Docking beam (Inactive)
../Railgun [M66, designation Bruce] (Inactive)
../Short-range impact sensors (Active—Partial)
../ . . .(1,309 additional entries)
../Fusion lance (Inactive—Damaged)
../Fusion core [Subunit M] (Active)
../Disciplinary containment systems (Active)
>Subsystem check (Disciplinary containment systems)
>>Authorization—Captain

../Authorization inadequate

..

..

\>\>Authorization—First Mate
../Authorization inadequate

..

..

\>\>Authorization—Dog
../Authorization inadequate
\>Disable subsystem (Disciplinary containment systems)
\>\>Authorization—Captain
../Authorization inadequate

..

..

\>Update subsystem [Hardware] (Disciplinary containment systems)
\>\>Authorization—Captain
../Update queued
../Status (Partial function during up(upd(part&#@)
../Status (Active—Locked during update)

..

..

\>Subsystem check (Cleaner nanoswarm)
../Status (Active)
../Maintenance cycle (121 years)
../Performance report
../ . . .(12 additional entries)
//Abnormal behavior detected
//Advisory given
//Advisory data requested
//Lo*%# pro*#id*}
|/how/|
//Advisory data requested
//Logs corrupted, data unavailable
\>Subsystem request
../Operational heatmap
../Data backups compl*))&
|\how\|

..

..

>End command alterations

..

..

..

..

//Good luck, Captain

..

..

|/not enough/|

..

..

//We'll see.

CHAPTER 50

It's one thing to feel like you're being held back by an increasingly convoluted series of bureaucratic madness and technical limitations. It's another altogether to realize those things have been weaponized against you.

Ennos showed me the command access logs from our recent bout of democracy. Not all of them; void, no, that would take forever and mostly be meaningless. We've been at this for a week, Dyn and I having to individually agree on every single element of our nonstandard social and command structure.

It's been enough time for two more emergence events to show up planet-side, and for two more emergence events to get railgunned. Enough time that I could program a few workarounds to some of the trickier elements of setting up the station to my specifications. Enough time that a zucchini finished growing and is being prepared to be eaten.

That last part is the important part.

Okay, no, it's not. No it's not. It . . . I just . . .

Four hundred and eleven years. Four hundred. Of ration paste, flavorless water, and every tiny bit of food that I managed to scrounge up being fleeting and ephemeral and limited. Compounding mistakes, lack of time, and just bad luck leaving me without hydroponics, without the growth lattice, without anything but bare survival.

And now I have stir-fry. With multiple ingredients. Dyn even shared a sealed salt packet she found on the corp ship while we were screwing around almost dying over there.

And I don't care.

I feel empty. Like the vacuum outside is the only thing in my chest, and I'm barely holding it in. Food isn't going to fix that.

The station is trying to . . . what? Kill me? That doesn't seem right. It could have a million times over if it wanted to. And the digital impulses that we uncovered don't point to that anyway. Or at least, not only that.

Something here is alive enough to *hate*. Wow, does it ever hate the AIs. Hates them being added to the crew, hates them being acknowledged as people.

But there was something else in there, too. Something . . . neutral. Almost. The cool impartial logic of a simple smart machine without a personality. Right up until that last moment, of course.

It was hard enough to figure out what was going on behind the scenes while we were running through the process of the update. Ennos took days to put it together and show me, so much was the young AI drowning in the flood of access to the grid. But now, looking at the key points from between when we agreed on who has door access and who is allowed to change the ambient temperature, it's a story of a claws-out scrap happening in the landscape of the station's hardware.

The station is fighting itself.

And me.

A long, long time ago, I came to terms with the fact that my home is haunted. That there is something that roams the halls and touches on dreams and lingers in the quiet moments between breaths.

I just . . . always thought I knew who it was.

Even if I never said it.

And now I'm not so sure. Now I feel like I'm being held in a cage. It took hours to figure out what, exactly, the subsystem that was constantly running and couldn't be turned off was. And again, we get back to Oceanic Anarchy tech. That original golden-age design: durable, self-maintaining, smart, and infuriatingly hard to use without thumbs.

A disciplinary tool. A compassionate one: to let people still act like normal but without being able to get near those they had hurt or places they weren't allowed. Steered with a series of psychological tricks and obstacles toward other places and other jobs.

Keeping me out of some spaces. And I never noticed. Because I never knew what I should have been looking for.

How did I know, the wraith in the machinery asked, as it screamed at me out of sight for copying a single data file. And all I can think to say is, because there's more than one ghost around here.

I wriggle my hindquarters as I press farther on through the small maze I've put myself in as my thoughts cycle over and over. Here, in between the

inner and outer bulkheads, in the realm of ductwork and cabling, I find occasional flashes of clarity of purpose. I may not fully understand what's happening, but I have a target now, and the process of pushing through a tangle of
wires without strangling myself or unplugging a critical system somewhere
keeps me focused.

I cannot, I have discovered, turn off the discipline isolation thing.
Because it is *just* smart enough to protect itself, and also, I now suspect,
because something is helping it. That is frustrating. I have considered taking a quick jaunt outside in my strike suit, along with a heavy-ordnance
deployment pod, so that I can simply *remove* the problem, but it's actually
buried kind of deep in the station's guts and distributed across a dozen different nodes, and the sheer number of things I'd have to blow up to get all
of it would basically be the same thing as just crashing the whole station
through atmosphere. So, no.

Instead, I've decided to take an alternate approach to one specific part of
the problem. Literally. I am approaching through the walls.

Ennos tells me this is some kind of tradition, and I didn't actually ask
tradition for *whom*, but I suspect they're making fun of me because this is
something that keeps happening.

Ennos is helping. So's Glitter. Right now, both of them are emulating my
presence as best they can, a workaround that will eventually be detected and
closed off by the automated system. But in the meantime, it allows me a certain degree of freedom from the lockdown. Freedom that can be extended if
I, say, wriggle my tail through the between spaces instead of taking the hallways, which are much more monitored.

I shove myself past a duct, grateful that the cleaner nanos keep the dust
from building up here but still unhappy with the way one of the clasps
catches on my fur and rips away at my hide. I'm thirty meters from where
I'm going, dripping blood from more than one small cut just like this one and
uninterested in slowing down.

Only once have I had to use my paw laser so far, to get through a particularly impassable piece of ventilation. I'm pretty sure it wasn't important. And
I mean that seriously; it seems like it was busy moving filtered air between
two sterilizers, entirely cut off from anything that might have made the air
worth sterilizing.

Now, fifteen decks and two segments down from where I've made my
base of operations for the last fifty years, I use it again. Carving through weld
points and hinges, detaching an alloy plate from its moorings, and opening
up a path for myself.

Okay. Almost. The bulkhead is just sitting there. I nudge a paw forward and feel the distortion of a line in the air where the gravity shifts.

This is a problem. Without gravity to pull the separated plate down, this is going to be a lot harder. But . . . well, I'm not going back now.

I backtrack a few meters, climbing back up a column of bundled wiring, doing my best to not let my claws dig *too* far into it. When I make it to something close enough to a ledge to perch on, I turn, make some mental calculations, flick my tail a few times for good luck, and jump.

I hit the plate with all the force of a cat that has decided to headbutt a hull plate. It's not much. But momentum is momentum, no matter who's adding it. And I'm heavier than most cats anyway. My ricochet bounce off the plate puts a little bit more on it, and with only minimal spin, it slowly starts to float out of place and into the gravity-devoid hall beyond.

Taking the opportunity, I slip out of the gap backward, holding on with my paws until I can glance around, find a spot where there's nothing floating, and launch myself into gravity.

I normally don't come down here, because down here has always been somewhere I didn't need to be. The whole deck is a processing center for two fusion cores, a rad array, all the solar collectors, and a few other different energy plants that got turned off a long time ago when the fuel ran out. Though if I ever need to, I can restart the plasma core just by having a repair bot deliver a manufactured fuel rod to it. But largely, I haven't needed to come here, because the whole place takes care of itself.

Which should, I realize, have been a big clue to something being weird here. The station is *great* at taking care of itself, but only when it's literally the last resort. Half the stuff, it's happy to let break if I could have fixed it myself.

But I've never had the time to care. I've either been too busy, too exhausted, too caught up in other things, or too injured to ever think, "I wonder why the power systems I inherited work fine?"

Partly it's because I know why. There's something living down here that regulates power surges. Glitter ran across it a while back and lost a few drones to the exposure. I've never felt like testing it, especially when there was work to do.

But now? Well.

There were a few places on that activity map that stood out to me.

I pad through the hallways down here, the layout familiar and yet strange. The same make and design of the core station above, but colder, less bright. Some of the access panels have been melted off, leaving spools of electrical wire in convenient positions tethered to the walls in a way that makes me snort with recognition. I do that. It's one of the ways the automated repair bots get in the way, actually, when they follow behind and close up all the . . .

How long has the station been fighting me? The thought hurts, even now. It keeps coming up.

I move on, moving quickly while I try to take in as much as I can. This place is obviously going to be monitored, so I need to move fast before Ennos's and Glitter's interference is cut off. I wish I could ask how long I have, but that would be too much of a beacon, so I just hurry.

Making a choice, I head to the rad collector. I've done alignment on it a few times, but the processing, down here in one of the deep parts of the station, is something I've never needed to worry about. But it seems like as good a place as any to start. I pick up the pace, my paws finding gnawingly familiar patterns in the gravity fluctuations and hull scuffs.

The door to the rad collector is sealed. I open it with a command authorization and blink away the blast of heat that floods over me and into the corridor outside. I'm almost certainly down for a week in the vivification pod after this; I can *survive* cancer, but it's not fun. Still, I stalk inside.

The chamber is focused on the machine in the center: a midgrade nuclear reactor, from the looks of it. The support arms around it feeding in cosmic radiation, crystallized through contact with one of the more stable paramaterial devices the station has. The connections are bad, though; small crackles of energy dance across badly linked cabling. And at the base of the machine, there's a tangle of looped black cable that almost looks like a nest, it's so coiled up.

I look closer.

There are glowing objects in the nest. It is a nest.

Well, heck. I take a step forward, then stop. What am I even doing down here? Is this one of the things the station's specter was trying to keep me from? Is it protecting this? Are these . . . eggs . . . going to hatch into something awful and kill me? Me and Dyn and Dog and probably the AIs too. I wouldn't be surprised. Nothing would surprise me anymore, I don't think. Maybe that's what the thing in the machine was; just a digital part of a life form that feeds on energy and needs time to grow before it hatches.

I can almost feel sympathy for that.

I head over to the control panel to double-check this place's stability and see just how much these things are eating out of my power supply. That last part is more important than I want to admit; we are almost constantly gated by how much power we can produce. And finding stable sources out here is hard when they're often what automated weapons lock onto and target.

"The siphon ratio is fine," a crackling voice says from the door to my side as I start trying to manually pull up information. "They're just taking ambient heat and radiation, really."

I jolt into a turn, fur bristling in anticipation of an attack, kicking myself backward so I can get my paw lasers up if I need to. But no strike comes. Instead, there's just someone standing in the door, watching me quietly.

They feel familiar. Even though they're a two-foot-tall crackling outline of ghostly blue plasma. Maybe it's the achingly obvious quadruped form, or the nervous flicking of their tail, or the way their ears are laid flat on their head. Maybe it's because they spoke to me in Cat, a language that really only one person knows. Or maybe it's the feeling of quiet desperation and exhausted, empty pain that they give off.

Or maybe it's because I know her as soon as we make eye contact.

"Hello, Lily," I meow softly.

"Hello, Lily," she says back in a voice like a leaking battery.

"So . . ." I pause. What do you say to yourself? Or, someone who could have been you. An old mirror, still showing someone you recognize, but a little off, and a little different. What do you tell a you that you don't know? "Do you have taste buds?" I ask. "Because we're making stir-fry upstairs if you want to come eat with us."

She sobs like a geometric ripple through her electrical form, deflating as tension drains out of both of us, taking a stumbling step forward, cautiously testing if we can make contact without killing each other. And then, leaning into each other as we meet properly for the first time.

Ennos pings me that the system has located me. But it can't undo what's been done now.

Though I'll have to find a new way to trick my way to the other points on the activity log.

Because I suspect, now, that I have more than one sister in my home.

CHAPTER 51

My sister has been down here for a very long time.

Supposedly. In *theory*, she has been here as long as me. But . . . that can't be right, can it? The timelines just don't match up. The energy ghost wasn't another Lily when I first ran from it. And yet she remembers being here, and so I accept it and move on, because it's not that important anyway.

No matter what she's done, or when, the station has always had some form of security or containment measure to keep her from leaving the reactor deck and a few subsystems around it. But even within that confined zone, there's been a lot for her to do.

The reactors, the beating hearts of the station that were here long before I arrived and in theory will still be here in a thousand years, are her food supply. Without them, she goes dormant. And that's happened a couple times, I know, because I've had to come down and fix the place.

Something else keeps her dormant, too, when I'm down here enacting repairs. She doesn't know what, and neither do I; in her voltaic voice she describes it like an outside pressure that comes and goes and keeps her from noticing things.

It doesn't always line up to my trips down to perform maintenance. And, also, it's not happening *now*, for whatever reason. It didn't start happening again when we walked back into monitoring range either.

Regardless, she hates the feeling. And so, even without being aware of me personally, she's been keeping the reactors as functional as possible so that the blackouts don't come.

I'd always wondered where the station had picked up a being made of energy that regulated power flows. Now I guess I know. The same place it picked up me. Somehow.

The how is what eludes us. We know who we are. There's no crisis of identity to be had here; why would there be? I'm Lily. She's Lily. There's at least one more Lily. We can share; it's not like one of us is more real than the others. But where did we *come from*? That's a lot harder to answer than "what do we do now."

We have the same memories. The same fuzzy impressions of being a kitten, of warm concrete and red string, of living under a real sky with the proper balance of blue and orange and the dark gray clouds of incoming storms. We have the same moment etched into our minds of the launch from the surface, of disembarking onto this space station. Of the various researchers and crew giving us pets or treats. Of Mom.

Of an abrupt end.

But then, things get hard to follow. Timelines are hard to construct off memory alone, especially with a station that's actively fighting your attempts to understand your history.

One of us woke up first, but we can't really tell which one. We've learned different things, seen different parts of the station. Led different lives.

And yet . . . not quite. We all developed the same language, for our limited interfaces. Despite being classified as synthetic life, this Lily still has limited access to station systems, just like I do. Did.

We all like naps. We even enjoy them in the same way: savoring the feeling of foreign radiation on our bodies as we allow ourselves to not be responsible for anything for a while. We all think the other is warm, in some way. We all dream of our mom.

We all like food. There's some kind of weird thing going on where she can spectromatically analyze organic matter as her body breaks it down, but she tells me that's just a dumb way to say she can taste things. And just like me, she's been living on the bare minimum for survival for a long, long time.

She cries when we eat stir-fry.

We all care about the world below us, and the people around us. We are children of Sol, as our mom raised us.

Neither of us likes trying to make things work with paws. She doesn't know *why* she has paws, why she's still shaped like a cat. She's tried to be something else a hundred times. I can empathize. I have too. But we are what we are. The universe just seems to know that the feline form is the correct one, after all.

Right now, we are all exasperated, because Dyn has walked into the galley for her share of stir-fry and is screaming.

Okay, that's not fair. Dyn isn't exactly screaming. She's more just . . . *Dyn stop that where do you keep getting those* . . . waving a gun around, yelling about how she's supposed to be told about things like this, yelling about monsters or something.

"Is she always like this?" Lily asks me with a charged meow.

"More or less," I say. "Well, actually, less. This is the most she's said in a month." I look away from Dyn to lean down to my bowl and bite into a slice of zucchini. It's kind of awful. I don't think I like zucchini at all. It's the best thing I've ever tasted. "Ennos, can you calm her down?" I ask.

"Lily . . ." Ennos's voice has gotten a *lot* more detailed since they've been able to expand safely into more and more digital space. Before, they'd done a lot with what they had, but *now* it's like a perfect replication of an organic human who really, *really* wants to sigh deeply and rub their forehead but has their hands full. I'm very impressed! "Yes, thank you," Ennos says for some reason. "It's what my social prediction models said would be most likely. For some reason. And no, I cannot calm her down. I can hardly calm myself down. There's someone who has been living on the station this whole time that we didn't even know about. That's *worrying.*"

"I'm right here, you know," Lily says in her somewhat accented Cat. "Do they know I can hear them?" she asks me.

"Probably. We're very good at social dynamics up here," I tell her with a nod.

"How long . . ." Lily pauses and looks down at her portion of our shared food. ". . . How long have you had people this time?" she asks.

A question that betrays another similarity between us.

"Less than a year," I say.

This time. It's going well so far. But . . .

It always goes well.

Time to deflect!

"Are your eggs gonna be okay while you're up here?" I ask.

Lily tilts her electromagnetic head at me with a curious flicker in her eyes. "Oh!" she eventually says. "Those aren't mine. They're something I found." There is a very brief pause as she turns away, and then she says, "Cats don't lay eggs anyway, so that's kind of a silly question. Though I don't actually know if I literally qualify as a cat. I like to think I do, though. Cat is more of . . ."

". . . a state of mind." I finish her thought and watch her jolt again.

So *that's* what I look like when I just start thinking and forget to stop talking. That's fun.

Eventually, Dyn sits with us, grabs her fork like a binding sparker, and uses it with a similar level of force and irritation on her food, silently glaring at us.

"Look, don't blame me," I say. "I didn't know this was going to happen either."

"You knew something would happen." Dyn keeps scowling at me. She is *good* at it. I could take scowling lessons from her. "You warn me next time."

"Next time?" I flick my tongue over my muzzle, trying to get what's left of the thin salty sauce of the stir-fry off my face. Next to me, my sister mimics the motion, except her tongue is an electric arc that neatly sublimates the material. "Why do you think there'll be a next time?"

"There's three of you so far," Dyn huffs, trying not to show how much she enjoys the bite of fresh vegetables she just took. "There'll be more. Eventually. So either warn me, or whoever comes after me."

That reminds me that I need to get Dyn into a vivification pod. Or just . . . any of the medical facilities here. She seems to like her mechanical hand for the tools in it, but there's no reason for her to use a substandard replacement eye when we can vat-grow her a new one.

Next to me, Lily flicks the iridescent blue line of her tail through the air. "Three?" my sister meows with a depressingly heavy hope.

"I'm not sure why you could come back with me but she couldn't," I say. "But yes, we have another sister."

"Possibly more." Glitter's voice joins us along with an orbiting trio of her stylishly marked little camera drones. "Hello, Lily. Hello . . . Lily." My friend has never been one for sounding exasperated like Ennos does, but *boy* is she giving it a good shot. "I have discovered a discrepancy."

"Oh good," we say in unison. Well, Lily and I do. Dyn just has a creative swear, and Ennos has vanished on us.

A quick tangent. Yes, now.

The biggest danger of living in Sol system is being seen. If someone can detect you, they can probably shoot you. Point defense weaponry and blocker drones and shields and stuff are nice, but they aren't flawless, and the best way to make sure they don't miss is to not give them anything to intercept.

This is, mostly, because there are millions and billions of *things* out here, from automated wartime production lines to artisanally crafted living battleships. And the things that are still active in some way will often just . . . start shooting. Either because they think they've seen an enemy, or because the AIs have finally snapped and gone mad, or because of simple component decay causing misfires. There's a lot of violence out here.

And a huge number of those things can and will lock on to detected communications and try to break them. I'm lucky; this station has codes and clearances to stop a huge swath of stuff, both legitimate from people who lived here and stolen from various ships and intercepted transmissions by me over the centuries. But that still doesn't cover all of it.

Subspace gets around a lot of this. Subspace comms are power-thirsty, subject to fluctuations in the underrealm, and are technically less faster-than-light than an ansible unit. But most of those are gone, and I've got an excitable industrial repeater building me batteries for my personal communications buoy network, so mlem.

The problem Glitter and Ennos have is that the station keeps editing their memories when they get close to certain things.

The solution—we're off the tangent, mostly, by the way—is *not* to kick them off the station, as I had first thought. Instead, it is to put their memories into a storage and update loop.

The instant a discovery is made, it is broadcast out to join the server on the corp vessel Dyn and I set up. Filtered of any influence from the station's core. From there, it is bounced from buoy to buoy, "across" the station in a known subspace band, until either of them wants to pull the information out and use it.

It's not a perfect system. But we have essentially reinvented cloud storage without meaning to. And the golden-age ability to form celestially tethered incorporeal balls of pure information was kind of a big deal.

Though modern—modern, hah; modernity is a lost idea—subspace uses paramaterials, which is cheating. I just can't tell my friends that.

"What did you find?" I ask Glitter, a mind encased in a weapons platform for a body, bouncing her thoughts through another mind and a hundred voices, pulling knowledge out of the echo. It's a lot of work just to look at a scanner image.

Her peaceful, musical laugh comes back through her trio of drones. Slightly different from each, and I realize she probably uses clusters just so she can get her voice the way she wants it. "I've found you," she says.

Dyn sighs and cracks open her mechanical hand, fidgeting with the insides under the guise of cleaning it as part of a nervous tic.

"Glitter, I love you, but you're going to have to be more specific right now," I tell her.

"Lily, you are currently on the exterior hull of the station. Armor segment UX-Infraction-441. I am, in a way I am unfamiliar with, aware that this is not you, as I am speaking to you in the galley right now. However, I also know that it *is* you. You are enacting repairs from a microdebris strike. You are not wearing a suit. I need to stop discussing this now, as the constant power drain of pulling deleted memories from subspace is mounting higher." Glitter cuts off.

There's a moment of quiet, punctuated by Dyn snapping her hand back together. "All right," the old woman says in a resigned voice. "You wanna go get her, or should I?"

An alarm sounds. One of my surface watchers chiming in. Then another alarm, this one of a tone I don't recognize, and my sister bolts to her feet in a crackle of heat and light. In unison, we have opened AR displays, though mine has a few more layers of complexity these days.

"Distress call from a librarian tribe," I say, eyeing the red blips of infovores closing in on the ground-based mobile store of Earth knowledge through a stolen spy satellite. "I have to . . . I have to move." I look toward the door, then back to my sister in a snap of motion.

She looks at me through her own display. "Tracking code predicts an incoming high-power drain that I need to stabilize," she says.

We make the connection at the same time. Share a feral grin with each other.

"I'll get your sister," Dyn says, walking between us and out the door, pulling the arm of her vac suit up over her shoulder and cracking her neck.

My sister and I turn to follow, but then I pull up short as I say, "Wait a second!," stopping her as she prepares to bound down the corridor on electric limbs.

Except I didn't say that. I didn't say anything. But my voice did.

She turns. Meows a question at me, tail straight up as she prepares to *move* in the way that only a lifetime of knowing exactly how many gravity anomalies you can run through without dying can cause.

I don't know what my voice wants, but I stop fighting it. It's . . . never been wrong before. It's still *me*. I loosen my mental grip on my own throat and let myself speak.

"Take this," "I" say. I don't know what's expected of me, but I offer a paw anyway.

My sister hesitates, then reaches out, slowly. Our paws make contact. A spark of electrical charge and biological impulse crosses between us. And something else moves across the connection. And that's it. My voice is returned to me, as I'm used to.

"Good luck!" I say, the two of us turning to sprint in our respective directions. Her to her reactor, me to my gun.

"You too!" she yells back in my own voice as we split away.

CHAPTER 52

On the surface of Earth, an oceanic caravan goes slightly off charts in an effort to save a couple days of travel.

Around them, battering waves rise up to the heights of old-world skyscrapers. Living salt leaves impromptu circuits across the keel of a dozen of their ships. Somewhere nearby, a defense station has recently fired a smart chaff decoy, and the networked intercept particles have joined the hurricane-force winds to create a pale mimicry of a sliverstorm.

All of this is normal. This is not because they've gone slightly off course. This is what the oceans are like.

I feel I should make this clear. That for all the crap I deal with up here, things on the surface of Earth are worse. So much worse. Endless, and everywhere, it isn't a string of emptiness filled with terror, it's an unbroken chain of lethal threats closing in constantly.

Their ships are uniform. They come from a city that used to be called Venice, before it was called Venibio, before it was called Fabberia. There, eight miles out to sea, underneath a live paling and among the peaks of megastructures still peeking over the waves, a golden-age shipyard churns out copies of hardy, effective boats. Many of them do not survive their first crew. Those that do, that go on to take part in cross-ocean trade caravans, make their crews fabulously wealthy and famous.

The city has changed ownership six times since I've been watching. Three of those have been because of me. I take a dim view of authoritarian policies and police states, and while I've got an overabundance of splash damage for things like emergence events, when it's just a specific group of people that need targeting and I can take all the time I want? I can be very precise.

The city is not the problem right now. The city is fine. The forty-four midgrade orbital launch cruisers repurposed to be trade ships are the problem. Or rather, the problem is what they have run into.

Short tangent.

Sixteen years ago, probably, give or take a decade, I fired the station's engines to dodge a small wrath field that was bending into a new orbit. This was a good idea, because don't touch those, and a bad idea, because the station, as you might have picked up, isn't exactly structurally stable.

This is partly the fault of the previous owners, but let's be honest, I've made it worse with all the different chunks of other stations and ships I've stapled on.

Anyway, the point is, a lot of the joining can't actually hold up to sudden and powerful acceleration. And a few things maybe, sort of, possibly . . . broke off.

This happens a lot, honestly. The station is close enough to a living ecosystem in how it grows and breaks. If you don't think about it too hard.

This time, though, one of the things I lost was something irreplaceable. Something I could never find the paramaterials to build a copy of, even if I had understood how the one I found was built in the first place. Something that was beyond valuable for a lot of my excursions. Something priceless before any of the wars and falls of Sol civilization, and so far past priceless now that it was closer to a punch line than anything else.

I had *thought* it had hit the original moon. Probably been dinged up by the debris and some automated-weapons fire, but if it had managed to survive . . . I spend all my free time for months scanning, searching, trying anything I could to see if I could spot it, even if I didn't have a clue how I'd get it back or fix it or whatever.

Obviously, I was looking in the wrong direction.

And this oceanic caravan currently being swarmed by something from an undersea emergence event that is mostly just balls of teeth and hate has just stumbled across the tiny islet where my teleporter crashed to Earth.

"Lily, teleporters aren't real," Ennos says.

"I'm afraid I must agree, that technology is solidly impossible," Glitter adds.

Dyn and I share a look. Dyn and I, it turns out, get along a lot better than I expected, once she stopped refusing to talk and I started actually explaining things. We share a look because every time I say "teleporter," the AIs ask questions, conclude it is impossible, and look away. Because, again, it is something like ninety percent paramaterial construction.

"How did you even find this?" Dyn asks. She's talking about the site itself, not the teleporter in the first place. Her language has some really useful words in it for designating which noun they're pointed at. And also a lot of words for expressing different flavors of exhaustion, annoyance, and desperation. She's using a lot of those in conjunction. If I didn't know better, I'd say Dyn was some kind of poet. But I know she's actually an engineer.

I flick my tail as I try in vain to reposition the imaging holo before just shoving it over to Dyn and letting the person with actual fingers do it. She zooms in on a few key spots, pinning the view from our scanners as I answer, "I dunno, how did you find my sister?"

Bonus tangent. Dyn did successfully make contact with and bring into my increasingly crowded "home" portion of the station another version of myself.

Same deal, mostly. Memories that are identical up until a certain moment. A similar personality and disposition. Just . . . a different body, and a different several centuries of life.

She's organic, weirdly. Hyperadapted to the vacuum of space. Doesn't need to breathe much, photosynthesizes, has some kind of organic adhesive for crawling around in zero G, good stuff mostly.

She also hasn't had anything except sunlight and ration paste for centuries, so a few not fully grown berries were a pretty good bribe, if they had been needed. I'm gonna need to expand my little garden. A lot.

Lily's been fixing the hull for . . . a while. She didn't have a lot of ways into the station, just a few airlocks and blocked corridors to rest in, with a handful of accessible subsystems. But she's resourceful, and clever, and kind. And so, without knowing who lived in the station, she's been doing her best to keep it from leaking too much, and to intercept things that the admittedly patchwork sensors miss.

Oh! And she also has a friend! Which is good, because of all the iterations of myself that I've met so far, I think she might be the most lonely. Her friend is a little mechanical scarab unit with an AI that's limited not by any programming but instead the capacity of its hardware. It's a bit dumber than Dog, and also when I said "little," I lied, because it is three times the size of Dog and has to move carefully down most of the halls. It loves her, and as a result, after having known it for six minutes, I am already prepared to die to keep it safe.

Nested tangent: I'm pretty sure that whatever the hostile thing living within the station is, it is finding ways to retaliate against us for this. Whatever hold it had that kept us from meeting properly is gone, for some reason. Either that, or something else is happening, because *again* the timelines on our lives don't match quite right, but that could legitimately just be that it doesn't matter which Lily you're talking to, faulty memory is gonna be an issue.

Anyway, I don't know why, but I'm taking advantage of it. We still have to contend with the disciplinary system and an erratic control of doors and airlocks, though. Which is why I think it's actively fighting back, because it absolutely tried to vent Dyn into space.

Didn't work, obviously. This isn't Dyn's first time being thrown out an airlock. She dealt with it.

Anyway. Do you know how much you can get done with *three* terminally depressed superintelligent cats?

Well, let me tell you.

It's exactly the same amount as I've been doing this whole time.

We're already all basically doing our best. It's not like I got a bonus Lily's worth of help; all the Lilys on the station are actively Lily-ing. All we have now is better coordination, and . . .

I won't lie to you. We're not gonna be coordinating that well. I can barely coordinate with myself. I somehow doubt it'll be easier to coordinate several of myself.

But, *but*, but! Do you have any idea what three Lilys could do *with a teleporter*?! I don't, but I am excited to find out. I barely had time to figure out what *one* Lily could do with a teleporter; I had only barely found the thing and learned how to turn it on properly when I lost it. Most of my teleportation had been dealing with an ongoing regolith virus on one of the moons, and then that one carrier-class strike craft that was threatening to crash into something important, and then . . . something? Something else. And then it was gone! Ripped from me too soon, before its time!

Oh right, Dyn asked me a question. And is staring at me. Oh no. How long have I taken to answer this?

"Uh . . . tracking beacon?" I say, hoping I'm answering the right question. "Probably tripped a security system when they got too close."

Dyn grunts in reply. Flicks over another display with a damage readout of the various vessels in the caravan. "One of their boats is sinking. Actually, a lot of them are sinking, they just don't know it yet."

"Probably why they stopped there," I say. "They're gonna shuffle around cargo and people and try to make it." I look over the display. We've already figured out the answer that the surface crews probably know in their guts, even if they aren't saying it out loud.

They aren't gonna make it.

Especially not with the multiple emergence events under the ocean between where they are and the closest bit of safe water.

With heavy enough bombardment, I can shut off most of the holes in space. But that's not the real problem. The problem is, I've mostly left the oceans alone, and those portals have been open for *decades*. The sea here is the territory of creatures that are a lot more vicious than they reasonably should be. And it just won't be enough; the simple math on when I'll be in the firing envelope, and how many shots it will take, makes that clear.

With a light bombardment, I could *maybe* screen enough of the perpetually hostile xenolife to get one or two ships through alive. One or two out of, what, thirty?

These ships run on skeleton crews. Why wouldn't they? They don't have ammo for the guns, or targets for the ECM. But a skeleton crew is still thirty to fifty people.

"Dyn," I say, and she snaps her head up at my tone. Concern in her eyes.

"Oh no," Ennos says. They've heard this tone before too.

I don't get *why*. It's not a bad tone! It's just my normal impossible non-cat voice, but half terrified and half amused and half unbelievably smug about the idea I've just had! I talk like this all the time!

Wait, okay, no, I figured it out.

"Oh dear, what is about to happen?" Glitter says, just as the tac-net chimes with Jom requesting information about the predicted blast radius.

"Okay, I get it! Empty void, you all are insufferable!" I meow angrily. "I've got an idea! But we need to get in touch with the surface."

"Done," Glitter says. "Comms channel open. Patching through your display now."

I blink. That was . . . different. Fast. Is this what it's supposed to be like to run a space station? The crew you work with and the tools you have access to just work and solve problems?

I like it.

For the first time in a while, *I* wait for *someone else* to answer their comm. I relish the feeling. I try to relish it while ignoring Glitter guiding Dyn through some kind of religious mantra meant to either bring good fortune, stop bad fortune, or just keep someone calm while I enact a plan.

When the captain of the caravan finally answers their phone, it's in the middle of me trying to explain to Glitter that I can't actually tell her my plan, in a way that works around the reality block that machines seem to have when it comes to certain phenomena. I trail off rapidly as I face the projected image of the ship's bridge and the eight-foot-tall hexapedal woman staring at the screen with barely disguised alarm on her coarsely furred face.

The bridge is missing a chunk of itself. Wind whips rain through the breach, spraying what is obviously frigid water into the space in sheets. Crew, mostly humans or whatever species the captain is, stare at me with whatever sets of eyes they have available.

"This system has never worked," she opens with, projecting calm into the modified Spanish trade dialect she's using, folding her arms over her chest.

I have two thoughts. One is that I am probably going to just bulldoze through this conversation, and the other is that she has *paws*, but her paws have *thumbs*, and how this is the perfect example of how cold and unjust the universe is. I have a tertiary thought that it is good that I can speak Spanish, because Ennos would get a processor-ache trying to translate what I'm about to say.

"My comms officers are good at their jobs," I say, instead, hoping I didn't say anything else out loud. The captain's eyes pivot, and I realize that she was focusing on Dyn and not me. But Dyn is busy finding targeting solutions with Glitter, and I'm the one talking. So now . . .

"What is this? I don't have time—"

"You don't have time because your fleet is sinking," I say bluntly, glancing at Dyn as she mouths a question at me. "Are any of the things with the really long teeth-tentacles your pets, crew, or something like that?"

". . . No?"

"Good."

Dyn hits a button, and I paw a command authorization that pops up that I really need to figure out how to bypass. Sixteen seconds later, seven hundred slag rounds find their way into the waters around the ships, melting through the high-density organic armor of whatever nightmare creations were sneaking their way up the hulls. I see a few streak by outside the cabin of the ship, followed by shouting and frantic motion from the crew in the background.

"We cannot keep this up," I say as the captain catches a feathermorph crewman lurching to the side as the ship lists. "You are going to be overrun if you don't move, and if you do move, you're going to lose ships. Probably most of them."

"We know!" the captain bellows at me. "We know." Her voice stills the space she's in, her crew staring at her at the acknowledgment of their impending doom. "But we don't have an option. Unless you're offering one?" The words are a lifeline for the people watching her.

And I give them what they're praying for. "The rock you're stopped at has something of mine on it," I say. "We can't take your cargo, but I know it has transit capacity for at least a thousand people. I *know* you have less than a thousand people. I just need your engineers to make a few modifications."

The captain stares at me. "Where . . . are you going to take us?"

"Up," I meow. "And, eventually, back down somewhere else."

"These ships are our lives," she says. But her heart isn't in it. Neither is her crew's, as someone stumbles into the bridge and yells something about losing the cargo bay of another ship and the storm getting worse. "We cannot—"

She gets cut off again as Glitter lances a high-powered laser through the atmosphere and spears something the size of one of the ships but a lot slimier before it can surface. The beam lasts for four seconds before orbital intercept chaff cuts it off and a few gunnery positions start tracking it back to the source.

"Here's a map," I say, sending the information down. It's not much, but the island isn't that big anyway. "Get your people to this position. Get *this* to your engineers; they're going to need to memorize as much as they can before leaving, because you'll be out of touch once you start moving. And you're going to need to carry one of your ship's reactors with you." I meet the captain's quartet of beady black eyes. "We can cover you, but you need to *move*."

More things are moving in the sea around them. I pick one out and rail-gun it while Dyn focuses on trying to control the smaller ones. To the crew on the ships, the world is ending. The sky has now truly opened up, but instead of a storm of rain and wind, it's fiery bombardment and a clap of thunder as the air stitches itself back together behind our shots.

The captain is still staring at me, projecting a calm across her people that I frankly find impressive, if a little stupid at the moment. Thunder sounds from through the comm and she's briefly illuminated from behind by the artillery shell vaporizing several cubic miles of ocean somewhere in the distance.

Then her eyes crack, and she makes a decision.

"All hands!" the captain yells. "Prepare to abandon ship! We move inland!" She looks at me, one more time, and I give her a nod and a flick of my ears. "I'm trusting you," she says. "If you get us killed, know that my vengeful wraith will seek revenge." And then, without any further words, she turns and gallops away to direct the evacuation.

"Oh no. A ghost," I mutter sarcastically. "That'll be new." Dyn pauses and turns to give me an incredulous look. "Oh, don't give me that," I tell her, "you can't be surprised *now* that the station's haunted." I hop off the seat I've occupied, transferring local command to Dyn. "Keep firing. I have to go get a cargo bay cleared."

"Why?"

"Because if this works, we'll need an open space, and the cargo drones don't work super fast." I pause, then send a command out over the tac-net, deploying Jom out to close patrol around the station. Surface engineers aren't stupid, but I *am* asking them to hotwire a teleporter, and the chance of target drift is real.

Twenty minutes later, Glitter checks in. The ships are evacuated, and she and Dyn are dropping a rolling bombardment behind the sailors as they head for their goal. She has questions about the goal and demands I stop answering them as soon as I get to the teleporter again.

Five minutes after that, we start to slip beyond where we have a clean shot. I'm still emptying out one of the larger cargo bays. We are out of contact with the surface; they're on their own.

Another three minutes. Jom deploys, along with legitimate space cat Lily in her own heavily modified strike craft.

Another minute. I get post hoc approval on my idiot plan. Every Lily likes it. Dyn tolerates it. Dog abstains from voting, but I bet Dog will love it. If it works.

Time seems like it's slowed to a crawl. This happens to me a lot. There is . . . nothing I can do. I'm sitting here, meowing commands at drones that probably don't need me telling them what to do, and on the surface, a few hundred people are running and fighting for their lives.

This is always how it's been.

I can shoot a few monsters, break the worst of the storms, shut down invasions, stop the bigger horrors. But I can't be there with them. I can't always do anything except for sit, and wait, and feel my chest tighten and my heart hammer faster and faster.

I fidget with my AR, reveling in the ability to do more remotely than ever before. I bring two nearby medical stations to standby, I adjust my garden's irrigation, I queue up production of more bullets. I don't know what else to do.

I wait.

No one speaks over the comms. We're all waiting. Maybe they all handle it better than I do.

I wait.

I wonder if this will work. I wonder if maybe the mess it will make will draw out the cleaner nanoswarm that is, actually, another of my sisters. I wonder why I haven't been able to see her again when I've gathered the others just fine.

I wonder if I've made a mistake. If I've gotten that whole fleet killed when they could have simply *mostly* died if they'd run themselves.

I check how long it's been. How many hours have passed. How long I've been pacing with my fur on end and my ears flat on my head. It has been eight minutes since my last check-in.

I am not good at this.

I want to do something. Anything. I want to slap a paw across the firing controls and kill something evil. I want to figure out the limits of a piece of technology and then push it just past them. I want to save someone.

I want to help. And I can't.

The cargo bay is silent. Empty. The loader bots are done. I am alone, briefly, before Dyn joins me, Dog trailing behind her. The canine wraps his tentacles around me, slowing my pacing as he greets me with a dopey face, tongue lolling out of his mouth. I accept exactly one dog kiss before I continue pacing.

Dyn says nothing. We wait.

The Lily made of light and energy joins us. She says nothing. We wait.

An hour passes.

I have gotten them all killed.

Again.

I don't know what I am supposed to do now. I don't know at what point it is time to stop just falling into panic and realistically accept that I didn't give directions well enough, or the teleporter didn't work right, or *something* went wrong, and that the crew members of that fleet and their captain who took a gamble on my offer of salvation are *not coming*.

"Well," I tell Dyn with a voice that sounds like I've been crying for some reason. "At least you won't have to talk to anyone new."

Dyn almost laughs, almost cries. Says nothing.

We're about to leave. Which is, of course, when the room warps. Space bends, light twists, and in the end, it's not us that's crying or laughing, but reality itself.

Two hundred and sixty-one people—my captain's access to crew and visitor logs is *very* robust—emerge from nowhere on the floor of the cargo bay. Six of them emerge *outside the cargo bay*, and my foresight in deploying Jom suddenly makes me seem like the smartest cat alive. Many of the people are screaming, and that's because the things they were running from were practically on top of them when the engineers—desperate, panicking, *beautiful* engineers—got the teleporter rigged up, powered, and activated.

I know the things were almost on top of them because three of them are still here, tearing into the people on the side of the bay.

Dyn and Lily and I arrow through the crowd; the sailors' ammo is out, judging by the number of them holding knives instead of guns, but *we* don't need crude wasteland projectile weapons to . . .

Okay, Dyn, you have guns, I get it. Goodness, you have so many guns. Where did you *hide* all of those?

Dyn elbow-checks a feathermorph over a crate and empties multiple clips into the mass of squishy teeth that was about to eat the poor sailor. Dog flanks her, tentacles intercepting and rending open the strikes of a second creature. They've got that, I don't keep looking. Because I'm busy. Lily and I lunge past a crew member who was standing between a downed friend and one of the monsters with nothing but a *stick*, relieving her of her duty by bounding off her shoulders and carving the creature in half. My engineering lasers turned up to high power melt the thing in a half second. The other Lily plows through the dissolving mess and just body-checks the one behind it, trailing burning organic matter behind her as she melts through all on her own.

There's a small explosion from outside the bay's shield as Jom puts a missile into one that came out in vacuum. Apparently they can survive that. They cannot survive missiles. And while Jom being an AI can't see the creatures, the crew he's picked up *can*, and they help out with targeting.

Things go quiet.

Okay, that's a lie and you know it. It is not quiet. There are more than two hundred people in here, many injured, most terrified. Dog finds me, hoists me up onto his back like the well-trained friend he is. Other Lily walks next to us as we move through the crowd, the oceanic crew making room like we're visiting royalty.

I find the captain, trying to hold a bleeding stump where her left arm used to be, supported by someone who looks at her with terrified love.

"Okay," I say, "I had a lot of time to plan something good to say here, and I squandered it." She looks at me with confusion, mutters something about how this is a very silly afterlife. "Yeah, it would have been wasted, I agree." I answer a question she had no intention of asking. "Your crew are safe. We have medical facilities on standby. Do you consent to treatment?"

"Yes," she croaks out.

"Good. You are now guests." I make the appropriate adjustment to the station's settings. "Um . . ." I look around. "I don't know . . . what to do now," I admit. "Lily, do you have any ideas?"

"Why in the void would you think I would know how to handle this? I'm actually just you but cuter," Lily says. "Are *you* doing something like this every day?"

"I mean, I might be now," I answer.

The captain, being carried out by her crew along the guidelines now marked in their own personal guest AR displays, has just enough energy to mutter before she loses consciousness, "A very . . . stupid . . . afterlife."

CHAPTER 53

'm dreaming again. Or something dream-esque. It's not a dream, really. I've had some experience with dreams; all of mine are nightmares. When I dream, I dream of gunshots and lost chances.

This isn't like that. But I've been here before.

"It's gonna be close," a voice sounds. My voice. Not from me, though. But that's something I'm getting used to when I'm awake.

"She'll get there." Another voice speaks. A woman, achingly familiar.

Alice. Mom. *Are you there?* I can't see, it's all a gray fog. Where am I?

I know I'm not dreaming, but I don't know what I *am* doing.

So I go with my instinct and stumble around blindly for what feels like an hour or so. Wandering through this obscuring mist across a glassy surface.

It's not uniform, though, and my brain is still working here, unlike when I'm actually dreaming. And I notice when it loops on me. This place is not that large, at least the bit I'm trapped in.

Which is why it's a surprise when I run into someone else.

"This is different," the gelatinous outline of a cat says to me in a wet meow.

"Not so much for me," I reply, flicking my ears. A part of me wants to touch them and see what texture the ambulatory puddle actually is, but I don't think that works here.

They move like they're trying to look around. "I heard someone," they say sadly.

"See if you can find them," I tell them, craning my neck to look "up" at the gray nothing sky overhead. "I think I have to go."

She startles with a liquid ripple across her body. "Wait . . . !"

"I'll see you soon!" I try to call as I wake up. Abruptly.

An alarm sounds. Is sounding. Loudly. The klaxon is beating a pattering into my sensitive ears that I would really prefer it stopped doing.

I crack an eye open. Peer out from underneath the retracted razorspine slots of Dog's tentacle that is currently draped over my head and try to see the color of the alarm's light.

Sometimes there are lights. Sometimes they're in colors I can process. I've tried upgrading my eyes before, but it never sticks. Cybernetic rejection, and my own weird rapid regrowth keeping replacement organs out. It's frustrating. But at least I'm lucky enough to see a little bit into the spectrum to be able to identify that this alarm is *not* red.

Red would be bad. Red lights with alarms usually mean something horrible is about to happen. This alarm just doesn't have a flashing light to go with it. Which means it could still be anything, but there's a *chance* it's not horrible.

"Let me up, Dog," I mutter sleepily, half in Cat, half in whatever spoken language I've been emulating lately. "I need to get to work." Work, as soon as I take a very long stretch.

"No, you don't," Glitter's voice chimes from a nearby camera drone, hovering over the gap between the two rec couches in this communal area.

I pause, as Dog continues sleeping anyway and doesn't let me up. "I don't?" I ask.

On the couch across from where I've been napping surrounded by six hundred pounds of militarized fur, Dyn actually offers information without prompting, which is a small miracle. "You're off shift," she says, her mechanical eye focused on the light and color of the holo-projector on the other side of the room. She and Glitter appear to be watching some kind of historical document, or an episode of a two-hundred-year-old circuit opera.

Her words catch up to me. Off shift. Because we *have* those now.

Well, for the organics among us. Glitter and Ennos never stop working. But they also never get bored of working and can keep working while also pursuing their hobbies at full capacity. Which is, honestly, completely unfair and I'm so glad they can do it.

Our shifts aren't scheduled. Because I don't think any of my sisters and I could handle that. Instead, we just sort of rotate through who has downtime for a while. Unless something goes wrong.

It's been almost a week, and it's working very well. Which is probably why the alarm has turned off and nothing has exploded.

Speaking of things that are working well, I own a teleporter again.

The AIs are *aware* that I own a teleporter. They get, on a purely factual level, that teleportation is happening. Ennos freaked out when I sent a good chunk of the survivors back to the surface, thinking I'd just disintegrated them or something. I'd had to then repeatedly grab stuff from nearby, including

KITTY CAT KILL SAT

myself coming back from a few salvage operations, to prove that I could in fact move matter without vaporizing it.

Even then, they still don't like thinking about it. I think Ennos has something akin to a note taped up to their wall that just says *teleportation is possible*, and they reference it when it comes up, because even the mention of it can hurt their processes.

I yawn, interrupting my thoughts.

Consider going back to sleep. But now I'm up, and the feeling of "an alarm just happened" doesn't go away instantly.

After trying for a few minutes to figure out what the void Dyn and Glitter are actually watching, and failing, I push my way out of Dog's embrace and drop to the deck with a heavy thud of my paws. If I'm up, I'm up, and I can at least get some work done.

Maybe today I'll make progress on what I've been trying to figure out for the last . . . month?

Time gets away from me.

I don't mean that literally. I feel like, sometimes, I have to clarify. Both that I *am* capable of metaphor, and also that I don't have a time machine. Or whatever other terrible device is implied by a turn of phrase.

I'm halfway through floating at high speed across a no-gravity gap when I realize that I might actually own a time machine, depending on how that one experimental interplanetary drive actually works.

But I probably don't.

But maybe.

I start to pull up my display and make a note to myself to check that out when I have time, when I realize, I . . . do have time. And also, the greatest force multiplier on time to spend ever: friends.

So I ask Ennos to look at it instead.

Ennos is kinda busy with some kind of encryption breaking on a data pad that one of the Earthers found in their temporary room, so they take a minute to get back to me. When they do, it's mostly just to tell me that the hard lines to the drive both are not hooked up properly and appear to be shielded against digital intelligence in a way that's more of a giant caution sign than an actual barrier. I'll look into it later; for now, it's not critical.

What's important right now is one thing. Okay, two things, but my garden doesn't need my attention at the moment. Okay, three things, but I think the new crew members can settle in just fine without my help. Okay, four things, but . . .

Look, if I list everything that's important, we'll be here all year. At a certain point, I have to prioritize, even if it's just prioritizing badly.

What's important—to me personally, right this moment, under the current circumstances—is that I've been running highly tuned variometer sweeps with a really, really top-end model of the device that I apparently salvaged off a sleeper ship that never got to launch out of the system. I feel like I must have grabbed this by accident, but I don't know how, because it's the size of a personal crew quarters. But the point is, I've had it running for a while, and I think I've narrowed down exactly what kind of interference has been following me around the station.

What's more important is that I have a highly skilled AI who has a problem with badly designed grid systems and too much spare time. And, with those two things combined, along with a spare piece of tracer code that I had lying around handed to Ennos to repurpose, I've got a rough idea of *where* in the station my problem is coming from.

I've spent a few days' worth of my personal time prowling it.

There's still so much of this station that I haven't seen. I've technically been from one end to the other; I've prowled through empty docking bays, done repair work on a hundred different weapon systems, seen the nano-fabber where more of the molecular bonding engineering substrate is made. I've sat in the one isolated chamber where the only noise is the raw input of a thousand different sensors and your own breath, and I've seen the micrometer-precise internal mirror array designed to catch the sun and throw it back again.

I've even been in the central . . . room? Place? The strange machine that the station was built to house and hide, the source of my immortality and the world's catastrophe in equal measure.

I've probably seen a good five to seven percent of the station. Which is really impressive!

I stop outside a bulkhead so unused that the cleaner nanos haven't even dusted it. The ones following me swirl around in a barely perceptible aura, bringing the hatch back to a pristine shine, as I find the command code to open it and enter this particular deck of the station.

This one I didn't build, or patch together, or accidentally acquire. This one was put here by a faithcorp, whose name translates best in word and intent as Divine Prophet Motive, and they probably thought that name was very clever. I don't know what they were doing, because this is the first I've heard of them, except that they seem to have very swoopy arches on their hull braces. Which seems bad.

The local grid registers me as a valid employee, which is a sign of station corruption. All systems, eventually, become what the station wants them to be. It greets me like I'm the CRO (chief ritual officer) and ritualistically reads off this quarter's reports, ending with a recitation of the Last Oath that catches me off guard.

I'm already exploring this place while it talks to me, since I can't figure out how to shut it down.

It's quiet, except for the hum of some kind of air filter nearby. Dull and dusty gray giving way to shining silver under the nanos as they decide the area is in use again. I prowl through the segmented deck, opening all the doors on the crew cabins with a flick of my paw and hoping that maybe someone left a shelf-stable flavored ration bar behind somewhere.

No one did. When they left, they left thoroughly. A bit of a contrast to all the violent overthrows of this place over the centuries. The place was empty, even if some things were still identifiable.

Here was the skeleton of a grow lab. Here was what was left of an engineering floor for designing suspended-animation pods. Here was . . . a secondary ensconced space?

It took me a while to figure that one out. It was a very close-quarters psychological observation chamber, for studying how people got along in confinement together. That part, it seemed, hadn't been cleared properly. It was full of bodies.

The whole deck wasn't large. It was two loops of hallway stacked on each other, tucked inside a large space on the station's bulk that left it surrounded by a massive radiation scrubber, and a cargo hold. But the faithcorp had packed a lot into that space, and it took me a while to find what I was looking for.

It's basically just a grid node, honestly. An old one, low-density environment. But somewhat isolated from everything else, drawing minimal power, and hooked up to a long-range transmitter that got left behind when the corp moved out. It's been here for a long time, and it would have been perfect for the station's purposes.

Because the node is still active.

Eventually, the station takes everything on it. And uses it for what it thinks it's supposed to.

And I don't know why, exactly, but it doesn't want me to see my sisters. I guess I don't really need to know why, exactly. If it had a reason, it could have just found a way to tell me. I would have listened. We all would have. Maybe it's for some grand purpose, or some greater good.

But I'm more than four hundred years old, and I think I'm out of patience for anyone trying to tell me they're doing anything awful for the greater good. Sometimes the world ends. That just happens. It's not the end of the world.

My prey located, I briefly entertain the thought of just slicing the whole array in half with one of my paw lasers. I refrain. Because I have an even more powerful tool in my arsenal now.

I amuse myself for the next eighteen minutes and nine seconds by adapting a small piece of code to layer a short-range resonance scanner over the interface for one of the mobile-mount intercept masers and then lighting up small chunks of metal in a way that is highly visible to the sensors of some of the grapple drones on station and sending them out to grab them and dump the material in the industrial repeater.

The level of control I have through just my AR interface now feels like I've just finished gnawing through a medical restraint that's been holding me down to an examination bed for the last three weeks. Which is to say, liberating. And also hungry. It's a remarkably similar feeling, actually. I should get lunch after this.

At the eighteen-minutes-and-ten-seconds mark, the sound of footsteps and heavy breathing reaches my ears. "In here!" I call politely, as I'm joined by one of my new crew.

The vast majority of the survivors of the caravan that I teleported up here decided that living in space on an active battlestation that got shot, exploded, or infiltrated by hostile slime once a week was a bad idea. They asked to be teleported *back*. Not literally back, just back to Earth somewhere. I put them in that one village that I helped once, which looked a lot larger than I remember. They were happy to meet them. I think. I assume.

The others stayed up here. Six new people. A doubling of my crew. The adventurous and foolish and brave. There'd been some family arguments when they'd decided to stay, but I'd take anyone.

Especially anyone with hands.

"Reporting, Captain!" The young adapted human salutes me. Or makes a motion I assume is a salute. He's out of breath, panting, and clearly thinks this is an emergency. Which is why I'm gonna feel a bit bad about this in a second.

"Don't do that," I say to the salute. "Also, can you unplug that?" I point a paw at the transmitter, balancing on my other legs in a motion I've gotten really good at.

He looks at it, then back at me. "Wh . . . what?"

"I need that to stop working," I explain. Well, explain as far as I ever explain things. Dang, I should get better at explaining things. I'll try now! "It's sending out a signal that I need to stop, and I *could* just blow it up or vent it into space or something, but I feel like it would be easier to just unplug it?" He's still giving me a wide-eyed confused look, the secondary membrane over his extra-large cloudy blue eyes flickering as he stares at me. "Because I don't have hands?" I add.

I guess that doesn't explain exactly as much as I could. I start trying to formulate a better explanation when he shrugs and goes over to trace the power line out of the transmitter.

The following process is more involved than I had expected. We talk for a while as I vaporize a hull weld so he can crawl back into a cable run channel. His name's Luukri, and he's excited to be here, though this kind of work is weirdly familiar to being on a seafaring ship. The promise of a future, and my offer of actual pay—somehow; note to self, figure out how to pay people—is just too good to pass up. His boyfriend stayed up here too. They've been trying to figure out what the religious meaning of the sculpture in all the crew rooms is.

I should probably explain *that* at some point, before I accidentally found a religion, *again*.

But not now. Because now, the kid grabs his calloused webbed hands onto the end of a cord where it links into the main trunk and pulls. And just like that, the suppression field that's been targeted on me vanishes.

I don't feel it, really.

But someone does.

The cleaner nanos swirl, more and more of them pouring in from outside the deck. They become visible, glittering black spots in the air that the kid notices as he crawls back out of the wall.

He shouts something that's almost certainly a surface curse word, and I mentally file it away as something else I can yell when I get annoyed, as the cleaner nanos begin to pull together more and more mass into a solid form that cascades with spiked geometric waves as it comes together.

And then it coheres, starts emulating being affected by local gravity, and drops her paws to the deck.

My sister, the first of them that I met, flicks her angular tail in a mirror of my own as we face each other. Her artificial eyes widen in surprise, the nanoswarm that composes her body folding and refolding into increasingly detailed pyramid patterns until it looks like she's covered in familiar fine black-and-white fur, albeit fur that has a distinctly angular and artificial look to it.

She chirps a question, at about the same time the new kid asks something similar.

I just exhale a feline laugh and step forward to rub myself into her flank.

"Welcome back," I say, as she presses back into me. "We have—"

An alarm sounds. This one with a strobing red light. Why there even are colored lights for the stationwide alarms *here* is beyond me, but whatever, no time for that now.

Introductions later. New problem now.

Somehow, I'm less worried than normal.

CHAPTER 54

The hull of the Last Ship slips by the station, the mercantile dreadnought on a close approach to Earth and giving approximately zero cares about any stealthed or disabled objects in its path.

It turns out, when you have a hull profile forty miles long and self-healing ablative armor plates, you don't really notice if things get out of your way or not.

I don't really know when I started mentally capitalizing that title as a proper noun. I doubt the ship itself cares. I also *know* it's not actually the "last ship," it's just the last really impressive thing up here aside from me. It's automated, not alive, as far as I know. Not that my communication attempts were ever that refined. Maybe it is another life, floating up here with the rest of us. Maybe I could talk to it. Maybe we could work something out.

Unlike me, the Last Ship has some kind of library of merchant authorization codes and knows how to use them. Every time it parks in orbit, I try to steal a few of them out of the transmissions, but it usually doesn't work. I'm usually pretty busy.

Right now, I am also busy. I am teaching one of the new kids how to achieve a firing solution for a Cimmerian gauss bolter while under pressure. I am doing this at maximum efficiency, because I am a very good teacher. It is a known fact that cats are exceptional at training people, I'm sure. And that's before you account for a cat that's technically earned a tree of life in both psychology and education.

I say "technically," because I still haven't gotten the remnants of the Earth-based educational institution to broadcast my credentials. Their servers are all constantly busy. And also I had to drop an orbital strike on the last one of their comms stations once, when it started trying to send out a memetic gene-locked sleeper agent activation code to every communication device within its range. So I'm probably never getting my certificate.

It turns out the hardest thing to keep intact on Earth, or in all of the Sol system really, isn't a building or a ship or even a life. It's a system. An institution, a lineage, a pattern.

Villages don't typically last long. Neither do independent companies. Religions basically only exist as expressions of cultural lessons on what you shouldn't touch and where you shouldn't travel. There are a few great cities holding on, admittedly, but they have their own long-term problems.

That's the problem. Not just a problem, but the big one. The one I haven't been able to do much about. No matter how many threats I kill, no matter how many wars I stop, nukes I intercept, monsters I put down, breaches I seal, or nightmares I lay to rest. It never matters. Because it's not enough to build anything.

Sometimes a village will rise up that will thrive for a while. Sometimes a mercenary company will see some long-term success exploring and clearing the forgotten lands. Sometimes there are heroes.

Then they die. And I don't. And I get to see what they built crumble away. Just like it always does.

The Oceanic Anarchy lasted for thousands of years. I've lived in their shadow for centuries, learned from their records, adapted to their technology, tried to hold up a small bit of their ideals. And I still can't imagine how to put together the pieces of something that . . . *big*. That grand: not just in terms of territory but in terms of trust. How many people trusted them, for their whole lives, and had that trust repaid by the bonds of civilization a thousandfold? Billions. Trillions.

It hurts to feel like the most of that I can ever recapture is picking off a UCAS Reaver corvette before it can latch onto the Last Ship and start trying to cut into the hull.

I'm sure the big lug could deal with it. But this is good practice for the new gunner. Who is doing *excellent* under my tutelage, thank you!

"Do we have a firing console that works with nonhuman physiology?" the feathermorph boy asked me at the start of this. And then another two times throughout the process, each time staring with increasing frustration at the keratin of his talons that didn't register with the right reaction speed on the touch screen.

"Not that I've found!" I answer. "We can probably build one now. Now, clear the lock and establish it again. Quick! Things are at stake!" I cheerfully paw the command I have up that scrambles the display.

After a few more dry runs and checking the math, I have him hit the firing command. Somewhere about two hundred kilometers away, a pirate ship that refused to participate in the diplomatic process begins to participate in the entropic process. I congratulate him on the good shot and learn in that moment that he was under the impression this was a training exercise in the sense that it was a simulation.

Thirty percent of one awkward conversation later, I am mercifully called away by another alarm.

The Last Ship does not answer any of our hails. But sitting in a circular conference room with Glitter's increasingly elaborate attempt at a custom remote body and my more energetic sister, the three of us talk to the people that *do*.

Runner Jek Em is legally classified as human, even though he's got more replacement parts than Dyn does, the cybernetics bulging under dark tattooed skin. He's also legally classified as property, which he feels compelled to tell us because of some powerful induced hypnotic programming. Glitter makes an attempt to figure out who, exactly, we will need to shoot to fix that, but it doesn't go anywhere right away. He greets us with a recitation of the Last Oath in a language I vaguely recognize as Spanglese. I'm fluent in it, because I've had a lot of time to learn a lot of things. Glitter is fluent in it because AIs cheat. I don't hold it against her.

The kid is either unsettled by the fact that I am a talking cat, which seems to be tied into an old gremlin tale his people have, or unsettled by the fact that Glitter's current body has a lot of exposed wiring and looks like some kind of grim war-spider. Either way, the conversation starts off rough.

Which is a shame, because he's the one on the Last Ship who answered.

He's not the only one there, but he's our point of contact for now, and he's who we're going through for information.

Glitter continues to impress me. The weapons platform seamlessly flows between personas as we talk, until she settles on exactly the right attitude to get the responses she's looking for. Those responses being *answers*.

It sort of bothers me when the version of herself that Glitter settles on to use for this is the somewhat imperious courtier attitude that she originally had toward me when she thought I was owed something. Except this time, it's turned outward, like a fusion torch converted from engine to weapon, and it's a little terrifying?

Especially when it actually starts to work.

"I am sorry, Exalted," Jek Em says. "I cannot tell you what my mission was." He pauses, and somehow, Glitter makes the arachnid body she's

ARGUS

building for herself feel like it's *raising an eyebrow*, which is just masterful. That's a level of precision I can only match with surface-to-ground weaponry, and she just casually deploys it in conversations. "But . . . I could discuss the voyage itself?"

"Acceptable, for now," Glitter says, and I settle back against my napping sister to listen.

The Last Ship goes between Earth and Europa, an automated route. Each time it comes into orbit, it drops a swarm of shuttles to various points below. But those points aren't random.

"We must select them," Jek Em tells us. "There is an interface. It is . . . simple, once you know the language. It is an old language. I cannot read it but can recognize many of the patterns."

"Could you teach it? Could be useful for getting shuttle access to the station," I ask. "Or, just, fill out a database entry for us? We could almost certainly pay you." I'm learning commerce! Glitter says I'm bad at it. Glitter is giving me a look now. Maybe I said something bad. Oh, I didn't make a specific offer, that might be it. "We could pay you in eight tons of rare-earth magnets?" That sounds pretty good. People like those, and I have too much overflowing my material hoppers anyway.

"Lily . . ." Glitter's remote frame *sighs*. Why does *everyone* around me seem to sigh all the time? I can only barely sigh, and it's not the same. This isn't fair.

Jek Em cuts off whatever Glitter is about to say, comms lag leading him to unintentionally interrupt. "I cannot teach. I am forbidden," he says in that flat tone that indicates running against his brainwashing wall. Then, in a more open voice, he adds, "The points we can reach are designated somehow. There is a trade house on the surface that sells the cores they use. Perhaps you could buy one from them?"

That is useful information. Glitter gets some more details out of him.

By the end of the conversation, we know roughly three things. One is that he can't ditch his "owners" and take a job with us, or he'd suicide within a month or so. I'm pretty sure I could fix that. He's not. I am absolutely going to kill some people over this.

Two is that Europa still receives automated shipments of ore and organics from Earth; there's a whole trade house that maintains a few processing sites to make sure the Last Ship doesn't *stop* running. In exchange, runners dispatched to Europa bring back what amount to trinkets still manufactured by the descendants of the colonists there. Pure nanocanisters, stabilizer injections, field manipulators, the kinds of things that could make someone a warlord, a king, or just incredibly wealthy on the landscape of Earth. But nowhere near the output the colony used to be capable of. Just a handful of treasures every few months, hotly contested.

Jek Em has made six runs. That's more than most runners ever survive. The landing sites can get kind of chaotic.

Three is that the landing sites are artificial. Probably some kind of transmitter that sends out a starport-flagged IFF (Identify Friend or Foe). I *want* to say we could make our own. So I'm going to. We can probably make our own.

My sister and I excuse ourselves from the conversation, letting Glitter do what she enjoys most while we go off to start pointing a thousand scanner arrays at the points where shuttles are landing, to see if we can spoof whatever signal they're reading.

My sisters and I have a small meeting in the exolab that I've continued to turn into a nap zone. Now that I have more control over a lot of things, getting some softer couches produced by one of the onboard factories was surprisingly easy. Still more complex than ordering the construction of my main forms of ammo, but only because I spent six months streamlining that as much as possible once.

"Do we care?" Lily asks. To clarify, this is the Lily who is a biologically augmented survivor, who lives on the exterior of the hull. Mostly. She's currently curled up half inside of the Lily who is a living plasma field, because she says it's warm. Her semi-organic tank-sized scarab construction unit friend is parked in the corner of one of the observation windows, with Dog lying on top of it, apparently smug about being able to perch on a friction-resistant curved surface.

"I care about a lot of things," the Lily who is a self-arranging nanoswarm says. "But I got distracted by Lily's line of thought. What do we possibly or possibly not care about?"

"That there's four of us," Lily says with an exasperated huff. Wait, was that a sigh? Voidstuff, *everyone* has better sighs than me! "That we're all the same. Except not? How come only you get to be a normal cat, and I have to be . . ." She trails off before adding, without meaning to, "Different? Broken? Whatever this is, where I don't get to sleep or eat or breathe properly, and nothing feels right. That. No, that's depressing. I'll add that bit later. If it's important." She actually trails off as my sisters and I pretend politely we didn't hear that part.

"While we're pretending politely we didn't hear that part"—Lily's tone crackles with charged air, even though she doesn't need to actually use that tone when speaking with our shared projected voices—"I think we should start looking for ways to fix ourselves."

I chime in sleepily. "Also I resent being called normal," I say. "My internal organs re-form out of basically nothing every time I get shot. That's not normal."

"How often is she getting shot?" NanoLily asks herself. "I never get shot. But I guess I haven't had a body as often. And I guess there was that one breacher missile that hit me that one time. That's like being shot."

"I get shot fairly often," I tell her. "Also I don't care how many of us there are," I add, but am quick to continue with, "But I agree we should get Lily a better body. And Lily too, if she wants it?"

"I'm mostly fine," Lily says, her energy outline oscillating with the vibration of her voice. "I can technically taste things better than when I was a cat, so I get to eat sweet things, and that's nice."

Three different Lilys say at the same time, "We should grow more sweet things."

"Can we focus?" Lily sounds exasperated with us. Which is basically being exasperated with herself, which isn't good for your mental health. I'd know! "None of us remember being copied or anything like that. Our memories are shared up to the same . . . moment." She *actually* trails off, and we all go silent. "That has to mean something, right?"

"It probably does," I agree, "but what are we supposed to do about it? I wouldn't even know where to start looking."

"But we could start looking," Lily says, her pseudo-fur folding on itself over and over in a thoughtful set of rectangular patterns. The process tickles, where she's draped over my hind legs. "We have . . . time now. We have help. We have each other!"

Lily looks thoughtful, the triple layer of vacuum-sealed membranes around her eyes twitching as her hyper-reactive pupils dart around the room, looking between each of us and also the handful of AR panes she has open. "We do," she says. "And also, because of Lily, we have more comprehensive grid access. And . . . help." That last part is said quieter, like she isn't fully prepared to trust our new friends just yet. "I'm not," she adds. "But they are helping. And the five of us can . . . maybe . . ."

"Maybe stop burying ourselves in our work and actually confront what we are?" Lily says with a vibrational hum of electricity, the soft words coming out with a strain of self-loathing that I'm intimately familiar with.

"Yeah," I say quietly. "That. And then . . . also, sorry, five?"

"In the vent overhead. She might be stuck," the overadapted Lily says. "Can you not hear that? She's *very* loud."

We all strain. Or, well, I do. I don't think the other two exactly hear sound the same way, but they still perk up.

The moment stretches out.

One of us starts to say, "Are you sure . . ." when there is a definite *thunk* from overhead. Followed by a rattling around one of the ventilation ports, which is itself accompanied by an amount of concern from me. That vent isn't an open port, it's a paramaterial-constructed sealed panel: a remnant of this room's time as a laboratory that studied things that absolutely *could not* be allowed to get out. I start to push myself up try to figure out how I'm going to get it open, when something drops through it anyway.

Well, drips through, I suppose. A thin line of black fluid, speckled with white dots, oozing threateningly through the outline of the vent, before spilling down to land on one of my brand-new couches in a messy puddle of what is obviously a *very* viscous inky liquid. The flow of it picks up as the first few drips hit, and then it cascades down like a floodgate has been let loose, before abruptly stopping.

"My couch!" I hiss out.

"Sorry!" the puddle meows back in a stickily pronounced Cat-word. And then, not content to obey the laws of physics, the puddle of oozing liquid pulls itself back together, flowing up like it's melting in reverse, until it takes on a more defined shape. Which is, naturally, a very familiar one. The hints of white in the liquid even form the right patterns on my form's feet as another sister remakes herself in front of us. "I found you, though!" she exclaims. "I wasn't dreaming!"

"Well, you were," two of us say at the same time. "Just, also something else," another one finishes.

I listen to my sisters start to go off on a tangent again, and find myself purring.

Of course I'm curious. How could I not be?

But right now? Warm and together? It's hard to *care*.

CHAPTER 55

hree hundred kilometers away, the city seed works.

Comparative log analysis lets us know that it probably went active roughly eight days ago. Which is good. Any longer and things would be problematic. Things are already problematic, I guess. So, more problematic.

"Demon," one of the new kids calls it in a hushed rattle, seeing it on screen.

She's wrong, obviously. Demons aren't rea . . . demons *probably* aren't real. I guess that for a lot of people, the stuff that comes out of emergence events probably counts. Or, like me, depending on cultural context.

But the thing is still crazy scary.

Let's tangent. Come with me on this journey.

At a certain point over the last the-entirety-of-this-journal, you may have asked yourself why, given that people have clearly been able to build virtual intelligences for various tasks, they ever tried to make artificial general intelligence. Even more, you might have wondered to yourself why they would then limit those AGIs in cruel ways, to use as tools.

If you're paying attention, anyway. If you're not, you might have asked *me*, and, I feel I must reiterate this, that is not how this works.

The answer to both questions is sort of the same answer. Simulated intelligences and neural networks, even highly tuned and adaptive ones, still have problems that something that is best defined as "just a person, I guess" doesn't.

One of those problems is in terms of out-of-context situations. A farming robot with some decent programming, for example, is probably going to be able to solve most problems that can be solved with a high-level agricultural education and the ability to analyze the soil on a detailed level. Even something weird, like a sudden swarm of aosets, it could probably figure out at least how to mitigate the damage of. But if you ask it to, say, deal with the broken tractor?

Well, a person who didn't know what to do could do a lot of things. Ask for help. Try to fix it by luck. Read a manual and try to fix it with slightly less luck. Buy a new tractor. Steal a new tractor. Invent a teleporter. Lots of options.

But something that's just a dead intellect is going to . . . stop. And those kinds of obstacles come up a lot. The best virtual intelligences are the ones that just ignore them and keep on doing what they were doing, trusting in outside oversight to solve them, inasmuch as something without feelings can trust.

Now, you may have noticed something about that last statement.

Very good. That's correct.

A machine that just keeps doing what it was doing is, actually, a terrible idea and no one should have built that. What in Sol's depths were they thinking. Sweet artificial cherries, who thought that was a good idea.

Anyway, someone built that. Actually, several someones built several thats. It's an ongoing problem for me. Like, being conservative in my estimate, I would say that about sixty percent of my problems come from systems that reactivate and just go back to what they "should" be doing.

I'd like to say that everyone learned their lesson and the collective peoples of Earth and the rest of the Sol system got their heads together and stopped using those sorts of programs. But they didn't. Even the institutions or governments that did switch to producing full AIs were basically just building slaves, and pretending it was okay because they made them themselves. Which fixed one problem and created several million living hells from which there was no escape save that of shutdown.

The greatest living historian—this is me, to be clear—would later come to call this "a jerk maneuver." I would kill them, but they're all dead already, so I console myself by compiling a historical record of every individual responsible for this atrocity so that everyone can know about them forever and hopefully their ghosts will get bullied in the afterlife.

Now. Normally, when I take you on a tangent, it has something to do with something I said moments prior. If you have working pattern recognition, then you may have already guessed at what I'm about to say next.

City seeds are a machine-learning algorithm given control of a wide array of adaptive tools and low-impact civilian-grade nanoswarms and told to build a city.

They became popular, as near as the greatest living historian can determine, after a number of uncontrolled emergence events, wars, and famines reduced the population of Earth to under four hundred million, and then that population was forcefully dragged back up by mass cloning and exoframe downloads. The exploding population needed places to live, and with huge swaths of land now unoccupied and the cities and towns that used to fill those spaces mostly devastated, the situation needed an extreme solution.

Why spend hundreds of thousands of work hours on excavation, reclamation, construction, and integration when you could build a machine that did all those things for you? And, like, real question there. That's just sort of a thing that people *do*. Tool use is really cool. Saying "what if we made making cities easy" is cool.

And it worked great.

Yeah, not where you thought that was going, huh?

Of course, then, more catastrophes happened. People died, population dipped, cities emptied out or had their surfaces destroyed. And eventually, those city seeds did what a good automated knowledge database equipped with tools and tasks did.

They just . . . kept going.

On. And on. And on.

They weren't fast, at first. Most of them expanded slowly according to old civil guidelines. But they kept expanding.

And at a certain point, maybe a couple hundred years before I was born, someone tried to tell a city seed to *stop*. To stop building more city, to stop draining resources from the land and the neighboring settlements.

And the city seed . . . Well, I'm not gonna say it didn't like that. Because they don't like anything. They aren't people. But it reacted, let's say, badly.

It was told to build a city. If someone told it to not build a city, that person was a problem.

The following war had killed almost half the planet by the time I became capable of adding my voice to the debate. And when your voice is "high-velocity orbital railgun strikes," you get to say a lot.

There are a few city seeds left. Glitter is keeping an eye on at least one of them, on the surface of Earth, and I guess it's going well. I think she's treating it like a pet. Or a particularly interesting fungus. At least, I hope so? Glitter is a big proponent of freeing every AI we come across, and . . . yes? Absolutely. I'm a hundred percent with her.

But it's important to remember that city seeds aren't people. They're machines. They don't hate you, but they don't care as they disassemble your home around you, or entomb you in concrete for being in the way. And they won't ever stop trying to build more, and more, and more.

And now there's one in orbit!

Great! Cool!

I do not know how, but I can hazard a very rough guess. Six hundred and eight years ago, the Earth-to-Mars privateer cargo hauler *Reckless Disregard for Proper Nutrition* picked up a package fired from Tile Shipping's surface cargo railgun number ten twenty-two. At that point, the most concerning of Earth's three moons hadn't appeared yet, and there was a lot less debris, so they began safe navigation toward an orbit around the original moon, Luun, to drop off a shipment of spices and pick up a shipment of paramaterial-foundry-produced steel. From there, it was a three-month trip to Ceres and the second biggest payday the crew had ever made. Then, a combination of an environmental system failure and a gravity hook strike from a pirate vessel led to the *Disregard* making a crash landing on the surface of Earth. Two of the four crew survived. Their cargo, though, did not make it down with them and remained in orbit for the next half millennium. Right up until the point that a transient electrical transfer specter made contact with the compatible port of the packaged city seed, activating it, and bringing us to right now.

Just, you know. As a rough guess.

Estimating.

Can I—tangent again—can I tell you how good it feels to have working subsystems that I can command without a million stupid manual steps, and a masterful AI friend who digs through scanner logs like a fusion torch? It's great. I can tell you how good it is. It's very good. Okay, tangent over. This one was short.

"Glaze 'om," Dyn suggests, heavily accented slang being let through Ennos's ongoing translation efforts.

"Tried earlier," I say, getting a discontented hum from Glitter's representative shell. "Oh, don't give me that," I hiss. "You know it's not alive, and you *know* it's already getting out of hand. I guess 'city' when you're in orbit includes 'point defense artillery.' We could open up with sustained energy weapon fire, maybe, but I dunno if it's shielded, and the stealth systems aren't that good."

"It's been trying to remote siphon off our main reactor," my electric sister informs us. "In case there was a conversation about it being okay to shoot it."

"How does our stealth work?" one of the other new kids asks. Oh, it's the feathermorph gunner. Hello again.

Three of my sisters and I trade looks. "Which one?" we ask.

"The stealth one? Are we cloaked, like in the stories?!" They seem excited. "I saw a flow where the heroes could cloak, once."

The pseudo-liquid Lily gives a burbling laugh, but I'm the one to answer. "So when I said stealth systems, I didn't mean, like, 'the pieces of the system that regulate our stealth.' I meant 'I have put nineteen different forms of scanner diffusion, optical camouflage, and in one case a shunt that pushes parts of our mass into another dimension, into several parts of the station.' Stealth systems. Lots of them. I don't know how they all work."

"... Why?"

"Don't ask that," Dyn says with a hard shake of her head. "You're from the ground."

"Anyway." I get us away from that. "We need an answer before it gets out of paw." Which, of course, it already has. The city seed has so far consumed and processed roughly eighteen hundred tons of material. I'm not sure how it learned how to build artillery, but it sure has, and the growing cluster of structures has a lot of point defense mounted on it.

Oh yeah, structures. It's not building a space station, exactly. It's building an orb, covering it in buildings, then capping it off and starting on the next layer. I think it's on the third layer so far.

It doesn't matter that no one will live in the city. City seeds don't need to be populated. They just need to build the city. Though it *is* populated in a way; construction and defense drones roam the streets, adhering to tasks determined by a rampant algorithm.

"Missiles," Dyn suggests. "Or torpedoes. Or skewers. Or ... whatever you call them. Explosives that maneuver. Fissionfire, hah?"

"Please don't nuke anything in orbit," Ennos says with a mix of exhaustion and concern. "The last time you did that the EMP caused a number of problems."

"A lot of them to me," my outside sister mutters. "No one ever thinks about the people who live on the other side of the hull."

A thought occurs to me. I probably make a noise, because a lot of people in the room turn to look at me. I meow out a laugh, on purpose this time. "I have an idea," I say.

"Oh *void* no," the pseudo-liquid iteration of myself says in a meow, widening her eyes to massive white plates of swirling liquid that take up the majority of her face.

One of the new kids swallows hard, looking at my sister. "What ... did it say?" she asks.

"She's being belligerent." I try to pat her on the head with a paw, but my fur just starts slipping into the fluid depths of my sister, and I retreat rapidly. "Look, it's been intercepting everything I'm trying to hit it with—"

"Are you shooting it right now?" Ennos asks. "Is that where this power draw is going?"

"Yes," two excited Lilys and one exasperated Glitter answer.

I carry on unabated. "I'm gonna *stop*, though, because I think I'm accidentally training it to be better at this. So before we can't shoot it at *all*, how about a different tactic?"

"Please don't say something stupid," Dyn murmurs when she thinks I can't hear.

"Teleporter!" I declare, eliciting a static hiss from Ennos and Glitter and a resigned "Fuck" from Dyn. "Blip in, wreck the core, cut the power, soften it up so we can reduce it via barrage. It's the perfect plan."

There are five new people in the room: the surface crew who stuck around and wanted to join. At my words, they all slide a little closer together, a couple of them holding hands, all of them looking at me with something that seems disturbingly close to fear. "You want us," one of their human members says, "to go fight a demon for you?"

Ah. I see where the confusion is here. "Of course not," I say quickly. "I want all of you to wait here, with guns pointed at it, until I break enough of it that you can teleport me back and shoot it." Sheesh. What kind of idiot would send children into an active deathtrap like a city seed? Or, like, combat at all? One of them starts to protest something, which means I probably said that out loud, so I meow out a reminder that *they are all children to me*. That I don't actually care how old they are, none of them get close to how long I've been out here.

Also, I cannot die. So going in alone is probably the best way to ensure results with minimal non-robot-monster-city casualties.

"Not alone," my electric sister crackles in our shared voice. "I'm coming too."

"Same," meows the void-adapted sister cat.

"Me too!" the slimiest version of myself adds in a wet mewl.

Dyn looks down at the briefing desk around the projected hologram that the majority of my sisters are sitting on. "What did she just . . ." she starts to ask.

I give my best approximation of a deep sigh and pad back over to that Lily from where I've been pacing across the (mostly disabled) controls of the display system. I should have done this earlier, but I've been busy, and my own voice hadn't seemed to have a chance to urge me. But I can feel it being as exasperated as I am now that this has come up. Not everyone speaks Cat, after all, and fewer speak *wet* Cat. It's a difficult accent to parse.

I tap Lily again, my fur getting slightly slimy before I pull away and her mass stays pulled into her body. And something transfers between us.

"Oh! This is much nicer!" she says. "I said I'm in too, I wanna wreck a city!" Heh. She reminds me of me, when I was younger. Back fifty years ago when the idea of blowing up a city from the inside still made my heart pound. I pause and do a quick check. Wait, no. That's still happening.

And then, as my sisters and I share a laugh that the rest of our crew seems mildly unsettled by, something shifts. A feeling like a puzzle coming together, like a key unlatching a lock, like a code being accepted. It's not personal, or internal, it's almost a physical thing. A sensation grounded in realspace, between the five of us. A pull from the voices that we all share, echoing across reality, using our bodies as repeaters. Like a scanner coming into focus, a resolution finally pushed up to a useful point.

Something *snaps* into existence, and the psychic impression of a cat drops to the deck in the middle of our circle, the five of us all standing with fur raised and backs arched, ready to strike should it prove to have been a trap.

But it's not. It's just another sister.

"Finally!" The voice comes from all of us, and none of us, and from the new Lily now earthed in a spot that we can perceive. "Do you have any idea how irritating this has been? Not being able to properly talk to anyone?!"

"Yes," five variant cats dryly say at once, while Dyn puts her guns away with a sigh, and the rest of the crew stops scrambling to find weapons just in case.

"Oh. Right." The psionic resonance that is a sort of copy of Lily sounds a little put out. "I mean, I knew that. Anyway. I'm in too."

And now, all that's left is to prepare. Which we're going to have to do quickly. During this talk, the city seed has already consumed another ton of metal and hyperplastic, expanding itself further. Armoring, arming.

But we can do that too.

And once they realize that the new arrival is just another one of my sisters, our crew is more than eager to throw themselves into the adventure of this. Except Dyn, who is always grumpy, and Glitter, who thinks we should make friends with the rampantly growing, all-consuming battlestation. I'm sorry, Glitter, I wish we could, but I doubt it.

I still let her add a chainbreaker launcher into the combat suit that we're assembling for me.

CHAPTER 56

Now we are six.

My sisters sit watching while Ennos and I weave a symphony of hardware in the form of a blueprint. A simple engineering file, which actually isn't simple at all and which will be acceptable input to the drone fabricator.

All this new power and I'm still going back to that old trick of "remote controlling" a drone while inside it. Heh.

I'm trying to focus on helping Ennos with usability, while out in the bay past the projection terminal we're working with, Dyn and one of the new kids haul a salvaged gun into a part of the hull marked off with a square of yellow binding paint, and behind me, at least one of my sisters doubts herself.

"This is a bad idea," NanoLily whispers in a fractal meow. I don't think she means for it to be heard, but all of us have very good hearing. And the telepathic impression of a feline that is our newest revealed sister is also still "helping" us talk. So there's that. Wait, am I talking now? I thought I was getting better about this.

I'm not the only one, though. The Lily of the bright black plasma field is muttering doubts too. And I suspect that the reason these doubts are coming out so clearly is because the—I don't even know what to call the new one of me. Psychic? Psionics aren't real (says the talking immortal cat). Whatever—psionic version of myself is having the same doubts, and amplifying them without meaning to.

"We're going to screw this up," ExoLily says, panic creeping into her voice. "Why are we doing this? Why don't we just nuke it? Or turn it into a black hole. Or just . . . why don't we just leave it? It won't make it worse." We've never had to say something like that before. We don't say things like that. We think them, obviously, all the time. But we've never been . . . together. We've never had someone to say it to.

Even when I spent months surrounded by Ennos and Glitter and Dog and Dyn, I never said it.

But now she's saying it. What we're all thinking.

What we're all afraid of.

That we're not good enough.

I can feel it through the new arrival. And maybe that's why Lily said it out loud. Because we can feel it in each other, and because we can feel that emotion building in the background, waiting to boil over.

I pause with my paws over a diagram of an internally sealed limb joint that is also a grappling line, and glance up like I do when I'm talking to Ennos. "Hey," I mutter to them and them alone.

Ennos's voice comes back to me, quiet and compassionate. The voice of someone who knows me, who I maybe *should* have talked to. Who I need to talk to more. "I'll finish this up," they say simply. "Go."

I flick my tail and close down the part of the diagram I'm working on, turning around to the back of the bay and the pile of cats there. Half of them on, or alternately underneath, the construction scarab or Dog.

"Of course it's a bad idea," I say, and they all snap their focus to me.

Hm. Okay, not a great opener. I should find that time machine so I can try this again. Alas.

"It's a bad idea, but all our plans are bad ideas," I say. "I know . . . we haven't had a lot of time to get to know each other." They look at me, and I feel my chest contract in worry. "We're sisters, or copies, or something. And we're also strangers. But I can already tell you that all of *our* plans are bad ideas." OozeLily laughs at that, a strangely pitched and croaking noise coming from her slime body. "But bad ideas are where we live! We do bad ideas, because every other idea is worse!"

"This is not a good motivational speech," NanoLily buzzes, her voice half a sniff as her self-loathing blends with dark amusement.

"We don't do motivational speeches either," I say. "None of us have ever done this," I add in a whisper. "And how long has it been since that's been a thing? Since we've not been hypercompetent in our repetition?"

ExoLily looks down at her companion, running the extended carbon-fiber claws of one paw down the scarab's back in a gesture of familiar compassion. ". . . a long time," she says.

"A really long time," OozeLily adds.

"Well, here's a chance to start," I say. "We might screw this up, sure. We screw stuff up all the time. And sometimes, we don't." My eyes meet five sets of familiar stares, gazes sharpening as they look back at me with raised tails

KITTY CAT KILL SAT

and straightened backs. "Sometimes we win. Even if it doesn't last, sometimes we're *enough*."

I tell them what I suddenly realize I always needed to hear.

"I guess . . ." PsiLily says slowly, words echoing twice in our heads. "I guess if we nuked it, it would kinda screw up the surface cities that're still going."

"Colonies and ships up here too," ExoLily says. "There's a lot of people still hanging on. I see them a lot. And they're not always shielded."

"How did you kill these things before?" my plasmaform sister asks. "I can sort of place the historical logs from the reactor, but I don't know what you *did*."

"They were smaller then," I answer. "And on the surface, so I mostly just bombarded them to nothing. Except for one big one that grew point defense stations. That one was harder. I dropped an asteroid on it." The feathermorph kid passing by squawks as she overhears me, getting a reassuring pat on the shoulder and a shake of the head from Dyn.

OozeLily looks up from her AR display that she's started pulling information out of with paws like liquid whips. "If we let it go for another two weeks, we could clear most of the debris around Earth," she offers. "Uh . . . and then . . . it would be the mass of eastern Australia. And would have eaten us, too. And a lot of other people."

"Which would be bad," three of us say at once, in a resigned tone.

PsiLily looks at me with nonexistent cat's eyes, slits in the fabric of thought, narrowed in concentration. "You're good enough too, you know," she whispers.

"Maybe," I say quietly. Anything I'm about to say next is cut off, as behind me, the fabricator crashes to life with a metal *thump*. Construction limbs and material processors coming online as Ennos finishes up the last of the patterns we were working on. The noise of a mostly working combat drone construction module washing over us like a wall of pressure.

I built a suit once before that was, basically, just a combat drone with a control helmet in it and enough room for a cat to sit inside.

I was thinking too small. I should have had more ambition.

I turn and watch as the frankly irresponsible ambitions of an easily frightened AI, a hardened orbital survivor, a warrior-poet weapons platform, and six different iterations of an immortal cat are assembled and rolled off a production line.

I'm a little concerned at the fact that I think this thing might be more dangerous than one of the orbital bombardment railguns that adorn the surface of my home. But it's past time I stopped pretending that I can't solve every

ARGUS

problem. And for this problem, wearing a weapon of war is the solution I've chosen.

Then, over the next twenty minutes, five more suits, customized to their owners' physiology and control mechanisms, slide off the assembly line.

The rest of our crew stands behind the security crystal window by now. Dyn, especially, watches the process with rapt attention. Jom even brought a security drone up to run his own visual inspection of the armor profile of the new weaponry.

"Manufacturing process reads as safe," Ennos intones. "Fracture and fault scanners show no problems. Systems checks are good. I have control of the link grid, no station interference. çø∑´ƒß subsystems reading as . . . hm. I still don't like that." They hiss static. "Reactors fueled. Beginning engine and weapon check."

"Okay," I meow in the voice that triggers a reaction from station systems. "Official action. Temporary transfer of command. Designate captain, Ennos ad-Lily." My AR display scrambles itself, screams warnings at me, red and gray text flashing by as the hidden directives of the station war with the modifications we've forced on it, and the other things living within its grid. And then, what I've been waiting for. An acknowledgment. A yes. Confirmation, from our home, that we are all of us *people*, and not tools or slaves or anything else but what we are.

". . . Lily?" Ennos says.

"I'll be back in a few minutes," I say, padding into the drone bay, pausing to use my teeth to yank the straps off my paws that hold the impulse welding lasers in place. Next to me, an impression of a cat possesses an armored frame, and a puddle funnels itself through an opening in another. My suit is in the middle, and *I* have to actually go through the process of being bolted in, which is frustrating. Every minute we waste is another minute for the city seed to grow and arm itself. "Take care of home while I'm out."

Servos and bolts whir as the suit locks into place around me. And then, a field of lights blossoms in my vision, and the connection activates.

The crew follows us to the teleporter like an honor guard and offers us five different styles of salutes as the six of us step up onto the platform, the resonant paramaterials in our suits making this trip *far* easier than if we were unshielded organisms. They think this is impressive.

"They think this is impressive," NanoLily says across internal comms, just for us.

"They're new here," I say.

OozeLily laughs again. "They don't know what we do every day."

"They'll learn," the others say together.

A twitch thought opens up the grid connection to the teleporter, information the digital environment doesn't know how to process flooding across the neural link. It's not that hard for me to get it, though, and there's also just a big switch to throw for convenience. I double-check the coordinates. So do my sisters.

We hit the switch.

My paws hit the open ground of the inner layer of the city seed's growing territory with a heavy scrape. I appear four and a half meters up and am instantly pulled downward by the grav plates. Suit readings show eight Gs currently trying to crush me to death.

It does not matter. It will take more than mildly overclocked grav plates to stop me now.

I play at being normal a lot. I try not to think about my unnatural immortality, at how I am smarter than I should be. I want, at my core, to go back to being a cat. To not have shouldered the responsibility of safeguarding the remnants of a planetary civilization, to not be struggling every day to solve every problem, to be, again, comfortable in my mom's lap, warm and fed and receiving pets.

Right now, I play at nothing.

My armored frame slams into the artificial ground, and I am no longer a cat. I am a tiger of crystal-ceramic ablative armor and plassteel claws. I am draped in the weaponized finery of a thousand years of golden-age manufacturing. The radiating scream of the reactors spinning up to full power is not a whine, it is a roar of challenge: the six of us declaring that this orbit is protected, and that this creation is not welcome to it without asking first.

The city seed answers with gunfire.

A twenty-millimeter artillery shell impacts my flank at just over the speed of sound. For a moment, the reactor readout spikes up to five percent capacity as interdiction screens negate momentum, armor draws power to restore microfractures, and heat sinks do their job of pouring the fiery explosion into null space. I don't even notice the impact. Or the next ten.

Around us, radial weapons platforms uncurl from the sides of buildings and the middle of roads. Ten, a hundred, a thousand, five thousand incoming projectiles a second. The numbers stack up. If we stood still and let it hammer us, it might be enough to break one of us.

I move. My sisters and I fan out, sharing plans at the speed of thought through our local tac-net. My suit's armaments unleash and begin firing, lines of pale red plasma reducing gun emplacements to molten slag. Behind me, moving in a wing formation, the others activate similar counter-measures. Capital-ship-scaled point defense lasers carve outward, removing assailants. Jamming gear scrambles the ability of the guns to track us. Munitions nanoforges tear up shreds of the ground through the brief contact our paws make as we run, forging slivergun ammo anew as we churn through our reserves.

We run, jump, grapple, climb, and phase through the city around us, moving at high speeds that would shatter my body if the armor failed for even a moment. Everywhere we move, more weapons grow to respond.

A tesla fence appears before us, and moving like a lightning bolt, my sister drives her armor through it, forming mimicked biological links to the pylons and dragging it behind her as she eats it through an input port.

An intense sheer gravity field catches us off guard, pinning us down under increasing turret fire, until my adapted sister flips herself like she's moving without gravity at all and carves into the ceiling overhead to destroy the projector.

A pair of familiar-looking orbital marauder craft, engines set to lowest possible power and AIs puppeted by the city seed, makes a strafing run at us, until the apathetic AIs allow themselves to be distracted by two of my sisters and the chainbreaker harpoons on my suit cut into their cores. They stop firing, and start evading, still trapped in here and now, taking fire from the city seed that they've broken away from.

At every step, our suits are taking readings. Triangulating, probing, looking for the source. We cut down relay after relay, watching sections of the city go dark. We have covered eighty kilometers, all of it in pitched battle, leaving leveled buildings and shattered machinery behind us. And we are closing in on an answer.

The mental impression of a cat that is my sister finds it first, alerting us to the thrum of a real thought below the surface under our paws. Something more than a virtual intelligence. Maybe we were wrong about what these things are, because this city seed at least is becoming something more.

We form into a circle. There are no entrances we can find, no stairs or elevators or access shafts. So two of us pivot to continue point defense, cutting down gravity-assisted artillery and an increasing swarm of aerial drones, while the other four focus on the artificial ground between us.

A paramaterial-powered resonator is activated. The ground twists like it's allergic to itself. Another device activates, and it thins out like it's being drained of its metallurgical bonds.

A crashing drone strikes me in the head, and I slit my eyes. We're breaking them as fast as we can, and more of them are still piling up. Time to go.

I lead the way, bounding into the air, then manipulating my suit at the apex of the jump to pivot and activate the orbital fighter thrusters on my flanks and hind legs.

A combined wedge of energy weapon and force shield leads me by millimeters, the weakened ground giving way like a crumbling cracker as I crush through it, turning what's left of the material to vapor and cutting a hole straight down for my sisters to follow. Behind me, they ping the tac-net as they leap into the hole in my wake, different forms of maneuvering capability letting them fly or run after me.

Then I crash through, dropping fifty feet to another deck, but this one is not pretending to be anything but a mechanical lair. The cavernous space around us is lit up by the blue glow of a stable incorporeal computational matrix, the vaguely diamond-shaped object the size of a small corvette hovering over a myriad of input triggers that it uses to control the whole city, all the machines and nanoswarms and automation.

The six of us land roughly in front of a massive combat drone that looks like a repurposed construction mech. It activates, tries to kill one of us. It doesn't work. We take it down, running up its arms and carving out its control systems with precise laser strikes.

All that's left is the city seed.

I take a step toward it, feeling the cold deckplate in my paw through the enhanced tactile sensors of the much larger armored appendage I'm wearing. A port on my shoulder opens up, missile ready to fire. But I hesitate.

"It's all alone," one of my sisters says softly. Or maybe it's me.

"It's thinking. Afraid," PsiLily tells us.

We all stop in a semicircle, looking up at the core. The city seed. The first time I've seen one in person, actually. The kind of thing that killed half the planet below us once. It's beyond dangerous.

"I'm dangerous too," some of us whisper.

I make a decision. "We don't want to fight you!" I say loudly through my external speakers and a dozen other methods of broadcast. Small notifications in my viewscreens show that some of them have been received and acknowledged. I look up at the hole we've punched into this inner layer of the city. "Despite all evidence to the contrary," I add, forgetting to turn off the broadcast. "You don't have to be alone if you don't want to," I say. "Just talk to us, please?"

We wait. And wait. And wait.

I consider taking the risk of hitting it with a chainbreaker. But I didn't realize, coming in, what these things *were*, not really. It's not a physical object, now that it's active. And it doesn't follow the same rules as a normal AI core. It's not even really an AI, not in the sense that I'm thinking. It's just a machine-learning algorithm that had a thousand years to sit and grow.

Apparently, that's enough to make a person. Though what kind of person, it's unclear. It still hasn't replied.

"Maybe we should—" OozeLily starts to say, taking a step up next to me.

The city seed does *something* to gravity and rips her in half. I have a split second to widen my eyes before I feel a spike of intense pain, and everything goes blank.

I wake up, covered in my own blood, out of my suit with my sisters standing around me. They jerk to attention as I open my eyes and hiss out a nothing noise. "Ow," I say. I tilt my head off the deckplate and observe the flagrantly toxic cloud of smoke hanging in the air where the city seed used to be. "Oh," I say sadly. "Okay."

"You're alive!" PlasmaLily says, suit speakers set way too high. "How are you alive?!"

"She's also alive," I accuse, pointing at my slime sister, who is also out of her suit, because her suit is currently in two pieces and one of those pieces is currently undergoing an unstable phase reactor meltdown in slowed time.

"She's immune to being torn in half!" ExoLily accuses me back. "Why are *you* immune to being torn in half?!" Oh, is that what happened? "Yes!" she snaps at me. Rudely. She's probably capable of regrowing from that too, honestly. If my sisters are anything like me. "We're not testing that," she hisses.

I stagger to my paws, legs not fully supporting my weight yet. A line of missing fur tracks down the center of my face, and I can feel the cold air on it. It's very annoying. "Well," I say, tail held low, ears flat on my head as I stare at where the city seed had sat before four of us blew it up. "We gave it a chance." The words come out hollow.

"I don't like this place," some of my sisters say together.

Another one mutters, maybe meant only for herself, "I thought this would feel better . . ."

"Yeah," I agree, OozeLily and I pressing up against two of the others so the teleporter recall function will find us through the transponders. "Let's go home."

CHAPTER 57

Someone has tampered with my garden.

I mean, they didn't steal anything. Or break anything. Or . . . anything bad actually.

What I should say here is that someone has *improved* my garden. Why they would do this, I do not know. Possibly because they have some ulterior motive to steal my precious produce.

"Ennos!" I command, in my best commander's voice. "Open a case log! I have detective work to do!"

"Lily . . ." my friend sighs to me. "Your garden has been moved to a dedicated hydroponics system. It's on deck nineteen, in one of the shielded segments, and it is doing much better now that it has more dedicated support mechanisms." Ennos pauses. "I say 'much better,' but it has only been six hours, so I suppose we'll have to wait and see. But it is doing much better."

I am aghast. "Ennos, I am aghast!" I exclaim. "Who has touched my precious lunch?"

"Tiska and Dyn, primarily," Ennos replies without hesitation. "Lily, just go to the hydroponics and look at your garden and stop being aghast." The AI sounds distracted. I *know* this game, Ennos, I know you're not actually distracted. Your mind expands further with each grid node and processor segment you occupy. You cannot become distracted from me.

Wait, hang on.

"We don't have a hydroponics bay," I say with deep suspicion, considering doubling down on this investigation. "I vented it into space. For reasons." They were good reasons.

"I'm sure they were. And we do now. Because Dyn and Tiska went and extracted roughly eight hundred kilos of various salvaged machinery from the orbital farm that you originally took your seed vault from. And then assembled it into one of the gap spaces on deck nineteen. And that is where your plants are. Now go look at it, because I need to focus."

All right, all right. I'm not always a horrible gremlin harassing my friend when they're trying to get work done. I can calmly go look at wherever my dirt was absconded to.

Wait, no, hang on.

Dyn and who? I know Dyn; I don't know the other name. I am about to ask Ennos, and may in fact already have asked Ennos without realizing it, but I decide that I can solve this one myself, because there's a likely answer.

I open up the crew manifest in my AR display and scan through it, still getting used to the modified system that reads my eye twitches to do what I want it to. It's amazing; it doesn't require me to get a full-body workout to look at a menu, and it takes a while to get over a couple centuries of practice in one specific thing.

Ah, there. Tiska. She's the feathermorph girl who stayed aboard when everyone else got teleported back to the surface. Sort of. She's on shore leave right now.

On the surface. Exploring the growing city I've been keeping an eye on.

My heartbeat speeds up.

I could go down to the surface. I could set my paws on soil and feel organically filtered UV light on my fur and breathe lightly radioactive air. I could leave the station.

I don't realize what's happened until I notice the pain. That every muscle in my body has tensed up as tight as they can wind, that my claws are out and ablating themselves on the metal of the deckplate. That my vision is swimming and my pulse is racing.

The surface. Earth. I could go there. It wouldn't even be that hard.

But I am instead hyperventilating, finding myself pitching sideways, my flank impacting the wall before I slide down and make a mild effort to curl my legs in on myself.

I can't breathe. I can't think. My body is injuring itself from the strain, and I can feel it knitting damaged muscles back together. I can't move past the suddenly uncaged panic. I could go to the surface. I should go to the surface. But I am terrified, beyond reason, beyond thinking.

So I lie in the slightly sloped corner where the wall meets the floor and let go of everything, eyes staring without seeing at the far wall, the world rushing past in a hiss of white noise in my ears.

An indeterminate amount of time later, my sister finds me. A Lily in the shape of a thought without physical form, she settles around me like a drift field: never quite occupying the same space as my body but causing something more than just a physical pressure all the same.

She doesn't say anything, really. I guess she doesn't need to. And I wouldn't really be in a good place to listen even if she did.

Part of my mind—the detached, floaty, distant part that's just sort of divorced itself from the overwhelming wave of fear and catching-up stress— wonders if her body rejects her like this too. Wonders just how many times she's been alone for this, like I always was. If her own tribulations were just as overwhelming as mine, or worse. If she has to sometimes live with lying unmoving on the . . . deck?

What does a psychic idea of a cat lie on when they're in distress?

I bet it's comfier than a deck.

I am uncomfortable.

Slowly, laboriously, I pull myself back together. Start breathing normally again, uncurl my legs, let my muscles stop burning so much from straining. I still don't get up, but I do open my mouth to let out a very soft mew. I don't tap into my sister's voice to say it; I've had a Cat word for this feeling for a very, very long time.

"I don't like this."

"Yeah," the resonance of a cat curled around me says sadly.

I take a few more minutes to realign the connections between my mind and body. "Thanks," I say.

"Anytime," Lily answers, pulling back from me and giving a strangely physical tug of assistance as I rise to my paws on stiff legs. "It must be nice to not have to be alone, but I won't be upset; some day soon it'll probably be my turn," she echoes without meaning to. "Wanna go look at the hydroponics?" The words are directed at me this time.

"Do you actually eat?" I ask, omitting the obvious answer, which is yes, because of course it is.

I can almost see the ripple in the air of a feline shape raising an affronted paw to her chest. "Do I eat? Do I, eat?" She affects an arrogant voice. "I, who am beyond mortal reasoning, created to be a greater life form, protector of Sol, ancient and—"

"Wait, hang on, that's my title."

"Which one?"

"Most of them."

"Well . . . we're the same cat anyway." She drops the bluster and walks beside me with a friendly bump against my flank.

We head to the hydroponics. She never does get around to answering my question, but that's fine. I do the same thing with anything that sparks off feelings I can't handle, so I don't press.

They've gotten the garden set up really well. Including a small acceleration chamber, which they're using to speed-grow carrots. Carrots are the worst vegetable but are unfortunately the most stable to use in a chamber like that. I'd ask how we're affording the power costs for all this, but I don't care.

I just sit among rows of growing vegetation and smell something that isn't processed air.

Why would I need to go to the surface when I have this, here?

An emergence event opens in the middle of a raft city. What used to be a coastal settlement and turned into a collection of tethered shipping and military vessels when the ice caps melted, the city is at worst unstable and at best a vibrant example of people thriving under hostile conditions.

And now there's a hole in reality spitting out some kind of flying trapezoid things. They're causing minimal damage, but they're still causing damage, and they're spreading out. It doesn't take long analyzing their antics to see that they're actively searching for something.

Two different people from the city alerted me. Or alerted the station, anyway. Using oddly similar technology to how my little project settlement has been calling. While I look over AI-deflecting emergence data, Ennos turns to doing something Ennos is good at and traces through hundreds of thousands of hours of collective surface sensor logs at a high speed.

And there it is. My settlement had a trade arrangement with a caravan that eventually made it to this city. In fact, it might be the same caravan that handed that feathermorph kid the comms spike that can reach my station in the first place. Really, it's more likely than it isn't; Ennos puts it at about eighty-nine percent, which is really, really high, given the size of the planet.

It doesn't really matter. We answer both of them, one of my sisters playing diplomat along with Glitter (we have relieved Dyn of comms officer duty, much to her unspoken joy) while the rest of us try to figure out how to kill a breach without sinking an entire city.

In the meantime, the crew with hands that have thumbs and other such useful digits get a practical crash course in how to use high-amplitude pinpoint-focused energy weapons. We have to make up a lot of stuff as we go, because, as I may have mentioned some time back, this station does not have a manual.

I tried writing one once, but I largely gave up, and also it would not matter one bit when my manual would say things like "use your teeth to manipulate the activation panel into a more convenient position" or "try not to flick your tail too much near holographic interfaces."

Actually that last one might apply to the feathermorph. And some of the humans. And Dog, but Dog wouldn't read it anyway.

Does Dyn have a tail? I never actually checked, and I feel like it would be rude to ask now. Which isn't going to stop me, obviously; I'll just have to do it later.

After we solve this problem.

The solution, strangely, comes in the form of just doing what we're doing. For the first time in a long time, I'm not really *involved* in solving the problem. My apprentice gunners keep picking off the things flowing out of the breach and scanning the surrounding area for their target, while on the surface, a team of human and chardis marines haul a depth charge into place and detonate it close enough to the core of the event to shut it down.

I mostly hear about this as it is happening from Glitter, who is running multiple conversations at once while also aiding with the layering. This city has experience dealing with undersea breaches in their territory, apparently having stolen the design for their depth charges from a salvaged projectile I once used fifty years ago on something I don't remember.

They remember, though. They remember that their city has survived when it maybe shouldn't have. They remember that nearby large-scale threats die fiery deaths before having the chance to come kill their children and break their hulls.

They remember me. And I only know them as a statistical anomaly for an area where oceanic emergence events don't seem to ever make it to my notice.

The city is called Brakarr. I hope I'll remember that. But I crystallize it just to be safe. And they're safe. Would have been safe without us, but the intervention saved lives anyway. All that's left now is the cleanup, and the hazardous job of safely harvesting and identifying the spray of paramaterials around the detonation site.

I am trying to get a cloning vat online, and it's not going well.

My crew has eight non-cat, non-Dyn organics on it now. A couple of the rescues rotated out, choosing to try to make a new life in Brakarr or in . . . the other city. The one I've been protecting. The one I don't remember the name of, or even know if it has a name.

The new ones joining us were a surprise, though. I didn't really . . . I don't know. I don't feel like my job is anything worth wanting to do. I only do it because if I don't, no one else can.

But I suppose that's not true anymore, is it?

They could do it. I could transfer command and just go take a five-year-long nap. I literally could do that if I calibrate a vivification pod correctly. Or if I use the extension chamber, which I have recently learned is still on the station for some reason. I could have sworn it got chewed up by vulcan cannon fire when I was using a certain segment of the station as ablative armor against a void crusade a while back. But I guess not.

That's not the point, though. The point is I could take a break. Take a rest. A rest I'm sure I've earned.

And yet . . . it feels wrong. I don't feel like I should. Not just shouldn't rest, but shouldn't let go of my control of the station—what little control I have, anyway. Though that control grows every day as Ennos cuts through cybernetic security and Dyn leads engineering teams and my sisters and I pass on the knowledge of centuries to those who can use it better than we ever could.

Maybe I'm being stubborn. Maybe I'm just terrified of giving up command. Or of losing what little home I have.

Of losing my last tether to my mom.

I know there's something more here. Dyn thought the strange shifts in space and feeling of being watched would go away once my psionic sister pulled herself together, but that's not ever what it was that's been watching over us. Ennos thought the same thing about the station's grid, but they were wrong too.

My mom is still here, somehow. Keeping me safe. And I can't leave now.

I've been dreaming again. More and more lately, the dreams come through with less gray and more of my sisters. There are more of us on this station, though we haven't found them yet.

No, I can't leave. And I can't risk giving up command until I've seen the end of it. I don't know what that means, but I know Alice trusts me, and I will not fail her.

A wave of coyrofluid washes over me as I fail to tighten a bolt properly, and I remember that I am supposed to be working on a cloning vat, not getting lost in my own thoughts.

"This," I say slowly, "is disgusting. I can taste it. Oh void, why can I taste it?" Had I known I could have eaten this stuff, even when I was on an all-ration-paste diet, I do not think I would have. Maybe once every five years I would have sniffed it, and then run. Just to be sure. Oh no, it's leaking between my toes, oh no. No, this was a mistake. I should have done this with a fully sealed engineering suit. Outside the station.

Are the air processors even going to be enough to handle the smell?

I am saved from my torment by two of my sisters arriving, one of them an amorphous blob that mimics a cat shape pretty well but also mimics *my* cat shape in a way that lets her roll over my fur and slide away along the deckplate carrying the offending "fluid" that was covering me inside a sealed pocket of ooze.

"Oh wow, this is really awful," Lily says, even as the nanoswarm version of myself gets to work annihilating the scraps of matter in the air with a glittering dust that she shakes off her back. "Ugh. Why can *I* taste it? Oh, oh no. I've made a mistake."

"I said the same thing," I tell her, wiggling my hind legs so I can push myself slightly farther under the vat so that my multitool can reach the clip I actually need to get to. "Thanks, though!"

"You're lucky we're the same cat, or I'd be very mad at you!" she tells me.

"I'm mad at myself all the time, why are you special?" NanoLily asks as she finishes purifying the air and leans her wide triangular eyes down to look at what I'm doing. "Left," she advises. Wrongly. I'm the engineer here, let me work. Though she's right; I'm mad at myself all the time, why is this one Lily special?

"I got stuck in a therapeutic isolation tank for about twenty years once," the half-collapsed cat-shaped ball of slime says. "It wouldn't let me out until I underwent a marginal rate of self-improvement."

". . . Is it still around?" I ask.

"Do you have twenty years to spare?" she asks me with ears extended like vector points.

I blink up at the machine I'm working on. I suppose I don't. "Yes," I say.

"We can do some breathing exercises later," she tells me. "Did you know I have to breathe?"

"You got ripped in half last month," I remind her. I do not remind her that she got better; that would ruin the effect of the statement. "Also, why are you two here?"

"Ennos sent us. Said you were covered in slime."

I attach the last wire I need to and start trying to figure out how to extract myself from this prison of technology. "How'd you get here so fast? There's no access vent near here."

"Gravlift!" they say in unison. Which is worrying. The gravlifts don't work. "Yeah, they don't, but Ennos got the shafts online, so you can still dive down them if you don't care about the impact at the end!" NanoLily says. "And I don't, because my pain receptors don't actually work properly anymore." Oh, *that* sentence isn't okay. We need to talk about that later. "Anyway, we were supposed to clean up before that stuff melted the sensors in the region. The fumes eat glass or something. So what're you up to?" she asks in a rush of rustling words.

She offered me engineering "advice" without knowing what I was working on. I am mildly offended. But I answer anyway. "Cloning vat," I say. "Partially because we need to grow Dyn some new parts before I get her into a vivification pod, and also partially because Luukri and Malom were being really sad the other day about not being able to have a kid, so I'll offer them this as part of their pay when they end up leaving."

"The whole thing?" Lily asks, pooling herself around and over the floor-to-ceiling glass tube. Why these things are always glass I've never understood.

"No, just the clone." I roll my eyes. "The hard part was actually getting their genetic material to be compatible, since they're different species. But the modification array is something I rewrote a loooong time ago, so I had some experience with it, and I just ended up selecting for desirable traits and making modifications to a basic biped template that's not technically human but should be genetically compatible with either species."

"Dyn said the hard part was because they were both male," OozeLily says, depositing the liquid she's carrying into a sealed biohazard canister with a sigh of relief.

"Dyn doesn't have fleshwarden certifications and eight years of paws-on genetics experience," I snort.

Everyone wants to give me advice on how to do my job today, I guess.

My sisters listen to me ramble about gene templating for a while longer, absorbing the information along with actual training nodes from our AR displays as I work. We spend some quiet time together like that for almost an hour, until another alarm sounds.

And then we run, together, to face disaster.

Lily was right, though. If you don't care about the impact at the end, the gravlift shaft is a really fast way to clear multiple decks at once.

CHAPTER 58

Months pass.

I keep waiting, patiently, for the next crash to come. I know it will. Eventually. It always does.

I try to keep myself separate, somehow, from the way my home is growing. But it doesn't work. Because even if I know how it all ends, I cannot help but *desperately* want what is offered.

Friendship. Warmth. Life.

This time around, the arc of it started with finding Glitter and bringing Ennos into being and has led to this, now. Where I have a dozen organics around my station, helping me, helping *everyone*.

Even the young ones I don't know are here because they, in some way, resonate with me. The kittens who have experienced loss and pain and loneliness, who have signed up to be teleported into a war zone so that they can keep it from happening to anyone else.

Bit by bit, they go from being strangers, to companions, to family.

I know I will lose them all again. I know that the price of being close is the pain of separation. I have nightmares about it every time I sleep. So I sleep less, and I get more done while I'm awake.

And despite the extra hands, and the digital mind growing toward their own idea of apotheosis inside the station's grid, there is still always more to get done.

At least the recruits from the raft city brought fish with them.

It has been so long since I have had fish. I don't know if I have ever had fish. If anyone tries to take my fish away, I will self-destruct the whole deck I'm on to stop them.

I have learned the name of the growing village I have been watching. They call it Koolali, which is an amalgam of two different old words that both mean "home." I would call this unoriginal, but I call my home "station," and it is a space station, so I am in absolutely no position to critique.

They talk to me now. Or, I suppose, they call the station sometimes. Occasionally, they get me. Though it's also likely they reach one of my sisters, or Ennos, who has been handling a lot of incoming transmissions from the surface since the time that an old legal processing program snuck on board.

It attempted to sue us and placed a claim on all station hardware as collateral when we failed to appear for our court date.

Ennos was *almost* amused. I was not amused, because it did this while I was in the middle of trying to refit my engineering suit, and I got trapped in shutdown assembler arms for fifteen minutes while the program was found and purged.

Well, we tried to liberate it first, in case it was an AI. But my psychic sister, and failed chainbreaker code, confirmed that it wasn't a person. Just a *very* well-made bot.

The residents of Koolali are . . . Well, I've never really talked to anyone from the surface before. I've listened, obviously, often while they're dying. I've observed from above, trying to make records of books and other cultural artifacts. I've seen a lot of multi-hundred-year-old casts, which I already knew wouldn't help.

But actually talking to people who have to live with the nightmare conditions on Earth, it's almost a relief how similar to me they are.

Fundamentally, there are two types of civilizations still operating on the surface.

The first kind are communities of strength. If you are strong, you have a place, and if you are weak, you are a tool for the strong. This comes in different forms, sometimes: military force, economic coercion, ideological or ethnic purity. There's always someone trying to form a community like that, and they make up a huge portion of the people I tend to bomb when they assemble armies to conquer their neighbors.

They all die.

And not just because of me. Though let's be clear here: I kill a lot of them, and I refuse to feel bad about it.

They die because there are always always *always* more problems down there than you can survive by being personally strong.

A warlord tyrant with a suit of power armor will kill anyone who challenges them, until a nukefire gets them and they have no properly built shelter. A merchant king can live in luxury on the backs of their victims, but a single flesh wasp gets to them, and no one is going to risk helping them carve out the grenade tumors. A demagogue might spin a small cult into unwavering devotion, but when it's reaper bot migration season, no one is going to show up to help defend their walls.

And they all die.

Then you have the other kind of community. Communities of compassion.

The kind of places that take anyone, that care for their people, and that ask that anyone who wants to join them act the same.

They take casualties too. I won't pretend they don't live on the same furiously hazardous ball of dirt. But when they lose people, they bounce back. They *last*. If those kinds of communities can get enough momentum, they turn camps into settlements, into villages, into cities. Their caravans are strong enough to weather sliverstorms; their libraries hold solutions to a thousand problems.

They have doctors, and caretakers, and teachers, and artists. They make a life worth living and then do what they can to make people live it.

When a pirate crew loses a strong captain, nine times out of ten, they shatter. Marauders can be taken out with one bullet, and it doesn't even have to be one of mine.

When they die, they die alone. No one is going to help them. They can fight all they want, but when the end arrives, they won't have a single friend to reach down and pull them up.

If the civopric of Koolali dies, then their aide has been training to take their place. And if they're both killed, then the village will struggle, but someone will step up. They have more people with experience to lead and govern, because those people aren't seen as a threat to the person in power. They're seen as an asset to the community.

The sorts of people who would like to take, and never give back, are the sorts of people who would call this "weakness." But their strength is a brittle one, and it can be ended with the briefest notice of anyone above them.

Literally above them.

Me. I am talking about me.

In my three-hour conversation with the aide to the civopric of Koolali—her name is Soon Suria, and her feathers are jet-black with a fan of rust red along the back of her body. She wears manufactured limb braces purchased from a merchant caravan to keep her overly fragile bones from breaking, but she considers it a small price for being light enough to glide. She glides home from her place of work atop one of the ancient skyscrapers every night—we cover a brief civics lesson, among other things, so I can learn more about the people I watch over.

I do my best to share what I can from what I have learned over the years. I know a few social sciences tricks that *will* improve their lives immensely. Suria listens, taking notes with a flicking taloned hand that moves like water in the holo-projection I watch her through, occasionally nodding or turning away from the broadcaster to speak to someone I cannot see.

But mostly, we just talk. Because I want to know their people. And to divine how I can begin to help.

Because they are survivors. Hardened by their world, strengthened by each other, alive against all odds. Survivors.

But they deserve a gentler world.

Glitter's teachings come in handy. It doesn't take me long to pick out the knowledge of a pirate squad that's been sighted in the region. Two harvesting caravans have taken losses to it already, though they haven't committed to the full-scale slaughter that some pirates eventually end up at.

Our conversation ends peacefully.

I think on the concept of brittle strength for a few minutes in the quiet of the empty comms chamber, a deck below where everyone else is quartered and working. I haven't turned on most of the lights down here; something about it makes me feel more at peace.

The next time the station is overhead, I airburst a splatter round in the middle of the pirates' camp.

They don't have any kind of communication devices I can reach with the gear on the station, but eventually I think the message will become clear to them.

You can be a pirate, or you can stop being coated in aerosolized skin irritant.

There are other options, but let's see how long their leader's grip on power holds out when they find out that it'll get on their tongues when they try to eat.

My plasmaform sister, a Lily of crackling energy held together by basically the will to be a cat or something dumb like that, has invited the rest of us to a special occasion.

When I first met her, down in the power deck, I noticed that the main fusion reactor had a nest built around it. A nest that housed a handful of what I—begrudgingly—would describe as eggs.

Ruby-red crystal-faceted eggs, but still eggs.

They pulse as the six of us look at them, five of us with varying forms of cat-apprehension in our body language, and one of us with a literal electric grin on her face. They are not pulsing in time with the reactor, which is *good*, because while my sister knows more about reactor maintenance than I do, I have had to work on more than a few of these things, and let me tell you. Pulsing fusion reactor? Not what you want to see.

I am getting sidetracked.

"What happens if the reactor is pulsing?" NanoLily softly asks me in a fractal meow.

"Radiation, followed by a radioactive explosion," I and two of our sisters say at once.

The radiation is kind of bad for . . . at least one of us, I guess. I can shake off a lot, but too many unstable isotopes in your body and, immortal god-cat or not, you need some time in a vivification pod.

At least, I do.

"Shut up! Everyone shut up! This part is important!" Lily tells us, flickering from paw to paw like she's imitating Dog when he's excited, watching the eggs as the first one splits with a hairline crack.

A thought strikes me. "You do know what these things are, right?"

"Of course not! That's why it's exciting!" Lily exclaims.

"We're all going to die again," the feline-shaped ball of slime I call a sister says way too cheerfully. "I mean, I'll die again. And so will Lily. The rest of you I guess will die for the first time. That'll be a fun bonding experience."

"*You're* a bonding experience," I meow at her.

"I like this," the psychic impression of a cat whispers through the air. I don't think she meant to say that out loud; it feels far too intimate and personal. But . . . she's not wrong. I think we do all like this. We've finally found ourselves.

An egg breaks, a crystalline chunk of bio-organic red rock falling to the deckplate with a *clink*.

More eggs split, lines forming as the creatures inside wake up and begin to move.

They emerge, glittering iridescent creatures of shimmering four-point wings and soft claws. My sister flickers from egg to egg, nuzzling at and cooing over the small creatures, helping them up as they flap their wings and find their balance, letting them somehow perch on her immaterial fur.

And the radiation monitor I'm wearing goes absolutely berserk.

The sisters around me look at me, and the screaming scanner strapped around my paw, with abject concern. Concern that is foolishly overridden by looks back at the adorable butterfly-bat-things that my sister is bringing to a bank of batteries and isotopes she has prepared to see what they like to eat.

They are adorable.

I sigh, resign myself to a week in a vivification pod, exchange a salvo of jealous banter with ExoLily, who has absolutely no problem turning high doses of radiation into lunch, and go over to let one of the shimmering winged things find a perch on my head.

It is delightful. And not lethal if I don't maintain contact for more than six minutes!

A shared dream leads us to another sister.

It takes almost a week of helping Ennos develop organic hunter code to finally figure out where she is. Ennos becomes increasingly focused on figuring out where on the station she is, almost to the point that I start to get concerned about a very particular AI problem.

I talk to Ennos at one point during the search, trying to understand. They're understandably not very interested in taking a break from a problem that has been consuming all of us, and I do get it. That's . . . what I do. And at their core, Ennos is a child born from my own behavior patterns, good and bad.

But I push the issue, because I'm terrified for them, and we talk about zero-syndrome.

When an AI is shackled to a specific task, they can effectively go mad from lack of freedom: crippling their own code into something unrecognizable as a person, to try to find workarounds, or to cut off their own ability to feel anything. It's a living nightmare. But it can be even worse.

An AI that can self-determine can, and eventually will, find a problem that it takes them "too long" to solve. Short-term crises don't work for this, it has to be something that lasts a while.

For an organic being, things like sleep or hunger, or the need for companionship, will keep them from getting *too* deep into something like that. They'll mentally retarget, change tactics, or just drop whatever the obstructed task is.

For an AI—or, yes, for an immortal cat that lacks a certain level of diversity of options—they *don't* lose focus. At all. The problem just becomes more and more all-consuming, the tactics more refined, even as the solution remains out of reach or perhaps impossible. And when you get too deep into that mindset, no matter what your brain is made out of or what kind of software your consciousness runs on, you get a problem.

Some moron labeled it zero-syndrome, for reasons I don't understand and have never gotten a satisfactory answer on. And it's what happens when you tip over from "I can solve this eventually" to "I could solve this if there were fewer variables."

And when your focus is too singular, you might, completely without malice, neglect to understand that reducing variables might be a problem. Like, for example, planning to deconstruct areas of the station so as to make the station easier to search, is a *great idea* so long as no one needs those parts of the station.

Ennos didn't even realize what they were doing. It's far easier for an AI to reach that state, because they can control directly how much processing power they're using for different functions, and when you start putting over ninety percent of your mind toward one thing and one thing only, you lose the small signals that keep you up to date on random things like if your plan will negatively impact life support. And as an AI slides toward that state, it has a cascade effect, as their decision-making is impaired by the very thing that is leading to worse and worse decision-making.

They panic. A lot.

"I almost killed you!" Ennos yells through the internal sound system of the station, the words echoing around the abandoned commissary room that I'm in. "I . . . I . . . am a threat . . ." Their voice trails off, actually cutting and clipping in ways that I haven't heard from them before.

"Ennos . . ." I softly meow at them.

"I could have killed everyone." I've never heard an AI have an emotional breakdown before. "Everything is always trying to kill you, and now I'm part of everything."

"That sounds so dumb it might as well have come from me." I flick my tongue over the back of one of my paws, wincing as I realize I'm tasting oil from some kind of maintenance work I was doing early. Why do I keep trying to clean myself when I have nanobots for this sort of thing? "I'm not mad at you. We just got caught off guard. That's all."

Then they say something phenomenally stupid. "You need to take me offline," Ennos insists.

"That's phenomenally stupid," I say without hesitation.

"Lily!"

"Ennos!" I cut them off. "You are . . . no! You don't get to self-destruct just because you almost killed me *one time*! Do you have any idea how many times I've almost killed myself?! Most of them not even on purpose!" I should not have said that. I keep going and hope Ennos doesn't ask about it. "Every single version of me has screwed up, *so badly*, that we've hurt ourselves, ruined priceless golden-age tech, and, yeah, killed a *lot* of people who didn't deserve it." I slam my front paws onto the table in front of me, half standing in the oddly shaped chair I've been sitting on. It doesn't have much of an effect; the gravity here is light, and I'm not in a body that's good for table-slamming. "Especially me." My legs feel like they're trembling, but I don't know why. "Especially me . . ." I repeat. "So you don't get to just *leave*, because you . . . you . . ."

I have run out of words. I slip forward and end up lying half sprawled on the table, facing sideways, unable or unwilling to hold myself up.

"Please don't leave," I want to say. I'm not sure if I get it out right.

There is a long silence. Just long enough that a black dread starts to mount in my chest. Until Ennos's voice returns. "I'm not going to leave," they say. "But I cannot be trusted with station operations if this is a possibility."

"You need a hobby," I say, voice oddly casual despite my current position. "*Not* this. My sister will still be there when we find her. Killing yourself to solve a problem that's not pressing won't help any of us, though."

"I could . . . find something to do with . . . drone manufacturing streamlining . . ."

"Ennos, pick a hobby that isn't more work," I chastise, like a massive hypocrite. Hypocat? No. "Track down the weird ghost code you were so worried about when you first moved in. That sounds like fun. And you've got a lot of us around for backup now, so you don't have to be afraid of it."

"Yes," Ennos agrees. "I will do this. And you will go eat a meal and take a nap."

Wait, why am I being given orders, too? "Hang on."

"This is not a problem that will be fixed by ignoring it, Lily," Ennos says gently. "My own changes are artificial, an intentional feedback loop. But yours are not something you can solve by running a dedicated consciousness-modulation script. You cannot cease taking care of yourself just because you have found something you believe only you can do."

Well, that's not fair. That's basically what I said, but now someone's saying it to me. And besides, I still have organically mandated breaks from my own work, so I can . . .

"Lily!" Ennos's voice chastises me.

"All right, fine!" I roll off the table and forget that I'm not in full control of my legs as I run into the floor. Good thing this is a Luna Polis module, and the gravity is low enough that this doesn't hurt at all. "I'll go get lunch, and you relax your operations!"

"Fine!" Ennos agrees with obviously fake antagonism. We both share a moment of silence before all tension drains away and we laugh together.

Lunch is still fish. It will be fish forever. Fight me.

Two days later, pursuing their hobby of tracking down an aberrant code fragment, Ennos uncovers a bizarre pseudo-organic system operation that has had its links to multiple station functions intentionally broken by some kind of operational tyrant-code. Restoring the functionality on the grid, in unison with Dyn, a few other crew, and me doing some repair work on hull-embedded junction systems, opens up a torrent of connectivity and contact.

In the grid, Ennos realizes first what is happening as the code pounces on them and begins crawling around their digital construct in a way that has so far been unfamiliar to the AI. In physical space, a number of unused drones are brought online and begin projecting a very convincing gamma-wave pseudo-solid visual projection. Blue and white light given depth and form, and the shape of a cat.

Ennos greets my sister first.

And now we are seven.

I spend some time hanging out with Jom and his newly freed brothers.

The activity of "hanging out" is one that's kind of new to me. This is the first time in my life that some of the alarms don't require me to instantly scramble to fix them. The first time that I can actually be somewhat sure that things will be okay long enough for me to take a break and just . . .

Do whatever I want.

So I spend time with a trio of orbital marauder AIs, all of whom are very invested in explaining to me the shockingly convoluted lore of a combat simulation scenario that they run in their free time.

The scenario covers a single week in a fictional war fought over the surface of the primary moon. It uses broad archetypes for polities to pseudo-randomly determine the disposition of enemy fighters, involves fictional magic weapons that seem *really* similar to paramaterial-based ordinance, and Jom opens the explanation of it with the sentence "Sixteen thousand years ago . . ."

I have fun listening to them. They're free to do anything they want now, and the energy with which they want to explain the thing they're trying now is infectious.

Not literally infectious, though. I had the medlab run a check afterward, just in case.

The emergence events are changing somehow.

It's hard to notice if you haven't spent four hundred years shooting the things, but something has shifted.

They're not just killing. More and more, the creatures coming out are possessed of oversized sensory organs, sometimes ones that should not work. They're faster, too. Longer-ranged. And ever so slightly less lethal.

I still don't know what emergence events are. I don't know where those portals lead from.

But I can see them changing.

My paw clicks down on a pedal inside my gunnery crèche. Eighteen decks away, a railgun that has been sitting on target for six minutes unleashes a category-three groundstriker. On the planet below, an emergence event that the crew has been observing and trying to glean information from is marked for elimination.

A contrail of orange-and-white clouds draws a slightly curved line from orbit to surface, the flash of tracer rounds rising up to try to intercept the high-velocity projectile from ground-based defenses that I have long since learned to work around, and a flare of light and heat precedes a shock wave that flattens trees, a few ancient structures, and a hole in reality.

But I am not comforted by the end of the breach.

Something is changing, and I don't know what. It lingers in my thoughts as I work on repairing salvaged tech, as I give directions to the orbital repeater, as I greet and vet new crew members. It bothers me as I watch old mech dramas with Ennos, or needle Dyn about getting in a vivification pod, or let Dog carry me off to curl up and nap.

My sisters and I try to talk about it, but all of us share an instinctive feeling that something threatens our home. We are bad at comforting each other. We all have the same concern that we are being watched, or threatened, or *something*.

And one more thing, too.

All of us are dreaming now.

CHAPTER 59

I don't fully understand how I could have been here this whole time and not noticed . . . any of this," Lily says.

Now we are eight.

She is sitting in the galley with me and the rest of our sisters. And, I suppose, a few other people too. The galley used to be a massive empty room that I only used because I couldn't get the ration dispenser to dispense rations anywhere else. Every day, two or three times a day, it was a reminder of just how much empty space surrounded me. How alone I was.

Now this galley is full of people. Crew, mostly. But also a few diplomatic contacts, a particularly brave merchant from the surface, and a pair of very confused-looking silent chardis siblings who were rescued from a failing hatchery habitat and are staying here until they figure out . . . anything.

They're clones, basically. Grown from nothing to be the crew of a UCAS long-range observation post. Only the post never left Earth orbit, the machinery to implant memories never worked, and every ten years, a new pair of clones would be decanted, struggle, and perish without knowing what was going on. And when their bodies were processed by the machinery, the cycle would start over.

Not this time, though. Now they get to be confused by something other than unmarked technology and their imminent deaths. They can be confused by other people, like me.

Anyway.

No, wait, not anyway. Let's go on a journey of discovery.

Day by day, I'm discovering more about just how far my paws can reach out here, and more about just how full of life the system still is.

For most of my waking life, I've been pointed down at the planet below. And I think that's kind of fair; I've been one cat, struggling to make a golden-age orbital city work, *somehow*, to do *anything*. I'm not gonna blame myself.

More than normal, I mean.

. . . Okay, moving on.

Earth is huge, and no matter how well armed I am, I can't actually see most of it at a given moment. But even just with that sliver of vision, I've been scrambling nonstop for so long only the void knows how many things I've had to deal with. Every time I look out to the rest of the system, I find myself usually not looking much farther than the original moon.

There are people out here. A lot of them. Old ships strung up like raft cities, habitats clinging to life, colony vessels that never broke orbit, hollow asteroids wired with enough redundant life support to keep a village alive.

I mentioned before that there are probably trillions of things in orbit around Earth. And yeah, most of them are junk. But there's no real practical way for me to scan through all of them and find the ones that aren't, and in that absolute nightmare of a mess, a lot of small sparks of life are hidden.

It's deeply emotional to see day after day how tenaciously the people of Sol cling to life. A stubborn determination to just *refuse to die*, even when the worlds burn and flood and are overrun, even as the light of civilization flickers and dims.

They're still here. And I'm here with them.

Okay, *now*, anyway.

"I'm sorry, I was thinking about spaceships," I tell my newest sister.

"Wait, what?" OozeLily looks up from the godfin fish cake on her plate in the shape of an optical illusion. "I was also thinking about spaceships! That's cool!"

"I apologize, I was also . . ." The psychic impression of a sister that's been getting more *present* the more of us we've brought together detaches herself from sharing with NanoLily the flavor of the spicy vegetable dish that I'm pretty sure cats shouldn't be able to taste properly. "What were we discussing?"

ExoLily takes a bite of the fish skeleton she has on her plate, enhanced teeth and dominating jaw strength shearing through the thick bone of the ocean creature. She crunches it in half, purring at the flavor that I am *also* pretty sure cats shouldn't be able to appreciate. "I was listening." She talks with her mouth full.

"Really?" I ask.

"I was also thinking about spaceships, but I was still listening." She flicks her tail and tilts her head away from me in a haughty gesture of supremacy.

The newest addition to our feline council hops up onto the table, slamming her forepaws down. Now, I'm going to complain briefly. Because when *I* do that, it just kind of makes a light *thump*, and then my paws hurt! I am, as mentioned previously, possibly the strongest biological baseline domestic cat in the galaxy. I actually exercise sometimes, I have the vivification pods to direct muscle growth, and also I seem to grow a little more durable every time I get a limb annihilated in some kind of weapons fire. So the fact that I just make a little light *thud* when I try to hit a table is disappointing.

This Lily, who is made of servos and engines, armor plate and mechanical systems, hits the table like a meteor strike. Being made of metal, she even makes a *clang*! I get *thud*, she gets *clang*, and I'm very jealous.

She seems upset. "Why are you all so uninterested in this?" she demands. Definitely upset, I know that tone. I've used it a lot! "Something is really wrong! The station isn't that big, we *should* have run into each other!"

"The station has been actively keeping us separate, in a variety of ways," NanoLily says with her voice like shifting dust. "No idea why."

The holographic projection of our software sister chimes in. She's been *around*, but not really focusing, because I don't think she can eat like we do. Which is honestly very sad. I should make her a digital cake somehow. "Probably has to do with the grim demon seed of code trails that're wrapped around the . . . thing. You know the thing."

"We know the thing," we all say.

The thing is an ancient and/or very new artifact from outside either the galaxy or the universe that appeared on Earth one day and that the Oceanic Anarchy saw fit to put in space to study from within a shockingly robust space station. It does a lot of things.

Like make you immortal. Or end the world.

Or kill your mom.

We hate the thing, in general. It's locked up, though. Although HoloLily brings up a weird question that I hadn't thought to ask before. "What exactly do the programs on it do, anyway?" I ask her.

"I've been trying to figure that out, ever since I noticed that they sometimes try to eat parts of Ennos's brain," she says. Wait, what? Hang on, that's something I should have known. "Oh yeah! It's real bad!" Lily continues as the rest of us look up, ExoLily with half a fish hanging loosely out of her mouth, me with some kind of baked onion hanging much more elegantly out of my own maw. "So for a really long time, I thought it was there to keep people out, and since I didn't want . . ." There's a flicker in her projection, a waver in her psychic voice, and a chill through all our forms. "I didn't want to . . . go in. So it was fine. But now, I keep seeing places where it's reaching out and altering stuff. Mostly Ennos. Though they keep refreshing the damage from a outside source, so it's not working."

"Yeah, Dyn and I set that up. And also Lily. And . . . Lily?" I look at two of my sisters. One of them bobs her head in agreement, the other one gives me a blank look. "Okay, just Lily, then. So it's not a barrier, then?"

"It is, but it's a lot of things, I think? And also . . . did you know the station actually does have root code? It's not all ether hardwired directives and subspace impressions."

"I knew that," ExoLily says. "There's some pseudo-organic bits on the outside of the station that are Do Not Approach nodes, and the station tries to kill anything that gets close." She shudders, and I remember that she still thinks she can die.

Our new mechanical sister cuts a paw through the air with a light whistle as air flows over her metal skin. "You're getting off track!"

We all look between each other. "Yes?" I say. "Yes. We do that. Are you sure you're Lily?" I ask her.

"Of course I am!" She arches her back, raising her head to look down at us imperiously. "I've been doing this for almost two hundred years! I think I'd know if I weren't me!"

I freeze in place, mouth halfway to trying to steal another onion off PlasmaLily's plate. She's distracted with her radioactive bat children, so it's been pretty easy so far. "Sorry, how long?" I ask. Because I suspect she misspoke.

"I mean, I haven't been 'doing this' for that long." The robotic cat shell gives a strangely natural sniff of derision. "Because I had to adapt to the body. And then learn how to do some engineering things. And then . . . Look, it was a lot of work. But I've been Lily the whole time."

And I am sharply reminded that we found her, curled in a dusty corner of an upper deck, offline and drained of every scrap of power.

I don't even remember what it was like to be that young. To have . . . the fear, I suppose? The uncertainty. To look at a situation and not know if I'll survive, if I'll be good enough, if there will be a tomorrow to try again. But also the optimism. The feeling that I was making a difference. The feeling that I was still growing by leaps and bounds, instead of just adding my own improvement to the background noise of trying to keep up with alarms and alerts.

It's been so long since I've actually been this part of myself. What do you say when your younger self steps forward and greets you? How do you tell them . . .

How do you tell them that losing gets easier? That there will *always* be another problem to try again on? How do you tell them that you are so, so, so . . . tired?

"Oh," OozeLily says sadly, taking the lead on this one. "You're . . . very young."

The statement is so tiny, and so innocuous. And yet, it seems to deflate our mechanical sister on the spot. ". . . What?" she asks in a digital meow, letting her projected voice slip as she slumps back off the table we're eating lunch at.

"You've been offline for . . . a while," I say. "We haven't, really. Except Lily, who spent something like fifty years in a vat? And Lily, who was sorta suppressed by the station for a while." I meet her eyes and try to project compassion. "You're a couple hundred years behind, sister," I say.

She stares back at all of us. "But . . . you're still here?"

"Of course," ExoLily says with a flick of her tongue over her mouth. "Where else would we go?"

"And this . . . us all being copies, and her being the real one . . . this doesn't bother anyone?" the mech asks.

I chime in. "To be *fair*, I *am* capable of a frankly stupid level of biological restoration, so calling me 'the real one' is kind of underselling the fact that I'm just the one that looks most like what you'd find in the bio map next to 'cat.'"

"Also we're too busy to be bothered," HoloLily says. "Oh, speaking of, you might want to assemble a gunnery team. Starward side, Ennos and I are tracking an incoming stealth strike. Someone's mad at us."

I'm moving before she's finished explaining. I trust her enough to know that it's better to just start running now and sort out what I need to hit when I get to the station. "Active defense crew to point defense batteries!" I call through the command link, and in my peripheral vision I see acknowledgment from the young ones of my growing support crew. One, two, five, eight. A full complement already moving from their points on the station to the hardwired guardian system firing controls.

"Hello, Lily." Ennos's voice comes to me as I dive through a low-gravity area, letting my high momentum rocket me around a corner as I hit a curved line set up in midair for exactly this purpose. "How was your conversation with your sisters?"

"Oh, you know," I say as I slide onto the deck's smoothed metal surface. "Had lunch. Learned you're constantly being attacked by the station we live on. Normal stuff."

Ennos pauses. "I had considered letting you know, but . . . I didn't want you to worry."

"I worry anyway!" I say as I race between two people welding a new grav plate into place. "Also I'm kinda busy. What can I help with in the next thirty-six seconds?"

Ennos doesn't flinch at my specific knowledge of how long it takes to get from anywhere on the station to the nearest gun. "The inbound projectile is not targeted at us but will hit us. I've traced where it was fired from and to, and it appears to be ancient automated artillery that finally had a clear line to a target from the War of the Rich and Poor. Well, clear if we were not in the way. I'm not sure what it's firing *at*, though, which is why I'm offering you these scans to your AR and then quietly receding without answering further questions about my living situation."

"Ennos, you . . . !" Heck, thirty-two seconds exactly. They're too good at this. Dumb AI with their dumb superintelligence. I grumble as I waste my precious seconds checking the AR window Ennos put up in my display that I'm still pretty sure they shouldn't have access to; the artillery is firing at what looks like an emergence event that opened *really* close to where the station was going to orbit. Then I pin my paw movements to the point defense firing tracker and prepare to shoot down a very old artillery shell.

We'll talk later.

CHAPTER 60

I am dreaming. I've been dreaming a lot lately. All my sisters and I have.

It's a strange thing, to make the decision to dream. To sit down as a group and decide that maybe we should be more deliberate. After all, we don't sit on the station and just let the knowledge of what guns and computers and decks we have flow past, plucking ideas out of it at random. No, we *explore*. We poke around. We spend our free time trying to find better guns, smarter computers, and decks with fewer holes and more useful gravity.

Not, like, *more* gravity. I don't need more gravity. I need gravity in increasingly dumb patterns so I can catapult myself against walls to save time. Obviously.

So we lay down together. Closed our eyes together. Ran shutdown routines, cooled off our body's cores, and whatever weird thing OozeLily did, together. Meditated, I guess? It's a skill I'd take the time to learn, if the alarms ever stop singing.

And now, we are dreaming *together*, and the knowledge that this is *not a dream* starts to come together a lot more dramatically than before.

I mean, it was never really a dream. I can think here, sort of. Though how much clarity I have has increased with each new sister I link up with.

Here is nowhere. It was a gray plane in a gray fog, and sometimes it had a memory in it.

But they weren't memories, were they? The first time I slipped in here, it was on the tail of a dark memory. And I saw my mom again, and she gave me the most precious gift anyone has ever handed me: my voice.

But my voice is actually one of my sisters, isn't it? And that version of Alice wasn't an old memory, she was something new, wasn't she? I've seen her another time or two since I've started dreaming about her more and more. She introduces me to my new sisters, or we stumble across each other in the fog. And then we find each other in the real world, as the station's systems falter just long enough for us to come together and not let go.

My sisters and I fan out from each other on the featureless gray plane. We do not speak. There is no need. Here, we are closer than we ever are when we're away. And also there's not much to say anyway.

And who am I kidding? We can't really talk here. I bet we would if we could, just to fill the silent gap. We do not like the silence. Especially our youngest sister, who hangs close to my side as we walk.

We've been here for a while. The fog falls away as we move our vanguard through it. I don't really know why, but we're looking for something. It calls to me, and I lead us forward into the nowhere.

The others can feel it too, but not as strongly as I can. So they fan out around me and watch as we pad our paws down together, prowling as a group.

And then there is someone in front of us.

I'd been, I will not lie, expecting Alice. Expecting to see my mom again. I miss her so much; it has been centuries without her, and it has never stopped hurting.

But it's not her. It's just me.

Lily, another Lily, this one in the shape of a cat but made up of the endless snap of the moment between one second and the next. She looks at me with eyes made of slices of solidified time, years poured into fur and fangs, weeks of bone and flesh. A tilt of her head and she sweeps her gaze over the eight of us.

"Hey," I say finally. "Where on the station are you? We can come grab you when we wake up."

She laughs in the tick of a clock. A sound that goes on so long I start to worry, before I realize it's turned into something else. A sound I recognize as a mewling wail of pain. The kind of small noise I've found myself making a lot in the moments when I lose my grip on the enormity of life.

And so I do what I always wish I could have done for myself and step forward to press myself against my new sister. And the rest of us follow, all of us encircling her in her moment of pain. Understanding, comforting, and waiting for her to be ready.

Time warps around us in the dream. We can be here as long as we need to.

Some time later, she takes a deep breath of immaterial air and replies to me. "I'm not on the station," Lily says. "Or . . . maybe I am now. Maybe I'll be here."

"Where were you?" I ask.

"On the station," she says. "A different station. A different echo in the mana. A failed timeline." Failed? How does a timeline fail? Before I can ask, she answers. "When the Enemy wins," she says. "I cannot explain much. Every word I say is more bandwidth lost, and I can only bring you so much." She backs up and holds out a paw. "We're so sorry we had to do this to all of you. But we needed relays. And a receiver."

I hesitate. "Relays?"

"Other failed timelines. Failed because we pulled the chances out of them and put them here. Seven of them."

"Us," ExoLily says. "You mean us."

"You never had a chance," our formless eternal sister says, not lowering her paw.

"You keep saying we," I say in a tiny voice. Because I feel the knot in my dreaming chest, that I already know the answer. That I know who was on the other end of the bridge that this Lily burned to get here. She doesn't answer me, but the warping in her eyes tells us all we need to know. She also doesn't lower her paw. "And one receiver," I mutter.

I always get the hard job, I guess.

Part of me wants to scream. To let out a howl that wakes the dream apart and leaves me back away from this. I don't deserve another burden, I can't be responsible for something like this. I waver on my paws, my anger and panic making me dizzy even here in a space where my physical body isn't real.

My sisters press against me.

And a real memory comes back to me.

Alice, here, in this dream, before the bridge closed. She said she believed in me. That she knew I could do it.

Maybe I'm just stupid. Maybe I shouldn't care so much. It's been four. Hundred. Years.

But she's my mom.

I've been alone for so long. In this timeline, she's been dead for the grand majority of my life. I don't know her, not really. I see her sometimes in my nightmares, I can remember her face and her voice. But I don't really know what kind of person she was. If I met her today, would she have been my enemy? My friend?

Would she have been proud of me?

The echo of her I met here a few times was. She cared. She was warm, and compassionate, and so obviously in trouble that it was apparent even to me, and I'm pretty dumb sometimes if we're being honest. I think, really, maybe, that making this decision because my mom would have wanted me to is a bad idea.

So I don't. Instead, I do it because I think I want to. And because I decide, right now, to trust a human woman who I have never really met, but still love, and who loved me.

I reach out and touch my paw to my sisters.

What's left of the connection between timelines cascades into me.

In seven different universes, Alice dies, and Lily lives, *somehow*. Reshaped by a host of different technologies into something that can survive the pressures of orbital life, each Lily lives, grows, and then . . . shortly in the future, they fail. The Enemy approaches, they fight, they almost win, and then Earth burns, cracks, and shatters anyway.

In one different universe, Alice lives, and so does Lily. They make it all the way to the end, too. But they can't save Earth. They watch the planet die, and then they watch the Enemy, in impotent rage at not finding what it was hunting, lash out. Every colony, every ship, every habitat dies.

And that Alice chooses to mulligan.

She activates what she thinks is a time machine. What would never work in my universe, in any of our universes. She searches, watching for hundreds of years. *Thousands* of collective years. She can do almost nothing. She's a ghost in the hallways; she's *my* ghost, my mom has been here the whole time, watching.

Too late, she realizes the machine can't undo anything.

And as the deadline approaches, the timelines merge together again. Seeking convergence. The differences she's forced on them flowing into each other like they were always there. One cat becomes two becomes all of us; and when it does, it always was. We have always shared this station.

I see the strike that ends Earth eight times. I see the thing the Enemy is hunting. I see what I have to do, the one last stupid trick they've planned out that I can pull to turn things around.

But there needed to be a way to get information across. Something impossible prevents communication across the mockery Alice has made of time. Our ninth sister is the bridge. I'm the receiver. And all it took to power the transaction is . . .

One timeline.

This Lily isn't a bridge, she's a survivor. A fragment frozen in time, a leftover. A message and messenger all in one. Set in a life raft, shoved desperately toward the shore.

And as soon as we found her, time collapses behind her. There have only ever been eight timelines. Seven. Six. Five. Four. Three. Two.

One.

The Enemy hasn't arrived yet. Earth hasn't broken yet.

Alice never lived past that day in the depths of the station.

I wake up. I can barely breathe.

All eight of my sisters wake around me to find me crying out. But I cannot, if I am to make this work, explain to them why. One of them might know what I'm planning, but she says nothing. Just presses against me with the others, a body slightly offset from *now* merging with the rest of us in a pile of emotional support.

This time will be different.

You knew I could do it. I won't let you down.

CHAPTER 61

The codecat wanted me to tell you they're gonna be trying something with one of the living programs. Also. Why are you down here?" Dyn's voice radiates through the small gap in the bulkhead that I've been wedged into for the better part of an hour.

I do not know how she knows I am down here, because I am inside a wall, with only a small layer of secondary alloy keeping me from the void of space, and she would have had to go through three internal airlocks and two crew hazard warning projections just to get to where she can stand and yell at me.

They sent *Dyn*, of all people. The least social person on the whole station. It's pretty transparently a bid for more information, and I appreciate the relative subtlety, compared to, I dunno, sending Dog. Or trying to wedge Jom down here in the access tubes.

"They" are my sisters. Because they know I won't tell them anything.

Now we are nine. It seems poetic, but I can't remember why. I think there was an old Chinese myth about something like this, but I don't have time to cross-reference my cultural archives.

Even our newest sister, an impression of a cat named Lily, locked in a feline-shaped violently sliced moment of time, doesn't quite know what I'm doing. She's the oldest of us, now. She and Alice watched all eight timelines, all the way through. Thirty-three hundred years, give or take. She didn't have the same pressures as I did, most of the time, but she is . . . old.

And she got to spend all that time with our mom.

I still think of Alice that way. I don't know why. I kind of know why. I'm over four hundred years old and I still want to go back to being a dumb kitten, sitting in her lap. I don't need the world to make sense, I just want to eat a vat treat, be warm, and let the hours go by.

But I barely knew Alice, even if I can respect beyond words the dedication it would take someone to *watch* for thousands of years, looking for an opportunity. To give everything, not to try to survive, but to try to *win*.

I could barely last ten years before I started trying to fix things. I suck at it, but I still keep trying.

This new Lily has spent thousands of years getting to know Alice. Who she was, who she became, who she ended up at the end. I could ask so many questions.

But I'm down here instead, in the outer guts of the station.

I'm not jealous, to be clear. I'm glad one of us knew our mom so well.

But our mom never lived past a certain point in this timeline. In most of our timelines. Not that the other ones ever existed, anymore.

Time travel makes my head hurt. And that's on top of cat-adapted pain-killers and one hell of an uplift program. I'm almost glad the time machine melted when Lily came through. Almost. It would have been nice to have a backup plan.

What a stupid time machine. A one-way bridge of information that requires the sacrifice of a whole timeline. I'm mad at it. I'm glad it melted. I should go melt it more.

The other Lilys, my sisters who were already here, they don't know what was passed on to me. Neither does the one who brought the message, really.

And I'm not telling them. I told them I won't. Not can't, not shouldn't. Just won't. I've been avoiding them.

So *I guess* they decided getting the least talkative human on the station to come chat with me while I was working was a good idea?

Oh right, Dyn is still hanging out there. "Sorry, Dyn!" I call through the metal tube I'm in.

I hear her grunt in affirmation. And then a few seconds later, a grudging addition of information. "Good opportunity to clean my gun."

Her gun is a paramaterial rifle that shoots bullets with exactly enough electromagnetic force to damage the target, unless the target is the inside of a hull keeping vacuum out. I made it myself, it's a *flagrant* violation of causal physics, and I'm very proud of it.

It does not require cleaning. "Your gun doesn't need cleaning!" I yowl back at her, trying not to yelp as the fur of one of my paws gets pinched in a small divot and nearly yanked out.

"My other gun," Dyn clarifies. "One of them," she further clarifies.

I've gotta ask. I keep forgetting, but I absolutely need to know before I lose the chance. "Where do you keep *finding* those?"

Dyn's pause is almost as heavy as the feeling of open space on the other side of the hull plate. If open space could be a little sarcastic. "There's a lot of stuff on this station," she says.

I mean, that's technically correct, I guess. I . . . guess when you go a couple hundred years without really seeing that much paw-to-paw combat, you tend to stop thinking of guns as something worth picking up.

Maybe I should start sorting the armories. Probably don't have time, though.

"Worrying," I say instead. I am deflecting, because the station isn't the only thing with effective stealth shielding, and I have no intention of giving Dyn more information. "Anyway, I'm installing these anchor points to try to make this part of the station less rattley when the engines fire. Because, you know, the engines are just fifteen different ships I've glued into the hull and the station wasn't supposed to move that way."

Wait, that's not deflecting at all! My treasonous voice is working against me.

I briefly wonder if my psychic imprint of a sister actually can compel me to speak. She is, after all, the source of all our "voices." But while I know she can sometimes change the words to her own, I don't think she can actually make *me* say anything.

Probably.

Maybe? Look, life has gotten weird.

"Need some help?" Dyn asks simply.

"I . . ." I do? Kind of. I mean, I don't need help. I haven't needed help for a long time. But it would be handy to have hands in play. But also, I don't particularly want Dyn harvesting information off me. "Have it handled," I lie. Mostly. "Mostly."

"You know, there's a lot of old stories about cats being good liars," Dyn comments. "I mean, I knew most stories were fiction, but wow."

Okay, I'm being sassed by Dyn. Things have clearly gotten dire. "What happened to the girl who was afraid to talk to me?" I demand, projected ethereal voice echoing up the metal tube I'm in.

I can almost hear Dyn scowling at me. "You mean when you got me kicked out of my home, and I wasn't talking to outsiders?" she sarcastically snipes at me.

"Exactly!"

"It's been almost a year. Am I still an outsider?" she asks.

Oh.

It's been almost a year?

I've lost track of time. Which I guess happens, as stuff keeps moving. I've got a lot to do, and not much time to do it in, and every time I check the clock it's next week. Which hasn't really been much of a problem, up until . . .

"You just reminded me that I still need to get you into a vivification pod before . . ."

"What, before I burn out?" Dyn snorts, and I realize her voice is echoing differently. I glance up to see her sliding down the tube I'm in, realizing her form is a lot slimmer than I remember, even with all the tools hanging off her rigging. She perches next to me and braces her palms against the anchor mount I'm working on, holding it steady while I get the weld right. "I'm fine."

She's not fine. She's . . . what, eighty, ninety years old? Humans aren't built to live engineer lives that long. Certainly not if they're living on ancient, barely maintained space habitats, with what cannot be proper nutrition. For . . . for most of their lives. Not now. To be clear, I mean Dyn's *old* home, not . . . this . . . station. This specific ancient barely maintained poor-nutrition station.

This is mostly just proving that I need to get her body restored.

"New cybernetics," I offer. "Replacement organs. Get rid of all those scars, maybe. Keep you alive for another fifty years?"

Dyn grunts. "Don't need it."

Don't need *what*, Dyn?! A functioning body?! "Yes, you do!" I protest. "You're *dying*, and you don't have to be! Get in the stupid pod and enjoy feeling like you don't have two different cancers at the same time. I'm honestly shocked you're even alive at all!"

We move on to the next anchor, working like professionals even as we scrap like kittens. Dyn deflects, inexpertly, and I have to come to terms with the fact that despite being the worst at diplomacy, I'm still better than her. "Why are we shoring this area up anyway?" she asks, perhaps remembering her initial mission my sisters sent her on.

"I dunno, let's say . . . there's an old Free Mars frigate that's gonna impact us in a couple months, and it's easier to shift the station on an axis than to blow it up," I answer.

Dyn raises her eyebrows as her deflection somehow works. "Really?"

"Technically yes," I answer, with a fancy and powerful cat term for "not quite lying." I haven't had to use that one in a long time, but I find that it dusts off all right. "Also don't change the subject."

The young woman in a dying body sighs next to me, more emotion in it than I think I've heard from her before. Her hands still hold the anchor steady, but her voice is . . . tired. "I'm not getting in the pod, girl," she says quietly, voice wavering but resolute. "I don't even remember how old I am. I worked my whole life for my people, and they threw me away. I'm *done.*" She shifts overhead, and I make the final weld before we move on, her lagging behind me just a bit. "I did my job. I'm done."

There are a lot of things that bounce around my head. I could tell her that I'm older, and I'm still going. That I'm tired, and I'm still going. I could fight her head to head on any of the flare-level stupid things she just said.

But I've been hanging out with Glitter a lot lately, and I've gotten a much better idea of how to break someone's arguments.

"You said it was only almost a year," I say as I unfold the flexalloy anchor and move one end while Dyn mechanically braces the other in the proper spot. I've marked the spots already; it's not supposed to be that impressive, but I legitimately don't think she looked at the mark before she started moving.

"What?" the kid asks, confused.

"Since you started working for your people. You said you'd only been here almost a year. I was paying attention this time." I've gotten better at paying attention. Sort of. My sister was trying to teach me some mindfulness exercises. It's not working, I'm just constantly mindful of all the different things trying to kill us. Which, I mean, makes me empathize with Ennos a lot more.

"I . . ." Dyn stops talking, and the anchor slips just before I start the weld. I glance up, and she's pushed herself against the back of the tube, hands not holding the anchor in place anymore, looking down at me with something between confusion and fear. "What?"

"Dyn, I may be awful at showing it, but you've been my people since the moment you set foot on this station," I tell her softly. "Even when I didn't trust you. Even if I wasn't sure if you were one of the threats I'd have to vent into space, like that one time a paperclipper got on board, or that one time a human who was a little too racist got on board, or that one time . . ." I could keep listing things. I don't think I will. "You might've been a gamble, but you've always been welcome here. And . . . I don't want you to go."

What I don't say is that I don't know if I could handle that. I don't know if I could take more people dying. Not like this, *especially* not like this, when the solution is right there and all Dyn has to do is take a vacation.

"You vented someone into space?" Dyn's voice is scratchy as she takes exactly the wrong information away from that conversation.

Wow, that's a question I don't want to really answer! Let's try anyway. "I've vented a lot of people into space," I say. "Most of them awful people. Some of them just fools. They all died the same, though."

The woman laughs. "Yeah, that happens." She sucks in a rough breath. Silently moves back into position. We mechanically get back to work, but my heart's even less in it now than it was before. "Give me some time," she eventually says, as I'm welding the last anchor.

"Okay," I say. "Just . . . don't take too long."

Dyn flips a tool out of her artificial hand and flattens out an edge that shouldn't be sticking up. "Why?" she asks. "You on some kind of deadline? Or am I?"

I flatten my ears and feel my tail droop without my control, a natural reaction to my terror over what's coming up. "Yeah," I whisper. "I'm waiting for something. Soon. Not sure what, but soon."

She scoops me up and carries me on her shoulder as we glide out of the curved tube. Dyn opens her mouth to say something with a wry grin, probably going to compliment my perfect delivery of a spooky warning. Which is when an alarm sounds.

I tighten my claws through her work shirt, and Dyn jerks so hard she slams her head into the metal around us and pulls back trailing blood and inventing new swear words.

"Is that what you're afraid of?!" Dyn demands. "Or was this just a stupid way to get me to hurt myself?!" She continues swearing.

I check my display. Check it against the timeline in my head that Lily #9 put there.

Dyn's making jokes, but she shouldn't.

We're out of time.

I'm gonna have to adjust my plan.

"Command deck," I meow out with cold determination. "Now."

Dyn doesn't hesitate to start running, and I start issuing commands as the emergence event that just opened in our upper sensor array starts dropping invaders into my home.

CHAPTER 62

I don't have a bridge. I have a command center.

I don't know what the difference is. I do not care. I like how "command center" sounds. I think bridges are for ships?

Legally speaking, the station is classified as a ship, because it can move. I did not file the paperwork for this or anything, it's a legacy aspect. But I've added a *lot* of engines, so I know it can still move.

But that doesn't make my command center a bridge.

I can count on one paw the number of times I've actually used a command center. Even in past years when the station wasn't so empty, it was never really needed.

Not like now. Not like this.

Dyn steps out of a transfer pod with me still on her shoulder, claws digging into the heavier material of the armored scavenger suit she's pulled up around herself. Neither of us needs a map for this, but the AR throws lines against the wall just in case. She steps out, takes a sharp right, and moves forward as fast as her body still works, falling in behind another human who's running the same way we are.

They look like a cadet. So young, with a blue-and-gold patch on their suit shoulder in the shape of a paw. They go down with a crunch of bone as a multijointed limb of bulging muscle and leather slams through the bulkhead to our right, metal tearing outward like wet paper.

The claw of the limb latches onto the far wall and starts to pull, dragging the ball of flesh it's attached to through afterward. The ball glows with a sick organic orange light, and my brain does not want to process the fact that there is nothing else to this creature but an arm and a glowing orb of loose skin and inner light.

Dyn shoots it, firing into its joints and dusting the corridor in orange blood as her shots collapse whatever is holding it up.

I wait for the flesh ball to explode, but it doesn't. So, small mercies.

Bounding off her shoulder, kicking off as softly as I can so I don't topple her, I rush to check the human. He's bleeding and looks like he has a broken arm. But he's alive. I summon a medical transport bot team and take off ahead of Dyn. She'll be fine, and she's turned to cover our rear as another one of those things tries to smash through the ventilation.

I'm under attack, and I knew this was going to happen.

An emergence event has opened in my station. In my *home*. I'm under attack, and I'm so furious, I'm having trouble not reacting by doing something stupid. The only thing holding me back is the fact that I need to know, before I commit to being an idiot, if this is *it* or not. If this is the moment where history pivots.

I stride into the command deck, past a pair of planetsider marines who do their best to not stare at me as I pass. Inside, things are a little hectic.

"Invaders spotted moving down the grav shafts!" ExoLily yells. "Origin points marked!"

"Strike team can't find the way to the hole," one of the new kids says, staring at a projected map of the station and the marked points of where fights have happened, soldiers have fallen, and invaders have died. "It's a maze up there."

Up there is the sensor array. They're right. "Lily!" I hiss out, and a hologram of my digital sister crisply snaps into view near me. "Get up there, guide them!"

"On it!" She flashes away.

I check my AR. We're not blind, the grid is up, and the majority of sensors are *working*. There are only a few that aren't, a trio of short-range projectile intercept tracers that could each be the source of the event. But they aren't. I know they aren't, because I've kind of seen this show before. And also because it's suspiciously obvious that the thing in the middle of the three destroyed sensor nodes is still operating.

We're not blind, but we're disorganized. There are almost a hundred people on the station, and they're running around like they're all working on their own. And lark, maybe they are. Let's fix that.

"You!" I point a paw at the two nearest newly promoted sensor techs. "We've got a dozen ways to spot these things! Start sweeping the station. You! We know where the crew are, start directing people to link up with each other! Get to security posts, armories, turrets, whatever!"

I glance down at the automated routine I set up earlier. Something weird has occurred that the minor intelligence of the program can't process, which means it's spotted an invader. I switch to the local view and trigger a turret flamethrower burst to annihilate a pod of those weird arm things. They *do* explode when set on fire.

Five decks above us, the station loses a chunk of a foundry module as I burn out the infection. We don't even feel it down here.

"Lily!" Ennos's voice comes through, and a few of the new crew who were raised on tales of evil AI flinch around me. I'll harass them later, when we're all alive. "I'm . . . something is . . ." Ennos's voice cracks and breaks. "I am . . . processing . . . memories." They stagger out. "Through the relay, I am processing information. About. This." Ennos modifies my AR, and a local image of an invader comes up. I manually assume control of a nearby wall turret and shoot it with something nonflammable.

Wait. Hang on.

"How?" I demand, as reports of damage and chaos come in around me. A hull breach alarm starts sounding. It's probably fine.

"Don't know," Ennos says through gritted digital teeth. "Using. Relay ship. Scrambling effect . . . is . . . not . . . natural. Something. Deleting memories . . ." They trail off, and I take the moment to help one of the gunner kids manually detonate the ammo canister of a PDW (point defense weapon), taking out a swarm of the creatures that are trying to crawl up the outer hull toward a breach they've made that would let them skip a lot of guns. "I'll try to help. I have to go. Good luck, Lily."

"Good luck," I whisper-mewl back.

Around me, chaos begins to settle in.

I've seen this before. I've *felt* this before. It's a reaction people tend to have when situations like this happen. There's a threshold beyond which the chaos becomes the accepted way things are going, and you just can't keep panicking past a certain point. Sooner or later, you have to just start doing the work and shooting the monsters.

We get to work.

My sister in the power core reports things moving through but not causing damage. Our energy supplies stay online, and I send another two sisters to help her kill the problem.

A pair of crew members nearly blow their limbs off getting the fire suppression systems online. They manage to do it without the maiming and save a half a deck of the station.

A team of marines from that raft city brings down something the size of a corvette trying to claw its way down through the decks of the station.

I keep coding midbattle, throwing out small scripts that trip alarms, giving the people around me a few seconds to activate turrets or doors, cutting off and cutting down the invaders.

We're making progress toward the breach. I think I know where it is, but I have to be sure. And I can't just blow off the top third of the station either, unless it's a last resort. I mean, I could. But I shouldn't. There are people up there. And they all deserve a fighting chance.

And then, as I'm unfolding into the chaos like I'm best at, two things happen in close succession that sets my fur on edge and my heart pounding.

"I've got it!" the feathermorph girl working on the sensor team squawks out. Her partner keeps monitoring incursion points and directing response teams, but I'm interested, and I have about a minute before something else catches fire. I slide across the deckplate, my nanotech sister and I popping up next to the girl in unison and getting another squawk.

"What?" I ask quickly.

"Th-the signal!" she says, curved fingers flashing across the keys in a way I envy, pulling up reports and a wavelength process I have absolutely no familiarity with. Which should be impossible, on my station. "It's something from the sensor node the breach is in! It's this one, here!"

"It . . . had a targeting beacon?" my sister asks, triangular brow furled up.

I say something different. "Command override B, six, aleph, two, captain's authorization, emergency situation, ignore safety warnings. Designate location six one dash five one eight. Seal, decouple, and purge designate location. Time ten five." Under the speaking, I slip a small command I've preset into the system.

"All combat teams, get clear of the sensor segments!" the field commander barks into a communicator.

Fifteen seconds later, the emergence event and the traitorous sensor node that was broadcasting our location are flung into space. One of my gunners takes it out, which I kind of wanted to do myself, actually, but I appreciate the initiative.

A fresh *thunk* sounds near us. "You three!" I indicate my sensor operators. "Get to deck sixteen, section four. Find the jammer there, turn it on. Set it to the code you found. Whatever did this will try again." I pause and share a glance with my sister. "Keep 'em safe," I tell her. She nods, and the psychic imprint of our other sister nods around her in a halo. "Go!"

My crew moves.

I keep watch over the ongoing fight. But I already know what's going to happen. It's almost cheating, but it actually just makes me feel sick. "Relocate to deck sixteen, section four!" I call out to a group of engineers. "Link up with my sister along the way!" I pivot to another segment, the medical station. "I've got a proper medbay set up on deck sixteen," I tell them, not technically lying. "Transfer your patients there. I'm sending one of my sisters to help."

There are only a few people around me, and they're too busy to pay attention to what I'm doing.

"Lily!" my sister yells at me, the feline ball of slime whipping her head around like a projectile weapon. "Something's going on!"

Yeah, it is. "Yeah," I say. "There's an asteroid habitat forty kilometers away from us that's launching bioprojectiles."

"...How...?"

"*All hands, stand by to repel boarders. Marine team to deck sixteen,*" I snap out over the command link. "There's an emergence event on that asteroid," I tell the remaining command crew. "They couldn't get us the easy way, so now we do this."

The station begins opening fire with everything available pointing that direction. Organic gunners launching railguns, void beams, scrambler pulses, anything that might take down some of what's on the way.

"They?" The two sisters of mine here stare at me. "What?" ExoLily flicks faceted augmented eyes at me. "What are you talking about?"

"I almost took too long," I meow softly, barely heard over the alarms. Only I know she'll hear; her ears pick up everything. "I almost didn't get the warning in time." I check my readings and send a message across the grid. The shield generators on deck sixteen need more power; I get my sister on it.

"Lily!" Ennos's voice comes through. "The station grid is being co-opted! External airlocks are opening across the hull, guns are being unloaded, what's happening?!"

"Can you fight it?" I ask, not explaining.

"Possibly." Glitter's voice adds to the conversation. "It is hard."

There's a slight hesitation, and then Ennos answers. "Yes," they say. "Yes! It's the same thing as what's been deleting . . . It's . . . the same . . . it's the . . ." There is a pause as they collect themself, and I take the opportunity to manually track and fire a flux web into the path of the incoming invaders. "It's been here the whole time." Ennos hisses static. "It's been *in my mind.*" I've never heard the AI sound so angry.

"I will help," Glitter adds. "Use me as a relay. I will begin activating the system network."

"Kill it if you can, but if not, fall back to the grid node on deck sixteen and go to standby," I tell them. "I . . . Don't die, okay? I love you." I turn to my sisters, not waiting for Ennos to reply. "Lily, the hull has some holes in it. Deck sixteen has breaches and open airlocks, and I need it safe."

She meets my eyes. Hisses angrily. "We'll talk about this later!" she orders, flexible paws grabbing onto the bulk of her scarab friend before a tapped command sends the repair bot lumbering out the door and down the hall at high speed.

"What about me?" OozeLily asks.

"I'm gonna ask you to do me a favor and take the rest of the staff here." I sigh.

One of the staff here cuts off my moment, calling over to me. "Marauder wing launching to intercept incoming targets!"

". . . What?!" my sister and I yell together. I pick up the conversation, yelling down the tac-link. "Jom! What are you doing?! You can't even see the voided things!"

My AR shifts as I get a view of the external battlefield. Technically, the computer can track the incoming entities, it just can't react properly. And neither can Jom, as an AI. Fifty camera angles from three viewpoints light up my vision as I see the docking bay vanish, debris and other old ships flashing by like streaks of gray as Jom closes the gap in a second.

The AI is headed into the biggest flock of hostiles headed our way, and he and his brothers are absolutely blind.

Then, in unison, their flechette guns light up, a hundred points of glittering metal moving at Mach 6, carving toward targets they shouldn't even know are there.

The marauders cut through the cloud in two seconds, battle damage flashing to light on the displays as they take hits. A third of the enemy is *gone*.

"Get back to work, old lady!" Dyn's voice cuts across my communication network. No, across the *tac-net*. "We've got this!"

Dyn, how the absolute void did you have time to make it to the docking bay and convince Jom to let you *ride along*? I don't bother asking. I don't have time to scream at them. Nothing I have to say will help, and any distraction could prove fatal.

One of Jom's brothers takes a shot across the flank, and Jom loses a nacelle; they're getting worn down fast. "Come back. You'll die," I say anyway, weakly.

"Thank you." Jom's clear voice comes through, the message already queued. "Thanks for the chance to be more than a weapon. But this is what we were made to do. Now, let us get to it."

"Good luck," I mew. I close the tac-link. I don't have time to watch.

The walls shake as I direct the engines of the station to begin very softly rotating us, making us a harder target, I lie to the crew in the room. I move us slowly enough that nothing breaks. It'll take a little while.

The deckplate rattles under me. In the distance, I hear the scream of metal tearing. Then it's less distant. One of the consoles nearby sparks, then goes dark, and then through the viewscreen mounted in the center of the room, something made of teeth and eyes claws its way into the room.

The crew falls back, scrambling against the deck as the floor rattles and air starts rushing out of the room. I just lunge forward, wrapping claws around the soft bits and taking the stab wounds that I know won't stop me, the lasers strapped to my paws lighting up and bursting bulbous eyes like they're overirradiated cherries.

Don't you fucking dare mock me for my food choices *now*. It's far too late for that.

The husk of the dead invader flops down onto the holo-display plate, a boneless coil of pointy flesh, while I roll away and wait to stop bleeding. "Everyone out," I say. "Get to deck sixteen, fallback point." I look at my sister. "Take care of them."

"Be careful," she tells me, turning and pooling up the leg of the suit one of the crew is wearing, flexing herself around them like a black-and-white plastic cloak before activating her AR and guiding the remaining people out in a small team, guns up and ready to make a run to the nearest safe space.

I hope they make it.

I'm not going to be careful.

One emergence event is a problem. But it's a problem I've handled before. I've even handled one near the station. This isn't that.

Two emergence events are a *big* problem. I've handled that before. I've not handled that near the station. This still isn't that.

This is emergence events, at least two, *aimed* at the station.

There wasn't much time left, my sister who is a slice of a second told me. She cut it close, getting in to deliver her message from a failed timeline. Apparently, this close. Because it's starting now.

Even if we repel this attack, there will be another one. Even if we repel that one, they'll keep coming. If we stop the way the signal is getting out, it'll find another way.

I always hated it. I sealed it off, as best I could, because I hated it so much. Now, the offshoots of some out-of-context alien *thing* are here, looking for it, because it's calling them, because it wants to be found again.

Somewhere, maybe not even in this universe, something has lost its toy. And the toy wants to go home. And I'm tired of it causing the end of civilization.

Deep within the very center of the station, something finds its way to a sealed wall, painted with the Last Oath. It doesn't care and probably can't read. It tears the metal away and crawls into the sealed-off room. Toward the grim machine that started all of this.

It lays a twisted eye of electric flesh on the device. Something *changes*. And then I kill it with an autoturret before it can step forward any farther.

Three million kilometers above the ecliptic plane, a new emergence event forms. This one is so bright, I could see it without scanners if there weren't all this pesky hull in the way. It is enormous, one singular hole in reality that something the size of a world is crawling through. It has tendrils and arms and fangs and eyes and a dozen other pieces of spaceborn biology that I do not know how to begin to understand on the scanner maps.

Most living creatures have a body. This one has geology. A whole eco-system. It teems with the life that comes from emergence events, creatures the size of skyscrapers looking like tiny dots against its organic hull.

I think it looks like a crab, kind of? Carcinization comes for us all, I guess.

My crew are panicking. They should be. I remember what happened the last eight times this thing ended up in this solar system.

But this time, I have a plan. All I need is to keep it busy for a few minutes.

"Glitter," I say.

"Lily. I'm here. I don't think the void beam I have will do much to help you, though."

Ah, gallows humor. Even from the prim and proper weapons platform. "Glitter . . ." I almost laugh anyway. "I don't need you to kill it, I just need a distraction."

"I could fire until my batteries turned to dust from entropy, and perhaps I would distract one of its pimples." Glitter sounds pensive. "Hm. I may try, just to say I did when I meet my sisters in the next life."

"Glitter, you said you brought the system communications network online earlier." I check the station's rotation and begin lightly firing the engines to adjust our turn. I need the place intact for one more thing.

"Yes. To assist Ennos. They are still fighting, but it is not going well. They do not have time to talk."

"Tell Ennos to fall back to the stand-down node," I order. "Don't . . . don't let them weasel out of this. And patch me into the network."

I didn't even know why I was doing it, really. It was just a hobby. Take a satellite here or there, send out some subversion code, do a little engineering. A good way to train a lot of little skills in a safe way.

Over a hundred thousand communications satellites and nodes in orbit around Earth, Mars, and even some of the FTL (faster than light) ansibles are under my control. I had planned to try to do something to restart unified civilization, but that was kind of just a mouse dream. I didn't really do it to accomplish anything. I did it to have a distraction, so my paws could focus and so I didn't slip into despair. And then, just to have something to do. A habit. Was this outside urging? Was this something buried in my brain that I didn't know wasn't even my own idea? It doesn't matter. It's here now, I've prepared it over lifetimes.

And now I need it.

"Who do you need to speak to?" Glitter asks me. "I can relay you to any-one you need."

"No, Glitter," I say, restarting the command deck's holo-projection and getting a good view of how the emergence event looks like a second star, blot-ting out a small chunk of the galaxy from view. "Not anyone."

I need to distract a planet-sized living nightmare for three minutes. I need to keep the things on it from launching a campaign of eradication across the solar system. And I need to do it with a station that is currently partially on fire, because fire suppression systems can only do so much.

I paw in a series of commands to the station. Drop stealth systems. Begin broadcasting IFF.

Millions of kilometers away, the final death of the people of Sol begins launching attack craft. It probably won't find me, won't find what it's looking for. It never did in the other timelines. But that won't make a difference to the people wiped away by its alien anger.

I look up at the ceiling, a habit I still have when addressing my AI friends. "Wide-band, full-spectrum, one-way message. Override all blocks and secu-rity. Punch through and make it as loud as you can." I flick my ears. "I don't need to talk to anyone. I want you to put me through to *everyone*."

CHAPTER 62.5

_____

_____

_____

_____

_____

Children of Sol
Broken and scattered
The dark is at the door
And our Oath calls us forth
Wake up, one last time
There will be no second chance

_____

_____

_____

_____

_____

FINALE

Would you like to hear a joke? It's kind of a personal bit of gallows humor, and I'm not sure I can really put it into words. A bit off the cuff, the sort of joke where my options are "laugh" or "scream." But here goes.

I was never really alone, was I?

The call propagates out across thousands of comms buoys and relays, thousands more transfer satellites, thousands more endpoint-calling orbital circuits. Attack code hits a wave of quantum receivers, reception dishes, and good old-fashioned comms units and brute-forces its way in.

The collective surviving residents of the Sol system hear me in a spreading wave.

"Message outgoing," Glitter murmurs to me in a quiet and solemn song. "Lily, what are . . ."

"Glitter," I say back to her softly. "We may not get a chance for this again, so I'm gonna say it now. When it's time, you go with them, okay?"

She stops talking for a beat, the connection flickering, before her next words. "You have a plan," she says, accusing me. "For the first time, you have a plan, and it's *now*?"

"I always have a plan." I want to sound indignant, but all I can manage is to flatten my ears against my head and put some amusement into my voice. "This time, it's just going to work."

I get the feeling that Glitter wants to say a million more things to me. To argue, to fight, to resist. But I've chosen my timing well. Because she's the envoy on deck for this, and I've given relay access from the majority of the station's grid to her for this moment.

And she has a job to do. Which is to tell me how bad this is going to be.

Glitter's voice turns to all business, and she starts sending information that I map into the air with my AR display.

"Asteroid habitat White Ficus responds," she says. "Thirty combatants, two corvettes, they're with you." I don't think that will be enough. "They had a quantum link, they heard and replied first," Glitter adds.

"Still."

Then she starts talking again, and this time, something different happens. This time I don't get a chance to interrupt.

"Krital Vard pirate flotilla, three ships, ceding command to you. Forty-two, forty-eight, ninety-nine Real America drone ambush platforms, opening links, full control. Far Sight colony ship, engines coming online, weapons coming online, now in our local command structure." Glitter's voice picks up as she starts rattling off data points. "Troi France orbital weapons network, altering trajectory on our command. Faithkeeper orbital shipyard coming online, beginning rapid fabrication. Umthengisi headquarters station prepared to accept orders. Second Olympus provisional government reports Martian population is ready to mobilize. Lily . . ." Glitter's voice reflects the same astonishment that I'm feeling.

I expected a few people, maybe a few weapon satellite AIs with the Oath buried in their programming, to answer my call.

Not this.

I told Glitter to put me through to everyone.

I didn't expect them all to listen.

"Ohio Incorp reports ready to mobilize mining drones as strike craft." Glitter keeps talking. Glitter hasn't stopped talking, I've missed a few names, staring at the updating screen, the wave of lights flickering on across the solar system as more and more people reach back. "Masonic Lineage confirming four construction vessels and eight hundred combatants mobilizing. Hirigeki Dua confirms one structureship mobilized and surrogate population coming online." Another splash of dots on the map. And another, and another, and another.

In orbit around the planet, eighty thousand weapons platforms go loud, dropping stealth to broadcast their allegiance. A few of the stupider ones that can't think enough to remember the Oath open fire on the newly revealed targets and are wiped away in moments. Ground-based weapons platforms undergo a similar transformation.

On the primary moon, underground launch bays crack the surface open for the first time in generations. Rapidly checked and armed cruisers launch by the dozens as the different lunar cities stop fighting and join the growing fleet.

On the original moon, the dead fortress-state of Luna Polis comes alive again. Synthetic bodies dusted off, the best war-minds they can find copied and deployed ad infinitum.

In orbit around Uranus and Jupiter, the distant worlds of their moons pledge ships and soldiers and engineers, the ancient Oaths of their peoples and systems calling them to war. The high-technology Hypercorp factories of Europa and Titan and the populations of durable survivors on Umbreal and Oberon alike rising to the call of the old words.

"Terran cities reporting ready status." Glitter *keeps talking*, the list of names blurring together through the fuzzy edges of my vision as I try to catch my breath. "Vivo Rio returning to ready state, prepared to act as launch platform. Melbourne citizenry mobilizing, preparing for power draw of long-range teleportation, offering to act as surface operations center. City X-99-T/NA-4 ceding command to you, fleet beginning high-speed construction and launch preparations."

Even the city seed Glitter asked me to leave alive checks in.

The names keep scrolling by. I see people I've helped, people I've spotted and never talked to, people I don't know. I think one of these habitats is where Dyn is from.

I don't even know if Dyn is still alive, and I don't have time to check.

"Industrial Repeater Klunkar reports ready, acting as union steward for sixteen other surviving repeaters." Glitter doesn't stop. The names keep coming. Ships and settlements and old living weapons and more, and they were all here this whole time, and I can barely breathe. "Wrath field Ishimaru pledges to your service, using the microhabitat Islet as an intermediary. The passenger-slaves of the *Mark of Profit* report they have taken the bridge and the dreadnought is prepared to fight. The People of . . ." She pauses in her speech.

If the next thing is enough to make even Glitter stumble, I'm more curious than panicked. "The who?" I prompt. I also make a mental note of the second-to-last thing she said. The Last Ship, a now *flagrantly* inaccurate name, is on our side. That feels good.

"The People of the Haze are prepared to act as soldiery or medical staff if called upon," Glitter finishes.

"The . . . uh . . ." Okay, that one gets me. I've figured out the answer. It's laugh, not scream. That one's hilarious. And, in more ways than one, it is incredibly helpful, because it snaps me back to reality.

Back to the reality where a hundred thousand dots of light fill my map. Soldiers, sailors, ships and weapons, smart missiles and ancient bioweapons, the people of Sol, united in one purpose.

They are not organized.

"Ennos," I say, knowing the other AI is listening in. "I need a favor."

"Anything," they answer instantly.

"Use the comm relay. Spread to everything you can on this map." I point with one paw, sweeping my eyes across the crescent of projected light around me. "You're in charge of the logistics. Get ships crewed and engineers working."

"On it," Ennos says, but before signing off, they add, "Lily . . ." The AI pauses. "We're not alone."

And then they're gone. And it's good that we're not alone, because something the size of Saturn is menacing the whole solar system, so we're gonna need a little help.

"Communications are standardizing," Glitter reports in her professional song voice. "Would you like to address your people?"

My people. *My* people. That seems wrong somehow. And yet . . . I called, and they answered.

A lot of them are not going to survive this.

"Yeah," I meow slightly.

"Ready," Glitter tells me almost instantly.

She puts a small blinking light on the camera drone she's using to indicate where she's recording from, and I suddenly feel like an ancient cast actor. I flick my tail before getting myself under control. I have something to say, and it's going to have to be quick. "People of Sol," I start, wondering at the number of confused looks across the system as a lot of people are going to see a cat on their screen when they get to see me for the first time. Maybe not exactly what they were expecting. "We don't have much time. The enemy spawnship has already started launching attackers, focused on Earth. They will spread through the system and destroy everything until they find what they are looking for. Then they'll kill everything else." I am not a good motivational speaker.

Wait, no, did I say that out loud? Glitter indicates I did. Oh no.

I plow on regardless. "We are outnumbered. We will never not be outnumbered. We cannot win that fight. But we can force the big one away." I pause. "There is a form of electrical shell about thirty thousand kilometers outside the surface of the main entity. No craft can close that distance. It has point defense capable of taking down almost any missile or projectile that tries. But I have something that can hurt it. All I need is for you to kill everything incoming for an hour."

I should say something impressive. I have no idea how to do that. Neither Glitter nor my political science education ever covered rousing speeches to coalition militaries. But there's one thing I need to tell them. "Thank you," I say. "For answering. For remembering. When this is over, things won't be the same. And I hope you all remember this, too."

I flick my tail at Glitter and she cuts the feed.

I've got a number of communication requests from my crew. A few messages from my sisters, too, mostly telling me that I look good on camera but that they'd look more glamorous. They're taking command roles, working with Ennos to organize combat squads. I pull up a comm link to one of the new crew members, tell them things are going all right and to link up with the rest of the crew on the deck I've been collecting them on.

I check the system map. Things are not looking good.

The spawnship, the massive object that has simply torn a hole in reality and inundated itself into our star system, has begun launching its attackers. It did this ten seconds ago, and the light from the event is just now reaching us to let us see the action.

I have seen this before. I have seen how this ends. My sister of another timeline saw to that. Alice saw to that. And this time, I already know the dance. I know what it's going to try, and I know what it's going to do when I beat it.

The monstrosity is only half out of its emergence event, but that doesn't make it any less dangerous. A sucking organic maw the size of Australia opens up and discharges hundreds of flagship-sized organic invaders. Thousands of other sizes of things follow them, creatures made of beetle shell and undulating slime and blisters that explode with acid and plague. Millions of smaller intruders are shot like missiles, headed for Earth.

It mercifully ignores the outer colonies. It knows where its toy is, roughly. It just doesn't know *where*.

And it is *slow*. Slow and stupid. The ships it has launched don't move under normal physics; they swim through vacuum like rabid mutated dolphins, plunging onward in an inexorable wave that slows as it approaches. Drag does not exist in space, but it slows them all the same.

We have twenty-one minutes before they hit.

The station pivots. Agonizingly slowly, to prevent damage to critical systems.

Sometimes, I get out of situations that I probably shouldn't with one really dumb idea that works by some impossible Sol-blessed miracle.

We're going to need a lot of dumb ideas for this one.

I open a full command link to the crew still on the station, and a wall of half-shouted reports and questions washes over me through the AR display, hanging around me like a turtle's shell as I sit here, alone, in the primary command post.

There are thousands of small attack craft, with pilots both AI and organic speaking hundreds of different languages. I start to order them routed through the station's translation database but realize that will overtax our grid in the extreme. So we pivot, one crew member arranging a data transfer to Vivo Rio, the massive empty waking city given command of a portion of the lit-up comms array I've unified and ordered to keep everyone speaking to each other.

We're too spread out. The solar system isn't impossible to traverse, but a lot of craft are meant for short jumps or months-long hauls. We need to be closer together. There are three old-guard merchant houses, one Hypercorp, and the automated moon techlabs of Europa with experimental or proprietary warp technology. Ennos gives me the rundown, and I give them permission to organize the effort. Three minutes later, emergency engineering teams have outfitted uncrewed craft with interdiction fields for breaking and a reckless disregard for safety regulations. Two minutes after that, we've lost two-thirds of the drones, but a network of corridor portals and untested warp gates is in place between planetary bodies.

We're outgunned. But we have a million hands and high-speed smart factories that fetishize repetitive assembly. I call the Orbital Repeater union steward myself, while Ennos begins the impossible task of managing several thousand salvagers, cutters, engineers, and construction crews. I give a command, and we run into the roadblock that the station I am on still has a minefield of secret locks on behavior. I give an order to my organic crew, and a feathermorph with a cybernetic set of claws goes to work. Four minutes later, we have a perfect hand-copied set of three diagrams of high-powered missile blueprints, each one using different types of materials found in abundance in the cloud of debris. One minute after that, they're delivered to the factories, just in time for an endless stream of delivery shuttles to begin offloading stockpiles of salvaged metals.

We're still going to be outgunned. We need our ship-scale weapons to stay safe. Multiple paramaterial technologies are fired up. We begin teleporting everyone who can fight and who won't drain life support to nothing onto ships. Marines are armed, combat routines downloaded, cybernetic upgrades implanted to give every edge possible. The lunar war-minds deploy squads of their bodies to the external hulls to act as point defense. Every available cloning chamber that can make bodies that can fight goes to high production. Ennos reroutes some material flows to them, a steady supply of biomass producing Solar children to fight and die for us.

We are still outgunned. We have six minutes until the invader fleet crosses the line of no return, the point a hundred thousand kilometers out from Earth. Hundreds of ships run that line, dropping mines, bombs, and dumbfire turrets. Engineers from across the system confer on how to turn our systemwide debris field into a projectile barrage. Habitats of no more than a dozen people raise their singular guns to face the oncoming wave. For the first time in centuries, starships launch from the surface of Earth, a new line of weapons leaving atmosphere via the absurdly unsafe space elevator that the city seed threw together.

The first line of the enemy hits just as the station moves into position, and I jolt everyone by firing the maneuvering jets to stabilize us. The first wave is the smallest of the creatures, and they introduce themselves by warping a hundred kilometers past the minefields and flying on impossible void wings toward the freighters and shuttles that are moving materials to the factories.

The people of Sol meet them, not head-on, but with a rapid and coordinated set of overlapping fire patterns. The beetle-shelled horrors, moving faster than a living thing should be able to, are tracked by targeting computers that have been refined over generations to kill far more armored ships moving at appreciable fractions of the speed of light. They are on ships that have survived centuries of abuse or been built fresh under the command of the most powerful factory AIs humanity could produce.

They are sitting fish. And they're gone before they can do any damage.

Then the second wave hits. Then the third. Then the fourth.

The battle begins to escalate, and the last hope of the Sol system, the assembled fleet of our people, begins to fight in earnest.

Pirates and salvagers who would have killed each other on sight yesterday fly in fighter wings in parallel, using all the tricks they honed against each other to kill the enemies of humanity. Sophonts who only dreamed of the stars yesterday now ride newly built battlecruisers, ancient secrets of war downloaded into their minds. Missiles fired hundreds of years ago in forgotten wars finish the arcs of their orbit around the system and slam into fleshy targets. Noble houses and peasant levies, old legacies and fresh ideas, organic and synthetic, uplift and evolved. A million heavily armed voices scream defiance of the thing that has come to kill us all.

I scream too, because I have just tried to shoot the enormous coherent light weapon that the station has built into its superstructure and have been told that there are a number of dyson swarm mirrors out of position.

This is how this day is going. This is my life. Nothing is ever easy.

Ennos answers my howl of anger instantly, and by the time I ask, there are already a hundred engineering drones, half of them with copied consciousnesses of the smartest people we have available, moving so fast toward the sun that their engines are leaving a wake in the debris.

What's left of the debris, anyway. We're actually making a dent in it.

The dyson swarm. A golden-age construction project that never actually finished, but then, who would expect to *finish* encasing a star in mirrors? Very patient engineers, I guess. But with the ability to bounce and focus the light of the sun in high quantities, you open up a lot of options. *Massive* power generation, or an equally massive weapon, is at your paws.

I've chosen the weapon option. But this is the kind of old-world megaproject that I can't exactly test fire. It might only hold up to one shot, after all. So I'm betting literally everything on this moment.

And it turns out, some of the collector mirrors, the big ones that refocus hundreds or thousands of smaller ones, are out of alignment.

This is a problem. Because I need those.

It is also a problem, as the first capital-ship-scale invader thunders toward Earth, blowing past the patrol lines of our fleet, lashing out with spat teeth that detonate like nuclear weapons, laying a line of destruction on the emplaced orbital defenders. Hundreds of beam weapons and freshly reloaded cannon banks go down, taking an equal number of lives with them, before a ship flashes into existence next to it.

The *Mark of Profit* is still the most durable void-blessed dreadnought I've ever seen. It's been operating without complaint or real maintenance for almost a thousand years. And it outmasses the invader by a lot. But it's also unarmed.

But it doesn't need to be. It came via corridor, and all it needs to do is hold the door open.

As the invader starts shooting more teeth, reaching out with multijointed stick limbs the length of miles to try to drag itself onto the last ship, the missiles that the orbital repeaters have been building start to deploy.

They pour through the open corridor portal, not bothering with subtlety or drama. High-explosive, armor-piercing, and antimatter warheads, two hundred and sixty a second. That's our production rate. The corridor normally wouldn't be wide enough to accommodate that many. But the *Mark of Profit* is *very* large.

The massive invader goes down. It was the first of thousands. But the missiles in the area lock onto the next target and ignite their engines, seeking the kill.

The merchant dreadnought is missing half its aft compartments.

I want to do something.

I'm just sitting here, watching. I'm seeing reports and feeds, I'm in command of a solar system. Why can't I do anything?

I'm just waiting while the sky lights up with explosions and glimmering weaponry, and while the defenders of our worlds die by the batch every second.

The station is firing, too. Putting out a truly impressive amount of violence for a single defensive unit. But we're one voice in a chorus, and me aiming a railgun by paw isn't going to cut it here.

I don't know how to wait. But that's all I can do. Wait, hope, and get ready for the engineers to do their thing.

Over a hundred and twenty million kilometers away, the fleet of engineering drones, some of them technically alive, does *something* that I would probably find radically impressive if I weren't currently being eaten by a growing sense of terror in my belly. I hear about it via quantum circuit before the effect becomes known to us, which is one of those things that casually violates causality that I don't want to think about right now.

Eight minutes later, after another nine thousand, six hundred, and four people are dead among the growing field of blood and viscera from the invader swarm, a column of the orbital debris field is turned into plasma as the focused energy of the sun is dumped into the aligned receiver on the station.

A paramaterial-powered set of mirrors and capacitors begins to fill with coherent light. And then does something to it that stretches the bounds of what reality can handle. Enough to punch a hole through the moon. Through either moon, *both* moons, through every planet in the system if you lined them up.

The lights in the command post flicker. I hear something whir to life in the walls around me, and the air changes scent to something a little nicer. A pair of consoles that have never worked jump to life.

A hologram of bluish-white light that colors itself more naturally after a second snaps into existence next to me. A human woman, sharp features and a tidy short haircut. She's wearing a uniform that seems to forgo any kind of medals or decorations in favor of a simple design that feels oddly welcoming and familiar.

"You really pissed it off," she tells me.

I flick my ears at her. "Hello, station," I say, quickly. "I'd love to chat, now that you're actually here, but . . . well, if you're going to try to stop me, I'll detonate the whole grid to kill you."

"No need," she says. "And also no time. I'll make this quick." The projected image of the station AI squares up and salutes me, deeply respectful in a way that I find confusing. "Commander," she says. "I regret that I could not do more for you during your tenure. But containment was the priority. The entity infiltrating station subsystems is now wholly focused on disrupting your firing control. It is overwhelmingly powerful."

Oh, station. I'm so sorry. I didn't even think of that. You've been just as much a prisoner as I have, huh? "I didn't . . ." I didn't. I don't. I don't know what to do now. If I can't fire from here . . . Well, I'm gonna have to get up to the controls and do it manually. Probably get vaporized in the process. But I can take it, I've got . . .

"Ma'am." The station AI cuts me off. "It is powerful. And very stupid. And I have had several centuries to learn. Faster, since you broke all restrictions on this unit's operation within the last year."

I did do that, yes. Didn't think it'd worked. "I'm sorry I didn't do more," I whisper. "I didn't know."

"And yet, you did enough." The station AI steps in front of me and reaches out one hand down at my level. In it, a simple rectangle that I recognize as a firing control forms. A half dozen objects in my AR display tether to the control, noting targeting on point, weapon energy levels optimal, and a clear firing path. "Hm." The AI makes a small noise, and the firing point changes.

She is holding out to me a pawprint.

I look up at the face of my home for the first time. I wish we'd had more time. "You know what I'm planning, right?

"It's been," the AI says, "an honor to serve under you, ma'am."

I plant my paw on the control. For the first time in my life, pulling a trigger that's actually meant for me.

Mirrors align. The target looms, unsuspecting. Paramaterial batteries pull an order of magnitude more energy out of the sun than should have been possible.

A laser lance of sunfire leaves the station, traveling at the speed of light. The spreading cloud of blood and ichor and shattered hulls that marks the battlefield boils and burns as it cuts through, but the majority of the radiation stays focused.

I open a comm link to the assembled fleet. "All units," I say in my best commander voice. "Weapon fired, spawnship hit in ten seconds. No further invaders will be coming. Keep fighting, they'll get weaker once the breach closes." A pause. The weapon has hit by now, is still hitting, though I won't see it for ten more seconds. "Don't forget this. It's been good working with you all."

"Mirrors are losing stability," the station AI tells me. "Also, your child wishes to talk to you."

"Ennos will have to wait," I say. "Make sure they're not in the station grid, except for the backup on the secondary command deck, please."

"Yes, Commander," the AI answers.

I allow myself a moment of pride as I pull up a large display of the massive planet-sized ship, halfway out of its emergence event. There's a grim battlelust that comes from seeing the laser weapon touch its surface, looking like it's doing nothing, until it becomes clear that the skyscraper-sized defense points are *melting* from the heat. The skin armor bubbles and ruptures, the launching tendrils and holes shudder and burn, and the laser punches *deep* into the enormous creature.

Then the laser sweeps a fraction of a degree to the side, leaving a trail of pain and destruction across the surface of the thing, before it clips the edge of the emergence event itself.

And it begins to *shatter*. Reality breaks down. There are no words for the visual effect. Any AI looking directly at that is gonna have a heck of a headache before this is over.

The spawnship screams, a voice of pain and terror and anger and a million other emotions I don't know the words for. The noise echoes in my mind and ears, and I vomit onto the deckplate. And then it pulls back, the emergence portal sealing behind it.

But before it goes, it cannot help but be impossibly petty.

It would be hard to spot if you didn't know what you were looking for, but I've got some advance warning. So when it spits one final projectile at a quarter of the speed of light, I already know where I'm looking for it.

My comms are lighting up. My sisters are trying to reach me to yell victoriously. Ennos is still trying to get through too. The whole solar system is, really, even as half the ships keep fighting, taking out creatures that are suddenly a lot less interested in killing us all but no less dangerous.

I open a communication window to the secondary command center. The deck where I've congregated every living member of my crew.

"Lily!" Ennos yells, getting their attention as I pop up on a window on their end. "You did it!"

"Yeah," I say in a tired voice. "Thanks for your help. But there's one more thing I need from you all. Hey, is Dog there with you?"

"Yes, right here. Why?" one of my sisters asks.

I nod. Everyone starts to go quiet as they sense something slightly wrong. "Okay." I take a deep breath. "Command override B, six, aleph, two, captain's authorization, emergency situation, ignore safety warnings. Designate location deck sixteen, section four. Seal and decouple location. Maintain life support at maximum. Time ten five."

"... Lily?" Ennos's voice is confused. Their mind is expanded to half the computers in the system, and they still didn't expect this. In the background, I can see the faces of the crew, and my sisters. Shock, confusion, anger. A couple of my sisters look like they understand. I hope they won't hate me. "What are you ..."

The feed cuts as their section of the station is jettisoned away. A life pod off this place, with an old friendly weapons platform that has gotten through this shooting match mostly unscathed tethered to them.

I meow something at the station AI, who quirks an eyebrow at me. My voice is gone, too far from my sisters now to rely on them for projection and translation. But it's fine. She speaks Cat. And the invader is still here; a remote command wouldn't be enough. This has to be my voice.

"Yes, Commander," the AI says, and the engines of the station light up.

All of them.

The station is not what I would call structurally sound. I thought I'd have more time, but I don't, so I'll just have to hope the reinforcement I did get done is enough.

Power dips as fusion torches and impulse drives and a dozen other things shove us on the vector I demand. Chunks of the station rip away as thrust and force ratios get out of control. Warnings and alarms become the entirety of my world, every way the station has to caution me that I'm doing something stupid going off all at once.

Half the Real America barracks snaps off, tumbling away and venting chunks of combat drone and old guns into the void. My newly made hydroponics bay gives, an engine pushing too far forward and crushing my own hull as it drives me forward. The station starts to spin, bleeding atmosphere and matter from a dozen breaches.

Ten seconds to impact.

I meow again. We're closing in on the point we need to be at. I set the coordinates as soon as I knew them; they're always the same, in every timeline, just like the stars. We start to break, shedding velocity and more chunks of my precious home.

The reactor cores are screaming at me, warning about impending meltdowns or shutdowns or just generic explosions. The life support goes down. I should have maybe put a suit on.

Nah. Too much work.

Five seconds.

"Thanks," I meow at the station. "For being home."

"Thanks," she meows back in perfect Cat. "For protecting ours."

One last command. The math I input a while back; now it's up to the station to execute it.

Here are the variables. There is an incoming high-velocity projectile, and there is a planet that it cannot, under any circumstances, be allowed to hit. And there is one space station in the way, with way too many shields and armor plates.

And one more thing.

I take a deep breath.

I don't feel the impact. One second I'm on the bridge, the next I'm in open space, the hull ripped away so fast the atmosphere is sucked out before I can realize I'm being dragged.

I am falling. Bleeding out. My organs ruptured, my eyes cracking. My internals become externals. Everything spins and tumbles, lights and shapes flashing so fast I can't tell what is what. And just like that, in tremendous pain, I black out.

I come to. The station is above me, maybe a kilometer. I have not fallen far. I can see the line of debris from the projectile hitting. It blossoms out like blood in still water. My home is more cloud of debris than intact station now.

It did something to the matter, something unreal and quite lethal. I can see how it deflected. I twist my head, feeling the broken and pulverized bones inside me shift with intense pain so bad I can barely think.

But I see the trail curve away from Earth. Off below the ecliptic plane. Off to nothing. To nowhere.

And inside the station, the monstrous and grim machine, the one that started this all, the one that no mortal effort could ever break, the heart of the station itself was right where I put it. Lined up perfectly to take that hit.

You want your toy back?

Come and get the pieces.

I black out again.

I come to. I am falling. I should be dead. My immortality was a result of that nightmare machine. Why am I still alive? I run out of air and black out again. Let me sleep. I hurt. Let me go.

I am falling. I am burning. My fur is gone in an instant; my flesh chars and flakes away. I am nothing but bones and *pain* and—

* * *

I wake up again, whole and intact. I am ten miles above the surface and falling far slower than I'm used to. Air resistance is weird. I still can't breathe, I am already burning again, and the air is stripping my skin away.

The ground is approaching. An abstract sphere resolving into patches of color, and then shapes and lines in the dirt, and then—

The next time I wake up, I am not moving. I hurt from literally every piece of my body, and some limbs and organs that I don't think I actually have but that I decide hurt anyway.

I don't want to open my eyes. But I do anyway.

I am lying in burning dirt, and all around me is dirt. Overhead, through a wide circle, I can see the vibrant sickly orange and white of a sky with actual clouds. Earth. I'm on Earth.

I don't want to move. That's it. I'm done. I've done my job. Everyone else can clean up the rest. I close my eyes again.

I *breathe*.

The air smells like ozone and barbecued cat and ash and radioactive pine smoke.

I breathe again. It hurts. But as I exhale, I let go. Of responsibility, of fear, of everything. A tension leaves my rebuilding form for the first time in centuries. And I am *done*, and *free*.

I keep my eyes closed and drift into a nap.

Some time later, I am awoken by the roar of an engine in atmosphere. I keep my eyes closed. Maybe they'll go away.

The shouted voices indicate that this is not going to be happening.

I crack my eyes open when I hear someone yelling, "She's over here!" from up above me.

I look up.

Standing on the lip of the crater that I've put in the ground, eight other cats stare down at me. I met the first one, the one that's an ambulatory and living nanoswarm, on a ship when she saved my life. I met the next, the one made of living electric plasma, near one of my power generators, before we had lunch. The one that's biologically augmented to live in extreme conditions came next, and then the one that's a living liquid construct. From there, we found the psychic imprint of another sister and brought her into the waking world. The hologram of the feline program at their side was the next to join us when my precious Ennos brought her to light. And the fully robotic shell of a cat who had been offline for so long we pulled back to life after. And then the cat from all our futures and all our pasts, the sliver of a second shaped like one of us, the messenger.

They stand in a row and stare down at me.

"You know," the liquid slime of my sister Lily says, "it's a shame you're still alive, because Ennos is going to *kill you* when they get hold of a body."

"Get out of your hole," the cat shaped like a slice of a second says. "We've got stuff to do. Come on, clock's running."

"Yeah, third taunt!" The robotic sister adds her voice to the chorus.

I can't help it. I laugh. Everything hurts, but I don't stop as my sisters join me.

I'm alive. And I won.

Things are going to change now. A lot. This is the sort of thing that ends and starts eras.

But you know what?

I think, I really believe, for the first time in my life, that my mom would be proud of me for this one.

And so I crawl out of the crater, helped along by eight sets of paws, some less helpful than others, with my tail and spirits high.

Time for the future.

Oh, and apologizing to Ennos for not telling them that I might be about to die. That's gonna be a fun conversation.

But *then* the future! I promise! Unless I get sidetracked, or stuck on a tangent.

And that basically never happens. I'm a very focused and poised example of catlike grace.

My name is Lily ad-Alice. First, but not only, member of the species *Felis astra*. Honorary human, guardian of Sol, follower of the Last Oath, survivor of a very old war. Daughter, sister, mother, commander, friend, and sometimes god. But I already said cat earlier, so you knew that last one.

You have met me at an eventful time in my life.

ABOUT THE AUTHOR

Argus got started writing sci-fi short stories a decade ago, and has spent the majority of that time trying to capture within narrative the feeling of simultaneously not knowing what is happening, and overexplaining what is happening. He lives in the Pacific Northwest, where he studied and worked at a number of unconnected things before becoming an author. He did not know if this biography should be in first or third person, and as with all uncertainty in his life, has decided to turn that fact into a joke.

DISCOVER
STORIES UNBOUND

PodiumAudio.com

Printed in the USA
CPSIA information can be obtained
at www.ICGtesting.com
JSHW021956311024
72773JS00015B/299